The Tontine

The

Tontine

A NOVEL BY THOMAS B. COSTAIN

Illustrated by Herbert Ryman

VOLUME I

DOUBLEDAY & COMPANY, INC.
Garden City, New York

With the exception of actual historical personages, the characters are entirely the product of the author's imagination and have no relation to any person in real life.

To my friends in the busy house of Doubleday, in particular those with whom I have worked closely over the years and all who had a part in planning and preparing this somewhat unusual venture.

CONTENTS

BOOK I

*A Very Bad Man Has
a Very Good Idea*

CHAPTER ONE

1

IT WAS in the year 1815 and the people of England were suffering from strange and unpredictable humors. The war against the French had been going on too long. A few months before, with Boney put away in Elba, it had seemed that all the dangers and uncertainties, and the hardships they had endured so long, had come to an end. Trade would revive and the luxuries from which they had been cut off and which they had missed so much would come back on the market. But the terrible Corsican had broken out and his armies were marching again into the Low Countries.

Englishmen loved a "little go" above everything and they had turned to the solace of gambling. The great ventures which had resulted in such unpleasantnesses as the South Sea Bubble were now prohibited by law and the state lotteries had been stopped. But private lotteries were proceeding merrily and all the men of England, and all the women too, were putting in their weekly dibs. Every owner of an oyster stall in London had his own little lottery and his customers not only got a plateful for threepence but a chance for five guineas if they drew the lucky number. A share in a drawing rode on every helping of rare roast beef served in the eating houses. The morocco men, who made the collections for bigger goes, took in half a million pounds sterling every year from domestic servants alone.

All this would soon be over. Parliament would get through with Boney and would come around to home problems again, and governmental brooms would begin on the gambling evil. But the tontines would keep right on, and this was natural enough. The tontine was a slow-moving affair and, on the surface at least, it lacked the evil features of the lottery. Men and women who put their money in tontines had to live out a good span of years to share in the heavy distribution of money and only in the final stages was there excitement for the public to share. Moreover they were a form of insurance and, for those who were lucky or, more accurately, who were healthy, they brought a fine income for the declining years. So the law would come down hard on the men who financed lotteries, and the pigeons and rooks who ran them, and would as yet turn no more than a dubious eye to the tontines.

It so happened, therefore, that on Sunday, June 18, 1815, a meeting was held in the drawing room of a gloomy old mansion on Grosvenor Square in London which the impecunious Duke of Outland had sold for a very fine price to a husky-voiced and highly suspect individual named Hark Chaffery. The latter was known to be a power in the shadowy reaches where men did not work but thrived on thievery and gambling and blackmail. Chaffery had come up from the kinchin lay, which was the lowest form of theft, to a monarchy in easy money and he had called a meeting of his henchmen to set into motion the greatest tontine the country had ever known.

This precious crew worked all day over the details and Chaffery himself, having a keen head on his puny, sloping shoulders, had proposed several innovations which delighted the shrewder of his men and were calculated to set the country into a flurry of eager participation. They never gave as much as a thought to the possibility, nay, the certainty, that on this very day the Duke of Wellington and his allied armies would face the dreaded Napoleon on a bloody battlefield close to the city of Brussels to which history would give the name of Waterloo.

2

At ten o'clock on Tuesday, June 20, Samuel Carboy started to walk to Capel Court, wearing a frown which added to the severity of his normally stern countenance. He proceeded at a slow gait, although it was certain he would be late for the opening, setting his feet down flatly and loudly as though providing periods for the sentences of his orderly thought. He paid no attention to the excitement in the streets which was mounting every minute and it might have been assumed that he was not going to the new Stock Exchange after all, for he passed by Shorter's Lane and turned into the Hercules Tavern. This would have been a miscalculation, however, for the men who built the new Exchange had provided quietly an extra entrance through this orderly and rather famous eating house. During each day, between the hours of ten and four, there was much running back and forth through the swinging door which led to the Floor, with pots of ale and tots of gin and glasses of brandy, not to mention the chops which members wanted broiled for them and the carrying of notes to such as had wandered into the tavern for a moment's rest. After the Exchange closed, the members would congregate there for a bite or even a deviled bone while Jack Prance and his singing quartet distracted them from unpleasant memories of the day. The place had a more than customary air of sobriety when Samuel Carboy entered. Ma'am, the only name ever applied to the female proprietor, sat watchfully at her elevated desk. The patrons looked glum and there was little talk going on. Carboy was not surprised at this. All England, he knew, had reason to feel glum at this moment; later there might be a change.

"Well, Mr. Carboy," said one of the patrons, who was seated in a corner over an early chop, "it seems the ironer wasn't up to it after all."

Carboy stopped and regarded the speaker with a disapproving air. "So, you believe this rumor, do you, Pinchley? Well, I have just this to say to you—and to all others like you. If the duke has met Napoleon," raising a clenched fist over his head to lend extra emphasis, "then he has smashed him to earth, never to rise again."

Pinchley indulged in a grin which contained a suggestion of sly triumph, as though to get the better of Samuel Carboy was compensation for the consequences of a national defeat. "There's no reason to doubt it. The Dutchmen came a-running through the streets of Brussels Sunday afternoon and yelling that Boney was on their heels. They'd threw away their guns in their hurry. A messenger arrived late last night as had seen them with his own eyes. No, Mr. Carboy, we might as well stand up to it. We've been beat and that's all there is to it."

"There's no word yet at Downing Street," declared Carboy stoutly.

Pinchley's sense of triumph broke out all over his face. "If you're so sure of this, Mr. Carboy, I suppose you're going to step in there and back your convictions by buying up everything?"

Carboy had been standing in an attitude which all his acquaintances would have recognized: feet planted wide apart, head held up straight, hands playing with the heavy gold chain across his waistcoat. He looked at the other man for several moments in a heavy silence.

"That," he said, speaking each word clearly and portentously, "is exactly what I'm going to do."

Near the door Carboy was stopped by another of the tavern regulars. "Samuel," said this man, who aspired to a closer acquaintance with the well-known Eastern merchant, "I know you had to put that Pinchley in his place. But, great gammon, man, the story is true! Boney has beaten us again."

"I don't believe it."

The other man dropped his voice to a lower pitch. "Listen to me," he said. "Nathan Rothschild just went in there. I didn't see him because he took the second door on Shorter's Lane but they say he looked gloomy. He didn't speak to anyone, and that's not Nathan's way. No, sir, it ain't; he's generally got a smile and a word for everyone. The story's got around that he's come down to sell everything he can get rid of—*before the bottom falls out!*"

"I don't believe it."

"Well, what about this? Your own partner has given instructions to his broker to sell everything he has."

Carboy threw back his head and laughed. "That," he said, "I can believe."

The Floor was in a state of turmoil when Carboy entered through the swinging door. It was a high arched building with galleries under the ceiling and massive pillars under the galleries. The pillars served another purpose besides that of holding up the building. Each was the center of a particular school of trading. Consols had three of them, banks had two, shipping lines and stagecoaches and private concerns had one each. There was one small support in a dark corner which had come to be recognized as belonging exclusively to old Heaven Beck, for it was here that he tied up the dog he brought with him each day for company.

The excitement was due, of course, to the still unauthenticated but, alas, well-supported rumor that Bonaparte had beaten the Duke of Wellington.

The members to a man were trying to sell, or so it seemed. Anyone who could get possession of a chair was standing up above the crush and repeating the usual formula with frantic vehemence: "I'm here. I'll sell. D'ye hear me? I'll sell. I've got consols and I've got bank paper and I've got shipping stocks. All I'm asking is *decent* offers. I'm not going to give these securities away." One member varied this by shouting in tones of intense indignation: "Come, men, come! You're English, ain't you? Do you want to take advantage of a temporary darkness on the horizon of Old England? Do you want to traffic in our momentary despair? Have you fallen so low that you have no feeling of shame? If you want to buy, come up now and buy like men. Support the market, if ye're honest Englishmen. D'ye want to drive prices down to nothing?"

A diminutive and sprucely dressed broker caught a glimpse of the grim countenance of Samuel Carboy and came over to his side.

"Samuel," he said, in as cautious a tone as could be employed and still be made audible in all that noise, "what is it to be today?"

The Eastern merchant looked down at him and said in much the same tone as he had used in the tavern, "Westerby, I'm going to buy."

"Buy!" The little broker's voice rose almost to a yelp. "Buy, Samuel? You're joking, Samuel. You're having me on."

"Westerby," declared Carboy, "our army under the Duke of Wellington could *not* be beaten by the usurper Bonaparte. I refuse to believe it. Make what you will out of these rumors. *I* don't believe them. Westerby, I am going to buy."

"But, Samuel, Samuel!" The broker was speaking now in a beseeching voice. "Haven't you heard about Nathan Rothschild? He came in here, looking like a death's head of gloom. That's *exactly* what he looked like. He stood about and said just exactly nothing at all. He kept tamping his hat down firmer on his head and looking very sick and glum. And then he turned and walked out. That means he's selling. If he intended to buy, he'd stay here and wait for his prices, wouldn't he? It stands to reason, Samuel, it stands to reason."

"Westerby, I'm going to buy."

They retired to a relatively quiet corner and Carboy gave the broker his orders. Westerby marked the prices down on slips of paper, shaking his head and making little clucking sounds of disapproval. At the finish he shoved the slips into the silver-embroidered pocket of his plum-colored coat. "It may be some time before they get as low as this," he said. "But they'll get there and you'll have what you want. You'll be ruined in the end, Samuel, mark my words. If you change your mind, get word to me fast."

Throughout this talk, Carboy had remained the very picture of confidence and imperturbability. When Westerby left, however, it was different. Carboy was human and doubts began to perch on his great solid shoulder and whisper in his ear, "Suppose these rumors are true?" He became a prey to doubts of his own. "If the duke *is* beaten," he said to himself, "I'll take a drubbing.

I won't be ruined because I'm buying outright. But if these damnable rumors are true, I'll be well clipped."

He began to pace up and down, his arms folded behind his back. The firm beat of his feet suggested confidence, a belief in the solidity of the wooden walls of the British fleet, in the unbreakable squares of red-coated infantry, in the omnipotence of the Iron Duke. But some of the scurrying, screeching, sweating mob saw that his brow was knitted in thought and they were sure they could read uncertainty in his eyes.

Prices continued to drop but they had not yet reached the levels set by Carboy. He stationed himself near the blackboard which occupied a large part of the wall space under the great clock. Here the figures at which deals had been made were hastily chalked up and then almost as quickly brushed off to make room for later quotations. The board was badly crowded since the directors of the Exchange had decreed that the names of defaulting members were to be legibly inscribed thereon in white paint.

To find some relief from the anxiety which was beginning to gnaw at his vitals, Carboy took advantage of a moment when Heaven Beck was not busy. Such moments were rare on a day like this. The galleries were filled with clerks on one side and patrons on the other and from both sides there was a steady dropping of notes to the Floor—confirmations of sales, new instructions to the Floor men, demands for information. It was the amiably obsequious Mr. Beck's duty to collect these notes as they fell and see that they reached the proper persons. Because he kept an eye always on the galleries, he had acquired a permanently arched neck and this accounted for his nickname. Around the noon hour, the nature of the missiles dropped over the gallery railings would change radically. The hungry men working upstairs would throw steaks and chops and cutlets to the Floor and Beck would collect them and see that they were taken to a small bakeshop owned by his brother where they would be broiled for a fee of one penny. His mind must have consisted of an infinitesimal number of small pigeonholes in which he could keep all these errands straight, for it was a fact that he never delivered a well-broiled steak to a clerk who had thrown him a cutlet, or vice versa.

Carboy maintained a certain note of dignity in everything he did and in particular he was addicted to the fine old English name of "mister." He did not like to be called Samuel or Carboy, even by his closest acquaintances (he had few if any real friends), and on occasions, when he had been addressed in this manner, he had been known to say, "Sir, you 'mister' me and I'll 'mister' you." He even extended the full dignity of proper salutation to one as humble as old Heaven Beck.

"What dog did you bring with you this morning, Mr. Beck?" he asked.

"The melancholy one, sir," answered the messenger, not daring to remove his gaze from the galleries.

Carboy looked into a dark corner behind them where he could see the long ears and sharply angled eyes of a veteran hound. "He does look a bit dismal, Mr. Beck," he commented.

"Ah, yes, sir. It's a trial to the poor fellow when I bring him with me. And yet, Mr. Carboy, sir, he would be offended if I passed him over and didn't give him his fair turn. He don't like being seen on the streets with me, sir. You see, Mr. Carboy, sir, he's a dog what has come down in the world. He'd been stole and an officer brought him to me instead of turning him in to the pound. We never did find out who he'd belonged to but, Mr. Carboy, sir, as sure as I'm standing here, that dog belonged once to a dook or a hurl."

"Well, a melancholy dog is the right kind to have here today, Mr. Beck. A good many of us are rather down in the mouth."

"But not you, sir, from what I hear."

So, the news of what he was doing had been spreading. Carboy did not know whether to be angry or pleased. This might hamper his efforts to pick up the securities he wanted at the prices he had stipulated and it might also make him the object of more ridicule if the rumor from the Continent proved true. At the moment, however, it gave him a certain prominence in the eyes of his fellows, and to this he did not object.

It was because of the uncertainty from which he could not escape that the Eastern merchant had fallen into talk with the messenger. Such trivial conversation could not be said to divert his mind but it provided him with a means of filling in time. A fluttering message from the clerks' gallery had taken Beck away for several moments and on his return Carboy asked another question.

"What do you call this one?"

"Well, sir, it's one of my little jokes, sir. You see, as he's so very melancholy, I calls him Hamlet." The messenger dropped his voice to a whisper as though he feared the brooding canine in the dark corner would hear him. "D'ye know what I think, Mr. Carboy, sir? I think he's ashamed of it. He thinks it's a vulgar name, sir, for a dog of his linige. He answers grudging to it."

"How many animals have you now, Mr. Beck?"

The messenger, still keeping his head thrown back so that he would not miss anything dropped from the regions above, counted on his fingers. "They grows on us all the time, Mr. Carboy, sir. When we got to ten, we said, no more of this. When it reached twenty, we said to ourselves, my brother and I, this is the end and no mistake. But somehow, sir, we've got sixteen dogs now and eight cats and one rabbit. Yes, Mr. Carboy, sir, it's quite a family. It keeps my brother and me busy all our evenings, brushing them up and looking after their little illnesses. Do you know what I think, sir? Every last one of the twenty-five of 'em prefers my brother to me. Do you know why, sir? Because he comes home with such a fine smell of cooking and frying and broiling about him."

"You know, sir," went on Beck, "we hope sometime to retire, my brother and me. We're saving all the time and it may just happen that a member here, sir, will say to me, 'Beck, if you have a few dibs put them on so-and-so,' and I'll make a pot of oof, sir. If that does happen, we'll take all our old fellows out into the country where we won't have to live in an empty warehouse with just a bit of yard full of rusty wheels and things. We're looking forward to it, sir. It will be so much better for them."

The hours passed, rapidly and noisily. A frantic body of men who owned stocks and bonds kept trying to sell at prices which would enable them to keep a roof over their heads while the buyers, a selfishly realistic lot, stood off at the sides and waited. None of the latter were prepared to buy until they could be sure the profits would raise fine, handsome roofs over *their* heads. Two topics of conversation monopolized all of them, apart from the chaffer of the market. Had any definite report come from Brussels? Was Nathan buying or selling?

Samuel Carboy stalked up and down and brooded. Was he being a stubborn fool? Would the roof of *his* house be torn away in this financial storm? Would the day come when his wife and his fine son and his pretty daughter would blame him for what he had done?

Westerby had been coming at intervals on excited tiptoe to press into his hands little slips of paper which conveyed the information that so many consols or so many shares of stock had been bought in his name at such and such a price. He was in so deeply now that he wondered if he should not begin to protect himself by selling. He acknowledged that it would be wise but he could not bring himself yet to the point of acting. It seemed like a betrayal of his belief in the inevitability of British dominance, of his faith in the Iron Duke.

At an early hour of the afternoon, just after Westerby had notified Carboy that the last of his buying orders had been carried out, after all the steaks and chops had been entrusted to the care of old Heaven Beck and had duly been fried or broiled and had then been consumed on the Floor or up in the dark recesses of the galleries, there came a loud sound of the Capel Court door opening and slamming shut and an outburst of excited voices. Then, with the suddenness of an earthquake and with all the force of a hurricane at sea, the Floor was filled with screeching voices and the sound of stamping feet. Hands were waved frantically in the air and men thumped each other on the back and shouted incoherently until they were hoarse. Some men went off to corners and sat down and some burst into tears; but in every mind, whether that of winner or loser, there was a sense of exultation. The country had been saved.

Official word had reached Downing Street. Napoleon had not defeated Wellington. The Iron Duke had won the victory—a smasher, sir, as the members confided to each other—and Boney at this very moment was racing for Paris with British cavalry at his heels.

Business went on, of course, more frantically than before. Prices went up, up, up. Pandemonium reigned as the few bulls waited to squeeze the last pound of profit out of this miraculous turn and the bears sought to recover at the most favorable terms the securities they had sacrificed earlier.

Samuel Carboy was one of those who found a seat for himself. He was not going to sell anything. His legs, which were noticeably substantial and strong, had suddenly begun to tremble. Westerby sought him out in the quiet corner he had selected.

"You're lucky, Samuel," said the broker. "But you've a right to be because you've got as much iron in you as the duke himself."

"Thanks, Mr. Westerby," said the merchant. "Do you know yet what Nathan was doing?"

"Buying. He was buying right from the start."

Carboy became aware, after the broker had left him, that the stool he had taken was close to Heaven Beck's dog. He saw, moreover, that Hamlet was sitting up straight and looking about him as though he understood what had happened and was as proud of the victory as any bellowing bull or wilted bear on the Floor. Carboy leaned over reluctantly, being a little afraid of dogs, and patted the loose skin of the canine's head. "Hamlet," he said, "I'm beginning to agree with your master. You're quite a fine fellow, sir. You're a regular John Bull of a dog."

3

Samuel Carboy's mood changed as soon as his legs recovered from their brief spell of shakiness. A sense of pride took possession of him. And why not? He had stuck to his guns as resolutely as Wellington's redcoats. He had refused to be stampeded by rumors or diverted by the almost unanimous pessimism of the Floor. He had bought while everyone was crying, "Sell!" He deserved his reward.

When the hands of the big clock touched four and the bell up under the roof gave the closing signal of two long and three short strokes, he got to his feet. His nankeen trousers had become hitched up over his high boots and he had to stamp his feet to get them down into place. His tie, which had been arranged hurriedly that morning, had slipped to one side and he had to struggle to get it straight. He gave the crumpled tails of his gray frock coat an impatient smoothing.

The members were streaming in a body through the swinging doors of the tavern and Samuel Carboy, holding his head high, followed along in the rear of the procession. He was always treated with the respect due his established position in the City but this evening there was a touch of deference in the way he was received. Groups seated at tables called to him to join them. Members who were still on their feet bowed to him and murmured congratulations. He seated himself finally at a table where half a dozen customers sat. He knew them all and did not mind the questions which were directed at him. Had he been in partnership with Nathan Rothschild all the time? Had he known of the semaphores the latter had placed all the way from the tip of Kent to a tower just outside the city so that the news could be received in a matter of minutes once the packet put in from Belgium?

Carboy gave one answer only. "I was not in cahoots with anyone. I backed my own judgment. That was all, gentlemen."

Jack Prance and his gleemen were on a raised platform at one end of the long bar and at intervals they obliged with medleys of popular songs. There was a formality about this part of the entertainment which never varied. As the last note died away the company would put down their glasses and applaud generously. Jack Prance would then step forward and bow and receive another round of clapping. After waiting until the last faint echo of a hand-clap had died, the leader would graciously nod to his helpers, who would bow once quickly before sitting down.

"One more go at it, Jack," called a customer, looking at his watch.

Prance never needed a second invitation, particularly on a memorable occasion such as this. He stood up and began on a song of his own composition which he called "Good Old London." In the course of it he would imitate all the cries of the street hawkers, the trumpets of the stagecoaches, the brisk orders of sergeants on parade. But he got no further than the first two lines which ran,

"Hark at me, friends, does anyone know
Why London is called Old Frog-and-Toe?"

when the same customer, who had asked for a final round of melody, interrupted him.

"None of that gammon, Jack Prance," he called. "We're Englishmen and
we've won a great victory. On a night like this, give us something to stir our
blood."

"That's the ticket," called another. "Give us 'The British Grenadier,'
Jack."

So Prance and his partners lined up and sang the words of that classic
marching song. The customers to a man rose and joined in. Even Samuel
Carboy, who did not know one tune from another, added a discordant rumble. At the finish they gave three cheers for the poor blind king and three
more for the Duke of Wellington and ended up with a hiss for the crushed
Bonaparte. All the company sat down then except Samuel Carboy, who was
fumbling with the buttons of his tight-fitting coat.

"I am leaving, gentlemen," he said. The pride which filled him, and was
threatening to burst through his skin like the gas from a Montgolfier balloon, caused him to go on. "This has been the great day of my life, gentlemen. My faith in our invincibility has been justified. I return to my home
and family with a strong conviction that such reward as I may have earned
is my just due."

It was still light outside and the streets were packed with demonstrators.
Flags had sprouted out from all the windows and rooftops. Bonfires had
already been lighted at street corners. Generous but perhaps shortsighted
donors had contributed kegs of beer which were being broached with noisy
approval. Parades were being formed under banners bearing hastily impro-
vised slogans.

Carboy stood outside the entrance to the Hercules Tavern and grinned
broadly at the antics of the crowd. "St. George for Merrie England!" he said
to himself. "Here we see it, the final manifestation of the never-say-die
spirit."

A beggar came up to him and began to plead in a whining voice. Carboy
had some loose coins in a side pocket but he felt that he knew the tricks of
the begging fraternity of London too well to feel any sympathy, even on
such a joyful occasion.

"Get out of my way," he said in a matter-of-fact tone. "You filthy dog."

4

The Carboy family lived in the country and occupied a flat in town during
the week, a rather small one at the top of a house on Duke Street. The
house was so tall that they could look out over all of the surrounding roofs.

As they had been renting the place for fifteen years, it was certain that they had seen many famous men in that time alighting from their carriages in front of Almack's and, with equal certainty, a stoutish lady with a lovely face waddling in and out of Pickering Place, whose name is recorded in history as Emma Hamilton.

Samuel Carboy was greeted at the door of the flat on this important evening by his wife. Mrs. Carboy was a well-set-up woman with good eyes and hair, although it might have seemed to some that her nose was rather prominent; an inheritance from her father, "Whip" Hanlon, a rough diamond whose fortune had been made, or so it was whispered, from black cargo. Carboy's eyes opened with surprise, for his spouse was handsomely attired in a blue satin dress trimmed with swan's-down and was wearing slippers with lashings of white and gold.

"Are we going out, Belle?" he asked.

His good lady gave her head a toss. "We were invited for dinner this morning," she said. "Or, let us say, we were *ordered*. To fill in, of course."

Carboy frowned. "The Graces'?"

"Yes. That woman again. Because she's the niece of the Duke of Outland and so plain she couldn't catch anyone but that social climber of a partner of yours, she thinks she can keep us at her beck and call." The daughter of Whip Hanlon flushed with resentment, recalling the years of condescension she had endured. "Sam, this is the last time. I won't take anything more from her after tonight—*or* tonight, for that matter."

"George Ninian Grace," declared her husband, "is not in my good books at the moment. If you want to let them have it, old girl, I won't object. Lay it on as thick as you like." The good humor roused in him by the thought of his wife dealing roughly with the genteel mate of his partner disappeared as he looked down at the clothes he was wearing. "These won't do, I suppose."

"No, they will not. And you'll have to be quick about changing. I ordered a cab to take us to Their High and Mightinesses and it'll be here in ten minutes."

"Come along with me then. I've something to tell you while I dress."

When they reached their bedroom, Mrs. Carboy said in an appealing tone: "Please, Sam, breeches tonight. George Grace always wears them. And I must say he looks handsome in them. It's not proper to wear those hideous long things."

Carboy grunted and reached out a pair of the long things from the wardrobe. Of course George Ninian Grace (he always called his partner Ninny in his mind and even sometimes in his speech) looked well in breeches. He had a good leg. His own leg, Carboy knew, was a strong and serviceable one but it was undeniably knobby. The battle of breeches versus trousers, which was being waged all over England, was based on this point. Men with well-rounded calves stood out for breeches, those who were bandy, or skinny or knock-kneed, demanded the right to cover their limbs decently.

"I will *not* wear breeches," he said positively.

"You are *so* stubborn, Sam. Your legs aren't really bad."

To conciliate her, he selected a frilled shirt with collar points which threatened damage to his eyes, and over a white waistcoat he slipped on a handsome evening coat of dark blue. As he struggled with the cravat, he told his wife everything that had happened that day. Belle Carboy listened in a state of speechless delight.

"Then—then—" she said finally, "we are rich, are we, Sam?"

"My dear Belle," declared the merchant, studying his appearance without much pleasure in the tall looking glass on casters which occupied a large part of one wall, "no businessman worth his salt ever allows his wife to know he is doing well until he is downright rich. I have been—ahem—prosperous for quite a few years, m'dear, although you've never had reason to suspect it." What happened today did not make me a rich man. It made me richer."

His wife's face lighted up ecstatically. "Then we'll build the new wing on the house? And have a proper dining room?"

"We'll have the properest dining room in all England. One with a minstrels' gallery, by gad."

"Oh, Sam, a minstrels' gallery! How wonderful! And you'll let me go it about the furnishings?"

Carboy's face relaxed into the first semblance of a smile he had displayed since climbing the laborious stairs. "Yes, Belle, you may go it." Then caution reasserted itself. "Within reason, of course, m'dear. Within reason."

"There!" Mrs. Carboy's tone expressed the disappointments she had suffered all through the years when she had had no reason to suspect the height of his prosperity. "You give with one hand and take away with the other. When I come into my own property, I'll show you, Samuel Carboy, what I mean by going it."

"If you have to wait for that father of yours to die, you'll be an old woman when you come into your property, Belle. And I'll be"—he puffed out his chest unconsciously—"the richest man in England."

At this point Mrs. Carboy remembered something she had intended to tell her husband as soon as he arrived. She spoke in a hesitant tone. "I had a letter today. From Allie."

Carboy was in the act of brushing some hairs from the lapel of his coat. He looked up sharply.

"What did Alfred have to say for himself?"

"Well—not much. It was just one of his nice affectionate letters. He—he says he doesn't feel disposed to go to Oxford in the fall."

Carboy's face turned a sudden shade of red. "Oh, he doesn't want to go to college! Fine, fine, fine! What does the young whippersnapper want to do? He tells me he doesn't feel the business is the place for him. He doesn't want to carry on a tradition of a full century and a half. Wouldn't it be a fine thing to have no Carboy to run things?" He was working himself up to a high pitch of indignation. "And he didn't feel disposed to be a soldier. You remember, Belle, that I offered to buy him a commission. But he wouldn't have any of *that*."

"I was against him going into the army," said Mrs. Carboy sharply. "I'd have scratched your eyes out if you had tried to force him in. Our handsome, peace-loving son in a uniform and teaching men how to kill!"

"If he had been in the army, he'd have had a share in this great victory the Duke of Wellington has won."

"And he would probably be lying dead on the field this very minute! Is that what you would like, you unnatural father!" The mother of the undecided Alfred was beginning to weep. "Let me tell you this, Samuel Carboy, I know he would have been killed! I went down to the greengrocers' late this afternoon and they said the loss of life in this battle was simply terrible. A fine father you are, wishing your son had been in it!"

"There you go, twisting what I say! All soldiers aren't killed when they fight a battle. Alfred would have come through. He's a Carboy, isn't he? The Carboys are lucky, as you ought to know. There's no French bullet made with the name of Carboy on it. And you know how the Graces have lorded it over us because their Julian is in the navy. He's only a year older than Alfred and they talk as though he's going to take Nelson's place. And *he* hasn't been killed, has he?"

"This terrible pride of yours! I believe you want your son to risk his life so you can go in and boast to that stupid partner of yours. What kind of a father are you, anyway?" She applied a handkerchief to her eyes. "Our fine, lovable Allie a soldier!"

Carboy was beginning to look abashed. "Come, Belle. You know I didn't mean it that way. I love my son, of course. Do you know what I was thinking as I drove home tonight? That I wished he had been there, right on the Exchange, so he could have watched me. It might have made him proud of me and—and that's a commodity he's been pretty short of."

"You just leave him alone for a while and he'll find out what he wants to do. I don't see any sense in him going to Oxford when he isn't going to be a rector or one of these men who stay there and teach and have to wear thick glasses because they read so much, and forget to get dressed for their classes. Let him have a little more time. He's a fine, clever boy and worth a dozen of this Julian Grace you keep throwing up to us."

"There, there, Belle. Stop your sniveling. We'll have to be starting right away."

At this point the sound of the *plop! plop!* of horses' hoofs rose from the street. They heard a muzzy voice say, "Whoa! Prinny!" The hoofbeats ceased in front of the house.

"There it is," said Mrs. Carboy. She reached into the wardrobe and produced a silk pelisse which she draped over one arm. A turban of the same color as her gown, with a white plume sticking up straight into the air to an almost alarming height, completed her costume. She slipped a hand under her husband's arm and led him impatiently to the stairs.

Her mind cast ahead to anticipated slights at the hands of her husband's partner and his demanding wife. "Niece of a duke, is she?" she said in a bitter whisper. "Well, he's the poorest duke in the country anyway."

5

The Grace family reversed the living arrangements of the Carboys. Their place was in the city, a large house on a short street near Swallow Place, a smug little street which drew distinction from its proximity to Hanover Square without involving its residents in the expensive level of living and the high social standards of that notable quarter. George Ninian Grace had often been heard to say, "I live just off Hanover Square," and to take a great deal of satisfaction out of it. In the summers the family moved to a small house which they rented from their kinsman, the Duke of Outland; a very convenient arrangement all around, for it was a charming place with a fine view, and the rent, as the impoverished old duke said, "came in devilish handy."

The Dowager Duchess of Abercorn was coming to the dinner and so was Sir Cully Granger, and so the Graces awaited the arrival of their guests in a certain state of tension. Grace himself, looking quite as distinguished in his black breeches and coat with its satin cording as Mrs. Carboy had intimated he would, interspersed his pacing about the drawing room with dashes into the dining room to make sure that the bench on which the claret was warming had not been placed too near the tiny fire (which had been lighted for this purpose solely) and to consult the butler on the question of how long it should be kept there. Anyone who knew that he had suffered heavy financial losses that day would have assumed that his lack of calm was due to that unfortunate circumstance, a view which his wife shared.

She was quite as plain as the daughter of Whip Hanlon had said. The hope had been in her mind as she dressed that the hint of a train on her black velvet gown would give her added dignity but, if the truth must be told, it did nothing more than accentuate the dumpiness of her figure. By adopting the latest "twig" (which was the prevalent word for fad) and wearing a monocle on a white ribbon, she had succeeded in making herself seem a little silly instead of gay and fashionable.

"Georgie," she said in an affectionate tone, "you must not let your troubles show tonight. You must seem brave and—and Spartan, my poor dear."

Grace was tall and just a little stooped in the shoulders, which circumstance was quite an asset, for it gave him some of the air of a scholar. His nose, which was long and well chiseled, lent an aristocratic tinge to his face but his rather mild blue eyes seemed to enter a denial. He paused and frowned down at her.

"Adelicia, are you referring," he asked, "to what happened on the Exchange today?"

"My poor dear, what else could I mean?" Her tone was full of solicitude. "I know how you are suffering. How we are both suffering. It has been such a dreadful day and yet we have to greet our guests as though nothing had happened."

"Yes, yes," muttered Grace. "I'm sorry, Adelicia, that you brought it up. I had succeeded in forgetting all about it. My concern, if you must know, was about the claret."

"They'll all ask for port anyway," said the ducal niece, with a resigned sigh. It was not easy for her to forget the losses they had sustained through what she could not help thinking of as her husband's pusillanimity. "George, is it going to make any great difference? Will we be able to keep the house?"

There was a trace of testiness in Grace's reply. "Of course, my dear. Our profits from Grace and Carboy will continue to roll in, won't they? They'll increase, I expect, now that Napoleon is finally beaten and our ships from the East won't be interfered with."

"Is that a coach outside?" asked Mrs. Grace, forgetting their less imminent problems.

It was a coach. The first guests arrived, another of the numerous Outland connection and his wife, who were greeted as Louis and Charlotte. A portly banker with a pale wife on his arm was the next to put in an appearance. He shook his head at Grace and clucked sympathetically. Several more couples came in, including a member of Parliament and his spouse, and then Sir Cully Granger, with his round stomach and round head surmounted by a fuzzle of white hair. An illuminative story about him was more than half believed among his acquaintances: that his knighthood had been due to some mixing up of names among governmental clerks. The Carboys were announced immediately after Sir Cully, and the hostess greeted them with a sigh of relief which she made no effort to conceal.

"Oh, Belle and Samuel! I was so frightened. I was sure you were not going to get here until after the dear viscountess. And that would have been such a great error, wouldn't it!"

"We had to hurry to get here at all," said Mrs. Carboy, her fingers twitching with a desire to sink themselves into the fuzzy headdress of her hostess. "You must remember, Addie, that we knew nothing of this dinner until after Samuel left for the office. He came home late—having been at the Exchange where he did so *wonderfully* for himself today—and barely had time to dress." There was a glint in her eye when she added, "It's unfortunate, Addie, that you feel it necessary to worry about the mistakes we may make."

Mrs. Grace may not have heard the speech through. She was studying Samuel Carboy in a state of puzzlement. "You did *well* on the Exchange, Samuel? I thought everyone lost because news came through that we had been beaten."

"I didn't sell, ma'am," declared Carboy. "I bought."

Dinner was served a few minutes after the arrival of a bent old specter of a woman who was so shortsighted that she mistook Carboy for her host and said, as she caught a glimpse of his betrousered legs, "My dear George, you really shouldn't, you know." The dear viscountess was to prove an even greater trial to her hostess than the late-arriving Carboys, for she kept screwing up her eyes and asking: "Who are all these people, Adelicia? I don't seem to know any of them."

"You know Sir Cully Granger, my lady," reminded Mrs. Grace.

The viscountess raised her voice. "Oh! He's here, is he? I suppose that means they haven't discovered their mistake yet."

George Grace proposed the health of the king and, after it had been duly honored, cleared his throat. "In view of the great victory our army has won, we should now drink——" he was beginning, when his partner interrupted him by rising to his feet.

Carboy looked at the severe and critical faces about him. He was fully aware that his conduct in thus injecting himself into the proper and orderly course of things would be construed as bad manners but this had no effect on him. He felt he was entitled to have his say.

"George," he said, "I would like to have the honor of proposing this toast. I suppose it's against the rules. I'm never quite sure what the rules *are* in a case like this but, whatever they are, I think I have earned this right. I had so much faith in our great military leader that I refused to believe the reports circulated this morning. I had no information by way of special packet or sent over semaphores as others are supposed to have had. I knew, I knew as surely as I am standing here, that Wellington could not be defeated on a field of his own choosing. We all knew that he had chosen the rolling country around Waterloo. I was so convinced he would win a victory that I went to the Stock Exchange and risked—not ruin exactly but the most serious losses—in buying the stocks which other men were throwing away. I threw my personal resources into the effort to stem the tide. That is why I have risen so unceremoniously to demand this right."

His host nodded his head, rather stiffly. "And now, having your permission," pursued Carboy, "I propose that we drink to that great man who confounded the rumormongers and won the decisive battle of all history. I give you His Grace, the Duke of Wellington."

When the glasses had been lowered, the viscountess was heard to remark in her penetrating voice, "George, who is that man?" The host whispered something in reply. "He seems to have a sound view of things, George," went on the dowager. "I heard today that many men, who ought to have had more courage and patriotism, went down to that place and sold everything they possessed. It's a pleasure to know one who didn't." She added, after a moment, "I have no sympathy with such cowardice, George." There was a moment of dead silence and then the member of Parliament saved the situation by beginning to talk of something else.

The dinner was reasonably successful in spite of everything. The viscountess asked for claret and was kind enough to say it was "just right," and moreover she relented by addressing a remark or two in the general direction of Sir Cully Granger. George Grace, who could talk well, roused himself to his very best efforts, winning many titters of approval from the ancient lady. The food was excellent. Samuel Carboy indulged his appetite to the fullest and had nothing more to say.

"I don't know, Samuel, why you had to start the dear viscountess to talking like that," said Mrs. Grace petulantly, as she responded to the Carboy farewells. "It was very awkward, really."

"It has been an awkward kind of day, ma'am."

"I suppose you made a great deal of money out of whatever it was you did."

"I was entitled, ma'am, to whatever I made."

"My poor George," went on the hostess, who seemed determined to vent her nettled feelings, "has always said you have a knack for making money. I must be frank and say it isn't one I can admire myself."

"Perhaps I had better be frank too," said Carboy. His mouth had set in an expression which the members of the staff of Grace and Carboy knew very well, sometimes to their discomfort and sorrow. "It's because of this knack of mine that a certain firm has been so prosperous. It's a knack that others in the firm may possess but which they certainly have never displayed and so it's something you'll never see at close range, ma'am. But you benefit by it all the time, ma'am. If it were not for it, would you be able to give dinners like this?"

"I suppose, Samuel, you're chiding me——"

"I'm giving you a piece of advice. It's this. Never bite the hand that feeds you."

The Carboys had little to say to each other on the drive back to their flat. The port, as usual, had induced in Mrs. Carboy a tendency to morose introspection. She kept going over in her mind everything their hostess had said to them and waxing more indignant with each hoofbeat. It was not until they went rattling across Piccadilly that she put her feelings into words.

"I'm sure that woman hates us," she said.

"She isn't capable of any deep emotion," declared Carboy. "She's just a petty and stupid creature. I wouldn't worry about it if I were you, m'dear. I hardly think we will have to go to their house again and be snubbed by them in front of their equally stupid friends."

His wife turned and stared at him. It was impossible to read her expression in the darkness of the interior of the cab but it was apparent from her voice that she had been aroused to a point of excitement and eagerness.

"Sam!" she said. "Oh, Sam! Is it to be soon? Is it really?"

Carboy did not respond immediately. He seemed to be thinking it over. "Well, yes," he said finally. "Very soon."

6

When they entered the flat a whirlwind in a flannelette nightgown flung herself at them, crying: "Hello, Mama! Hello, Papa! Here I am. And aren't you glad?"

Mrs. Carboy looked at her daughter Isabelle with a stern eye, completely overlooking the beauty of the girl, with her eyes half closed from sleep (but even more attractive because of it) and brown curls disheveled under a lace nightcap.

"I don't know about your father," she said in a sharp tone, "but I am not glad at all."

Isabelle took her father's hand fiercely in her own and laid her head against his arm.

"I didn't want to go to Miss Bordley's old school, Mama. It was you who picked it out. It was you who had it all arranged before I knew anything about it, or my dear Papa-sy either."

Mrs. Carboy's feeling began to verge on a sense of outrage; she stepped across to the fifteen-year-old child and gave her a shake which dislodged her from the sanctuary of her father's arm.

"Isabelle," she demanded, "what have you done? No evasions, mind. No holding back. Tell us everything, young lady, because I mean to talk to Miss Bordley and I'll get at the truth anyway."

The girl made no answer. A sulky look had taken away much of her natural charm. She snuggled back against her father's side.

"Come, Isa," said Samuel Carboy in a placatory tone. "Tell us what happened. You mustn't be afraid."

There was another moment of silence. Finally the girl said, "I kicked her."

Mrs. Carboy flew into a temper at this piece of information. "You kicked her! You dare to stand there and tell me that you kicked Miss Gertrude Jane Bordley! You ungrateful child, you—you hoodlum!"

"Yes, Mama. Right on her skinny old shin."

"But why? Why? Whatever could have induced you to do such a dreadful thing?"

Isabelle established herself in a chair and tucked her heels up under her. Now that the truth was out, she seemed very much relieved. She pouted out her pretty lips and addressed herself to her father.

"She never liked me, Papa. She said mean things all the time. She said I was not bright at my lessons. And I *am* bright—when I want to try. She knows that. And when I caught Nonnie Hill-Barrows over the ankle in a game of shinty, she said I did it on purpose."

"And did you do it on purpose?" demanded her mother in a voice which indicated that her patience had been drawn out very fine indeed.

Isabelle pouted again and said: "Yes, I did. I hate Nonnie. Most of the girls hate her. Her uncle does something at court and she thinks she's better than the rest of us."

"How did you get here?"

"I came in a cab. That mousy little Miss Ginley, who teaches history, came with me."

"And your clothes?"

"They were packed by the maids and put in the cab with us."

Her mother looked at her with a face which grew redder every moment. "They don't want you back then. Well, you get off to bed now, young lady. We don't want to hear anything more out of you, *if* you please. Your father and I will have to talk it over and then, of course, Miss Bordley will have to be seen."

"Papa!" cried the girl. "Don't let her send me back to that school. I don't like it. I'm very unhappy there. If she sends me back—I'll kick Miss Bordley again."

"You go to bed this instant."

Isabelle obeyed her mother with a final appealing look over her shoulder for her father's benefit. It was apparent even in the bagginess of her nightgown that she was a very tidy little bundle of femininity indeed. It was also very apparent that she was completely aware of this and intended to take every advantage of it.

Samuel Carboy busied himself in preparing glasses of brandy for himself and his wife, making quite a thing out of testing the water in the kettle to see if it were hot enough for the purpose. He was dreading the outbreak which he knew to be coming.

"Well, Samuel Carboy, I hope you're satisfied!" said his spouse, stationing herself at his elbow and glaring at him indignantly. "Spoiling that child the way you do! If you would just save some of the affection you waste on her for your fine son, it would be better for all of us."

"I try to be fair to both of them. You know I do, Belle."

"This is the third school she's left under disgraceful circumstances. Where are we going to send her now? She is going to be finished right and graduate somewhere."

"I don't keep the names of girls' schools in my head. I have more important things to occupy myself. Such as making a great fortune for you and our children to enjoy. Making it when I had to stand out against the opinion of everyone. Only two men in England had the backbone to do the brave thing today. I was one. Nathan Rothschild was the other."

"I know, Samuel, I know." His wife's tone became more restrained. "I think I was chiefly angry with the child because she selected this day of all days to do this dreadful thing."

"Dreadful? I'm sure that old spinster had been giving her plenty of provocation. I know when I was a boy I kicked teachers on the shins. Many times."

"I see the child comes by it honestly then." Mrs. Carboy took a sip of her brandy and water. It seemed to have a soothing effect on her. "Well, we'll have to do something about it tomorrow. I'll talk to Miss Bordley. Will you come with me?"

"No. You can handle the situation." Carboy tossed off his glass, replaced it on a shelf and yawned. "I'm going to bed now. This has been the hardest and busiest day of my life."

CHAPTER TWO

1

The firm of Grace and Carboy had been in existence for more than one hundred and fifty years. It had been formed in the early days of active trading with India and farther east, and from the very first it had been a profitable concern. It had established a record even more unusual than this long run of mounting success; there had always been a Grace and there had always been a Carboy, one of each and no more. At first the Grace interest had predominated, the first Carboy being a sea captain with experience in the trading methods of the East but little capital. Gradually, however, the junior interest had grown, the Carboys being men of energy and initiative and the Graces being gentlemanly and somewhat averse to the rough-and-tumble of business.

Nearly a century after its founding, the firm had become an equal partnership. The two partners of that particular period, being in thorough accord and desirous of establishing their comfortable and well-paying enterprise on a basis of perpetuity, had entered into an agreement which was to be binding on future participants. The firm was not to be allowed to pass into alien hands unless there ceased to be either Graces or Carboys to carry it on. It was decided between them, and solemnly signed and attested, that in case the partners of the future fell into such lack of harmony that to continue in business together would be impossible one must buy out the other. Only as a last resort was the house to fall to outside interests. This arrangement was not proof of a David and Jonathan relationship between the two men who made the agreement. It was, in reality, the basis on which many partnerships of the day were formed.

Although the partnership had thus become one of even share and control, the respective parts of the families had never changed. The Grace partner always had the big center office with a personal secretary, a cheerful fire blazing in the fireplace in cold weather, a string of visitors who dropped in and chatted over tea (at office expense, naturally), and the right to speak for the firm on any matters which did not concern important things such as business and profits. The Carboys had always attended to the more prosaic affairs such as the buying, the selling, the keeping of books, the management of the staff. The Grace played the gilded figurehead, the Carboy worked hard and long to make the money on which both families lived.

Oddly enough the Carboys had never openly objected to this unfair arrangement. They never quite lived down the bluff old sea dog who had represented them in the forming of the business. The Graces, on the other hand, lived on the very dim recollection that the first of them belonged in a many-times-removed way to the minor nobility. The Grace wives had always been condescending to the Carboy wives. The scale of living of the Graces had always been above that of the Carboys.

The oddity of this tacit understanding became particularly apparent when George Ninian Grace and Samuel Carboy found themselves representing the two families. Carboy, as has perhaps become apparent in some degree at least, was a man of quite extraordinary ability, the possessor of remarkable judgment and a driving, blistering will. George Ninian Grace was different in every respect. He was a pure dilettante who believed he would become a great painter if he could ever get the time to develop his gifts (he had all the time in the world actually) and who wasted his days in perfectly inconsequential hobbies and interests. Samuel Carboy worked early and late. George Ninian Grace fell into the habit more and more of absenting himself from the handsome center office. It was strange that they reversed themselves in the matter of political beliefs. Carboy was a rock-ribbed conservative, a Billy Pitt kind of man. Grace had been a Fox liberal, an amateur Jacobin and an admirer of Napoleon Bonaparte.

Owing to the abilities and the energy of Samuel Carboy, the firm had achieved new high levels of prosperity, even though most of the Continent was cut off throughout the period of the Napoleonic Wars. This had not stimulated his partner to take a more active share in things. On the contrary, the additional profits had led Grace to participate even more in outside activities. He was, as Mrs. Carboy had pointed out, a social climber.

His one effort to share the increased responsibilities had come about some years before and had not been exactly successful. There had been some trouble with a native ruler of one of the smaller Indonesian islands. A sailor on a G. and C. trading vessel had carried off a native girl, or some such trifling matter. The shah or emir or sultan of the island (George Grace never did discover his proper title and called him any one of the foregoing as the fancy seized him) decided nevertheless that the company ships should be banned forever from trading with his people. It was decided in London, therefore, that some unusual means of placating him would have to be found. Things were in a turmoil at the time and Samuel Carboy knew better than to leave the conduct of the business in the hands of the ineffectual George Ninian Grace. It would be better to let the latter try his hand at playing ambassador. It was not hard to persuade Grace to undertake a mission of such dignity and he set out at once in the most comfortable of the trading vessels with his wife, his son, a nurse, a secretary and a cook; and a great supply of gifts for the irate ruler. It always thereafter remained uncertain whether he actually succeeded in seeing the dusky potentate or whether he dealt only with underlings. He was rather vague about the whole thing. All the gifts had been distributed, however, even though he came back without having reached any agreement for the lifting of the ban. He did not return empty-handed. He brought with him a great bronze statue of the heathen god Taku which he had purchased at considerable expense.

Samuel Carboy looked at this trophy and whistled with dismay. "The god Taku, eh?" he said to the beaming homecomer. "An ugly critter, isn't he? What are you going to do with him? Set him up in your drawing room?"

"No, no!" protested Grace. "I didn't buy him for myself. I bought him for the company."

"By gad, did you now," said Carboy. "And how is Old Dust-and-Dung going to be of any use to us?"

Grace was, among other things, an avid student of history. "It's this way, Samuel," he said. "There was a time when every place of business in London and every house had a sign instead of a number. If we had lived then we could have used this for our identification. The Sign of the Bronze God. A very original and notable thing, it would have been. Don't you agree?"

"How long ago was all this?"

"Oh, many hundreds of years ago."

"Well now, see here, George, we're living in the reign of George III and our exact location is very well known to anyone. In fact, we have a number."

"True," said Grace. "But we can still use it to make our house stand out from all other importing companies. It will be our trade mark. We'll set it up at the entrance."

Carboy gave the statue another look, a startled one. "This thing? Thunderation, George, it's so ugly it will scare away customers."

"Nonsense," declared Grace in a tone which said that Carboy was incapable of appreciating the finer things. "It will draw them like a magnet."

"Have it your own way then. We've sunk a healthy hunk of money in it and I suppose we ought to try to get some of it back. Unless," hopefully, "you would agree to having it melted down."

"Certainly not," declared Grace, thoroughly huffed and not realizing that his partner had put the suggestion forward in all seriousness.

So the god Taku stood for many years in all his ferocity and ugliness at the entrance to the offices. It became one of the familiar sights of the Ludgate Hill section. The business continued to prosper and perhaps Grace said to himself that he had been right and that some of the prosperity was due to the magnetic qualities of Taku. He never volunteered this opinion, however, in the presence of Samuel Carboy, whose aversion for the thing did not abate and who never called it anything but Old Dust-and-Dung. It would have required constant cleaning and polishing to keep this huge mass of bronze in good condition but, as such details were beneath the notice of George Grace in his fine office and because Samuel Carboy refused to do anything about it, the statue remained the butt of wind and rain and snow and dust as well as providing a home for the birds of the neighborhood, which built nests in the god's Medusa-like hair. Poor Taku became a very sorry-looking old god indeed and no doubt was very unhappy so far away from the blue skies and the sunshine of the land where he spent his first years. He must have resented the attentions of the city urchins who never acquired any proper awe of him and even took to shying rocks at his head. They finally succeeded in making a dent in his nose, thereby changing his whole appearance. He ceased to be a ferocious god of the woods and looked instead like a broken-down old city derelict who had been robbed of his clothes and in sheer desperation had draped himself in a torn sheet.

2

The offices of Grace and Carboy opened at seven o'clock and it was seldom indeed that Mr. Carboy arrived later than seven-thirty. When he failed to put in an appearance on the morning after his spectacular success on the Exchange there was much anxious speculation in the open rooms where clerks plied their pens as well as in the dark cubbyholes where minor officers labored. Had success gone to his head? Was he arranging for the investment of the vast sums he had made by his daring plunge?

The truth of the matter was that Mr. Carboy had been treated to a surprise at breakfast. He had come into the dining room on the very dot and he had finished his first cup of tea and was spearing with his fork at the bones of a kipper when his daughter entered the room. She greeted him cheerfully. "Good morning, Papa. May I join you for breakfast?"

Carboy's surprise was heightened by the way she had elected to garb herself. It was apparent that she had succumbed to the military influence, for over a pretty frock of pink muslin she had donned a Wellington mantle of black. It was becoming—there could be no doubt of that—but there could be no doubt either that it added several years to her age.

"Isa!" said Carboy, replacing his fork and staring at her. "Do you know that thing makes you look like a grown-up woman?"

"Do you really think I do?" The girl's dimples showed in a manifestation of delight. "That's the way I want to look. I've been trying so hard to."

"Are you aware also that the cloak you've got on belongs to your mother?"

"Yes, Papa. She'll be very angry when she finds out. But I won't be here."

"Are you aware—er—finally—that such cloaks are for evening wear only?"

Isabelle seated herself at the table. She curled up her nose at the kippers and said: "Boiled eggs, please, Papa-sy. Two. I'm hungry. And I can't eat them if they're too soft. May we have some marmalade?"

Carboy rang the bell for the one servant they kept in town, a prim woman of indefinite age whose name was Higgins. "Marmalade for Miss Isabelle. And two boiled eggs, four minutes."

"I know *everything* about clothes, Papa. You need never tell me anything about them. Of course, a Wellington cloak should be worn in the evening. But hasn't he just won a great battle, and shouldn't we do something about it? All I can do to celebrate it, Papa, is to wear a Wellington cloak. Besides, as you said yourself, it makes me look older. I almost think it makes me look a marriageable age."

Carboy was disturbed at this. "Nonsense! You're still a little girl at school. At least, you *should* be at school. You won't look ready for marriage for many years yet."

Isabelle tossed her head as she reached for a piece of toast. "Now *that* is talking nonsense. Of course I look marriageable. There's been one man already who would have liked to marry me."

Her father took serious alarm. "A man wanted to marry you? Who was he? Whoever he is, by gad, I'll call him out. I'll ruin him. If he holds a post of any kind, I'll see to it that he's discharged."

"Don't get so excited, Papa," said Isabelle calmly. "It was just our Latin teacher at Miss Bordley's. Such a nice little man with *such* a curly mustache."

"So, it was just your Latin teacher! I'll see you don't put a foot inside of that place again, no matter what your mother says or does."

The girl was now eating toast and marmalade with an almost greedy appetite. It must be mentioned that a small dab of the marmalade had attached itself to the tip of her nose. "I thought you would feel that way," she said, between bites. "All the girls were madly in love with him. Lor', how jealous they'd have been if they'd *dreamed* he preferred me."

Higgins brought in the eggs and Isabelle reached for one and cried out immediately: "Ooh! I've burned my fingers!" Carboy was staring at her in complete bewilderment. He had lost all interest in what was left of his breakfast. There was silence while the girl with great care chipped off the top of an egg.

"See here, Isa," he said finally. "I—I don't know what to make of all this. I suppose it's a sign you're growing up. I—I don't like it. And what did you mean when you said you wouldn't be here when your mother finds out you're wearing her cloak?"

Isabelle looked up from her egg and gave him the benefit of her very best smile; and to do her credit, and in spite of the dab of marmalade, it was the very best of all very best smiles which had been put on for certain purposes all the way down the ages. It was a dazzling thing, in fact, for a girl of her years and inexperience.

"I won't be here, Papa," she said. "Because I'm going out with you."

"With me?"

"With you, sir. I've never seen your offices, have I? I think it would be nice if I went with you this morning to the place where you do such very wonderful things. And if you took me all around and I met all your clerks and things."

The cragginess of Carboy's face melted away in a smile such as he had not employed for many years. "Why, yes, my pet. It would be *very* nice. We'll start as soon as you're through with your breakfast."

It was apparent as soon as the cab had crawled up the hill that there was something different about the offices of Grace and Carboy. Samuel Carboy stared out of the cab window in astonishment and sprang out as soon as they reached the door. "Binns!" he shouted. "Binns! Come here at once!"

In response to this choleric summons a small man came skipping out of the front door. His high bald dome and mutton-chop whiskers made him look like the popular dog of the moment which was called a Blenheim.

"Yes, sir. What is it, sir?"

Carboy raised his cane and pointed it at the statue of Taku. "That, Binns. What's been going on here?"

Someone had at last found a use for the bronze god. A large bill, printed in the blackest of type, had been pasted on the front of Taku's sole article of apparel.

"It was this way, sir," explained Binns, who acted in many capacities, as doorman, porter and general factotum to Carboy himself. "A man of Hark's came by this morning with a bundle of these bills under his arm——"

"A man of Hark's? Do you mean, by any chance, Hark Chaffery?"

"Yes, sir. He works for Hark Chaffery. And a swaggering, nasty sort of fellow he is. He sees me at the door but all he does is wink at me and say, 'Here's a good place for one of these blarsted things.' He has a pot of paste in his other hand and a brush and he swops a lot of it on the statue and has a bill stuck down afore I can say another word. I tells him this is private proppity but that doesn't concern him in the least, sir. He says, 'Another word outa you, m'lad, and over the Embankment ye go and plump into the river. Ye'll be sunk so deep, they never *will* find you.'"

Carboy began to splutter. "Such confounded impudence. I'll have something to say about this." Then he stopped and his mood changed. He stopped frowning and found room on his face for a trace of a smile. "Binns, leave it there for the time being. I want Mr. Grace to see it *when* he arrives."

Carboy walked over to the statue and ran an eye over the bill. Under a heading in black type,

THE GREAT
WATERLOO TONTINE

he read that a committee composed of men he knew slightly, and not with complete approval—Sir Sockden Deane, Bart., Baron Aldwych, Sir Humphrey Waystreet, Jenkins Store, M.P., among others—was launching a tontine for the greatest of all patriotic purposes, the care of veterans of the army and navy, the brave men who had won the battles of Waterloo and Trafalgar. There would be eight classes in the tontine and, as each was closed out in due course of time, the capital would revert at once to such control as might be designated so that the veterans would have the sole benefit.

Quite apart from the patriotic purpose for which it had been conceived and launched, it was pointed out further, the venture would be found so favorable to investors, so new, so sound, so truly extraordinary in every way, that no man with a guinea in his pocket or an ounce of sense in his head could refrain from entering himself or some member of his family. The yield would be unusually attractive to the individual sharers for this reason

and that, explained at some considerable length in an excess of black type and with rather more than the usual sales fervor.

Carboy shook his head in reluctant admiration. "Clever," he said. "Damme, if it isn't very clever. The name now—the Waterloo Tontine. Who will be able to resist that? And all this about the care of wounded veterans. *That* will bring the investors in if anything will. They'll fairly drip with sympathy. The thing has been timed to perfection."

He turned to Binns. "You're sure this fellow was hired by Chaffery?"

"Dead certain, sir. I've seen him about. He boasts of it, sir. A thorough-going bad 'un, sir."

"But why would he be pasting up signs for this?"

"I'm sure, sir, I don't know."

"Are there more of these bills around?"

"Yes, sir. All over the district. I hears, sir, they're pasting them up everywhere. Even on public statues and on private gates and pub doors, sir."

"Who does the pasting up?"

"Why, sir, it's been the same one. Helped out by others, in course. All of them on the kedge, sir."

"The kedge? Does that mean something? That they are criminals, by any chance?"

"Well, I supposes so, sir. They makes a good living, shall we say, sir, without ever doing a tap of honest work?"

Carboy was shaking his head as he turned in at the front door. "This is strange," he was thinking. "I don't understand it at all. I'm sure Chaffery isn't using his mob at idle moments in such honest work as billposting. This will bear looking into."

3

When they reached the somewhat dark and somewhat humble office where Samuel Carboy labored so steadily and to such good effect, he said to the doorman: "Binns, take my daughter to the salesrooms. She will want to see everything, especially the silks and satins and all the Eastern jewelry. When you're through there, make a tour of the place. And now send Flinch in."

When Mark Flinch, the chief clerk, put in an appearance, Carboy motioned him to draw up a chair. "Mark," he said, "I think you know London as well as anybody alive. Every little nook and cranny. And every person of any consequence."

"I've lived in the city all my life, sir. It'll be hard for you to believe this, sir, but I've only been out of the city three times in my life. Always on Sundays it's been and I can't say, sir, that I enjoyed it very much. Yes, I know London. I could give Jack Prance some pointers about *that*, I think."

"Tell me about Hark Chaffery."

"Chaffery, sir? Well, you know, I'm sure, that he's top man in the lotteries."

"Yes, I've heard that."

"They say it's just a beginning with him. Anything crooked, sir, he's in it. He's been so smart that the law has never been able to get at him. Everything is done by his henches. He lives like a gentleman himself. Has a big house in the city, drives out with two footmen and tucks a napkin under his chin and powders into eight courses every night of his life."

"But I thought most of the lotteries were privately run."

"No, sir. He plans them, he controls them, he makes the deals, and he pockets all the profits."

"How is that done?"

"Well, sir, it's done this way." The head clerk was reveling in this chance to show his intimate knowledge of everything that went on in his beloved London. "He sends a hench to a little fellow running a beefsteak-and-kidney-pie shop. 'You're in it,' says the hench. The little fellow says no, he's out of it. He doesn't want any fancy goings-on going on about his place, not him. 'Hold your lip, you cheap little clack box,' says the hench. 'Didn't ye hear me say ye're in it? All ye got to do is give us five pund for this chance and ye give it out that every customer gets a number and the lucky one will get another five pund—which you'll put up, in course.' So the customers pour in to get their cuts of pie and their numbers. And do you know what happens then, sir? One of the mob is handed the lucky number which is going to be drew and he picks up the five pund. And then he takes four pund to Hark. It's all very neat and shipshape, sir."

"That's all I wanted to know," said Carboy. He was thinking: "It's all clear enough. This mob leader is promoting himself out of the little game into a very big one. He's going to run a tontine, with a few titled pigeons to lend it respectability. Now a tontine is well within the law but *he* will find some way to steal all the proceeds. This will indeed bear looking into."

"There's that case, sir, at eleven o'clock," said Flinch. "The maritime rebates, sir. Crown vs. Johnstoun. Judge Jeffrey Pound is trying it."

"I must drop in and hear some of the evidence. If the decision goes as I think it will, we may have to change some ways of doing things ourselves." Carboy looked down at the surface of his desk which was quite bare. "No mail? Has Dobling got it again?"

"Dobling's got it, sir."

Dobling, Reginald of that ilk, acted as secretary to Mr. Grace. He was a college man but had failed to make any practical use of his knowledge and had fallen as low as the occupancy of a clerical sinecure. He spent his time in the office, for the most part surreptitiously reading the classics, Grace having little work for him to do. Realizing the need to cover up his employer's lack of participation in the activities of the firm, and his own enforced but very much enjoyed idleness, he had fallen into the habit of taking the morning mail into the center office on the pretext that Mr. Grace must look it over first. After a certain interval he would return it to Flinch with a condescending remark such as "Nothing to disturb us there, Flinch, so we leave it to the staff." It was a favorite device of his to issue out and demand a certain file of letters. "Mr. Grace wants to be thoroughly familiar with this," he would say. The documents he obtained in this way were generally kept for some time, hidden away in a desk drawer or deep in a letter press. If they were needed he was likely to refuse until "our study is completed." It had reached the stage where, when anything was missing, the office force would agree that "Dobling's got it." And generally he *did* have it.

Carboy got to his feet. "I'll attend to this," he said grimly.

The center office was unusually large, with a high ceiling and an enormous fireplace under one of the handsomest mirrors in all London. George Grace's desk would not have been out of place in the study of a prime minister, a magnificently carved specimen of seaweed mahogany. Even

Dobling's desk, which occupied a corner, was much finer than the one which served for Carboy. The carpet was so thick that the heaviest-footed subordinate could cross the room as silently as a cat on the prowl.

Dobling looked up indignantly when Samuel Carboy entered without knocking. His lips opened to voice a complaint but he thought better of it in time. Carboy crossed the room and stood beside the desk of the secretary, looking down angrily at the pile of letters reposing there.

"Give me the mail, Dobling."

"Sir," in a tone of protest, "it is Mr. Grace's intention to look it over first."

"When will he be in?"

"I am not in his confidence sufficiently to say, Mr. Carboy."

Carboy reached down with both hands and scooped up the mail. He scowled at his partner's secretary. "Now you listen to me, Dobling. You are not to touch the mail again. If you as much as lay a finger on it, there will be an explosion which will blow you right out of this window behind you."

"I shall speak to Mr. Grace about this," declared the secretary in a rebellious tone.

"Speak to Mr. Grace by all means. I intend to speak to him myself. Let me know as soon as he comes in."

Dobling got to his feet with a show of righteous indignation. "Sir," he said, "Mr. Grace will let you know when he is free to see you."

Carboy was on his way to the door but at this he turned and studied his partner's secretary with a look which indicated that the promised explosion was not far off. "Dobling," he said, "you're a queer one. You're downright odd. Damme, if I don't think you're more concerned about upholding your dignity than holding onto your job."

"My ability to hold onto my job, Mr. Carboy," declared Dobling haughtily, "is no concern whatever of yours."

"Perhaps it is, Dobling. Perhaps it is. We'll see. Soon."

Isabelle returned to her father's office in a state of enthusiasm over the velvets and velours she had seen, and the ostrich plumes and the mandarin gowns. Carboy got to his feet at once.

"Now we're going to court, Isa," he said. "It's only a few blocks away and we won't stay more than a few minutes. Then we'll have some lunch and I'll put you in a cab for home." He paused and indulged in a sly wink. "Will it be safe for you to go home then?"

Isabelle caught his conspiratorial mood and smiled delightedly. "Oh yes, Papa. If I know Mama, she's at Old Bordley's this very minute. The storm will be over when I reach home."

Carboy thought it incumbent on him to adopt a more properly parental attitude. "You know, Isa, you were very wrong about this," he said in a reproving tone. "You must be more careful at the next school."

"Papa, I don't want to go to any more schools. I think, really, that I've outgrown them."

"You're going to a school, young woman, and you might as well make up your mind to it."

"Oh, lor', Papa, don't you start lecturing me. If what I did was wrong, I expect to be wrong an awful lot of times."

4

The judge was an old man with heavy jowls and small eyes imbedded under cavernous brows; an ill-tempered old man, as was immediately apparent. He was scowling when Carboy and daughter entered, and the slight noise they made in reaching seats close to the railing caused him to scowl at them.

"There's too much noise in this court," he said in a tone which could only be described as snarling. "Tell them, Crier, that I'll have them all out if there's as much as another whisper."

Carboy was watching a tall young lawyer who was standing at the counsel's table with a number of large lawbooks under one arm. It was clear that this neophyte was resentful of the judge's irritability. He remained without moving, looking up at the bewigged figure on the bench until his immobility brought the judicial eyes around in his direction. Holding his position for a second longer, he stared back, then raised his arm to the level of his shoulder, thus allowing the ponderous volumes to fall. They landed on the floor with a thud which resounded throughout the court with the unexpectedness of a roger's blast. It was so deliberately done that the spectators held their breaths in anticipation of thunderbolts from the bench.

The young lawyer bent over to retrieve the books and then placed them on the table.

"I regret, m'lord," he said, "that my arm lacked the strength to hold these volumes which are so necessary to the argument we shall present in due course."

The judge's scowl had taken on a still more ferocious aspect. "Let us hope, for the sake of your client," he growled, "that your argument will prove stronger than your arm."

Carboy had noticed some things about this disturber of the peace of the court. His arm, contrary to what he had said, looked capable almost of assuming the task of Atlas, and his profile was that of a perfect Greek statue. At this point the young lawyer turned his head, however, and the newcomer was shocked to observe that the other side of his face was marred by a birthmark of violent purple from temple to chin.

Carboy wrote on a slip of paper, "Who is that?" and handed it to an acquaintance close at hand. The acquaintance, careful not to attract the attention of the choleric judge, scribbled his answer on the sheet and passed it back. "Jonathan Bade," he had written. "A good man." Carboy nodded his head with satisfaction. He had been hearing good things of this Jonathan Bade.

The young lawyer had plunged into a dissertation to which Carboy listened with the closest attention. It was not only well phrased but it had an originality and ingenuity of approach to the legal problem at issue which made it seem penetrating as well as forceful. The merchant found himself nodding in agreement at the end of each passage.

Isabelle began to show signs of impatience. "The air is very unpleasant in here, Papa," she whispered. "And the face of that old man up there is unpleasant too." Even the fact that she was attracting a great deal of admiring attention did not compensate and she fidgeted about in her seat until her father was compelled to give her a promise of departure as soon as he could scribble a note.

The message he indited, using his knee as a pad, was to Jonathan Bade, Esq.

> I have not had the pleasure of meeting you and would like to suggest that you permit me to correct this by calling on you at your offices at four o'clock this afternoon. There is a matter I would appreciate the privilege of discussing with you. Your servant, sir,
>
> *Samuel Carboy*

The note was passed across the railing and reached the hands of the lawyer when he took his seat. He read it and then turned in the general direction where Carboy sat, revealing in doing so the full ugliness of the one side of his face. He gave a nod of assent.

"I am very hungry, Papa," said Isabelle when they reached the street. "I think I should like a cutlet and a thick slice of steamed pudding."

"I know exactly the place for that," answered her father. "Everyone was looking at you in there, chickabiddy. That cloak makes you look so grown up that they were puzzled as to who you might be."

The girl was only faintly interested in the opinions of the middle-aged men who had surrounded them in court but she made it clear that she had watched the young lawyer. "What a dreadful thing, Papa," she said. "He looked so handsome at first that I was thrilled and excited. He looked like the kind of man a woman of the world could fall in love with. But when he turned! Ugh, what a dreadful scar!"

"He's a young man of great promise," said her father. "I think he may be useful to me."

They were each handed lottery tickets as they entered the eating house Carboy had selected. Remembering what he had been told, he took both tickets, tore them in two and threw them under their table.

5

Jonathan Bade's quarters consisted of a rather large dark room, untidily filled with books. There was a small alcove which gave the impression that

it was used as a kitchen. The owner of these far from impressive accommoda-
tions was hastily making up a couch, on which he had slept the night before,
when Samuel Carboy entered.

"I hope you will overlook the state of things here, Mr. Carboy," he said,
offering his guest a firm hand to shake. "I am a bachelor, sir, and get along
as best I may."

Carboy found it possible to like this young man in spite of the scar. His
eyes were clear and direct.

"I came, Mr. Bade," said Carboy, "because I have been hearing the best
of reports of you. And also because I considered your argument in court
this morning uncommonly good."

"Thank you, sir. The point at issue was, without a doubt, one of interest
to you."

"Quite."

"If you would like a cup of tea, I could have it ready for you in a minute.
Or would you prefer, sir, a whisky and water?"

"The whisky, if you please."

The whisky proved to be hidden away behind a pile of lawbooks and the
search for clean glasses was rewarded finally in a nest of dishes left over
from a meal of the previous day. Carboy watched the young lawyer as he
thus slowly got together the ingredients for the drinks. "That smart little
minx of mine was right," he thought. "That fellow would be oncommon
handsome if he didn't have that abominable birthmark."

"This is a curious thing, Mr. Carboy," said Bade, handing his caller a
glass and seating himself on a rickety stool beside the chair on rockers in
which the merchant had been ensconced, "but it so happens that you are
the first client—if you *are* a client—to call on me here in what purports to be
my office."

Carboy looked surprised at this piece of information. "How is that?"

"Because of my sensitivity, Mr. Carboy—my foolish sensitivity, you may
say. This!" He raised a finger in the direction of his disfigured right cheek.
"You see, I realize fully the effect this has on people—this gift which nature
bestowed on me. It startles people who see it for the first time. I recognize
the look which comes into their eyes and I—well, I don't seem to get accustomed or reconciled to it. I decided I would live my life in seclusion
and for three years I did nothing but work on briefs which were sent me.
I never left this room except at night when I could take my exercise with
impunity."

For several moments he remained silent, ruminating undoubtedly over
the unfortunate combination of circumstances which had forced this kind
of life upon him. Then he proceeded more slowly with his explanation.

"An opinion developed among some of those I worked for in this way
that I prepared good briefs. Why, they asked me, shouldn't I sometimes
follow things through in court? I thought it over. I thought it over most
seriously. Finally I decided that it might be less unpleasant to appear in
court and to stand before large numbers of people than to meet individuals

face to face. I gave in; and for several years now I've been pleading in court rather frequently, as I think you know.

"But up to this minute, sir," he concluded, "I've appeared only in cases confided to other hands. I have no clients of my own."

During this explanation, Carboy's eyes had been turned away from the speaker and had been fixed on a clotheshorse over which were draped a blue coat with steel buttons, a quiet blue, however, pepper-and-salt trousers, an elaborate dressing gown and a very handsome scarlet house cap on the order of a fez. The young lawyer had his streak of vanity, he concluded, in spite of everything.

"You may have a client now, Mr. Bade," said Carboy. He crossed one knee over the other and leaned back in his chair which responded by creaking alarmingly. "I'm hard to please in lawyers. When they tell me a thing can't be done—and they're always doing *that*—just because it never has been done, I become furious with them. When they say a plan of mine is impossible but don't prove to me that it is, I get even more angry. Lawyers, my young sir, are cowards. They are afraid of the past. They are like ostriches with their heads stuck in legal sands. When you handed it back so impudently to old Jeffrey Pound, that squeaker and bully, I said to myself, 'Sam Carboy, this may be the man for you.' I've been making some inquiries about you this afternoon and what I've been told amounts to this: you're not afraid of the past, you're not afraid of anything, of man, God or devil."

Bade had taken a sip of the whisky in his own glass and had put his glass aside. It was not good whisky and did not merit more than a sip, although the caller was drinking his with seeming enjoyment. Bade looked up at his prospective client and shook his head deprecatingly. "I don't believe, Mr. Carboy, that I'm ever afraid of men or devils," he said. "But God —ah, sir, that's a different matter. I have a great fear of God, sir. I'm a stout enough believer, for one thing, and for another I've been shown some evidences of His power. Why should I not be afraid of a Hand which can send me into the world condemned to solitude, cut off from the pleasures of society, refused the greatest boon life has to offer—love, romance, a wife, children? The power, not always benign, which did this to me could do other things. I think of the future with dread because of this prospect. I might, for instance, be robbed of my sight and my mind like poor old George upon his throne. I think I may truly say that I love God but of this there can be no shadow of doubt, I am afraid of Him."

Carboy nodded his head with sudden vigor. "I'm most oncommon glad to hear you say so, Mr. Bade. You see, I've got plans in my head which will take a lot to carry out—vision and courage and a trick of seeing new ways of doing things and finding, damme, some new meanings in the laws perhaps. I'm not content to go lumbering along the old roads, Mr. Bade. I've got new destinations in my mind and so I'll have to find new roads to them, or get someone who *can* find them. But I don't ever want to go too far. Those who help me and advise me must fear God and the law of the land as much as I do." He gave his head another series of emphatic nods. "We'll have to do a lot of talking, Mr. Bade, but I'm saying right out in meeting now that you may be the man I'm looking for."

The lawyer was so interested in the discussion that he had forgotten his physical disability. He was watching the merchant with intent eyes.

"This is all very interesting, sir," he remarked. "It begins to sound like an invitation to sally out on an adventure. Or perhaps more nearly to take to horse at dawn and ride to hounds over frozen roads with all the bugles blowing loudly."

"No bugles, Mr. Bade," said Carboy quickly. "What we do, we'll have to do without much noise. Until it's done, sir. *Then* we may give a blast or two on bugles."

"At any rate, it sounds most interesting, sir. I shall be happy to continue the discussion."

When Carboy got to his feet an hour later, it seemed almost certain that they would get together, that the young lawyer who had dared to create an uproar in a court presided over by old Jeffrey Pound would lend his courage as well as his legal talents to help along some at least of the ventures which were hatching in the aggressive and acquisitive mind of Samuel Carboy. Nothing had been settled, of course, for Carboy never rushed into things. He would think it over, he said as he shook his rumpled nankeen trousers back into place (they *were* a nuisance, he conceded) and took his departure. "That young fellow's got what I need," he said to himself. "He's got some grand ideas. He'll do more than shake his head like that old fool of a Craver and his young fool of a son. He'll do more than growl and say No, no, no! I think I must try him at any rate."

CHAPTER THREE

1

George Ninian Grace was ill for two days, so it may be assumed that his losses had cut more deeply than his nonchalance at the dinner party might have suggested. On the third day he put in an appearance just in time to partake of the tea which was served each afternoon in his office. As he spread jam languidly on a perfectly browned crumpet, he listened to a bitter complaint from the devoted Dobling.

"He's been on the rampage, sir," said the secretary.

"Who, Dobling?"

"The Grumbler, sir. The Growler. The Great Panjandrum of his own election with the great large button—not being content, mind you, with a small one—on top. He's been giving me orders, sir. I'm not to touch the mail in future."

"Indeed!" Mr. Grace sipped his tea with an outward show of his usual composure but his cheeks had flushed. "I don't like this sort of thing, Dobling. I don't like it at all."

"He gave me orders, sir, that I was to let him know as soon as you arrived. I said you would notify him when it would be agreeable for you to see him."

"You seem to have acted with your usual good discretion, Dobling," said the senior partner; for such the Graces in the firm had always considered themselves. "I shall have a talk with Mr. Carboy."

He was to have the talk much sooner than he had supposed. There was a quick and determined knock, and, before Dobling could do as much as get to his feet to answer, the door opened and Mr. Carboy stepped into the room.

"I heard you had arrived, George," he said. "So I came right in. I want to talk with you."

"But, Samuel," protested Grace, "I've just started my tea."

Carboy looked across the room at the secretary, who was keeping his head discreetly lowered over some more or less imaginary work but who seemed to be finding it hard to suppress a slyly triumphant grin.

"Finish it while we talk, George," he said to his partner. "This matter won't wait, I'm afraid. Not even for tea and crumpets and"—glancing appraisingly at the tray—"and the most expensive marmalade to be had. It's important, George, and it's confidential. I think Dobling will have to step out."

"Very well," said Grace. "Will you oblige us, Dobling?"

When the door had closed on the secretary, Carboy took a chair beside the desk of his partner. He had made up his mind to come straight to the business in hand.

"George," he said, "we've come to the parting of the ways."

The frown which settled over Grace's face made it clear that he did not fully grasp Carboy's meaning.

"The parting of the ways? Great Constellations, Samuel, what are you talking about?"

"Us. The firm of Grace and Carboy. It can't go on any longer this way. I'm completely and bitterly dissatisfied with our arrangements."

Grace replaced the crumpet he had been holding on the plate in front of him. He touched a napkin quickly to his lips and then dropped it over the unfinished food.

"Do you mean you are going to leave, to—er—pull out?" he asked. "Why, Samuel, I wonder if this place could run along on an even keel without you. I do indeed. For both of our sakes we must talk this over in the fullest and frankest way. It should be possible to—to assuage your dissatisfaction."

"You don't seem to have grasped my meaning." Carboy was finding the urbanity of his partner most trying. "I am not talking of leaving the business necessarily. Although it might come to that."

"Well," said Grace, with a laugh which contained a small degree of condescension in it, "you can't mean that I'm the one to leave. I assure you, Samuel, that nothing of that kind has ever entered my head or ever will. Nothing in the world could induce me to give up the business which my forefathers started."

"*Our* forefathers, George." Carboy's manner was getting gruffer with every word he spoke. "My forefather, the old sea captain, brought the idea to the first of the Graces. It's true they did not start as even partners but a generation or two adjusted that. It has been an even partnership ever since— in some respects but not in others which are most important."

"Put things in plain words, Samuel. What do you want?"

"I'll put it in three words, all very plain. Buy or sell. We can't go on as partners. That's certain." Carboy paused to give careful consideration to his words. "I will give you the price at which I am prepared to deal. It will be my price whether I buy or sell. You may recall that this is in accordance with the articles of partnership."

Grace's face had turned white. He was realizing at last what was in his partner's mind. He said, with an attempt at firmness: "I have no desire to do either, to buy or sell. Where does that leave us?"

Carboy leaned forward belligerently. "You know where it would leave us, I would go to court and force a dissolution of the partnership. That also is provided for in the articles of agreement."

A feeling of panic had now taken possession of Grace. "That would be very bad for both of us. You must see that as well as I do."

"I realize it fully. The business would be broken in two and we would divide what we got for the sale of the stock on hand, the ships and the real estate. The good will would belong to us equally. I would start in business for myself and you would probably do the same. We would begin to cut each other's throats. I'm sure that in your mind you agree I would be more expert than you at the business of throat cutting. . . .

"If it comes to that, George," he added after a moment, "you will net much less that way than you would by selling out to me. Less than half, I assure you."

Grace fumbled with some papers on the desk. He gathered them up with an unsteady hand, sorted them over and then dropped them into a side drawer of his very expensive desk.

"What are you prepared to offer?" he asked finally.

This brought an unexpectedly violent explosion from Carboy. "Damme, man, do you think I'm prepared to shoot a figure at you at this early stage? I'm not simple enough for that, even if you're simple enough to expect it. No, no, I will go into things carefully and deeply and then I'll send you a letter, stating the figure at which I'm prepared to buy or sell."

"It—it surely doesn't need to come to this," said Grace, with a nervous attempt at a laugh. "Why are you so sure it is necessary to destroy a business which is running beautifully? There must be ways of correcting whatever it is you object to."

"What I object to? Is it necessary to put it into words? It comes down to this: I do all the work, you sit around and do nothing and get your half of the money I make—which is a very great deal every year. You get the icing, I get the dry ends of the cake. We can't compound a situation like that."

"Surely—surely, there must be some way. What *do* you want?"

Carboy gestured with one hand to express his skepticism. "You wouldn't even listen to my conditions. What would you say if I demanded that you content yourself with something less than half the profits? That this big office be mine, as the working head of the concern? That you take mine or one we could arrange by knocking out some partitions——"

"You need not go on," declared Grace stiffly. "I most certainly would not consider any such conditions as that!"

"I favor a clean break myself. As I said at the start, it has come down to a case of buy or sell."

Grace remained silent for a long time, his head bowed over his desk. One of his white and well-cared-for hands rested on the mahogany surface. Carboy saw that it trembled.

"Samuel, Samuel!" said Grace finally. "You seem determined to press me back against the wall. I'll make every effort to purchase your share because to—to sell is unthinkable. But this catches me at a difficult time. As you know, I took a loss on the Exchange in the panic about Waterloo. Not as much as some people seem determined to make out, mind you. But enough to make me think carefully about a step like this. You would, of course, allow me time."

"All that is provided for in the partnership agreement."

"I'm not as familiar with the papers as I should be perhaps. What do they allow? Six months?"

"One month."

Grace fell into another long silence. The line of his back and the tensity with which his hands were locked together suggested desperation. They had been friendly enough as young men and for a moment Carboy felt sorry for him. This feeling was quickly dispelled, however, because Grace's mood changed suddenly and unexpectedly. He sat up straight and glared at his partner. When he spoke, there was a distinct note of pettiness in his voice.

"I see through you, Carboy," he declared. "There's malice in this. And envy."

"If I feel malice and envy, you have yourself to blame," answered Carboy.

"And you've waited until I have temporary losses to hamper me. You strike me at a vulnerable moment. It's not a pretty thing you're doing, not a pretty thing at all."

"Do you admire the selfishness you've shown all these years? Are you proud of repaying my industry and ability with nothing but condescension?"

There was silence between them for a moment and then Carboy began to feel a return of the pity he had experienced before. Grace, he knew, was helpless in a situation like this. He knew nothing of business; had never tried to learn, in fact.

"Let me give you a piece of advice, George," he said. "I give it in all honesty and without any of the malice and envy you say I feel. Don't mortgage everything you own to buy me out. I would set myself up in opposition at once. Do you seriously think you would have any chance against me? You wouldn't, George. You would steer yourself right on the rocks."

"That," declared Grace with a sudden show of spirit, "is a matter of opinion."

"George!" said the other sharply. "Let's get some common sense into this discussion. Look at yourself for a moment as other people do. Think of the way you've treated me. We could have compromised our differences if you had seen how absurd things were and had come to me. You didn't; and now nothing in the world will divert me from my purpose. George, you wouldn't have the faintest idea of where to start if you were left here alone. Don't you suppose I have my plans all made? If I walk out of here, I'll be under way in less than twenty-four hours. Those who have been dealing with Grace and Carboy have in reality been dealing with me. Very few have even seen you. They would follow me in a body."

Grace looked about his large office. He looked at the mirror over the fireplace, at the portrait of his father on the opposite wall which had been painted by the great Benjamin Wilson, at the handsome paneling of the walls and the stout beams in the ceiling. He was beginning to realize how much he loved the room. It had been to him the perfect expression of his well-ordered existence. Could he leave it to this blustering man who had been his partner so long?

"Very well," he said, rising to his feet as an indication that he did not intend to discuss the matter further. "Send me your letter. I will give the matter immediate consideration. I will let you know my decision as soon as possible."

Carboy, dismissed, left the room in a ruffled state of mind. His ineffective partner had managed to have the last word. He felt that, in some way, he had been put in the wrong.

2

Three weeks went by. Carboy knew that Grace was striving desperately to raise the capital needed to buy him out. The latter had been to a number of banks and had discussed the situation with many of his friends. Carboy knew also that he was not meeting with any degree of encouragement. He was well liked but in the City he was known as a charming and cultured man who had no knowledge of business at all.

During these three weeks Grace had not visited the office. He was furious with his partner and declared openly that he hoped never to see his face again. He was telling stories around which were not intended to improve Carboy's reputation. In this endeavor he had some small measure of success, for men are only too prone to accept gossip inspired by hatred. Carboy paid no attention to what was going on. He was convinced that his reputation would stand the embittered assault of his partner.

In the meantime Dobling sat in idleness in the big office and smiled slyly when he thought of what was going to happen. He had every confidence that his employer's connections would make it easy for him to raise the needed capital. Very soon there would be no Carboy around the office and he, Dobling, might become the power behind the throne. He even went so far as to drop hints to that effect.

"I know how you've laughed at me," he said to members of the staff. "'Dobling's got it,' you've said. Well, Dobling's going to get it from now on. What am I going to get, do you ask? I'll tell you. I'm going to get power. You'd better start worrying about what may happen to all of you. I'm not one to forget easy."

Three days before the month allowed for a settlement had expired, Carboy had a caller of considerable importance. He was deep in an accumulation of mail at the time and not paying any attention to his daughter, who was sitting in a corner and enjoying snatches of a lurid-looking novel she had brought with her. Miss Bordley had proved obdurate and, as Isabelle had been ejected from three schools, it had not yet been found possible to get her into another of the standing on which Mrs. Carboy insisted. Finding her mother's temper short under these circumstances, the girl had fallen into the habit of paying visits to the office where her father welcomed her cordially if somewhat absent-mindedly. She had arrayed herself this morning with particular care in a dress of blue dimity with a fashionably high waistline; in which she fancied, and with good reason, that she bore some resemblance to Napoleon's beautiful sister Pauline. She was giving more thought to this point, in fact, than she was to the novel in her lap. Her eyes were fixed on her boots, which had blue fabric tops and were very neat and fetching indeed.

Flinch put his head in at the door. "A caller, sir, Sir Theobald Gardiner."

Carboy looked a little flustered for a moment. What did Sir Theobald Gardiner want with him? The caller was a very wealthy man with interests in Jamaica. He owned a large county seat and a town house and was very high up in social circles. The thought crossed Carboy's mind, "Grace has sent him."

"Show him in, Flinch."

Sir Theobald was in his middle forties. Being a widower with no children, he was the object of more feminine wiles and contrivings than perhaps anyone else in the kingdom. This gave him a wariness which had finally spread to his business dealings.

"You are—er—Carboy, I take it," he said, staring at the merchant through a monocle of most unusual size.

"Yes, Sir Theobald. Will you take a chair?"

The baronet sat down but did not proceed at once with his purpose in calling. He had seen Isabelle sitting in her corner and swinging one foot back and forth with the ease and nonchalance of a lady of fashion. He stared at her for a long moment through his monocle.

"George Grace came to see me yesterday," he began finally. "We were at Eton, y'know. I always liked him. Still do. We discussed something that might interest you."

"I'll be glad to listen."

The first feeling of awe which Carboy had experienced at the arrival of so great a man as Sir Theobald Gardiner had vanished. The baronet, as he had expected, had come on business and there Carboy could meet him on much more than even terms. He studied his visitor, noting the perfect cut of his claret-colored trousers and the tightness they showed at the knee, the neatness of the straps over his boots to hold the trousers in place, the handsome fit of his gray frock coat and its double lapels, the immaculate cravat in which his longish jaw was almost buried away from sight. "He's as much of a fop as I've always heard," thought the merchant.

"I'll have to tell you everything, Carboy," said the baronet, withdrawing his eyes with some reluctance from the corner where Isabelle sat. "George wanted me to make him a loan or invest some money with him in this business. To help him buy you out, in other words. I said no. Quite firmly. I'm fond of George but I have no faith in his ability to make a proper use of the money he was asking. I know, of course, that you have a sound business here and it so happens that at the moment I have some idle capital. I said to George that I might be interested on one basis. If you should decide to incorporate and offer shares to the public, I might be willing to take a slice of it. My attitude would depend on one thing, naturally. That you remain the active head of the business."

"That is very flattering, Sir Theobald. If we were to follow your suggestion, who would be president?"

"You—perhaps."

"Sir," said Carboy, "I am laying plans to allow myself a much wider participation in business. I aim to branch out in many directions. There are several words which will have no place in these new activities. 'Perhaps' is one of them."

"Quite right, Carboy. Shall we say 'definitely' instead?"

"A much better word. Would it be possible for me to acquire a controlling interest?"

"I will now use the word you seem to prefer. 'Definitely' not."

"That is clear and to the point. Let me explain my feelings about this, Sir Theobald. I expect to have very wide concerns but nothing will ever be allowed to change the business in which I have spent all of my life to date. It must remain as the solid, unchanging core of everything. I would never consent to any arrangement which might result someday in alien control. I will not consider a plan which leaves me without full authority." He leaned back in his chair and gave some further thought to the possibilities. "How did Grace respond?"

"At first he said no, that the breach between you could not be healed——"

"That is true. He has been blacking my character all over London. Would you forgive that if you were in my place?"

"I'm not sure. My skin is thin enough but when important considerations are concerned I can overlook a great deal."

"Do you know how things were being managed here?"

The baronet smiled. "I don't suppose I know the full details but I've heard enough to realize it was unfair—to you. But, of course, George didn't see it that way. It seemed to him that the Graces had always been entitled to have things their own way. When we spoke about it—and this was only a few days ago—he was still in a wax over what he called your ingratitude. He said firmly that he would not come to see you. That's why I'm here this morning."

"I hear he doesn't hesitate to call me a thief publicly. You see I have friends in the City too and everything he says comes back to me. I wouldn't see him if he did come."

"He'll be disappointed. But he *has* been waspish. I told him so. I told him he seemed bent on self-destruction."

The baronet smoothed his mustache thoughtfully. His black hair had a wide streak of white through it, beginning with his forehead, and the thin fringe of whiskers which bounded his cheeks had become pepper-and-salt. In spite of these evidences of advancing years—partly, in fact, because of them—he was a remarkably handsome man. After a few moments he nodded his head.

"Well, we're not getting together on my plan," he said. "I shan't urge it on you. Perhaps I'm proving a poor ambassador for my old friend in not striving to persuade you. But can I, a stranger, say anything more when you are completely antagonistic to the idea?" He gave his head a negative shake, and then almost immediately smiled. "I must confess, Carboy, that I was looking forward to having some small hand in a lively business such as yours. You see, I've been one of your solid investors, depending on land and the consols for my income. I was saying to myself that it would be exciting to have a fling at something different."

"Sir," said Carboy, "a fling, if conducted under the right auspices, would be profitable as well as exciting."

Gardiner rose to his feet and Carboy followed his example at once.

"We'll meet again, I trust," said the visitor. As he drew on a glove, his gaze wandered to the corner where Isabelle was sitting with her eyes lowered over her book. "Am I permitted to say that you have a charming daughter?"

"My little girl is returning to school in the fall but in the meantime she sometimes pays me an unexpected visit. Isabelle, this is Sir Theobald Gardiner."

The girl stood up and dropped a curtsy. It was so gracefully done that the visitor's good opinion of her continued to mount.

"I am sure," he said, "that Miss Isabelle will soon complete the conquest of her books and begin on the conquest of everyone she meets in the pleasant life ahead of her. I am to be numbered among the first."

"It's kind of you to say so, Sir Theobald, but you mustn't turn her head," said Carboy.

When the visitor had gone, Isabelle turned furiously on her father. "Papa, why did you have to say I was going back to school? I've made up my mind not to. And calling me your little girl! Really, Papa!"

Carboy paid no attention to her. He stood beside his desk in a semitrance, smiling and nodding to himself. He said aloud: "This settles things. Grace is desperate. He's made his final play and it has failed. Now he'll have to come to my terms."

"Do you think, Papa, you should treat me like a child? Shouldn't you answer when I speak to you?"

"What did you say, Isa?"

"I was trying to make you see— Oh well, what does it matter? But I must say, Papa, it was most unfeeling and unfair of you."

"You mustn't go drawing conclusions from a polite speech made by a man who came to talk with me."

"Papa," said the girl, "he was talking to you but he was looking at me. He was looking at me most of the time. You know, Papa, two people can sometimes get quite well acquainted by just looking at one another and not saying a single word. Sir Theobald—and, oh, isn't he handsome, Papa!—did more. He paid me the nicest compliment I've ever had."

"What nonsense are you talking, child?" Carboy was too deeply concerned with the conclusions he had drawn from the baronet's visit to pay much attention to his daughter. He began to pace up and down the restricted space in his office. "He has just three days more," he thought. "He'll wait until the last day and then send me his letter, accepting my terms."

"I'm not talking nonsense. I'm trying to make you realize, Papa, that I've just met one of the handsomest of men and the most eligible in the whole country and that I made a good impression on him. Which *proves*, Papa, that it would be very foolish to send me back to school in the fall. I'm not your little girl any more. I've grown up. Perhaps it would interest you to know that every girl at Old Bordley's would give anything for the chance I've had today. We talked about such things all the time; and we all agreed it would be quite easy to marry a man as old as he is—when he's so very handsome and so well dressed and so *very* rich."

Her father's thoughts had gone far away from her again. He made no reply.

3

On the last day under the partnership agreement, Samuel Carboy received the expected letter from George Ninian Grace. It was short and bitter but, as far as Carboy was concerned, eminently satisfactory.

Sir:
    In accordance with the terms under which our partnership has ex-

isted, I accept the offer you make for my share in Grace and Carboy.
I do so with the conviction that you are taking advantage of my position, a temporary one I assure you, and that your conduct throughout
has been unfair, grasping and in a high degree ungentlemanly. Inasmuch as I shrink from visiting again the offices which my family
established, and as I wish to spare myself the need of setting eyes on
you, I am sending movers to collect for me my personal belongings.
They will follow on the heels of this note.

I conclude with the hope that the health of the concern will not de-
preciate under your sole and unguided control.

To this, sir, I subscribe myself,
George Ninian Grace

Carboy had no more than finished perusing the letter when a rap came on
the door and Flinch entered. The head clerk seemed on the point of bursting
with excitement.

"Sir," he said, "there's movers here and they say they're to take everything
in Mr. Grace's office."

Carboy nodded. "The partnership has been dissolved, Flinch," he said.
"From now on I'm sole owner. I don't want the movers interfered with in
any way. But, Flinch, keep an eye on what's happening. If there's anything
you don't understand or don't approve, let me know."

"Yes, *sir*."

In ten minutes Flinch was back. "They're taking the desk, Mr. Carboy. I
remember distinctly passing on the bill when it was purchased for Mr. Grace.
Here it is, the bill. I had it looked up. The desk, sir, is the property of the
company, not of Mr. Grace."

Carboy found himself confronted with a difficult situation. From the day
the desk had been installed in the center office, he had admired it, had
coveted it, had looked forward to the time, distant perhaps, when he might
sit behind it himself. He was fully aware that it had been purchased by the
company. In fact, he knew the price paid to the last shilling. Should he
further antagonize Grace by claiming it and putting in the latter's hands a
weapon for more damaging talk? Or should he take the generous course by
standing aside and allowing the desk to be removed?

The acquisitive instinct in the new owner was so strong that he had to
force himself into saying, finally: "Let them take it, Flinch. I prefer not to
interfere." He had to check himself from countermanding the order almost
immediately, however, the words rising abruptly and involuntarily to the
tip of his tongue. The more generous instinct continued to prevail and he said
instead: "Urge them to take that monstrosity at the entrance. It belongs to
the company but I will be glad to make him a present of it. If they refuse,
sell it for old metal or have it melted down. I don't want to see it there
another day."

He rose from his chair soon after and visited the center office, which was
now practically empty. Dobling still sat in his corner, however, biting his

nails as he cogitated bitterly on his folly in so openly backing the wrong horse. Carboy spoke to him briefly and left the room, closing the door after him.

He met Flinch in the hall. "Well," he said, "Dobling's got it."

"He's got what, sir?"

"His discharge. And now, Flinch, come with me. I want to give you instructions for a new sign. It must be a very handsome thing and you'd better hire an artist to do it. I don't want any of these daubers who make signs with a few swishes of the brush but at the same time, naturally, I don't want to pay through the nose. Don't go searching through Soho for another Rembrandt or Holbein. You realize, of course, that the wording will be changed. It's to be Carboy and Company."

CHAPTER FOUR

1

The Carboy house in the country stood on a pleasant bend of one of the small rivers and it had some size and dignity; but it had never completely satisfied Samuel Carboy. Higher up in the hills, with its chimneys and roofs visible in the distance, was a much larger and much older house known as Beaulaw Hall and he had spent many covetous moments gazing in that direction and thinking how much better it would suit him. Now that fortune was beginning to shine on him so conspicuously, he decided on a bold move. Instead of fulfilling the promise he had made his wife of adding a wing to their own residence, he sold it, at a reasonable profit, and bought Beaulaw Hall instead. A park went with it and many fine acres of grazing land on the hillsides and a charming old garden hidden behind a wall of brown brick. There went with it as well a deep sense of importance and squireship.

One afternoon in early August the coach from London stopped at the nearest village, and Samuel Carboy alighted in a pair of shiny Wellington boots. His feet touched the paving stones in the yard of the coaching inn with the stride of a conqueror. That evening there was to be a housewarming, with all his relatives and a few friends and neighbors invited. The chief factor in his sense of pride was, however, a deal which had been simmering for the purchase of three rival importing houses, none of them as prosperous as Carboy and Co. but nevertheless with good connections and small shipping lines of their own. All that stood in the way of the final scribbling of signatures and the fixing of the seals was a small matter of additional capital. He had no doubts whatever that he could raise the required amount.

He looked over the nearest gable of the old inn and winked at the sun. "They'll all sit up pretty straight when they hear about it," he confided to the best of all astronomical neighbors. "But it will be like the grinding of John the Miller, it will seem small, small, small when I get around to doing the great things which buzz in this head of mine."

He then saw with satisfaction that the coachman he had hired the week before, an Irishman named Daniel Groody, was waiting for him under the rear archway. The phaeton, which had been acquired with a great deal of pride because it had the new and expensive elliptical springs, did not show as much as a speck of dust, and the harness on the pair of bay horses was as shiny as a Bow runner's buttons. Groody stood at the front wheel with a wide grin of welcome on his face and a whip over his arm.

"Good day to you, Mr. Carboy," said Groody in a voice as broad as his grin.

Carboy nodded with satisfaction. "You have things looking shipshape, Groody. Quite spick and span." Then he motioned toward the coach. "I've a heavy cargo for you."

The guard had been unloading an assortment of baskets and parcels from which protruded such welcome articles as the black necks of wine bottles and odd shapes of imported fruit, not to mention a well-iced cask of shellfish. A company of four were scrambling down from the top, looking very red of face from so much unaccustomed exposure to the sun. They revealed themselves as none other than Jack Prance and his three gleemen.

Groody looked doubtfully at this quartet and asked, "Might they be guests of yours, Mr. Carboy?"

Carboy nodded his head. "They're singers. They'll keep us amused this evening."

Groody's air showed an increase of doubt. "It's all-overish they were to begin, I'm thinking. And now what with a good shaking up in the coach after a pint or two and the sitting up there in the sun—well, sir, they do seem a little coxey-loxey already." The coachman then gave a cheerful smile and nodded his head. "A pleasant thing it must be to hear them, sir."

"You'll have that pleasure tonight, Groody," said Carboy. "I haven't got a full staff yet. There will be a footman later to help the butler but tonight I'm going to have you in to give him a hand. Bringing in the plates, whatever he asks."

Groody ran a hand over his long upper lip. "Well now, sir, it's handy I am with the horses. But I'm not sure of chiny."

"You'll have to be sure," declared Carboy. "We'll use the Bow service tonight."

His grandfather, who had been disposed to financial rashnesses, had invested some money in the porcelain factory at Stratford le Bow and, when it failed, had salvaged from the wreckage a complete table service of the best ware. It had been one of the chief prides of the three Carboy wives who had owned it in succession; and so zealous had been their care that not so much as a chip or a scratch marred a single piece.

Groody was now shaking his head over what his employer had called the cargo. "If it's taking these four chaunters we are, sir," he averred, "it will be best to make two trips of it. If they could be warned not to put in the time with another shant of the bivvy, that is."

But Jack Prance, who came up at this point, said that as far as he was concerned he was accustomed to tight fits; as indeed he was, having only two rooms to live in and a large wife and six children. The others felt the same way, so they managed somehow to crowd themselves into the seat. The baskets and packages had been stowed away by some kind of magic and Mr. Carboy had his foot on the steps. He would have hoisted himself up beside the coachman immediately if the inn groom had not come over to them in a state of excitement.

"It's him, sir!" he exclaimed, pointing at the occupant of a dogcart which had wheeled creakily into the yard. "It's the Duke of Outland, sir!"

Mr. Carboy dropped his foot from the step and walked around the carriage to get a better look. The driver of the dogcart was an old man with untidy white whiskers, wearing a shaggy coat which probably was made of fustian and which certainly had seen better days—much, much better.

Perhaps this is as good a time as any to remark that at this particular moment in history, more than at any other, the people of England stood in awe of their peers. They loved a lord, they burbled over a baron, they thought an anemic earl more interesting than a famous prime minister pronouncing on points of foreign policy, they mulled over each known minute in the life of a marquis. And as for a duke, it can only be said that they were completely flabbergasted at his magnificence.

"That's Old Sheppy!" said Carboy in a bemused tone.

"Yes, sir, Mr. Carboy, sir, that's Old Sheppy hisself," confirmed the groom.

"Blow me tight!" gasped Jack Prance.

Daniel Groody was the only one who failed to react properly to the occasion. One look over his shoulder sufficed for him. "I'll lay two bob," he muttered to himself, "you could haul that doddy up by his heels and shake a young gopher or a bullfrog out of his clothes." He turned his attention to Duke, his favorite of the pair of horses. "You're a juke as is a juke," he muttered. "Ah, Juke, you've a fine glossy coat and you're a fine glossy fellow, and when it comes to blue blood, I lays my shilling on you."

Mr. Carboy, his curiosity sated, was in his seat. Groody gave the reins the smallest hint of a tug which the bays understood, for they set off at a brisk pace.

"May I say, sir, it's your son, Mr. Alfred," said Groody in chatty tones, "that's got the fine hands for this. What a rider to the hounds he'll make!"

Carboy grunted, "I'm glad to hear it." He then settled down into the cramped space at his disposal and said nothing more during the ride to the Hall.

2

At this very moment the son and heir of the Carboys was demonstrating that he had a pair of feet for hill climbing as well as a fine hand for the reins. He was making his way in a great hurry along a curving patch which ended on a rocky crest well above the subdued August current of the river. On this crest stood what was left of a Norman church.

When he came in sight of the moldering tower of the church, he began to run so fast that he reached the entrance in a breathless condition. His cheeks were red with the exertion and his wavy yellow hair was standing on end.

"Nelly, Nelly!" he called. "Are you there? Are you safe?"

A voice from within, the kind of voice which suggests that its owner must be very attractive indeed but often proved itself a delusion and a snare, answered at once. "Yes, Allie, I'm here. You're late. I've been here a long, long time."

"I had a bad time getting away," said young Carboy, blinking in the gloom of the interior, which seemed very cool and sepulchral after the blaze of the August sun.

Even the difficulties in which his eyes were involved could not prevent him from seeing almost at once, however, a slender figure seated on an overturned slab of stone. No delusion or snare this time! The owner of the voice was a young and pretty girl with dark hair and eyes of that very decided blue in which Ireland seems to excel. Her nose had a freckle or two, and was much improved thereby, although it had started out quite well, and there was a commendable roundness to her cheeks. A very pretty girl, in fact.

"Oh, Nelly!" said the boy. "I was frightened! Nelly, this place is haunted!"

The girl, who was dressed in blue ticken, a coarse and cheap fabric which could look well only when draped on a neat figure and had a hard enough time even then, got to her feet in a hurry. Her feet looked small though encased in shoes with blunter toes than the fashion of the moment decreed.

"Haunted?" she said. "Do you mean there's a ghost here?"

Young Alfred Carboy was glad of the honest excuse afforded by her alarm to take both of her hands reassuringly in his.

"I wouldn't have asked you to come here if I'd known about it. It was the groom told me and that was what kept me late. I guess we had better get out of here fast."

"Yes, Allie," said the girl. "I guess we had."

They left the shade of the ruinous walls and ran, hand in hand, to a safe distance where they could look down on the stream below. Here they were out in the warmth and security of the sun, and the terror they had felt in the gloom of the old church slipped from them at once. They seated themselves on the edge and the girl promptly withdrew her hands from his.

"Tell me about the ghost," she said. "Is it a lady with a dagger who murdered her husband? Or is it a nobleman who lived a very wicked life?"

"Neither," said the boy, watching her face with an expression on his own which said that he would be content to go on like this forever and never ask for anything better. "This ghost is quite different. It's an old priest who did a lot of good and can't bear to leave his church because he loved it so much. Sometimes, so the groom says, when the wind is strong enough you can hear

him intoning the service and"—his voice dipped a notch or two—"and sometimes you can hear *other voices joining in!*"

The girl indulged in a pleasantly high laugh which carried a definite note
of relief. "I wouldn't have run away if I'd known it was the ghost of a nice
old priest," she said. "You can't be afraid of one like that."

Alfred was not as sure of this as she was. "A ghost is a ghost," he said.
"The groom says if you see him and let yourself answer when he speaks,
you vanish and you're never heard of again. Perhaps it's the voices of those
who did speak which can be heard joining in the services."

The girl seemed very proud of her dress, which clearly was a new one.
She patted her skirts into place and seemed very conscious of the cuffs on
the sleeves, which were turned back far enough to give a full view of a pair
of good elbows. Her expression had changed, however, to one of extreme
gravity.

"Allie," she said, "I know it was wrong of me to meet you here. I must
never do it again. Here or—anywhere else."

The boy looked most particularly boyish as he listened to what she said.
Her gravity did not seem to disturb him much.

"It's hard to believe that I saw you for the first time just six days ago," he
said. "I'm talking to your father and you come out with a message for him.
He says, 'Well, here's my little girl.' I take a look at you and I say to myself,
'She's nice.' Then I take a second look. 'She's pretty and she's sweet.' Then
I keep on looking and I say, 'She's *wonderful!*' That was just six days ago
and now, Nelly, I know that I love you. I guess I shouldn't say that, but the
truth of it is, I'm clean off my head about you. But I'm not asking if you feel
the same way about me because that—well, that would be putting the nags
to the gallop, wouldn't it?"

"Oh, Allie!" said the girl. "You shouldn't have said that."

He seemed a little puzzled. "About the nags?"

"No, no. About—about loving me. It made me very glad to hear you say it
but I—I'm not sure you really mean it."

"You'll find out I really do, Miss Nelly Groody. And now I guess you'll
take that back about not seeing me again."

But the coachman's daughter shook her head. "No, Allie. What you've said
makes it still more necessary for us not to meet like this again. . . . It's
wrong. My father works for your father—and you know what *your* father
would say if he knew. There would be serious trouble for all of us."

Alfred Carboy shook his handsome head. "I would tell my father the
truth." His eyes were filled with resolution. "I would stand right up to him."

There were several moments of silence while the girl tried to find the
right words to say. She kept her eyes lowered and with her fingers she
smoothed a place in her skirt which showed a hint of a crease.

"It's like this, Allie," she began finally. "My father is a poor man. A
coachman can't be anything else but poor, can he? But with Daddy we never
know what is going to happen. He always says what he thinks, even when

it's about his employers. He says it right to their faces. How many times do you think we've moved that I can remember?"

Alfred considered this for a moment. "Four times?"

"Eleven." Her expression carried a suggestion of all the trouble this had meant for the family of the irascible Daniel Groody. "It's not because he isn't a good coachman. He knows more about horses than anyone, I think. It's just the things he says. When he comes home and tells my mother about the conversations of the day and he begins, 'And I said to him, "It's a mighty funny thing about you, mister——,"' she doesn't wait to hear any more. She just goes and begins to pack the boxes because she knows we'll soon be moving again. But when he says, 'I told him right to his face I wouldn't take that from anyone,' why then she begins to cry because this generally means there will be no separation pay; and it's so very hard to move without separation pay."

"Then you mean you can't see me because your father might lose his job?"

Nelly nodded her head reluctantly. "It's partly that. You see Mama wants to stay very much this time. She has rheumatism and sometimes we're put in damp houses and then she suffers a great deal. But the house your father gave us is dry and warm, and Mama is very happy about it. Just this morning she said, 'You keep a tight rein on that tongue of yours, Daniel Groody.' It's not so much the money this time because Papa has inherited some from his old uncle Shamus in Ireland." She mentioned this with an air of pride. "Oh, quite a lot of money, it is. Two hundred pounds. That's a very great deal, isn't it, Allie?"

The boy nodded. "Yes, Nelly."

"It was because he fell heir to the money that Mother was able to get me this dress. It's the finest dress I've ever had. I'll have to take it off before she catches me wearing it like this. But I did want you to see me in it."

"I think it's the prettiest dress I've ever seen." Then he added in a sympathetic tone of voice, "You do have a bad time of it, don't you?"

This seemed to her rather in the nature of a reflection on her parents and she flew to their defense. "I'm very happy in most ways. We're a most affectionate family. I don't want you to think I'm complaining." She rose to her feet. "But I'm sensible enough to know, Allie, that nothing but trouble can come of meetings like this between you and me. I've had no education except I can read and write. I've never read a book, because there's never been one in the house. Doesn't that show you what I mean? We must be sensible. We must indeed, Allie."

"I can't be sensible where you're concerned, my sweet little Nelly. There's no use asking it."

"At any rate we must be sensible enough to go home now. You must go first. I'll not start until you're out of sight. No one must see us together."

The boy got up reluctantly. "Whatever you say about that."

The coachman's daughter took the seams of her full skirt in her hands and dropped him a curtsy.

"Good afternoon, Mr. Carboy."

The boy grinned. "Good afternoon, Miss Groody."

3

The carriage had not returned from the village when Alfred Carboy reached the stables. He said to himself as he hurriedly saddled his horse, a trim little black, "I'll ride out and give them a welcome." Accordingly he came galloping over the East Meadow as the well-filled equipage arrived at the stone gatehouse.

"Hurrah!" he shouted, loosing his lasso from the pommel.

Groody raised his whip in response and one of the gleemen answered the greeting with a reverberating "Halloo!" of his own. Alfred tapped a heel gently into his mount's ribs and came charging after them. He was twirling the lasso in the air now and shouting excitedly.

"Hello, Father! Did you have a nice ride out from town? Did you bring everything? There's going to be a high old time tonight, isn't there?"

"I brought everything on the list," shouted Carboy in response. Then he became anxious. "See here, young fellow, don't go twirling that thing at us. You'll do some damage if you don't watch out."

"Ah, sir!" said Groody. "It's nothing he's ever roped with it. He likes to swish it around and pretend he's good at it."

But there's always an exception to a rule and always a first time for everything. Before he heard his father's admonition, Alfred had loosed the rope. It came snaking lazily through the air and by some unhappy chance landed over the head of Jack Prance. As it tightened over his shoulders, the singer let out a frightened squawk. It proved to be a perfect cast, lifting Prance out of the crowded seat with a strong backward tug.

"Help!" cried the leader of the quartet in frantic tones.

Groody brought the carriage to a stop with an expert pull on the reins but it was too late to prevent the famous soloist of the Hercules Tavern from leaving the company and ending up in a clump of privet beside the drive. It was, fortunately, a sturdy specimen of its kind and it cushioned his fall. Nevertheless he settled down into the greenery until nothing of him showed but a frightened white face and two agitated feet in rusty Wellingtons with well-patched soles.

"Are you hurt?" asked Carboy anxiously.

There was much threshing about of legs and arms and finally Mr. Prance emerged from the hedge and got his feet on solid ground.

"Tag me, Toby!" he ejaculated, trying to release his arms. "What happened? How did I get all wound up like this? For a second I thought Jack Ketch had me."

Young Alfred, very contrite, freed his arms of the rope. Prance's eyes surveyed his nether portions and he let out a sudden bleat of dismay.

Samuel Carboy asked in a still more anxious tone: "What's wrong, man? Have you broken a leg?"

"It's not my bones, sir. It's my trowsis. There's nothing left for me to sit down in."

"Are you all right except for the trousers?"

"I think so, sir. Lumme, was I taken aback!"

Carboy turned furiously on his son. "You rascal!" he bellowed. "You thoughtless young scoundrel! You might have killed the man."

"Yes, sir. No, sir." Allie was too taken aback himself to know what he was saying. He stood by his horse's head and wound the rope up into a small ball.

"Don't you 'no, sir,' me!"

"I'm sorry, Father," said Allie, very uncomfortable and red of face. "I didn't mean to do anything. I just let it fly for fun."

"Fun, eh? Give it to Groody, young fellow."

The exchange was carried out, with obvious reluctance on the boy's part.

"Now then, Groody, I want you to burn that thing. We'll have no more of this nonsense." Carboy glowered at his son and heir. "You're a young simpleton, that's what you are."

"Yes, sir."

"You did it on purpose."

"No, sir. It was an accident. I've never roped anything before."

"Well, you'll never do it again. I will see to that. We're going to have a serious conversation before this day's out, young man. I'm going to cut your allowance off for a month."

"You can't do that, sir."

Carboy bellowed, "And why can't I?"

"Because," explained the boy, "I've no allowance to cut off. You cashiered me for a month when you were down last."

"So I did," Carboy scowled. "Well, damme, it'll be two months now. You won't have a shilling to your name for the whole of your summer holidays." He motioned in the direction of the stables. "Ride back and leave the horse for Groody to attend to. I want you to go straight to your room and say a prayer of thanks that nothing worse came out of this. And get this through your head: I'll have no further foolishness of any kind out of you."

"Yes, sir."

Allie sprang into the saddle and rode off. Jack Prance climbed stiffly into the back seat and settled down among his fellows again.

"Do you feel all right now, Prance?" asked Carboy, glancing over his shoulder.

"I think so, sir." The soloist spoke in a cheerful tone. "I'm kind of a tough 'un, Mr. Carboy."

"That's good. You'll get a new suit of clothes out of this."

Carboy watched his son riding ahead of them up the drive with a dark air. But after several moments his mood changed. There was even a hint of reluctant approval in the wink he suddenly bestowed on the coachman.

"Groody," he said, "you were right. The boy *does* ride well. He rides oncommon well. Just like a—well, you know what I mean, one of those half-man and half-horse creatures."

Out of the depths of his lack of schooling and his slimness of knowledge Groody managed to produce the right word. "Would it be a centaur now that you're meaning?"

"Yes, that's it. The boy rides like a centaur, Groody." He indulged in a half chuckle. "I can't help feeling proud of the young rascal. But," turning a sharp glance sideways, "don't you go telling him I said so."

4

The members of the quartet, discovering a need for slumber, were accommodated in the haymow where, no doubt, being well trained in precision and unity, they snored in close harmony. Samuel Carboy made a brief tour of inspection of his new domain and came back in a mood of high elation. Everything he had seen had pleased him, particularly the park, which was baronial in its dimensions. He stood on the drive and looked up at the high roofs of the Hall, at the massed chimneys, at the stone carvings over all the doors and windows, at the play of the last rays of the sun on the glass of the tall oriel window.

"This is an out-and-outer," he said to himself. "Getting it will always be the great moment of my life."

When he reached the small room which he regarded as his study in competition with his wife, who insisted it was a strawberry parlor, he found that amiable lady awaiting him with what proved an interesting sheaf of news.

"Sir Theobald Gardiner sent over a note," she reported. "He's staying at Outland Park and he persuaded His Grace to let him join us here for dinner tonight, if we have a plate for him."

"Splendid!" exclaimed Carboy. His eyes glistened in the anticipation of a real triumph. "He's been nibbling and now I think he's ready to bite. You gave him a nice polite reply, I trust, m'dear."

"I did," answered his lady. "And now what do you think of this? There's a rumor that George Grace is taking a long lease on a house owned by the duke—the stone house with a high porch at Willikin's Elbow—and is going to settle down there permanently. He's going to make do on what he has. That at least is what I've been told by that reliable little gossip, the curate. The curate even told me how much rent George is going to pay. He, the curate—"

"Whose name, if you must go on forgetting it, is the Rev. Diggory Weather-Townsend."

"Altogether too much of a name for such a funny little man. Well, your Rev. Mr. Weather-Townsend says that George is going to devote himself at last to his painting."

An unexpected scene of gravity took possession of the man who confidently expected to build on the elimination of a useless partner a career of titanic proportions. He would never forgive Grace for the trail of bitterness he had sown through the banking offices and the countinghouses of the City but, nevertheless, he felt a stirring of regret.

"It may be what he should always have been doing. Who knows, I may have jolted him into his right sphere."

"At any rate you jolted him out of the center office which he had no right to in the first place," declared Mrs. Carboy, who had not relented a jot. She added suddenly: "Isabelle's sick. She was taken down with the measles yesterday."

"I *am* sorry." This was in the nature of an understatement, for Carboy intended to turn the occasion into an impromptu testimonial dinner to his own pyramiding greatness. He wanted his daughter on hand to see and hear and remember. He added, with a glum nod: "I believe Sir Theobald will be as much disappointed as I am. He always asks about the minx. On your way out, Belle, tell that butler fellow I'll have a whisky and water. I'll have it here. And without any delay because I'm thirsty."

His wife gave him a hard look as she reached for the purple velvet bell-pull. "You'll have to get yourself accustomed to all this grandeur, Sam," she said. "And, by the way, there's someone waiting for you. A barrister. He drove over from Reading."

"Then that ratty-looking stanhope on the drive is his. Did he say what he wanted?"

"I haven't spoken to him. Do you want him sent in?"

"I suppose so." Carboy had hoped for a short rest before dinner and he resented the dimming of this prospect. "But I won't order a whisky for him. Any man who arrives at such an hour can drive home thirsty."

The barrister's name proved to be Rankster and he proceeded to business as soon as he had ensconced himself in a chair, using a form of address which might be termed explosive.

"I've come about the Waterloo Tontine," he said. "Do you know that it is positively—*sweeping*—this country? It is, sir, I assure you that it is."

Carboy shook his head. "I was introduced to this Tontine in a curious way and my acquaintance with it ended there. I've been too busy with more important matters to pay any attention to such things."

"Sir," said the barrister with a dramatic gesture, "this is the biggest 'go' yet. They've opened four offices in London to accommodate the people who want to buy."

"How much money has come in?"

"Millions, sir, millions. Over a thousand shares have been sold in Manchester already. They're clamoring for the chance to get in up in Yorkshire. It's the same thing—let me see now—up in Glasgow and, yes, sir, as far north as Fife and Aberdeen where they don't—he, he!—take naturally to any kind of financial risk. The shares, sir, are going like hot muffins."

The barrister had drawn out a small book from a pocket and was flipping over the pages rapidly in his search for facts.

Carboy smiled. "A morocco man, I see."

The lawyer looked offended. "Not quite, sir. I've been given charge of presentation and sales in the Oxford district. I'm having quite a success, sir. I rather think you'd be surprised if you saw the list of those who are going in. Oddly enough the chief interest seems to be in the class which might conceivably interest you, Mr. Carboy, the twelve to eighteen years. Things are really going in that classification. They're boiling, sir, boiling. I've sold eighteen shares myself and my assistants have accounted for a round dozen. Your partner has put his son in. I beg your pardon, sir, your former partner."

Carboy's interest had been casual up to this point. Now he sat up straight in his chair and stared at the voluble barrister. "Are you telling me that George Grace has entered his son Julian?"

"Indeed, yes, sir. He signed the papers yesterday and gave me the hundred guineas."

Carboy said nothing for several moments but his mind had been busy. "There you see the real Ninny Grace!" he said to himself. "He throws away most of his patrimony on the Exchange and then hopes to provide a future for his son by buying him the shakiest kind of an annuity. The whole thing's a gamble but he seems to regard it as an investment. He'd rather do that than start in and work for his family."

"Would you be interested, Mr. Carboy, in putting your son, or your daughter, or both, into the twelve to eighteen?"

Carboy took a long sip of his whisky and water. "Before answering you, Mr.—er—Rankster, I'm going to ask you a question of my own. What part is Hark Chaffery playing in the Waterloo Tontine?"

"Hark Chaffery, sir?"

"Hark Chaffery. I have reason to believe he's interested in it."

"Well, sir, I don't know, I'm sure. He may have bought a share for himself."

Carboy swept that possibility aside. "Listen to me, Mr. Lawyer. Chaffery never puts in. He's interested only in taking out."

The expression on the face of the barrister suggested that a hostile foot was trampling on something which might turn out to be his financial grave. "Sir! Are you suggesting that Hark Chaffery has had a share in the organization of the Waterloo Tontine? That is an absurdity, sir. It has been organized for benevolent reasons, as you must surely have heard."

"Yes, I've heard that too. But I don't believe it entirely."

"Sir, the lottery king of London would be sadly out of place on our board, which consists of men of the highest ideals and the most philanthropic aims. Haven't you seen our list of sponsors and committee members—Baron Aldwych, Sir Humphrey Waystreet, Jenkins Store, M.P., Sir Sockden Deane——"

"Yes, yes, I've seen the list. I've seen all those names on many lists." He leaned forward and nodded his head confidentially. "Keep your ears open and your eyes too. You don't want to be involved in anything shady, I'm sure." Then he paused. "Mr.—er—Rankster, who acts as your chairman?"

"I believe it's Sir Sockden Deane."

"I know him. I think I could go straight to him if needs be. Now, Mr.—er —Rankster, who's your secretary?"

"A very good man, sir. Experienced in the Irish tontines. His name is Charles Wogan Finnerty."

"I think," declared Carboy after some cogitation, "that I've heard of Mr. Finnerty. Is he sometimes called 'Slab'?"

The barrister nodded reluctantly. "I've heard him referred to by that name. May I repeat that he's a most excellent man for the post?"

Carboy leaned back in his chair and took a nip of the whisky. "Mr.—er —Rankster, have you been in the London offices of the Tontine?"

"Yes, Mr. Carboy. On several occasions."

"I've been wondering, sir. I've been wondering if you happened to meet anyone there besides Mr. Slab Finnerty. Someone who might conceivably be—well, sort of keeping an eye on things."

The barrister hesitated. "Well, now that you ask, there was on each occasion a man in the offices whose—whose official station I found a little puzzling. A curious-looking man named Downs."

"Downs." Carboy repeated the name as though it had touched lightly some chord in his memory. "Why do you describe him as curious?"

"Well, sir, he was white all over. Even his eyelashes. There's a name for it, I think."

"Albino?"

"Yes, that's it."

"Did you talk to him?"

"No. Not directly. He listened while I talked to Mr. Finnerty."

Carboy remained in thought for several moments. "It's just possible that I'll have some business for you. No promises, mind you. But I'll think it over and let you know in a couple of days. And now I would offer you a whisky but you have so far to go that I'm sure you want to be on your way."

5

The dinner was going very well indeed. There had been toasts and Sir Theobald Gardiner had been quite witty while Whip Hanlon, Mrs. Carboy's father, had surprised everyone by making the table rock with his down-to-earth witticisms. The mutton was rich and fine, the roast beef was tender, the capons roasted to a perfect crispness, the wine completely to the satisfaction of the most difficult in the company. Daniel Groody had not dropped a single plate. Jack Prance and his men in the minstrels' gallery—this most perfect and complete of houses boasted of one—had kept the table in stitches, particularly when the leader had sung his best solo, which he had written himself. It began:

If poor Jack Prance had got his chance
   Tonight he'd sing afore the king.
(Spoken) *Meaning no offense to present company.*

Samuel Carboy was the best satisfied of them all. Before dinner he had talked confidentially with Sir Theobald Gardiner and the latter had expressed his desire to have a financial share in the new shipping amalgamation. They had, in fact, reached a thorough understanding and had come out to dinner with the baronet's hand familiarly and even affectionately on his host's shoulder. The guests, who had been assembling while they talked, had been properly impressed with the perfections of Beaulaw Hall. Yes, it had been very close to a perfect dinner.

"I heard something this afternoon," said Carboy, waving away a third helping of Yorkshire pudding but allowing his glass to be filled. "George Grace has bought a share in this Tontine for his son."

At the other end of the table on Mrs. Carboy's right, Sir Theobald Gardiner nodded his glossy head. He was at his magnificent best; his breeches displayed a perfect pair of legs, his coat was of black velvet, his waistcoat white silk with gold buttons, the lace of his cuffs fell as low as his well-groomed knuckles. "I heard about it," he said. "In fact, George told me himself. I couldn't help feeling it was an odd thing for him to do. But it seems clear enough that the whole country is going mad about it. The patriotic touches in the prospectus seem to have done it. The money is simply rolling in."

"Yes," said Carboy slowly. "But I—I happen to know something a little disturbing. It may be necessary to take a hand in it to get matters straightened out. Perhaps you and I, Sir Theobald, if you have no objection to a good dust-up."

"None at all," said the baronet heartily. "I enjoy a fight. I was a good boxer once, you know. I take it you have something up your sleeve."

Carboy nodded his head. "I rather think I have."

"Sam," said a clergyman cousin, sitting halfway down the board, "what are tontines? I've been hearing about them all my life but, as you know, I've no head for that sort of thing, and I never have got it straightened out."

"Well, Edwin, if you have any idea of buying into one, I would advise against it," said Carboy with a grin for the benefit of the rest of the company. "Might lose most of your skin, old boy. You see a tontine is called a form of insurance, on the annuity order; but actually it's a gamble. Hardly for the cloth, eh, Sir Theobald?"

"It's a clever scheme. But certainly *not* for the cloth."

"If any more of you are in the dark," said the host, glancing about him, "I can explain how it works in a few words. Generally there are six or eight classes, starting with children and winding up with people over fifty-five. Each class is run separately. Suppose we consider boys and girls from twelve to eighteen years. They are entered by their parents at one hundred guineas apiece. For twenty years—that's what they call the tontine period—the money is kept in active use and the profits are applied to the principal, except, of course, such sums as are needed to pay operating costs. At the end of the tontine period the total has rather more than doubled. At this point the payment of interest begins. Each participant gets an equal amount.

"And now," went on the host, his face expressing the interest he felt in any scheme as neat as this, "we come to the gimmer. When the holder of a share dies or falls out of sight, his part of the interest reverts to the others and his payments thereafter are divided equally among all the survivors. As the years pass and the members begin to die off faster, the survivors begin to enjoy handsome incomes. It becomes fantastic as things narrow down; because, you see, the full amount must be paid, no matter how few there are to receive it, even when there is only one recipient left. There was one case, I think it was in France, where the sole survivor was an old woman. She had paid a small sum to get in but during the last few years of her life she had an income of close to"—he looked about him solemnly—"of close to twenty thousand pounds a year."

"Twenty thousand pounds a year!" exclaimed Whip Hanlon in an awed voice. "That's a lot of dimmock."

Sir Theobald consumed a final forkful of the sage and summer savory stuffing, sighed in repletion, and proceeded to take the discussion into his own hands.

"Do you know, Samuel," he said, "that I've come close to going into one of these tontines several times? What held me back was the infernal slowness of them. You have to wait until you're ready to die before you know if you're going to be one of the big winners. I like my fliers to be quick—the start, the horses in the backstretch, the struggle up to the tape. But you have to concede that the final stages of a big tontine can be very exciting. Do you know the story of the two old men in France who survived the rest of the field? A capital story, this one. The first of the old men belonged to a noble family, an impoverished set who had been existing for several years on his share. The other was a doddering old notary in a small town. The noble family resented the stubborn way in which the notary insisted on living and standing in their way. Feeling ran high. It ran so high that the citizens of the small town had to organize to protect their man. They took turns standing guard over his house at night, four at a time; loaded pistols ready and a signal arranged which would set the church bells to tolling if the other side tried violence. *They* considered trying it but got a firm hint from someone high up to drop the idea. So their man died and the notary lived on for three years. He had no family so he endowed the village in some perfectly jackassic ways."

The company was listening in an absorbed silence.

"But you have to go to the Irish tontines to get real excitement," went on the baronet. "They always run books on the outcome, of course, and they get into a positive frenzy during the last stages. Do you recall the story of the four old women? This one ran out half a century ago and it reached a point where only these four decrepit, ignorant crones were in the running. They were all women of very modest means. The betting got so furious that all of them had to be guarded. A man was caught one night climbing through the window of one of them, with a knife in his belt. He had bet everything he owned on another one of the four and was planning to slit the throats of the three in turn. The old ladies didn't seem to care very much, being so very old; but not too old to have carriages of their own, and companions, and four big meals every day. Then a doctor tried to bribe three of the cooks to slip some poison into the food they prepared. The news leaked out and he had to run off to South America. Just got away, at that, the officers arriving at the pier as the vessel warped out of the harbor. One of the cooks was supposed to have tried it but his mistress took a dyspeptic turn and didn't touch the poisoned dish."

"Which one of the old ladies won?" asked a cousin.

"Oh, the doctor's choice. But he couldn't collect a shilling on his bets. South America was too far away for that."

As the talk went on Carboy had been looking about him: at his wife's father, that toughest of octogenarians, at his wife, whose gros de Naples dress was cut low enough to display a healthy as well as handsome pair of shoulders, at his uncles and aunts and cousins, all of them very bobbish in a hard-bitten, apple-cheeked, full-waisted way. He was finding justification for the course he had in mind.

"Cousin Edwin," he said, addressing the clergyman relative, "would you consider us a long-lived family?"

"I would indeed, Samuel," answered the clergyman, who was already, as Mrs. Carboy remarked later, a little coxey-loxey. "No Carboy ever dies under eighty. No, sir! Those who don't reach ninety are the weaklings."

The head of the household turned suddenly in the direction of his son. "Alfred," he directed, "stand up!"

The son and heir of the family was startled at being thus signaled out. He rose slowly to his feet, wondering which one of his sins had found him out and whether he would have to expiate it publicly.

"I've had a change of mind," declared Carboy, looking about him sternly as though challenging anyone to deny him the right. "I'm going to buy a share in the Waterloo Tontine for my son. I have two excellent reasons. The first stands here before you. Have you ever seen a better physical specimen than this son of mine? Go over and try his muscles, some of you. All of you, if you like. Have you ever seen a more handsome and healthy complexion? He'll live to be ninety at least, this son of mine will. At any rate, I'll swear to this: he'll outlive the cub of a certain man whose name won't be mentioned, except that he's already put down his one hundred guineas on *his* son."

Alfred, blushing and looking thoroughly uncomfortable, decided to sit down at this point.

"Alfie!" said Whip Hanlon suddenly. "Stand up again."

Alfred got up, more embarrassed than ever. Mr. Hanlon rose to his own feet. He was a handsome old man in a florid way, with white hair and a well-trimmed beard. What was more, he was wearing breeches and displaying to view thereby the most enormous calves undoubtedly in the whole of England.

"This boy is my grandson and my namesake. I'm very proud of him. I agree with Sam that my grandson will live to a ripe old age. If," with a broad grin, "he should get to be eighty and show signs of not meaning to reach ninety, I'll be right on hand, ha-ha! to take steps. I'll cut him out of my will, damme if I don't!"

There was a loud roar of merriment at this, the old man laughing more than any of them.

"Stand up straight, Alfie," he went on. "Square your shoulders and throw out your chest. I want them all to see what a handsome fellow my grandson is."

"Yes, Grandfather," said Alfred. "Why don't you go into the Tontine yourself, Grandfather? You'd be sure to win it."

Everybody laughed again and the old man slapped his huge thigh and said proudly: "That's my Alfie. I tell you he's a smart 'un."

"The second reason," went on Carboy, when he was able to get the floor again, "is this. I'm going to apply for some changes in the organization and, in order to have any standing in court—well, I think I had better leave it at that. At any rate there is going to be another entry—a likely winner, I think."

There was loud applause around the table at this. Before it subsided, the baronet rose to his feet. "I don't wish to dampen any of the enthusiasm of our worthy host," he began, "but the figures show that most tontines are won by women. To take care of this, I am going to risk a hundred guineas myself for a share and I am going to nominate for it a very young lady who

has already insinuated herself into my heart by her charm and her exceptional beauty but who, because of a minor ailment, is not present this evening. If her parents have no objection, I desire to enter—Miss Isabelle Carboy."

The applause grew so loud at this that Samuel Carboy found it hard to make himself heard when he rose to propose a toast. "Ladies and gentlemen," he said, pitching his voice high, "I ask you to drink to the expectation that my two children will have for their declining years, in addition to what I shall leave them myself, a splendid income received from the decision we have just reached. I desire to couple with this sentiment the name of Sir Theobald Gardiner to whom we are so very much indebted."

Daniel Groody had been carrying in the Bow dessert plates, filled up high with the very finest of all sweets, a suet pudding stuffed with raisins and covered with that great benefaction to humanity, a foamy sauce, and over all, perfect lashings of the richest cream. He had heard every word said on the subject of tontines and he was feeling happy because it had enabled him to make up his mind on a most important problem.

"So, it's a long-lived family they are," he said to himself. "Is it, then, they've never heard of the Groodys of Donegal, not to speak of the Phelans of Killarney, where my mother came from? Is it they've never heard of those four ancestors of mine who lie in a row in the little churchyard, and them so tall you have to measure careful with the eye or you'll be trampling on their feet? It's marked plain as plain, their ages, and the youngest is ninety-two. Now that's the stock we come from; and a great shame it is that all four were bachelors.

"And it's beauty too, is it?" he went on, distributing the dessert nimbly under the unfriendly eye of the butler, who had been born in London and had no faith in foreigners of any kind, Scotch, Irish, Welsh, or even the rough-speaking men of the north and west. "Then let them think of this. My little Nelly is prettier and healthier than any of them. Miss Isabelle, is it now? Well then, we'll just take a hundred of the fine round jingling fellows me uncle Shamus left me and we'll enter Miss Nelly in this Tontour, or whatever it's called. And someday, the blessed Lord willing, she'll be driving in her own carriage and living like a queen."

The guests were drinking another toast and all of them were standing up and singing. Groody stood and waited, a suet pudding in each hand and a cream jug hooked in one finger.

"It's a great piece of luck that I found it out in time," he said aloud. So much noise filled the room that no one heard him. So he went on: "I didn't know what to do with it, this fine handsome lot of blunt. But now it's a relieved man I am because I know exactly what to do with it and I'll have no more burning of holes in my pockets."

6

When the ladies left the gentlemen to their wine, they did so regretfully because they knew that Jack Prance and his men would now begin on the coarse parodies of popular songs for which they were famous, such as "Here's to the Maiden of Blushing Fifteen" and "Oh Dear, What Can the Matter Be?" The son and heir of the house, knowing that he would not be missed, proceeded on a stealthy errand of his own. He stole out to the kitchens and found his way to a small room behind a hatch where Nelly Groody was washing dishes all by herself, looking very small behind such a mountainous heap of crockery.

"I hate to see you doing this," he said.

"It's just for this once," she answered cheerfully. "Being such an important occasion, everyone had to help."

"Just the same . . ." He looked about him to make sure that he had not been followed and then, being in a great hurry, did not finish what he had started to say. "I came to tell you I have a plan. I'm always thinking of plans, Nelly. You see, I'm named after my mother's father. He's always called Whip but his name really is Alfred. He's going to leave me most of his money. Do you know what I'm going to do with it? I'm going to start a big horse farm, the biggest in the world, and I'm going to take your father in with me as a partner. There can't be any objections then if I marry the daughter of my partner. It's done all the time. Isn't that a wonderful idea, Nelly?"

"Yes, it's wonderful, Allie. But please run along now or you'll get yourself in a most terrible row."

"The cook saw me coming in but she only grinned and winked. I think she's romantical-minded and likes to think I'm in love with you. She won't tell anyone I'm here. And here's some more news. Father has put me in this Tontine that's being started."

"Oh, you'll win it, Allie. I'm sure you will."

"Yes, I think I'll win it all right. But it won't do me much good because all the others will have to be dead before I collect the full amount. I mean it won't do us much good because you'll be an old lady then too. But you'll be my wife and I'll be as much in love with you as I am now and I'll buy you a diamond necklace or something just as fine."

"You do think of such sweet things to say, Allie." She stopped and listened. "That's my father's step. He won't know you came here to say you would make him a partner. All he'll know is that you shouldn't be here and that it will cause trouble. He may get angry and break all these dishes. Allie, you can go out this other way."

Allie decided that the time had not come to discuss partnerships with her short-tempered father. He went out the other way, saying as he did so: "I would like to break all the dishes too. So you wouldn't have to put your pretty hands in that dishwater."

CHAPTER FIVE

1

Samuel Carboy went for a walk next morning with his guest, Sir Theobald Gardiner. The latter would have preferred to ride but the owner of Beaulaw Hall had to acknowledge that he was not much of a horseman.

"I'm very much afraid, Sir Theobald," he said, "that it would be a case of Jack Gilpin all over again. Wasn't that the name of the fellow in the poem?"

Gardiner began to recite from the poem in question, with a rapt look on his face.

> "John Gilpin was a citizen,
>   Of credit and renown;
> A trained band captain, eke, was he
>   Of good old London town.

"What a splendid poet Cowper was! I considered his death nothing short of a national calamity."

"Well," said Carboy, "this Gilpin couldn't ride a horse and neither can I."

They fell immediately into conversation after that, their tall beaver hats bowed as they strode along, their high boots (which were covered clear to the ankles by their trousers) creaking a little on the rough country paths which they selected.

Carboy began to tell his companion his reasons for believing that Hark Chaffery and his organization of thieves were behind the Tontine. He had nothing more to go on than the evidence of the posting of the notice by a Chaffery henchman on the bronze robe of the god Taku and the information he had gleaned during his talk with the lawyer Rankster; but this seemed to him sufficient to warrant the start of a careful investigation.

"Now let us suppose, Sir Theobald," he said, "that this fellow gets tired of the few guineas he picks up in each of the hundreds of eating houses and in the scores of barbershops and hairdressing parlors. Let us suppose as well that he's willing to be relieved of the danger he runs as the head of a criminal mob. He wants to pull off a final coup, one so big that it will bring in the cooters," the term most commonly used on the streets for sovereigns, "by the million. How would he go about it?"

"I'm sure I don't know, my dear fellow," answered the baronet. "I'm afraid I'm somewhat deficient in an understanding of the criminal mind."

"They're not so different. I think I can trace the thoughts which run through the mind of our shrewd Master Chaffery. Being accustomed to making his money in the little goes, he would turn to the respectable big brother

of the lotteries, the tontine. He would then get together a group of decoys
—with titles, of course, like Aldwych and Deane and Waystreet—to act as
a board and lend an air of supposed respectability to the proceedings. They
would have no power, of course. All they'd get out of it would be a couple
hundred cooters apiece and a substantial slice of the disgrace later. The
money as it rolled in would be deposited at once in the Bank of England
and converted into consols. But would it be? Frankly I doubt it very much.

"I think," he went on, "that Master Hark Chaffery, that clever little man,
hasn't deposited as much as a crown piece in the bank. I'm sure he hasn't
bought a single government bond. The money is being stored in some convenient way as fast as it comes in. When enough of it has been accumulated
to make the kill worth while, Master Chaffery will scoop it up and decamp
to the Continent. There he'll spend the rest of his days, with race horses and
mistresses and a big palace to live in."

Gardiner turned a startled pair of eyes on his companion. "Damme, Carboy, I believe you're right. I believe that's exactly what this miserable fellow
intends to do. It's genius on your part to understand everything so clearly.
Positively, it's genius."

"Now then," continued Carboy, feeling a desire to puff out his chest at
his companion's praise, "since the criminals are moving in on such a respectable business as the running of tontines, I rather fancy, Sir Theobald,
that the time has come for respectable business to move in on the crooks.
Business will have to be represented, mind you, by men of a realistic turn
of mind."

"Oh, quite," said the baronet.

"We'll have to get definite evidence—and I don't think that will be hard—
and go to the proper authorities with it. The money will be seized and
deposited in the bank and the books will be taken over as a first step."

"And that," said the baronet with a sigh of regret, "will be the end of the
Tontine."

"Not at all!" cried Carboy. "Let us suppose that a million guineas have
been collected. It may be a great deal more, as a matter of fact. Are we
going to send all that back? Are they to be disappointed, all these hopeful,
eager people who are taking this chance that they will live long enough to
be big winners? No, no, we can't disappoint the public. The realistic businessmen who will be put in temporary charge of the reorganization—you
and I, Sir Theobald, I rather think—must not be as selfish and hard as that.
The Tontine will be regularized and put under strict and permanent supervision. The realistic businessmen will step out, after being suitably reim-
bursed, and the Tontine will roll along for another sixty or seventy years."

"And what will the realistic businessmen get out of it? A matter of, say,
a good round thousand pounds?"

Carboy shook his head. "A percentage. You see, if it got out that we were
being paid, say, three or four thousand pounds, that would look to the public
like a great lot. There would be an outcry. People would say, 'We're being
robbed!' There would be so much talk about it that we would be cut down

to an honorarium. Sir Theobald, you say you want to learn how things are done. Well, this is the first lesson: never get yourself in the position of having to accept an honorarium. You could starve, sir, on honorariums. You will fail, you will see your house taken over your head, you will see the doors of the poorhouse opening up in front of you, if you let yourself be paid in that currency. The honorarium, sir, is suitable only for clergymen, professors, poet fellows and authors who can always be fobbed off easily. No, sir, what we want is a percentage. A very small percentage. So small, in fact, that everyone will say, 'Why, how generous these men are to accept a poor thing like half of one per cent for getting at the truth of this swindle. Give them a vote of thanks in the House, knight them, present them with diplomas all done up with gold seals.' But on a small percentage, Sir Theobald, I rather think we might bring in for ourselves as much as—say—ten thousand pounds apiece."

The baronet turned and looked rapturously at the head of Carboy and Co. "I sit at the feet of the master," he said.

On their return the conversation had veered to matters of much less consequence. Carboy was plowing along with tired feet when he noticed his companion stop for a moment and wave his hand. He stopped also and, looking about him, concluded that the baronet had waved at one of the upper windows of Beaulaw Hall.

"The little baggage!" said Sir Theobald. "I trust, Carboy, you won't object to my referring to your daughter in that way? I used the term with the utmost respect and admiration. A hand was waved to us from one of the windows and I am—shall we say, fatuous?—enough to believe it belonged to that very handsome child of yours."

"If it was Isa, it means she's getting better."

"I hope so. I trust, my dear host, that she will be well enough to put in an appearance before it becomes necessary for me to leave."

"That will depend. It will depend entirely on whether she looks well enough after her short bout with the measles. That little baggage, as you call her, is just as realistic as we'll have to be when we match our strength against the well-trained crowd of Hark Chaffery, Esq."

2

The horses had to be fed at seven o'clock so Daniel Groody was an early riser. This meant that his daughter, who got his breakfast for him, had been up at an even earlier hour. It was a few minutes short of six-thirty when she brought in from the tiny kitchen a rasher of bacon, three buttered rounds of toast and a bowl of tea.

Her father grinned and tossed two small coins in the air with one hand, catching them in the other. "More than the least he could decently give me," he said, "but less than I hoped to get, my little dickeybird." He slid the money into a pocket. "I dropped never a dish."

He began then to indulge in a series of facial grimaces, winks, grins, frowns and nods, which were intended quite clearly to mean something. Accustomed as she was to her father's eccentricities, the girl found this particular demonstration of them beyond her understanding. She looked for an explanation to her mother, who had just come into the room.

"Daniel Groody, will you stop acting like a monkey in a cage?"

Mrs. Groody was a neat woman who almost ruined her natural comeliness by a perpetual air of gloom. On this occasion her expression suggested that word had just been received of deaths in the family, that the roof might be expected to blow off the house at any minute and that there was every indication of a divine intention to fix an irrevocable date for the end of the world.

"Helen Groody," she said in a decidedly alto voice, "your father has something to tell you but doesn't know how to go about it. He'll be expecting me to do it for him."

The head of the family beamed. "If it's so good you'll be, Armanda," he said.

"Daniel Groody," declared his wife, "you know I don't approve of this. I'm against it from every standpoint. It will take more than half of what's left from the inheritance left you by your uncle Shamus. If we go in, we'll never see a shilling of it again."

"Nelly will," said the Irishman. "That's what I want to do. To protect her."

"Daniel Groody, you know she'll have to live to a good age before she gets anything out of it worth mentioning. It's a gamble, Daniel Groody. I," with an increase of sternness, "do not believe in gambling. Most particularly as the rest of the money is burning your pocket as well. At least it would, if I didn't have it in *my* pocket. I've got everything in my pocket if it comes to that and I'm not sure at all that I'll let you have the money for the tontine."

"Oh," said the daughter. "It's about the Tontine. Does Father want to put me in? Is that what this is about?"

Daniel Groody had become very tense all of a sudden. He said in a suspiciously quiet voice, "Is it that you won't let me have this money that you're saying, Armanda?"

"Mother!" cried the girl in sudden alarm. "You mustn't make Father angry! You know you mustn't!"

The coachman took a step nearer to his wife. "Are you saying I'm not to have my own money to do with as I please?"

"Daniel Groody, we'll have none of your tantrums now. Don't come a step nearer to me. Do you hear me?"

"I'll be thanking you for the money then."

"Give it to him, Mother!" cried Helen. "Father, you mustn't get so angry about things. You frighten the life out of me when you do."

"Helen Groody, I think you're in this with him. You're both ready enough to see that I get no good out of the money. I'm just his wife. I can slave all day long and have nothing to show for it. *My* future is not being thought about. I can starve in my old age for all he cares, as long as his daughter is provided for. Oh, I'll give him the money for the Tontan or Tontour or whatever it is. But the rest will stay right where I've put it for safekeeping. I'm not going to let Daniel Groody get his hands on that."

Her husband's manner relaxed at once. He looked at Nelly and gave her a relieved wink. "Well, child, it's settled then. You're to be put in against the son and daughter of the house. And beat them both you will or my name's not Groody and I don't have four uncles as lived to be over ninety. You'll be writing the letter for me to the lawyer man this very day."

Two days later Samuel Carboy heard about this unexpected competition and he did not like it at all. His dislike increased when he was told something else, that his son was making a practice of seeing a great deal of the coachman's daughter. "I'll attend to that young man," he said grimly. "And I'll attend to Groody." He tramped in high dudgeon to the region of the stables where he found Groody burnishing a piece of gear and singing " 'I'd give my pipe, I'd loan my bowl,' " in a high and quite melodious voice.

"See here, Groody, this won't do," said the proprietor of Beaulaw Hall, "it just won't do at all."

"What is it you don't like, Mr. Carboy?"

"Why," demanded his employer, "did you put your daughter in the Tontine? This isn't the kind of thing you should be doing with your money, if you *have* the money."

"I have the money, Mister Carboy."

"Groody, this kind of thing is for people of ample means. A hundred guineas, man! You can't afford to go gambling this way."

"Can't I now? Is it my own money or isn't it?"

"It's your own money, of course. But don't you see that you shouldn't go in when I do? It—well, it makes the thing seem ridiculous. People will laugh at us. They'll say you're aping me."

The stillness of manner into which Groody was likely to fall when his fighting instinct was aroused became quite apparent now.

"It's a funny thing, Mister Carboy," he said. "It's a mighty funny thing if any man living or dead can tell me what I'm to do or not do with my own money."

Carboy realized now that he had not expressed himself well, that he had gone further than he intended. Groody was a good man, and he did not want to lose him. It might be a difficult matter to get as good a man at the same money.

"What I meant to say, Groody, was that you ought to have consulted me. I could have told you better ways of making that bit of money of yours work for you than putting it into a gamble like this. What's bothering me is that I'm afraid I'm responsible for getting you into it. You heard me talking about it and you decided to follow my example. That makes me feel guilty. Isn't it so?"

"It is so. I'd heard a bit about them but I didn't know how they worked.

It was your talk and that of the man from the juke's place that made me see what a fine chance it was."

"Well," said Carboy, "it's done now and can't be changed. I hope your daughter lives long enough to get a lot of money out of it." He stopped at this point and his brief moment of good nature ended. "But there's something else and this won't do at all. I'm told that my son has been seeing a lot of your daughter. I'm putting my foot down about that right here and now."

It was clear that this did not suit Groody any better than it did his employer.

"And I put my foot right down on top of yours!" he said. "It's the first I've heard of it and I don't like it at all."

"I don't want him to get himself entangled in any way now," went on Carboy in a tone which had shaded to sullenness. "Oh, he'll do it, of course, sooner or later. Human nature, I guess. They must have their fling. It will cost me plenty to get him out of the messes he'll get into. But it would be plain negligence to let it happen right under my nose."

"And a sharp nose it is, Mister Carboy. I don't want my daughter in a mess any more than you want your son. But if it happened it's not a penny we'd be taking from you— What is it I am saying? *If it happened!*" The coachman's tone had changed to one of self-condemnation. "My little girl is as clean and pure as the snow or the fine white angels up in heaven. Nothing can happen where my Nelly is concerned. Why have I let myself speak as though I thought it might? A fine father I am, thinking and saying such things or standing by while you say them! . . . Just the same we'll have no more foolishness of any kind. If she speaks to your son again, it's the back of my hand she'll be feeling."

Carboy had allowed the deep expression of feeling on the part of this coachman to go unnoticed but he fastened on the last words.

"That's good. That's the attitude to take. If you keep your eyes open there'll be no trouble between us."

The mood of deep depression which preceded action was descending on Daniel Groody. Under the circumstances, it was well that his employer added in brisk tones, "Well, I must let you get back to work"; and betook himself away.

But what the two fathers had called foolishness was not to be prevented as easily as they imagined. The house occupied by the Groody family was a stone cottage on a rise of ground behind the stables. The next morning, after carefully scanning the surroundings, Alfred Carboy mounted his little black mare and came riding out on the nice bit of flat meadowland which provided the Groody family with a pleasant outlook. He saw the daughter of the family at once, of course, but pretended not to have done so. Instead he began to put the mare through her paces, sometimes riding at a full gallop, sometimes slowing down to allow of some fancy stepping. Once he stood straight up in the stirrups and once he dropped the reins and rode with his arms crossed on his chest. He was, in fact, doing a first-class job of showing off before the lady of his choice.

Nell Groody was sitting on the small porch, shelling peas. She was keeping her eyes on the basket in her lap, so that her long black lashes were like shadows on her cheeks. It must be explained further that, as the day was very warm and she had not expected anyone to see her, she had yielded to temptation by slipping off her shoes and stockings. Her feet looked almost as small and quite as white as a child's and it would have been difficult for anyone to see them without proceeding to name the toes after the order of the very old nursery rhyme—Harry Whistle, Tommy Thistle, Harry Whible, Tommy Thible, and little Oker Bell.

The equestrian brought the horse to a stop in front of the cottage and sprang to the ground.

"Good morning," he said in a low tone.

The girl pretended surprise. "Oh! Was it you riding out in the meadow?" Then she gave vent to a giggle. "You're a *wonderful* rider. You're—well, just *wonderful*." Then a sense of alarm drove the pleasure from her face. "Allie, you shouldn't have come here. You'd better go away at once."

She became aware then of the nakedness of her feet and tried desperately to slip on her shoes. Alfred Carboy grinned and called upon a much more recent slang expression.

"Never have I seen a prettier convention of ten," he said. "I could kiss every one of them."

"Allie! Please! You must go away at once."

"Yes, I know." But instead of moving, he gave his head a determined shake. "But they're not going to let me see you. I've had my orders. I won't see you again for a long time, a very long time, and I must be sure of one thing before I say good-by. You do like me, don't you, Nelly? You—perhaps —love me?"

Mrs. Groody called from the back of the house, "Helen Groody, who are you talking to?"

Nell was reduced already to the imminence of tears. "Allie, you *must* go away. Father has been so angry with me. I'm sure your father is just as bad. I've been told I mustn't see you or speak to you."

"Helen Groody, who's out there with you?" The reason that Mrs. Groody found it necessary to call instead of coming out to investigate herself was that she had been caught in the act of dressing.

"I'll go," said Alfred, smiling with the greatest fondness on the terrified girl. "But not until I've heard you say it."

"What is it I must say?"

"That you love me."

Nell got to her bare feet, holding the container of unshelled peas in one hand. "Oh, I do, I do!" she whispered. "I shouldn't say it, Allie. But I do. So very, very much."

Young Mr. Carboy smiled triumphantly. "That's what I came to hear. Good-by, Nelly, my darling one. Don't let them tell you it's—it's impossible.

Don't believe them if they do. We love each other. Never forget that. You keep on loving me and I'll keep on loving you and someday I'll come back and I'll just whisk you up in my arms and carry you off to a parson."

The sharp impact of Mrs. Groody's heels could be heard on the hall floor, advertising the fact that she had finished dressing and was coming out. "Now then, Helen Groody," she was saying, "your father will limb you for this."

Alfred Carboy turned, waved once, mounted his horse and rode away across the meadow.

CHAPTER SIX

1

Hark Chaffery was not getting the satisfaction he had expected out of owning the house on Grosvenor Square which had once belonged to the Duke of Outland. It was a difficult neighborhood for his henchmen to reach without attracting undesired attention. Nor could the fact be overlooked that the other residents of the square had not taken to him. This had been demonstrated most unmistakably soon after he had moved in.

Up Downs, who was in charge of the morocco men, had been responsible. He had convinced Chaffery that it would be the right thing to give a whooping soiree—Downs's own expression—and invite all the neighbors to attend.

"These bleeding dukes won't come to see me," Chaffery had protested.

But Up had been sure they would. "Curiosity," he said, giving his head a brisk nod. "Curiosity will do it, Hark. They know who you are. They'll come swarming in to see what you're like."

"They'll come to laugh at me, if they come at all."

"No one ever laughs at you, Hark."

Mr. Downs, it should be explained, did not get his nickname from the fact that he was taller than anyone else on the kedge where scrawniness was rather more the order. He received it when Chaffrey stumbled on the fact that away back in the good old days, when the crooks of London were well organized and had a sanctuary called Alsatia into which officers of the law seldom went, the leaders had been called the Upright Men. This had hit him on his funny bone and he had laughed in a high-pitched key. "Me an upright man?" he chortled. "Nah. But we could pass it over to someone. Downs, now. But we'll just call him Up." He laughed again and slapped his spindly thigh. "Up Downs. That's a good one. That's funny. Laugh, all of you." So they all laughed heartily and Downs became Up Downs for the rest of his life.

Great preparations were made for the entertainment of the Noses (one of Chaffery's favorite words) who lived about the square on which stood the

Van Nost statue of George I. Outland House occupied a corner and so was
not closed in tight with the other houses but had a bit of garden of its own
and a stone fence. Its view of the statue, it should be added, was rather
more concerned with the tail of the horse than with the imposing countenance of that great monarch. The arrangements were placed in the hands of
the most expensive caterer in London, who had supplied roasted capons and
ducks and great pink rib roasts of beef and hams which looked as bristly
with cloves as a porcupine with quills. There were mountains of sandwiches
and platters of wonderful cakes and tarts and confections. There was enough
wine to satisfy a whole company of five-bottle men and plenty of more serious
vinous fare.

Waiters were sent in and a score of musicians with their violins and bull
fiddles and pipes and horns. Finally a reluctant Jack Prance and a fearsome
trio of gleemen had been hired to do the entertaining. All in all, it was going
to be a great occasion.

But no one came. The curiosity on which Downs had counted had not
been strong enough. There was nothing but a great silence in the lofty hall
with its arching stairway and in the high-ceilinged and very gloomy drawing
room and even in the dining room where the hired staff had congregated.
There had not been as much as a single footstep on the paved area in front
of the house. The footmen stood about morosely in the glory of their scarlet
liveries. Jack Prance and his men looked more frightened by the minute.
Not a bow had been drawn across the strings of a fiddle.

By ten o'clock it was clear that the defeat was complete and decisive.
Hark Chaffery acknowledged to himself that for once in his life he had failed.
It was clear from the sag of his sloping shoulders and the limpness of his
chest that he was taking it badly. His small black eyes darted this way and
that, with a reptilian hint to them, and his fingers began to tap his forehead,
a sure sign of trouble ahead.

"Might as well wind up this glorious occasion," he said finally. He motioned in the direction of the dining room. "What am I going to do with
all this stuff?"

Someone suggested, "Let us work on it first and then send the rest to a
'ospital."

Chaffery glared. "Stow that!" he said bitterly. "Food that's been scorned
would poison them at the 'ospitals. I've a better idea myself. I'm going to
show the Noses what I think of them. Here," motioning to the head waiter.
"Take all the food out to the street and set it afire. Make a real bonfire of it.
I don't want any of the Noses to miss it."

A good supply of kindling and paper was taken out to the road and a
roaring fire built, on top of which all the fine food was piled, all the iced
cakes and the berry tarts and the sandwiches made of white bread and the
joints of cold meat and the roasted chickens and spiced condiments.

Chaffery walked to a window. "Some of them are joining in after all,
blast their eyes!" he muttered. "They're standing at their doors and windows

and wondering what it's all about." He turned and glared at his henchmen. "I hope they see in this how much I hate them."

He walked back to his chair and motioned to Jack Prance. "Come on, you. Sing something. You're being paid for it."

"I hopes so," said Prance. Then he added hastily, "Yes, sir. In course, sir."

"Are you caper merchants too?"

"No, sir. We don't dance. None of us."

"Then sing."

The quartet sang a song they had prepared for the occasion. It was not one of their best performances. They were in a highly nervous state and their voices may have quavered a bit. Chaffery had been informed of the usual procedure, however, and he acted accordingly. At the finish he laid aside his glass, to which he had been applying himself ever since the frost set in, and applauded. Jack Prance stood up on legs which trembled and gave a bow. He sat down in much quicker time than ever before and his men established an all-time record in getting on their feet and off again.

Chaffery glowered over his glass. "All right. You've sung and we've listened, now then, have you chaunters ever sung for these people?" He made a gesture with his free arm to indicate the square.

Prance thought it safer to assent. He gave a quick nod.

"Then tell me this. What's the most you've ever been paid for singing before a"—all the bile which the fiasco had stirred up in the lottery king became evident in his tone of voice—"before a bleeding duke, or a grinning earl, or a stinking lord?"

Prance had never sung before a duke or an earl or a lord of any description but it did not seem wise to say this. He proceeded to draw a figure out of his hat, as it were. "Three canaries," he said, meaning pounds.

Chaffery motioned to a man named Hoppy who acted as his almoner or his lord privy nurse, whichever seems the better description. "Give him six," he ordered. "Twice as much as he ever got from any of the high and mighty Noses. And now understand this, I want it told around. I want people to know that Hark Chaffery has a generous side to him. I want it told around to the discredit of the bleeding dukes and lords. I want you to talk."

"Yes, sir. We'll talk," Jack was fairly sweating with fear because the sum he had invented was costing the terrible Hark Chaffery so much.

"Now clear out of here, all that don't belong." Chaffery reached again for his glass. "I won't be able to go to sleep unless I get myself well plowed."

The imported helpers departed. The fire on the road died down. The honorable lords and ladies of the square were no longer watching. Chaffery turned his attention to his own people. He had taken to drinking gin straight from the bottle and by this time he was as well plowed as a seeded field.

Suddenly he cried out in a high screech, "Downs! Where's Downs? Bring that specimen of underdone white meat to me at once."

When the palpitating director of the morocco men had answered this summons, Chaffery glared at him in silence for several moments and then raised a forefinger.

"It was you, Downs, you told me to give a big blow. You said they would all come. You said they would be curious. More—more—moreover," he finally got the word out in full, "it was you said no one would dare to laugh at me." He raised both hands in the air. "All London will laugh at me now. My own men will snicker behind my back. I've been humilated." He liked to use long words but sometimes he overlooked a vowel or put his money on the wrong accent. "I've been humilated, I tell you. You come over here, Up." He pointed at a spot on the floor directly in front of him. "Right here. I've something to say to you."

Up Downs placed himself on the exact spot to which the index finger of the lottery king had pointed.

"I don't like being laughed at." Chaffery's voice rose to a still more shrill pitch. "I don't know what to do. I feel as if knives are cutting and whirling and snipping inside me. There's going to be suffering for this, and you're going to do most of it. Unless—unless you can turn the laugh on them. I don't know how but you've got to bring the Noses here to see me. Here, do you understand? To see Hark Chaffery. I want them all. And I want their wives with them, all dressed up to the nines and painted to the teeth. I want h'ostridge plumes and monocles and snuff and high hats. Do you understand? Then get to work."

2

His neighbors would not come to see him but Chaffery did not lack for visitors. He suddenly became very busy after the Battle of Waterloo had been fought and won and all manner of people called on him beside those who belonged. Some were barristers, some were bankers, some were businessmen. They came and went, as often as not after dark had fallen. They were always in a great hurry and they had no desire, it was clear, to be observed.

Samuel Carboy's housewarming had been held on a Wednesday. On the Saturday morning of that same week a strange visitor came to see Hark Chaffery. He was a little man who wore a hat drawn down over his brow and, in spite of the warmth of the day, a coat which fell below his knees. He was a bent old man and he walked slowly.

He did not attempt to enter by the front door but shuffled around humbly to the rear. When he had rapped on the door twice a voice inside said something which would have been unintelligible to anyone else but which elicited from the old man the words, "Barge along, Bob." The door opened at once to admit him.

This, it may be explained, was a holdover from the already mentioned early days when the criminals of London had a government of their own and laws and rather picturesque customs. They still believed it necessary to have passwords and had fallen into the habit of using the last lines of popular songs, the first half to be given and the response to be the last half. There had been an occasion not long before when the words "What my *tongue can never name"* had elicited the response *"Tol de rol de liddle lol."*

The old man took off his hat when he found himself in the kitchen, revealing a benevolent cast of countenance under a great mop of white hair. "Strike me lucky!" said one of the household, a footman. "It's just old Byron."

Byron the Sniveler was the acknowledged king of the beggars of London but this did not win him any great measure of respect. After all, the beggars cadged for what they got. They did not wrest their gains from the public by force or clever stratagem. They never found themselves at odds with the law unless they became involved in other illegal activities. Nevertheless Byron the Sniveler was a great artist in his way. Each night he stood in the region of the theaters, bent over so that his face was rarely seen. He never addressed any of the ladies and gentlemen as they stepped in and out of their carriages. Occasionally (he was very patient and watched for the best opportunity) they would hear a sob. Those who knew him would laugh and say, "There's the Sniveler at his tricks," but this did not happen often because the old man strove to work only on strangers. Whenever anyone felt impelled to stop by a sense of pity, they were lost; for Byron the Sniveler had some of the poetic instinct which might have been expected in one of his name and could tell a story calculated to melt the metal heart of a kingly statue. It was well known that he had accumulated many tens of thousands of pounds in his day.

"Splints!" said the old man sharply, addressing the footman. The latter had earned his name by starting on the hospital lay, which meant he had robbed the pockets of the victims of accidents.

"Yes, Sniveler."

"I want to see Hark."

"I'll tell him you're here, Sniveler."

The old man said in a voice from which all trace of benevolence had departed, "Oh no, you won't, Splints! You'll take me right up to him, Splints. And there'll be no announcing so he can go dodging away into some hole."

The old man, followed by the reluctant footman, shuffled into a small room on the ground floor where Chaffery was already deep in work. He was wearing a morning jacket with elaborately padded shoulders to give him an appearance of girth and it was noticeable that his slippers had high heels. A steaming cup of tea stood beside him, and a plate of muffins. Up Downs was standing in a corner like the dunce of a class though he lacked the cap.

"Hark," said the king of beggars, "we're beginning to hear things. We hear that money's rolling in. That it's being lugged in every day in bags and barrels and boxes."

Chaffery looked up casually and coldly. "Oh, we're doing well enough, I guess."

"We hear," went on Byron, "that already as much as a million pounds has come in."

A flush took possession of Chaffery's face which did nothing to improve its natural ugliness at all. "A million cooters? Is that all? Have you heard too that we've been offered the crown jewels as security for the shares the king is taking? Do you know we've been given a mortgage on the Tower of Lunnon by the Home Sec'tary?"

Byron the Sniveler looked Chaffery full in the face. Everything about him had changed and he seemed all steel and greed.

"Hark," he said, "you're the Chair. You're top man of the Six. You have the last word. But we don't like what's going on. We don't care for this silence that's suddenly closed down on everything. Chaffery, we want to know how things stand. It's our right."

"You'll know, Sniveler, as soon as there's anything to tell."

"We believe there's plenty to tell right now."

The head man of the kedge turned slowly to his visitor. "Listen to me, Byron," he said, leaning back in his chair and surveying the king of the beggars with a cold air. "I started on the kinchin and I mizzled umbrellas. That's being at the very bottom, isn't it? But I came up fast. I've got to the Chair. Do you know why? Because I think. I think more than all the rest of you put together. I think of new schemes. I have angles, slants, dead-ons. I make money for all of us. But there's one more reason and it's the most important of all. I have everything worked out in advance always. I stick to my plan. Byron, I've got all my plans made this time and I'm sticking to them. According to my plans, it's not time to give out a word. Things are going well. I'll tell you that much and no more."

The Sniveler returned the cold glare of the occupant of the Chair with one that equaled it in glacial quality. "You've said your say," he stated. "Now I'll say mine. I'm here for all of us. I'm speaking for Mace-or-cue, Slums, Crimp and the Hedge. We want you to call a meeting."

There was a long moment of silence. Chaffery's fingers were tap, tap, tapping at his forehead.

"Well, that's going a bit far. It's not quite regular, you know." He paused. "When?"

"Tuesday. At two."

"Here?"

"No. You know where."

"Very well, Sniveler. I'll call the meeting."

Chaffery sat very still for a long time after the old man had left the room. His face still carried an angry flush.

"It's my plan," he said finally. It was clear he was not addressing Up Downs so he must have been talking aloud for his own benefit. "I thought of it. I saw the big chance. I worked out all the details. It's mine from beginning to end. But now they want to have a hand in it, these cheap fogle hunters, these smooth whites, these bungling flashmen! Well, I won't give in to them! I'll tell them so when I see them."

While this soliloquy proceeded, Downs looked like a boy with something burning the tip of his tongue. He raised first one foot and then the other. He was breathing hard. Finally he could contain himself no longer.

"You better walk soft, Hark," he said. "You heard what he said. It's a demand. You know what can happen when they get rough. You ought to after what you did yourself to Driver Pollett." Then his own grievances came pouring out. "You're the head of the Six but you ought to give some thought to the rest of us. Look at me. I've been watching the offices of the Tontine on top of everything else. I've never worked so hard before. And what do I get? I get nothing. It's a long time since I've had as much as two bob in my pockets. The rest of us has got rights too but you forget all about us."

Chaffery did not seem to hear him. He kept on in muttered undertones. "Why doesn't Slums attend to his houses and his women? Why can't the Hedge give all his time to taking the profits on what other men do? Why do they have to come edging over my line?" Then, with a suddenness which almost caused Downs to jump out of his dead white skin, he swung squarely around. "So! You've got a grievance, have you? I'm the one with a grievance, I'll have you know. My own people have been preaching. They've been telling everything they know. And I'm the one that knows you've got the loosest gab of all, Downs. I'm going to get to the bottom of things and I'm not going to lose any time about it."

CHAPTER SEVEN

1

Samuel Carboy reached his office on Monday morning as the clocks were chiming seven. He walked into the center room with a sudden loss in the confidence of his gait, due to not being entirely accustomed yet to the new order. The handsome desk he had coveted had been replaced by one of even greater resplendence, a brown mahogany piece with a high gilt rail and a rather elaborate inlay. He flipped over the letters on the green leather surface until he came to one postmarked Dublin.

"Ha!" he said in an expectant tone. He opened the letter and scanned its contents with mounting satisfaction.

Mark Flinch had followed him into the office and it was apparent he had matters of importance to discuss. "Later, Flinch, later," said Carboy. "Have you ever heard of a man named Downs? I'm inclined to think there's an individual of that name connected in some ways with the Chaffery crowd."

The head clerk nodded. "I've encountered the—the individual, sir, once or twice. A very queer one, sir. Looks like a stalk of celery, he's that white. He gives you the shivers, sir."

"Could you get in touch with him?"

Flinch pondered over the matter. "I think so, sir."

"Ask him to come here and see me. And there's to be no clacking about it in advance."

"I can't promise to produce him, sir. But I'll try."

It proved an extremely hot and uncomfortable day. By five o'clock Carboy, very limp of collar himself and getting short of temper, told Flinch to send the staff home. The latter nodded thankfully. "They're wore out, Mr. Carboy," he said. "It's hot as a h'oven in the front office and the pens—well, sir, there's no reason not to be frank, sir—the pens are lagging a bit."

It was just as well that this little concession had been made to the weary staff. At five-thirty a tall figure, looking a little like a white wraith, dodged across the mews on which the offices of Carboy and Co. backed, and let himself in through the back door. It was dark inside and for several moments he did not move.

"Who's that?" asked a voice from the room beyond.

"Who's asking?"

Flinch came to an inner door and blinked at him. "Oh, it's you. We're expecting you."

Downs was feeling the need to be extremely careful. "Who's around?"

"Everyone's gone but Mr. Carboy himself. Come along, will you? He's waiting."

Carboy was lighting his pipe when the two men entered his office. Downs, suddenly apprehensive, showed a tendency to hang back. The proprietor of the business stared at him over the bowl.

"This is him, sir," said Flinch. "This is Downs."

"They call me Up Downs," said the visitor with a feeble hope that it would put things on a free and easy basis.

Carboy laughed. "Well, Mr. Up Downs, you've been a great deal at the offices of the Waterloo Tontine." He waved in the direction of the door where Flinch was lingering. "Get along. This is confidential. Now, Downs, I asked you here because I thought you might like to make some money."

"I need money," answered Downs. "I need it bad."

"I have questions to ask you. If you answer them honestly—and I have ways of judging if you *are* honest—I'll pay you well."

"How well is—is well, sir?"

Carboy reached into the semicircular wall of brown cubbyholes ringing the desk and drew out a bag which clinked. He proceeded to make a pile of twenty-five guineas.

"That's pretty tall, isn't it?" he asked.

Downs studied the mound. Yes, it was tall, he said to himself. Chaffery was a hard master. He didn't let his men get their hands on very much. Up himself had been getting along on very short rations since he made his great mistake about the Noses. He was too much of a bargainer, however, to let the man behind the desk see how much of an impression the tower of guineas had made on him.

"If the profits in some lines I know about," he said, "was to be piled up, they'd be as high as the Tower of Babble."

"These are yours," said Carboy. "I'll hand them over now on your promise to answer my questions. If what you tell me warrants it, I'll give you as much again."

Downs could no longer restrain his desire. "When you've been short a long time, there's a nice feel to gold," he said. Suddenly he reached out with hands cupped together. "Start at your questions."

2

Carboy made two calls after concluding a highly satisfactory session with Up Downs. The first was at a tall house just off Cavendish Square; a rather dingy residence which managed, because of architectural peculiarities such as very tall and very narrow windows and a front door lacking a transom, to look furtive. Sir Sockden Deane, its owner, was obviously puzzled, and not at all pleased, when he discovered the identity of his visitor.

"It's late, Carboy," he said.

"Not too late, I sincerely hope," answered the visitor. "I have information for you which I think you'll want to hear, early or late. It's about the Tontine."

The baronet responded in a sharply suspicious voice. "Yes? What about it?"

"It's wrong, Sir Sockden. All the apples are rotten under the top layer. Do you know that a very clever but far from respectable individual named Chaffery is behind it?"

The baronet, who had wispish red whiskers and eyes which were too closely related, looked startled at this. Even if he had been entertaining suspicions of his own, he did not relish having the matter called so brusquely to his attention.

"Nonsense, Carboy. This is—this is absurd. The plan was originated in the most regular way. We held a meeting——"

"Who called it? Did you?"

"No. I—I'm not entirely clear at the moment as to who called it. But it was well attended. A fine body of men, sir. All of them filled with a consuming desire to establish what will be, I am sure, a great charitable institution."

"You are now chairman of the committee, I believe."

"I am. A post, I may say, which carries great honor with it."

"But certain to be the first target if things go wrong." Carboy was saying to himself, "This fellow is not only crooked but stupid as well." He studied the weedy figure of his host and his gorge continued to rise. "Let's not beat about the bush, Sir Sockden. You have a secretary who seems to be rather completely in charge of things. A certain Charles Wogan Finnerty."

Deane nodded his head. "A good man. Experienced. In the Irish tontines."

"Perhaps too experienced, Sir Sockden. Would you care to look over a report I've had on him?"

The baronet took the letter which had arrived from Dublin that morning but did not read it at once. He was studying his visitor with an aroused and antagonistic air.

"I don't understand this at all," he said. "Why are you—shall we say, sticking your nose into something which doesn't concern you one damned bit?"

"Put it any way you desire. Perhaps I'm actuated by a wish to rescue you from what may prove a very embarrassing position. Perhaps I'm not. But I *am* concerned about the conduct of the Waterloo Tontine for good and sufficient reasons. I advise that you read this letter before we say anything more."

Sir Sockden Deane read the letter and his face seemed to become rustier and his stooped figure weedier as the contents sank in. He remained silent for several moments, tapping the edge of the missive against one finger.

"H'm. It seems possible we've been reposing more confidence in Finnerty than his record warrants."

"Is the money which comes in—and I understand it's literally pouring in—used at once in the purchase of consols?"

"Of course."

Carboy now delivered his heaviest broadside. "Not a shilling has been so employed," he said. "It's still held in the form of currency. It could be removed, if anyone of felonious intention were in a position to get his hands on it, without any great difficulty."

"A serious statement, Carboy. What authority do you have for it?"

"My authority," said Carboy, "is of the best. I don't need to go into particulars because I can see by your face that you believe what I've told you. The point left to be discussed is, How do you go about safeguarding things? I certainly don't need to point out that your position would be most precarious if the money was stolen."

The baronet pawed nervously at his thin and sandy side whiskers. "Come to the point, sir. I know you have something to suggest."

"Yes. You have authority, as chairman of the committee, to call a meeting at any time. The resourceful but not always scrupulous Mr. Finnerty—it's too bad, isn't it, that he bears the name of that splendid adventurer, Charles Wogan?—is very conveniently out of town. That gives you an opportunity, sir, to call your meeting and accomplish the first step, which is to discharge Finnerty."

Deane frowned uneasily. "Have you any idea how much business there is to be attended to at the Tontine offices? The place is like a madhouse."

"I am well aware that a successor would have to be appointed at once. You will need a man who is able, fearless and, in all things, expeditious."

"And," there was a dryness in the baronet's tone, "you have a candidate to propose for the post, no doubt."

"I have. A very able man, and a fearless one. A young barrister, sir, Mr. Jonathan Bade. I've had occasion to make use of his services and I have the sincerest respect for his capacity."

The baronet gave his head a single affirmative bob. "A good enough man, I believe. Have you reason to know that Mr. Bade would agree to being saddled with such a difficult task on short notice?"

"I think we can depend on it that he will."

Deane, most clearly, was unhappy over the situation. He looked out of the single narrow window which admitted light into the gloomy little study where they sat. His bushy brows drew down closely together.

"You will be telling me next, Carboy," he said in sulky tones, "that we must act quickly."

"In half an hour, sir. I have messengers available to carry the word to your members. I assure you there's not an hour to be lost. Not a minute."

3

The second call was at the headquarters of the Bow Street magistrates. Carboy had been there on a number of occasions and on errands of various kinds; and he had always been irritated at the lack of order, not making allowance for the fact that the officials of this noisy and ill-smelling institution had been gradually finding themselves saddled with the whole problem of law and order in London.

It seemed busier this afternoon than he had ever seen it. In the center, behind flimsy railings, sat the presiding magistrate of the day. Outside the rail sat the plaintiffs, defendants, witnesses and spectators, all very quarrelsome and vociferous. One of the runners, attired in the red waistcoat which had earned them the name of Robin Redbreasts and with the gilt crown of his baton protruding from one of the pockets, was standing at the entrance to the inner area. He seemed a jaunty sort of individual, his black felt hat cocked at a decided angle and his gloves as white as a bridegroom's.

Carboy addressed himself to the runner. "I must have a word with the magistrate," he said. "On a matter of the greatest importance and urgency."

"It's His Worship, the Honorable Dawson Climber, sitting today, sir. As you see, he has a visitor. Miss Harriette Swain."

Carboy knew a great deal about Miss Harriette Swain and the crusade she waged for fallen women. He glanced with interest at the comparatively young lady, who nevertheless had streaks of white in her black hair, sitting beside the magistrate and speaking with great earnestness. She was handsome, he conceded, much too handsome to be wasting her life on a Cause.

"If Miss Swain knew the nature of my visit," he said, "I am sure she would yield me His Worship's ear."

"I will speak to him, sir."

The runner entered the enclosure and whispered to the presiding official. The latter in turn spoke to his visitor. Miss Harriette Swain smiled, nodded and rose to her feet. As she came directly toward him, Carboy had a chance to see that his first impression of her looks was most amply borne out. She was rather tall and most becomingly attired in a dress of blue chintz and a cottage bonnet under which her intelligent eyes sought his quite frankly. She stopped beside him.

"May I speak to you, sir?" she asked in a beautifully modulated voice which had aided her a great deal, he knew, in the many platform appearances she found necessary. "I am Harriette Swain."

"Samuel Carboy, ma'am, at your service."

She had a very light pelisse over one arm and both hands were filled with tracts. She offered him one of these.

"I trust, sir, you will read it, if you find the time. Or rather, *when* you find the time. I feel it is important and worth your attention."

"Perhaps, ma'am, perhaps. I am indebted to you for allowing me to speak at once to the magistrate."

"Your errand being an urgent one, Mr. Carboy, I will detain you no longer."

The Honorable Dawson Climber was a stout and irascible-looking individual with a nose like a gouty toe. He had started to scribble some notes with a squeaky pen, no doubt reminders of the information he had received from the head of the movement to redeem the women of the underworld.

"A remarkable woman," said the magistrate, looking up and nodding. "I've known her and admired her all her life. An unusual combination, sir, of sweetness and resolution. I trust you will find it possible to contribute something to the great cause she directs."

"The world, Your Worship, is full of great causes," declared Carboy stiffly. "A man can't support 'em all. Still, I may be able to spare her a guinea."

"A guinea, sir!" said the Honorable Dawson Climber, raising his eyebrows. "I was thinking of something rather more substantial. Ten guineas, twenty, perhaps even a hundred. She's in a very great need of money."

"A hundred guineas? Come, Your Worship!" Carboy seemed both shocked and amused. "Will you agree if I say two?"

The magistrate bobbed his head. "Two, then. And now, sir, what can I do for you?"

Carboy dropped his voice to the level of discretion. "Sir, you can prevent the most diabolically daring and clever attempt at a theft in the whole history of crime."

It was the magistrate's turn to express surprise. The end of his flamboyant nose twitched uneasily. "The crown jewels?" he asked.

Carboy shook his head. "The funds of the Waterloo Tontine. There's a scheme on foot to decamp with all the money which has come in. I don't need to tell you how much *has* come in, I'm sure."

"Cartloads!" said the magistrate in an awed tone. "Everybody I know has gone in. I invested a hundred of the best myself, entering my young grandson. Named after me, and a fine young rascal he is. I hear you're in, Carboy, and your former partner. It has become a matter of patriotism to be in." His tone suddenly developed heat. "I want the whole story as fast as you can give it to me. Sir, I'll see that a lot of them are hanged if they steal our money!"

Carboy seated himself beside the desk of the presiding official and whispered to him at some length, retailing the evidence he had gathered to connect Hark Chaffery and his lottery aides with the Tontine. The magistrate nodded his head repeatedly and seemed in full accord with what Carboy was suggesting.

"The board is meeting now," concluded the latter. "They will put my man in to take charge temporarily. What remains to be done is to make it impossible for anything to be removed from the offices in the meantime."

The magistrate responded briskly. "I shall assume the responsibility for doing that at once. I'll send over four of the runners to take things in hand. One will stand outside each door and the others will be inside the offices to keep an eye on what goes on there." He raised his voice. "McDad!"

The runner who had greeted Carboy on his entrance made his way again inside the railing. He stood stiffly at attention beside the desk.

"McDad," said the magistrate, "I'm placing you in charge of an operation of the utmost importance. You will select three men and bring them to my office. There you will receive your instructions."

CHAPTER EIGHT

1

The next morning Carboy was summoned to Bow Street by a hurried note from His Worship, Mr. Climber. The latter was seated in his office, a dingy little receptacle for files of documents with or without seals, when the merchant was ushered in.

"Our morocco monarch doesn't let any grass grow under his feet," said the magistrate, with a hint of official relish in his voice. "He's struck back at us. Downs is dead, sir. Murdered in cold blood last night."

Carboy did not at first exhibit surprise and certainly his face gave no indication that he felt any regret for the fate of the man he had persuaded into selling information. It was clear, however, that on second thoughts he did not appreciate the speed of Chaffery's retribution. He was asking himself, undoubtedly, where the next blow would fall.

"Fortunately, Mr. Carboy, his own ticket has come up. A warrant is out for his arrest."

The merchant nodded with quick satisfaction. "Are you free to tell me what has happened?"

It was raining heavily and even the radiance of Mr. Climber's nose did nothing to relieve the dinginess in which they sat. The magistrate hunted for a report on his desk and then tilted back in his chair as he perused it.

"There's nothing to hold back, sir. Let me see. It was seven-fifteen this morning that the body of Downs was discovered. In a warehouse a block from London Dock. The body had been dragged there and was partly covered with fagots. Anyone who knew Downs would have sworn he hadn't more than an ounce of blood in that whole dead white body of his but it seemed he lost several quarts of it in the course of dying. They'd been pretty thorough with him. A bullet in his neck and a mashed-in skull to make sure."

The magistrate's voice took on then a note of satisfaction. "You saw Miss Swain here yesterday. She'd come in to report that one of the girls she was sheltering had hopped it. Name of Stassie Cole. A doddy wench who used to be seen with Pillbeck Carter. Well, she was found this morning in a rooming house in Soho. It was the greatest good luck, sir, that we had the report of her disappearance and that we set out to find her. The first thing she told us was she had spent several hours during the evening with Downs." He made a gesture with one finger across his throat. "Pillbeck's gone, as you probably remember. Hanged. So the girl took up with Downs, who had your money in his pocket and wanted to spend more of it. She left him early because, in her own elegant diction, he got as drunk as Davy's sow. By this time, of course, we knew that Downs was in the hands of the Cold Cook, and that we had a real lead. We questioned her fully. She finally divulged that Belter Kelting had been hanging around during the evening and keeping an eye on them."

"I know that name. A bad one, isn't he?"

"The Belter has been a bad one from the day of his birth. We've had him here several times on suspicion of murder but he has always been as sly as a fox. He's never been convicted on any charge. But this time it was different. He had been on the pipe all night and when they brought him in he was mops and brooms. Excuse me, sir," continued the magistrate with an apologetic air. "I spend all my days here and I've fallen into the habit of using some of this confounded lingo I hear all the time. What I meant to tell you was that Kelting had been smoking opium and that his nerves were in a jangled state. He could hardly sit still. Under these circumstances, he did badly under the questioning. We had it out of him in no time at all. He killed Downs. I think he must have disliked his victim because he talked as though he had enjoyed the job. Having put his own head in the noose, the Belter lost his nerve entirely and ended up by acknowledging that he was acting on orders from Chaffery. There was a suggestion also of a dislike for the head of the mob. He didn't seem content to swing unless Chaffery swung with him."

Carboy gave a low whistle of satisfaction. "You must feel very pleased, Your Worship, that things have worked out so well."

The magistrate nodded. "As I said before, it was luck. It all went back to that report we had about the girl from Miss Swain. Well, that's the whole story. Except that half a dozen of the runners are on their way now to the house on Grosvenor Square. It will be the first arrest ever made in *that* neighborhood."

"Do you expect to get more evidence before they go to trial? You'll need more than Kelting's word to convict Chaffery. He goes to great lengths to cover up his tracks, I hear."

The magistrate was not entertaining doubts about the conclusion of the case. "Kelting's confession will enable us to get to the bottom of things. I assure you that Chaffery's head is in very serious jeopardy this very moment. And a good thing it will be for all concerned, Mr. Carboy, if we convict him this time. If he isn't convicted, he'll hit back hard."

2

There was a leak somewhere at Bow Street, for Hark Chaffery got word of what was happening. He was sitting down to a late breakfast in his scarlet dressing gown and tasseled fez when the news was whispered in his ear.

He sprang to his feet, spilling his cup of tea all over the table. "I warned that clacking fool not to go on the pipe!" he cried furiously. It was clear that he was frightened as well as angry, for his face had turned a tallowy white.

"Breezer!" he said to the man who had brought the word. "How much has the Belter told them?"

"I don't know," was the answer. "They know that Downs is dead and they have the Belter in irons. But there's a lot of excitement at Bow Street. They're on their way here by this time."

"He's caved. The Belter has caved right in. Breezer, go down to the head of the square and keep your eyes open. Let us know as soon as you see the runners headed this way."

The man Breezer departed in a hurry as though glad to be out of this ill-omened house. Chaffery believed that the iron sway he had exercised over his henchmen still held but there was a look in the eye of Master Breezer which said that he was never coming back; nor was he likely to wait for the arrival of the runners.

Chaffery turned then to the two men who had been sharing breakfast with him, if anyone could ever be said to share even as small a matter as a slice of ham with him with any degree of fairness. "Jack!" he said. "Get on with your part of it. You're to see Conkey and tell him to have the cart ready. I'll follow you in two minutes. See that there's plenty of straw to hide in. We'll go straight to the docks because the barge will be our safest stall for a day or so."

The man departed with as much celerity as Breezer had shown. Hoppy had left the room and he now came back with a bundle of clothes in his arms. Chaffery talked as he dressed.

"Did Jack get off?"

"Yes, Hark. I saw him cross the square when I was upstairs. He was running."

"The fool! He'll give it away." A frightening thought took possession of the king. "Hoppy, do you suppose he's so anxious to save his own skin that he'll cut and run for it? That he won't go near the stables at all?"

"All I know is he's a stinking lag and coward." Hoppy himself was not exactly a picture of resolution at the moment. He swallowed hard and then added: "The rain's stopped and the sun's out. A nice day for a hanging."

"Keep a hold on yourself, Hoppy."

The head of the mob had already slipped into clerical trousers and was nervously fitting a hat of ecclesiastical cut over his brow. Hoppy buttoned up the gaiters with fingers which bungled and slipped. The result was not going to be very successful, for the cloth neither became Chaffery nor did it do much to conceal his identity. When the operation of dressing was completed, he looked exactly what he was, a furtive and desperate character disguised as a clergyman.

Either the leak at headquarters had not been prompt enough or Officer Jerry McDad, who had been sent to make the arrest, had acted with rare expedition. Before the king of the lotteries could slip out at the back door and make his escape through the carriage house, a loud knock sounded on the front door. Hoppy looked at his master for instructions.

"Better go," whispered Chaffery. "It may be some of our own people."

Hoppy went to the door and spoke the first half of the day's signal through the keyhole: "*He heaved a Sigh.*" The caller did not respond with the other half: "*And died for Love.*" Instead there came an even louder knock and the most dreaded of all demands, "Open in the king's name!"

Hoppy went stealthily out through the kitchens, Chaffery following on spidery tiptoe. A cautious glance through one of the windows brought a frantic signal from Hoppy to his master.

"Too late!" he said in a frightened whisper. "The Redbreasts are out there."

At this point Chaffery proceeded to demonstrate why he had obtained control of the lotteries and had then gone on to the Chair of the Six. All trace of fear left him. His eyes narrowed to slits and his movements showed both determination and resolution.

After examining the priming of a pistol, he went to an embrasure in the drawing room which commanded a view of the front porch. Raising his weapon, he aimed with great care.

The explosion was followed by shouts and the sound of scrambling feet on the stone entrance steps. Chaffery threw the pistol down with disgust.

"Missed!" he said. "I've always wanted to kill one of the vermin and here I've gone and lost my last chance. I managed to crease him; that's all I get out of it."

After testing the chains across the front door, he joined a group of his people who had come in mad haste from different parts of the house after the explosion. There was a stout woman who obviously was the cook, two housemaids, two footmen and the man Hoppy. Chaffery looked them over with a brooding eye.

"It's come," he muttered. "Two days more and I would have been away. And then it would never have come. Two days too soon!" He spoke up then for the benefit of the white-faced group. "We're in serious trouble. Now then, no screeching or crying. It won't do any good. The house is surrounded. If it's any consolation to you, it's my fault. I should have left Downs alone until more important things had been attended to. Well, I didn't. When I heard he had clacked, I couldn't get a moment's peace of mind until he cocked his toes. He could have been killed to my complete satisfaction later. And here we are, and we can't get away. We still have a choice. We can walk out and let them take us. Or we can fight it out and get ourselves killed."

A loud voice from somewhere on the outside demanded that they lay down their guns and surrender.

"Not me," said Chaffery. "I'm not going to let them hang me. They won't have the chance to stand Hark Chaffery up at the Old Bailey. They won't take me to be preached at in chapel with an open coffin right there in front of me to be stared into. They won't keep me in chains until the morning when they walk me out to be hanged with all London watching." He shuddered. Then he regained his resolution and turned to one of the footmen. "You, Hinchey, are you ready to walk out under a white flag?"

The footman, who was unusually tall and conspicuous for the fine cut of his long legs, gave his head a sullen shake. "I can't let myself be taken. They've got too much on me."

He had been a rainbow (the slang term for a footman, which stemmed from the brilliant coloring of the uniforms they wore) with a very rich family in the north and the contour of his legs had led to trouble involving the mistress of the house. The others all knew it would be a case of hanging if the police got their hands on Hinchey.

Splints, the other footman, had less to fear. He said: "I don't want to stay and have my head blew off. I'm ready to walk out."

So were the two housemaids, who were fluffy-headed little creatures and had been selected for other duties beside the housework. Chaffery had expected them to leave. A lack of morals was the most serious charge the police would have against them.

The cook was a Frenchwoman who had escaped to England after getting into some very serious scrape in her own country; something in the line of poisoning, it had been whispered in the ranks. Her black eyes and hair, the dead whiteness of her skin, and the extreme arch of her hips made her resemble a spider.

"I stay," she said. "Better to die quick than be sent back."

"Madame Ragoo stays. And wise she is because the French have nasty ways of dealing with women. Sometimes they burn them at the stake. So that makes four of us." Chaffery pointed at one of the maids. "Pull off a white petticoat, Sally, and we'll hang it out from a bedroom window. Then the three of you who want to risk the mercy of the law can walk out through the front door."

This preliminary step was accomplished without any trouble or delay. The sound of voices on the outside when the trio emerged indicated that by this time the runners were in full force. Chaffery looked at his remaining companions.

"The best we can hope for is to be killed before they get in. We might as well sell our lives at a good price. Can you shoot, Madame Ragoo?"

The Frenchwoman shook her head. "I have great fear of the pistol, please, Mister Chaffery."

"Still you can stand at a window and blaze away at them. If they shoot you, you're in luck." He handed her a pistol. "Go to one of the front windows and don't be afraid to show yourself. I'm going to the window on the upper balcony. You two place yourselves wherever you want but keep right on spraying lead at them."

The sudden outburst of shooting from the house caused the runners to take shelter behind trees and on the balconies of nearby houses. The Duke of Lanstrow, roused from a late sleep, was astonished to find two runners at one of his bedroom windows. The wife of the Honorable Freddie Farady, who was a great beauty, was disturbed at her toilet by officers of the law taking possession of the next room. Pistol fire began to rain on Outland House from all directions. There was a constant splintering of glass and the puff of pistol smoke from the windows of the beleaguered mansion.

Madame Ragoo had taken her instructions literally. She exposed herself so openly that she went down at the first volley. When her companions in jeopardy found her later, she was already completely beyond the reach of French justice. Her figure, sprawled out on the floor, still had a suggestion of the spider about it.

Chaffery on the other hand seemed to have a charmed life. He stayed for the better part of half an hour at his post above the balcony and had the satisfaction of knowing he had scored a hit on one of the officers in the street below while nothing more serious had happened to him than dust in his eyes from masonry chipped by the flying bullets. He was still there when preparations were completed in the street below for the use of a battering ram in breaking through the front door. Firing a final shot, he went downstairs and found that both of his male companions had joined the Frenchwoman in achieving the security of death.

The king of the lotteries now faced a grim decision. If he stood his ground when the door was broken through, the police might oblige by killing him. He was certain, however, that they would strive to avoid this. It would be a great feather in their caps if they could take him alive and have him paraded at the Old Bailey. Reluctantly he decided to take things into his own hands.

He made his way on legs which seemed determined to balk at the duty his will was imposing on them to the small room off the end of the hall which was called the study. Here he proceeded to discard the clerical garb.

"They'd laugh at me if they found me in these," he said to himself. "I won't have that. I won't give them a chance to say that Hark Chaffery wanted to run away."

The glass in the window of the study had been shattered and lay all over the floor. The curtains remained drawn, however, and very little of the bright sunshine which had followed the rain made its way into the room through the small rents caused by the bullets. Chaffery undressed in the dark and put the clerical garments away in a drawer where, he hoped, they would not be found.

He seemed determined that there should be some degree of dignity about his death. Although a crashing sound from the front of the house gave warning that the runners had broken in, he allowed himself time to don his handsome dressing gown. He then went to the mirror over the mantelpiece and restored order to his hair by running his fingers through it.

All this had consumed more time than he could allow safely. The door was given a violent outward yank and a voice cried, "He's in here!" as he raised the pistol to his temple and pulled the trigger.

3

Being both hard of hearing and shortsighted, Lady Twiverly did not realize at first that the reason her impatient tugs on the bell brought no results was because the house was empty. This knowledge came to her when she hobbled with her cane in the direction of a draft and found the front door open. The two footmen of the establishment, in their fine gold and mulberry liveries, were standing on the front steps.

"What is this, what is this, what is this!" cried the testy old lady, pounding her cane down very hard.

"Excuse us, m'lady," said one of the pair, "but all hell has—I mean, m'lady, there's trouble on the square."

"Trouble? What trouble?" She squinted about her and frowned. "It seems to me there are many people on the square this morning."

"All Lunnon is here, m'lady. The runners come from Bow Street to arrest Hark Chaffery for murder——"

"For murder? What murder? Tell me at once."

"I don't rightly know, m'lady. But it seems that Hark wouldn't let the Robin Redbreasts in and so there's been a great to-do—pistols being shot off all over the place and people killed and wounded. Three has been took to the 'ospitals by reason of getting in the way of the bullets and they say as Hark hisself has been killed in there——"

"Dear me, dear me! I always miss everything. I'm going over. Come, both of you. One on each side of me."

It seemed as though the footman had not been guilty of exaggeration when he said that all London had come to the square. It was literally black with people who had been attracted by the sound of the pistol shots. Every window on the square was occupied and every doorstep. The crowd was so thick that two men had climbed up on the equestrian statue of George I and a boy was clinging to the horse's tail. It would have seemed impossible for an elderly woman to make her way through such a dense mob but Lady Twiverly managed it. Perhaps there was something in the impatient tap of her cane which had the same effect as the sound of a leper's bell or it may have been the commanding tone of her voice. "Come! Come! Come!" she kept repeating. "Out of my way, out of my way!"

When she reached McDad, who had remained in charge of operations, she plucked at his sleeve. "Officer! Officer! Is he dead?"

"As dead as mutton, lady," answered McDad cheerfully. His hat was gone and there was a deep red groove on his forehead which bore witness to how close Chaffery had come to ending his connection with Bow Street for all time.

"Then I'm going in."

"Lady," said the officer, "no one can go in yet. We're waiting for the coroner and the four 'ternity boxes——"

"Four? Are there four of them dead? I must go in, Officer. I think I have a right. I'm Lady Twiverly and he invited me once to a reception. I didn't go. Nobody went and he got angry and burned all the food out on the road. I'm sorry now I didn't go. I think he must have been an interesting man."

"It would be an unpleasant sight, m'lady," said the officer.

"Would I want to go in if I thought it would be a pleasant sight? Come, Officer. Didn't you hear me say I'm Lady Twiverly?"

McDad hesitated, then motioned to the runners who were maintaining a line in front of the house. Lady Twiverly was allowed to enter, the footmen trailing after her.

"Well," said a very pleasant feminine voice, "as you've let her in, I'm sure you can't refuse me. I'm Mrs. Farady."

The famous society beauty had finished her toilet in record time and was attired in a delightfully cool-looking lavender dress which did not quite reach the ground and allowed glimpses of a neat pair of shoes with black velvet bands strapped over an equally neat pair of ankles. Under a wide-brimmed leghorn hat, she looked about her as though saying, "Take full advantage of this privilege, good people, because I'm *never* seen out this early in the day." Somehow she had collected escorts, all of them young and dressed most monotonously in black tail coats and square-flapped waistcoats.

McDad could not think of any reason for refusing this demanding beauty who clearly was someone of great importance. "Very well. Mrs. Farady and escort."

"Escorts, Officer," said the lady, her tone conveying her resentment of his lack of notice. She went through the line, taking four young gentlemen with her.

This brought demands from all the residents of the square, who announced their names as though going to a reception and passed through the guards. The crowd hooted and complained bitterly at such discrimination. The sightseers did not remain inside the house long. They came out almost as fast as they went in, the first being Lady Twiverly, who was muttering to herself: "I'll give Old Sheppy a piece of my mind if I ever see him again. Making that terrible creature a neighbor of ours!" The last had vanished by the time the coroner arrived and the supply of rough pine coffins had been carried through the door.

Anyone who understood the whole situation would have realized that Up Downs had thus succeeded, although at the cost of his own life and those of four others, in following out the orders given him. He had brought the Noses of the square to see Hark Chaffery. Some of them had brought their wives but if Chaffery had been there to see he would probably have complained that they were neither dressed to the nines nor painted to the teeth.

That they took no more than one look at what was left of the king of the lotteries and then left rather hurriedly would have brought some satisfaction to the departed morocco man.

CHAPTER NINE

1

In midafternoon, after a long day spent in a stagecoach journey which had begun at five in the morning, Mrs. Samuel Carboy arrived in London with her two children. She had decided to come for several reasons, all of them having to do with Alfred and Isabelle. The former had taken to fast riding and was trying hard, or so it seemed to her, to break his neck. She knew also that he was still much concerned over the coachman's daughter, even though he might not be seeing her. As for Isabelle, she was bored and difficult in the country. There was nothing for her to see or do and, unfortunately, no girls of her own age and station to help her in conquering the monotony.

As Alfred sprang down from his seat on top, a groom touched his cap and said in a cautious undertone, "Mr. H'Alfred Carboy, sir?"

"Yes."

"Gentleman in h'uniform asks will you be so good as to step into the coffee room."

Alfred, not knowing what to make of all this mystery, indulged in an uncertain frown. "What's his name?"

"Didn't say, sir. Just would you kindly step in."

"Does he belong to the police?"

"No, sir. No runner about him. Blue serge and fine big buttons. The navy, sir."

So the son and heir of the Carboys walked into the coffee room to be greeted by a young officer who sprang up from his table and said, "Midshipman Grace presents his compliments."

A delighted grin swept over Alfred Carboy's face. "Julian!" he said, shaking hands. "Well, draw it mild, if you haven't turned into a likely-looking young Nelson."

"Yes, here I am," said Julian Grace. "Expect to be out of the navy very soon. They're going back to peacetime and it's just as well because I've got some plans of my own."

They shook hands a second time, smiling at each other more broadly than before. "I wonder, Allie," asked young Grace, "if your father would be as angry as mine if he knew we were still good friends?"

"We'll always be good friends, you and I, Jule. I don't mind telling you that I think my father was a bit highhanded in the way he went at it."

"Well," conceded the heir to the Grace fortune, or what was left of it, "I always did think my father knew nothing about the business. I didn't think he should have taken so much the best of it and keep throwing on the dog, the way he did."

"We'll let it stand at that," suggested Allie. "It's done now and can't be undone. They were both at fault. But, old sea dog, tell me how you knew I was on that coach?"

"I've been in town three days and I've come over here each afternoon, hoping you might put in an appearance. I wanted to see you—and Her."

"Her?"

"Isabelle. Your young sister. Surely you knew I was always moony about her? I saw you both as soon as the coach came in. She was at the window and she bowled me right over. How she's grown up and what a beauty she's become! I'm afraid I'm done for this time."

Allie laughed, scornfully. "Isabelle? Why, you cupboard-head, she's just a brat in pigtails still! Well, she doesn't wear pigtails any more, it's true. But——"

"She's beautiful!" Grace was speaking in an awed voice. "Give her another year or two and she'll be the toast of England. It frightens me to think how many men will be in love with her. What chance will I have?"

"None," declared young Carboy with the easy cruelty of youth. "What do you suppose your parents and mine would say if they heard you talking like this?"

"I don't care. I'm quite mad about her, and that's the truth."

A look of gravity had taken possession of Julian Grace's face. He was a pleasant-appearing young fellow, a little on the dark and poetic side. It could not be denied that the uniform he was wearing brought out his best points. It was the regulation thing for midshipmen: a tall black hat with gold trimming on one side, a square blue coat with an abundance of gold buttons on its collar of white as well as down the front and on the cuffs, a trim pair of white trousers, and a gold-headed sword swung from his belt. It was clear that he fancied himself in it and he was even inclined to swank a little; but no one could blame him for that, nor for humming between snatches of talk a catch from the tune of "A Right Little, Tight Little Island" which had been written when Napoleon was threatening invasion of England and was still a favorite with navy men because it was the wooden walls of the fleet which had made Boney give up the idea.

"Well," said Grace, "she's just fifteen and that may give me a chance. Something will turn up. I don't know what unless I should become a naval hero. I'm hoping that I will. . . . Well, this brings me to what I want to tell you. Allie, I'm going to South America. My family don't know it—but I am. Do you know what's going on there?"

Allie looked puzzled. "People are living there."

"There's half a dozen big countries and they're colonies of Spain. The

Spanish government has treated them all badly and they are fighting for independence. There's a certain man"—he dropped his voice to a dramatic whisper—"a very great man who can't be mentioned although in the navy we think he's the greatest sea fighter alive today. He's been invited to go out and take command of the fleet of the brave colonists."

"An Englishman?"

"Of course. I said he was a great sea fighter, didn't I? All this is very secret and nothing will be done for quite a while. But if this great man goes to South America, I'm going to try for a place with him. They say there's a chance for fame and fortune—and I'm going to need both if I'm to marry Isabelle. They say there will be big prize money and huge estates to be awarded and titles and whole counties full of fine cattle——"

"That's it!" cried Allie with sudden excitement. "I knew there was something about South America. The pampas. That's where I would like to go. I want to have land, stretching to the horizon, and great herds of horses and cattle."

"You come with me, young fellow, and you'll get them." Grace became very serious and businesslike. "I'll let you know as soon as I get my plans made. If I have to go before you're ready, I'll get word to you somehow. If you follow me, go first to Brazil because it isn't a Spanish colony. Yes, that would be the plan for you. Go to Rio and wait for word from me."

Allie remembered suddenly that he had not come to London alone. "Help me, Davy!" he said. "Mother will think I've run away or something. I'll have to go back right away, Jule."

They shook hands for a final time. "I guess it was a good thing our fathers broke up the firm," said young Grace. "You and I wouldn't have done very well with it when it came into our hands. I think in a way that's a compliment for both of us. We're made for other things. We'd have driven the business in one direction only."

"Right into the ground," agreed Allie with a grin.

"Yes. Right spang into the ground."

There could be no doubt about it, they were a pleasant pair of youngsters: both tall, both a little on the rugged side through addiction to games, filled with good spirits and brimming over with a sense of friendship. The feud between their fathers, they hoped, was not going to drive them apart, although if pressed to it each of them would have fought loyally for the rightness of the part his own sire had played. Each of them understood this and they had kept away from the issue after the first expression of neutrality.

2

Mrs. Carboy and Isabelle went to the offices of the Tontine, to which they had been directed by Flinch. Mr. Carboy was not there, however, when they arrived, and a tall young man rose from the desk he was using in the center of the main room to introduce himself as Jonathan Bade and to inquire what could be done for them. He maneuvered himself so that only the left side of his face could be seen and Mrs. Carboy was astonished at the severe perfection of his profile. Isabelle, who remembered him from her day in court, felt again the stirring of an interest in him and said to herself that she must have been wrong in thinking that a mere birthmark could destroy the effect of *such* a divine forehead, *such* a lovely nose and *such* a manly chin; but when he was compelled to turn and she glimpsed the purple ugliness of the other cheek, she knew she had been right after all and banished him from her thoughts.

"We are expecting Mr. Carboy at any moment," explained Bade. "He's in court over the details of a new arrangement for the Tontine. I am very sorry that we have no separate room where you could wait. We're very crowded here, as you see, and the best I can do is to have chairs placed for you."

"Thank you. We don't want to put you to any trouble." Mrs. Carboy paused and glanced about her at the dinginess of the room and at the flying fingers of the clerks. "Then there have been developments today?"

"Yes, Mrs. Carboy." The young lawyer indulged in a brief and rather unhappy smile. With the acute sensibility which his physical disability had developed in him, he knew what Isabelle had been thinking. "It has been a day which will long be remembered, a day of excursions and alarms, and there has been, to top it off, a battle between the Bow Street runners and the myrmidons of Mr. Hark Chaffery. The runners had all the better of it and four of the lottery men, including Chaffery himself, are dead."

"How wonderfully exciting!" cried Isabelle. "When did this happen?"

Despite the futility of it, Bade still contrived to give them no more than momentary glimpses of the right side of his face. "It is hard to believe, ma'am, that such a melodramatic event could happen on Grosvenor Square. But it did. Chaffery occupied a house on the square which he had purchased from the Duke of Outland."

"His Grace," said Mrs. Carboy in a tone which tended to exclude the duke from any possible share in the blame, "is a neighbor of ours."

"So I understood."

The chairs were placed and the ladies sat down. They proceeded to ply the lawyer with avid questions about the day's happenings. Isabelle sat forward on her chair and her brown eyes sparkled with excitement and interest. She repeated several times, "Oh, why wasn't I there!"

Samuel Carboy came in shortly after, accompanied by Sir Theobald Gardiner. He looked blank when he saw his wife and daughter seated just inside the door, having had every reason to believe they were safely ensconced at Beaulaw Hall.

"Well, my dear, what brings you and the kitten to town so unexpectedly?" he asked.

"We made up our minds last night and caught the early coach. Allie came with us, of course, but he's abroad at the moment on mysterious errands of his own."

"Indeed," commented Carboy. "And why should they be mysterious?"

"Oh, Samuel, we've been hearing all about what's happened today! I'm so glad it wasn't necessary for you to take part in this dreadful battle."

"My dear," said Carboy dryly, "I have a well-ordered conception of my personal responsibilities and I may tell you that I don't consider it necessary for me to assume at any time the duties of a Bow Street runner. Sir Theobald and I have spent a large part of the day in court."

"And I may say most successfully," declared Gardiner, bowing to his partner's wife and then allowing his eyes to kindle a little as they rested on the daughter of the house. "I'm glad to see you both in such excellent health and spirits."

"The Court," explained Carboy, including Bade in the audience he was addressing, "has decided to relieve the members of the original committee from the need of further participation. They have been praised for their efforts and presented with two hundred and fifty guineas apiece. The affairs of this—this new concern have been placed under Sir Theobald and myself as trustees until everything has been put on an even running basis."

"And will you both get two hundred and fifty guineas?" asked Mrs. Carboy.

"The matter of remuneration is of no importance, my dear, in our case," explained her husband. "We are undertaking it as a public service. I suppose when we have it on an even keel there will be some small reward for us. Based on a very, very small percentage."

Isabelle looked up quickly. "But sometimes, Papa, a very, very small percentage can mount up, can't it?"

Carboy and the baronet exchanged delighted winks which meant: "Listen to that! She's not only pretty and bright. She has a keen eye for business."

"I trust, Bade," said the merchant, "that everything has gone well here."

The lawyer nodded. "I think you will be glad to know, and you also, Sir Theobald, that nothing had been removed. Not as much as a scrap of paper." He got to his feet reluctantly, knowing it had become necessary now to speak to them confidentially and that he would have to stand out in full view. "They had been storing the money away in many odd places and in ingenious ways but I think we've located every piece of gold and every note. The total will prove rather staggering, I think. They're working on it in there now," motioning over his shoulder at a back room. "Two of our best men are with the officials from the bank. And there's a man from the Stock Exchange to see that the conversion into consols is handled right. We mustn't run the price up by rapid buying."

"Decidedly not," said Carboy. "Is it going to be as much as we anticipated?"

"More. Considerably more." The training of the pleader was beginning to assert itself. Bade gestured with one arm. "Make no mistake about it, gentlemen, this is Tom Tiddler's ground. We've been picking up the gold and silver from every nook and cranny. Fortunately for us, Tom himself was not able to be here to interfere with us."

"His capacity for interference," said the baronet, "has been done away with in the most thorough manner. A lucky thing all around."

"I was hoping, my dear," said Mrs. Carboy, seeing that the men had drawn together into a group in a most masculine and exclusive way, "that you would be able to escort us somewhere for tea."

Sir Theobald took it on himself to answer. "My dear lady, if your husband shows any reluctance, I shall be most happy to take you and Miss Isabelle to tea. I know the most charming place for the purpose. It is quiet and the crumpets are always toasted just enough and the sweets are delightful beyond description." He turned to Carboy. "If it will be any inducement to you to come with us, it is quite possible to get something more stimulating than tea."

"That settles it. I'll be glad to join you."

Jonathan Bade cleared his throat. "I have some interesting figures if you would care to see them before you go. About the tontine."

Both men showed a desire to learn the nature of the statistics on the slip of paper the lawyer was holding in his hand.

"Well, let's take the last class," said Bade. "The old codgers over fifty-five. Oddly enough there are more than nine hundred of them entered already. The interest payments will begin at once in this class, so it is like an annuity. It won't be much at first but as the old boys drop off the payments will grow fast. In another twenty-five years they may all be gone and the capital can be handed over for the care of the veterans. It will be rather handsome at that. At least ninety thousand pounds.

"But the real interest will be in the one your children are entered in, Mr. Carboy, twelve years to eighteen. The number of entries is really astonishing. There are at this moment—and, of course, they are still coming in and will continue to do so for some time—exactly five thousand and sixty-three."

"Over five thousand!" Carboy whistled. He turned and looked at the baronet and it was easy to see what was running through his mind. Why had he left it to an underworld rat like Hark Chaffery to see that this was truly an El Dorado?

"Sixteen of them have died already. I suppose it will take at least sixty-five years to bring this race to an end. By the time the capital is paid over for the veterans, there won't be more than a midshipman or two still surviving from Nelson's fleet and perhaps a drummer boy who stood up with the thin red lines at Waterloo. But there will be other wars in the meantime and thousands of more veterans. This class will bring a huge capital for the hospitals—nearly a million pounds."

"It's really very exciting," commented Mrs. Carboy.

"Yes, ma'am, it is indeed." Bade forgot his scar for a moment. His eyes sparkled as he proceeded to draw a picture of what this meant. "I think the most tense moment in a foot race is when the runners are standing, expectant and motionless, on the line, waiting for the signal. Picture in your mind this race we are starting. The line runs clear across the face of England. Nay, it is longer than that, for it must overlap into Scotland and even across the Channel where the entries are coming in thick. What a starting line it is! There are six thousand runners that we know of now, and more to come. Think of them toeing the line, all of them excited and keen to start. Handsome, sturdy boys, so many of them from the best families. And nearly as many girls. Nice girls, all of them, I'm sure, some plain, some pretty, a few lovely—but none as lovely as Miss Isabelle, none to be spoken of in the same breath with Miss Isabelle—and they are just as eager as their brothers in the line. And every one of them, every one of the six thousand, is sure he or she will win."

Isabelle had been listening with the deepest interest. Her brown eyes sparkled, her lips were slightly parted, and when she spoke it was in almost ecstatic tones. "Oh, I want to win!" she cried. "Do you think I'll have a chance?"

Her father came over and patted her cheek. "Of course you'll win, my pet. We'll never let *you* get sick. If necessary we'll pack you away in cotton wool and have doctors around in droves to fend off all diseases."

This idea did not find favor with her. "No, thank you, Papa. I'm not going to be wrapped up in cotton wool. And I'm not going to be sick again. I was sick last week and I didn't like it at all. No, Papa, if you please, I'm going to *live!*"

Jonathan Bade turned around fully to watch her, his eyes showing that he was beginning to feel deeply about her, even as early as this. "Yes, she'll cut a swath in life, this beautiful, eager young creature," he was thinking. "Ah, if I could only go along with her!"

Isabelle went on to expound her full idea of what she expected out of life. "I may have a career on the stage. I can dance. You should see me dance. Perhaps I'll have engagements at Covent Garden. And I've decided to play this new game. Is it called golf, Papa? There was a man near the Hall yesterday and he carried a stick and he was hitting away at a small ball. I was out for a walk and he asked me if I would like to try. So I did and I hit the ball so hard it went right out of sight." She burst into delighted laughter. "I think he was angry. He said, 'There goes my ball, so I guess that's the end for today.'

"But none of that's going to count very much," went on the girl. "I'm going to court. *That* is really what I'm most interested in. I'll have to wear *very* expensive dresses, Papa."

"And what about marriage?" asked Sir Theobald, who had been watching her intently and listening to every word.

"I've thought about that too, of course. More than anything else. I'm going to marry a duke. I don't think that anyone else will quite do."

The baronet thoughtfully smoothed his silky mustache. "A duke? That's looking high, isn't it? Well, and why not after all? I guess, Carboy, we'll have to find a duke for this young lady of yours."

Carboy had not been listening as closely as the others. He now asked a question of Bade with a frowning preoccupation. "What will the yield be, based on these figures?"

"I am inclined to think, Mr. Carboy, that the final survivor in the class can count on a yearly income of over twenty-five thousand pounds."

Carboy gave vent to a low whistle. Even with the ambitious plans in his own mind, it seemed to him that an income of such proportions would be like a substantial slice of the national debt.

BOOK II
The
Tall Young Men

JULIAN GRACE fell under the spell before his feet touched the soil of Jamaica. The merchantman on which he had shipped arrived at the entrance to the crescent harbor in the early hours of evening and the melodious voices of the crew who were bringing the pilot out could be heard clearly at what seemed an impossible distance. The young passenger stood by the rail as the darkness thickened about him and watched the small, twinkling lights of Kingston across the bay. The soft air wrapped him about like a scented cloak.

A man beside him said: "We've passed the spot where Port Royal slid down into the sea more than a hundred years ago. They're still there—the houses and the prisons and the churches. The natives say that sometimes the tolling of the bells can be heard, summoning the shadows of the dead people to service."

"It's their own voices they hear," declared Julian. "I've never heard sweeter music than that song they're singing."

Nothing that happened thereafter could dissolve the spell, even though it seemed an endless time that he waited in Kingston for further orders to reach him. The days fell into a close pattern. He wakened long before the warm Jamaican sun could make its appearance over the Blue Mountains. He bathed in cold water and dressed himself in white cotton trousers and waistcoat, and a coat of bright blue cloth. Then he went to his door and clapped his hands for Noel. The latter was always within hearing and in a matter of minutes he would arrive with a broad smile and a large tray of food.

The young visitor from England and the servant of fourteen or so had been on the best of footing ever since the evening when Julian had landed from the merchantman and found his way to Harty's Tavern. Here the round black face of Noel, wreathed in a smile of welcome, had won his immediate liking. The servant had said: "I'se N'ile, I'se you' boy."

Breakfast varied little: a cup of coffee, a ripe banana, a plate of paw paw, three thick slices of toast and a fried egg. His thoughts as he dealt with the food (Noel standing by and watching for the merest hint of a wish, "Muff'n, suh? Jam, suh?") were inevitably with the perplexing situation in which he found himself; the visit he had paid to the revolutionary envoy in London, the eagerness with which his desire to enlist in the fight for Chile's freedom had been received, the urgent suggestion that he start for the west before the Foreign Enlistment Act could pass the House of Commons, and the instructions which had brought him here to Kingston to wait. He had been informed most definitely that he would receive word quickly as to the next step. But the days rolled by, changing into weeks, and nothing had happened.

It was his custom, immediately after disposing of every scrap of the breakfast, to sally out into the streets of the city, where the air was still cool and invigorating, and walk from end to end of the harbor, his eyes scanning the water line for the first sight of an incoming ship.

On the morning which rounded out his three weeks of waiting Julian said to Noel, "If nothing happens soon, I'm going to take the first ship back to England."

Noel shook his head. "See the candlelight befo' you blow out match."

"That's all very well," grumbled the former midshipman, reaching for his white hat which sported a rim at least ten inches wide. "You have a proverb for everything. But here I am, with nothing to do. For all I know, I've been forgotten."

Noel did not understand what it was all about but he grinned cheerfully and asked, "What M'ss'r like fo' him dinner?"

"Not beef. Not lamb. Not veal." The meats on the island, Grace had discovered, were tough and stringy. "Tell you what, Noel, you get me some chicken and rice. A whole leg, mind you, and a good slab of the white meat. And I'll have a good stout pudding to top it off."

Noel's dark head nodded in ecstatic approval. "That m' good, M'ss'r. Empty belly glum, full belly laugh."

As young Grace trudged down Harbour Street, he saw just ahead of him the tall young man with the red hair. Every day now for over two weeks he had seen the same thin figure taking much the same course as he did and gazing just as intently out to sea. The stranger paused to glance in the window of a clothing shop and so allowed Julian to overtake him. The latter, convinced that the delay had been a deliberate invitation, decided to address him.

"Sir," he said, "I think you are English. And I'm pretty sure you've been in the navy."

The stranger turned from the uninviting display of cheap goods in the window and faced him. He was about Julian's own age and pleasant-looking, with an eye the color of the sea under sunlight, and a mop of unruly red hair. There was a slight dent in the bridge of his nose, as though he had run foul of a capstan bar or something equally unyielding, but this, oddly enough, tended to give him a bold, even a rakish, air.

"Yes, I'm English," he affirmed. "And I *have* been in the navy. So have you, for that matter. No mistaking the roll in the gait, is there?"

They confronted each other for several moments of careful scrutiny and then indulged in reciprocal smiles.

"It may be," said Julian, feeling his way carefully, "that we are here on the same kind of an errand. But I was given very strict instructions about talking to strangers and keeping a still tongue in my head."

"Quite," said the other. "Suppose we leave it that an unexpressed agreement has been arrived at between us? I'm going under the name of Johnson but my name is *not* Johnson and never was. Perhaps you have an alias too."

"I'm calling myself Jackson. It was *their* idea, not mine. Unimaginative beggars, aren't they?"

"Do you suppose we would be breaking our promises if we dropped these silly aliases just between the two of us?"

Julian Grace thought this over carefully, for he had given the most solemn assurances to the Chilean officials from whom he had received his instructions and his expense funds. He was convinced, however, of the honesty of his new acquaintance. "I think," he said after a moment, "that we could introduce ourselves properly without—well, shall we say, breaking our sacred vows or blackening our honor? I'm Julian Grace."

"And I'm Cymric Forster. At your service, my dear Grace."

"My father," went on Julian, feeling that something further by way of identification was needed, "is George Grace, formerly of Grace and Carboy, Eastern merchants."

"Of course," said Forster. "Ludgate Hill. The Sign of the Ugly Giant. It's been taken down, hasn't it? I don't remember seeing the old fellow the last time I passed that way."

"Moved off somewhere. My father sold his interest in the firm nearly three years ago and it's now Carboy and Co. He lives in retirement in Berkshire. A stone house at Willikin's Elbow, part of it fifteenth century. I suppose it's an interesting old dump but it's dashed cold and damp at times. I've been thinking I would prefer one of these houses we can see back of us here in the hills. I'm told they are little bits of paradise and that they get their share of the trade winds."

Forster drew out a handkerchief and mopped his brow. "Paradise? Seems more like the other place to me."

"My father has gone in for painting," went on Julian. "Landscapes in oil. He dabs away all day long and I've never been able to make head or tail of anything he does. There's a lot of other artists around there and they get together and jabber about their work. Damned if I don't think they're all a little misty in the tops'ls."

"I'm a h'orphan," declared Forster with a grin. "We have a servant named Amstery who swore I'd always been a h'orphan. At any rate I never saw either my father or my mother, and my older brother died before he was old enough to be put into trousers. There's a bit of property for me when I get the bags off in another year. Nothing princely, mind you—just a small block of consols or something and a place in Yorkshire rented at sixty pounds a year. An uncle acts as my guardian. He's a parson and a blasted old hell-relisher if there ever was one. He made no objections to my taking on this little business we have ahead of us and I think he's counting on my getting a Spanish bullet in my head before we're through."

"All we seem likely to get," declared Julian bitterly, "is holes in the seat of our trousers from sitting around and waiting. I've had three weeks of it."

Cymric Forster whistled with dismay. "Three weeks! Do you suppose they've forgotten us?" His eyes had taken on a hot, reddish glint and it was clear that it was not his way to accept things calmly. "This is a rum state of things. . . . Look, Grace, there's a sail off there to the east."

Julian shook his head. "A fishing boat. That's all."

"Huh! Another day of the hope-deferred stuff." Forster mopped his brow again. "I've an idea, my friend. Fellow I've met has a shop just a block away from here. It's the coolest spot in town. He handles the sales for his father's rum mill and any time you go in a black hand shoots out at you with a glass in it. The finest, swizzlingest, rib-ticklingest drinks in the world. He's a splendid fellow and wants to join the army of Bolívar in Colombia but his father has put his foot down on *that*. He, the father, says he's willing to go on managing the stillhouses up in the hills and putting up with the smell of the cane juice and the scummings but that he, Ambrose, must go on doing the selling. Let's go over and see him."

"What's his name?"

"Ambrose Brinker. He's creole—born on the island, you know."

2

"Dunder! Two glasses," said a cheerful voice from the shadows. There was a fine rich smell of molasses pervading the shop. It was dark and most heavenly cool.

Dunder had both hands out in a trice with a long glass in each. They sat down and began to talk while they sipped their drinks. Forster had not been guilty of the slightest degree of exaggeration, for this was indeed a drink to tickle the ribs. As his eyes became accustomed to the darkness of the interior, Julian saw that Ambrose Brinker was a tall and rather stoop-shouldered man in the early twenties, with a pale complexion and a pair of twinkling brown eyes sunk rather deep under his brows.

"Gabstock," said the host, addressing Forster, "is the swizzle to your taste?"

"It's perfect, Clink."

While Julian was puzzling over the form of salutation the two acquaintances had used, Brinker turned to him and smiled in the most friendly way.

"I've seen you," he said. "Wandering around town and looking very unhappy. Don't worry too much about it. You'll get your instructions any time now, I'm quite sure. I figure you'll be picked up at one of the ports on the north of the island, St. Ann's probably, and taken from there to Rio."

For a moment Julian was too astonished to say a word. Then he managed to stammer, "How—how do you know so much about me?"

Brinker laughed. "The whole island knows. We've had a dozen here before you—brave young crusaders who wouldn't have been let out of England if the guv'ment had known what they were up to, just because the Spanish guv'ment had lodged a complaint about neutrality and all that nonsense. Why, say, a block down the street you'll see a sign which says Gabstock and Clink. They're in the rum wholesale trade and they're my competition. Even Gabstock and Clink—and they're the stupidest pair on the island, including Dunder, who's not bright as a sunrise exactly, and all the inhabitants of Nanny Town—even *they* know that your name isn't Jackson."

"In that case," said Julian with a laugh, "I guess there's no particular point in concealing the fact any longer that my real name is Grace. Julian Grace."

"That," said his host, "is the one thing we didn't know. Glad to make your acquaintance, Grace. Does the drink please you?"

Julian indulged in another long and delicious swallow. "It pleases me so much," he declared, "that if I was foolish enough to have another—which I won't be—I would go right out on the street and shout my name to the world and where I'm going and who I'm going to fight under—if I fight under anyone."

"Thomas Cochrane," said Brinker. "And a great man he is. I could talk by the hour about the exploits of Thomas Cochrane. I even have some theories about that great secret of his, the method he suggested to the Admiralty for polishing off the French in quick order."

Julian gasped. "You've heard about that?"

"Listen to me. You *must* go down the street. You'll find both Gabstock and Clink outside, waiting to drag into their shop any customers on their way here to deal with Brinker and Son. *Even* Gabstock and Clink will tell you that Thomas Cochrane has been given the command of the fleet of the revolutionists in Chile to fight the Spanish."

With an abruptness which threatened the safety of the contents of the glasses held in his guest's hand, Brinker suddenly sprang to his feet. "I know the sound of those wheels!" he cried. "I could tell them if artillery was passing at the same time."

Forster winked at Julian, as their host made a precipitate rush for the door, and then motioned him to follow. The latter did so slowly. He was thinking: "I could recognize any wheels which were bringing Her nearer to me. And there could be a whole battery of artillery passing too."

The sun had been climbing in the meantime but there was an unexpected breeze to alleviate the heat. The air was as soft as a caress, the trees with their gorgeous blooms rustled softly, the magic of the golden island was at its peak. Julian stood under the canvas projecting out over the front of the shop and thought of the last time he had seen Isabelle. It was, he calculated slowly and sadly, over two years since that last blessed glimpse had been allowed him. She had driven in to Great Beaulaw with her mother to take the coach to London, looking very lovely and grown up in pink muslin and one of the delightful little bonnets which were generally called kiss-me-quicks. Ah, how he would have liked to kiss her, not quickly but lingeringly and hungrily! She had seen him and had waved behind her mother's back, a gay little signal which had sent his heart right up into his throat. Ever since he had been thinking about it and wondering just what she had meant. There had been encouragement in it; of that he was positive.

Daniel Groody had been doing the driving, although it was being whispered around the countryside that he and his employer were not getting along well for reasons which were public property.

"Isn't she beautiful?" said Ambrose Brinker in a tone of intense awe.

A vehicle had drawn abreast of the shop, one of the type known as a kittereen, a gig with a high pole, on top of which was an umbrella to protect the lady on the back seat from the sun. Usually the umbrella was ineffective because it was not large enough and was placed at too high an elevation to assure protection. This one, however, was a very special kind of kittereen. It was, in the first place, quite obviously new and had gay red stripes on its wheels whereas most kittereens on the island were decrepit old veterans which squeaked and swayed with alarming hints of approaching dissolution. In the second place, it had a very special umbrella, as wide as a beach shelter and capable of affording shade to more than the slender lady and the small girl who sat under it; with stripes to match the wheels, moreover, and a gay fringe around the edge.

If the vehicle was somewhat on the garish side, the lady herself was quiet and composed and very lovely. She was as dainty as a water chick and the possessor of the largest dark eyes which could conceivably be accommodated in a face as small and heart-shaped as hers. Her dress, while simple, was a dream of good taste, made of beige silk with trimmings of brown. Her hat was brown also and cone-shaped, with small yellow rosebuds. Her gloves might almost have been designed for the small blonde child sitting beside her.

The occupant of the kittereen turned in their direction for a moment as she passed. She bowed to Brinker and smiled. The face of the young merchant turned pink with gratification and delight.

"She remembers me!" he said in low but fervid tones. "My divinity remembers me! I make no effort to conceal my feelings now. I love her. I love her madly and devotedly."

"Who is she?" asked Forster.

"She's governess to the children of Mr. and Mrs. Chester Soames of New Orleans. They arrived about a month ago and have rented a house in the outskirts while arrangements are made to accommodate them properly up in the hills. Chester Soames has bought a lot of land up there and intends to settle down. The wife's an invalid." He watched the kittereen receding up the street. "The governess is French, Mademoiselle Philline."

"You're quite right, Brinker," said Forster. "She's beautiful."

"Everyone admires her. And yet there's a pretty general opinion that she has a slight—a very slight mixture of blood in her veins."

"A quadroon?"

"No, a mustee, more likely, the child of a quadroon mother by a white father. That's getting so close to the vanishing point that the child of a mustee by a white father is considered white legally."

"You are well acquainted with the lady?"

Brinker shook his head. "I've met her twice, both times on matters of business. They needed a supply of good wines and she came in to place the order. I hadn't seen her before and, when she came into the shop, I was so overcome I could scarcely talk. My fingers seemed incapable of writing down the order. After she left, I realized she had omitted rum from the order and I added by way of compliment a stone jug of our own special brand— all done up in paper and tied with a blue ribbon. A few days later she dropped by and thanked me. Ah, how prettily she did it! They had enjoyed the rum, she said. I got myself in hand and we talked for a time. When she left, I knew I was lost. I was deep in love and I kept saying it was a foreordained matter. She could so easily have been directed to our rivals!"

"You really seem to be in a desperate state of mind," commented Forster.

"I would marry her tomorrow—if she would have me. I'm ready to risk everything. I'm ready to toss my future to the winds, to lose my standing, my inheritance. Yes, I am indeed desperate." He turned abruptly to Julian. "Have you ever seen anyone so beautiful?"

"Yes," answered Julian stoutly. "There's a girl in England more lovely even than your Mademoiselle Philline. I love her so much that, if I thought I had no chance of winning her, I would rather not return from what— what lies ahead of us."

"You lucky dog! Loving an English girl of the right social stripe. I'm assuming that such is the case."

"Oh yes. But I'm not as lucky as you think. Her father and mine are mortal enemies. We would have to run away because our families would never consent to a marriage."

"*Does* she love you?"

"I have no reason yet to believe so." Julian heaved a deep and heartfelt sigh. "I'm afraid my chances are pretty slim. She has suitors by the score. A duel's been fought over her. At least it would have been fought if the parents hadn't interfered."

The kittereen had vanished up the street and the men who had rushed out from all the shops and offices along the streets to watch it pass had returned to their work, refreshed and edified no doubt by this glimpse of the fascinating governess. The three young men went back to their seats and their unfinished drinks.

3

Julian had invited his two new friends to join him for dinner at Harty's Tavern. Noel had seen to it that the chicken and rice were supplemented with a platter of lamb chops and a magnificent pudding of a creamy batter in which almonds nestled while bananas rode a positive tidal wave of whipped cream on top. The host had discovered that madeira was the wine

Jamaicans preferred and he had selected the brand with great care. It was a successful dinner from every standpoint.

"You know, perhaps," said Brinker when the last trace of the pudding had vanished (much to the regret of Noel, who had kept an admiring eye on it all through the meal) and they had settled down seriously to the wine, "there's a great deal of unrest among the natives. They're demanding their freedom and, in time, they'll have to be given it. Of course we go at things like this slowly and carefully. There have been mutinies in the past, quite horrible little bloodlettings. We don't expect any more of that dish and yet the spirit in the air now is—well, it's pretty ugly."

"What's causing it?" asked Julian, who had developed a feeling of pity for the lot of the unfortunate people during his brief stay on the island.

"We can't be sure. But there's one theory that this black king on Haiti who calls himself Henri I is determined to drive white people from all the islands. He's supposed to be training agents and sending them out to stir up feeling. I think there's something in it. We have a fellow up at the stillhouses named Josipher. He has a splash of white blood in him and he's a born troublemaker. My father has caught him spreading tales about the heaven on earth King Henri is setting up. If he had his way, there would be a King Josipher right here in Jamaica. He's run away again." He put down his glass with sudden decision. "I've an idea. Dunder tells me that Jubilee Gaff is going to play somewhere tonight along the water front. I suggest we go and hear him. You'll have a surprise, I promise you; and you may get as well some idea of how things are among the natives."

"Who is Jubilee Gaff?" asked Julian.

"The mystery man of the island. Quite a few years ago he hobbled down out of the hills, carrying a queer instrument he had made for himself. He said he'd come to 'mak moosic.' He wasn't a runaway slave. At any rate no one has ever claimed him. All the black people seemed as though they had been expecting him and they came out in great crowds whenever he played."

"I would like to go," said Julian eagerly. "I'm sure it will be something to remember."

Dunder led the way to an abandoned warehouse on the water front. It was large and there was a strong aroma of molasses about it still, although it was so old they could see the first stars of evening through holes in the roof. It was so well filled when they arrived that they had difficulty in finding standing room at the back.

A shambling figure in a ragged coat and patched trousers came out from somewhere and mounted a rickety platform at the other end. The banjo was in his hand.

"Jubilee Gaff," whispered Brinker.

The old man crossed one knee over the other and began to play. At first he strummed slowly and the airs he evoked from the strings were different from anything Julian or Forster had ever heard. Julian, who was passionately fond of music, stood in a bemused state as things began to achieve a meaning for him. He found himself transported to a land where naked tribesmen danced in wild abandon and went furiously out to war with javelins in their hands; a wild, gay people in a black land.

Then the note changed suddenly and took on a throbbing tension. The sadness deepened until it was possible to feel the terror of the barracoons and the despair of the captives herded into them. Julian had no difficulty in knowing what the old minstrel was about now, he was reciting the tragedy of the black race. It was possible to see the filthy slave ships breasting the rolling seas, to hear the crack of the overseer's whip and the moans of the sick and the dying.

There was a long silence after the gnarled fingers ceased to pluck the strings. Julian's feelings exploded in a heartfelt "That was wonderful!" He nudged Brinker's elbow and asked in a whisper: "Tell me something more about this strange old man. I've never heard his equal."

But it was not Brinker's elbow he had encountered. The latter had vanished and Julian found that he had spoken instead to a lady wrapped up almost to the eyes in a dark pelisse. She turned toward him and he saw that it was Ma'amselle Philline.

"You want to know about this old man?" she whispered back. "I will tell you what his own people say about him. They say he is the spirit of the black race and that he has been sent to keep them from forgetting the land from which they came, and how they were made slaves by the white men."

They looked at each other for a moment in silence and then Julian nodded his head and said: "It's not hard for me to believe that, ma'amselle. His music is like the voice of a prophet."

"Thank you, m'sieur. Thank you so very much."

He was surprised at the fervor in her voice but before he could say anything more there was an interruption at the other end of the room. Jubilee Gaff had disappeared and the platform had a new occupant, an exuberant lady with a broad black face and a voice which seemed to rattle the loose timbers of the roof. Everyone began to laugh almost at once, even Ma'amselle Philline.

"This is Coromantee Kate," she said.

Coromantee Kate began by telling Annancy stories at which she laughed as loudly herself as her hearers. The Annancy she depicted was a sly and mischievous fellow who always got the better of everyone, particularly the white overseers, and it was easy to see that the crowd loved him as well as the narrator. At intervals she would pause to go through a curious ritual, slapping her ample hips, weaving her hands back and forth in front of her, patting her cheeks and bobbing her head.

"I cannot laugh at this Annancy, m'sieur," said the governess. "I wish that she would sing instead. Ah, how she sings!"

In a few minutes the black entertainer began to sing some of the best known of the songs of the plantations, "Me go to Ricky-lan-jo" and "Eyes come Shine!" The crowd had been pensive and silent while Jubilee Gaff plucked the strings but they had become boisterous at the first glimpse of Coromantee Kate. They weaved their hands in concert with hers, they tapped their ears and slapped their behinds. They sang after her, "Eyes come Shine." There was not a care in the whole warehouse save on the smooth white brow of Ma'amselle Philline.

"See them! How they laugh!" she whispered. "How gay they are, although there is no happiness in their lives and no hope for them in the future. Ah, the brave, black people!"

Dunder, who had been missing also, materialized at Julian's elbow. He began to whisper. "Suh, M'ss'r Brink say come away at once. Dey's trubble. He say bring white lady to shop. He say danger fo' white lady."

Julian looked at Ma'amselle Philline, whose eyes seemed suddenly to have become quite enormous in her white face.

"Did you hear?"

"Yes, I will go with you. At once, if you please. I think I know what it is."

She left the warehouse behind Julian, taking great pains to keep her face muffled. On reaching the street the two Englishmen stationed her between them and she placed a hand under each of their arms.

"You are both very tall young men," she said. "Should I be afraid when I am with you? And yet I think we must, as M'sieur Soames sometimes says, put the best foot forward."

They reached the Brinker shop without any interruption or delay. Dunder, moving with nervous speed, proceeded to close all the windows and to bolt tight the storm shutters. It was not until he had done this that he lighted the first candle. Needless to state, it became stiflingly hot and they sat in a silent group in the greatest discomfort. It was clear to the Englishmen that Ma'amselle Philline was in a highly nervous state. Her face was pale and she started at every sound.

Ambrose Brinker came in through the back entrance and, at the sight of the still figure of the girl, he gave vent to a gusty sigh of relief. "Good!" he said. "The Lord be thanked for this. A great weight has rolled from my back."

He seated himself in front of Ma'amselle Philline and smiled at her reassuringly. "Have you any idea what I must tell you?" he asked.

She nodded her head silently.

"It's true, then, that you were born Lucie Hortense Manion and that you lived on the island of Barbados?"

"Yes, m'sieur. It is true."

"And that you were the property of a Barbados merchant named Barton Skill?"

"Yes, m'sieur." She shuddered perceptibly. "That terrible old man! I ran away at the first chance."

"You were recognized in the crowd tonight. A sailor from Barbados was there and he made for headquarters at once to report you and claim the substantial reward that Skill offered years ago. I was there when he came in."

Forster said, with a puzzled frown, "I saw you go out but had no idea what you were up to."

"I had something to report myself. I had seen Josipher standing at the front near the platform."

Ma'amselle Philline, who had been sitting with her gaze averted, raised her head at this point. The paleness of her cheeks had given way to a flush. "What chance have we?" she asked in accusing tones. "Slaveowners stand together everywhere. In all the islands it's the same, and in the United States. Even, they say, in England. So that other owners will respect *their* property, they hurry to report any runaways they see. Do they think of the degradations which drive slaves to risk the consequences of flight? No, it's all a question of property, of class privilege." She turned bitterly in the direction of Brinker. "You heard about me because you were there to report another slave."

"One who belongs to my father," answered Brinker mildly. "This is the third time Josipher has absented himself. My father takes him back each time and doesn't punish him excessively. Shouldn't I have gone?"

"I suppose the number of lashes he gets is increased each time he runs away!" The girl shuddered again but after a moment began to speak in a more normal tone. "If you are surprised because I have a French name and accent," she said, "I will tell you I was born in Haiti. My father was French and a rich landowner. My mother was one of his own slaves. She was a quadroon. I never saw her but he told me she was very lovely and had a white skin. I was only a few years old when he had to leave the island because of the rebellion of the slaves. He was a royalist and so he didn't go back to France but settled in a trading business in Barbados. His wife wouldn't let him take my mother but he insisted on taking me. His wife was

so angry about it that he placed me with a poor white family. I couldn't go to
a school but he paid for me to have private lessons and he even taught me
some himself. Then he died and his wife destroyed the paper he had made
out, giving me my freedom, and she sold me to this man."

They had all been listening intently. "How did you manage to escape and
reach the United States?" asked Brinker.

Her manner became antagonistic again. "I don't dare tell you the rest of
the story. You're a slaveowner and you might cause trouble for those who
helped me to escape."

Brinker looked hurt. "I don't think I deserve that. I'm trying to help you."

"You're all against us. Because I have a small trace of black blood in my
veins, you are ready to send me back to that loathsome old man——"

Brinker leaned close enough to her to reach her shoulder and give her a
peremptory shake. "Lower your voice," he said sharply. "Come, get yourself
under control. You'll give yourself away, and all of us with you, if you talk
this way. Now, ma'amselle, I have your interests at heart and I am going to
break the law by trying to get you safely away. Are you listening to me? Do
you believe what I'm saying?"

The girl struggled to regain her composure. After several moments she
touched her eyes with a dainty wisp of handkerchief and sat up straight in
her chair.

"I believe you, m'sieur. And I'm sorry for what I said. It was fear which
put such words on my tongue—fear of what they would do with me. You
will forgive me?"

Brinker's face lighted up with a smile. "Of course, ma'amselle. And now
let me tell you what I propose to do. We must stay here for several hours.
Long enough, at any rate, for the hunt to come to an end. Then we'll escort
you to a house in the suburbs which is owned by an elderly relative of mine.
She'll take you in and keep you until the excitement dies down. As soon
as it seems safe, we'll take you north to my father's estates. From there we
can put you on a ship for Boston. At Boston you will be free." He turned
to the others. "Are you willing to help me in this?"

Julian and Forster said, "Of course," in unison.

"Then," declared Brinker, "we must compose ourselves for a long and
uncomfortable wait. It won't be safe to show a light."

4

The next three days passed quietly as far as the conspirators were concerned. The town seethed with excitement over the discovery that the beautiful governess was an escaped slave. An active search was kept up. The women
of the town were openly jubilant, the men regretful but firm in the conviction that she must be apprehended and sent back to her owner. Brinker
reported to Julian that the cause of all the commotion had regained her
composure in the security of his ancient cousin's house and that the latter

had taken such a fancy to the girl that she would defend her to the last gasp.

"Are you making any headway with her yourself?" asked Julian.

Brinker shook his head glumly. "Very little, I'm afraid. You see, I'm a slaveowner and secretly she fears and hates all of us. I hoped at the start that she would relent but now—well, I've just about given up hope."

On the third evening Noel put his head in at the door of Julian's room. "Ship come tomorrow, suh," he announced.

Julian sprang eagerly from his chair. "Has it been sighted?"

"No, suh. No one see yet. No one but Jubilee Gaff. He see."

"What foolishness is this?"

"When Jubilee Gaff say he see, he see. You watch, suh. Jubilee Gaff say he see ship. Tomorrow ship come." He remained in the doorway while he fumbled mentally for words. "Suh, you take me?"

"Noel," said the young Englishman, who had received rather broad hints before of the servant's desire to accompany him, "you can't go where I'm going. But this is what I'll do. I'll come here on my way home and we'll see then if anything can be done about you."

Noel still hesitated in the doorway. "You no forget, suh?" His broad face was the picture of woe. "N'le want to go ver' much."

The ship did come, a merchantman from Liverpool. An hour after it put in, an underofficer arrived at Harty's Tavern with a letter for Robert Jackson, Esq. It contained the long-awaited instructions. He was to leave at once for St. Ann's on the north shore of the island and present himself at the home of Timothy Ballard. There he was to remain as a guest until he could be taken off on a Portuguese ship sailing around the Horn for Santiago.

Forster had received similar instructions. Accompanied by Brinker, he came to the tavern in a state of high elation and found Julian packing his belongings. His capacity for picking up information made him the bearer of one important piece of news. "This Timothy Ballard," he said, "is the wealthiest planter on the island. Why do you suppose he's in this?"

"All the sympathy here is with the revolutionaries."

"Well, they say he's fabulously rich. Among his most prized possessions is a beautiful daughter. Which one of us do you suppose she'll fall in love with?"

"It will have to be you, my old redhead," said Julian.

"You're a dashed good-looking fellow, Grace. I think I'll drop the information early that your heart is already set on someone else. Sort of clear the air, that way."

"She'll probably be a spoiled and hoity-toity brat and will think us beneath her notice. And there are more important things to talk about than the fancies of an heiress we've never seen. Can you be ready to leave today?"

"It's all arranged," declared Forster. "I've seen to everything. We leave at noon. A guide and horses will be ready for us here."

Julian did a few steps of the hornpipe. "So, we're off, my hearty," he said jubilantly. "We'll be admirals when we come back, with our bags full of gold, and our hands full of land grants and medals. We'll snap our fingers at heiresses."

"Quite," said Forster. "They'll come down in droves to meet the ship and they'll send us notes on scented paper; and we won't even give 'em a wink. But just the same I'm a bit curious still about this Ballard heiress."

Brinker was looking quite down in the mouth. "Do you know what the governor's council has done? Made it a prison offense to harbor an escaped slave, with a fine of one hundred pounds as well. My poor old cousin doesn't possess one hundred pounds. I've already written to my father, explaining about the guest he's going to have, and when he hears about *this* he'll be in a state of mind. Wouldn't be surprised if he cuts me out of his will. Ah, the things we do for love! And my beautiful Lucie doesn't give me as much as a sweet smile."

"She'll come around, never fear," said Forster.

Brinker held out a hand to Julian. "Good-by, Grace. I hope you get better treatment from the girl in England." Then he turned to Forster and grinned. "Good-by, Gabstock."

Forster shook his hand vigorously. "Good-by, Clink."

5

The guide, a white man named Clasher, had a tendency to talk. Before they passed the palm-fringed avenues which led through the outskirts of Kingston he had told them of a dozen or more young Englishmen who had passed through the island on their way to fight for the revolting colonists. According to him, they had met with unfailing bad luck. One of them had "rotted to death in a Caracas prison." A second had been "hangit by the Spaniards without benefit of clergy." A third had been "cut to bloody shreds with a machete." It did not make cheerful hearing, but when they reached higher ground and could feel a breeze on their backs, the guide became less lugubrious and spoke enviously of the good pay. "Might go myself," he averred, "if they want anyone as has druv mules."

By midafternoon they were high up in the hills. The road wound in and out and up and down. Sometimes they rode beside streams which had been reduced to mere trickles, sometimes they were so high up that it made them dizzy to look back over their shoulders. There was lavish beauty everywhere. Julian had read about the trees of the tropics and he picked them out with a lively interest as they passed: the balata, the lancewood, the pimento, the lacebark, the palmetto royal. The poinciana tree was to be seen everywhere among the taller green of the others and so laden with red blooms that the long seed pods left over from earlier seasons were almost hidden from view. The ferns by the side of the road brushed their shoulders as they rode by and songbirds in all the thickets piped their hearts out in an ecstasy of welcome.

Timothy Ballard was not at home when they reached his low stone house after a half-mile ride from the entrance gate. Mrs. Ballard welcomed them with a smile in which languor and curiosity vied. She was a pretty woman with dark eyes and determinedly blonde hair.

"I can't send you to your rooms," she said. "My husband hasn't decided where he wants you to be. Well, he will be here soon and in the meantime," brightly, "we can have a nice talk."

They sat down in an alcove at the rear of the wide central hall and the visitors drank long rum punches while Mrs. Ballard talked.

"I must warn you about Mr. Ballard," she began. "You mustn't mind his manner. He's gruff but at heart he's really quite gentle. And please keep this in mind. He's not tall and he's inclined to be sensitive about it. I wish you would consider his feelings by—by saying nice things about Napoleon, who is short too, or any other great man you can think of who wasn't tall. It might be wise, if you don't mind, not to speak about height unless he brings it up. But," with a sigh, "he will. Perhaps you would sit down as much as possible, so he won't notice and—well, you might slouch a little."

They assured her they would do everything to consider their host's tenderness on the subject and she went on then to talk about many things, coming back always to what, most clearly, was a favorite topic, the difficulty of raising children in the tropics. Her eyes misted over with tears when she told them that, of the eight girls she had brought into the world, only two had survived. There had been no boys. This, she averred, had been a great pity in many ways because boys seemed better able to withstand the conditions.

"It's always the first year," she said, with a doleful shake of the head. "They have so many troubles then, the poor little dears. And it gets so hot in summer. I've done the best I can, goodness knows, and after all it was Queen Anne, wasn't it, who bore seventeen and couldn't raise one? It can't be the fault of our doctors. A queen wouldn't have been so unfortunate, because she would have the very best, wouldn't she?" Aware, perhaps, that her reasoning was becoming a little involved, she concluded, "It may be that eight is too many in sixteen years.

"I like to think," she went on, "that my six little darlings are allowed to keep each other company up there. You see, they died at almost the same age and it would be *such* a good arrangement, wouldn't it? I think it's being done that way because I see them often in my dreams and always there are just six of them and no more. They look so pretty together and their wings are so new and neat and white! It's a matter of great pride to me that they always seem to be wearing the white bonnets I made for them, with blue ribbons under their chins."

An interruption occurred when the older daughter came in and was introduced as Constance. She resembled her mother in languor of manner but she was disturbingly pretty, with quiet gray eyes and two honey-colored pigtails, one on each shoulder. Julian remembered that his friend had expressed himself as interested in the Ballard heiress and so he kept an anxious eye on Forster while they were being introduced. His anxiety proved to have a sound basis, for he saw the latter go down for the third time without even a struggle. "He's hooked!" he thought. But it did not seem a matter to be concerned about, for the girl was as amiable as she was pretty.

The second daughter, Winifred, came in later; a plump and dark child of eleven, who seated herself in front of Julian and plied him with questions. They were direct and personal questions and covered a wide range. At one point she startled them all by remarking, "I think this one is a more bea-utiful young man than the other one."

Everything that was said served to create a picture of Timothy Ballard as the sun around which the household revolved and the two visitors were not surprised when they heard a deep and masterly voice raised at the back door. The owner apparently had discovered their guide, who was staying over the night. "So, it's you, is it, Clasher!" he exclaimed in an exasperated rumble. "I've half a notion to throw you off the property, you slinking hound!"

"Oh dear!" said Mrs. Ballard.

The master of the household was halfway through the door when he saw his wife and he began to admonish her. "Now, Lydia," he exclaimed, "you've been talking about *them*. I can see your eyes are fairly swimming with tears. Damme, m'dear, you'll get one of your blasted headaches again."

He was surprisingly small to be the possessor of such a big voice. His head was completely bald and he had an ample spread of mustache of the type which would be known later, when the bicycle became popular, as the handlebar. Perceiving that the guests had arrived, he walked over to them with hand held out. Julian, who was nearest, found his fingers crushed in a vise.

"Gad, you're a pair, you are!" said Ballard in a dismayed tone.

"No comments, Timothy, if you please!" cried his wife. "Our guests are very tall and they're very, very nice. We like them, don't we, Constance?"

The older daughter said, "Oh *yes*, Mama," in a very sweet and earnest tone.

"It's a great inconvenience to be so tall, sir," said Forster. "They laughed at me all the time at school. If I had my choice, I'd be a more normal height."

"Would you now? That's interesting. I suppose you'd consider Napoleon more nearly normal, wouldn't you? Or Admiral Nelson, or Alexander the Great? There were hundreds of great men who were under the average."

"Timothy," said Mrs. Ballard, "our guests haven't been shown to their rooms yet, because you did *not* say where they were to go when you hurried off this morning in such a temper to raise a fuss somewhere or other."

The face of the small martinet took on an apologetic expression. "My dear boys, I beg your pardon most humbly," he said. "We must attend to this at once. Now let me see. I think, Grace, we'll have you in Napoleon Bonaparte. And Forster shall have Alexander the Great." Feeling an explanation was necessary, he added: "We have so many bedrooms that names are necessary to tell 'em apart."

The house, being all on one floor, had not seemed large as they approached it but they discovered now that it was quite astonishingly roomy, one apartment opening out of another and wings shooting off in most unexpected places until an effect like a maze was created. Julian was escorted through the library, a very large room with drawn curtains to give it a scholarly atmosphere perhaps. The books were contained in metal cases raised off the floor to protect them from the destructive interest of insects. His suite opened directly off the library and on entering he found himself confronted with a large portrait of the conqueror now securely caged on the island of St. Helena. There was a plaque under the painting inscribed in large letters:

Napoleon Bonaparte
At the age of 32 years
FIVE FEET AND ¾ INCHES

The bedroom was large and airy, containing a four-poster bed amply shrouded with netting. It had, he found to his amazement, a bathroom of its own and a niche for shaving enclosed with tall mirrors and a battery of sconces containing at least a score of candles.

There was a black servitor in attendance who said: "Hot wattah laid on, suh. Jus' time fo' a splash, suh."

Julian would have liked to take full advantage of such remarkable luxury but his valet would not allow any dawdling. He was hurried into his trousers and bullied into his coat. His tie was pulled into place in a jiffy and with a triumphantly expert flourish. In no time at all he was dressed and in the hall. Here he met Forster who, quite obviously, had been turned out with equal expedition.

"I've learned something," whispered the latter. "Alexander the Great was just five feet tall. An odd way to get your education, what?"

Timothy Ballard was waiting for them, very sleek in a dark blue coat and white waistcoat. "Young men," he said, "I'm going to pick your brains. I want to find out what is thought in England about business now that they have peace."

"I don't know much about such matters, sir," said Julian. "But I've heard my father talk. He was an Eastern merchant but he's retired now."

"And what does he think is going to happen?"

Cymric Forster had drifted over to join Mrs. Ballard and Constance. This left Julian to face the questioning alone, backed up only by a recollection of his father's vicariously acquired information.

"My father thinks the country will have many black years, probably as many as ten, because of the expense of the Napoleonic Wars. For this reason he's glad he retired when he did."

"That's very interesting. Very. I think, Grace, your father must be a man of vision and common sense. His views coincide with mine quite closely. Is he, now, as tall as you are?"

"Oh no, sir. I would say he's about your height."

"I would like to know your father, Grace. I would indeed."

Forster was having equal success with the ladies. Mrs. Ballard's comely

face was animated and Constance was smiling, frequently and, it seemed,
happily. The child Winifred had already been sent to bed. She was not, at
any rate, in evidence.

6

The two volunteers remained in the luxury of the Ballard ménage for ten
days and it was apparent from the start that Cymric Forster had fallen in
love with Constance and that she reciprocated. They went for long walks
together in the cool of the morning and were inclined to be silent and preoccupied when in the company of the others. Mrs. Ballard saw the way
things were going and she must have been pleased because she said nothing
to Mr. Ballard, fearing perhaps that her choleric spouse would be opposed to
the match. The head of the household was taken by surprise, therefore,
when Forster bearded him in his office and asked for permission to pay his
addresses to his daughter. Constance, accompanied by a palpitating train of
supporters, remained in the hall after the door closed behind him. She did
not actually stoop to listening at the keyhole but she came close to it. Her
mother stood behind her in a state of the greatest anxiety and Winifred was
in a condition of unabashed excitement farther down the hall. It seemed to
all of them that the heavy bass voice of the household god lacked some of
its rumble and bluster and this clearly was favorable.

The two men emerged finally from the office with composed faces. This
was a decidedly good sign.

"Hullo!" said Mr. Ballard, surprised to find the hall so well populated. He
looked sternly at his wife. "I've something to say to you. In the privacy of
your boudoir."

"Lydia," he demanded, when they reached this most tastefully appointed
apartment, "did you know of this?"

"I—I suspected, Timothy."

Ballard frowned. "For the first time in my life I'm at a loss. I am positively
undecided. It's not the kind of match I've wanted for our sweet Constance
but the young man seems reasonably eligible. Oh, I went into everything
with him. He has some property and his family is good. Well, it came down
to this: I didn't say no to him but I refused, I refused in no uncertain terms,
to allow an engagement until—until he comes back from the fighting."

He began to pace up and down the room, with long and therefore slow
steps. "If it comes to an engagement—and, mind you, I'm not committed
that far—it will be for one reason only. His inches. Yes, m'dear, it may hinge
on that point. It will be a great relief to me to know that my grandsons will
never suffer as I've done."

This might be the paternal understanding but on the feminine side it
was considered settled. The quiet Constance would marry her redheaded
suitor when the campaigning was over. She was radiant with happiness, and
laughed and talked more than she had ever done before. Mother and daugh-

ter had long, serious discussions, mostly on the subject of clothes, and from these Winifred found herself excluded. She came indignantly to Julian about it.

"I've made up my mind," she said. "When I'm married, I'll keep it a secret. I may even elope. But anyway I won't let them help me. I'll—I'll exclude them. That's what I'll do."

"How soon is this going to be?" he asked with a smile.

"I hope to marry young," announced the child. Then her face clouded. "But, of course, I may not marry at all. I'm not going to grow up pretty like Constance."

"Well, now, I'm not at all sure about that. Let me have a good look at you. Turn your head and let me see your profile. Now the other way. H'm!" He pretended to be giving the matter careful consideration. "Do you know what I think? I think, in the first place, that you're going to be tall and slender. You'll be dark, a real brunette, and your hair will be straight and glossy. I won't be at all surprised if you turn out as pretty as she is." He was becoming carried away by his enthusiasm. "You may even be prettier, if that's possible."

"Oh, if *only* you're right!" sighed the girl.

"But there must be no eloping, mind you. When you get married, it must be done in style."

"My father," said Winifred with seeming irrelevance, "has miles and miles and miles of land. He's *very* rich."

On the afternoon of the tenth day a note was delivered to Forster from Ambrose Brinker. He had arrived safely at his father's plantation in the hills, and so far all was well. He wished them a good voyage and a glorious return.

"He's managed it," said Forster. "They've arrived there without being seen. And so far, I judge, his father isn't of a mind to turn them out. The more he sees of Ma'amselle Philline, the more he'll be inclined to help her escape."

On the evening of the same day, word was received that a Portuguese ship would be close offshore during the early hours of the night and would take on the two passengers for Santiago. Immediately there was much scurrying in the household and much packing of baskets with good wine and food to supplement the sparse fare they would find on board. Constance and Cymric were permitted to spend a half hour alone in the library, which was the most secluded room in the house. There was a suspicious mistiness in their eyes when they emerged. Mrs. Ballard was weeping openly into her handkerchief and even Mr. Ballard cleared his throat and hemmed and hawed as he said to his daughter, "Come, come, my child. Come, come, now."

As the two young men mounted horses in the darkness to ride to a cove several miles east of St. Ann's, they heard Constance call in a muffled voice, "You must return soon, my love." Then the deeper tones of Winifred's voice were heard. "I'll be more grown up when they come back and Mr. Grace may want then to marry *me*."

CHAPTER TWO

1

Nell Groody had an excuse for being up and out of the house by five-thirty this lovely morning in early October. There had been a slight touch of frost and the grapes were ripe on the hillside; already turned, in fact, to a beautiful blue which young sapphires have perhaps before they reach that dark perfection of maturity. She was swinging a basket in one hand and keeping an eye on the narrow path which crawled up the other side of the hill from the Oxford road.

"Hello!" said a voice from somewhere among the vines. "We *are* prompt, aren't we? Five-thirty, it was to be—and here we are."

"Allie!" said the girl, beginning to take bunches from the vine and laying them carefully in the basket with a hand which trembled. "It's so nice to hear your voice."

"And is it nice to see me?" His face had come into view several rows beyond where she was standing. "They can't see me here so I'll wait until you join me to show you how *I* feel about it."

"It's been so long," said the girl in a whisper. "I was excited almost out of my wits when Cook at the Hall handed me your note. But, Allie, wasn't it very dangerous? It had to go through several hands."

"Perhaps. But I had to see you and so I decided to take the risk. Do you have to strip all the vines between us? I'm getting pretty impatient."

"I must have a full basket when I go back. Allie, why did you take the risk?"

He answered in an eager voice. "I have a plan. A great plan, and I have to tell you about it. You look very sweet and pretty in that cute little bonnet. I can hardly wait to kiss you. Aren't you going slow with the picking on purpose?"

"Perhaps I am. What *is* the plan?"

"Do you remember that I told you my grandfather Hanlon is going to leave me most of his money? Some time ago, when I gave in about going to Oxford, I told him I didn't see how I could get along without my horse. We talked it over between us and agreed not to say anything to my father because it would just make him angry. My grandfather said he would give me a horse and keep it stabled close to town where I could get it any time I wanted to."

"So that's how you got here. I wondered."

"I tied it back in Waster's Spinney. Well, this is the plan. I'm going to tell Grandfather Hanlon that I can't live without you and that I want to take you somewhere—South America or Canada or even Australia—where I could get a lot of land and horses and cattle. I'll ask him to give me some of the money now. I think he'll agree."

"Oh, Allie!" Nell made her way around the last row of vines which separated them and arrived breathlessly beside him. Her eyes had lost in her excitement the gray blue which went so well with the blackness of her hair and had become almost a match in color for the grapes in the basket. "Are you sure he'll agree? It would make me so happy!"

"Happy enough to kiss me?"

"Oh yes!" Her arms went around his neck and for several moments they neither spoke nor moved.

"You see, this makes all the difference," she said.

He looked a little doubtful at this. "Does it?"

"Don't you see, Allie, that when there's a chance you'll be able to marry me after all it's proper for us to meet? At least, it's different than before when it all seemed so hopeless. To see you then was—well, it was foolish, at least, wasn't it? It was certain to cause talk. People were sure to believe the worst of us. Now at least we know, between us, that we have an honest reason for meeting."

"But not quite as honest as you think, my sweet. Could you be persuaded to let me kiss you again?"

She could, it seemed. There was another long moment. But when she took a step backward, not a very long one, her eyes had a troubled look.

"I'm in such a difficulty. Father and Mother are against my seeing you because they say it can come to no good. Mother wants me to go into service somewhere nearby but Father is against it. He says his daughter is *not* going into service, that he can support me without that. But, Allie, if—if we have to part—and Father dies, what happens to me then? I'm afraid Mother is right. I should be in a position to earn my own living. Are you going to speak to your grandfather soon?"

The boy nodded emphatically. "The next time I see him. His place is quite close to Oxford and I can get out to visit him sometimes over weekends. That's what I'll do, and I know he's going to say yes. So, my pretty Nelly, you must *not* worry about the future." His eyes lighted up and he reached behind him where he had concealed a parcel in the vines. "I've got a present for you. It's pretty, I think. A cashmere shawl."

Nell squealed with delight when she saw it, for it was most certainly the loveliest shawl in the world.

"It made a hole in my allowance," said the boy. "But I don't care about that. I'm glad you like it."

"It's simply lovely." Nell's pleasure was beginning to diminish a little, however, as doubts assailed her. "But what—what am I to do with it? I can't let anyone else see it. They would know it came from you."

"Oh, hide it among your things and just wear it when I can see you in it.

Such as that wonderful morning when I'll be here to tell you that Grandfather Hanlon has agreed to give us the money."

"Oh, Allie, Allie, you don't understand. You must think I'm in the same position as your sister, who has dozens of dresses, and clothespresses of her very own. It would be easy for her to hide a shawl away where no one would see. But Mother and I share a drawer in our one chest. I have one other dress and three pairs of stockings and a few other things. That's all. Mother would have her hands on the shawl in no time at all if I put it there."

This, clearly, was a difficulty he had not foreseen. He thought the situation over and asked, "Isn't there some place in the attic?"

"Perhaps." Nell put all doubts determinedly behind her. "Don't worry about it, Allie. I'll find a way. And I love it. It's so beautiful. It's the loveliest thing I've ever seen."

She draped it across her shoulders and the boy was so overcome at thus seeing her arrayed in a splendor of his own contriving that he gazed at her in speechless wonder. She removed it then and, producing some pins (any woman can always find pins for an occasion), secured the shawl to her petticoat where it was hidden from sight. The petticoat was a plain one and without a single frill but the intimacy of all this was almost more than he could stand.

"Oh, Nelly, Nelly!" he said. "I love you so much!"

There was in her attitude a more common-sense approach to their problems than he seemed to have acquired. "Why," she asked, "do you think your grandfather will be willing to have you marry me?"

"Nelly," he said in a whisper, "I'll tell you a secret. Grandfather was getting pretty well along before he married and then he took a maid in his own household. I heard this recently and I made some inquiries and found it was true. It was a very successful marriage, mind you, but my mother has tried to keep it quiet. Well, as he did the same thing, he should be favorable to us, don't you think?"

"It seems," said the girl, from whose voice all the animation had been lost, "that you and your grandfather have tastes in common. You are willing to look far beneath you. That was what you meant to say, I think."

"Nelly, *please!* I didn't mean it that way. I—I simply told you what happened. The family thought they had to keep it a secret because she worked for him. Of course there was talk at the time." He came to a guilty stop. "I'm making it worse. Now you are angry with me."

"The family would never be able to keep me a secret, Allie. There would be a great deal of talk."

"Now you're *very* angry with me." In search of self-extenuation, he added: "But I did get up at three o'clock and climb a wall in order to ride over and see you for just a few minutes."

Nell was on the point of tears. "I know, Allie, I know. It was sweet and wonderful of you to do it. And you brought me this beautiful shawl. I don't know why I should feel bad about it. But I do. I'm sure things will go wrong."

"No, they won't," he declared. "I won't let things go wrong!"

There was an attempt at stoutness in his voice but they looked at each other for several moments in a state of mutual misery.

"I don't see why this sort of thing makes a difference," he said finally. "It makes me sick to hear Mother and Isabelle talk about this and that. They're snobs, that's what they are. Well, I must start back. I'll be here a week from today. Same time and same place. And I'll be able to tell you then what Grandfather thinks of the plan."

"Yes, Allie," she replied with sudden meekness. "I'll be here. And I don't know how I'm going to exist until I know."

2

Alfred Hanlon lived some miles north of Oxford and a little to the west somewhere in fact between Hagley Pool and the ruins of Godstow Nunnery. This was romantic country, for at Godstow the Fair Rosamond had lived out her life in meditation and, perhaps, in repentance, and the countryside thereabouts was full of associations with history and poetry. But neither High Squires, a stone house behind a very high wall where Hanlon lived, nor old Whip himself added anything to the poetic associations of the district. High Squires was a gloomy place both inside and out and its owner, who had been interrupted at breakfast over a dish of chops when his grandson paid him a call, was looking very sleepy and sulky in a worn and stained dressing gown. His nightcap was still on his head and his feet were bare.

"Alfie, my boy," he said when he had listened to his grandson's story, "you're a young ass."

"But, Grandfather——"

Hanlon held up a huge, gnarled hand. "Let me have my say, Alfie. It's natural enough for a young fellow like you to enjoy a romp. But why must you marry the girl?" He took a deep pull at a stone mug filled with something suspiciously like beer. "Who is this little hussy who has you fairly panting for matrimony?"

Alfred Carboy explained again, going into still more enthusiastic descriptions of Helen Groody. His grandfather listened as he crunched the meat from the last of the chops.

"That's what you said the first time." The old man wiped his hands on the tail of his dressing gown. "The coachman's daughter, eh? I begin to see your motive in coming to me, young fellow. You think I'll be sympathetic because it happened that I married a coachman's daughter. Actually old Pandle wasn't quite up to that. He was just a second groom." He glared at his grandson from under his heavy white eyebrows. "Is that what's in your mind?"

Allie had the good grace to show some embarrassment. "I—I expect so, sir."

"I'll have to set you right," said the old man after a moment. "Yes, I married the daughter of a groom. Wouldn't be surprised if my reasons were very much the same as what's in your head this very minute. My Charlotte was a plump little baggage with a swing to her and rosy cheeks. I was getting on in years and I was really mad about her. She made me a good wife. The marriage, I have no hesitation at all in saying, was quite successful from my standpoint. But, my boy, it was all a mistake as far as she was concerned. You see, she couldn't bring her old friends with her when she married me and no one on a higher level—not that I was so damned high—would have a thing to do with her. Your poor grandmother had a very lonely life. And, Alfie, it will always be the same."

"But, Grandfather, I want to take Nell to some other part of the world. That would make everything right."

"Except for your mother, who would eat her heart out with you so far away. And what about me? I haven't got so much longer to live and I like to see my grandson once in a while." He rose grumblingly to his feet. "Put this silly idea out of your head, my boy. Your father is going to make himself a great figure in England. One of these days they'll give him a title. Don't you want to share in all this? It will be better than getting yourself roasted to a cinder raising sheep in Australia. As for the girl, there will be plenty more of the kind along."

The old man was not satisfied, however, with the look he saw on his grandson's face as the latter left the room. "That young rooster is going to make a fool of himself if something isn't done about it," he said to himself. He stumped stiffly on his bare feet up the stairs to his bedroom. He sighed as he faced the necessity of getting himself ready for a trip. "Can't leave this to Samuel to handle. He shows no sense where the boy's concerned. A fine, sensitive boy like my Alfie can't be ordered around. I'll have to go and see this girl's father myself."

3

Daniel Groody did not object to his daughter making a shilling or two in various ways around the place. It was the need to wear a uniform, to curtsy, and bob her head and take orders from everyone, most particularly to be called Groody, which he could not tolerate. It happened, therefore, that she was in the north orchard picking apples when Alfred Hanlon was driven into the coach yard at Beaulaw Hall and announced his desire for a few words with Daniel Groody. When she returned in late afternoon, in a cart with half a dozen other pickers and many baskets filled with the red apples of fall, the Groody household was in an uproar. Her mother, in a suspiciously calm manner, was packing, and her father, his eyes still emitting sparks, was pacing up and down and giving audible expression to his outraged feelings.

"I must take my daughter away, must I?" he demanded of the world. "Did he think I would scramble on my knees for the miserly hundred pounds he offered me?"

"What's wrong with a hundred pounds, Daniel Groody?" Mrs. Groody gave vent suddenly to her feelings. "It was enough to buy your daughter a place in this tontine, wasn't it? And now you're taking her away for nothing at all, aren't you?"

Groody disregarded her and turned instead to his daughter. "I said to him, 'I'll have ye know I was left twice as much, Mister Hanlon,' I said, 'by my uncle Shamus in Ireland.' And then I shook my fist in his face and said to him, 'If you offered me ten times as much I would throw it back at ye. Oh, I intend to take my family out of here,' I said, 'but it's not a shilling I'll be taking from you for the doing of it.' And then I said, for good measure and to let him know how I felt about him, I said, 'To hell with you, Mister Hanlon,' I said. 'And to hell with Mister Carboy. And to hell with his son!' "

"But did you have to follow him all the way to the Hall, Daniel Groody?" demanded his wife bitterly. "Did you have to insult him and say he made his money taking slaves out of Africa and he had to keep a high stone wall around his house because he had so many enemies? Did you have to wave your arms at Mrs. Carboy and shout that she could have her son back for all of us?"

Nell intervened at this point. "Oh, Father, did you say that!"

"He did. And he said worse things, if you want to hear."

"I don't, Mother. Please, I don't want to hear any more."

Nell was thoroughly sick at heart. This, she said to herself, would put an end to everything. Whatever small chance there had been before of a happy way out of her difficulties was gone now. She was sure she would never see Allie again. She put her bonnet on a hook and began to set the table for supper, her eyes downcast and clouded with unhappiness.

"We're moving again and it's all your fault, Helen Groody," declared her mother. "Nothing would do you but you must go on seeing him and getting yourself talked about and disgraced. And your sensible father threw the money back in his face. A hundred pounds may look very good to us before we get ourselves settled under another roof."

"I wouldn't touch his dirty money!" cried the head of the family.

"I saw him once only," said Nell in a weak voice. "He rode over from the university and I talked to him for a few minutes. Was there anything wrong in that?"

"There was everything wrong in that, Helen Groody, and you know it. Hadn't you been told a dozen times not to see him? And now we'll find ourselves, as sure as scat, in a house with a roof which leaks. And my rheumatics will get bad again. You won't be satisfied, either of you, until I'm dead and laid away in the grave."

"Please, Mother! I'm feeling very sorry for what I did. And I'm—I'm so unhappy I don't care what happens to me now." She began to cry silently as she carried in the few dishes needed for their simple supper and started the kettle to humming and bubbling on the hearth. "There's no hope for me now. My chance for happiness in life is gone."

Daniel Groody's mood changed at once. He lost all belligerence and there was a sick look on his face as he watched his daughter. "I didn't want to hurt you, my little girl," he said in a piteous tone. "It's biting off my tongue I'll be doing if what I've said has made you feel so bad. May the saints look down on us and forgive me! It's thoughtless I am when the temper's on me." He walked over to her and touched her beseechingly on the shoulder. "But I couldn't let that old tarragon speak ill of my own little girl, could I now? Was it silent I ought to have been when he as good as called you a loose woman and to my very face?"

Nell tried to achieve a smile for his benefit. "It isn't your fault, Father. I should have been sensible and seen it would come to this sooner or later." She laid a loaf of bread on the table and a plate with three very small slices of ham. "Sit down, Father, and have your supper."

"Yes, Daniel Groody, sit down," said his wife. "There's no telling when we'll be having another meal, now that you're out of work again."

He sat down and struck the top of the table with the handle of his knife. "Out of work!" he cried. "Who said I'm out of work? I'll have you know that Squire Clarken of Little Shallow has been at me to go with him. He's seen me driving to the coaching inn and he likes my style, and the way I handle the horses. Just this day two weeks back it is that he said to me, 'Any time you want to make a change, Daniel Groody, come to me.'"

His wife asked suspiciously, "What kind of house goes with the job?"

"It's small, it is indeed. And it's thatched."

"Daniel Groody, it will be damp! I just know it will be damp."

"Mother," protested Nell. "We'll have a house, won't we? And that's the first consideration. Come, sit down and have your supper. I'll draw the beer for you and Father. That will make you both feel better."

CHAPTER THREE

1

Alfred Carboy's two years at Oxford had been more successful than might have been expected in view of the reluctance with which they began. Only because it was a choice between college and Ludgate Hill did he make his decision and set off for the necessary cramming to Dear Old Diggory's. John Eustace Diggory Bland had so many connections in high places that gradually he had become known universally by the nickname he had earned when he was himself a student at Oxford. He owned an island on the Kennet River with a handsome old Queen Anne house of red brick, filled with paneled rooms and bookcases in the most unexpected places; a cricket field, moreover, and boating facilities. More important than anything else, he kept a staff made up of three of the most expert crammers and so could get the dimmest kind of candidate over the entrance hurdles. Dear Old Diggory, who never did anything more fatiguing than cleaning his pipe and lighting it, strolled about the grounds, sighed at the exertions he saw put forth at the nets, spoke affably to the boys under his care, and charged their fathers a most extraordinarily high rate.

Alfred was a quick study and had just managed to scrape through.

He had not become a Smart but inevitably he was drawn into Horse where his unusual riding ability made him a popular member. All in all he had been reasonably content, a state of mind which ended abruptly when he learned that the Groody family had left Beaulaw Hall as a result of the visit of his grandfather. He fell into a despondent frame of mind then and even began to drink a little, an excess he had carefully avoided before.

He was in a receptive mood, therefore, when Boots Cope and Riddell Gilson, the acknowledged leaders of Horse, came to him with a problem.

"It won't do, Carboy," said Cope. "It won't do, you know. Rid and I have— well, by gad, we've gassed it about, and we've come to—— It comes down to this, Carboy. It won't do, really."

Alfred Carboy was completely mystified at this. "What are you talking about, Boots?"

"The Smarts! Damme, man, if we don't look out they'll—I say, if we don't do something—damme, the Smarts will be having everything their own way."

Alfred turned to Rid Gilson for fuller elucidation. "The Smarts," said the latter, "are starting to lord it over us. You must have heard what's been going on. You've been dashed standoffish for some silly and unsatisfactory reason or other, and moping around like a sick loon but, by gad, you must have heard something."

"I heard they gave a party."

"It was more than a party, my dear old fellow. It was a declaration to the world, by gad, that Smarts can do no wrong. Did you know they smuggled three Toasts up to Lordy Hamp's rooms? No chaperones, mind you. All three from the most respectable families in town. Nice, silly girls, dressed right up to the nines. Some of the younger Smarts, having less restraint and *savoir-faire* than the older men, started pawing at the Toasts. Then they got to tearing off sashes and the like. By gad, one of the gals was stripped down to a single petticoat by the time she got home. There's been a terrible to-do about it. If the families of the three hadn't wanted to keep the whole thing dark, there'd have been some cashiering done. But nothing *has* come of it and so the Smarts have become unbearably insolent, by gad."

"I heard all about that," conceded Alfred. "But I wasn't much interested."

"Not much interested!" cried Gilson. "All of Oxford has been ringing with it!"

"Nothing else has been talked about," added Cope. "Not in right circles, you understand."

"The Smarts have been winning, too," said Rid gloomily. "A first in fencing. Three debates. They're sweeping us up on the end of a broom. They're gobbling up the Freecynics and they even talk of reviving the Banterers. I tell you, they're going it. And what are we doing? Nothing. Nothing at all. Just sitting on our balloon butts and doing abso-lutely nothing."

"It's—my dear old fellow," declared Cope, "it's—it's infamous!"

"It comes down to this." Rid Gilson raised a forensic forefinger. "It's boots and saddles, my men. We must be up and at 'em, as the Duke said. Action, by gad!" He dropped his voice a peg or two. "In other words, we must give a party."

"That's it, my dear fellows, a party!" said Cope.

"One," went on Rid, "which will make theirs look as tame as tea and crumpets with the dear vicar. We won't have Toasts. We'll have girls of the town. Out-and-outers. We'll smuggle them in. Rosie and Ardelia and the Belle of the Ball. We'll have enough to drink to set this whole building afloat."

"It sounds like a good idea," commented Alfred without any particular enthusiasm.

"Isn't your blood racing with excitement?" demanded Rid. "You'd better start to boil and bubble, my lad, because we need you in this. We need you badly. In fact"—he paused and looked about him at Alfred's untidy but unusually capacious sitting room—"we need your rooms."

Alfred was floored by this statement. He looked at his two visitors in a far from co-operative spirit. "You want to give the party here? But why? I can't afford to buy all the drinks. I don't know these ladies of the town you're talking about."

"We need your rooms because they're perfect for the purpose," declared Rid emphatically.

And he was right. Alfred had been given the privilege of the most visited rooms in St. John's College. They faced on the street and they were up just one flight. There was, moreover, a solid standpipe climbing the wall within an inch of the sill and an obliging architect had, for some good reason no doubt, arranged for narrow brick ledges in the wall at easy intervals. It was a simple matter for anyone who had been locked out to ignore the entrance and the necessary explanations there by climbing up to Alfred's window, which was never locked. They went through his sitting room every evening in a steady procession, thus reaching their own diggings safely and escaping the inquisition of the gate. This had become such a general practice that their stealthy footfalls did not disturb his slumbers any more than the gentle and thrice blessed rain from heaven.

"By gad, old man," said Rid Gilson. "We'll have to bring the little dears in through your window anyway. Listen, dear old fellow, we'll supply the drinks and the bread and butter and the round of beef and the ham. We'll invite the guests and we'll arrange for the girls, and pay 'em, by gad! We'll supply the ropes to haul 'em up and the willing arms to manipulate the ropes. Is it, then, asking too much that you supply the rooms?"

Alfred was in a state of mind where he did not care much what might happen to him. Nell had been taken off somewhere by her irate parents and he might never see her again. His grandfather, on whom he had been sure he could depend, had done this to him. Ahead of him stretched an endless succession of blank days. He was sunk in apathy, life was ashes in his mouth.

"All right," he said to his two visitors. "We'll have the party here."

2

The leaders of the Horse had counted on a small attendance, eight or ten of the choicest spirits and no more, but this was soon found to be impossible.

Rid Gilson and Alfred received the chosen few in Alfred's rooms while Boots Cope remained on the street below to superintend the hoisting operations. The ropes had been ingeniously arranged to allow the crew above to do the raising easily and at the same time provide some degree of comfort for the hoistees. A whistle from below announced the arrival of the first of the petticoated visitors. Three of the youngest guests lowered the ropes and then began to haul in with much puffing and heavy breathing. A tall and arching pink plume came into view.

"It's Belle," said Rid Gilson. "I hope the old girl's in a good mood. She can get positively ugly when she wants to."

But the Belle of the Ball was not in a good mood. She was a statuesque blonde and of a solidity which made lifting her no simple matter. The trio tugging at the ropes did not succeed in easing her over the sill with sufficient finesse. She landed, in fact, the wrong way up; her back on the floor, and a pair of large white legs, only partially covered by stockings, kicking wildly above her. It became apparent also, when she had been helped to her feet, that her finery had suffered in the mischance. Her skirt had been split from top to bottom. She faced the discomfited group in a fury.

"If I thought," she stormed at them, "that you did this on purpose, you snotty young cupboard-heads, I'd raise such a fussation that all the skinny-legged duns and fullows and chuncellors of the cullidge would soon be outside that door!"

"It was an accident, Belle," pleaded Gilson. "You'll get a new dress out of this. That'll make up, won't it?"

"I'll pick it out myself," she warned. "And charge it to you, Master Gilson, never fear. It'll be a downer, that's what it will!"

"And now, sweet lady, a little refreshment perchance?" Rid was striving hard to smooth the ruffled plumage of the first of the feminine visitors. "If you will deign to state a preference in drinks——"

Belle looked at him with a scowl. "Fancy talk!" she scoffed. "They's lots of things I don't like but there's one thing I don't like more than all the other things I don't like. And that's fancy talk."

"I hereby beg your pardon. Plain Saxon words it shall be from now on."

"Beef," declared Belle. "And beer."

Another whistle sounded below. The hoisting squad rose to their feet and began to lower the ropes. The Belle of the Ball put down her sandwich and her bottle of beer and rose to her feet, careless of the fact that in doing so she revealed a Junoesque thigh for all to see.

"It was not so stated in so many words," she declared, looking bitterly at Rid Gilson, "but I was led to believe I'd be the only lady visitor." She pointed in the direction of the window with an accusing finger. "If that's Ardelia being hoist up, mark my words there'll be trouble here tonight."

Unfortunately it *was* Ardelia. To make matters worse, she was lifted through the window with the greatest ease and so landed on her feet like a bird; a bird of some bizarre tropical variety, red of head, green and gold of plumage and furious of temper. She stood still and glared at Belle.

"This place reeks of cheap perfume," she said. "Don't go putting that winder down. We got to get some air in here."

Belle lifted the empty beer container above her head. "When I swings a bottle," she said, "them as has good sense don't linger in my vucinity."

Ardelia looked at the table loaded with provisions and decided against the beef. "I'm seeing too much of that commodity right now," she declared, staring a second time at Belle. "Ham for me. And whoever pours the whisky for me needn't be too delicate about it."

"I wish to point out early, Ardelia Teakle," said Belle, "that when you get yourself plowed you ain't a h'ulevating sight."

"I'll answer *that* when I've had my second," declared Ardelia. "Not before. What I say then will be worth coming through two winders to hear."

A third whistle below provided an opportune interruption, although it directed the wrath of the Belle of the Ball in Gilson's direction again.

"More?" she said. "This is no longer a mere insult. It's a pusitive h'utrage."

"It's just Rosie," said Gilson.

Rosie arrived like another bird, which did nothing to placate Belle, who was still suffering from the effects of her undignified landing. The newcomer was a dark little bird, slender and neat and vivacious. She waved a hand at the company in the best of spirits.

"Hello, my dear, dear boys!" she called. "Why there's my very sweet Cedric and my nice, quiet Buck. And I see my dashing Rid."

"She's trying to make out she's the sweetheart of the hull cullidge," declared Belle darkly.

"But who," went on Rosie, catching sight of Alfred, "who is this? Who *is* this bee-uteful young gentleman?"

"Don't you know him?" asked Rid, surprised that any member of Horse had been around so little.

"Know him? No, Rid. I've never even seen this gentleman. Has he been hiding from me?"

"If he has, he's certainly been found now," declared Rid. "His name is Ralph Roister Doister."

Rosie stepped up beside Alfred and placed her hand under his arm. "I don't think his name is Ralph and I'm certain that—that other name you gave is just silly. I believe he's the handsome young man I've been hearing about, who rides so *very* well. I believe his name is Alfred Carboy." She looked up with a flicker of her eyelashes. "We're going to get along very well, aren't we, Allie?"

Not knowing what to say under such circumstances as these, Alfred asked the girl about her desires in the matter of refreshments.

"Oh, nothing much, my nice Allie. I eat so very little. But I do want a little gin." She held up a hand with thumb and fingers parted to indicate a measurement. "A tot, perhaps. Or, let me see. Perhaps a jolt would be better. In fact, why don't you and I start out on a basis of frankness and helpfulness, my new friend? What I'd really like is a good splash of it."

The success of the party came even more seriously into doubt when the window was opened from the outside and a head with a reddish mop of hair appeared therein. The owner of the reddish hair climbed into the room with an air of surprise at finding it so well tenanted but displayed an immediate determination to partake of the refreshments. He was followed soon after by a plump young fellow in a mulberry coat. A third and a fourth arrived. The planners of the party had overlooked the fact that Alfred's rooms were the route taken by late students. No amount of expostulation could move the newcomers; a party was in progress and they were going to stay.

Belle did not like the way the party was going. She got tipsily to her feet. Taking an empty beer bottle in one hand, she gave it an experimental swing.

"I had friend once," she declared in a thick voice, "said lady should de-

fend herself with buttle. Break buttle first, he said, and swing—swing with
buth hands."

Alfred Carboy had escaped from the attentions of the pre-emptive Rosie
and was standing back against the wall. He was still suffering so acutely from
the blows fate had dealt him that he was able to follow what was going on
with a degree of detachment. He smiled when he heard the Belle of the Ball
ranting in a combative voice about being a lady but his amusement diminished when Ardelia chimed in with doubts on that score. This, he knew,
meant trouble. There was an immediate grapple between the two town girls,
with frantic reaching for hair to pull and faces to scratch while both embattled voices were raised in screams of rage.

The man nearest to him said, "Now there *will* be trouble," and began to
make his way to the door. This aroused Alfred to the need of taking action
but he did not see what, under the circumstances, could be done. Rid Gilson was endeavoring without much success to separate the embattled pair.
The room, Alfred observed, was thinning rapidly. In fact, by the time the
knuckles of authority sounded on the panels of the door there were no guests
left save Rid and the three women.

The porter had enlisted the backing of two dons in black gowns. The trio
stared into the room with eyes which expressed astonishment as well as
official indignation.

"Three!" said one of the black-gowned officials. His voice suggested that
he was gargling rather than speaking. This had nothing to do with his sense
of outrage; it was his normal method of expressing himself. He turned with
high disapproval on the porter. "How do you explain their presence here,
Parchley? This—really, this has to be seen to be believed, it has indeed.
Three, by Jove! How did they dare?"

"They didn't come in at the entrance, sir. I'll swear to that."

"Mr. Gilson, these are not your rooms," said the first speaker.

"No, Mr. Fortescue."

"They're my rooms, sir," said Alfred.

"And you are—eh, Carboy, I believe. Will you tell me, sir, what this
means? Three women in your rooms and all this loud and vulgar screeching!"

"A—a party, if you please, sir."

"How," demanded Mr. Fortescue, "did these women get here?"

"Through the window," explained Alfred. "With ropes, sir."

"Ropes! This is a most flagrant breach of the rules, sir. Did you do the—
the hauling personally, Mr. Carboy?"

"No, sir." After a moment's pause Alfred concluded that he had not been
completely honest in his response. "But it was done with my knowledge and
consent, sir."

"Ah, quite. We do not need to ask you if there were more guests. The
clatter of their departing heels sounded in our ears from every direction.
Do you care to give us the names of these others who were—shall we say?—
enjoying the pleasures of this delightful social occasion?"

"Oh no, sir, I couldn't do that."

"I didn't expect you would. Porter, I think you had better take steps to escort these alien guests to the street."

Parchley threw the door open with one arm and motioned brusquely with the other. "Come on, the lot of you!" he said. "We'll be having no more noise out of you three brims."

With the porter out of the way and the women consigned to their habitual background, the streets of the town, Mr. Fortescue suggested that Gilson accompany him and his colleague to his rooms for a closer examination. After hemming and hawing further, he added: "You will remain here for the time being, Mr. Carboy. You understand, of course, that in the morning you will be summoned to make your explanation before the president."

Despite his indifference to most things about the life he was being compelled to live, Alfred felt a sinking of the heart at this announcement. He was certain of the outcome: he would be sent down. What other punishment could there be for the great fault of which he stood guilty? He had never felt any urge to enter fully into the life of the university or to struggle for leadership in studies or sports but he was shocked at the certainty that his college career would end in this humiliating way. What would his father think? What would he do? "I may be cut out of his will," he thought. This was a particularly grim prospect since his grandfather Hanlon, on whom he had always counted, had deserted him. The future looked dark indeed.

CHAPTER FOUR

1

The house at Squire Clarken's was as small as Daniel Groody had hinted and fully as damp as Mrs. Groody had feared. The latter was in a bitterly complaining mood late one afternoon and it so happened that the head of the family made the mistake of selecting this juncture to bring a stranger home with him for a bite of supper. The stranger, moreover, was a gypsy; a young gypsy with a roving eye and a musical instrument over his shoulder. He was most elaborately attired, a cluster of shilling pieces serving as buttons on his purple-braided maroon coat and pennies fairly rattling on his beige waistcoat.

"It's a new friend I've brought," said Daniel Groody in a casual tone. "And that's a banjore on his shoulder."

"It could be the very harp that King David played on before Saul and I'd still say he's a dirty gypsy!" cried Mrs. Groody.

"Come, come!" protested her spouse. "That's not fairly spoken. It's descended from ten kings he is, and he has a generous tongue in his head for everything Irish. His name is Faden Jock."

"Then you and your Faden Jock and all ten of his kings can have supper at the inn. I'll be feeding no gypsies tonight, Daniel Groody."

The gypsy undoubtedly heard what was being said but he gave no sign. As he entered the room his eye had fallen on Nell, who was sitting in a corner sewing on a piece of linen. He had watched her with an eye which kindled warmly. He now took a few steps in her direction.

"Little Flower," he whispered, "how did it happen that you grew in this tight little niche?"

He was handsome in a dark and rather oily way and Nell had taken a dislike to him at once. It was clear that he was aping the royal manner of the great gypsies, some of whom wore Spanish gold pieces for back buttons and spaded guineas and half guineas on their coats. She lowered her eyes to her work and said politely, "Good evening, sir."

"Ah, how beautiful you are, my sweet gazi!" went on the visitor in a cautiously low tone. "The fairness of gorgio women has been known to drive men like me mad. Little Flower, it must be that you feel drawn to me. Just a little, perhaps? When she made no response and continued to keep her eyes averted, he shook his head in pity. "Always so cold, the gorgio women! Always so afraid of life! They do not know what they miss. Pretty Flower, Pretty Flower, you should know what it is to have a gypsy lover!"

Daniel Groody had been whispering to his wife and had succeeded in bringing her around. She stepped over to the visitor and said with a nod which she strove not too seriously to make friendly: "The words I spoke were not meant to give offense, young man. I am happy to have you with us for supper."

The gypsy bowed. "Handsome mother of a very lovely daughter, I thank you for your kindness. Perhaps what I have to tell you will make up for the inconvenience of my presence. I hope you are tar'blish, madame."

"I am not well, sir. I am never well."

"I am sorry to hear it. I think it possible some of the secret remedies of my people would serve to make you better."

Mrs. Groody shook her head stubbornly. "I'll not put any of your heathenish medicines in my mouth. I would expect the good Lord to punish me if I did."

"You must have a more open mind, madame. You think of us as wanderers and, perhaps, as thieves. You do not seem to realize that we are the oldest race in the world. We know many strange and wonderful things which are withheld from all others. I, madame, am proud to be a gypsy."

Fortunately a very good meal had been prepared. There was a beef and kidney stew, well seasoned with herbs, and a loaf warm and crusty from the oven, and a small bottle of red wine. The guest partook liberally of everything and, while he ate, talked in a steady stream. His eyes, however, seldom strayed from the quiet girl who sat opposite him.

"It must be known to you, madame," he said, "that we have the gift of second sight. Not all of us, naturally. The gift is not soiled and made common by general usage. But always there is one who can read the future as though it had been written in fair print on a white page. Of those so gifted none has been so well endowed as the Lady Margilda whose caravan travels in our train."

"She is with you now?" asked Mrs. Groody, whose interest could be caught at once by such talk. She had eyes now for no one but the young gypsy.

"Yes, madame. The caravans tonight are drawn up in a circle around hers in the Danegeld meadow. The meadow, as you doubtless know, belongs to the Squire Clarken, who is a loud and ugly-spoken man and will probably order us to leave in the morning. Leave we will, if the Lady Margilda is not able to find in his past something he would not care to have discussed openly." He paused and nodded his head at Nell. "Your daughter, madame, who is so beautiful that my head swims with delight when I look at her, is clever also. I can read it in her eyes and the line of her brow. She is quite deedy enough, in fact, to manage the shop in the village of Little Shallow."

"The shop in Little Shallow!" cried Mrs. Groody. "Young man, don't you know that it belongs to Mrs. Parker? Though it may be you've never heard her spoken of by any name but Mrs. 'Enry. Let me tell you Mrs. 'Enry would like to catch anyone trying to run her store for her! She's a sharp one, even if she is so fat she can't take a step by herself. She can swing that cane of hers!"

"Mrs. Parker, madame, is dying."

Mrs. Groody's eyes opened wide at this. "I didn't know she's been ailing," she said.

"Mrs. Parker is so huge that she could have every disease known to man under that skin of hers and no one guess it. This trouble has been bringing her time close for many months. She will die of it tomorrow."

"How can you sit there and say such things!" cried Mrs. Groody. "It fair gives me the creeps to listen to you."

Faden Jock lowered his fork and stared solemnly at his hostess. "Madame, I am doing no more than repeat what the Lady Margilda has said. She has never told us anything that did not come true. That very stout lady will start tomorrow afternoon on a very long journey—to a place where she will not be known either as Mrs. Parker or Mrs. 'Enry and where perhaps she will be called to account for all her harshness and her meannesses in life."

"You will feel very silly tomorrow, young man, if she doesn't die after all."

"I can tell you the exact hour when the black wings will brush her shoulder, madame."

"When?" asked Daniel Groody eagerly. He had been listening with ears which seemed to twitch in the immensity of his interest.

"At five minutes after three," stated the young gypsy.

Nell had been in Little Shallow several times and knew the shop, which happened to be the only one in the village. It was a frame house of no great size with a large front window in which a dusty assortment of the goods for sale shared the limited space with cobwebs and a few ancient decorations. She had entered once only and it had seemed to her that the loud bell which rang as soon as she opened the door was unnecessary because Mrs. 'Enry herself was always in the shop; a woman of such extreme obesity that a special chair had been constructed to accommodate her. Mrs. 'Enry kept a cane across her lap with which she pointed out the objects her customers desired. They had to help themselves, even to scooping up and weighing the sugar or tea or coffee and wrapping it up; but no one ever dared take more than he had specified because the shopkeeper's eyes, deeply embedded though they were in the huge surface of her face, were sharp and observant. There was a till beside Mrs. 'Enry and she made change with hands which seemed absurdly small at the ends of her enormous round arms.

Faden Jock addressed himself directly to Nell for the first time. "How would you like to own that shop," he asked, "when Mrs. Parker has departed this life?"

"Own the shop!" Nell's tone made it clear that she realized the utter impossibility of such an idea.

"You are surprised, miss, but is it not true that your father has enough money to make the first payment?"

"Her father," cried Mrs. Groody, on the defensive immediately, "has no money to buy shops with!"

Faden Jock pouched out his lips and gestured with both hands. "Please, my nice new friends, understand this about me. I am telling you only what the Lady Margilda has herself told me. Little Flower, did you not lose a hair ribbon a day or so ago?"

"Yes," answered Nell. She had been greatly disturbed over her loss, because hair ribbons were great events in her life and not to be lost lightly.

"It was found and came into the hands of the Lady Margilda. Enough of you clung about it still for her to learn many things about you. She saw that you have, under that quiet manner, a decided gift. A gift for managing things. She learned also that your father has a matter of fifty pounds or more in his possession——"

"Lies!" cried Mrs. Groody. "All lies, young man! Daniel Groody hasn't fifty shillings, let alone fifty pounds. And even if he did, do you think I would consent to having him throw it away in such a crazy scheme as this? Buying a shop, the very idea! You might as well tell him to buy the Tower of Lunnon."

The young gypsy paid no attention to her outburst. "The Lady Margilda told me also that Mrs. Parker's son will arrive tonight to be with her in her last moments. He comes from Yorkshire where he has a sound business of his own. But he's a hard man and Lady Margilda is not sure how good a bargain can be made with him for the property. He's also an impatient man and he will want to get back to his own business right away. Lady Margilda told me to make it very clear to you that he will accept fifty pounds to bind the bargain."

"Young man!" exclaimed Mrs. Groody with a frightened look. "What is all this you are telling us? I think you must be the Devil himself!"

Faden Jock winked covertly at Nell. "No, madame, I am not the Devil. But I know there is one. I have seen him with my own eyes."

"You have seen the Devil?" asked Daniel Groody in a thoroughly awed voice.

"Several times. And a very handsome old party he is. I think when he was young he inclined rather to my line of looks. What a way of dressing he has and what an impression he makes on the ladies! It's always been at race tracks where I've seen him, because the Devil has a weakness for horses." His manner grew more serious. "But I want you to understand this, all of you; the gift which Lady Margilda possesses does not come from him. What's more, it's never used to further his purposes."

The senior Groodys were listening quite literally with bated breath. Only once did Nell disturb the semicircle her eyelashes made on her cheeks as she bent over her work. It was a quick glance she gave their guest and a far from favorable one.

"I don't believe a word he's said," she thought. "The very idea, telling us he has seen the Devil! I think he's a kind of devil himself, and a very sly one. He has some scheme up his sleeve to cheat poor Father out of what he has left of the money." She possessed a certain degree of belief in the prophetic power of gypsies but none at all in the honesty of Faden Jock. "And yet," she said to herself, "how did the Lady Margilda know about Father's fifty pounds?"

All her life she had been interested in shops. She had always begged to go with her mother on the rare occasions when Mrs. Groody had discovered a need to go shopping. There had been a fascination for her in the fine stock displayed, so rich and expensive and new, in the brisk talk going on between the clerks and the customers, in the clink of coins dropping into the till. Yes, she realized fully that she had often longed to work in a shop, to wait on customers, to wrap up parcels neatly, to figure prices and make sales. So she listened to every word the gypsy said and in the end she half believed that the Lady Margilda had seen into the future and for some reason had sent Faden Jock to tell them of the opportunity.

The gypsy got to his feet and swung the banjo over his shoulder. "I must be on my way," he said. "The Devil likes to get out on nights as dark as this and he leaves a smell of brimstone wherever he goes. I think it probable he'll be waiting around anyway to whisk Mrs. Parker off with him. I'll give the old gentleman a wide berth if I see him." He winked at Nell as he passed her, and whispered: "Some night you will let me sing you a love song, Little Flower. I will melt that hard little heart of yours."

The argument between Daniel Groody and his wife began as soon as the door closed on Faden Jock. "We will buy the shop for the child," declared Daniel. "It's just as the Romany lad said, she has a chuff side to her and she'll make a lot of money for us out of the little business."

Mrs. Groody's lips were drawn down tight. "It's not as much as a penny you'll get out of me, Daniel Groody."

"It's her future I'm thinking of. This will make her safe and comfortable in her old age."

"You've robbed me already of a hundred guineas to take care of her future," declared the wife. "And what about my future, Daniel Groody? It won't matter to you if I breathe my last in an almshouse just so as the child can wear silks and have cream in her tea."

Nell did not join in the discussion. She distrusted Faden Jock too much to have any real belief in what he had told them. She tried to bring the debate to an end and, failing in this, she laid her work aside and went off to bed.

2

At an early hour the next morning Squire Clarken came to the stables and called out to Groody to saddle the roan. "I'm going down to order those thieving gypsies to be off," he said with a hard grin which made it clear he relished the task ahead of him.

And yet when Nell returned that afternoon from an errand to one of the outlying farms, she found the gypsy caravans still drawn up in a perfect circle in the Danegeld meadow. She stopped in considerable surprise.

"That's queer," she thought. According to her father, Squire Clarken had fully intended to harry them off the place early that morning. She found herself wondering if the Lady Margilda had discovered some circumstance buried in the squire's past and had made a bargain with him. After a moment however, she discarded that possibility and concluded that the Romany people had wheedled an extension of time out of the choleric Mr. Clarken.

It was then that she noticed the old lady standing in the entrance of the rather ornate caravan in the middle of the circle. She was old and her eyes were filled with tragedy and yet she was still strangely beautiful. Nell caught her breath as she watched her. "It must be the Lady Margilda," she thought. And then she told herself that there could be no evil in this gentle old woman and that everything she said would be the truth. She was convinced now that everything would come out as the Lady Margilda had predicted.

It happened that a few hours later another errand took her by the kitchen garden and she paused to see the late flowers which were blooming abundantly; great clumps of beautiful asters, tight little button dahlias, and the ubiquitous cosmos. The cook, spying her wind-tossed hair from one of the kitchen windows, put her head out the door. Her arms were white with flour to the elbows and her face was rosy from the heat of the fire where a roast was turning.

"Have ye heard the news, Nell?" she asked. "About the old woman?"

"Do you mean Mrs. 'Enry?"

The cook nodded. "She gave her last gasps this afternoon."

"Oh, Cook, please," said Nell. "Did you happen to hear when she died? I mean, the exact time?"

The cook gave her head a satisfied nod. Of course she knew the exact time. She always knew such things. "She drawed her last breath, Nelly, at exactly five minutes past three."

So, the Romany lady had been right! If she had known the time when the old shopkeeper would die, it stood to reason that everything else she had said was equally true. Mrs. 'Enry's son *would* accept fifty pounds down to bind the bargain!

Nell hurried home. Her mother was sitting in a rocking chair in one corner of their tiny sitting room. Nell remembered how terrified she had always been when her father would get into one of his tempers and stalk up to his wife in that light-footed way he had, his hands stretched out as though ready to take her by the neck. How many times she had found it necessary to interfere! She was thinking, *He* could get the money from her.

"Mother! You must listen to me. We must *not* lose this chance because of your stubbornness. Mrs. 'Enry is dead. Her son is here and he's going to sell the business. I'm going to see him tonight. Do you hear me?"

"I don't hear a word you're saying, Helen Groody. You needn't waste your breath because I'm not going to listen."

And then Nell discovered something about herself which later gave her much cause for alarm. She found herself stalking up to her mother with the exact gait her father used. What was more, her hands were stretched out in front of her. A temper in her, the existence of which she had never expected, had risen to white heat.

"You *will* listen to me, Mother! I must have the money. I want to do this for your sake and for Father's. *Take that look off your face and get the money for me at once!"*

"Helen Groody!" cried her mother in sudden alarm. "You're a true daughter of your crazy Irish father. Don't you come a step closer or I'll scream."

"Scream as much as you like! I don't care. You will get that money right away or I'll do something I'll regret as long as I live. I won't have this great chance lost because of your whims, even if you are my mother."

She was so close now that she could hear her mother's frightened breathing. Mrs. Groody suddenly threw her hands up in front of her face and capitulated. "I'll get the money," she said. "You look ready to scratch my eyes out. Upon my word, child, I believe you would."

She got to her feet and went to her bedroom. "I'll give you the fifty pounds. And when I die of a broken heart you'll know it was all your doing."

"Your heart won't break, Mother," said Nell. She was feeling suddenly very limp and weak. "I'm giving you a promise. I'll work so hard to make the shop a success that you'll live in comfort for the rest of your days. You won't have to do a tap of work. And I'll turn over a share of the profits to you every week until the fifty pounds have been paid back fifty times over."

"Fine words! That's all I'll ever get out of you."

3

Mrs. Groody sat in the chair her husband had painted for her, and rocked comfortably. From the window in which she had stationed herself she could see all the way down the road running through Little Shallow. The main part of the village was on the top of a gentle hill and the street rambled downward in a pleasant and easy way, lined by cottages behind stone walls over which the heads of fall flowers protruded in great profusion. A church was shared with the nearby village of Carnwood and so had been built halfway between the two. She could see the spire above the trees in Gipland Spinney and, as it was a Sunday, the sound of the bells came faintly but melodiously to her ears. She could see people who had made a late start hurrying down the street to avoid being behindhand for the services. A sense of complete well-being took possession of her.

Her husband had been allowed the morning off as no one from High Squires happened to be going for the morning devotions. He was in the shop at the front of the house, looking over the stock with Nell. Mrs. Groody could hear every word they said as the door was partly open.

"It's a very small stock, Father," said Nell, her voice showing the extent of her disappointment. "Half a barrel of flour, a quarter of a barrel of sugar, a *very* small supply of tea and almost no coffee at all. Those candies she kept for children are old and flyspecked. There are no fancy things at all. Will you take a look at this pail of salted fish! Did you ever see anything more horrible?"

"Well, my girl," said Daniel Groody in a cheerful voice, "we'll just have to crawl until we learn to walk."

"Father, I've been doing a lot of thinking about this business of ours." It was clear from the tone of Nell's voice that her thinking had been of a serious kind. "Where did Mrs. 'Enry get these supplies from? Are there big shops which sell goods to little shops?"

Anyone who knew Daniel Groody well would not need to see him at this point to be sure he was scratching his head in a puzzled way. "Are there now? I'm thinking, Nelly, there must be. I've seen fellows driving by in vans and carriages and boogies, all loaded up with goods. I always thought they sold to houses along the road but perhaps they sell to shops instead. They're called bagmen and that must mean something." He paused and, when he continued, his voice had taken on a rapt tone. "Ah, what a fine life it is for a man to live! Driving about the country with a horse and boogie!"

"These big shops which sell the supplies must be in the large towns," went on Nell. "In Reading, for instance. Father, do you suppose you could get a day off and drive me to Reading to see what we can get? We *must* have a better stock than this if we hope to make any real profit."

Mrs. Groody began to rock slowly because she did not want to miss a word. She was sure in her mind about what was coming.

"I could get a day off. Just let the squire say no to it and he'll get a piece of my mind."

"He will not!" cried Mrs. Groody in a sudden and bitter resentment. "You'll keep that mouth of yours shut tight, Daniel Groody, and not be losing another job!"

"Whether or not, it's to Reading we'll be going someday very soon. But, child dear, what would I be saying to the men in the big shop? I can talk to horses and make them understand me but I can't get any sense out of businessmen. All I could do would be to twiddle my cap and stare at 'em."

"Don't you worry," said Nell in a confident tone. "I'll do the talking. I've been going over it in my mind and I know exactly what I'm going to say to them."

Mrs. Groody was rocking very slowly now and saying to herself: "The first word they utter about needing money, they'll find they've got me into a real ferrick this time! I'll stamp on the floor and scream! I'll give them a piece of my mind, and no mistake. Not another penny will they wheedle and scroup out of me."

"Do you know anything about bills, Father? People run bills at shops so it stands to reason that little shops must run bills at big shops. There must be credit in business."

"Credit in business? Well, now, I don't know about that." Daniel Groody, without any doubt, was scratching his head a second time. "It's never a word I've been hearing about credit." The tone of his voice changed to one almost of pain. "How can the likes of us talk about bills and credit to the men in the big shops? It can't be done, Nelly, it stands to reason it can't."

Mrs. Groody was wishing she possessed a cane or had a broomstick in her hands to assist in the demonstration of protest she would soon be displaying.

"I can talk to them," declared Nell. "I've been thinking about this too and I know how to go about it. Oh, I'll get the credit, you may be sure. And now here's another thing. We could get the post office if you had a horse and could drive about the country, delivering the mail."

"With a boogie of my own?" It was clear that the head of the house had been transported to the heights by this prospect.

"Well, in time. At first you could ride the horse and carry a bag over your shoulder for the mail." Her voice lost some of its tone of confidence. "Father, when we open the shop tomorrow there will have to be money in the till so we can make change. Have you any in your pockets?"

"Tuppence. But you can have it, child."

"I've got tuppence too. I'm afraid that won't be enough."

This was the point for Mrs. Groody to explode into wrathful denial but much to her own surprise she did not say a word. A realization had suddenly come to her that it was going to be very pleasant living in this dry house with shingles on the roof instead of thatch. She had never known a finer prospect from any window than the view of the village street, with people walking up and down, and the church spire in the distance. It would be nice to have neighbors so close at hand and to hear the jingle of the bell when people came in to buy goods and to pass the time of day as well.

To her still deeper amazement she did not stamp her feet on the floor and cry out in a rage. Instead she heard herself saying: "I've got two shillings in change. Will that be enough?"

And then suddenly she was aware that the door from the shop had been opened wide and that they were staring in at her. Daniel Groody was a picture of astonishment, his broad and humorous mouth as wide open as his eyes. Nell's face was shining and her eyes were at their very darkest blue.

"She's for us!" cried Daniel Groody. "All the time I'm worrying about her and I lay awake at nights thinking, 'Is she for us or is she agin us?' I was sure she was agin us. But, child dear, we didn't need to worry. All the time she was for us and not agin us."

"Mother, Mother!" cried Nell, running into the room and throwing her arms around Mrs. Groody's neck. "Oh, this is wonderful, wonderful! We're going to all work together after all. I'm so happy."

CHAPTER FIVE

1

The City offices of Plumbottom and Hook, Bankers, were very dingy indeed. There was a sign hanging over the entrance which, through long exposure to the elements, had lost one B and one K and in general had become indecipherable. The front of the building was of white stone but it had never been scraped and the soot of the City had gathered deep upon it. There was a tiny room just inside the door where customers waited until they were escorted to whichever cubicle they were to go in that great rabbit warren of tiny rooms. Each office contained a little middle-aged man who seemed as bloodless as the entry books over which he labored.

There were six partners in Plumbottom and Hook (the banking law allowed no more, for some reason) and because of a whim of Mr. Plumbottom's they occupied a large room jointly. Mr. Plumbottom had a large desk closest to the fireplace. Four other partners had small desks in a row and it is perhaps needless to state that the one who held the fewest shares of stock was the farthest away from the fire.

Late one afternoon Mr. Plumbottom, who was very shortsighted, was deeply absorbed in some documents on his desk when it was announced that a visitor wished to see him. Without looking up, he grunted that Mr. Eaveright would attend to the matter.

"Mr. Eaveright is not here, sir," said the attendant.

The head of the bank squinted at the desk nearest him and discovered that it actually was empty.

"Great gad, Frisbie," he said. "Where is Mr. Eaveright?"

"He's gone for the day, sir."

Mr. Plumbottom looked startled because it was much too early for anyone to depart, even a full-fledged partner. "Mr. Calker, then," he said.

"But Mr. Calker has gone for the day also, sir."

"What!" The expression on the president's face suggested that some strange epidemic, which he did not understand at all, had visited the establishment. This conviction grew on him as he discovered in turn that the other two had gone for the day, Mr. Sykes and Mr. Hoare.

"This is odd!" he muttered, holding his temper in check with difficulty. "Damned odd! Frisbie, who is this visitor demanding so rudely and insistently to see a partner?"

"Mr. Samuel Carboy, sir."

"Carboy!" Mr. Plumbottom turned a choleric color. "I haven't spoken to that man for ten years. I don't intend to renew my acquaintance with him now. Send him away."

"Not so fast, if you please, Mr. Plumbottom." Samuel Carboy had expected some such response and at this moment he appeared in the door of the holy of holies where the partners usually sat in solemn conclave. "I recommend strongly that you hear what I've come to say. It's a matter of the greatest importance."

The banker glared at him. "Humph!" he said. After a moment's reflection he waved a hand in Frisbie's direction. "Leave us."

"I come, Mr. Plumbottom," said Carboy, "to suggest that you call a meeting of your board tomorrow morning."

The effrontery of this proposal caused the banker to glare at him furiously. "Do you refer," he demanded finally, "to Plumbottom and Hook?"

"I am referring to Plumbottom and Hook."

"Now see here, Carboy. I don't know what's back of this outrageous suggestion but damme, sir, if you think——"

"I'm one of your shareholders, Mr. Plumbottom. In fact I have acquired a controlling interest."

The banker indulged in a loud and angry neigh. "What absurdity is this? No one could take the control away from me, not even if he bought out each one of these four."

"I've done that, Mr. Plumbottom. Each one was quite glad to sell and to accept shares in a new banking amalgamation which I have under way. Each of them has been very much against the—the policy which has cut the profits of Plumbottom and Hook to the vanishing point. Perhaps they haven't dared express their dissent but it has been very deep-rooted, sir. The sixth partner did not hesitate to express her feelings. She said you were ruining the bank with your stupid and bungling management. Pardon me for speaking in such terms but I am using her exact words. I refer, of course, to the widow of your late partner, Mr. Theobald Hook. She also has sold to me, thus giving me a clear control."

There was a long silence during which Mr. Ernest Plumbottom breathed with dramatic heaviness. He was a corpulent man with black eyebrows and mutton-chop whiskers; a perfect sample, one might have said, of the banker type.

"I suppose," he said finally, waving a hand at the row of empty desks, "that this explains their absence."

"Yes. I had conveyed to them my desire for a private talk with you this afternoon."

There was a still longer pause. Mr. Plumbottom had turned a gray color. His fingers pawed nervously at his watch chain.

"This is hard to believe, Carboy. We've hated each other all these years and I suppose this is your way of taking it out on me. You want the satisfaction of throwing me out of my own bank."

Carboy dismissed this suggestion with an impatient wave of his hand. "I don't let likes or dislikes influence me. I have no hesitation in saying that I dislike you, Mr. Plumbottom. I have small regard for your capacity as a man of business. The only reason that I'm interested in this bank at all is that my partners and I have acquired many companies in various lines during the past few years and we're very much in need of a bank of our own. We intend to make many changes here. You seem to have taken a pride in making it look like a secondhand furniture warehouse or a rag and bone shop. We're going to admit some light—this new plate glass, in fact—and we'll tear out a lot of these partitions. There's going to be a touch of dignity about the place from now on."

"And where do I fit into these ambitious plans of yours for a concern which you don't yet control officially?"

"You have a choice, Mr. Plumbottom. You can sell out to us, accepting payment partly in cash and partly in shares in the new concern. Or you can keep your holdings, converted into the new stock. If that's your preference, you'll continue as chairman. You'll have a fine office and you'll preside at all board meetings. A carriage will always be sent for you to bring you down to the annual meetings and to take you home. Each year you'll be voted a bonus of one hundred guineas and a pipe of canary or something of the kind. Your portrait will be painted by a good man, and at company expense, to hang in the board room. You can, in fact, continue to throw on all the dog you want. But," emphatically, "you will have no authority and no duties. You'll never dictate a note or sign a letter. And I'll expect you to show me the ordinary civility of calling me Mr. Carboy. Is that clear?"

Nothing could have been stated with more clearness. Mr. Plumbottom asked for time to think things over. Carboy said, "Three days," and gathered up his gloves.

In three days he had his answer. Mr. Plumbottom had decided to remain and serve as chairman of the board.

2

The renovations had taken a month. At the end of that time the once dingy offices of Plumbottom and Hook had blossomed into the freshness of new paint, the up-to-dateness of wide windows with plate glass, and the opulence within of fresh carpets and attendants in livery. A new sign bore the name, The Trafalgar Bank, and if this did not convey to all and sundry a suggestion that this was an institution of the most solid principles and the most worthy traditions, the names of the officers would undoubtedly suffice. Lord Charles Strongarm was the president and Sir Arthur Crust vice-president. Strongarm and Crust! Strength and frugality! What better guarantee could a bank offer the public? Samuel Carboy, who had selected them with that thought in mind, often chuckled to himself over it.

The month, of course, had brought other changes. The Trafalgar Bank might be organized on a basis of solidity without change but the seasons were beyond control. Snow had been falling for three days. It lay deep on the streets. It had drifted into all the alleys and courts, concealing much of their ugliness, and it covered window sills and filled gutters and eaves. The

City did not like it. Men went to work with blue noses and collars turned up to protect their ears, complaining bitterly of the discomfort. Only the crossing sweeps were happy about it. Their voices had a cheerful note although their breath froze in front of their noses and their hands were chapped and cold. They had a few extra pennies in their pockets every night and that was compensation for everything.

Samuel Carboy had a suite of offices on the second floor. The headquarters of Carboy and Co., which he had never expected to leave, were too far removed from the busy center of his new trade empire. Accordingly a Mr. Morkerson sat in the large center office over which there had been so much bitterness, and acted as managing director of the parent company.

The morning of the great day when the bank was to have its formal opening, with a luncheon in the board room and a most distinguished list of guests, Samuel Carboy stood in front of his fireplace and toasted his back most comfortably while he talked to Sir Theobald Gardiner. The latter, who was the possessor of a neat wit, was to preside.

"Sir Theobald," he said, "you are right, of course. The bankers of London are right. The press is right. There *will* be a depression, and a severe one. We'll have to pay for the way we chucked money around in beating the Corsican. But you're wrong in assuming that it will soon be on us. I guarantee—and I speak after the most profound study of conditions—that the trouble won't begin until the early twenties. That leaves us about five years in which to reap a harvest."

Success was having its effect on the Eastern merchant turned industrialist. The Carboy chin had acquired an additional layer, the Carboy mid-section was putting an increasingly heavy strain on his waist buttons. No pickpocket could rob him of his watch because it would have required the efforts of a steam hoist to dislodge it from the tight pocket in which it reposed. His manner had become more brusque and assured, not to say pontifical.

"Since Waterloo," he went on, "we've had nearly seven thousand failures. That's not strange with the public clamoring for wild schemes in which to lose their money. Why, damme, Sir Theobald, there was a mad Frenchman in here yesterday who's trying to launch a company to drain the Red Sea and dredge up the gold and silver that the children of Israel lost in their crossing! The investors have no faith in solid stocks but they'll risk their money in any silly bubble. When it comes to industrial stocks, it's sell—sell— sell! It's just like that day on the Exchange when they thought Boney had beaten the Iron Duke. Well, we've been doing as I did that day—we've been buying. We've picked up sixteen companies at bargain prices. They're key concerns and by acquiring them we've got a foot in every industrial field in the United Kingdom. With the five more years of continued free trading which I guarantee, we can put all our companies on such a solid basis that the winds of adversity, when they begin to blow, will play harmlessly about our ears."

"By gad, Carboy," said Sir Theobald admiringly, "you're a Napoleon yourself. A Napoleon of industry. You know, that's good. I may use it today."

His manner acquired a renewed touch, however, of the anxiety which had prompted the discussion. "I hope you're right about all this. We're in most infernally deep."

"And we'll make ourselves infernally rich and powerful."

Jonathan Bade put his head in at the door. "The cloth has been laid below and the first guest has arrived," he announced. He consulted his watch. "The prime minister will be here in a very few minutes. He's bringing a member of his cabinet with him—I don't know which one—and six members instead of the four we requested."

"Now *that* is positively gracious of the old boy," declared Carboy.

"More good news," said Bade. "The governor of the Bank of England has sent word that he's been able to put off his other engagement and so he's coming too."

Carboy got to his feet with alacrity. "This, damme, is going to be the most auspicious opening any bank ever had." He looked with a hint of concern at the lawyer. "Are we going it with the food?"

"I hope the prime minister doesn't have to do any more speaking today. He wouldn't be likely to sparkle after the way we're going it. Sir Theobald selected the wines himself."

Carboy drew back at the door. "Sir Theobald, I hope you'll have some nice things to say about our officers. Everyone in the City knows they are old dunderheads and we must present them in as good a light as possible. Butter them up like a pair of baked parsnips right straight from around the roast."

The baronet nodded. "They'll fairly drip with it by the time I'm through with them."

"Will you mention that we've chosen Nelson's ship as our trade mark?"

"I'm building my peroration around it."

"All that plate glass we've put in," declared Bade, "is enough to make the public do pitchpolls in sheer eagerness to deposit their money with us. There never was such plate glass, I assure you. Not a crack, not a seam, not a discoloration. They shine as bright and clean as the morning of victory. People, finding it possible to look in and see business going on inside and the clerks driving away with their pens, will say, 'Here's one bank with nothing to conceal.' "

They hurried downstairs in order to take their places at the head of the receiving line. They had barely done so when an outbreak of cheering in the street marked the arrival of the Earl of Liverpool at their door, the prime minister who had succeeded, in spite of his lack of political genius, in bringing the country through the last stage of the great crisis.

The meal had progressed to the sweet course when the prime minister leaned closer to Sir Theobald Gardiner, on whose right he sat. "This man Carboy must be a 'straordinary fellow," he whispered. "His climb has been —well, quite unusual, hasn't it? But I must say he's a confoundedly silent fellow. I've hardly had a word out of him."

Sir Theobald smiled as he whispered back. "Overawed, my lord. After all, to sit beside the head of His Majesty's Government is quite unusual for a man who's spent his life in trade. At his best, my friend Carboy talks with great force and conviction."

"Indeed. I take it, then, that the taciturn Mr. Carboy has qualities which do not show on the surface."

Sir Theobald allowed his voice to drop still lower. "Will you permit me to make a prediction, my lord? Samuel Carboy will soon be the richest man in England. I have no hesitation, in fact, in going a step further and saying that he will be in time the richest man in the world."

The earl took a quick glance at his host on the other side. "Egad, are you serious? I fail to remark in him the outward evidences of such potential greatness."

"Nothing can stop him." Sir Theobald hesitated before continuing. "My lord, he has a fine broad shoulder, my friend Carboy. The exact kind of shoulder, in my humble opinion, on which the blade of the royal sword might fall with all due fitness. He deserves to be Sir Samuel, my lord."

The prime minister took an approving sip of the madeira and sighed because he dared not risk another helping of the pudding.

"I'll give the matter some thought," he said finally. "In fact, I may go so far as to say that I'll discuss him with my colleagues. You appreciate, I trust, that he has made many enemies."

"You, my lord, have risen to the top in the political world without creating enemies. But I assure you that it's impossible to do so in the fields of finance and trade. Sometimes, as you know well, the enemies a man makes are the measure of his greatness."

"Quite, quite. But in some ways it's a bar to advancement!"

"I am sure that my friend would be very happy to make a suitable contribution to any cause, or fund, which might be stipulated."

The prime minister nodded his head slowly as he took another sip of his wine. "I see. I shall remember what you've told me. It's not impossible that —that something will be done. As you say, he's a man of real substance." The ministerial resolution weakened at the sight of the pudding being handed around to others along the board. "Dammit, I *will* have another slice. It's most 'straordinarily well spiced."

After the distinguished guests had taken their departure, Samuel Carboy and Sir Theobald exchanged congratulatory glances.

"We've scored a success," said the latter.

"It seemed so to me. The prime minister enjoyed himself. He certainly powdered into the mutton."

"Samuel," said Sir Theobald in a confidential whisper, "I put the suggestion before him."

Carboy turned immediately, his eyes showing a sharply aroused interest. "You mean——"

"Exactly. The matter of a little tap on a certain shoulder. He promised to take it under consideration. I rather think, Samuel, that it will go through."

He added as an afterthought, "Of course it would cost something in the way of a contribution."

Carboy shrugged his shoulders easily. "I expected that. I'll be willing to do whatever is customary. In fact I'm prepared to do things handsomely. I appreciate how much of an honor it will be." His companion was surprised to see that his eyes had filled with moisture. "It will make me the happiest and proudest man in the world."

"You've got to expect that it will take some time. He must speak to his colleagues. As you know, they don't rush at things." Sir Theobald changed the subject then to ask, "Have you had any further word from the boy?"

"Another letter came yesterday." Carboy's manner had changed abruptly. He was frowning. "He still doesn't say where he is. But he assures us that he's well and that we needn't worry about him. I wish I knew where the young rapscallion is and why he's playing this trick on us."

"That's easy to understand. He thought he was going to be sent down from Oxford and he was ashamed to come home. Give him a little more time and he'll come back of his own accord."

"I hope you're right. His mother's almost beside herself and even old Alfred Hanlon is getting querky about it. I'll have to get that young man to work or he'll be landing in some serious trouble."

"Easy, Samuel, easy. The boy's going to need your sympathy and understanding."

"The way I feel at present," declared Carboy gruffly, "I haven't much of either commodity to offer him."

3

Not a day passed without some dealings on the Stock Exchange but Samuel Carboy did not go there himself. Jonathan Bade had acquired new offices from which there was a view of the Exchange and on days when the dealings rose to a high peak Carboy would settle himself there; and clerks would run back and forth like aides-de-camp on a battlefield, carrying to him slips with information and taking back other slips on which he had scrawled his instructions. His name was now spoken on the Floor with almost as much awe as that of Nathan Rothschild.

He invaded the Floor only once during these days, and none of the busy habitués of the place would have believed the reason which took him there. It was a good quarter hour before the opening bell was due to sound and he sought out, not the busy brokers or the financial figures who stood about and muttered together in low tones as though everything they said had a godlike quality of importance, but that most humble of Exchange employees, Heaven Beck.

"Good morning to you, Mr. Beck," he said. "By the way, I've never understood the reason for that name they've tagged on you."

"Well, sir, Mr. Carboy," said the messenger, "someone remembered that

in the old days, the very old days, sir, priests were sometimes called heaven-
becks, just as poundkeepers were called harmon-becks. So, seeing as my
name was Beck and I'd got myself this crick in the neck, partly by staring
up all the time and partly because of the rheumatiz, they started to call me
Heaven Beck."

Carboy digested this information for a moment and then gave his head a
nod. "Come over to your corner for a moment, Mr. Beck, I've got something
to tell you."

The corner, as usual, was occupied by one of the Beck dogs, a potbellied
little fellow with a reddish coat and whiskers to match. They found stools
beside the canine and sat down.

"What's *his* name?" asked Carboy, looking at the dog as though he distrusted his pacific inclinations.

"He was so small and rambunctious when we got him, sir, that at first
we called him Boney. But will you believe it, Mr. Carboy, the others understood about the name and they didn't cotton to it. They began to pick on
him. So we had to get another one for him and now we just call him
Bouncer."

"A good name for him, I'm sure. I'll appreciate it, Mr. Beck, if you'll
keep an eye on him while we talk. I don't want him doing any bouncering
around me." Then he lowered his voice. "You spoke once of investing your
savings when the right time came. Are you still of that mind?"

Beck's face reflected his knowledge that he had suddenly come face to
face with fate. He turned rather pale and gulped as he answered. "Oh yes,
sir, Mr. Carboy."

"You'll respect what I'm going to tell you? No running around and asking
other opinions? No hints or winks or suggestions to others?"

"You can depend upon me, sir. I pledge my word most solemn."

Carboy looked about to make sure that not another pair of ears were
within hearing distance. "Have you been watching Highcastle Ltd.?"

"I have that, sir." Beck made sympathetic clucking noises with his tongue.
"What a great pity, sir. It's been like Humpty-Dumpty, sir, falling clean off
the wall, hasn't it?"

"Now, Mr. Beck, I've a suggestion to make. Get every scrap of capital
you have at your disposal. Beg, borrow or steal as much more as you can.
Well, forget the stealing part; that's just a figure of speech, do you understand? But you must get together as much as you honestly can and sink it
all in Highcastle Ltd. at the opening."

Beck's mouth fell open. "Highcastle Ltd., sir? Why—why—it's been falling for a month. Every day it goes lower."

"It will reach its lowest point at the opening today. Buy Highcastle, Mr.
Beck. At the opening, mind you. Not a second later. Get your order in now."

The messenger had turned a tallowy color. Like most men who dream of
the great moment when opportunity will present itself, he was completely
unprepared and unnerved.

"Yes, sir," he stammered finally. "I'll do it. But I'm scared, Mr. Carboy. I'm plumb ratcheted and tozed, sir."

"Every shilling. Every bent penny. Every brass farthing. Get your brother's savings too. This, Mr. Beck, is the chance you've been waiting for all these years!" Carboy shook an admonitory finger at him. "Take my word for it. And keep a still tongue in your head."

"Indeed, yes, sir. Every shilling, sir? At the opening?"

Carboy got to his feet. "Don't go into this if you have misgivings. But if you let your fears get the better of you, you'll miss the greatest chance in a hundred years."

He made a quick exit then before any of the eager occupants of the Floor could buttonhole him. For the next hour he was busy with detail and attending to the many slips which reached him from the Exchange. These messages made it clear that what he had predicted about Highcastle Ltd. was being most amply borne out. After opening at a disastrously low figure, the stock had suddenly given itself a shake, gathered its cerements about it and emerged from the grave into which it was being shoved so unceremoniously. It had gained in an hour a matter of six points and the entire interest of the Exchange had now been transferred to it.

"Funny thing happened over there, sir," said one of the messengers, delivering a note to Carboy. "To old Beck, sir. Never made a mistake in his life before. Never handed a slip to the wrong party, sir. Always knew which beefsteak belonged to who. Today, sir, he made four mistakes in the first ten minutes after the opening. Notes were getting into the wrong hands. There was a regular to-do about it, sir. It was concluded, sir, that he was ill and he was told he had better get himself a rest. He went over and squatted down beside the dog. I had a look at him, sir. He was as white as a sheet and shaking like a man as has seed a ghost."

At noon Carboy questioned the same messenger about the condition of Beck. "A meer-aculus recovery, sir," said the man. "He got took better all of a sudden, old Beck did. Right now he's doing his work as sharp as a knife. And—you won't believe this, sir—he's *whistling*."

After the last stroke of the bell announcing the close, Samuel Carboy started over and found a completely exhausted Beck standing near the pillar where his dog was chained. The messenger had difficulty in using his voice.

"Oh, Mr. Carboy, I've been looking for you for the last two hours. I wanted to know if I should sell. It kept going on up and there I was with a fine, clean profit. I was sure, sir, I should take it and get out."

"Sell?" Carboy looked at him with the amazement St. Peter would unquestionably display if a newly arrived soul, after being admitted, had come back and tapped him on the shoulder to say, "Well, St. Peter, I've seen what it's like inside and now may I got out and look at some other places?" "Mr. Beck, you didn't sell, did you? Damme, sir, you surely weren't foolish enough to do that."

Beck shook his head. "No, sir, I didn't. But I wanted to. It kept going up and I had a great profit and I kept saying to myself, 'You silly muggins, get out before they change their minds.' But you hadn't said anything about when to sell——"

"Good. Now, Mr. Beck, get this into your head. Never sell this stock. Keep it to your dying day." He let his voice fall. "It's going to become more valuable all the time. Things are going to happen in the woolen trade and we're getting all old established concerns like Highcastle together in a plan to make wool cloth on a big scale. 'Wool for the World' is going to be our slogan. The shares you hold—I don't know how many you bought and I don't care—will be doubled and tripled and quadrupled in course of time. Hang onto it and you'll end up a prosperous man."

Beck responded in an awed whisper. "Sir, it's like a dream. I've pinched myself a dozen times to make sure."

Carboy had become aware that Bouncer no longer looked hostile. He was wagging his stub of a tail. "Damme, Mr. Beck, I think this dog knows what has happened."

"Of course he does. They always do, these poor old stray fellows. Bouncer will be thinking all the way home of the farm he'll have the run of before long and he'll nearly drag my arm out in his hurry to spread the news among the rest."

CHAPTER SIX

1

Mrs. Derek Slingsby had taken inside seats on the Brighton Diligence (Crossweller, Rogers, Norris, Blackin & Co., Proprietors) to London for herself and her daughter. Being what might be termed an assertive type of woman, she studied the dingy lawyer, who occupied the rear seat with them, with a far from approving eye before scanning the three passengers facing them, with their backs to the horses. These were even more questionable: a businessman in a small way and a huge overcoat, a dapper man with a roving eye, and a woman whose respectability seemed decidedly open to debate.

"My dear," she said in an audible tone, "this is not going to be a pleasant trip for us. Where *do* such people come from?"

"Mother," whispered the daughter, who was rather pretty and had not given the other occupants of the inside the benefit of a single glance, "did you notice that young man?"

Mrs. Slingsby's disapproval of things in general became concentrated in the highly annoyed gleam she turned on her daughter.

"Young man?" she said. "What young man? Speak up, Nancy. What low creature have you been noticing now?"

"The upper Benjamin on this coach," explained Nancy. "The guard, Mother. He's sitting outside now and doing that tootling on the horn. But he's not low. Mother," in a still lower tone, "I know him."

"You do not know him! No daughter of mine could know the—what was that vulgar name you had for him, child?—the upper Benjamin on a Brighton coach."

"But, Mother," persisted the girl, "there's something queer about it. It's very mysterious. Do you remember hearing me speak of Isabelle Carboy?"

"The daughter of this man who's buying up everything in England? The new millionaire? Yes, my child, of course I remember."

"Well, when Isabelle and I were at Miss Bordley's together—I hated her because she was so pretty and so smart and so everything—she had me to tea with her parents once. It just happened that her brother was there that day. He was at Clutterhaugh but he had been given the day off and had come into town. He looked so handsome in the bowler hat and pink tie. There's nothing better-looking than what they wear at Clutterhaugh, is there?" She dropped her voice so low that her mother had to bend her head to hear. "Mother, the upper Benjamin is Alfred Carboy!"

"Nonsense!"

"It's not nonsense. I would know him anywhere. There, that's him playing on the bugle now."

"Nonsense, I say. The son of a millionaire would never be playing 'Old Towler' on a Brighton coach for the amusement of a lot of cheap bagmen and lawyers."

"Mother, when we stop at Croydon for lunch, I'm going to make sure. Oh, isn't it exciting? I never thought I would see Allie again. Not that he paid any attention to me when I did see him. It was a pose with the Clutterhaugh boys. Women played no part in their lives."

It had begun to snow when the smoking horses came to a stop in the coach yard at the Fox and Hounds. The face of the mysterious upper Benjamin appeared in the window of the coach. "Time for lunch, ladies and gentlemen," he said. He opened the door, let down the steps and stood to one side to lend a hand to the ladies in their descent.

"Oh, Mother, it is Allie Carboy," whispered the excited girl. "Isn't he simply handsome? Mother, I'm going to stay behind and speak to him. I must."

"Do they expect me to walk through this snow?" demanded Mrs. Slingsby. She glanced about her indignantly, her skirts clutched in her hands and raised just sufficiently to allow a glimpse of shapeless felt overshoes. No one, it seemed, expected her to do anything. She could have remained where she stood like another Lot's wife until the lunchtime was over for all anyone connected with the coaching business cared. The driver, looking like a scarecrow escaped from a wheat field in four overcoats and with bands of hay fastened around his legs for warmth, made at once for the common room where a beefsteak and kidney pie and a pot of ale awaited him. The guard was busy taking out of the boot the luggage of the passengers who were not continuing into the city. After a moment the indignant lady raised her skirts a few inches higher and waddled inside.

Nancy approached the guard and said in a careless tone: "Oh, guard, there's a hatbox I'm very much concerned about—— Why, Allie Carboy, what are you doing here?"

Alfred straightened up and looked at her from under his low-crowned white hat. "My God, it's little Nancy Slingsby!" he exclaimed. "I *am* found out. See here, Nancy, you've got to give me your promise. You won't go telling on me. You see, I've run away from college and I don't want to go home yet. I've got to make a living some way. You will promise, won't you?"

"Of course, Allie." The heart of the heiress to the not overly large Slingsby fortune was palpitating with excitement. To share a secret with Allie Carboy! To be in a position to render him a great service! It was all too wonderful for words. "Of course I'll keep this to myself. But—but—isn't it kind of funny of you to be doing this?"

"I was heaved out of Oxford," he said gloomily. "I'll have to go home soon, I suppose. But not yet. It'll take a matter of months before the pater's willing to look at me without a headful of foul ideas. Like having me go into his office and learn the business his way."

"Your secret is safe with me, Allie. But"—she indulged in a giggle—"fancy you all dressed up like a guard on the Brighton Dilly!"

Mrs. Slingsby was seated in one of the small dining cubicles and had ordered corned beef for both of them. Nancy did not like corned beef and she picked at her food with an indifferent air.

"Mother, I had a talk with him. I've promised to tell no one."

"My girl," said Mrs. Slingsby, laying down her fork, "you surely know your mother well enough to realize that I will not be bound by any silly promises you may have made. I know my duty when I see it. This very afternoon I shall make a call on Mrs. Carboy, with whom I have a bowing acquaintance, and I will tell her *all*."

Nancy was horrified. "Mother, you can't!" she wailed. "You can't betray me this way. Allie will never look at me again."

"It's more important for Mrs. Samuel Carboy to look at me again than for her son to look at you, my girl."

And so it came about that when Alfred Carboy rode into Piccadilly three nights later, his high boots splattered with mud and snow in the folds of the cape on his box coat, he found Alfred Hanlon waiting for him in the coaching office.

"Well, Alfie!" said his grandfather, grinning at him affectionately. "You're caught out, my lad. Whatever got into you? Not that I'm blaming you. I'm sure you had your reasons. When I was a boy I did plenty of damfool things myself."

The youth realized that he was not entirely unhappy at being found out. He was growing tired of the hectoring of the driver and the complaints of passengers and the discomfort of sitting up above the boot and sounding his "old yard of tin" in rain and snow. It had to end sometime.

"Well, Grandfather," he said, grinning back, "you've got me. Are you going to turn me over, bound hand and foot?"

"I'm going to hand you over to a waiter, Alfie, my boy. He has a slice of roast beef for you and a pint of beer. How does that sound?"

"Grand," said Alfred.

"You get started on the victuals while I go in and attend to such matters as your resignation and the collecting of what pay's due you. Crossweller, Rogers, Norris, Blackin & Co., Proprietors, had better not try to hold out as much as a penny. I'm spoiling for a good go at somebody."

2

The Carboy family now occupied a house much closer to Hanover Square than the one of which George Grace had been so proud. It was quite imposing, constructed of red brick with graceful metal balconies at each of the windows and a door of such magnificence that a plebeian hand would have paused before using the massive silver knocker. When the prodigal and his captor put in an appearance there, they were met by a footman in knee breeches and plush coat. This apparition made no effort to conceal his dismay over the wide, low collar and the rough suit of clothes Mr. Hanlon was wearing and the state of Allie's boots.

"Mr. Hanlon, sir, and Mr. H'Alfred, sir," said the footman. "The master and mistress are entertaining at dinner. A large and important party. Twelve, sirs, no less."

"No need to worry about us, Copsy," said the old man. "We got no desire to join the party, eh, Alfie? We've dined, very comfortably. Just smuggle us upstairs and then whisper to both Mr. and Mrs. Carboy that we've arrived. We'll wait until the guests have gone."

It was a full hour and a half before the carriage wheels of the last to depart had crunched their way through the snows of Salsify Street. In the meantime Alfred Hanlon had engaged the close companionship of a bottle of brandy and young Alfred had curled up on a sofa and gone soundly to sleep. Samuel Carboy was the first to arrive upstairs and, contrary to expectations, he was smiling when he came in.

He said, "Ha, Father-in-law," and walked over to the sofa. Here he stood and looked down at the limp figure of his son. It seemed to him as though a weight had rolled off his shoulders. It had been there, unexpressed, for the whole time that the boy's whereabouts had been a mystery. No hint of the anxiety consuming him had been given and he had met his wife's agonized appeals for action with a gruff "Oh, he'll turn up, never fear." No one had guessed the state of his feelings and there had been a general conviction that his absorption ·in business had resulted at last in a hardening of the heart.

Mrs. Carboy followed him into the room, her skirts rustling in her hurry. She ran to the sofa and went down on her knees beside it.

"Allie, Allie, my little son!" she cried. "Have you any idea of the suffering you've caused your poor mother?"

The youth stirred, rubbed his eyes and drew himself up to a sitting position.

"Say, I had no idea it would feel so good to be home," he said, giving his eyes a final brush of his knuckles and smiling first at his mother and then at his father.

"Bless you, Allie, do you mean it?" sobbed Mrs. Carboy. "Are you truly glad to be back? Will you promise never to do it again?"

Samuel Carboy had seemed at a loss for words. At this point he interjected: "Well, Alfred! We're back again, are we? Are you feeling well?"

"Yes, Father. Quite well."

"Then it's true," said the mother. "What that silly girl and her pushing, climbing mother said about you. You actually were a guard on the Brighton Dilly."

"Yes, Mother. It was fun at first. And I did pretty well, what with my pay and the capping."

"Capping?" Samuel Carboy frowned. "Do you mean the tips?"

"Yes, Father."

"You actually accepted gratuities from the rabble riding in your coach?"

"Well, yes," said the boy. "I had to live and there I was, doing them all a service. So why shouldn't I take the money?"

Old Alfred agreed with this. "Why not?" he asked.

"I hope," said Mrs. Carboy, "that you didn't take anything from that dreadful woman."

"No, Mother." Alfred grinned. "She didn't offer anything." He went on then to talk about the work he had been doing. "I'd have liked it better if I'd been doing the driving. We had good, sound horses and I got fond of the poor old fellows. Barney was my favorite. I wish I could buy him and get him out of that grind. Seven miles one way at top speed and then later in the day seven back. It's hard on them, I can tell you. Sometimes we got a bolter but none of them were jibbers or pluckers."

"You had better put all that out of your mind," advised Mr. Carboy. "A more important point is this. Do you want to go back to college?"

Alfred had been told by his grandfather that the action at Oxford had not been drastic but this had not created in him any desire to return to the halls of learning. The shake he gave his head, in fact, was emphatic in the extreme.

"It would be waste of time, Father. I'm not cut out for a scholar. I would come out with a little Latin and a dash of literature and in no time at all it would all go right out of my head."

"When you were a little fellow," said Mr. Carboy, "I used to think of sending you on the Grand Tour. But the wars didn't stop and it was impossible for an Englishman to travel on the Continent. It still is, I'm afraid. Certainly it wouldn't be safe to go through France or Spain or Germany. Italy, perhaps. Travel is broadening and I'm wondering if we should send you up through the Scandinavian countries, with perhaps a dip into Russia."

Alfred was sitting up very straight now and it was apparent from the light in his eyes that he was very much interested.

"Nothing to see in the northern countries," declared Grandfather Hanlon. "They live in darkness half the time. Much better to send him on a Grand Tour of the Americas."

"Yes!" cried the youth. "I would like that."

"There's something to be learned over there." Mr. Carboy, it was clear, was also rather taken with the idea. "What parts would you like to visit?"

Alfred had his answer ready. "Rio," he said. "I would like to go to Rio first and then afterward to the United States."

Inasmuch as something had to be done with the son and heir of the family and as a tour of the Americas had no obvious disadvantages, it was decided after very little more discussion that this was the best course to take.

"It's customary to send a companion along," said Samuel Carboy. "A tutor. We'll have to make some such arrangement, I suppose. The boy can't start out alone." Suddenly he gave his thigh a satisfied smack. "I have it! The very man. Chave. The Rev. Abel Chave."

As no one else had ever heard of the Rev. Abel Chave, the head of the house proceeded to explain. "We were boys together. He was kind of a poor coot and so his parents sent him through for the Church. He wasn't even good enough for the Church and he's been doing some tutoring. I wouldn't consider him except that he *has* been to the Americas and would know his way around. And he's a good scholar. What's more, he won't be too expensive." He indulged in a moment's calculation. "All his expenses, of course. Perhaps a new suit of clothes. And ten pounds a year."

"Ten pounds!" Mrs. Carboy spoke in a startled tone of voice. "Isn't it rather small, Samuel?"

"He's out of employment at the moment, as I happen to know. His income is exactly nothing a year. Ten pounds a year is ten pounds more than nothing a year, isn't it? A handsome increase, in fact."

Grandfather Hanlon was on his son-in-law's side on any point of this kind but he intervened with a suggestion. "Make it twelve, Sammy. A pound a month. Sounds better."

"Very well, Father-in-law. Twelve it is."

Alfred had been showing some anxiety over the turn things had taken. He now asked, "Will I like this Mr. Chave?"

"You don't need to like him," declared his father. "He's just going along to keep an eye on things and manage the trip for you. I remember now that I never cared much for him. I used to boot him around quite a bit when we were boys together."

The youth swallowed the necessity of traveling in the company of the Rev. Abel Chave but he now proceeded to take a stand on a matter of much greater importance. "There's one thing I must do first," he said. "Please, it's very important. I must see Nell Groody before I go. Open and aboveboard. I want to go right up to their house, with you knowing all about it, and her parents as well. I've got to tell her myself about this long tour. I can't go away for a year or two without saying anything to her."

"Why not?" demanded his father.

"Write her a letter," suggested his grandfather. "A short one. Just 'Dear Friend, I'm going away. Good-by.' Something like that."

"No letter!" declared Samuel Carboy emphatically. "You can't tell what silly notions jurors will get. A pettifogging lawyer can take the most innocent letter and read all sorts of things into it. If anything has to be done—and it seems all poppycock to me—he must see her himself. And with no witnesses, mind you!"

Mrs. Carboy entered the discussion at this point. "I think he had better see the girl if he won't be content about going away otherwise. But he must make us a promise. He won't make *her* any promises. There must be no talk about waiting for each other. No sentimental nonsense of any kind. He'll explain, and then he'll say good-by, and that will be all. Are you willing to make us such a promise, Allie?"

The boy nodded. "Yes, Mother."

"But will you keep it?" demanded his father.

Mrs. Carboy took it on herself to answer this. "You ought to know by this time, Samuel Carboy, that when our son gives his word he keeps it. Now that he's promised, I'm content to have him go and see her."

As Mrs. Carboy was tying the strings of her nightcap she said to her spouse, who was already in bed and on the point of falling asleep, "That's nicely settled, I'm glad to say."

"What?" he asked, blinking at her.

"About Allie. Let him have a year away and he'll forget all about her. I know him well enough to be sure of that."

"I think you're right, m'dear."

As she blew out the candle she said in an accusing tone: "You did a great deal of talking at dinner tonight. Lawsy, I couldn't get a word in to save my life."

"What if I did? I had a lot to say."

"Well," said his wife, "I must say it surprises me the way you're coming out. People are beginning to look up to you. And once you get your knight-hood——"

"I guess," he commented with a satisfied yawn, "you won't mind if I talk their heads off then, eh, Lady Carboy?"

3

Alfred Carboy had visited the shop at Little Shallow several times during the incumbency of Mrs. 'Enry but he hardly recognized the place when he arrived there several days after the talk with his parents. It was evening but the place was well lighted by large candles with hurricane shades. When he entered, he was surprised to find that the interior had been newly painted and that the stock was fresh and inviting. The rickety counter, which had been the sole equipment in Mrs. 'Enry's day, had disappeared. There was a new one, containing glass receptacles labeled "tea" and "coffee" and "salt" and even much more inviting information such as "ginger" and "coconut" and "cinnamon." There were no less than three wheels of cheese on display and a small counter for rolls and bread fresh from the oven. The varieties of candy on view had been causing excitement among the youthful population and even those who had attained to courting age. Everything, in fact, was spick and span; and, of even more importance, there was a hint of prosperity in the air.

Nelly looked through the door leading from the family living quarters and flushed when she saw who it was. When she came into the shop, followed by both of her parents, she was trying to smile but finding it hard on account of the sense of formality his letter had created.

"Good evening," said Allie. "I—I sent Mr. Groody a note."

"I had it," answered the head of the family, giving his head a stiff bob. "So, here you are. And here we are."

"I wanted a chance to talk to Nelly. As I had been told I must never see her again—even by Nelly herself—I didn't want to come without your consent."

"Do your parents know you are here?" asked Nell.

"Yes. I told them about it at the same time."

There was a long pause. Daniel Groody looked first at his wife and then at his daughter as though asking, "Well, what do we do now?" Mrs. Groody frowned but said nothing.

The visitor was gazing at Nell as though he had never seen her before. It was not only because her gray kerseymere dress was neat and trim and her white collar was adding a softness to the line of her throat. A change had come about in her as well; she seemed more alert, more assured, and she moved quickly and with decision. Her eyes met his squarely and, although he felt that he could read a message for him in their depths, they did not show any of the maidenly confusion which might have been expected. She was a new person, in fact, and quite different from the apprehensive country girl he had known.

"I think Mr. Carboy has something to tell me," she said to her parents. "We can sit here in the shop and I'll attend to any customers who may come in."

Mr. and Mrs. Groody took the suggestion and returned to their sitting room behind the store. Alfred did not seem pleased at this arrangement.

"I hoped, Nelly," he said, "that we could go out for a walk. We could talk freer then. It's turning cold but I don't think you would mind it much."

"I don't dare leave the shop in their care," explained Nell in a low tone. "Father gets all flustered when it comes to making change and he always suggests they pay the next time they're in. Then he forgets to tell me about it. As for Mother, she's sure I don't charge enough for anything and she puts the prices away up every time she tends shop. There would be no business left at all if I let them have anything more to do with it."

Alfred had seated himself on the other side of the counter and was smiling at her across it. "You're different," he said. "You're very different. And I think I like the new Nell even more than the one I knew before."

She was studying his face with serious eyes. After a moment she said, "I don't think that's what you've come to tell me, Allie."

He shook his head. "No. I came to tell you that I'm going away. For a year or even two. As I don't want to go back to Oxford, my father is sending me to the Americas with a sort of a tutor. I'm to keep my eyes open and see everything, and then come home to fit myself into something."

"Have you given up your idea of having a large farm and raising cattle and horses?"

"Only for a time. Father won't hear of it now. I must wait until I'm in a position to assert myself."

Nell lowered her eyes and began to speak in a restrained voice. "I think this tour you're to take has another purpose as well. They hope you'll forget all about me, so that you'll come home cured. Isn't that so?"

"Oh yes. They make no bones about it. They're still against us. Before they agreed to my coming tonight they made me promise not to—well, not to say any of the things I want to say."

"If you promised, Allie, there will be no use asking what it is you want to say to me, will there?"

"I suppose not." He leaned his elbows on the counter and looked at her with intense earnestness. "Nelly, Nelly, they've put me in a pretty difficult position, haven't they? I can't pour out all the things I've been thinking. I must just sit here and look at you—and say nothing."

The poise she had displayed at the start was beginning to desert her. She looked at him with a hint of tears in her eyes.

"They've been very clever, Allie," she said. "They've made it so I can't say anything to you either. All I can do is—sit here and look at *you*."

Their eyes held for a long time and then Alfred began to smile. "Perhaps this is the best way after all. I'm poor at saying things. I always get mixed up, don't I?"

"What are you going to do while you're away?" she asked after another long pause.

"Travel around. Talk to people. Go into shops and banks and business offices and keep my eyes open. That's all I'm supposed to do. But I have another idea. The colonies in South America are still fighting for their independence from Spain. I'd like to have a hand in that."

The reserve which Nell had been struggling to maintain deserted her at once. "No, Allie, you can't! There's no reason for you to fight for people you know nothing about. So many young Englishmen who went have been killed already. They all seem to be killed sooner or later. Allie, Allie, put this dreadful thought out of your mind. For the sake of your parents as well as—for me."

He seemed surprised at her vehemence. "There's not as much danger as that. A friend of mine, Julian Grace, has gone already. He's the son of my father's old partner, and they hate each other but we're still good friends, Julian and I. We talked about it before he left and I promised to join him if I could get to America. And now I'm going to have the chance."

"Have you heard from your friend since he left?"

"No. I don't know where he is. He was to leave word for me at Rio de Janeiro. That's where I'm going first."

There could be no mistake about the depth of Nell's feelings at this point. Her eyes had filled with tears and she regarded him in a state almost of desperation. "Allie, you must give this idea up! It's not fair. Your friend was in the navy and so it's different with him. He's trained to fight. But you're not, Allie. You won't like it—and it would be your luck to be taken a prisoner or killed. I know there will be a tragic ending if you do this!"

Alfred noticed that she was trembling and concluded that this was not due entirely to her emotions. The room was getting chilly and he was finding it hard not to tremble himself. "Isn't it too cold for you?" he asked, looking at the chimney where the small fire, which had been burning when he arrived, had finally died down.

"I don't want to ask Father to bring in more wood. He takes so long that we won't have a chance to talk at all." She smiled then and rose to her feet. "I know what to do about it." She was gone from the room for several moments and, when she returned, she had his gift wrapped snugly about her shoulders. The shawl was fitted over her neck and arms and even about her waist and this made her seem very slender.

Mrs. Groody came into the shop on her daughter's heels, carrying a tea tray and a plate of small cakes. Alfred had been in such a hurry to ride over that he had failed to make his customary enormous dinner. He enjoyed the tea and helped himself to the cakes with an appetite hardly in keeping with the errand on which he had come.

The almost brooding air with which Nell watched him passed unnoticed. While Alfred sipped his second cup of tea, she tried to escape from the unpleasant train of thought which had taken possession of her, by speaking of the problems of the shop. "We're doing well. Oh, quite well. It hasn't been possible yet to lay anything aside because the notes to the wholesale houses have to be taken care of. So far we've been able to meet them and I've stopped worrying about that. At first I used to lie awake nights, wondering how we would pay the bills when they fell due. But even when things seemed most desperate I kept on buying. You see, the stock had to be made attractive if we ever expected to build the business up."

Alfred finished the last cake. "You seem to take it seriously," he remarked. "I must say it's hard to see how you can get so interested in a little shop like this."

"I love it!" exclaimed Nell. "It's mine. Mine to direct and watch and labor over. I think I feel about this store the way your father does about all the companies he is buying."

Alfred laughed. What she had said was preposterous. His father's interests were enormous. Samuel Carboy was the most talked-about industrialist in the whole kingdom. He directed banks and owned great fleets of ships, and men trembled at his words. How could all this be compared with a little village shop where people came for small quantities of tea and sugar?

He did not put his thoughts into words but Nell knew what was passing through his head. The look she bent on him would have made it clear to anyone more observant that she had indeed changed since he had seen her last. She had changed in her outlook as much as she had in person.

"You don't believe what I'm saying, Allie, but I know that I'm right. If you let yourself become deeply concerned about small matters, they may turn into important matters in time." In an effort, perhaps, to convince him of this, she continued: "As soon as we've saved enough, I'm going to build a new wing. It will be fitted up as an eating room and there will be a kitchen behind it. I'll have a cook and we'll serve meals to travelers. Little Shallow has nothing but that pub down the hill, the Pig and Porcupine, and the food sold there isn't very inviting. Do you know that Little Shallow is famous for its pork and mushroom pies? I'm going to make a specialty of them and after a time perhaps travelers will go out of their way to stop here. Oh, I have lots of plans! When you come back from America, Allie, you won't know this place."

Alfred had been thinking how pretty she looked in the shawl he had given her and how absurd it was for her to be so interested in her business venture.

"I'll be back sooner than you expect," he said. "That is, of course, if I don't meet Julian Grace or get some instructions from him. If *that* happens, I'll have to go, because it was a compact between us. If I don't hear from him, I'll be back perhaps in a year. When I do get back——" He came to a stop and looked at her with an air compounded of longing and guilt. "I mustn't say what I was going to, Nelly. But the plans I have in my head for when I get back won't have anything to do with running a shop—or buying up companies like my father, for that matter."

The girl's first impulse was to say, "I hoped you would tell me that," but she had been learning to school her emotions in the short minutes they had been together. She replied, instead, in a quiet voice, "I'm glad you'll be back so soon."

Alfred's face began to glow with the exuberance he usually displayed. "What's a year? Nothing! The time will fly, Nelly, because we'll both be so busy. I'll be a world traveler when I get back and my head will be filled with ideas. And a year may be enough time for you to get this important business going. Perhaps you'll be a lady of property and you won't look at a poor suitor like me."

Nell was thinking, "If he really loved me he wouldn't let his parents tie his tongue in this way." She wanted to say, "Allie, I love you so much that I can't let you go. I'll never change. I'll go on loving you as long as I live. Oh, my dear one, you have no idea how deeply you've made me love you!"

A conviction that she must not take the initiative held her back. If anything of the kind was to be spoken, it must come from him.

All that she allowed herself to say was, "We can't tell what a year will do, can we?"

"No. I guess we can't. We'll just have to wait and see."

Her mind filled with rebellious thoughts. Why should she remain silent while their chance for a life of happiness together slipped away from them? She understood only too well the dangers of separation. He would be changed when he came back. She continued to regard him with desperate appeal in her eyes, hoping that he still might decide to defy his parents. But Alfred was brushing his lips with a handkerchief and did not read the message she was striving to convey to him.

Seated in the kitchen, drinking their tea and nibbling at the cakes, Mr. and Mrs. Groody heard the talk in the other room go on for several more moments. It was evident to them that the tones used were more subdued. They looked at each other as though to ask, What has happened between them? Then Alfred appeared in the doorway between the two rooms.

"I think I told you in my letter that I was going away. I leave for Rio in a few days, so I won't see you again. I hope you'll be happy and prosperous here."

After he had gone Nell remained in the shop for a longer time than seemed necessary. They could hear her poking at the faint evidences of life left in the chimney. She turned the lock in the door and then the lights went out one after another, very slowly, it seemed. When she appeared in the doorway, she kept her eyes lowered but her father's quickness of perception led him to see that she was on the point of an outburst of tears.

"Whatever it was he said to you, childie," he declared, "it will be all for the best in the long run. That stuck-up son of a thieving father! It's glad I am that he's going away so he won't be here to upset my little girl!"

She looked up at them then and tried to smile. "I'll go straight to bed if you don't mind. The entries in the books can wait until the morning when I'll feel more like it." She turned and walked toward the narrow stairs which led to the low-ceilinged upper floor. "You're going to get your wish, Father. I—I am quite sure I'll never see him again."

CHAPTER SEVEN

1

The voyage was a rough one but the last of the tall young men to go to the Americas in search of enlightenment and adventure proved himself a good sailor. Alfred Carboy had grown considerably as was evident when he

stood on the quarterdeck beside the captain, who had taken a fancy to him
and encouraged his company. The commander was not a small man by any
means but the young passenger was a full head taller. The voyage had done
him much good; his color was fresh, his gray eyes alert, his hair the warm
tint of ripe corn. He had become so handsome, in fact, that every feminine
eye followed him on his rambles around the deck.

He was seldom in his cabin except to sleep, the Rev. Abel Chave having
proved himself a far from diverting companion. The clerical failure was a
sallow little man with a stomach as hard and round as a beetle's and a
biliously saturnine eye. Fortunately for his charge he was a very bad sailor
and so kept to his berth, where he yawned and groaned all day but always
did justice to three square meals and sometimes four.

Alfred's first step after they had settled themselves in comfortable quarters
in Rio was to go to the post office. There was a large public room with a
score or more of bulletin boards along the walls and a row of wickets at
one end. Each bulletin board, he discovered, contained lists of the mail
received from one country, with the names to whom the letters were addressed. Opposite each name was a narrow slide with a numbered panel.
People were taking these panels and presenting them at the wickets.

His own name was on the English list and he carried his panel excitedly
to one of the clerks. The missive handed him was from Julian Grace. It
informed him that he, Julian, was on his way around the Horn with another
Englishman, one Cymric Forster from Yorkshire, to take service in the
Chilean navy under the great British admiral, Thomas Cochrane. Alfred's
heart gave an exultant leap as he read. He decided without a moment's
hesitation that he would follow his friend to Chile. He felt sure that his
father would not object to such a change of plan because he had once been
anxious to buy a commission in the army for his son. The Rev. Abel Chave
could be paid off and sent back, and a good riddance to him.

This mood was of short duration, however. A glance at the postmark revealed the fact that the letter had been waiting for him the better part of
a year. There had been no word of developments off the Chilean coast but
it was clear enough that it was too late now to seek a part in the campaign.

The two weeks that Alfred remained in Rio with his mentor and guard
were dull and uneventful despite the fact that he dragged the reluctant
Chave everywhere, even to Man John Byway where the ministerial nose
curled up in shock and dismay at the open efforts of the dark little women
to gain his attention. The only incident which bordered at all on the adventurous was when they watched a native funeral and Chave allowed a
mourner to press a lighted candle into his hand. His acceptance carried a
penalty with it, that he must contribute a coin to the cost of the obsequies.
The frugal soul of the traveling companion rebelled and it was only when
he realized that some unpleasant surprise in the event of failure to pay was
being prepared for him that he brought out his purse. With beads of per-
spiration covering his brow, he produced the smallest coin it contained and

then hurried away, muttering in agonized tones: "Why should this calamity have been visited on me? I am ruined! I am lost!"

On the last evening of their stay the Rev. Mr. Chave developed a hoarseness in his throat and decided it would be unwise for him to venture out into the night air. He preached at Alfred as he sat with his feet in a tub of hot water, his nightcap already pulled down tightly over his brow.

"You must eschew the haunts of sin," he orated in his best pulpit manner. "Flee from the wiles of the harpies who infest the streets. Let not your eyes rest on their voluptuous forms. Only if you pledge me your word to behave yourself as a gentleman and a Christian will I consent to let you roam this city of gilded sin alone."

"Vincent Klimstad is calling for me," explained Alfred. Klimstad was the one acquaintance they had made, a young American in the consular service. "You have my promise, sir. There's no need for you to worry about me."

This was quite true. He did not take any interest in the gambling establishments of the city nor could he be carried away by the painted faces of Man John Byway when his mind was filled with the image of the gentle girl he had left behind him in England. He was still sure in his own mind that his devotion to Nell Groody would not waver during the period of his travels.

Vincent Klimstad, a stocky young man with a lively black eye, was waiting for him when he went downstairs. The American looked surprised and pleased when Alfred announced that a rumble in the pipes of the dragon would make it possible for them to venture out into the city unattended.

"Splendid!" cried Klimstad. "I was wondering how we could get free of the brave Chave. We have an adventure on our hands this evening. Well, not an adventure exactly, but something which may prove very interesting."

The Englishman's eyes lighted up at this announcement. "What have you in mind, Klim?" he asked eagerly.

But the young consular agent had no intention of letting the cat out of the bag at once. All he would say was: "We're going to call on a lady. A very lovely lady, Carboy. She wants to meet you because she has a favor to ask. It would be unfair to the beautiful creature to tell you anything more." Then he seemed to go off on another tack entirely. "First we're going to a theater. There's something good playing here. A French farce. Quite naughty, I hear. It's a French company so I hope you can follow the language."

"My French is practically non-existent. We had a Mousser to teach us at Clutterhaugh but he was an émigré and talked all the time about French politics. I didn't learn much from him." Alfred accompanied this negative report, however, by a positive nod. "But that won't be any drawback if the company's a good one. I can follow the action. Matter of fact, Klim, I have an idea in my head that I'd like to be an actor. I was in a play at Clutterhaugh—a beastly thing in blank verse, written by one of the masters—and the fellows all said I was pretty good. I played the villain."

The French farce did not prove amusing at all. The situation was old and the dialogue, as far as Alfred was able to judge, stilted. The hero had a black beard and the heroine was a veteran of long standing. Even the breeches girl, who was always counted upon to give a lift to the dullest of farces, was heavy of mood and thigh. When the curtain dropped on the first act, the two young men looked at each other and shook their heads.

"Tedious," said Klimstad. "Well, we shall now proceed to the adventure I promised you. If you'll be so obliging, look back of you along the row of boxes. Third from the right."

Alfred's eyes found the box in question. It was occupied by a lady in a silver gown, sitting close to the railing. She was alone and he thought her quite lovely. She was fair with a cluster of blonde curls above a slim brow and her eyes were a deep blue. A large emerald dangled on her throat.

"La Bellilote," said Klimstad.

"Who is La Bellilote?"

"Come, come. Don't play the innocent on me, young Mr. Carboy. Surely you remember about her. She was Napoleon's mistress during his campaign in Egypt."

"I had just been born when that happened. Say, she must look a lot younger than she is. She's a topper, isn't she?"

"She fell in love with the Man of Destiny but he treated her pretty shabby. Never saw her after he returned from Egypt."

"But he must have been generous with her. Look at those diamonds!"

"Fakes! That's not a real emerald. It's a very good imitation made from the shell of a green beetle. She's pretty hard pressed at the moment."

Alfred was still very much puzzled by the presence of the emperor's paramour in Rio. "But what's she doing here?"

"Didn't I say she fell in love with him? Now, if you draw a line straight from this city across the Atlantic, what do you strike? St. Helena! Rio is the nearest point to that stinking hot island where they're keeping the Man of Destiny caged."

"I guess her being here is a proof of devotion, all right," said Alfred.

"It may be more than that. Come along, she's expecting us in her box."

On the way upstairs Klimstad explained how the invitation had come to be made. "I met the lovely little creature through a wild Irishman who got into difficulties here. His passport was no good and he couldn't get away. I'm afraid I—well, I permitted him to get American papers. Before he left he introduced me to La Bellilote. I saw her again last night and I happened to mention you. She begged me to bring you around tonight. That's all I know."

They found themselves in almost complete darkness when they entered the box, owing to the fact that a curtain had been drawn across the front. An arm moved in the gloom and a piping voice said, "Names, pleeze." It was a Mazombo footman, very small and ugly and very gaily attired in a long green coat.

"Mr. Klimstad and Mr. Carboy."

La Bellilote turned at once and smiled at them warmly. She extended a white arm as they advanced into the light.

"I was afraid you were not coming, M'sieur Kleemstad. I was saying to myself, 'Pauline, you must reconcile yourself. You are growing old and men no longer care to see you.' I was feeling very sad about it. And this play is so very, very dull."

Klimstad bowed over her hand and said in clumsy French: "You need never have such fears as that, Madame de Ranchoup. May I present Mr. Carboy?"

The lively blue eyes under unexpectedly dark brows studied Alfred intently. "He is young and very handsome. You said he was young, M'sieur Kleemstad, but you did not tell me he was handsome. It is a pleasant surprise. I am sorry he is leaving so soon."

"Come, Madame de Ranchoup," said Klimstad pointedly. "I thought it was because he was leaving that you wanted to see him."

She motioned Alfred to take a chair beside her and then subjected him to a close and intensely serious look. "You will forgive me, m'sieur? I must get to know you quickly." After a study of several moments she smiled. "I like you. You have gray eyes. That is good, I think. I have known so few men with gray eyes and they have all been brave and honest. I am sure you are both, m'sieur Carboy." She turned to Klimstad with an apologetic air. "The curtain will go up in a very few minutes. Would you think me very . rude if I asked to speak to M'sieur Carboy alone?"

"Then you had better take the back of the box. There are too many eyes

on you here, madame. I'll stay and amuse myself by watching the audience. It won't be very amusing, so please come back as soon as you can."

It became apparent when La Bellilote rose to her feet that she was even smaller than she had seemed at a distance. She barely came to Alfred's shoulder, even with the aid of her close-curling pompadour. Her dress was a Parisienne triumph with a flaring skirt which contained no more than four tucks (in France, ladies of fashion were wearing eighteen tucks in honor of the return of Louis XVIII to the throne) and had a sprig of violet in each. There was an unquenchable coquetry in her very fine eyes as she laid a hand on the young Englishman's arm and led the way to the rear of the box.

The footman, who was coal-black and as wizened as a sapajou, lighted a candle in a wall sconce and then drew out chairs for them.

She began to speak in low and hurried tones. "M'sieur, I have made up my mind to trust you. I am sure you will respect my confidence in this matter which is of such very great importance—to me and to many others."

"I haven't any idea what it is you mean to tell me," said the youth. "But I give you my word to respect your confidence fully."

She nodded her head and smiled at him warmly. "I am sure you will. This is what I am asking. That you will take a letter to the United States for me."

"That doesn't seem to be asking much."

"But, m'sieur, the letter is of such importance that it would be a catastrophe if it reached the wrong people. You see, I am holding nothing back. I am putting myself in your hands."

Alfred felt some surprise at the seriousness of her attitude. "I suppose it's because you don't want to trust it to the mails here?"

"Yes, m'sieur. You must have seen how things are handled. It's an easy matter to examine mail which doesn't belong to you. I don't dare send this letter in the usual way."

"Where do you want me to deliver it?"

"To the captain of one of these strange new ships. I think they are called steamboats. You have heard of them?"

"Oh yes!" the youth responded with sudden enthusiasm. "I'm very much interested in steamships. I wanted my father to build a line of them and let me run it. . . . But he said I was too young and that anyway they weren't ready for commercial use yet. My father, madame, is a great businessman. He'll be running steamships before very long. And railways too. He keeps an eye on everything."

"This one runs from Philadelphia to a city called Trenton. The captain is a Frenchman and a very, very great sailor. His name is Jules Achille Gouvet. It's my hope that you will deliver my letter into his hands at Philadelphia."

Alfred agreed without any hesitation. "I'm sailing direct to Philadelphia and I'll be glad to take the letter for you. And I'll"—he hesitated and then straightened up with juvenile seriousness—"as it's so very important, I'll guard it with my life if necessary."

She gave his arm an ecstatic squeeze. "Oh, thank you, thank you, m'sieur. I will have every confidence in my brave messenger. May I give you the letter now?"

She opened a silver bag and produced a missive of some thickness, addressed in a neat hand to Captain Gouvet. The youth placed it in an inside pocket.

The footman threw open the curtain with a flourish and a deep bow. "Act starting, pleeze m'd'me," he said.

Klimstad left his seat at the rail and felt his way back to them in the darkness.

"Had enough of the play, Carboy?" he asked. "I'm content to leave without finding out if the husband discovers his wife's lover in the locked closet or if the comte succeeds in his fell designs on the pretty niece. Besides, we seem to have accomplished our main purpose in coming here tonight."

"Yes, m'sieur," said La Bellilote. "My heart goes out to both of you." She looked up at Alfred from under the longest lashes he had ever encountered. "How can I thank you? Someday, perhaps, things will be again—as they once were. I will be in Paris and you will come there on a visit, and you will call on me. Then I shall be able to tell you how much I appreciated what you are doing for me tonight."

She hesitated briefly and then resumed her chair. From her handbag she produced, after much searching, a tiny pair of gold scissors with jeweled handles. With these she ripped one of the violet rosettes from her skirt and held it up to Alfred.

"You are English," she said, "and so, I fear, you have no love for the emperor—for Napoleon. Still, I beg you to take this little reminder of our very brief acquaintance. Violet is the color of the Bonapartists and we who love him call him Papa Violet. Did you know?"

Alfred was looking with dismay at the rent in her skirt. "Madame, you've ruined your gown!" he said. "And it was such a beautiful one."

She smiled and shook her head. "Oh no. Adversity has made it necessary for me to become expert with the needle. When I get home tonight I will repair the skirt and sew in another rosette. It will never show."

"I hope," said Alfred, as he and his companion turned to leave the box, "that someday I'll be able to accept your invitation and call on you in Paris."

"Young donkey!" said Klimstad as they made their way slowly down the dark stairs to the exit. "She'll never get back to Paris unless Napoleon is restored to the throne. Do you want that to happen?"

2

Alfred Carboy and the Rev. Abel Chave disagreed on the question of taking the steamship which ran daily on the Delaware River between Philadelphia and Trenton.

"Puffing, smoking, belching abominations!" said the clergyman. "Why don't you want to travel in a coach behind well-trained horses? It's the way God intended us to go."

Alfred had an ulterior motive for wanting to take the steam packet. Quite apart from the letter in his pocket which must be placed in the hands of Captain Gouvet, he was consumed with a desire to ride in one of the new ships.

"I don't think God's against steamships," he protested. "I think God's always on the side of progress."

They were sitting in the common room of an inn in Philadelphia. Their bags had been carried out and the bill had been paid. All that remained for them to do was to wait for the conveyance to be announced which would take them to the coaching office or to the wharves where the steam packet left for Trenton. The clergyman, who had eaten an enormous breakfast and was feeling belligerent as a result, glared at his charge.

"Did the children of Israel cross the Red Sea by steamboat?" he demanded to know. "Did they journey over the Jordan River by steamboat? Was it on a steamboat that Elijah was taken up into the clouds or was it in a chariot of fire? Did the cedars and the gopherwood for the Ark come down from Lebanon by steamboat? Listen to me, young man. The Lord made us and He made horses and He made coaches and He made chariots of fire. But He didn't make steamboats."

Alfred looked at his mentor without any attempt to conceal the distaste he was beginning to feel for him. "It was my father's idea that I would learn things by coming to the Americas," he said. "He told me when we left that he wanted me to keep my eyes open. That's why I intend to take this new ship. It will be an experience and I'll be able to tell my father what I think of it."

"I refuse my consent," said the Rev. Mr. Chave.

Nevertheless he departed alone on the New York coach while Alfred made his way to the docks. The *Black Bull* was tied up at her moorings but smoke was pouring from the stack and it was apparent that she would be leaving soon. A porter carried his luggage across the gangplank and deposited it on deck with a thud.

"Two hog," he said, holding out a hand.

"Do you mean twenty cents?" asked Alfred indignantly. He resembled his father in some respects and one was an unwillingness to be cheated. "No two hog for you, my friend. One hog."

"Two hog!" screeched the porter. "I lugged the stuff here with my own two mauleys and I takes nothing less than two hog."

A member of the crew with some authority—there was no way of telling what his rank might be from the nondescript uniform he wore—bore down on them in a towering rage.

"One hog for you!" he cried to the porter. "It's the usual, ain't it? And git off this ship fast, ye dirty hickjop!"

The porter made his way reluctantly to the gangway. Here he turned and shook a fist at them. "A ship, is it? Ye call this cantankerous a-bomination a ship?" When he reached the dock he swung around with renewed boldness to shout at them: "Git a sail! Git a sail!"

The officer had been superintending the loading on board of large-sized rocks which were being piled up in pyramids at intervals along the deck. He gave Alfred a wink and resumed this somewhat unseamanlike occupation.

"Sir," said Alfred, "I would like to see Captain Gouvet."

"So you want to see Captain Gouvet, do you?" The officer indulged in a laugh. "Lots of people want to see the captain. But how many of them gets to do it? I'll tell you, young fellow. None."

"But I have a letter to deliver into his hands," protested Alfred. "It's important and I can't give it to anyone else."

The officer scratched his head. "Then you'll have to wait. Getting this vessel a-started is a job and the captain won't likely appear on deck until we're on our way up the river. On'y one thing will bring him up then."

"What is it, may I ask?"

"You'll see, young gem'man. You'll see in plenty of time."

The steam packet began to move. A convulsion, which caused passengers to clutch frantically for rail or stanchion or even another passenger, shook the vessel. A roar like the first rumbling of a volcano issued from somewhere down in its bowels. It snorted and balked and a great volume of smoke poured out of the smokestack. The whole thing seemed highly undignified to the watchers on the dock, who doubled up with laughter and shouted derisive remarks, some even going to the extent of cocking snooks at the departing leviathan.

Alfred was the only passenger on board who seemed to be enjoying the excursion. The women and children had taken refuge in the salon and were huddling close together. The men for the most part had remained on deck but were finding it a strenuous method of displaying their boldness, for with each switch of the wind or change of direction a blast of sparks and hot ash and clouds of smoke would swirl down on them from the smokestack. Whenever this happened, there would be a scramble for the other side of the deck to escape. Alfred watched this game for several minutes and then clutched at the arm of the officer who had befriended him in his altercation with the porter.

"I say, Mr. Officer, wouldn't we be saved all this if the smokestack was made a little higher?"

The officer stopped in his tracks and regarded him bitterly. "So. Have we got so few troubles that now we got to listen to fool suggestions from passengers? A higher smokestack, you say? How would it be if we brought the sun and the moon and the stars down closer to us at the same time so we could navigate easier? How do you know we wouldn't get lopsided and topple over if we had a higher smokestack? Just tell me that, young fellow."

Alfred brushed some hot ash from his hat and commented mildly, "Almost anything would be better than this, I think, sir."

He had been told that he would discover in time the only thing which could bring Captain Gouvet on deck and he now had the privilege of observing what it was. Several sailing vessels had come out on the river and were tacking back and forth, and even cutting across the bows of the *Black Bull* in a highly uncomplimentary fashion. Every time that one of them succeeded in this, all of the men aboard the skittering ships would shout loudly: "Git a sail! Git a sail!"

When this had happened several times there was a loud roar from below and a stout man with a long spade beard and a braided cap appeared on deck. He ran to the nearest pile of rocks and began to throw them at the encircling sailboats. Between heaves, he would pause and shout at them: "Heads of cabbage, sons of pigs! Get a sail, is it? I'll show you that you can't cast foul aspersions on the greatest invention since Noah built the Ark!"

When the captain had made his third trip to the deck, Alfred got his courage up to the point of approaching him.

"Are you Captain Gouvet?" he asked.

The bearded officer with the braided cap nodded his head. "I'm Captain Gouvet," he affirmed in a booming voice. "What do you want with me, young man?"

"I have a letter for you. I was told it must be handed to you and no one else."

The captain's manner changed and became somewhat calmer. His fierce black eyes studied Alfred for a moment and then he said in a tone of voice which carried a hint of politeness in it, "Come with me." He led the way to his cabin and closed the door after him.

"Now, what letter is this, m'sieur? Who does it come from?"

"It was given me at Rio. By a lady. She said I was to place it in your hands."

"By a lady, m'sieur? What was this lady like?"

"She was quite beautiful, sir."

The captain's eyes began to burn in the intensity of his interest. "Did she have fair hair, m'sieur, curling up on her forehead? Was her figure——" He began to make motions with his arms to indicate the proportions of the lady in question and the fineness of her curves.

"Yes, Captain. The lady had a very fine figure."

"Ah, m'sieur, I have heard it said she is one of the most beautiful of all women. Someday, if I have luck, I hope to see her in the flesh." He accepted the envelope and turned it over in his hands several times. "Now I have it, m'sieur, and you have done your duty. My thanks, m'sieur. *My* duty calls me to the bridge now." He gave his head a defiant nod. "We are in an experimental stage, m'sieur, and there is no telling what may happen."

That he had spoken the truth was apparent some time later when the *Black Bull* finally came in sight of the tall bluffs which one of the passengers identified as the approach to Bordentown. There was a sudden explosion below decks, followed by loud cries of pain and fear, and the sound of scurrying feet. Although the excitement seemed to die down after the first few minutes, the engines ceased to function and the ship began to drift about aimlessly in the middle of the river.

A member of the crew appeared at Alfred's elbow. "Are ye the young fellow as saw the cap'n in his cabin?" he asked. "Very well, then, ye're to come with me."

Below decks Captain Gouvet was sitting on a barrel while two of the crew knelt in front of him in an effort to bind one of his feet in long strips of cotton. When he saw Alfred coming down the ladder, the captain motioned to everyone else to get out of hearing.

"M'sieur," he said with a wince, "as you see, my foot has been scalded in a little difficulty with the engine. It had been my intention to remain over an hour at Bordentown and take a carriage to the comte's to deliver the letter. But this is now impossible. It is true I could send one of my officers with it, or my personal servant. But, m'sieur, I have given the matter much thought and it seems to me the best substitute I could find would be the one who brought the letter all the way from Rio to deposit it in my hands. That is, of course, if M'sieur is prepared to undertake it for me—or, shall we say, for the beautiful lady with the bewitching curls and the so lovely figure? I fear, m'sieur, it would mean you would have to stay overnight in Bordentown. There is a good tavern. The Indian Arms. You would be comfortable and you could catch the coach for New York in the morning."

Alfred was beginning to wonder about this transaction in which he had become involved. It seemed now to smack of mystery; worse, even, of conspiracy. Was there something illegal about the information the letter contained? Would it not be wise for him to bow quietly at this stage and have nothing more to do with it?

Still, there was an adventurous side and he did not want to go on about his affairs (particularly as he had no affairs which counted) and not learn anything more of the mysterious letter. He was being asked to take it on the second lap of its journey and this on the surface was innocent enough. Why should he become squeamish at this point?

"I'll take it, Captain," he said finally.

"Bon! Bon!"

Captain Gouvet was in great pain. While they talked, he had been grunting and groaning and shifting his injured leg as though his sufferings might be alleviated by this means. He clutched his black beard with one hand while he reached in a pocket for the letter with the other.

"They need not make any point of what has happened to me, m'sieur," he said with a tone of mounting impatience. "There are accidents on sailing ships also. Masts break and fall, and men are killed. There is a sudden wind and someone falls from the shrouds and is never seen again. Legs do not get scalded in sailing ships, it is true, but worse things are happening all the time on the seas."

"Quite true, sir. Who is to receive the letter?"

"The Abbé Force. Do you know who he is?"

"No, sir. It's the first time I've heard the name."

"The Abbé Force is a French churchman. He is a man of remarkable parts but it is quite true that nothing is known of him outside the boundaries of France."

"And where do I find the Abbé Force?"

"He is staying at the moment with the Comte de Survilliers, who has an estate beyond Bordentown. It is called Point Breeze. Do you know who the Comte de Survilliers is, m'sieur?"

Alfred shook his head. The name meant nothing to him.

"It is a title adopted by Joseph Bonaparte for reasons which, I am sure you will agree, are obvious enough. The former King of Spain came to America after Waterloo and brought most of his fortune with him. A shrewd man, Joseph Bonaparte, the shrewdest of the whole family, even more than Caroline. It's a lucky thing that he is, because his gold is keeping many famous soldiers of the emperor from starving. They gather around him at this fine house he has built for himself at Point Breeze." The steamship captain looked closely at the young Englishman before continuing. "The abbé is waiting to receive this letter."

"It must be important."

The captain gestured with one hand. "Who knows? The abbé is a man who understands how to look after his own best interests. I have speculated, m'sieur, as to the contents of this letter and have reached one conclusion only, that it is no concern of mine." There was another pause while the injured man writhed with pain. "I have instructed one of my officers to see you ashore with your belongings, m'sieur, and to start you on your way."

The officer was an American. He grinned at Alfred and winked as they waited on the dock for the luggage to be brought off. "Going to the Cump's, eh? Nice time to pay a visit. They say the two princesses, his daughters, are with him right now. Handsome gals, both of them. Better watch out, young fellow. You know the reputation of the Bonaparte women. Are you going to the Indian Arms? Good place. Food is fine and the rooms are clean. But watch out for Charlie Hosking when he gets to making out his little bill." An admiring shake of the head. "He's a good 'un, Charlie is. Nothing so simple as adding for Charlie. Multiplying is more in his line. Puts a downer on the bill if you as much as squint at a towel or lean heavy on the butter knife. Even oliver-skulls is extra."

"Thank you," said Alfred, smiling in farewell. "I'll add up the bill before I pay. But I don't think I'll have the pleasure of seeing the lovely princesses. I won't be in the place more than five minutes."

"From what I hear," declared the officer, "the Bonaparte women never need more than five minutes."

3

There was only one conveyance at the dock, a high carriage with a seat in front for the driver and a second seat in the rear capable of holding two stout men or their equivalent in women and children. Half of the back seat was already occupied by a man muffled up in a green coat with a black cape and nothing on his head whatsoever.

"Cap'n Griffen's for the Indian Arms but I'll drive first to Point Breeze," said the driver. "The cap'n won't mind."

"Absolutely not," said the first passenger in a decidedly English voice.

Alfred climbed up beside the accommodating Captain Griffen, discovering him to be a middle-aged man with a face which gave the impression of having been shaved all over. This curious effect was due to a complete lack of hair on his bare head and to the practical non-existence of eyebrows. When their eyes met, the young Englishman found that his fellow passenger was regarding him with a shrewd twinkle.

"Good day, young sir. My name is Tobias Griffen. I'm a British officer but I might as well tell you myself, before someone else does, that I've been out of uniform for some time. I was attached to the embassy at Washington and they put me to work on that nonsensical business in Mexico a year ago. You recall it, no doubt."

After a moment's thought Alfred gave his head a nod. "I think you mean those Bonapartist generals who were scheming to seize Mexico. They were going to get Napoleon out of St. Helena and make him the Emperor of Mexico. Was that it?"

"Exactly. As the British government has been saddled with the responsibility of keeping the devil caged, my superior said to me, when it was all over, 'My dear Griffen, you show a turn for this beastly sort of thing, so from now on the honor is all yours.' I've been here ever since, keeping an eye on these honorable gentlemen you propose to see."

Alfred felt a slight tingle of apprehension. How did this strange individual come to know so much about him? Not only that but Captain Griffen was watching, in the interests of the British government no doubt, the activities of Joseph Bonaparte and his household. What kind of a hornets' nest was this in which he had become involved?

"My visit, sir," he declared, "will be a brief one. I'm to see one of the guests."

"The Abbé Force." Captain Griffen nodded his head. "Curious fellow, the abbé. I'm sure you'll be much interested in him, young man."

"Not at all, sir," declared Alfred. "I never expect to see him or hear of him again."

"Nevertheless he is one of the great characters of the Bonaparte era. I might even say he was their mystery man. He had no official position but it's quite certain he had a great deal of influence with Boney. I've reached the conclusion that Boney used him as a check on Talleyrand. At any rate he always had a not too clean finger in the diplomatic pie. Some say he was Bonaparte's familiar devil, the imp who whispered in his ear. Certainly there was always a whiff of brimstone about the fellow."

Alfred made no comment. He was thoroughly convinced by this time that his best policy would be to say nothing at all.

"Yes, he was a well-hated man, the Abbé Force. He was a wolf, a weasel, and a great gray fox, all rolled into one. He was a sort of Olivier le Daim, if you like, with more than a touch of Machiavelli thrown in. A paragon of evil, in fact; if you'll forgive such a contradiction in terms." He broke off suddenly. After a moment he began to whisper in order to avoid being overheard by the driver on the front seat. "You're a British citizen and so I would be justified in demanding that you turn over to me the letter you're taking to the abbé. But I'm not going to do it. All the schemes they're hatching at Point Breeze to get Boney free are quite absurd. The British navy patrols the island so well that he could never be brought out. And, as it happens, I have other ways of finding out what's in the letter. Under the circumstances I'm not going to place you in an embarrassing position by making any demands on you. You got yourself into this in good faith and didn't know what it was about. But I do want to give you a word of warning. Get away from the place as soon as you've dropped the letter into the oily palm of the great gray fox. Never mention what has happened to a single soul, not even your parents at home."

Alfred looked at him with serious misgivings. How did it come about that a British agent making his headquarters in Bordentown in the United States knew so much about his movements?

Captain Griffen guessed what was passing through his mind. "We have agents in Rio, to keep an eye on things. One of them sent me a letter by the same ship that brought you and I received it this morning. He knew all about our pretty La Bellilote and the letter she confided to your care. It's all quite simple, really."

Then he raised his voice again and began to speak of other matters. "Some curious goings-on at Point Breeze. The comte hasn't been content to build himself a rather imposing home. He's honeycombing the grounds with secret passages."

"Secret passages?" Alfred exclaimed. "That seems strange, sir. How does he intend to use them?"

"No one can be sure. But, of course, we can guess. One of the passages runs all the way from the house to the river. It comes out on the bluffs and has an iron grating to close it in. Anyone wanting to make a quick exit could get to the river in a few minutes."

"Do you suppose," asked Alfred, his eyes widening, "they've dug it out to use in case they *do* get Napoleon off the island?"

"Well, that's what some people think. It's even whispered about that down under the house they have some secret rooms. All very snug and comfortable, and very hard to locate if you don't know the secret. It's said they have a lighting system down there and some way of ventilating the rooms. There's a regular library and a wide bed and one of those French sabot baths. Do you know the kind? It's shaped rather like a shoe and you put your feet down into the toe, and it has a padded rest for the head. It's true that Napoleon has always been partial to this kind of a tub. But this is all hearsay. I thought you would be interested."

They had been passing a long stretch of park land, closely fenced in, and at this point they came to high gates of wrought iron above which an enormous eagle spread its metal wings. There was a two-story stucco house of square construction at one side of the gate and a guard in a sky-blue uniform on the steps. He came over slowly when the carriage came to a stop.

"What is it you desire, messieurs?" he asked. Then he caught sight of Captain Griffen and his eyes took on a hostile gleam. "You will drive on, if you please. We tolerate no spying or snooping here."

"T'other gent'man has business with the Abbé Force," said the driver, motioning over a shoulder with his thumb.

The guard walked over to the carriage and looked up at Alfred. After a moment of anxious scrutiny he asked, "What is it you wish to see the abbé about, m'sieur?"

"I have a letter for him."

"If M'sieur will give me the letter, I will myself personal see it is delivered to the good abbé."

Alfred gave an emphatic shake of the head. "I must give it to him. Otherwise it won't be delivered at all."

The driver began to turn the conveyance with impatient flicks of his whip. When the operation had been completed, he addressed the guard in gruff terms. "See here, mousser. We haven't all day to stand palavering with the likes of you. Either you say you'll see the young gent'man gets in or we'll drive back to the inn and send a note to the cump, complaining about your conduct. Which is it to be?"

The guard pawed at his whiskers with indecision. Finally he said with a doubtful shake of his head, "He may get down. I shall keep him here until a messenger can be sent to the château, to learn the wishes of the abbé in the matter."

"That's more like it," declared the driver. He turned his head and nodded to Alfred. "Down you git. Will you be wanting me to come back later?"

"How far is it to the Indian Arms?"

"Matter of a mile and a half, roughly speaking."

"Then I'll walk it." Alfred drew a coin from his pocket and handed it over. The driver looked at the money, gave a satisfied cherk and then flicked his whip over the backs of the horses. Off they went, a small cloud of dust gathering behind them. Captain Griffen, who had neither moved nor spoken, did not even raise a hand in a gesture of farewell.

Everything inside the stone walls which enclosed the domain of Joseph Bonaparte seemed strange and foreign to Alfred Carboy. The servant who came to escort him to the house was attired, probably by choice, in a shabby infantry uniform; and he had never before seen such baggy trousers nor a cap of such height. Voices reached them from various parts of the park and the words they used were unintelligible. The artificial lake they encountered on their way was larger than any he had ever seen and the presence of gondolas, seemingly straight from Venice, made him more deeply aware of an alien background. Even the presence of clumps of small white violets along the side of the road added to the effect.

He understood just enough of architecture to realize that the house was of French design. The stone walls were covered with white plaster and there were iron gratings over the windows of the lower story. The wings were so wide that the house, in spite of the squat tower at the entrance, seemed low-slung. It was gracious in its effect rather than imposing.

The house faced the park and Alfred could see the gardens stretching back of it toward the river. The keeper of the gate had talked to him while they waited and had said that they were modeled after the Escorial in Spain where Joseph had once reigned as king.

The young Englishman had not expected to find the new establishment of Napoleon's oldest brother as impressive as this. "They seem to live in state," he remarked to the servant who strode ahead of him.

The latter did not understand. "The weather is good, yes, m'sieur," he answered in French.

A man in a black and white livery was standing on the stone steps at the entrance. As Alfred approached, he came sharply to attention.

To compensate for his ignorance of French, the young Englishman spoke slowly and distinctly. "I have letter," he said. "For Abbé Force."

The servitor, who had an empty sleeve and a face which had been tanned to the consistency of leather, answered with equal care. "The abbé, m'sieur, has not roused himself from his afternoon nap. He does not often sleep so long. Will M'sieur leave his letter? Or is his desire to deliver it personally?"

"I must see the abbé. I would like to wait until he is up."

"I will speak to Monsieur Maillard. Perhaps he will take it on himself to waken him." The old soldier grinned in a friendly way. "They talk, talk, talk. All through the night. And they drink while they talk. So it follows that during the day they are certain to need these very long naps. . . . In the old days it was different, m'sieur. The bugles sounded at daybreak and we were only too glad to get to sleep as soon as we could."

"I judge you've seen much service under Napoleon."

The man's eyes lighted up. "I fought in nearly all the great battles with the emperor. I started with the march from the English Channel. I wore out my shoes and was wearing wooden soles bound with rope before we got our first look at the Osties. Ah, m'sieur, what a surprise it was for them! They didn't believe we were within a hundred miles of Ulm, but there we were, all around them. I was at Austerlitz, m'sieur, and Jena too. I was at Wagram and it was there I lost my arm. I missed the Russian campaign but I got back into it later."

"Were you at Waterloo?"

The soldier's expression changed at once. In a frigid voice he said: "Does M'sieur mean Mont St. Jean? I was there also. We never speak of that one. How badly the emperor was served by his marshals!"

The sound of carriage wheels was heard from far down the driveway and in a few moments a span of laboring horses came into view. Behind them was a heavy vehicle in which three men were seated. One of the trio stood up and gave a loud halloo.

The shout brought an immediate response. Servants came tumbling out through the front door, women as well as men, shouting with abandon. One of the maids had a mop in her hand and she waved it above her head with great enthusiasm. A footman cried in an ecstatic voice: "*Vive Lallemand! Vive Gauthier!* Ah, the good Monsieur Pigeon! He sticks to his vow."

"He won't have to go bareheaded long, Achille," said another manservant. "We will have the emperor back on his throne before so very long."

Heads began to pop out of windows along the front of the white house, and voices cried, "*Vive! Vive!*" The man standing in the rapidly approaching carriage wrapped a newspaper into the shape of a trumpet and emitted through it a very good imitation of a bugle call. A small man with uncovered head (Monsieur Pigeon, without a doubt) stood up beside him and blew kisses with both hands. Dogs began to bark at the stables and the maid with the mop indulged in an excited jig step. At the edge of the drive a small boy with an iron on one leg jumped up and down in spite of his lameness and cried in an ecstasy of emotion: "Bravo! Bravo! Bravo!"

"What is it all about?" asked Alfred of the custodian of the entrance.

"It is just a welcome for our brave comrades, m'sieur. They have been away for three days."

Monsieur Maillard appeared at this moment, a harried individual, teetering on nervous high heels. "I will have the abbé wakened," he said to Alfred. "Provided the matter is one of urgency."

"I believe the matter to be of importance," declared Alfred.

A footman was summoned and given instructions to waken the sleeping churchman. Monsieur Maillard then escorted the visitor inside and asked him to be seated. The entrance hall was quite impressive, as Alfred discovered at once. It rose the full height of the house and there was an elaborate marble stairway branching off on each side. There were many statues and the walls were covered with tapestries which were very old and worn.

"We live simply," said Monsieur Maillard in a mournful tone. "Eight footmen only! Actually, m'sieur, no more than eight. Maidservants we cannot keep long. We have thought of bringing out girls from France to take places in the household and to make wives for our men. But the men—I assure you, m'sieur, I am speaking the literal truth—seem to have a liking for American women. Why? I do not know. I need not speak of the times when the household was royal but at Morfontaine, before we went to Naples, it was quite different. Ah, how different, m'sieur! A guest then had a suite of apartments with a staff to attend his needs. He had"—he began to count on his fingers—"a valet de chambre, a lackey, a coachman, a groom and a jockey. A chariot and a gig and riding horses were at his disposal. He was given a catalogue of the library and each morning there were lists of those who would be present at each meal and the dishes to be served. For the entertainment of guests there were theatricals, four billiard tables and all the equipment for rouge et noir, pharo, la roulette and biribi."

As the major-domo talked, Alfred became aware of a small dark head
and an observant pair of eyes in the shadows above the marble balustrade.
It was a very pretty girl of perhaps seventeen years, dressed in riding costume and with a scarf of a rich maroon satin wound about her throat. She
did not turn away when her presence was thus detected but continued to
study him seriously.

"Her Royal Highness," said Monsieur Maillard, looking up to see what
had attracted the visitor's gaze, "is very curious."

The face disappeared then. Alfred would have liked to ask many questions
about her but decided it would not be proper to display curiosity. At this
moment the word came that the abbé was ready to receive his visitor and
the young Englishman was escorted up the staircase and along a high-ceilinged hall so encumbered with paintings and statuary and crystal chandeliers
that it seemed like a museum. Everywhere about him in the gloom he could
hear the ticking of clocks. A slender figure whisked out of sight at the far
end of the hall as he advanced.

The abbé received him in his bedroom, into which the faintest light managed to filter through shuttered french doors. The air was decidedly heavy.
When the visitor's eyes became accustomed to the gloom, he saw that the
abbé was seated in a chair beside the bed. He was a massive man with a
round head and a brow so denuded of hair that only a few sandy whisks
showed above the horizon. He was in a nightgown, a thing of immensity,
and beneath its not too clean hem his legs were spread out in a relaxed
pose.

"I am informed," said the abbé in a scholarly tone, "that you have a letter
for me."

Alfred was now capable of observing the room in detail. A table at the
churchman's elbow was piled high with books and papers and the feathered
end of a quill pen protruded from somewhere in the midst of them. The
abbé had been reading in bed, for a portfolio of documents had fallen to
the floor, spilling its contents about. A robe of rusty black was hanging over
the end of the bed.

The visitor, feeling the keen eyes of the churchman on him and both
chilled and repelled by them, drew the envelope from an inside pocket and
placed it in the abbé's hands. "It was given me, sir," he said, "by a lady in
Rio de Janeiro with instructions that I have followed. Captain Gouvet was
injured today and could not come. I've brought the letter to you at his
request."

The clerical eyes, set closely in the abbé's broad pudding of a face, lighted
up in a brief and not too convincing smile. "You are welcome, sir," he said.
He turned the envelope around in his hands, scrutinizing the condition of
the seal with unabashed thoroughness. "I am much relieved to have this
letter, my young sir. The lady was well, I trust?"

"Quite well, I think, sir."

The abbé beamed. "A very lovely little person. And with the staunchest
heart. I am fond of her."

Alfred had been occupying a small gilt chair while this brief conversation progressed. He now got to his feet. "I have completed my errand, sir, and must be on my way."

"Come, come! Not so fast, if you please. I am interested in you and even more so in your name. Are you related by any chance to that remarkable man of the same name who is doing so much to reshape the industrial face of England?"

Alfred looked the surprise that he felt. His father's name could not be so familiar here in the wilds of America that an old French priest would know of him. "My father is Samuel Carboy," he said in a hesitant tone.

There was a moment of silence while the abbé took his turn at thinking. What strange coincidence, he asked himself, had brought the son of Samuel Carboy into the household of Joseph Bonaparte on an errand concerned with the secret activities of the Bonapartists? His mind veered immediately in another direction. If they should succeed in their plans to replace Napoleon on the throne of France, the most pressing need they would feel would be for peace with England. Men like Samuel Carboy, who were taking advantage of the conditions in the world of business, would have everything to gain also by keeping the two countries from flying at each other's throats. The lucky chance which had brought this boy to Point Breeze might be converted to their own best interests. It might be possible through the agency of the son to plant certain thoughts in the mind of Samuel Carboy.

"Must you be in such a hurry?" he asked. "You have done me a service and I cannot let you go like this. You must remain to share our evening meal and spend a night under the comte's roof. He will not be content if he is robbed of the chance to speak with you. The company will, I assure you, be diverting."

Alfred gave hurried thought to the advice of Tobias Griffen. "Get away from the place," that strange individual had said, "as soon as you've dropped the letter into the oily palm of the great gray fox." Well, the letter had been delivered and now he must heed the well-meant advice of the English officer.

"It is kind of you, sir," he said, giving his head a shake. "But there are reasons why I can't accept. My bags are at the Indian Arms. I must be off at a very early hour of the morning. Nevertheless, I am greatly indebted to you, sir."

His inclination had been all toward staying. To sit at the table of the man who had occupied two thrones, Naples and Spain, to see his two lovely daughters, to hear the talk of the old soldiers who were staying under the roof of Joseph Bonaparte! It would be something to remember all his life.

The abbé sensed his feeling and brushed aside his objections with the wave of a pudgy hand. "A carriage will be sent for the bags at once, M'sieur Carboy. It can be arranged for you to leave as early in the morning as you may desire." He twisted in his chair and pointed to a bellpull on the wall. "It is out of my reach. Will you oblige me by giving it a vigorous yank? Keep on yanking at it. The servants are not always disposed to heed a single summons."

CHAPTER EIGHT

1

An hour later the heir of the rapidly accumulating Carboy fortune was ready for dinner with the Bonapartes. He had been told that the rule in this curious household was to wear breeches in the evening. Luckily he had brought a pair with him. It was apparent, as he stood at a window of his spacious bedroom and gazed down at the blackness where bobbing pinpoints of light marked the passage of boats on the river, that there was nothing of Samuel Carboy's lumpiness of limb in the long and handsome legs of his tall son.

Now that the decision had been made and he was due to appear in a very few minutes in the drawing room below, where an ex-king and his two princess daughters would receive him, Alfred was experiencing a sense of real elation. He knew that he was looking well. His black coat fitted him perfectly. His ruffled linen was spotless and he had succeeded in tying his cravat under the lethal sharp points of his starched collar in the accepted manner. He was not too much concerned over the probability that his tongue would desert him. The less he said under these circumstances the better.

"It wouldn't be hard to talk to that cute one who was staring at me in the hall," he said to himself. His thoughts, he realized, had been almost continuously with the Princess Charlotte since it had been settled that he was to spend the night under a quasi-royal roof.

A bell from somewhere in the stillness below gave a faint tinkle twice. Alfred felt a tightening in his throat. He tugged nervously at the tails of his coat to make sure they were in place as he turned and walked toward the door. "I wish it was customary to ride up to the table on a horse," he said to himself with a regretful sigh. "Then I would know what to do."

The trumpeter on a clock above the fireplace blew eight times as he entered the long drawing room. A sallow lady in green, who had once possessed some beauty and whose eyes indicated an interest still in fields where beauty counts, came to meet him at once.

"Well!" she said, stopping short and regarding him with surprise. "How very young you are! I expected someone much older. You are a boy; and, I may say, a very handsome one." Her eyes dropped to survey his nether appointments. "How well you wear them! It's quite a rare thing, I assure you. If evidence is needed, just take a look at that display of mature knobbiness and unlovely shins over at the fireplace." She paused and indulged in a nonchalant gesture. "You must pardon me for speaking out about such things. I make a practice of being frank. It's the one trait a middle-aged woman may employ with any chance of success. So you mustn't be disturbed or shocked by anything I say—I am the Comtesse de Valain and I am going to take an interest in you this evening which may even seem motherly."

Alfred had been watching the group around the fire in their flamboyant uniforms and wondering who they were. He brought his gaze back to the lady in green and gave a deep bow. "I am greatly honored, Comtesse. I am Alfred Carboy. I feel so unsure of myself that it will be a matter of great relief to me if you will be so kind as to—to take me in hand."

The comtesse lowered her voice. "Don't be afraid of anyone here, Mr. Carboy. Look again at that group. They're a stupid lot, I assure you. As for His Majesty"—she used the form of salutation, to which Joseph Bonaparte had once been entitled, in an openly careless tone—"you needn't be afraid of him either. He's rather kind. But when you see him at close range—how very dull and uninspiring ex-kings can be! I could write a whole book— and someday perhaps I shall—about the little sillinesses of our good Joseph. He likes huge mirrors, draped with sky-blue satin. The house is full of them but four more arrive tomorrow from New York. I have three in my room already. He also has a passion for clocks and for trimming trees. If you should be weak enough as to bring up the question of tree pruning to him, he would talk to you all evening. Finally," she added, "his taste in mistresses is quite appalling."

Alfred had decided that the Comtesse de Valain had been born in America. Her voice had all the intonations he had detected as soon as he stepped off the ship at Philadelphia. Her use of the Anglo-Saxon word "mister" had seemed to him a further proof. He found himself liking her in spite of the frankness she seemed to consider a virtue. Her eyes, which were dark and animated, had a friendly look.

"Will the two princesses be with us tonight?" he asked.

"Yes, indeed. We still keep up a pretense of royalty, so they will sit at the head of the table with their father. I'm going to take you with me to the very foot. As a matter of plain common sense as well as for your own good." She gave him a warm smile. "Have you stumbled on the truth yet? That I am an American?"

"I rather thought you were."

"My voice gives me away. I was born Cissie Cotton in Virginia but I never seemed to acquire the charming drawl of the South. I suppose a New England ancestor put in a claim to my vocal cords. The Cottons were never wealthy and it was considered that the daughter of the family had done very well when she married the Comte de Valain, a French planter in Haiti."

"Haiti?" said Alfred eagerly. "I hope to go there before my tour ends."

"I have no such desire," declared the comtesse. "I was in Paris when the native uprising took place on the island. My poor husband was killed, in some revolting way. Somehow the Valain estates were not recovered and now they never will be."

"You must have been in Paris at the time of the Terror."

"I lived through the whole of it. I never knew a moment's peace of mind.

There I was, a widow with a title but not a sou to my name. I don't think I can be blamed for going with the tide. I belonged to a circle which included Josephine and the delightfully immoral Thérèse Cabarrus—you know who I mean, Our Lady of Thermidor. I didn't drift with the tide *they* took; but when Josephine married Napoleon, I attached myself to the rising star of the Bonapartes. Now here I am, attached to the Bonapartes still, even though the star has fallen right out of the heavens. The good Joseph finds me useful and, being a frugal soul, he pays me as much as a footman or an assistant cook."

She noticed that his eyes had gone back to the group at the fireplace. "I see you are interested in our heroic refugees. Well, the stoutish one on the right goes by the name of Gauthier. But that's not his real name."

"I saw him arrive this afternoon," said Alfred.

"That's Marshal de Grouchy."

"De Grouchy!" The young Englishman stared hard at the man who had failed to come to Napoleon's aid at the battle of Waterloo.

The American-born comtesse gave her head a toss. "I don't know why he dares come here after the terrible way he behaved at Waterloo. He goes everywhere, trying to explain himself. No one listens. Or if they do, they laugh at his reasons."

"Do you mind telling me who the others are?"

"The tall one beside De Grouchy is General Lallemand. He has just arrived from Texas. Next to him is that stupid Monsieur Pigeon. If he didn't own an acre of real estate on the water front of Marseille, they wouldn't tolerate the little pest. Why doesn't he go back to his dragon of a wife and his six children? Or, at any rate, to his deserted mistress in Paris who writes him every week in a most pathetic hand? I suspect that his loyalty to Napoleon is a matter of convenience."

"The other one, the dark man on the left, must be Colonel Lebaud. I've heard a lot about him."

"None of it good, I'm sure," said the comtesse tartly. "He rode in the great charge at Marengo and he's talked of nothing else since. Except, of course, his conquests."

Alfred was looking very much taken aback by the frankness of her comments. She detected his disillusionment and hastened to add: "There will be a better lot here soon. Some brave soldiers with fine records, not blowhards like Lebaud. And there will be diplomats on a higher level than the Abbé Force and some financial men, of course. I'm afraid I shouldn't be telling you all this."

"I already know something of what is going on."

Monsieur Maillard appeared in the doorway at the far end and announced, "His Majesty the King."

A plump man who might at first glance have been mistaken for Napoleon walked slowly and stiffly into the room. A second glance dispelled the first impression completely and quickly. There was something about Joseph Bonaparte which suggested the ineffectual. His face was amiable, his waistline had the slightest touch of the comic about it, his calves had in their unusual fullness a hint of youthfulness. He was dressed magnificently and yet with good taste. His breeches, which fitted him tightly, were of white satin, his square-tailed coat was lavender with white pockets, his waistcoat the faintest shade of lemon. A single jeweled order was suspended around his neck.

Alfred asked the comtesse, "Is it customary still to address him as king?"

"They do it here," she whispered in response. "I think it's the rule in the households of monarchs who have lost their thrones. It relieves the dreariness. It means nothing, of course, but they cling to the form even if they have lost the substance."

Joseph Bonaparte said, "Good evening," in a bland tone of voice and walked to a chair near the fire. "We have had a pleasant day, messieurs," he added, seating himself. "It was most stimulating in the woods. It would do some of you much good if you would shoulder an ax and join us."

"Follow me," whispered the comtesse to her young charge.

They walked together to the other end of the room and came to a halt in front of the good-natured ex-king. At close range it could be seen that Joseph was quite fatigued after his day in the park and might be expected at any moment to fall off into slumber.

"Your Majesty," said the comtesse, "I desire to present a visitor, Mr. Alfred Carboy. He arrived today on a mission to the Abbé Force. In presenting him to you, I am acting for the abbé, who is indisposed this evening. He has asked me to apologize and explain the reason for his absence."

Colonel Lebaud said in an audible whisper, "The good abbé may be indisposed but I saw his tray going up and it's clear he has not lost his appetite."

The ex-monarch indulged in something between a laugh and a titter. "There is an edge of ill nature to everything you say, Colonel Lebaud," he remarked. "We are sure the abbé is genuinely fatigued. The fruits of his amazing activity are to be seen every day in the stream of letters he sends out."

"If the pen is mightier than the sword," declared the colonel, emboldened to further efforts, "then the abbé is the mightiest warrior the world has ever produced. Fortunately it isn't true."

"But ink is sometimes a more effective weapon than gunpowder."

"The emperor," declared the soldier brusquely, "conquered the world with the sword."

Joseph turned at this point to nod and smile at the visitor. "We are being very rude," he said. "M'sieur Car-bpfmm stands here in our presence quite neglected while we argue among ourselves on such futile matters. Will you pardon us, m'sieur? We are happy to welcome you and to thank you for the service you rendered us."

The Englishman bowed but said nothing, winning by his reticence an approving nod from the comtesse.

The voice of Maillard was raised a second time. "Her Highness, the Princess Zénaïde."

The older daughter of the family entered the room with a gentle rustling of silk skirts, and with a smile and bow for her father and the company about him. She was quite delightful-looking. Her hair was honey-colored with faint glints of gold in it, her eyes were a rather gay light brown, her complexion was fresh. That she was a general favorite was shown by the warm smiles with which she was greeted by the company.

"Her Highness, the Princess Charlotte."

The young Englishman turned his head at once and saw the girl who had stared at him from the dark upper reaches of the hall come into the room. She was quite young but she managed nevertheless to invest her arrival with some of the drama of a stage entrance. She had the beauty of languorous black eyes with longer lashes than nature could ever be expected to create and a skin with the faintest hint of ivory. Her gown was white with a decidedly bouffant skirt and red rosebuds peeping out from each flounce. The bodice was tight and allowed full display to the prettiest of shoulders and arms.

"The little hussy!" whispered the comtesse, with a trace of amusement as well as annoyance in her voice. "Dressing herself up for a state ball! She must have heard you were here. Certainly she wouldn't do all this for these spavined old veterans."

Joseph said something unintelligible, nodding first to the Englishman and then to each of his daughters in turn, thus providing an introduction. He then rose and said in a delighted voice, "We detect a note of invitation in the Maillard eye."

The major-domo inclined his head ceremoniously. "Dinner is served, Your Majesty."

The king led the way alone into the dining salon, his daughters following him together. The comtesse, who was the only other lady present, came next on Alfred's arm, and the rest of the company straggled along after without any attempt at order. The salon was highly imposing. There was a portrait of Napoleon over the fireplace. Half a dozen long mirrors (with blue draperies, of course) hung at intervals on the walls. Two enormous chandeliers were suspended from the ceiling over each end of the table, the sparkle of their brilliant prisms rivaling the light from scores of candles. Hothouse flowers were massed in the center of the tables. At the head, where Joseph would sit, was a small gold vessel filled with the white violets which were blooming so profusely in the woods.

"I hope you are hungry," said the comtesse to Alfred. "The food will be superb."

2

The food was superb but the young Englishman paid small attention to the dishes laid in front of him; the fish, as white and delicate as sole caught right off the cliffs of Dover, the small steaks, covered with a sauce which ordinarily would have caused him the greatest delight, and a dessert which was new to him and went by the name of ice cream.

He did little more than play with his knife and fork as his eyes rested on the trio at the head of the table: the portly onetime king talking and laughing with the honey-colored princess who sat on his right, and with infinitely more interest on the younger daughter who occupied his left. The Princess Charlotte was as little concerned with food as he was. She had a paper in front of her and seemed to be writing on it. Her dark eyes were lowered and her extremely long lashes shaded them as she bent to the work.

Occasionally she raised her eyes and stared hard at Alfred as he sat beside the comtesse at the far end of the table. When this happened he would feel emotions which he had never experienced in such degree before; an excitement, an exhilaration, a desire to be capable of holding her regard—perhaps for all time.

"I must say this about Charlotte," declared the comtesse, as though she had sensed what was in his mind. "She's clever. She's artistic to her finger tips. I sometimes think she's got all the brains in the family. No, I must take that back. Joseph has ability of a kind; he would make a good president of a bank, for instance. As for Zénaïde, she's sweet and gentle and I love her. She's going to make a wonderful wife." Her eyes moved again to take in the bent dark head of the younger daughter. "Charlotte thinks the Bonapartes will come back into power. She dreams of the day when they'll rule the world."

The dinner came to an end finally. Joseph Bonaparte glanced at each of his daughters to let them know that the royal appetite had been thoroughly appeased, then rose to his feet. The princesses followed suit and the guests rose from their seats with some slight fumbling of feet and chairs. Joseph bowed and said: "The rest of the evening will be spent in our study where the presence of some of you may be required. In the meantime we leave you to your wine." Then he bowed again and left the room, his daughters following him.

The comtesse remained standing. "You carried yourself well," she said to Alfred. "I was quite proud of you. It will be necessary for you to remain here a time, although I must leave, of course. Are you much addicted to wine?"

The Englishman shook his head emphatically. "It makes me dizzy. I think it's a beastly habit."

The comtesse gave him an approving smile. "How glad I am to hear you say so. I suppose you'll come to it in time and perhaps get to be one of these gross creatures called five-bottle men. Well, stay long enough to have one glass of wine with these worthy gentlemen who are going to settle down to a long evening of disgusting indulgence. Then betake yourself to bed so you'll be ready for your early start in the morning. I won't see you again."

"You've been very kind to me, Comtesse. I'm most thankful to you."

The comtesse indulged in a somewhat ironic laugh. "You'll take one memory away with you. A very lively princess, who may make a name for herself in history, has stared at you all evening like a sly little cat eying a fine big mouse. Or rather, I think, a secluded princess of centuries ago, watching from a window in a Norman castle a tall, blond Norseman riding by. It's something for you to remember, at any rate."

Alfred drank his glass of wine, made his excuses to the rest of the company and left the dining room. It was his intention to go straight to his room, write a letter to his mother (making no mention of this unusual experience which was now coming to a close) and then retire for the night. At the top of the marble stairs, however, he was stopped by a servant who said in a labored attempt at English, "Young M'sieur come."

"Come? Do you mean you want to take me somewhere?"

The man did not understand. He stumbled over some words and finally said, "Abbé Force."

"Very well. Take me to the Abbé Force, if that's what you mean."

The abbé was sitting at a writing table, his corpulent form wrapped in a brown dressing gown which looked like nothing so much as the hide of a grizzly bear. His feet were naked.

"M'sieur Carboy," he said, laying down his pen, "I have been asked to give you a message—and this." He held out a roll of stout white paper, held by a bow of violet ribbon. "Before you look at it, I must make some explanation. I—I have an ally in this house. There is one person to whom I can talk without reservation and in whom I can confide. I have received many favors at the hand of this ally of mine—small favors, it is true, but sufficient to make it necessary for me to reciprocate on occasion. Because of this, I am doing my friend a favor now." He cleared his throat and folded the fingers of both hands together, not caring seemingly that some of them were wet with ink. "First, you had better undo that ribbon and look at the paper. Then I shall deliver the message."

Alfred unrolled the sheet. A gasp of astonishment escaped him when he realized what it contained. It was a picture of himself, done with bold and skillful strokes of a soft pencil. He studied it with the most intense concentration. It was, he thought, a quite remarkable likeness, although his height had been slightly exaggerated and an almost Grecian beauty had been conceded to his legs. So this was what the Princess Charlotte had been so busy over during dinner! This was the reason, moreover, for the long and intent glances she had given him.

"I can guess what it is, young sir," said the churchman. "The princess draws with remarkable skill."

Alfred was reading a few lines written on the edge of the paper. This was rather difficult, for the princess' ignorance of English spelling had necessitated some corrections. This was what he read:

A likeness, and a good one, I think, of an Englishman who was presented to us this evening. It is just as he looked, standing in front of our father; such a tall young man and with hair like gold!

Charlotte

"Against my own judgment," said the abbé, "I must now give you the message. Hearing that you are to leave early in the morning, the Princess Charlotte has asked me to arrange a meeting. She has things to say to you, I believe. Fearing that a meeting between you would almost certainly be misconstrued, I suggested that she permit me to speak with you and convey your answers to her. It seems, however, that some of the points at least are of the kind which cannot be discussed through a third party. She came to me as soon as dinner was over and she is now waiting."

It is easy to believe that the mind of the young Englishman, on hearing the information thus conveyed to him, was in a turmoil. There is always a certain freemasonry among the young. A spark passes from eye to eye which can be much more effective than mere words. By some such means of communication Alfred had known that the princess was interested in him but it had never entered his mind that it might lead to anything like this. What were the matters she wanted to discuss?

"You may have heard talk of underground passages and secret rooms in this house," went on the churchman. "It is true that the Comte de Survilliers —I prefer to use the name by which he desires to be known on the outside— has had tunnels constructed, one of them at least of considerable length. It is also true that he has a secret chamber but the belief that it is a part of the tunneling is erroneous. I am under compulsion, M'sieur Carboy, to give you information which is supposed to be most closely held. Before I go any further, I must demand a pledge of you. I must ask, m'sieur, that not a hint of what you may see or hear will ever pass your lips."

"I most solemnly swear, Your Excellency."

"The secret room is of easy access when you know the location and the mechanism," declared the churchman. "That is as much as I dare divulge and I must ask that you permit me to bind your eyes."

He rose from his chair and fitted his splayed feet into slippers which had been lying on the floor beside him. Looking more than ever like a shambling bear, he found a black mask in a drawer of the table and shuffled over to his visitor. He proceeded to fit the mask over Alfred's eyes and to knot the ties most securely.

"I consider it highly desirable, m'sieur, that you continue to wear the mask during the course of the interview," declared the abbé.

"I am subject to your commands, Excellency."

The abbé took him by the shoulders and turned him around a number of times. Even had Alfred desired to keep himself clear on the point of direction, he would have been quite at a loss when this safety measure had been completed. The abbé left him then and walked apparently to one of the walls of the room. There was a sound which suggested the friction that ensues when a well-fitted wooden panel is turned.

"This way, if you please," said the abbé. "Go slowly and feel the way with your feet. There are three steps to descend."

Alfred followed these directions. He had not been told to stoop but, conscious of his unusual height, he did so instinctively. His feet had no difficulty with the steps, which were shallow and broad. He heard the panel in the wall close behind him. He remained where he was and waited.

"If M'sieur will now remove the mask," said a voice of attractively modulated depth.

Alfred hesitated. "I was directed by the abbé to keep it on," he said.

He heard a low laugh which had the same suggestion of huskiness as the voice. "When you passed through that door, m'sieur, you ceased to be subject to any order from the good abbé. May I suggest that you now consider my wishes only?"

"I am at your service, Your Highness."

Raising both hands to the back of his head, he was discomfited to discover that the churchman, anticipating some such contingency, had knotted the cords most effectively. His fingers, lacking vision to guide them, made no progress at all.

"It seems," said the princess, "that you need assistance." There was a rustle of silk skirts to indicate that she was crossing toward him. "That abbé! He must always try to impose his will. M'sieur will please come a few steps because the light here is rather dim. Now, as you are so *very* tall, you will, perhaps, kneel?"

Alfred obeyed, going down on one knee. He could feel deft fingers working on the knot and he became conscious of a perfume much more enticing and seductive than anything Grace and Carboy had ever brought from the

East. The cords yielded and the mask was removed from his eyes. He rose
to his feet and turned.

He was aware of two things at once: of the close proximity of the Princess
Charlotte, her eyes bright and even excited, her lips slightly parted; and of
the curious nature of the room in which they stood face to face. As the princess has appeared several times in the course of this narrative, it may be wise
to begin with the background of their meeting.

Alfred had seen "hides" in English castles and had always been surprised
and rather dismayed at their bareness and lack of all comfort. The secret
room which Joseph Bonaparte had contrived in his American home was completely different. It was small enough but most luxuriously furnished. The
walls may have been of cold brick but they were hidden by velour hangings
with battle scenes of the Napoleonic era embroidered on them and an
abundance of tassels of gold thread. There was not only a couch of good
width but a rather ornate desk with two deep chairs beside it. A half-open
panel at one side gave a glimpse of a small toilet beyond, which contained
a sabot bath. In the ceiling was a grating which provided outside ventilation
and even a small share of light. A dozen or more candles burned in side
sconces. In such a well-equipped nest a refugee could hide away in com-
parative ease and security.

Alfred did not take in all these details at once. His first glance, and many
succeeding ones, had been at the Princess Charlotte, who was standing in
front of him with the mask twirling idly in her fingers.

"I did not fully realize how very large you are," she said. "I fail by several
inches of coming to your shoulder."

"My height always makes me feel awkward," he responded.

"No, no. That is very wrong. M'sieur moves with the grace of a panther."
She laughed lightly. "I am quoting from a book when I say that. I have
never seen a panther."

She seated herself in one of the chairs. The visitor disregarded her invitation to take the other, however, and remained standing. He felt very unsure
of himself. What did royal etiquette demand of him under these circumstances? Was it proper for him to speak only in response to questions from
her?

The princess had not changed from the white gown she had worn at dinner. With quick movements of her small hands she spread the artistically
gored and embroidered skirt so wide about her that her visitor caught a brief
glimpse of a jeweled slipper of quite diminutive size. Drawing herself up-
right, as though conscious of the need to maintain the dignity of her rank,
she spoke first of the short time they would have. "They are always concerned about me," she said with a dissenting pout of her lips, "when I try
to steal a few moments for myself. I am in quite a difficult position because
there is so much I must say to you."

If Alfred had been older and more experienced, he might have suspected
that the first sentences she proceeded to use had been prepared and, even,
rehearsed.

"Everyone says of me that I am a true Bonaparte," she began. He had been surprised from the first moment at her command of English but a certain stiffness and conscious precision began to show now. "I *know* that I am. Perhaps you will laugh at me for saying this, m'sieur, but I think that I have a great deal of the emperor in me. I never do anything until I have thought it out with the *utmost* care. But at the same time I know by instinct at the very first what it is I want. That also is like the emperor, who never stopped at anything to get what he desired. I never hesitate to say what is in my mind; and the emperor, I may tell you, was *devas-tating* in his frankness. This is necessary when you are of royal rank and others cannot speak frankly to you. Please forgive me for saying all this when we have so little time to talk."

The young Englishman was watching her closely, his mind less concerned with what she was saying than with how she looked. "She has the loveliest eyes in the world," he thought. "How dark and lustrous they are!" He was surprised to realize how easily and completely he was yielding to the fascination she exerted. He had wasted no time in falling in love with Nell Groody but that had been quite different from what was happening to him now. He felt that he was being carried away by a force he could not resist. As he watched the play of emotions on her eloquent features and the graceful movements of her hands the desire to resist became steadily less.

"You must know, of course, what concerns us all here," she continued. "Every loyal supporter of the emperor wants to see him escape from that terrible island. That woman in Rio is very active in it, the one who entrusted the letter to you and so was responsible for your visit here." The expression in the eyes beneath the deep black lashes changed suddenly. "Why was she so sure she could trust you in a matter so very vital and secret?"

"I don't know, Your Highness."

"Had you seen her often?"

"I saw her once and I talked to her for a few minutes only. I was taken to her box at the theater on the night before I sailed for the United States."

"Did you admire her very much?"

"I thought her beautiful, Your Highness. For a woman of her age."

Charlotte's brief surrender to suspicion came to an end. She laughed, with a husky catch in her throat. "But it was a good thing, m'sieur, that you saw her once only," she said. "She's a fascinating woman. But I must not in-terrupt myself in this way. The poor abbé is, no doubt, so highly anxious that he will come in and insist on dragging you away. Before"—she became completely grave—"before I have said the important things.

"It is this way. My father is sure that Napoleon's escape can be accom-plished. All these great talkers below are certain of it. The Abbé Force is doing everything he can to make it possible. But I am certain of this: the abbé has his doubts. He is a realist and he knows how ill the poor emperor is, and how closely the island is watched by the terrible English ships. I am the only one who speaks out and says, No, no, it is impossible, it is a dream which cannot come true. And so the abbé and I, who are much in accord on most things, are in this respect looking far into the future.

"We know that Bonapartism is something which will go on and on. It is not just being loyal to the emperor. It is a movement of people and races. Even more than that, it is a way of thinking. The Bonapartes will rule in France again. Nothing can stop that, nothing, nothing! As it cannot be Napoleon himself, I am not sure who will lead the way. There is a cousin, Louis Napoleon. He is a son of Queen Hortense of Holland, and he is very ambitious although he is young. Perhaps he is the one, and if this comes true I may have to marry him. It may be a woman. Why should it not be? There have been empresses who ruled as well as men. There was Catherine the Great of Russia and there was Isabella of Spain." Her eyes were burning now with the intensity of her feeling. "Why should it not be me? I am the truest Bonaparte of them all. I grow more like the Emperor each day. The Abbé Force says so; and who knows better than he? I think—I am sure that if he had the selection of a successor he would choose me."

Alfred was watching and listening with amazement. This was not the Princess Charlotte who had been developing in his mind as a result of his brief glimpses of her, impetuous, foolish and self-willed but so attractive and fascinating. Why was this intensely ambitious woman revealing her thoughts to him?

A sound reached their ears from some part of the house beneath them, a loud murmur of voices and much moving about. The princess rose to her feet and faced him at close range. There was such a disparity in their heights that she had to throw her head far back to look in his eyes. She stood in this attitude for several moments.

Alfred felt an impulse to take her in his arms, to touch the crisp curling hair on her rather broad brow. All other thoughts had been driven from his head. His meetings with Nell Groody, which had filled so large a part of his thoughts on the long sea voyages; Nell in the haunted church, in the buttery at Beaulaw with steaming dishes piled up around her, in the vineyard on that memorable morning when she had declared herself, the new Nell of Little Shallow, so cool and businesslike and rather aloof, in her tiny shop; all such thoughts had vanished from his mind.

"They will be looking for me," whispered the princess. "I think I should go now, my tall Englishman. But before I do"—she placed a hand on each of his shoulders and raised herself up on her toes to bring her eyes on more of a level with his—"I must say something else, something which is quite as close to my heart as the future of my family. If you had the desire to say what I am going to, you could not; and so I must be the one to say it. I will have to marry someone of equal rank, of course. That is inevitable. I have known it ever since I was a small girl and I have never felt any reluctance until this moment. Already they are looking for a husband for me. The Abbé Force writes letters about it all the time. I will do whatever is necessary. It is my duty. But—but the very first moment I saw you this afternoon, standing there in the dark hall and listening to that bothersome Monsieur

Maillard, I knew you were the only man I could ever love. Are you surprised
that I dare say this? I have no hesitation about it at all. You see, my tall one,
this may be the only chance I will ever have. I cannot let you walk out of
my life without knowing." She paused and then her eyes widened in a smile.
"How did you like the sketch I made of you?"

"I cannot tell you how proud it made me, Your Highness."

"And the likeness? You think it good?"

"It's a work of art. But, Your Highness, it flatters me. Am I to keep it?"

"Of course. I hoped you would want something to remember me by if—
if things do not come out right."

"I would value it more than anything else in the world!" declared the
Englishman fervently.

"Then," said the princess, speaking rapidly and in low tones, "you must
listen very carefully. Even if I am not destined to be the one who wins back
the throne, I will always have power. I will have my own guards. You must
serve with us—with me. What a handsome officer you would make! You
would always be near me and I would never love anyone else. I swear it.
You must give me your promise now. If you refuse, I shall throw myself at
your head—more than I am doing now! I shall wrap my arms around your
neck and never, never let you get away from me."

"But, Your Highness," protested Alfred rather faintly. "I am English. How
can I serve in a foreign army? Even if—if it is *your* army?"

"The emperor had men of all races serving with him—Germans and Rus-
sians and Turks and Italians—and, yes, even Englishmen. Why, then, should
you hesitate? True, I would have a husband; but that need not matter. The
Bonapartes have caused many scandals in the past. Why not another? Now
I am being as frank as the emperor; and I am afraid you are shocked, being
English."

"Must you leave so early tomorrow, my tall one?" she asked after a moment of silence.

Alfred hesitated. "My traveling companion is in New York and is expecting me there at once. I don't want him getting into a blether and writing
letters home. Or, worse still, going to the police to have me traced. He's a
great soft donkey and I don't know what nonsense he might try."

"It is clear you do not really love me yet," said the princess, regarding him
with serious eyes. "But another day might make a difference. A week? Ah
yes, M'sieur Al-fred, you would love me then." Her eyes had something in
them now of the conquering Napoleonic light. "And so you must stay. It
is settled. You will go to the inn and write a letter to this soft donkey of
yours which will keep him quiet. Each day you will go for a walk at a certain
time. Let us consider when—I think it should be at half past two. . . .
Please, my tall one, do not think I am giving you orders. I am a Bonaparte
and we are managing people. It is a habit with us to speak this way. And, of
course, we *are* good at—at arrangements. So, at two-thirty. Most of the men
here take a nap after lunch and it will be a safe time. Follow the road from
Bordentown and just before you come to the line of my father's land there

is a small road leading down to the river. They have a strange name for it—
Upsa Daesy Lane. If I am free my maid will be waiting on the lane for you.
She will bring you to a place where we will not be seen. If you do not meet
her, you will know that something has gone wrong. Is it all understood, my
Pantagruel, standing up so high above me?"

Alfred had found that he was no longer afraid of her. She was, after all,
a small girl who had inherited an instinct for management. He rather liked
this, and was even amused by it.

"It is understood," he said, smiling at her.

"If it should happen that you are seen with the maid, you must let it be
known that your tryst was with her. She will be punished in that case but
it is the only safe way. I make it up to her. She has always been a kind of
whipping girl for me. There! I have given you all the orders and I will stop.
Someday, perhaps, you will give orders to *me*. I think it might be good for
me."

She fitted the mask over his eyes and tied it behind his head. This much
accomplished, she allowed one hand to smooth the hair on his brow. "There,
my tall one, you must go now. But tomorrow you will saunter down the
lane and somewhere near at hand I shall be waiting for you."

"Yes, Your Highness."

"The first step is right behind you. Tap twice lightly on the panel. Until
tomorrow, my sober Englishman."

3

"The mask is tied with a different knot," said the abbé, his hands fumbling with the task of removing it. He gave a noisy sniff. "The princess tied
it for you. I recognize her perfume. Does she think her old abbé has lost
his powers of observation?"

Alfred was a little abashed when the black covering had been removed
and he faced the accusing eyes of the old churchman. "You are leaving in
the morning," said the latter. When the young Englishman made no response, he turned slowly and looked him over with deliberate calculation.
"I would advise against a change of plan. It will be in your interests to leave
when you intended. And, M'sieur Carboy, I am certain you would be wise
not to come back."

A sound of voices raised in song reached them from the direction of the
dining salon. It was a dirgelike air and the abbé frowned impatiently when
he recognized it.

" '*Champ d'Asile*'!" he said. "They are filled with self-pity, these great
heads of the ox. And so they always sing this song, always when the bottle has been making the rounds. Do you know the words? Listen."

> Hear the story of our sorrows and our woes.
> Savages, we are Frenchmen!
> Have pity on our glory.

"They should not sing of their glory but of their folly," continued the churchman. "Their folly, M'sieur Carboy, has been to live too long and too well on the bounty of the emperor. It was Napoleon who brought wealth and position and fame to these strutting peacocks. They did little to deserve the rich rewards they received, the titles, the estates, the gold, the handsome wives. And now they are sitting around and doing nothing while they wait to see him back on the throne. If it happened, they would rush away on the first ship and squat themselves down before the trough again. Make no mistake, young Englishman, the Bonapartes will rule again. But it will be too late to get this soft-witted crew out of their threadbare coats and back into gold braid.

"*Their* folly is selfishness," he repeated. "What kind of folly are *you* contemplating? It would be quite easy for you and little Princess Slyboots to get yourselves into serious trouble." He gestured broadly, causing the sleeve of his heavy robe to fall back almost to the shoulder. "Suppose you do not go away, or suppose you do go but come back. There are many good reasons why either course would be most obnoxious to all of us. We want no kind of talk. A scandal might be fatal to our purposes." He pursed up his thick lips. "If you are around here longer, it is likely that a quarrel would be forced on you. Are you a good pistol shot?"

Alfred gave his head a negative shake.

"Have you skill with the sword?"

"No, Excellency."

"To fight a duel then would be a very sad thing for you. You would stand no chance against a man who has made killing his chief concern. Lebaud, for instance. I have acquired a liking for you and I would prefer to save you from getting a lead bullet through your heart or a lethal sword thrust through the ribs."

Ordinarily the shrewdest of men, the abbé had made a mistake in thinking that Alfred Carboy could be frightened away. The latter flushed and drew himself up to his full height. He bowed to the churchman.

"Thank you for the advice, Your Excellency. I am returning now to my room."

The tone of voice employed shook the abbé's confidence. Had he failed to win his point, after all? He looked with a frown at the retiring back of the tall visitor. "The Princess Lolotte is waiting for me to let her out," he said.

CHAPTER NINE

1

Old Sheppy, otherwise the Duke of Outland, looked at Near Sandiwell and shook his head. "That left wing is going to cave in if something isn't done about it," he muttered to himself. "What a nuisance, what a damned nuisance! The whole roof is bad. Will Georgie Grace pay for the repairs? He should, in all decency, because I'm letting him have the place practically as a gift. But he won't. Not Georgie. I'll have to scrape the money up somehow. It's just one cursed thing after another."

The duke was driving his dilapidated pony cart and looking fully as shabby himself. It may seem hard to believe that a ducal hat would have a hole in the crown but it is a fact that his had; and it had been a cheap and unfashionable hat to begin with. There were patches at his elbows and knees and it was doubtful if a worse pair of shoes could have been found by inspecting all the chimney sweeps in London.

Mrs. Grace was in the garden, picking spring blooms for a little lunch she was giving that day. It was not her head that he saw first and, in fact, he took umbrage at seeing her at all. He had been hoping to whisk in and out and so escape her endless complainings.

"Uncle Sheppard!" she called, straightening up and waving a handful of flowers to make sure of his attention. "I'm so glad you're here. The water came down the dining-room walls again last night. You ought to see the state the room is in."

"Curse the state the room is in!" protested the duke. "I came to see Georgie. On a very friendly errand, I may say; and I don't want damp walls shoved into my face this way."

"But, Uncle, something will have to be done about it. We can't go on living like this."

"Why don't you put buckets under the leaks in the roof? You ought to see the state we're in at Outland Park; and we go on living somehow. Though why we do is more than I can see. Where's George?"

"Painting. As usual. You can have no conception, Uncle, how hard he works. He's at his easel morning, noon and night."

"He might find enough time to put those buckets under the leaks," grumbled the duke.

When the crotchety peer had shambled through the side door, Mrs. Grace returned to her task. The encounter had irritated her to such an extent that she fairly tore the flowers up by the roots. "He treats us like paupers," she said to herself indignantly.

The Duke of Outland found George Ninian Grace in the library, which he had converted into a studio. The walls were covered with old books in bindings which were crumbling away and the moldy smell they exuded vied with the odor of oil paints and turpentine. Grace was not a tidy man to begin with and he had succeeded in turning a once gracious room into an artistic shambles. Three easels with unfinished canvases stood in as many corners. The floor was covered with paper to catch the flickings of paint which flew about in the frenzy of inspiration. Here and there finished paintings had been propped up in front of the books. The visitor studied these and his jaw fell. His eyes registered a kind of furious disbelief.

"By gad, George!" he said finally. "I see you're going to make a damned fool of yourself again."

George Grace had risen from the folding chair he used for his work. He had a sense of pride which balked at accepting criticism, even when it came from a ducal source. His face turned red with vexation.

"Sir," he said stiffly, "I am not aware that I have ever—er—made a damned fool of myself, as you so graciously put it."

"By gad, you have! If letting your affairs get into such a mess that you can be shoved out of your own business isn't being a fool, then I know nothing whatever on the subject of idiocy."

Grace began to clean his brush on a piece of rag with fingers which trembled.

"And what new piece of idiocy on my part do you foresee?" he asked.

The duke made a circular motion with his right arm to indicate the row of finished paintings. "This blasted nonsense. These cursed daubs. Damme, I think you have no regard for public opinion at all, Georgie. People who see these nightmares will think you're in your dotage."

George Grace was so infuriated that he could not speak for several moments. "Sir," he said in a voice which seemed to choke him, "I will endeavor to contain my proper resentment and explain to you what it is I'm striving to attain in my work. Will you be kind enough to come over to this window?"

When they reached the window they had a clear view across the southern section of the Vale. There had been a heavy downfall of rain during the night and the air was now fresh and cool. It was so clear that across the Vale they could see White Horse Hill with the strange stone outline of a huge galloping animal on its steep slope. The White Horse has been a puzzle down through the centuries, a rare chance for speculation on the part of historians and scientists. The people of Berkshire are properly proud of this mystery, perpetuated by some strange race far back in the past.

"What do you see?" asked Grace.

"By gad, Georgie! You're treating me like a backward child in a charity school with your questions. What do I see? I see the White Horse. Is that what you mean?" He promptly launched into a reminiscent strain. "Would you believe that I helped in the Scouring in 1780? I was as strong as a young bull then and I was the first to toss my hat in the ring afterward. I was an Old Gamester even then and they came against me in the backswording, three of them, one after another. I broke the skin on all their shins with the greatest ease and everyone yelped, 'Good for ee, Young Sheppy.' I still have the silver-laced hat I won that day."

"Does that figure up there look like a horse?"

The peer hooted contemptuously. "Of course not. It looks no more like a horse than I do."

At this George Grace raised his voice in triumph. "And yet for centuries men have been staring at it or climbing up to see it closer—savages, untutored men, as well as the men of today. In all that long procession down the years not one has ever failed to recognize it as a horse." His eyes lighted up. "There, sir, *that* is art! It's not necessary to trick a thing out in full detail. You do no more than suggest your subject and everyone at a glance will see what it is you intend to convey. You paint an object as you see it yourself." He gave his head a nod which had a faint trace of smugness over the neat way he was establishing his point. "That is what I'm doing."

"Now, Georgie, you know how dangerous it is to get my temper up. I can't control it when anyone tries to twist things around to put me in the wrong. You call that queer animal up there a specimen of art? I call it the attempt of savages who didn't know any better." He nodded his head vigorously. "Do you know that once I got so mad at Prince Frederick that I took after him with a riding crop? If three court officials hadn't held me back, I would have taught him he couldn't talk that way to a British peer."

George Grace knew all about this famous occurrence. All England, in fact, remembered it very well. The high regard in which Old Sheppy was still held was due to the effort he had made to discipline one of the highly unpopular sons of King George III.

"Don't poison my ears with any more of this blethering foolishness," went on the peer. "And the next time I come, oblige me, my dear fellow, by having all this junk taken out to the ross heap. Today I've come to give you a very important piece of news. Cythian Fordyce is dead."

George Grace was not particularly interested in this important piece of news. He knew Cythian Fordyce, who had been the member for Little Grimditch for as long as he could remember. He had never liked Fordyce, considering him pompous, ill informed and blind to the responsibilities of his position. He gave his head a nod and waited.

"When these cursed fellows in the Commons get to shouting their heads off about rotten boroughs, it's Little Grimditch they have in mind as much as Old Sarum. Well, I suppose there's some reason to it because we've got no more than four voters. The point is this, Georgie, I have the nomination in my pocket and I'm thinking of putting you in to take his place."

This put matters on a different basis at once. George Grace forgot all about art and his theories on the subject. He followed the duke back from the window and they seated themselves on a settle near the fireplace.

"Sir," said Grace, "I would esteem it a great honor. It was one of my first ambitions to sit in the House and take a part in public affairs. I had a gift for words, I may say. But I gave it up long ago. It was certain I would never have the time for it. Now that you mention this possibility, I feel the same urge taking possession of me. I have the time now and I would strive to make myself a useful servant of the king."

"The way I look at it," said the duke, "is that you'd have chances to get your hands on a little blunt now and then. You get paid to sit on committees. But whether you catch the nod of the big fellows for that or not, there are always new boards and companies being started where they need names. All a member has to do is nod and they hand over a hundred guineas, two hundred, three hundred. It's all very tidy and comfortable, Georgie. And, of course, there's no need for you to sit in the House much. If the majority is small, the whips may crack down on you and insist that you appear for divisions. But that doesn't happen often."

"If I receive this honor, the only thought in my mind will be of the responsibilities attached to public office," declared Grace.

"Quite," said the peer. "But save all that for the hustings, my boy. The important thing is to pouch the blunt. To have your palm ready when some- one wants to pour the fine, tinkling guineas into it."

The Duke of Outland rose to his feet. He looked with dismay at the size of the hole in his hat. "I wish I could take the seat myself," he muttered. "The first thing I'd find a hatter fellow and get myself a new one. I wore this hat when I was on night patrol at the Channel, watching for Boney. That was fifteen years ago."

2

The Duke of Outland left Near Sandiwell by a rear door. He slithered around the troublesome left wing, keeping an eye open for his equally trouble- some niece, and reached his pony cart without any delay. With surprising agility, he sprang into the seat, brought out his whip, called, "Up and at it, Marmaduke," and was off with a furious creaking of wheels. George Grace watched his departure from the library window, his eyes showing no interest in what they saw. He turned when the pony cart reached the road and left the house by the same door.

Near Sandiwell stood so close to the water at Willikin's Elbow that at times the little river lapped the stone steps of the kitchen. Each spring the stream indulged in a rampage and invariably selected the Elbow as the most convenient spot for overflowing its banks. The house enjoyed the full benefit of these freshets and had even been known to have four feet of water on the ground floor. The suns of summer were seldom capable of re- moving the dampness completely or of driving out the odors of mildew and decay. On the other side of the house, however, there was a hill high enough to scoff at the yearly furies of the usually gentle little river. There had been occasions when the occupants of the house had found it necessary to seek sanctuary on the crest of the hill. It was there that George Grace betook himself after his interview with Old Sheppy.

From the top of the hill there was a splendid view of the White Horse. But the amateur artist, who had drawn on this mysterious reminder from an earlier age to such good effect in his delineation of the true meaning of art, did not now give as much as a glance at it. Instead he looked off in a northerly direction where his eyes came to rest on a high ridge from which projected the ruined tower of a church; none other than the haunted edifice where Alfred Carboy and Nell Groody had kept their first tryst. Some distance back as years go, there had been a village around the church on the crest and, although it had disappeared so completely that not as much as a foundation stone remained, it was still the excuse for the parliamentary borough of Little Grimditch whose four remaining voters, all of them sheep farmers, had sent Mr. Cythian Fordyce to the House of Commons for so many terms.

George Grace studied the horizon in that direction for some minutes and when he returned to the house there was a light in his eyes which had been long absent. He held his head high, and his feet seemed to tread a fleecy bank of clouds.

"Uncle Sheppard got away without seeing me again," protested Mrs. Grace when they met at the path leading to the rose garden. "I so wanted to see him. Something *must* be done about the bathtub. What is the sense of having one when the water must be carried from the river, heated in the kitchen and then carried to the tub which is on the opposite side of the house?"

"My dear," said Grace, paying no attention to her complaint, "if that girl has any free time today, I would appreciate it if you would have her clean up the library. I want her to dry my brushes and pack them away with the paints somewhere. Then I want her to find a dry place to store the pictures I've done."

Mrs. Grace found it hard to believe her ears. "Georgie!" she exclaimed. "Do you intend to give up your painting?"

"For a while now. I won't have any time for it, my dear. And to be frank with you, I'm a little out of conceit at the moment with this sort of thing. I am going to make a confession. I discovered as soon as I took a brush in my hand that I had little gift for drawing. I think I have a good color sense and an instinct perhaps for composition, and so I did not regard my lack of skill in draftsmanship as necessarily fatal. Still it drove me, I suspect, to the kind of thing I've been doing.

"Well," he went on, "enough of that. I'm going to devote myself to politics in future. I'm going into the House. Your uncle has decided to put me in for Little Grimditch."

"Oh, Georgie! That's wonderful." Mrs. Grace gave her hands an excited wave in the air and there was a trace of color for once in her plain face. "I'm so happy! I know you'll be a great success in the House. I'm sure you speak better than any of the men in the Cabinet. It's a good thing Mr. Pitt isn't alive or you'd even floor him. And there will be money as well? Will there, truly? I mean will it bring us an income?"

"Your uncle says it will. There are ways of making money, it seems. Prerogatives, you know. Fees and so forth. Your uncle says you can pick up the blunt—his own word for it—with both hands. But, my dear, it's not the money which attracts me. It's something quite different." He had been striding ahead of his wife but at this point he turned and faced her. He continued in low, tense tones. "It's power. The power every member has; to ask questions in the House, to call attention to things, to have committees of inquiry appointed. My dear, I am going to devote myself in the House to hounding a certain man right out of public life. Samuel Carboy thinks he's through with me. Ha, I'm just beginning. He's going to find out how tough and disagreeable I can be when I'm roused to a fighting pitch!"

Mrs. Grace's face had gone pale with excitement. "Do you really mean, George, that you'll attack him in the House?"

"That's exactly what I mean. I'm going to give him no peace. The first question I'll ask will be how much he and that turncoat friend of his, that fellow Gardiner, are getting out of the Tontine funds. I'll ask if there is any need now for the trusteeship—or whatever they call it, I'm never sure of such things—to be continued. And that will be no more than a start. I'm going to ask questions about all this buying up of businesses, this combining of factories, this merging of shipping lines. I'm going to question the advisability of this method of creating large concerns on the ashes of small industry."

He was talking as though he were already on the floor of the House and had the pillorying of Samuel Carboy well in hand. Raising both clenched fists in the air, he made a vow. "I'll never leave him alone. I'll attack him. I'll let the country see what he's trying to do. I'll drive him out of business. I swear to devote myself to one thing from this moment forward, the complete undoing of this upstart who is building a fortune out of what he stole from me!"

"Yes, Georgie, yes!" cried Mrs. Grace. "Show him no more mercy than he showed you."

A red wagon turned in from the road and came at a spanking gait up the drive. They could read the words *Haste, Post, Haste* in large letters on one side.

"Good day, ma'am and sir," said the driver, pulling up beside the couple. "There's quite a little mail for you this fine morning."

Mrs. Grace in a preoccupied manner took the sheaf of letters he held out. She was looking curiously at the mailman himself. "You're new, aren't you?" she asked.

"Yes, ma'am. My first day. Name's Groody, ma'am."

"Your name is familiar, Groody."

"Perhaps it's because my daughter runs the shop at Little Shallow. She's had a sign painted six feet long, H. GROODY. You've been seeing it maybe, ma'am."

"Yes, that's it. I've seen the sign. Your daughter, Groody, is making a very good shop out of it."

"It's as smart as a fox with two heads that my daughter is, ma'am. Begging your pardon, of course, if I seem too boastful."

Mrs. Grace was ready to begin on a long interrogation. "You were employed once by Mr. Carboy, I believe," she said.

"Yes, ma'am." Daniel Groody was turning the mail wagon on the narrow drive and found it necessary to keep his eyes on what he was doing. "Good morning, ma'am and sir. It's a pleasure it will be to serve you."

"His opinion of Sam Carboy would be worth having, I think," declared Grace, watching the swiftly receding wagon. "Someday I'll stop him and ask a few questions."

He was interrupted by a wild shriek from his wife. Ordinarily the most staid of women, she seemed at this moment to have gone slightly insane. She waved her arms above her head and even indulged in a dancing motion with her feet. She was crying in a high-pitched voice: "Georgie! Oh, Georgie! I'm so happy I want to scream."

"My dear," expostulated Grace. "Have you taken leave of your senses? Suppose anyone should see you."

The house was in such a secluded position that they were not likely to be seen by anyone except the great White Horse up on his hillside; and it was doubtful if this little domestic tableau would hold any interest for him after his long centuries of guardianship over the wide Vale.

Then he saw that his wife was clutching a letter in one of her hands. "Is there news?" he asked with an immediate increase of interest.

"Yes, George!" she exclaimed. "It's from Julian. It's from our son. A letter —in his own dear handwriting! Oh, George, he's alive after all. He's alive, do you hear me? I've been fairly sick with worry for months, ever since all the fighting took place and we had no word from him. I never expected to see him again."

She drew out a handkerchief and wiped her eyes. "My darling son, my own Julian! I was going mad with fear."

"I confess that I felt the same way, my dear. I never said anything because I didn't want to disturb you."

She looked at the postmark and then emitted an ecstatic squeak. "He's in London! Do you hear that, Georgie? He's back. He's safe. The dreadful sea can't get him now that he's on dry land. Oh, how wonderful, how wonderful!"

She had dropped the other letters in her excitement and they were scattered on the grass about her. Her husband, knowing that she would proceed with the reading of the letter and convey the news it contained in her own way, stooped and proceeded to retrieve the mail.

"He's well, George. He says so in the very first sentence. How thoughtful of him. To know how anxious I would be about him." She was tearing through the letter at breakneck speed, her eyes darting from page to page. Her hands were trembling so much that it was hard for her to read the words. "He fought under Cochrane all through the campaigns. He must have been very brave, George, because he was given land. A whole ranch, George, as long as from here to Oxford. He sold the land before he left the country and he's got the money with him. How wonderful it is. It passes all belief."

There was a long pause as she slowly read one of the pages and then turned back to read it again. When she looked up, her manner had become more composed. "The government, George Grace, is going to honor our son too. He had an appointment yesterday at the Admiralty and so had to stay over in London. He hopes something is going to be opened for him at the Admiralty. Oh, what good news it all is!" She stopped suddenly and then emitted a delighted screech which topped all her previous efforts. "He's arriving tomorrow. He'll be on the Wantage coach."

George Grace shoved the other mail carelessly into a pocket and held out a hand for the important one. "May a mere father now have the privilege of reading what his son has to say?" he asked. His wife handed the letter over with reluctance. "You must be quick about it, George. I've only skimmed it so far. I want to linger over every word."

"There will be no time for lingering over anything today, my dear," said Grace, not raising his eyes from the handwritten pages. "We must give our hero son a royal welcome. A roast of beef, no less. I'll go to the cellar in a minute and select the wine. Should we invite anyone to join us?"

"No, no. Not the first night. I want the dear boy all to myself."

"That girl will have to get to work in real earnest. The place must shine."

"Would you have time," suggested Mrs. Grace with some hesitation, "to rub down the walls in the dining room? I was telling Uncle Sheppard how damp they were but he paid no attention. It will need a strong pair of hands."

"I was never noted for the strength of my hands, my dear. In any event I won't have the time. I have many things to do."

CHAPTER TEN

1

The coach for the west, by way of Wantage, was due to leave at 5 A.M. and Julian Grace rubbed his eyes as he waited in a corner of the cobbled yard at the Bell Savage. He had spent a long evening with some navy friends and it had taken all the will power he could summon to get himself out of bed in time. He was in uniform and looked handsome even when he yawned.

The luggage had been packed away and the driver was standing by the front wheel, and cracking a whip impatiently, when the booking clerk appeared in the door of the waiting room with a sheet of paper in his hands.

"Ye can't go yet, Jemmy," called the clerk. "Them two inside ladies ain't arrived."

"Inside ladies nor outside gem'mum don't count with me, Booking," declared the driver in a loud voice. "I leaves in two minutes and I hopes they ain't arrived when the two minutes is up. They're all blasted nuisances, these inside ladies, and if I had my way, Booking, they'd be muzzled and handcuffed afore being allowed on."

The crisis thus forecast was avoided fortunately by the arrival, within the two minutes stipulated, of a cab with a feminine head peering anxiously out of the window on each side.

"It's them, Jemmy!" called the booking clerk, sounding very much relieved. "They'll be having lots of bags, Guard, so you'd best get busy with them at once."

Deprived of the chance to stand up for his rights, the driver mounted to his seat and tucked a cover over his knees. "Just like the perverse creatures," he muttered. "Two seconds to spare. And so I can't drive off and leave 'em flat."

The booking clerk hurried over to the cab and offered an obsequious arm to the middle-aged lady who was struggling to get out on one side. "We held 'er for you, ma'am," he said, expecting thanks and handsome capping all around.

The lady gave him an icy stare. "It's a good thing for you that you did," she declared. "I'm Mrs. Samuel Carboy and I expect coaches to wait for me."

The driver said in discreet tones to the upper Benjamin: "Hell-fire and heeltaps, Benjie, it's Mrs. Carboy herself! I thought it was only a duchess." Then, for the information of the other, he added in a whisper: "Sam Carboy owns this line. Bought it in a week ago. Whew, that was a narrer one!"

The mention of the name Carboy brought Julian Grace to a dead stop as he was preparing to mount to the top on the other side of the coach. He paused with one foot on the step and saw that the second of the late arrivals was none other than the divinity whose lovely face had never faded from his mind during the whole of the two long years he had spent in the Americas. Isabelle was wearing a sheath dress of gray muslin with a blue velvet tunic reaching almost to her knees. Her hat was high and gay with ostrich feathers fluttering in the breeze, and her gloves and shoes were trim and fashionable. She looked more beautiful than ever.

Young Grace watched her from his secluded position on the opposite side of the coach, his face flushed, his eyes sparkling with excitement, his heart thumping as it had never done when Spanish bullets had rained about him.

Isabelle was not in a very good mood. She was still sleepy and rather more than a little sulky as a result. But it must be acknowledged that petulance seemed to become her. The knuckles she raised to mask her yawns were white and dainty and so there was no reason to complain because her lips could not be seen. Her nose and her arched eyebrows more than made up for this, without any mention of her eyes, which were so warm and lovely that the young sailor felt his knees go weak and had to support himself against the side of the coach.

"She's going to travel with me!" he breathed to himself ecstatically. "Of all the dozens she could have taken, she has chosen this coach. It's a sign. It means the gods are with me. They're going to give me my chance after all."

He waited until the two ladies had entered before undertaking to climb to his seat on top. As he ascended he touched the body of the coach with a reverent hand because of what it now contained.

Because of the early hour of their departure, and the pace at which the driver set the six horses, it was chilly work sitting on top. Feeling the need for a stimulant, Julian Grace got down at the first stop and entered the inn. The brandy served him was raw and he had difficulty in swallowing more than a few mouthfuls. The result was that he had to run when the guard signaled departure by tooting on his horn "Oh, Nanny, Will Ye Gang wi' Me?" He scrambled up the steps in such a hurry that he had resumed his seat before becoming aware that there had been a change in the arrangements during his absence. The fat bagman, who had been beside him on the first lap of the journey, had moved forward, and he now had as his partner a slender vision in blue and gray with ostrich plumes which bobbed at every movement of the coach.

"Good morning, Julian," said Isabelle.

"Isabelle!" he ejaculated. "What great luck is this? Are you going to Wantage?"

She nodded her head and, because they were sitting so close (shoulder to shoulder, in fact), he shivered with delight as the ends of the ostrich plumes touched his ears. "*Wasn't* it lucky that I began to get a headache inside and persuaded Mama to let me come up here? She wouldn't have allowed it if she had known the pleasant surprise I was going to have."

"Do you really think it pleasant?"

"Julian! Of course." She turned and smiled at him, and the radiance of the smile caused him to catch his breath. "I might as well confess that I saw you as I was getting in. Fortunately I had enough presence of mind to call Mama's attention to something else and so she didn't get a glimpse of you. You'll have to fairly fly down when we reach Wantage. If she sees you, I will be in a pretty fix. You've no idea how hard Mama can be."

They had arrived at a hill and the horses had to tug and strain to drag the heavily loaded coach to the top. The ascent was so steep, in fact, that the top passengers had to clutch the sides and backs of the seats to avoid falling over backward. Isabelle had one arm of the seat to rely upon but she further assured her safety by slipping her other hand under Julian's arm.

"Oh-h-h! This hill always frightens me," she said, her fingers tightening their grip. "I'm frightened even when I'm inside. It's really quite terrifying out here, isn't it?"

The hill might be steep but it was not high and, to Julian's intense regret, the coach soon passed over the crest and went bowling along as easily and rapidly as before. Isabelle sighed and removed her hand from its anchorage under his arm.

"And now," said Isabelle, whose color was most becomingly high because of the exposure to the wind, "you must tell me everything. You'll soon find out, Julian, that your papa and mama, and mine, are just as angry at each other as ever. I won't be allowed to see you. That's why I took that most convenient headache. I knew this was our only chance." She paused and frowned as a thought occurred to her. "It's really very funny that Mama believed my story. I've never had a headache in my life. She must have had something else on her mind. Oh yes, I know what it was. She had a letter from Allie before we started for London. She must have been thinking about it because she seemed very worried. She just nodded when I said I would have to take a seat here." She added, glancing up at him quickly and then turning her eyes away, "This will be the last time I'll ever see you, Julian."

Julian was beginning to regain his self-possession. "Oh no," he declared. "You're going to see a great deal of me. I'll attend to that. I've got all manner of schemes in my head for seeing you without our parents hearing of it."

"Just the same, we had better take advantage of this chance. I want to hear all about your adventures in South America. Mama and I were at a tea yesterday and there was some talk about you. One lady said she heard you were a hero and that you behaved so well under Lord Cochrane that the government was going to reward you. Mama sniffed but I listened to every word with, oh, such great interest. Is it true, Julian? Were you a very great hero?"

Julian dismissed this with a laugh. "Cochrane was the hero. He's the greatest man in the whole world, I think. All I did was obey orders. I was in some pretty brisk scraps."

"Go on! Go on! That's what I want to hear about."

So, as the horses strained up the hills and galloped furiously down them, and the other passengers grunted and dozed and talked in monosyllables and indulged in lunches out of paper packages, Julian Grace told Isabelle Carboy of the adventures in which he had participated. The most exciting part of his narrative had to do with the capture of the forts defending Valdivia. Julian had commanded one of the parties which had gone ashore in the darkness one night.

"We surprised them," he told his companion, his enthusiasm growing as his memory went back. "We captured the forts in turn and that gave us command of the city. We drove the garrison up into the hills. It was fast work and we only lost seven men." He stopped suddenly when he reached this point. "One of those killed was my friend. His name was Cymric Forster and we were together at Jamaica while waiting for the ship to take us around the Horn." His eyes filled with tears and he spoke in a whisper. "He was a wonderful fellow. One of the bravest men that ever lived. Always the first into action and cheering the rest of us on. One of the Spanish garrison fired his gun at random as he was turning to run away and the bullet hit poor

Cymric between the eyes. He must have been killed instantly." There was a long pause while he winked back the tears and sought to get firmer control of his voice. "He was the best friend I ever had. No one ever had one like him. When I saw his body stretched out on the wet stone floor of the fort, I sat down and cried. I was wishing I had been killed with him, so we could have started out on the last adventure together."

"Cymric Forster?" Isabelle's brow was knitted in thought. "I've heard that name. I think he must have been related to one of the girls at school."

"That seems unlikely. The only relative he ever mentioned to me was an uncle who was his guardian, an old curmudgeon." Julian sighed deeply. "I had to go on, of course, as though nothing had happened. I took a hand in the capture of the *Esmeralda*, the Spanish flagship, and I was present at the capitulation of Lima. That ended the war or at least it assured freedom to the colonies."

Isabelle had been listening intently. Her first question was one that Samuel Carboy himself might have asked. "Did you get your share of the rewards?"

Julian nodded. "There was a large sum of money voted to us and I was to have an officer's share. But it was never paid. They gave us land also. Fortunately for me, I sold my land to a member of the Junta who paid me in gold. It wasn't much but the Junta revoked the grants soon after. The man who bought my land had found some means of holding onto it. Cochrane got nothing for himself and he even had to fight to get the men their arrears of pay. I was one of the few who came home with any money."

"How much?" asked the practical-minded Isabelle.

"Four hundred pounds. My passage home was paid so I had most of the money jingling in my pocket when I stepped ashore at London." He stopped at this point and his face resumed the gravity it had worn when he spoke of his dead friend. "I intended to stop in Jamaica on the way home but the only ship I could get was not making any stops. So I couldn't tell the Ballards about poor Cymric. I wrote instead."

"Who are the Ballards?"

"Timothy Ballard is one of the wealthiest planters on the island. We were his guests while we waited for a ship to take us south. Poor Cymric and Constance Ballard fell in love with each other and they were going to be married."

"She was a great heiress?"

"Yes. There are just two daughters, so they're certain to inherit large fortunes. Constance was a sweet and beautiful girl and I'm afraid she'll be heartbroken."

"You said there were two sisters. Did the other one fall in love with you?"

Julian smiled. "Winifred was only about eleven. I think she'll be quite a beauty when she grows up."

Isabelle knitted her brows again. "But why did the older sister fall in love with your friend and not with you? Was she a little blind?"

"Haven't I said that Cymric was the most wonderful fellow in the world?

He was handsome and gay and amusing. It was the most natural thing in the world for Constance to love him. Besides"—his eyes now looked straight ahead of him and his color had become high—"I wasn't interested. I was in love with someone at home."

"Why, Julian, you surprise me! I thought you never took a romantic interest in any girl."

His courage came back at this point. He turned and looked straight at the face so close to his shoulder. "I think you know, Isabelle. I think you've always known that—I am in love with *you*."

Isabelle looked down. "Yes, that's true," she said. "I've always known that you liked me better than any other girl. And I've always been very glad."

There was silence between them for several moments. The coach went through a small town with a flourish of the trumpet in the hands of the guard. Small boys ran after them, screaming like mad. An old countryman in a smock and a market cart had to haul his horse in to the side of the road, and he shook his fist after them and expressed his opinion in toothless annoyance.

Julian began to speak in a matter-of-fact tone. "I went to the Admiralty yesterday by appointment. They have a post for me. Not an important one but there's a chance to advance and there's quite a decent salary. I'm to take a month's holidays and then report for duty."

"Will you be sent off to sea?"

He shook his head. "It's a staff appointment. In the event of war, I would be assigned to a ship but there's a feeling of gloom at the Admiralty on that point. They think there will never be another war now that Boney is beaten; and they're very unhappy about it. Of course, a staff post has one advantage. A man can marry and settle down."

"But," commented the girl in equally casual tones, "you won't think of that for years and years."

There was no longer any hint of hesitation or timidity in his eyes when he turned toward her at this point.

"I'm thinking of it *now!*" he declared. "Don't you realize, Isabelle, how much I love you? I—I—if I thought there was no chance for me, I swear I would get a pistol and blow my brains out!" The ears of the corpulent bagman sitting in front of them twitched and he turned to look at them over his shoulder. Julian waited until he resumed his former position and then continued in a lower voice. "And, Isabelle, I can support a wife. I have this post at the Admiralty, I have money in my pocket, I have the very best connections. I expect to be an admiral someday. Oh, I know I'm not a great catch——"

"But, Julian, my dear," whispered Isabelle, "I've always said I would never marry anyone under a duke."

The young officer, taken down considerably by this frank admission, gave a rueful laugh. "Well, I don't think I can quite achieve that. It's impossible to get to be a duke nowadays. Oh, I know that Wellington did; but I'm not a Wellington exactly, and I'd need a great war and a lot of luck even if I

were. But I think I'll get to be a knight, at least. Lady Grace. That wouldn't
be bad, would it?"

Isabelle slipped her hand under his arm again. He promptly interlocked
their fingers and gave hers an ardent pressure.

"Now, Julian," she began, "you mustn't think I'm calculating or merce-
nary. I like you *very, very* much. I think I like you better than anyone else
in the world. But Papa and Mama would never give their consent and your
parents would be just as much against it. We know that. I—I am very much
afraid, dear Julian, that this is nothing but a lovely dream."

"But we can marry without their consent," protested the young officer.
"People do it all the time."

"Do you mean—*elope?*"

Julian reached an arm behind her shoulders with the intention of drawing
her into his arms. The bagman was staring straight ahead. They were occupying the back seat and no one could see them but the rustics who stood
by the side of the road and cheered the coach on.

"Yes, that's what I mean. Elope! Thousands and thousands of couples
have run away. Why can't we?"

"But," she protested, wriggling clear of his arm, "they would bring us
back. You know Papa has a coach built like the one Napoleon used, and he
can travel like the wind. He and Mama would be on our heels at once."

"Have you ever heard of Gretna Green?"

"Do you mean," she asked, her eyes round with excitement, "that you
would take me there?"

"Yes, my darling, that is what I mean. There's no use speaking to our
parents because we know in advance what they'll say. We'll just be very
cautious and give them no reason to suspect. In the meantime I'll make all
the arrangements. At the appointed time I'll meet you with a coach and a
driver *and* a chaperone—I have an aunt who will go with us, she's a very
sweet old lady and she will love you—and off we'll set for Gretna Green."

There was a long silence following this declaration. Then Isabelle began
to speak. "You mustn't try to rush me into saying yes. You're being most
terribly impulsive. You have a month's holidays and we can see each other
often, I think—and then we can see how we feel at the end of that time. I
think it's sensible to allow ourselves that much time to make up our minds.
Don't you?"

"No! I don't need the millionth part of a second to make up my mind. It's
made up already. It has always been made up, from the first time I saw
you when you were a little girl—the most beautiful little girl in the whole
world. I don't want to wait a day more than is necessary to make the arrangements. After all, my sweet one, I must have you as my wife when I
settle down in London at my new post." He paused and then said in a
recklessly loud voice, "Don't you know how maddeningly lovely and desirable
you are?"

"Oh, Julian, you are so rash!" sighed the girl. "And I *do* like you so much!"

2

Julian reined in his horse and put out a hand to help Isabelle. This was in no sense necessary; she was a splendid horsewoman and perfectly capable of handling the liveliest of mounts but he was filled with a desire to be of aid to her. They had turned up a familiar road, one which ran from the main highway and went on up into the hills through a rather thick cover of trees. It was a little-frequented path and they chose it for that reason.

"This is our third meeting," he said. "Three meetings in ten days. It seems very little!"

"Yes, Julian. But I must keep at my golf in the mornings and when Papa's home he likes to bowl on the green in the afternoons. It's hard to find time for other things."

"Do you read much?"

"Books! Lor, Julian, no! I can't be bothered with them."

He smiled at her as though she had said something wise and fine, being at the stage where even her faults delighted him. "But, darling, it's time to get something decided. If we are going to run away and get married in time for me to reach London to report for duty—well, we must make our plans at once." He paused and reached out to touch her hand. "You get more lovely all the time."

This was true. Her meeting with Julian and her surrender, partial at least, to the normal emotions and desires and longings of youth had given her an expression of happiness which she had never worn before and which unmistakably added to her natural beauty.

"I see I must tell you everything," she said with a sigh. "Before you came back and we met on the Oxford coach—perhaps it would have been better if we hadn't!"

"I have decided opinions on that subject," declared Julian.

"Well, before I was foolish enough to deceive poor Mama in that way, a man had proposed to me. I didn't refuse him. I said I must have time to think about it. I haven't seen him since but very soon now he'll be expecting his answer. He must have an answer before I can seriously consider anyone else. Even you, Julian."

"Is he a duke?" belligerently.

Isabelle shook her head. "No, he's not a duke. But he *does* have a title."

"I suppose he's a silly viscount or a stuck-up baronet. I can see him without any hints from you. He's a whiskered dandy, a spindle-shanked old beau. He's over sixty, I'm sure. He's a widower, with a whole brood of stuck-up and venomous children. Perhaps he even has grandchildren."

"I won't speak to you again if you make such unkind remarks!" cried Isabelle. "He is *not* old. Of course, he's a lot older than I am, and he was married once before. But he has no children and it's really silly of you, Julian Grace, to speak of grandchildren under the circumstances. He's a very handsome man. He's wealthy, of course, and he stands high at court. No one could ask for a more eligible and agreeable husband."

"He's fifty, if he's a day."

"He is *not* fifty."

"Then he's in his late forties. He's got rheumatism, I'm sure. And he sniffles."

"He does *not* sniffle, Julian Grace! He's a charming man and he's very much in love with me. What more could I ask?"

Their horses were moving slowly up the steep road, nuzzling at each other and enjoying this unwonted ease. Straight ahead of them they could see a small house set back a little distance from the road, from which came a sound of barking dogs. They had ridden this way on several occasions but had been too concerned with each other to pay any attention to such an insignificant place.

"What more can you ask? You can ask for romance, for youth, for happiness! What happiness can you hope to have with an old fellow like that? It's always a mistake, Isabelle. Especially for a girl who can have any man she wants in the whole country."

"I like him—very, very much."

They lapsed into silence at that, a somewhat sulky silence as far as Julian was concerned. It lasted until they came abreast of the house. The stillness was punctuated then by the loud barking which had been heard farther down the road. The sound now took on the proportions of a canine pandemonium. Dogs came racing down the road from the house, the yard and from the adjoining woods. They were of all breeds and sizes. But they seemed friendly.

"This must be the place," said Isabelle, bringing her horse to a halt. "Dear me, what a lot of them! Papa knows the man who lives here. He used to be a clerk on the floor of the Stock Exchange and Papa did him a good turn. He told him to buy a certain stock and it went up and up and up, and the poor little man made so much money that he was able to retire. He brought all the dogs with him."

The dogs were cruising about them at top speed, jumping up at the horses and barking to attract attention, all in complete amiability. The door of the house opened and a voice of command reached them. "Down, old fellows, down! Is this any way to behave? Down, I say."

The barking ceased at once. The dogs stopped their antics and stood about quietly while the owner of the voice came to the road through a well-tended garden. He proved to be a man of somewhat advanced years who walked with his head at a stiff angle. He bowed to them and smiled.

"I must apologize for my friends," he said. "They don't see much company and it excites them when they do."

"Are all these your dogs?" asked Julian in astonishment.

"All of them," proudly. "You can see they are of many kinds but they have one thing in common. They were all strays. I can't bear to see a dog or a cat without a home; and my brother, who lives with me and shares the responsibility, feels the same way."

"How many have you?"

"Well, young sir, I haven't counted lately. We expected to have fewer when we moved out to the country but it has worked the other way. We have more than ever. There are plenty you haven't seen in the house and barn. And, of course, we have cats, and a rabbit who was wounded and can't run, and an opossum and a family of young owls in the barn."

Julian frowned with a degree of disbelief. "But do they live together in peace? Can you keep the dogs from worrying and killing the other animals? It seems impossible to me."

The man smiled. "They are all friends," he declared. "I assure you we never have trouble with them. They quarrel a little over food, of course. Even a dog, who will lay down his life for his master, is not at all generous about his bones and the meat in his own particular platter."

"My father," said Isabelle, "is Mr. Samuel Carboy. He knows you. I think you must be Mr. Beck."

"Mr. Carboy!" exclaimed the man. "He is my benefactor. I will never be able to thank him enough for what he did for me. He is, my pretty child, the patron saint of this establishment. We remember him always in our prayers, my brother and I, and we have taught all these fine old fellows to sit up and bark once, by way of a salute, whenever they hear the name mentioned. Just watch if you please."

He held up a hand to attract the attention of the canine train and then said in a distinct voice: "Carboy! Carboy!"

The dogs responded exactly as he had indicated. They assumed sitting positions and, raising their heads in the air, gave a single bark in unison as a salute to the bringer of prosperity and the father of security.

"Yes, miss," he said, smiling with gratification, "that's what training can do. Will you and the young gentleman come in and see our rather unusual establishment?"

Both thought it would be interesting to observe a household of this curious nature at close range. Julian tethered their horses to the fence and they followed Beck inside. The front door admitted them into a good-sized room which contained, as their host had said, many other dogs. There were stalls along all the walls, each containing a mattress and a plate with its owner's name on it. There was also a round-faced little man hanging over the fireplace where the kettle was beginning to hum. The latter took one look at the visitors and scuttled from the room.

"That's my brother," said Mr. Beck. "He's very quiet and doesn't like company. He always runs away."

The dogs had followed them inside and had joined forces with the rest of the pets. A pair of pointed ears showed above the rim of a basket on a side table, a proof that cats when in the company of dogs, even the most friendly ones, prefer high places. Several bird cages were suspended from the ceiling and a snuffling sound coming from under the only couch in the room could probably be attributed to the opossum.

Isabelle was looking the canine company over with lively curiosity. "Which one is Bouncer?" she asked. "I mean the one who was with you the day when Papa gave you the information about that stock?"

Beck walked over to a chair in one corner which was occupied by a dog of melancholy expression and advanced years.

"Here is the poor old chap," he said. "He hasn't much longer to go and he knows it. I don't think he minds so much, Miss Carboy. Do you, old fellow?"

The dog slowly raised a paw and extended it to his master. The latter took it in his hand and gave it a solemn shake. "I'm glad he did that. It means he forgives me everything. You see, miss, it came out a short time ago that he had been a show dog once. I found a bow of blue ribbon and poor old Bouncer—we called him Boney once—pounced on it as though it belonged to him. He took it right over to his bed and I really believe he was thinking it ought to be tacked up above him. Oh, he had been accustomed to that sort of thing. He was very proud of it. But some of the younger dogs, who didn't like being lorded over, stole it from him and tore it into shreds. Well, he'll be passing along soon. I think he expects to regain his former station in the paradise that old dogs go to. You believe there's such a place, don't you, Miss Carboy?"

Isabelle hesitated. She had never given the possibility any thought and she was not at all sure she believed. Julian had no such doubts.

"I believe it," he said. "I'm sure there's a paradise for horses."

Mr. Beck then poured tea for them and produced from an oven at the side of the fireplace a tray of buns. At least they looked like buns; but when Isabelle, who had always been a rather greedy eater, bit into the first one she emitted a shriek of delight.

"They're wonderful!" she cried. "Why, they're not bread. They are made of crust, and they're crumbly and filled with the most divine minced meat!"

"My brother makes them," explained Beck. "He was a cook, you know. Ah, how well we live on the little dishes he concocts!"

The smell of the hot food caused a restiveness among the canine occupants of the room, leading in no time at all to concerted begging and the emission of sharp barks of entreaty. The master of the household took a pipe from his pocket and elevated it in one hand. The shuffling and the noise ended at once. Every dog in the room stood still and watched him.

"It's my way of letting them know I'm displeased," he explained. "It wouldn't be nearly as effective if I got out a whip and lashed at them. When I raise my pipe they know there will be trouble if they don't watch out. They quiet down at once."

He proceeded then to tell his guests of the eventful day when Samuel Carboy had persuaded him to buy Highcastle Ltd., and of the exciting hours during which the stock had climbed and climbed. "I still have it," he said with an air of pride at the finish. "It brings in a fine income. Enough for my brother and me, and all our poor old friends, to live on. I'll never sell it—unless, of course, Mr. Carboy should come here and say, 'Mr. Beck, the flush days are over and it's time to get rid of those shares.' Ah, what a great man your father is, young lady!"

As they rode back in the first approach of dusk Julian realized that it was for him a case of Now or Never. He would not win her if he allowed this moment to slip by. Keeping his horse down to a walk, he leaned over and took one of her hands in his. She was wearing gloves with high cuffs and a beaded fringe.

"Darling Isabelle," he said, "we have only another hundred yards to go. Then we come out into the open again; and you will turn one way and I'll turn in a different direction. It can't go on that way, you know. If I leave you now without a final effort, you'll marry that doddering old beau with his money and his title." He reached out suddenly and gathered her into his arms. "Darling, throw away your doubts!"

"It's easy for you to say that," protested Isabelle in a muffled voice. "But it's hard for me to—to make my choice."

"This isn't an easy situation for either of us." He decided then that the time for words had passed. He kissed her fervently, then with great gentleness. He kissed her so often that they lost count, if either of them had any thought of counting, which may be designated as extremely unlikely.

Isabelle did not attempt to turn her face away or to free herself. After a moment she raised an arm and placed it around his neck.

"I've won!" thought Julian exultantly.

"Oh, Julian, I *do* love you," she breathed. "It's very wrong. It's very foolish. I shouldn't love you. But I do!"

CHAPTER ELEVEN

1

Samuel Carboy had always openly professed his contempt for Napoleon Bonaparte but secretly, of course, he had admired him and had realized the scope of the Corsican's genius. He had conceived a great admiration, for instance, for the famous coach which the emperor of the French had designed for himself so that he could travel rapidly over the continent he had come so close to conquering. The new titan of British industry had to do a great deal of traveling also—from factory to factory, from branch bank to branch bank, from one end of England to the other—and he decided that in this respect he could borrow a leaf from the voluminous Napoleonic book.

Accordingly he had a carriage built for himself along the lines of the French demi-calèche. The body rested on four wheels, the rear ones being twice as high as the front, and it was slung on an elaborate system of springs which made it ride easily. Every inch of space inside had been utilized.

There was a bed which folded back under the seat when not in use and a desk lid which could be used for writing, complete with all necessary supplies. There were, of course, an infinity of small drawers and pigeonholes in the oddest places as well as the most obvious, so that all reports and memoranda could be kept close at hand. A cupboard, neatly fitted in with the rest, held a supply of food. A lantern hanging from the ceiling provided light.

In a similar carriage, drawn by six horses, Bonaparte had dashed at mad speed over the face of Europe. Sometimes he had a secretary with him, sometimes his great chief of staff, Marshal Berthier. The latter would ride on the same seat and take down notes on the plans which poured from that ingenious and machiavellian mind like a boiling cascade. The emperor dictated all through the hours of darkness, while the carriage swayed and rocked over steep roads in the hills and dangerous descents into the valleys, and Europe slept uneasily in expectation of the dread plans he was concocting. As soon as he was through with a report, he tore it into small pieces and consigned it to the darkness of the road behind him.

Samuel Carboy felt justified in providing himself with a copy of this famous coach. He did not believe in ruling his rapidly growing empire from an office in London. He wanted to see everything with his own eyes, to meet the men who were supposed to follow out his orders, to make sure that they did so in accordance with his explicit directions. He had to be continuously on the road, particularly in the central and northern counties where the industrial development was most marked. He did not, however, model himself in any other respect on the great Corsican in the use of his coach. He never tore up a report. As soon as he was through with it, he filed it carefully away. He contented himself, moreover, with four horses and so never equaled Napoleon's eaglelike flittings. Napoleon, it may be interesting to note, rode on one occasion from Dresden to Paris in five days.

On the evening of the third day after the visit paid by his daughter and her escort to the house of the brothers Beck, Samuel Carboy returned in his coach from an extended tour of the west. He had expended his energy in a most prodigal way and so his first glimpse of the lights of Beaulaw Hall caused him to feel a glow of content.

"Ah, how I'll enjoy the luxury of sleeping again in my own bed," he said to himself. "Perhaps I'll be able to allow myself a few days' rest."

A smile of satisfaction settled on his face, partly due to his anticipation of a short spell of ease, partly due to the successes he had scored on the tour which was now coming to an end.

2

Mrs. Carboy received her lord and master in the hall. It was quite lofty, extending the full height of three stories, with a massive arching stairway. An oriel window on the first landing gave plenty of light in the daytime but at night reliance had to be placed in a chandelier which hung high above the entrance. The hall was in partial darkness, therefore, when Samuel Carboy came in and he did not detect the worried look on his wife's face as she greeted him.

"Back again, m'dear," he said cheerfully. "Good results. They were hustling all along the line. Next time I'll give 'em a surprise visit and perhaps I'll catch 'em unprepared."

"I'm glad you're back for dinner, Samuel," said his wife. "I have such a good dinner. And Sir Theobald's here. He wants to see you at once." The tone of her voice in saying this caused him to stare at her sharply. "I don't know what it is he wants because he hasn't told me anything; but he seems disturbed. I tried to talk to him in the library but he kept pacing up and down and I don't believe he heard a word I was saying."

"I'll go in at once and see what's wrong with him."

"Be quick about it," cautioned Mrs. Carboy. "We don't want the dinner spoiled. There's sole and a prime roast of beef. And such a berry flawn!"

The baronet was standing in one of the window embrasures when Carboy entered the library. He came forward with a reluctance which the latter did not fail to note.

"Sam," he said, "I've something to tell you and—damme, I'm sorry I must do it."

Carboy's first thought was that some one of their many schemes had fallen through or that an unforeseen loss had been sustained. He looked at his partner with immediate concern and said: "Out with it, Sir Theobald. I guess it's not so bad that I can't take it in my stride."

"You won't like it," warned the baronet. "It has to do with your title. Everything was going well. There has been some opposition but I had every assurance that you would be on the list. Yesterday I was summoned to Downing Street." He shook his head and frowned down at the floor. Then he burst out: "Sam, it's a damned shame! I can't tell you how badly I feel."

A quarter of an hour later, with the butler hovering in the background and giving his throat a preparatory cough, Sir Theobald came out. "Ma'am," he said, "your husband desires a word with you."

Mrs. Carboy looked at him apprehensively. "I know something is wrong. Is it very serious?"

"Serious enough, ma'am. He prefers to tell you himself."

Carboy was pacing up and down the room when his wife entered the library. She knew he was in a towering rage because he kicked the rug in front of the fireplace every time he reached it. His hands were under his coattails and he was holding his head down.

"That son of yours," he said in a grating voice, "has become involved in a pretty mess."

Mrs. Carboy caught her breath. "Oh, Sam! Has anything serious happened to him? I think I'll die if he's hurt or ill."

"Your son is not hurt and he's not ill. I am the one who must pay for his folly. I am the one who is being hurt."

The mother of the absent Alfred dropped into a chair, her weight making it groan and creak. She put her hands over her eyes and began to weep.

"Is there a woman in it? Oh, Allie, Allie, what have you done to make your poor mother suffer this way?"

"There's a woman in it!" affirmed her husband grimly.

"Is it going to cost you much money to settle?"

"Money be damned!" ejaculated Carboy. He reached the rug in the course of his pacing and kicked it viciously. "I'm not getting the knighthood. Because of the scandal that boy has got himself involved in, the prime minister says he can't nominate me."

"But—but, Sam, what is it that my poor Allie has done?"

He paused in his pacing and stared at her with eyes which suggested that he himself found it hard to believe what he was going to tell. "He got himself mixed up in a Napoleonic plot in America. Do you understand the full infamy of what I've just told you? My son has done this to me! I, who backed Pitt through his whole career, who always stood against any peace with the Bonaparte usurper, who risked my fortune to show my belief that he could not beat an English army under our own great general, I have this happen to me. My son, bearing my name, has engaged himself in some fool conspiracy to get Napoleon off St. Helena!"

"I don't believe it!"

"I found it hard also to accept such—such an incredible thing. I told Gardiner that I didn't believe it. But, unfortunately, the information comes from Downing Street. A British agent, who watches the activities of Joseph Bonaparte and the crew he has collected around him at a place called Bordentown, has sent a full report to the Foreign Office. It seems that the boy was entrusted with an important letter by an ex-mistress of Napoleon's at Rio de Janeiro——"

Mrs. Carboy interrupted defiantly. "That is absurd! How could Allie make the acquaintance of a mistress of Napoleon's?"

"An excellent question, my dear Belle. I'm going to put it to that boy as soon as I see him—which won't be for a long time." He gave a short, wry laugh. "Whether we believe it or not, he took this letter and delivered it to the Bonapartist crew who have built themselves a mansion in this small town in the United States. He delivered it in spite of the fact that the agent saw him first and warned him not to."

"Did he know what was in the letter?"

"The agent, a British officer named Griffen, thinks not. But he soon had an opportunity to discover what an infamous lot he had fallen in with. He stayed overnight at the Bonaparte house and dined with the so-called royal family. He heard the drunken officers discussing their nonsensical schemes and singing their foul army songs. And then, it seems, he did something much more dangerous and damning. He conceived an adolescent passion for Joseph Bonaparte's younger daughter. Why in thunderation, Belle, does the young fool let his romantic feelings get him involved in so many silly scrapes?"

"He's young, Samuel. And there has only been one other. The Groody girl, you must admit, was pretty and rather nice."

"Damme, I don't understand him at all. Why, instead of posting off for New York at once, as he was expected to do, he hung around the place for a week. Griffen reports he was seeing the girl—she's called a princess because her fat dotard of a father was illegally hoisted onto two thrones by Napoleon, Princess Lolotte, a heathenish name—he was seeing her a very great deal. There's a place near the mansion which is called, actually, Upsa Daesy Lane —but there's no need going into all these details. He finally had a row with one of the gang, a Colonel Lebaud. The Frenchman went at him with his sword drawn and Alfred—this is the only part of the story which gives me any satisfaction—seized the broken limb of a tree and broke the damned frog's sword off at the hilt."

Mrs. Carboy, her cheeks flushed, her eyes flashing, cried out: "Good for my son! That was courage for you. Sam Carboy, you have to own up that you're proud of what he did."

"I'm proud that he displayed real courage. What has always galled me about that boy is his lack of common sense and ambition, and all other proper qualities. Well, he *had* to leave after this fracas and so he joined Abel Chave in New York." A flush as noticeable as his wife's appeared on the cheeks and heavy jowls of the financier at this mention of his son's custodian. "That was my mistake, letting a stupid creature who couldn't hold a job as a curate take my son in charge. It seems Chave was afraid to travel on a steamship. Alfred, quite properly, was very much interested in it and set off alone while that cowardly fellow went on to New York by stagecoach. All the trouble started right there and so I place a share of the blame on that damned stickit minister's shoulders. Chave stayed in New York with his runny nose buried in the Greek classics while our son got himself into trouble. I'm going to bring Chave home by first mail and then I'm going to kick him out into his chronic unemployment with the ten pounds I owe him in his pocket."

"I disliked the man," contributed Mrs. Carboy, happy to enlarge on any point in her son's favor. "I distrusted him. He had a sneaky pair of eyes. And I don't believe he ever bathed."

"That's not all," went on her husband, his mood reverting to the gloom he had first displayed. "Some churchman in the Bonaparte household—an abbé, or something of the kind, a conniving, underhanded fellow—entrusted the boy with another letter. It was to be placed in the hands of a French agent in New York. By this time Alfred must have known what was in their minds but he was so infatuated with the daughter that he agreed to deliver the letter. He was staying at the same inn as Captain Griffen and the latter went through his bags and clothes before Allie left and got his hands on the letter. It gave away some valuable information about the plot they were brewing up."

Mrs. Carboy was holding a handkerchief over her eyes by this time and giving full reign to her emotions. Between sobs, she said: "My poor Allie!

All alone, with no one to help him and advise him, in that strange land!
No wonder he's got into trouble. Why did you send him away, Samuel?
Why were you so cruel to him?"

Carboy gestured angrily. "I refuse to accept any of the blame. Well, there
it is. Downing Street has the whole story. It will get out, of course, and it
will be a black mark for all of us to share. And I have lost my knighthood."

"Oh, Sam, Sam," sobbed his wife. "I'm so sorry about that. I know how
much you were counting on it."

After a pause of several moments Carboy began to speak in a lower tone.
"Belle, it was the great ambition of my life. I wanted a title more than I
wanted wealth, I think. Sir Samuel Carboy. It had such a fine roundness
to it! I didn't want to be one of the last to go in to dinner for the whole of
my life. I wanted a decent seat instead of always being in the middle of
the table. I wanted these high-nosed bankers and men in the City to address
me as Sir Samuel. It would have meant so much to both of us."

Forgetting her own feelings for the moment, his wife saw that there was
actually a tear on each cheek. She had never known him to display so much
feeling in all the years they had been together.

"Well, the chance is gone. Those who hate me will always have this weapon
to use if the suggestion ever comes up again. It isn't just the matter of the
title; they'll use it all the time. There will be whispering about me and
charges and innuendoes. As for the title, Belle, the chance will never come
again."

"But, Samuel," said Mrs. Carboy, "I'm sure you're not going to take it out
on the boy. You're not going to cut him off?"

He indulged in another wry laugh which was almost like a snort. "Belle,
don't you know me better than that? Do you think I'm like the hardhearted
father in a cheap melodrama? I'm a man of some intelligence and decent
feeling, I hope. Alfred is my son and, no matter what he does, I'll never cut
him off with a shilling or drive him out into the storm. But, Belle, I'm going
to discipline him. What he did over there makes it certain that he needs a
sharp lesson if he's ever going to amount to anything in this world. While I
was waiting for you to come up, I was thinking it over; and I reached a
conclusion about him. He can't be allowed to come back at once, not with
this cloud hanging over him. I've decided he must stay away for at least three
years, by which time most people will have forgotten about it. I'm going to
write him tonight and give him his orders. Oh, I'm not going to mince words,
Belle. I'm going to let him know what a cruel and terrible thing he has done
to us. I'm going to send him one hundred pounds. And that, m'dear, is all
he will receive during his three years of exile. What's more, when he returns
he must pay his own passage."

"Samuel, Samuel, you are being too hard on the poor boy!"

"Hard? The time has come for him to learn how to make a living for
himself. Perhaps in the process he'll get a little common sense knocked into
him."

3

Dinner was not a very convivial affair. The soup was cold, in the first place; but then it generally was well chilled because it had to be brought from the distant kitchen wing, necessitating the climbing of one flight of stairs and the passage of three halls. The sauce for the sole was not a success. It was not until the roast beef appeared, in fact, that the spirits of the trio picked up a little. The roast was brown and crisp on the outside and pink in the middle, and the Yorkshire pudding was a complete success.

"Samuel Carboy, Esquire, apologizes for his lack of spirits," said the host, glancing at Sir Theobald Gardiner, who had turned his attention to the roast beef with the heartiest of intentions. "I'm afraid that's all the name I'll ever have. Knighthoods must be seized like—what is that expression?"

"Are you referring to the bald spot of opportunity?" suggested the baronet.

"That's it. You must seize it the first time it offers itself. I'm very much afraid the chance to be knighted will never present itself again."

Sir Theobald said: "Have I your permission, ma'am, to read something from a report? It's of interest to all of us." He drew a paper, folded into a small square, from a pocket of his waistcoat. "I have here the latest figures on the Tontine. In the class which concerns us nine hundred and two of the contestants have died already."

Mrs. Carboy looked shocked at the figure. "Isn't that very large? And all of them so young!"

The baronet dissented with a shake of his head. "No, ma'am. The teens are a dangerous time. Young people die off in droves. Consumption, diphtheria, typhoid fever, accidents. Eighteen of them were killed in the hunting field, six of them girls. I knew one of the girls, a stunning little creature. Eleven were drowned. One swallowed a needle and died of convulsions. One was so overcome with passion for a virtuous barmaid that he took a shot at her—it went wide, fortunately—and then blew out his own brains. Not much to blow out, I guess."

"Rather better than I expected," commented Carboy.

"Samuel!" ejaculated his wife. "Do you mean you're glad so many have died, just because they're in a competition with our children?"

"Well," said Carboy listlessly, "it doesn't matter much how fast or how slow they drop off. It's only the final survivors who count."

The baronet summed the matter up. "By the time the youngest of the class have reached the twenties, there will be a total of two thousand or more dead."

At this point there was a sound of barking dogs from the main drive and a man's voice raised in direction. The trio at the table looked at each other with puzzled frowns.

"Has the hunt club changed its hours?" asked Carboy.

The butler came in and stationed himself at the owner's right hand. It was clear that his dignity had been ruffled.

"A person to see you, sir. May I state my opinion that his errand cannot be of sufficient importance to disturb your dinner, sir?"

"Does the fellow insist on seeing me?"

"Yes, sir. He is most insistent."

"Why do you think so poorly of him?"

"Well, sir, he drives a most curious cart. I am sure he made it with his own hands and that someday he will come to a tragic ending, sir, when it collapses under him on the road. Moreover, sir, it is drawn by two animals of a most unusual size and hairiness. They might be lions and on the other hand they might be dogs. I have been quite unable, sir, to reach a conclusion on the point."

"Dogs? I think I know the man. He wouldn't come at this hour if he didn't have something serious on his mind. With your permission, m'dear, and your indulgence, Sir Theobald, I think I'll look into this at once."

As he had expected, it was Heaven Beck. The latter was standing beside the cart, which had been drawn up before the main entrance and which, as a matter of fact, *was* of home manufacture and owed much to pieces of rope and strands of wire. It was clear to Carboy at once that his visitor was in a disturbed state of mind.

"Mr. Carboy, sir," began Beck, "I am told I have taken you away from your dinner and for that I am indeed very sorry."

The owner of Beaulaw Hall was so much interested in the dogs attached to the cart that he paid no attention at first to his visitor.

"Extraordinary!" he said. "Where did you get the beasts? Don't tell me, Mr. Beck, that they were strays on the streets of London. What a riot they would have caused there!"

"They are of a French breed, sir. They were owned by an old widow woman in Kent and when she died the executors didn't know just what to do with them. The police were called in and they brought them to me. They are very fine fellows, Mr. Carboy, and as strong as horses. Their names are Jacques and Hippolyte."

"What brings you here tonight, Mr. Beck?"

"Sir, my errand is either of no importance at all—in which case I will most humbly beg your pardon—or it is so vital that it will brook of no delay. Mr. Carboy, your daughter honored me with a visit a few evenings ago and, with your permission, I should like to say that I regard her as an angel, sir—a rather modern type of angel, sir. I have such regard for her that I hesitated to come tonight and it was not until I considered how much more I should consider your interests, sir, above all others, that I saw my duty clearly."

"Come to the point, Mr. Beck, come to the point."

The friend of strange dogs hesitated. "Sir, I am very much afraid your daughter is eloping!"

"My daughter eloping!" cried Carboy. "Nonsense, Mr. Beck. Stuff and nonsense! My daughter is paying a visit at the home of a friend."

"Mr. Carboy, when your daughter was at my place she was accompanied by a very handsome young man. He was, I learned later, the son of your former partner, Mr. George Grace."

"My daughter was with Grace's son! Mr. Beck, I don't believe a word of it."

"I assure, sir, I am speaking the truth. I liked them both very much, thinking them the handsomest couple I had ever laid eyes on in my whole life."

It was growing dark outside but sufficient light reached them through the oriel window above the entrance for Carboy to read sincerity as well as anxiety on the face of his visitor.

"One hour and twenty-five minutes ago, sir," said Beck, consulting a rather battered watch without chain or fob, "I saw them drive by my place in a large carriage. There was a driver at the reins and young Mr. Grace was sitting on the box beside him. I saw the face of your daughter, sir, at the window. I couldn't be mistaken about *that*, I do assure you. When she realized that I was watching, she drew her head back. There was an elderly lady with her inside. The carriage, moreover, was loaded with bags and luggage of all kinds. They were going, quite certainly, a long distance."

"In what direction were they headed?"

"For the north, sir. They were making for the Oxford road."

"Gretna Green!" cried Carboy. A sense of conviction had engulfed him. He called to the butler, "Fleck, come and hold these spirited steeds!" and then he led Beck into the hall where he ensconced him in a chair. "Wait here, please," he said.

When he broke the news to the silent couple at dinner, his wife pushed her plate away from her and repeated the word he had used: "Nonsense!" Sir Theobald Gardiner said nothing but it was clear that he was very much disturbed. He was holding a wineglass in his hand and, with a carelessness quite foreign to him, he spilled some of the contents on his ruffled shirt.

"You know, Samuel, that Isabelle is visiting with an old school friend near Reading. She took a number of bags with her this afternoon as she had been promised there would be much social activity. This dog man must be mistaken."

"I wish I could be sure of that."

Assailed by a sudden fear, Mrs. Carboy sprang to her feet and started to leave the room. "I'll go up and see what she took with her," she said.

Left to themselves, the two men regarded each other with somber eyes. "I'm afraid there's something in it," declared Carboy. "And yet it seems unbelievable. My little Isabelle has always been perfect in every respect. Has she thrown all her sensible ideas about the future to the winds? The Grace cub won't come in for anything worth mentioning; and I've heard her say many times that nothing under a duke would satisfy her as a husband. Damme, Sir Theobald, am I another Job that all my misfortunes must come down on me at once?"

The baronet had been studying the red stain on his ruffled bosom with a hint of distaste. He looked up at his host and it became evident that he was fully as concerned with the tidings as either of the girl's parents. "I don't believe it," he said. "I—I have reasons for thinking that Isabelle would not be guilty of this great folly."

Despite this reassuring speech, Carboy gave the bellpull such an impatient jerk that he tore it away from the wall. When the butler obeyed the summons in as much of a hurry as the dignity of his office permitted, he said: "Get out my carriage. Fresh horses, of course. Tell Humpster I'm sorry but he'll have to be ready to leave with me at any minute. If he hasn't had his dinner, tell him to pitch in at once." He waited until the butler was out of earshot and then turned to his guest. "Sir Theobald, if it's true, I'm going to follow them. I must save the child from the consequences of this outrageous mistake."

When Mrs. Carboy returned, they knew from the expression on her face that it was true. She was breathing hard.

"That daughter of yours has run away," she said to her husband. "Everything she valued has been taken. All her best dresses and her jewelry and even a few miniatures. I suspect that her maid, that sly little slut of a Parker, knew all about it. She tried to deny it when I questioned her but I could tell from her eyes she was lying to me."

"Your son and my daughter!" said Carboy slowly. "They seem to be determined to rob us of what we value most in the world. The boy—well, I never have understood him. But Isabelle—why would she do such an insane thing? There's never been any romantic nonsense about her. Her ambitious ideas have always been a source of real delight to me. I believed her when she talked about the kind of marriage she wanted."

The baronet had risen from his chair. They realized, to their surprise, that his face was white. It was clear that he had something to say but he hesitated and ran a finger nervously over his upper lip.

"Samuel," he said finally, "I have a favor to ask of you. Let me go with you."

Carboy was taken by surprise at this request. "It will be a long pull, I'm afraid," he said. "They seem to be heading for Gretna Green. We may have to drive all night in order to overtake them. It won't be easy."

"I have a reason for wanting to go," said Gardiner. "What that reason is I'll explain later. But I most earnestly beg you to let me share your ride."

"Then have your valet pack a bag for you at once. You'll need it before we're through with this."

"At once," said the baronet. He glanced down at the stained ruffles. "I must change my clothes. I shouldn't care to visit a poundkeeper like this."

He took a few minutes only and had rejoined them when the butler entered with the announcement, "Your carriage is ready, sir."

CHAPTER TWELVE

1

The two men sat hunched together, shoulder to shoulder. The carriage swayed and jolted and creaked. Here, on the edge of the Vale, it was all up and down. One minute the horses would be straining to reach the top of a hill, the next they would be going down at a mad pace and the driver would be feeling nervously with his foot for the brake. Samuel Carboy began to talk in a tone which betokened puzzlement.

"Sir Theobald," he said, "I'm not surprised that my son has got himself into trouble. He's—well, I might as well come right out with it—he's weak. I've tried to tell myself that it was just the irresponsibility of youth but now I have to face the truth. He's never going to amount to anything. I used to think he would settle down but I've given up hope of that. He'll never be a credit to me. There's just one thing to do with him. Put him on a horse. When he's got a horse to ride, he's happy. But, damme, Sir Theobald, a man shouldn't spend his whole life on the back of a horse. He can't look after his affairs on a horse. He can't be a worth-while citizen on a horse. Sometimes he's got to get his feet out of the stirrups and under a desk. Sometimes he's got to agree that a man's shoulders are made to carry responsibilities and not just to wear fancy riding jackets."

There was a long moment of silence. Sir Theobald smoothed the ends of his neat mustache and stared straight out into the blackness. His interest in Alfred Carboy, it seemed, was slight.

"But with Isabelle," began Carboy again, "it's a different matter. Damme, Sir Theobald, I worship that child! I've always been so proud of her. She's so bright and gay, and so sound at the core."

"Like a well-cut diamond," contributed the baronet, sitting up straight and showing an immediate interest in the conversation.

"Exactly. Like a well-cut diamond. Hard, it's true, and sharp at the edges. But with sparkle. Ah, such a real sparkle!"

Sir Theobald drew a sigh from deep down inside himself. "And so beautiful," he said. "So very beautiful!"

"Why," demanded the distracted father, "has she done this? Has she taken leave of her senses? I'm sure she can't love this young cub. It would be easier to understand, and a lot easier to forgive, if she had run away with a damned groom or a chuckleheaded cornet of horse with no chin. But the son of Ninny Grace!"

"Easy, Samuel, easy. This is not—er—irrevocable, you know. I'm sure we'll be able to make this little charmer of yours see the light—if we catch up with them in time. So don't get excited about things, Samuel. Keep a cool head."

Another carriage came tearing out of the darkness to meet them. Humpster slowed down and took the side of the road to let the stranger pass. The wheels ground through sand and stone, and the body of the coach jerked spasmodically on its elaborate body of springs. A spatter of pebbles rained on the window as the two ships passed in the night.

"I hear," went on Carboy, in a tone which evidenced a deep inner disgust, "that Old Sheppy is putting George Ninian Grace in for Little Grimditch. A fine member of the House he'll make! I can hear him now, making precise little speeches in his precise little voice. Rubbing his white hands on a scented handkerchief, so very genteel, and smirking and nodding—and talking a lot of weak-spined nonsense!"

"You know him very well," declared Gardiner. "And so do I. But I think I know him better when it becomes a question of what he'll do in the House. He may smirk and nod as you say—but he'll have something to talk about, never fear. Us. You and me. He'll be pitching it into us, never fear."

"You can't pitch hay with a one-tined fork," said Carboy in a contemptuous tone. "I've no fear of what George Ninian Grace may say or do. And I'll tell you what I'm going to do as soon as we catch up with these crazy young loons. I'm going to kick the backsides of Grace's son right out of the coach!"

The baronet nodded his head. "Oh, by all means, Samuel. Kick the backsides of this boy as much as you like. The thought of him being soundly kicked is one which gives me a great deal of pleasure, I confess. Kick him once for me, Samuel." He paused and gave his mustache another smoothing. "And while you're doing the kicking, I'll talk to Isabelle. Let me handle that part of it, Samuel. I think I can manage it better than you."

Carboy studied him curiously, at close range because the side lights did little to illuminate the interior of the coach. "Well," he said, "just as you want it. You're more diplomatic than I am."

An hour passed. Humpster, who had been driving all day, opened a slot in the roof and called down to them in a weary voice: "I'm getting most oncommon sleepy, Mr. Carboy. Mind if I sing to keep myself awake, sir?"

"Go ahead. It's a good idea. People will think we're a party of drunkards on our way home."

So the coachman sang in a voice far removed from the key and thumped his feet against the box to keep himself alert. Carboy said to his companion, "Might as well do some work." He supported himself with a side strap and struggled to his feet. From a pigeonhole he produced some papers. He drew a pillow and a rug from another compartment and offered them to his companion. "Better make yourself comfortable and get some sleep," he advised.

2

Samuel Carboy kept at his scrutiny of the papers until he became aware that the light of dawn was showing through the windows of the carriage. Humpster had not been singing for hours but every few minutes he had kicked his heels against the back of the box to keep from going asleep. There was something rhythmic about this regular *clump, clump, clump*. Carboy had been aware of it all through the night but had not allowed the sound to break his concentration.

He glanced over his shoulder at Sir Theobald Gardiner. The baronet was snoring in a gentle and thoroughly refined way.

Carboy got to his feet and snuffed out the light above him. As he did so there was a sound of horse's hoofs beating loudly on the road and a voice commanding the carriage to stop. Humpster reined in so abruptly that the coach veered drunkenly to the side. Carboy leaned against the glass and peered out. He could hardly believe his eyes when he saw that the rider, who had commanded them to halt, was wearing a mask.

"Strike me pink!" he cried. "It's a holdup."

"What? What did you say?" Sir Theobald struggled up slowly to a sitting position. He rubbed his eyes with the backs of his hands.

Carboy of a sudden had become very tense and still. He glanced quickly at his companion and motioned with a thumb at the glass. The rider with the black mask was staring in at them.

"What nonsense is this?" demanded the baronet petulantly. "Someone's playing a trick on us. The holdup went out of fashion long ago. After—after the last of the bandits, whose name eludes me, was hanged." He knocked on the window with his knuckles. "Get along with you! We want none of your tomfoolery. We're in a hurry, my man."

The masked rider yanked the door open. He indicated that they were to get out.

"Are we going to stand this kind of treatment?" demanded Gardiner, turning to Carboy. "I must say it goes against the grain to take orders from cattle like this."

"Lots of things go against the grain these days," declared the highwayman. He motioned to his empty left sleeve. "I lost my arm at Waterloo. What is my reward for fighting for my country and getting crocked up? My wife and my two little sons go hungry because I can't get work."

Carboy got down first, aware for the first time of the cramped position in which he had spent the long night. The road was low at this point and heavily wooded on each side. A high ridge showed above the tops of the trees off in the distance. He scowled at the mounted figure.

"Good morning, Mr. Carboy," said the highwayman. By his voice, he was not an entire stranger to education. "I was sure it was your carriage. It's pretty well known on the roads. You whisk through these parts like the spirit of Boney rushing to battle."

"Yes, I'm Samuel Carboy. If that means anything to you." The magnate continued to frown. "See here, we're in a desperate hurry. Get along with whatever you have in mind so we can be on our way."

"It's a case of forking over, Mr. Carboy. We'll have your cash, *if* you please. Your watch also and that ring on your finger. Your friend here will fork over also. He's a dressy old dog, isn't he? I expect we'll do rather well out of him."

"Didn't you hear me say we're in a most damnable hurry?"

"Yes, I heard you. It's an odd thing. All the coaches on the road tonight seem to be in a hurry. Just half an hour ago there was one on the back road. Because they *were* taking the back road, I was not surprised when I found they were eloping. A handsome young couple. They were very disturbed when I made them stop. The old lady with them screamed at me that she'd see me hanged in London for my pains. But the girl was very pretty and the young man was quite decent so I took five quid and let them go on their way."

There was no hint on Carboy's granite face to indicate that the information thus given him was of any importance. He had already concluded that he was dealing with an amateur highwayman. If he were to drop a hint of his intention of overtaking the young couple the man in the mask might be capable of cutting the traces and leaving them stranded by the side of the road.

"So," said Carboy, "you made a deal with them. Why not make one with us? Here's what I'll do. I'll pool my money with that of my friend and we'll —er—fork over twenty pounds. You'll have our word that the transaction will be forgotten. If you strip us of our jewelry, you'll have to take it to some stinking crook in London who'll give you little enough for it. You run the danger—even the certainty—of being caught that way. What do you say? Our way and go in peace? Or your way and be hanged?"

"Your offer is low," said the masked man. "Niggardly, in fact. I'll take thirty."

"Twenty-five. My last word. If you agree, we'll never tell anyone what happened to us. If you strip us of all our belongings and delay us now, we'll report to the police at the nearest town."

"Done!" The man reached out an eager hand. "Give me the blunt and I'll be off. This is the easy way and even Davy's Sow would have enough gumption to take it. I have never seen you, my fine gentlemen. You've never seen me. There was no holdup. No money has changed hands. We just met in the glorious light of the new dawn and called a greeting to each other as we passed."

The money was passed over. The man in the mask counted it carefully and then stuffed it in a pocket of his coat.

"What's the next town?"

"Wellingborough. Straight ahead."

Carboy saw that the highwayman's horse was a serviceable animal but shaggy of mane and unkempt of tail. It looked much more suited to dragging a plow than galloping over the roads at night with a mounted posse in pursuit. Carboy looked at the highwayman himself in search of corroborative evidence. It was not hard to find. The mask was carelessly tied. The pistol, carried in the left hand, was not being managed with ease and nonchalance.

"I am coming to believe," declared Carboy, "that you are telling me the truth. You've been driven into this. I suspect, in fact, that this is your first venture in crime."

There was a moment of silence and then the highwayman laughed. "You are right, sir," he said. "I made up my mind to it at eight o'clock. The bareness of the family cupboard, when the question of supper arose, was the last straw. I made this mask from the trimming of an old hat of my wife's. Then I—well—I borrowed the horse. I haven't done badly but I'll never go out on the road again." He paused. "Had you known all this, Mr. Carboy, you wouldn't have given in so easily, I'm afraid. You wouldn't have forked over the twenty-five quid without some kind of a struggle."

Carboy gave an unwilling nod. "You are quite right. I think, my friend, I would have been inclined to give you a tussle."

"Everything I've told you is true. I was a soldier and I lost an arm at Waterloo."

"Aren't you concerned over what we may do now? Are you certain still that we'll abide by our promise and not go to the police in the nearest town?"

The man in the mask laughed a second time. "There's a deal of talk about you nowadays, Mr. Carboy. Some think you ought to be clapped into jail to keep you from gobbling up this whole little island known as England. But all agree you are not a quibbler or a liar. You've said you won't do anything to set a posse on my heels, and I believe you. I'll restore my fiery steed to his rightful owner and the duties to which he is more accustomed. The mask will be most carefully destroyed. I don't expect to have any qualms or fears on the score of what you will do, sir."

"You speak most damned well for a common soldier."

"Perhaps I was an uncommon soldier," carelessly. "I've had a little education."

Carboy was pleased at the confidence thus displayed in him but this was not enough to rid him of a sense of defeat. This confessed amateur in the role of highwayman was having all the better of it, in addition to the tangible gain of twenty-five pounds.

"You have my money in your pocket. And that, I assure you, is not a point that gives me any satisfaction whatever. I don't enjoy giving away money. But I didn't part with it through fear of the pistol you were brandishing in the window of the carriage. I'm not a coward. I gave it to you because I thought you had earned it. You won't believe this, young man, but I paid you for value received." He gestured brusquely. "Don't delay to figure that out. Be on your way. We must be on ours."

When Carboy climbed back into the carriage, he found that the baronet had preceded him and was busy with a pencil and the back of an envelope.

"This will do it," said the latter, nodding his head with satisfaction. "Ex-soldier. Lost an arm at Waterloo. Has wife and two sons. Lives hereabouts. Out of employment at present. With that much to go on, we'll have him laid by the heels in no time at all."

Carboy thumped on the box and called impatiently: "Humpster! Put them at it! We must get to Wellingborough without delay. Put them to the gallop." He turned then to his companion. "This has been a stroke of luck. If this fellow hadn't held us up, we would never have known they took the other road. We'd have got ahead of them. We would have been the ones to get to Gretna Green. Young Grace would have heard about us driving furiously on ahead of him and he'd have had the sense to turn off and get some unscrupulous parson to perform the ceremony. And all England would have laughed at us."

"That's true enough, Samuel," declared the baronet. His eyes were angry and his face a shade of red which had nothing to do with the sleep from which he had so recently wakened. "I dislike intensely being made ridiculous. This fellow held us up at the point of a pistol and made us give him practically all the money we had. The valuable information he gave us is beside the point. He's a thief and I'm going to see him tried at the Old Bailey and hanged as he deserves!"

The driver had taken his instructions literally and had put the tired horses to the gallop. The coach was rocking from side to side as they descended a steep incline. It was not until they reached level road again, and had slowed down a little, that Carboy was able to address his companion.

"I'm sorry, Sir Theobald, but I must put my foot down in this matter," he said. "You must have heard everything he said. Well, I've given my word and I must see that it's kept. If it will make you feel any better, I'll repay you out of my own pocket. But there must be no move made to set the police on his trail."

The baronet pocketed the envelope with his notes. "It's not the money," he said with a pronounced suggestion of sulkiness in his voice. "I can't abide being made sport of by a cheap plow hand."

Carboy shook his head emphatically. "In the days following Waterloo, I laid the foundation of my fortune on the Floor of the Exchange. At the same time I was paving the way for some profitable deals in which you've participated. And all the while this poor fellow was lying in an army hospital with his arm shot off. Doesn't that entitle him to some consideration? If not, I put it to you that we must keep our main objective in sight. If we waste time swearing out an information against this fellow, we may fail to stop the elopement. They'll give us the slip if we wait on anything else."

Most reluctantly, Gardiner drew the envelope from a pocket and tore it into bits. "The elopement must be stopped," he conceded. "Nothing else matters. I would have sworn that revenge was the most powerful of all emotions but now I realize that it isn't. Love is the strongest."

3

The first inn they visited, which was called by the natives the Red-nosed Parson although the sign creaking over the door said the Chess Player, contained the runaway party. Julian Grace was standing in the lobby, looking very white and unhappy at being discovered. At the first words, "Well! Here they are!" spoken in Samuel Carboy's loudest voice, the young lover was joined by his aunt Josephine, who literally popped out of a room on the ground floor. The chaperone was a sweet-looking old lady with the mildest of eyes and a tongue like a steel file.

"Mr. Samuel Carboy, is it?" cried Aunt Josephine, drawing herself up to her quite inconsiderable height. "You will please address yourself to me. So, you are the man who treated my poor cousin George Grace so shabbily! You are the man who is stealing so many other concerns! You are the spider, the thief, the oily scoundrel——"

"Yes, ma'am," said Carboy with a savage nod of the head. "Yes, I am the man. I am everything you say, if you prefer it that way. But I have nothing to say to you, ma'am. What I have to say is for the ear of this young scoundrel who has tried to steal my daughter!"

A voice joined in from the landing of the stairs. "Really, Papa! Must you shout so loud?"

It was Isabelle and it was apparent that she had been trying to get some sleep. Her hair was disheveled and she had one hand over her mouth to conceal the yawn she could not suppress. Even under these circumstances she looked beautiful.

She flushed a little and drew back when she saw Sir Theobald Gardiner behind her father at the foot of the stairs.

"Isabelle!" said Carboy sharply. "I must say that your conduct has been so outrageous, so unfilial, so unexpected——"

Gardiner laid a restraining arm on his partner's shoulder. "Samuel, Samuel!" he protested. "We had an agreement, if you recall. You made me a promise."

"Yes. I did. But I—I think it necessary to speak to my own daughter and let her know how shocked I have been by her conduct."

"Speak to her later, of course, but our agreement was that I would talk first." Gardiner looked up at the figure near the head of the stairs. "Am I asking too much, Isabelle? I have something to say to you, dear child, which may prove in the best interests of all of us if you will listen."

Julian's face flushed angrily. "You have no part in this," he said. "Surely, Isabelle, you agree that this is a matter which concerns us only. Not even your father. And certainly not—not this stranger."

"But he's not a stranger, Julian," protested Isabelle.

Julian, trying to appear cool and collected and to carry off this most painful situation with dignity and firmness, was flushing like a schoolboy and finding difficulty in choosing his words. "Is he—is he the man you told me of?"

Isabelle nodded and yawned again. She seated herself on the stairs and supported her head on her hands. "That dreadful ride!" she said. "I'm not sure I'll ever get over it. Tibby, I think I would like to speak to you first."

"Tibby!" cried Julian. "Who do you mean?"

"She means me," said Sir Theobald Gardiner triumphantly. He walked to the foot of the stairs and held out a hand to assist her in descending the rest of the distance. "Come with me into the parlor, child. We'll be able to talk there."

"Julian Grace, are you going to stand by and let this happen?" demanded the belligerent Aunt Josephine. "Are you going to let this little creature——"

"She's not a little creature!" cried Julian, still more disturbed and unhappy. "She's the most beautiful woman in the world. I love her to distraction!"

"We've had our trip for nothing, my poor, penniless boy," was the unsparing response he received to this outburst. "I'm sure she's got her eye on that rich old man."

"I'll have the carriage brought around," exclaimed Julian, "and I'll pick her up and carry her off in spite of them all!"

But he knew that it was too late for that.

4

"How can I look you in the face?" asked Isabelle, sitting beside Sir Theobald in the tiny parlor. "How stupid and silly you must think me!"

"Stupid? Silly? No, Isabelle, you are adorable." He looked at her steadily. "Let me talk. And while I talk, be content to listen. I think I can help you make your decision."

"Yes, Tibby." She sighed deeply. "But I *have* been stupid. I am very much ashamed of myself."

"My most beloved little Isabelle, I want you to believe this: if you desire to marry this young man, I will not only withdraw and so make it easier for you but I shall strive to smooth the path for you. With your parents and even with the Grace family as well. I mean it, little Isabelle. He's a fine young fellow. He's handsome. And so very young! It may be wiser for you to have a husband more your own age."

"Oh, Tibby, Tibby!" cried Isabelle. "You are so kind and so good and so wonderful! Why didn't you talk to me like this before?"

"But how could I? I did not know about your young man."

"I don't mean that. I mean, why didn't you let me see how you feel yourself?"

Gardiner smoothed his glossy black mustache and regarded her with a puzzled frown. "But, my Isabelle, my little pet, surely you know that I'm madly in love with you!"

"I thought so. I hoped so. But you didn't *speak*. When Julian began to make love to me, I told him something that wasn't true. I said there was another man who wanted to marry me and that he had proposed. I thought it would make him see he had no chance. But instead it made him still more pressing."

The baronet gave his head a shake. "My child, I see now that I've been remiss. But consider the difficulties of my position. A middle-aged lover is always at a disadvantage. He feels awkward and he's afraid that people will laugh at him. So he holds his feelings in and tries to seem dignified. He hopes that the—the object of his affections—will know how he feels without being told."

"Oh, what a mistake. What a great mistake!"

"I've been the stupid one. And now, I suppose, it's too late."

"Tibby, no!" cried Isabelle. "I knew this was wrong almost as soon as we started. I began to dislike that fussy old woman more every minute. And in the darkness of the coach I would look at Julian sitting there beside me, and I would wonder. He seemed a complete stranger to me. I couldn't understand why I had agreed to run away with him. I wanted to be back— oh, how I wanted to be back at home with my dear papa and mama."

"Did you—did you think of me?"

"Oh yes. And I was ashamed to think of the opinion you would have of me."

"Would you have married him, if we hadn't come?"

She shook her head. "No. How could I? I realized that I didn't love him and that I didn't even know him. I'd have run away a second time, I suppose. From him."

Sir Theobald drew himself up with a sudden return to his usual dignity of manner. "I shall speak to your father. And ask his consent to paying my addresses to you."

Isabelle's beautiful brown eyes began to sparkle. "Yes, Tibby, you must speak to him. But when?"

He rose to his feet. "Now. At once. Of course we'll have to get rid of those people first. I'll send them packing and then I'll speak to your father. It will be settled by the time you've had your bath and come down for breakfast with us." Suddenly he lost all dignity and said in a whisper, "Oh, my darling, I love you more than any young man ever could!"

CHAPTER THIRTEEN

1

Julian Grace, the most unhappy man in the world, would have been glad if the story of the interrupted elopement could have been kept a secret. But Aunt Josephine would be neither cajoled nor threatened into keeping a still tongue. In a matter almost of hours the countryside was buzzing with the news. People began immediately to take sides. The women stood almost solidly behind the Grace family, calling Isabelle a hoyden who didn't know her own mind and her parents a pair of ill-bred upstarts. The men, with an eye to the future perhaps and a hope of favors to come, were more inclined to take the Carboy side. They smirked and winked and agreed among themselves that the little minx was the high-steppingest filly in the county.

The wedding was to take place in early June, and a full month earlier the issue was brought right out into the open. Mrs. Grace was giving one of her rather dreary teas (to quote some of her very best friends) and, naturally, the question came in for much discussion. All of the ladies present knew the Carboys and all of them had received invitations. Who were going to accept, who refuse?

Mrs. Grace's hands shook with emotion as she poured the tea and passed the rather scantily filled plates of sandwiches and cake. "I have just one thing to say," she declared in a voice which trembled also. "Anyone who goes to that wedding will never be received within these walls again."

"Really now, Addie," said a cousin who also was related, much more distantly, to the great Outland family. "Do you think you should say that? I mean—this taking of such a definite stand, is it wise?"

"It has never been possible for you, Fanny, to take a stand on anything," asserted the hostess with more than a hint of acid in her tone. "Now I am different. I have never, never refused to declare myself. And here we have an issue which affects all of us. I can only repeat what I said before. Our friends must choose between us, between the Graces and the Carboys. There is no middle ground."

"But, Addie," spoke another of the guests who, it was clear, had mixed feelings. "This—this might be—shall we say embarrassing?—for some of us."

"If it is embarrassing for you, Millie, declare yourself now." Mrs. Grace waved her teaspoon in the air like a gage of battle. "You must stand by us or stand by them."

A new voice, a timid one, put into words the thought which was in all their minds. "Will His Grace stand with you? I mean, are you sure he feels the same way about it? He's rather a friend of Sir Theobald Gardiner's, isn't he?"

Mrs. Grace laid her spoon down. She glanced about the circle of faces. She was not sure, now, that all of them were her friends. At least she was not sure they were her friends to the extent of willingness to do battle for her on any issue which might arise.

"Do you suppose," she asked, "that my uncle Sheppard is not a believer in family solidarity? I am certain that he will have too much regard for *my* feelings to treat the invitation—which, no doubt, he has received—with anything but the contempt it deserves."

That seemed to settle the matter. If the Duke of Outland refused the invitation, then the marriage of Isabelle Carboy to Sir Theobald Gardiner would be attended by few, if any, of the true elite of the county. Perhaps a slight doubt lingered, however, in the minds of some of the ladies who had listened to Mrs. Grace's ultimatum. "Oh dear!" whispered one of them to her nearest neighbor. "If we could only be sure! He's such a contrary old dear."

2

A fortnight before the event, the prospective bridegroom came down to Beaulaw Hall unexpectedly. Samuel Carboy was at home and received him with a glum countenance.

"These damned cackling old hens!" he said. "They've got the whole countryside stirred up. There's a regular campaign going on to keep people from coming to the wedding. I don't give in easily, as you know; but, by gad, Sir Theobald, I'm beginning to think we'll have a pretty slim attendance. Poor Belle is in tears half the time."

Sir Theobald brushed the matter aside with airy confidence. "I wouldn't worry too much, Samuel," he said. "I came down to get things straightened out. But there's something else we must talk about first. Would you in the meantime let Isabelle know that I'm driving her over to Outland Hall this afternoon for tea with His Grace? I'll want her looking her best, of course. Not," emphatically, "that there's any difficulty about *that*. The divine child would knock the wind out of Old Sheppy if she went in rags and tatters."

"I'll convey your wishes," said Carboy. "And then I'll join you in the library. Help yourself to the whisky. Or Fleck will get you a capital bottle of madeira if you prefer it."

The information which was causing the baronet much concern did not seem to affect Carboy. The latter paid more attention to his glass of whisky (he was getting more addicted to that variety of drink all the time) than he did to Sir Theobald's story.

"Well," he said at the finish, "suppose the honorable member for Little Grimditch does get up on his hind legs and attack us for our connection with the Waterloo Tontine? We've expected all along that he would. The sooner he gets what he has to say off his delicate little chest the better."

The baronet refused to regard it as lightly as that. He gave his head an ominous shake. "I hear a committee will be appointed to look into things. They'll find nothing, of course——"

"Not a thing!" declared Carboy. "We've been careful to handle it in the most businesslike way. Not an unnecessary penny has been spent."

"It's the matter of our percentage that they'll attack."

Carboy frowned thoughtfully. "I wish we had forestalled them by voluntarily giving it up. We've done pretty well out of it and could have afforded to let it go. Well, it's too late for that."

"What I dislike is the publicity that the investigation will cause." Sir Theobald made a grimace of distaste. "George Grace will have plenty of uncomplimentary things to say about us, and that is what people will remember and believe. A complete vindication will do us little good. And that's not the worst of it, Samuel. Broker is going to have *his* say too."

"James Borrow Broker? That flannelmouth! What's he got to do with it?"

"He sits for a constituency in the Midlands. He's going to talk about conditions in the factories. I hear he's been going around on a tour of inspection and is ready to fire a broadside at employers in general and us in particular."

"Has he visited any of our factories?"

"Of course. You're going to be his main target, so he would be certain to get the kind of evidence he'll need."

Carboy finished his whisky and set the glass down hard. "Is he going to harp on the pay they get?"

"That will be his main line of attack, I fancy."

"Let him rant. What we pay our employees is a matter between us and them. What's the House of Commons got to do with it?" He leaned over and gave his companion a reassuring pat on the shoulder. "Don't be an old woman about it. You'll be in Italy on your honeymoon and I'll be here to bear the brunt of it. I've got a strong pair of shoulders, you know. All the Ninny Graces and the James Borrow Brokers, and all the simpletons in the House and the gabbling Mrs. Malaprops in the country, will make no impression on me."

"I'll feel that I'm deserting you."

"I'm much more concerned about the wedding than with what my one-time partner is probably saying this very minute on the Floor of the House. This is the greatest event in my Isabelle's life, and I don't want her feelings hurt in any way."

It was the baronet's turn to display confidence. "Now *there* I can take things in charge. Do you suppose my little pet has had time to get ready? We're due to have tea with His Grace in an hour. We mustn't be late."

"I'll order the carriage around at once," said Carboy. ·

3

Isabelle Carboy had never seen Outland Hall. In this respect she was no different from most people. It was hidden in a tangle of wood and not even the tip of its famous dome could be glimpsed from any road. She saw, first, the medieval gatehouse around which the drive now circled because it was dangerous to venture under this crumbling pile of masonry. The front façade of the house itself was startling in its originality and ugliness. Inside it was rather Nero-esque, as someone had remarked once, with very high cold ceilings and rows of high pillars.

They were received in a small parlor where three sober masculine figures clustered in front of a tiny fire: Old Sheppy himself, his son and heir Lord Blettor, and his grandson, whose name was George Frederick Louis Manly Wilkins Gorse but who was called Young Chip. A far from trim butler escorted the visitors in, carrying at the same time a tea tray and a plate of thick sandwiches.

"By gad, Tib, the Carboy girl *is* a beauty," said the duke, taking Isabelle's hand and kissing it through his white mustache. "I heard she was but, damme, I wasn't prepared for this. You're a lucky dog. And you, my dear, are the most charming visitor we've had in these empty halls for many a long day."

Lord Blettor seemed to agree with this unreservedly. He was a bleak man with a bald head and a withdrawn smile. Young Chip, who was probably fifteen, stared at her with an enthusiasm he had reserved up to this time for dogs and white mice.

"Sit down, my dear," went on the peer. "Here, we'll share this seat close to the fire. The rest of them can stand about as they wish and worship you from afar. Now let's talk about what interests me most. Sports. They tell me you ride like a hussar and can hit a golf ball right out of its cover. Capital, my dear, capital!"

"You've been a champion yourself and so it's most generous of Your Grace to say such nice things about me."

"Ah, that was so long ago!" The duke sighed. "But you should have seen me at the backswording when I was in my prime. I broke a young farmer's shinbone once and had to pay him a pension for a matter of twenty-seven years. That was just one of the things that has helped to keep my head in financial chancery all my life."

No fault could have been found with the way Old Sheppy had arrayed himself for this occasion, save perhaps that the knees of his plaid trousers were a little worn and his collar frayed. His son was neatly but plainly dressed. There was a patch on the knee of Young Chip's knickerbockers. Isabelle looked about her and reached the conclusion that all three fitted into the house perfectly, in its present condition at least. The room where they sat was dingy and bleak. Someone had burned a hole, perhaps with a poker, in a corner of the painting hanging over the fireplace. Around the edges of the firebox were shreds of paper and discarded envelopes and tobacco tampings and faded flowers. The rug was pitted with holes and at some time a puppy had tested his teeth on the edges. There was a saddle in one corner; to which, Isabelle suspected, it had been hurriedly relegated on their arrival.

The duke helped Isabelle to a sandwich consisting of a thick slice of meat between two slabs of bread.

"Corned beef," he explained. "The only kind of sandwich worth eating. They were never served in this house while my wife was alive."

"Mmmm! It's so good," declared the girl, sinking her white teeth into a wedge-shaped piece.

Old Sheppy was very pleased that she liked her sandwich. When she asked for a second one later, he went right over into her camp and never left it. "Any girl who likes corned beef sandwiches will make a fine wife," he said to the baronet.

Then he realized for the first time that Gardiner wore a glum expression.

"What's wrong with you?" he asked.

"I'm a little worried. Your member is taking the bit in his teeth."

"*My* member? Do you mean Georgie Grace? Is he making an ass of himself again?"

"Well, that remains to be seen. He's speaking in the House soon on the subject of the iniquities of certain financial figures. Chiefly myself and Isabelle's father."

"The Divinity gave many gifts to Georgie but completely overlooked common sense." Old Sheppy turned back to Isabelle. "When I was a boy the king was George II and he didn't speak English well. Once he took it on himself to pay his respects to the arts by saying, 'I hate all boets and bainters.' I've always agreed with that sentiment but now I'm adding to the list. I'm beginning to hate all boliticians." He laughed even more loudly at this sally than any of the others. "I think we'll have to groom Young Chip for that seat. Do you know, he already has his eye on it. He's even prepared a manifesto on the subject, giving his qualifications. He wanted me to have it printed and distributed but we couldn't afford to do it."

Isabelle had been conscious that the boy's eyes had never left her since she entered the room. She smiled at him now and sent him into such a state of physical shrinking that his head seemed about to vanish from view like a turtle's down into the collar of his ill-fitting coat.

"I'm sure," she said, "that Master Chip will make a good member someday."

"But sooner or later he'll have to sit in the House of Lords and *that* will take the starch out of him." The duke raised the lid of the teapot and squinted at the contents. "I hope you like your tea strong. Will you pour it, my dear?"

While Isabelle performed this function with graceful movements of her hands the old duke proceeded to talk about the problems of his unusual household.

"When we have visitors, they have to take us as we are. It's strange there isn't a woman here because there always were plenty of girls in our family. I had eight sisters. They're all dead now, poor things, and so no feelings will be hurt if I say that I detested the lot of them. They got themselves married off—a duke's daughter can always get a husband—and proceeded to bring daughters into the world. There are Gorse nieces and grandnieces all over the kingdom, and an unattractive lot they are in the main. But there are none here. Blettor did his duty and brought a hundred thousand into the house with his wife, who was a daughter of Manly Wilkins the banker. But the hundred thousand wasn't enough to salvage this sinking ship and it will devolve on Young Chip to marry a girl with a real bouncer of a fortune.

"Well, here we are, the three of us, without a feminine hand to ease our burdens or bring the light touch of charm into our barren existence. And damme, if it isn't a grand way to live! At least I thought so until I saw this charming and beautiful young lady who is going to throw herself away so blindly."

The baronet smiled. "I trust Your Grace will be on hand to witness the act of throwing away."

Old Sheppy frowned uneasily. "Damme, Tib, I can't be sure that I will. You see, I haven't bought myself any clothes in ten years. It may even be longer. I'm a pretty seedy old party; and so I've fallen into the easy and pleasant habit of going nowhere."

"Isn't it time you got yourself all fitted out for another ten years of easy and pleasant living?"

"If you go through my pockets, Tib, it's shillings and pence you'll come up with, not pounds or guineas. I'm dragging bottom at this exact moment; and it's a pretty sorry, muddy job."

"Your Grace," said Gardiner, "the trouble with you is that you're a great gentleman but not a man of the world. Let me make a suggestion."

He dropped a hint to Lord Blettor that Isabelle would enjoy a personally conducted tour of the great rambling house and the heir of the family led her away with the utmost willingness. Young Chip, to whom the absence of his new divinity would have been like a physical pain, followed on their heels.

"Your Grace," said the baronet, taking the seat Isabelle had vacated and speaking in confidential tones, "tailors are always in need of important patrons to keep themselves in the swim. Now, take my people, Slingcott and Stork. You would say they are about the best, wouldn't you?"

The old peer almost smacked his lips at the thought of the outstanding coats, the remarkable trousers and the resplendent waistcoats produced by the firm in question. "I've always heard they're the best. And I have the evidence in the way you look yourself, Tib. Damme, if you're not a regular sonnet in silk and broadcloth."

"Very well. Here we have Slingcott and Stork, at the top of the heap. But if a new firm gets started and men whose names mean something begin to go to them, where will Slingcott and Stork be? They know how the land lies,

Your Grace. If they could say that you had put yourself in their hands—and then you began to make appearances, looking like Prinny in his younger days—it would be like stumbling over a gold mine for them. I'm sure they would be willing to fit you out and not charge you as much as a shilling."

The old duke had listened with avid interest. "By gad, Tib," he said, "the idea of being well turned out again appeals to me. Are you sure they wouldn't send me a bill?"

"I'm positive of it. But I'll make a personal point of speaking to them. If they say yes, we'll have you down in London by the first coach; and looking like Beau Brummell in time for the wedding."

"Do you suppose they'd make something for Blettor and Young Chip as well?"

Gardiner hesitated. Then he threw caution to the winds and nodded his head. "I'm certain they would."

But when the rest of the party returned from the tour of the house, Young Chip, his round face red with embarrassment, unexpectedly refused to consider the idea of going to London for clothes. When pressed for a reason, he swallowed several times and said, "Because I'm not going to the wedding."

"Now see here, young fellow," said his grandfather sternly, "this isn't handsome behavior. Why do you say you won't go?"

If the boy's face had shown embarrassment before, it now gave proof of positive suffering. He made several efforts to speak before finally managing to say: "I think I—I could tell Miss Carboy. But I couldn't with all of you around."

So on the way to the entrance, when the time had come for the engaged couple to leave, the boy fell behind with Isabelle.

"Now, Chip," she said, "I want a satisfactory explanation out of you. Why do you dislike me so much? Because you must, you know, if you won't come to see me married."

"Oh, Miss Carboy! I—I——" He fell into incoherence for a moment but finally regained some control of his tongue. "What I mean is that you—that you are making a *terrible* mistake. You mustn't marry him. You're so young and beautiful. And he's old. He's much too old for you."

Isabelle indulged in one of her most charming laughs, a tinkling ripple of sound. "Now, Chip, that's not fair. Sir Theobald is a delightful man. He's handsome and amusing, and I'm *very* fond of him. He's not really old at all. Is that the only reason you won't come?"

"No," said the boy. He dug his knuckles down into his pockets, and he dragged his feet and twitched his shoulders, all symptoms of youthful indecision and agony of spirit. "Did you hear what Grandfather said about me? That I'd have to marry an heiress with a real bouncer of a fortune? Well, it's true. And you're the only young and beautiful heiress I've ever seen. Why couldn't you—well, why couldn't you sort of back out of this with old Tib and—well, wait a few years? There isn't any great difference in our ages, is there? Three or four years, perhaps."

"Or five or six. Chip, can it be that you're proposing to me?"

The boy's round face went scarlet. But this was a matter of such earth-shaking importance to him that he checked the impulse to run and hide. "Yes, Miss Carboy. I don't want to marry any heiress who comes along. I want to—to marry you. If I can't, I won't marry anyone. I'll go off to war and get myself killed." After a pause, he began to speak in an almost wheedling tone. "As soon as Grandfather dies I'll be a lord. And later I'll be a duke."

"Chip," said Isabelle in a confidential whisper, "I'll tell you a secret. I've always wanted to marry a duke."

"Then—then—oh, Miss Carboy, is it settled?"

Isabelle shook her head. "No, Chip. You see, I would be twenty-five at least before you could think of getting married. And that means I'd be an old maid. You wouldn't marry me then. Nobody would. I'd be left on the shelf. I'll tell you what we'll do. We'll make a bargain between us. We, the duke-to-be and the heiress, will keep track of each other. Who knows what may happen in the years to come?"

"Yes!" said the boy. "Something will happen. And someday I'll marry you."

"And you'll come to my wedding?"

After a few moments the boy nodded his head. "I'll be as mad as hornets. But I'll be there."

CHAPTER FOURTEEN

The day of the wedding was perfect. A warm sun seemed to hang over Beaulaw Hall and to select that one spot in the world for the benefits it bestowed. There was not a square inch of cloud in the sky when Sir Theobald Gardiner arrived in a great hurry in a coach, with his secretary and his valet and a great mass of boxes and bags. He should have been as happy as the birds which sang in the hedges and clustered in the treetops; but instead he looked distrait, even worried. The reason came out at once when he encountered his prospective father-in-law.

"Is it certain that the duke is coming?" asked Carboy. This speculation, on which so much depended, had not been out of the minds of any member of the family for weeks, although Isabelle herself had professed confidence.

"The only thing surer is that the sun will rise in the east tomorrow," said the baronet. He fished in a pocket of his coat and produced a sheet of paper with a commercial name at the top. "This is why I know. I received this bill from Slingcott and Stork yesterday. I'm not sure whether His Grace was inno-cent enough to think they would supply him with clothes free of charge or whether he understood that I would do the paying. In either case, he hasn't allowed any scruples to hold him back. Listen to this." The ruffled peer began to read from the list in his hand. "Two frock coats. A dozen shirts with ruffled bosoms. Two hats, both beaver. Six pairs of trousers. Six waistcoats, in assorted colors, and damnably expensive. Six pairs of shoes—highs, Wellingtons, and pumps. A dozen handkerchiefs. A tweed hunting suit. Two tweed caps. Gad, Father-in-law, the old dotard has really been going it. He's got himself well bubbed, sartorially speaking. A regular damned spending spree."

Samuel Carboy began to laugh. He threw back his head, in fact, and roared with delight. "Good for Old Sheppy!" he said. "I admire the old coot for getting his full pound of flesh. And, of course, Sir Theobald, you know as well as I do that it's worth what it has cost you."

Samuel Carboy had another talk later in the morning. It was with Jonathan Bade and it was something both men were due to remember as long as they lived. Knowing the tendency of the young lawyer to hide himself away, Carboy went to his bedroom and found him staring out of the window with a heavy frown.

"Why so glum?" asked the industrialist. "It's a beautiful day; and it's going to be one filled with pleasure and satisfaction for all of us."

Jonathan Bade turned a slow eye in the direction of his employer. "Yes," he said in a flat tone. "It's a beautiful day."

"I've had a peek at the bride," declared Carboy proudly. "She's going to look her best."

"When even a plain girl can become lovely on her wedding day, it's natural that the divinely endowed Isabelle should achieve a miracle of radiance."

Carboy looked at him with his first stirring of interest in the lawyer's feelings for the daughter of the house. Then, abruptly, he changed the subject.

"I've got some questions to ask. Grace is bringing up the matter of the Tontine in the House today. You've assured me all along that we have nothing to fear, that every blankety legal cord has been properly knotted. Are you positive of this? Do you feel safe in saying there's nothing they can get their hands on?"

"You have nothing to fear," answered the lawyer. "The slate is clean, the books are open for the whole world to see. It has been handled in a clean and businesslike way from beginning to end. Since Hark Chaffery vacated the scene, it has been in every respect a model operation."

"Good. I'm delighted to hear you say so. You see, Jonathan, I have a curious feeling about the Tontine. I believe somehow it's going to be very important to my children in the end. I can't put into words just what it is I feel. Well, so much for that. Now for the other matter. Did the letters come?"

Bade walked to the table and took some envelopes from a dispatch case lying there. "Yes. They're here. I've gone through them. You can have the Persia and Muscovy Co. if you're prepared to pay the price."

Carboy looked at him with a puzzled frown. "The price? There's been no talk of price yet. There can't be any until they reach an agreement with us."

"I was not thinking, sir, of the price in pounds and shillings," declared Bade with a deep sigh. "There's another price involved here. The price in damage to the spirit, in loss of inner content, in the destruction of certain ideals. *This* price is extremely high."

"Now see here, Jonathan." Carboy placed himself directly in front of the lawyer and spoke in accusing tones. "I've known you were against the deal. You've put all manner of obstacles in the way. You were slow at finding the legal angle which is now going to enable us to take the company over. What's wrong with you? Why are you getting so squeamish all of a sudden?"

"The reason is simply stated. Legally we're on firm ground. Morally our feet are in a quagmire. We have no right to take over this concern."

"We've taken over scores of concerns!" exclaimed Carboy. "Why should we hesitate now?"

"There's a difference. A very great difference. All the difference, in fact, between right and wrong. In every other case we were in a position to do something for the company we engulfed. There had always been mismanagement or carelessness at the top. Or there was a clear indication that certain evils in the trade could be corrected only by amalgamation." He paused and studied the industrialist with a steady eye. "But the Persia and Muscovy is a self-contained corporation which is being well managed and is not only making money for its owners but is providing satisfactory employment for several thousand men. We know that the relationship between owners and labor has been cordial. It's true that the flaw in the charters which we've discovered gives us a loophole. But why should we interfere when things are going along so well?"

"I need the company!" declared Carboy. His face had turned a mottled red as it always did when he met opposition.

"The empire you have established—I dislike the word 'empire' but where can I find a better?—has got along so far without it. It will continue to do so. I can see no need for this particular addition."

Carboy had taken to pacing up and down the room. Each time that he turned he paused and glowered at his legal adviser. There was a threat of trouble in the heavy way he planted his feet and menace in the slow turning of his eyes.

"Put it this way, if you like," he said. "I want this company. I want it more than any I've added yet to my holdings. It's not the greedy desire of a boy for a stick of candy. I happen to know that I can accomplish some remarkable things if I have control. It will be most useful to me." He stopped his pacing to propound a question. "Isn't that reason enough?"

"No," answered Bade. "Not nearly enough. It was all the reason Napoleon needed for some of his conquests, that's true. But you hate Napoleon and dispute his reasons and methods. You don't want to do anything that might provide reason for comparisons between you."

"Then let me put it this way. I may not need the company but I want it! Must I explain my motives further than that?"

"There's no reason why you should. I'm only your lawyer." Bade looked the industrialist squarely in the eye. "But, Mr. Carboy, I remember distinctly the first time we met. I remember every word said. Most particularly I recall you saying, 'Those who help me and advise me must fear God and the law of the land as much as I do.' Do you recall saying that, Mr. Carboy?"

"I said what I believed. I haven't changed. There's nothing illegal in what I propose to do."

"No, Mr. Carboy. The law is crystal-clear and you will stand in no danger of going to jail. But your conscience is another matter. Can you explain your motives to your conscience, sir?"

"I have already done so," declared Carboy shortly. "My conscience finds no fault."

"Perhaps it is getting blunted. A blunt conscience is a dangerous thing. Consider, sir, Pontius Pilate."

Carboy made no comment at once. He was breathing hard and giving other indications of a rising temper. He resumed his pacing, giving an occasional angry glance at the lawyer.

"I am going to repeat one other thing which was said that day," declared Bade. "It was something I said. I was pleased with the prospect of becoming your legal man and I remarked, 'It begins to sound like an invitation to sally out on an adventure.' Well, sir, I begin to dislike the flavor of the adventure. If you take forcible control of Persia and Muscovy, I shall turn my horse about and ride home. The adventure, as far as I am concerned, will be over."

The mottled red of Carboy's face grew deeper, and his hands trembled. "I should boot you right out. But I don't think I will. You're a valuable man in spite of your silly doubts and cavilings. It's getting clear that I'm going to lose my son. I lose my daughter today. Can I lose you at the same time?"

"I'll be happy to stay. On one condition. That you go back to the basis on which we started. I've never budged from it and I never shall."

"Bade," declared Carboy, "you're asking the impossible. Who am I to say that I will or I won't? I've learned one thing, that a man can't control his destiny. Here is the plain truth: I've ceased to be the master of the business, I've become its servant. I sometimes grow weary of all this growing, this buying of more companies, this getting more involved in banking and shipping. But can I stop? I can't. An iron hand is directing me and all I can do is obey. In other words, my boy, the time comes when a business rolls along of its own momentum and can't be stopped or controlled according to the childish doubts and beliefs of weak men." He paused and then added with some reluctance: "I'm getting to understand Napoleon better. He summoned the whirlwind and then was forced to ride along with it. I'm beginning to feel already the tugging of the whirlwind I've conjured up." There was a still longer pause. "We'll have this out later. It's not a day for bitter disputings."

As they talked they had been aware of great confusion in the house. There was continual running up and down in the halls and the sound of feminine voices raised in practically all the emotions: delight, doubt, uncertainty, fear, and sometimes even pain. The house was packed with servants, many of them engaged only for the occasion, and continual mistakes were being made. Loud voices reached them from the enormous marquee which was being raised on the rear lawn where the yeomanry would be regaled with beef and beer. Carriages were driving up in great haste and dashing off again. The voice of Mrs. Carboy could be heard in obviously happy direction of all this activity.

"I'm trying today to do my very best for my little girl," said Carboy. "The worst of it is that you can't do everything yourself and so be sure it will be done right. That fool of a Fleck must carry the bride's cup at the head of the procession, filled with rich wine. It's a splendid silver bowl and it cost me a pretty penny. I'm sure that idiot will drop it. I've asked him a dozen times if he feels equal to it, and each time he gets more unsatisfactory and evasive in his replies." Carboy looked questioningly at the attire of the lawyer, which had nothing festive about it. "Isn't it time you were getting ready?"

"I'm not going down."

"Why not in God's name? Is it because of this quarrel between us?"

"No, I made up my mind about it last night."

"Is it that old reluctance to having people see you? I thought you got over that long ago."

Bade hesitated. "It's partly that, I guess."

Carboy walked to the door, saying, "Well, whatever it is, pull yourself together and get down in time. I know you like my little Isabelle."

"Yes," answered Bade, beginning to gather up the papers on the table. "I do. But I won't be present."

CHAPTER FIFTEEN

1

Alfred Carboy brushed his suit carefully. It was not his best one; *that* had gone two weeks before and, as he was a poor hand at bargaining, had brought him precious little. To come quickly to the point, it was the only suit he had left; he had also one hat, one pair of shoes, one shirt, and, to vary the monotony, two cravats.

Having finished the brushing, he dressed himself and then looked in the cracked mirror over the dilapidated washbasin. "You've come down in the world and you look it," he said to himself.

With a cautious glance over his shoulder, he drew a bottle of ink and a pen out of one of his pockets—they belonged downstairs and Mrs. Lagg, the landlady, would have gone into a rage if she had known he had them—and placed them on the rickety table beside his bed. He proceeded then to write two letters. They were not long but he took time over their composition.

When they were finished he addressed them in the clear and scholarly hand
he had been taught at Clutterhaugh. Oddly enough he addressed each of
them in the same way:

> Mrs. Samuel Carboy
> Beaulaw Hall, Berkshire
> England

This done, he sighed unhappily, pocketed the two letters, and rose to his
feet. He counted his money and then indulged in a frowning calculation.

"There's just enough," he thought. "A dinner at that little restaurant off
the Bowery. No wine, the money won't stretch that far. I'll have to be content
with beer. That will leave me with a quarter for a gallery seat in a theater.
Then I'll sign on with the first outgoing ship, if I can. Or—well, we'll come
to that later."

He did not get much pleasure out of his dinner. The veal cutlet was too
thick and too tough, the vegetables were soggy, the dessert was a tasteless
concoction made of corn. He tipped the waiter fairly but not generously,
looked at the time, and walked out into the street.

"What an ass I've been!" he thought as he turned west in the direction of
Broadway. "When I got the pater's letter and the hundred pounds, I should
have got on the first boat and gone home to have it out with him. But I
was too proud and I wanted to show him what I could do. How was I to
know that they only raise cattle somewhere off in the West and that riding
a horse won't get you a job in New York? I still had enough left two months
ago to get back somehow—but still I stayed. I didn't want to turn up like the
Prodigal Son. And here I am, with all my clothes in hock and a single quarter
in my pocket. What would Lolotte think if she saw me now?"

The Princess Charlotte, he knew, had been packed off to Europe as soon
as they had discovered the nature of her interest in the young Englishman
who had brought the letter from Rio. Did she ever think of him? At best it
would be the most fleeting of thoughts she would give him. The dark-eyed
princess was too realistic to retain any interest in a passing romance.

And Nell Groody? His thoughts were more often with her than with the
vivacious daughter of the ex-King of Spain, and they were always heavy with
a sense of guilt. He had written her one letter only and that had been immediately on his arrival at Rio. It could not have been a very satisfactory
letter for her to receive, because he had no knack for putting words together
and he had not been able to think of much to say. Poor Nelly! She was still
running her little shop, and waiting. Waiting for him! If he managed to get
home someday—tears came into his eyes whenever he thought of the comforts
of Beaulaw Hall and the loving kindnesses of his mother—he would not be
able to redeem himself by marrying the daughter of his father's onetime
coachman. That, he knew, would be the last straw as far as Samuel Carboy
was concerned. He would be cut out of his father's will and cast adrift for
the second and last time.

At any rate Nelly had a roof over her head and a warm bed to sleep in, and that was more than he had. Mrs. Lagg had made it clear to him that afternoon that he must produce some part of his back rent or never return.

Despite the grimness of his prospects and the bitter reflections which filled his mind, he found his steps quickening as he reached the section where the theaters were located. He did not intend to visit the fashionable Park Theater which had just been reopened on a larger and grander scale than before. He doubted if a seat could be secured there for as little as the solitary coin in his pocket. There was a small house off Broadway which would suit him better in every way. It had a flaming Liverpool lamp suspended over the entrance and an exciting sign in the largest and blackest of letters which announced to the world that the Marcus Aurelius Wallace Repertoire Company was offering new plays, direct from London, and many sensational effects. He was willing to confess to himself that the classic offerings at the Park, such as *Othello* and *School for Scandal* and even *Lionel and Clarissa*, were too dull for him. The little Globe and the Wallace players would be more in his line, more likely to make him forget for two hours the grim alternative he must then face.

He found that he was much too early. The door of the theater was still locked and he could see through the glass a bleary-eyed old woman giving the floor of the vestibule a belated mopping. Hoping to see some of the players arrive, he walked around into the dark alley where the stage door would be located. He had seen many stage doors in his time (it was almost a tradition at Clutterhaugh that a senior must have theatrical experiences) but this one was the grubbiest and least impressive he had ever encountered. There was a sign under a small lamp, a rickety flight of six steps and a man squatting atop them. He was a fat little man, not very clean, and he was chewing tobacco with a rhythmic motion of his jaws. He regarded Alfred with a jaundiced eye.

"You're way ahead of time," he said. "Hell, the play won't be over for three hours. Who you after, little Emmy or the Great Beauty with the Haunting Eyes?"

"I'm after no one. I—I just thought I might be lucky enough to see some of the company going in. I'm going to buy a ticket as soon as the doors are opened."

The liverish eye looked down at him skeptically. "I know you cullidge fellas too well to believe *that*. I think you've been taken by Emmy and her legs." Then a new thought took possession of him. He removed his own legs from the railing and seemed prepared to get to his feet. "Say! Are you stage crazy? Do you want to be an actor?"

"Yes! To both questions." Alfred began to experience a sense of excitement. Had he suddenly stumbled over an opportunity? Was it possible he might be offered a chance with this great repertoire company? "I would like a position as an actor very much."

"Ever done any acting?"

"Yes. I acted in all the school plays. I was always the villain."

The man spat viciously at an open barrel of garbage. "Ach! Pooh! Don't let Weeping Wally know that, if you get to talk with him. Better no experience at all than these ampature things." He got to his feet and began to climb down the steps with a twitching gait. "Come over here into the light. I want a good look at you, young fella."

When Alfred stepped close enough to be inspected, the doorkeeper whistled. "Whew! You're big, ain't you? You're no cullidge man, you're a reglar Vicking. If the Great Beauty lays an eye on you, it's leads you'll be playing, and God help us all. That ain't what I got in mind for you."

"Are you the manager? I'm afraid I've been making a great mistake. I thought you were the doorkeeper."

"Lissen. I *am* the doorkeeper but I'm nearly everything else as well. I'm the stage manager, and I'm Props and I'm Baggage and I'm Lights and Giblets. I'm everything that Weeping Wally ain't. When you come along here tonight, I'm sitting here and wundring if I'd have to play the part myself. My name is Samson, young fella, and I don't need a haircut and I didn't kill the Philadulphians, and so we'll consider all them questions asked and jewly answered. Around here they call me Samp and let it go at that."

"I think I understand about Lights, Mr. Samson, but did you say—Giblets?"

Samson nodded. "You see, we're living in at the moment. Things ain't going so well because the Great Beauty with the Haunting Eyes must play Juliet and she turns up her nose at *Bessie from Birmingham* and *Follow Me, Ferdie.* So the ghost takes a vacation and don't walk. We sleeps right here and gets our own meals. I buy the food and it's giblets I pervide oftener than the chicken. You get the point?"

Alfred wasn't sure that he did but he followed the general factotum up the steps when Samson motioned him to do so. They found themselves first in a drafty anteroom from which a glimpse of the bare stage could be had, set for the first act with a potted palm, a moth-eaten couch and three chairs. Samson turned down a narrow flight of steps and they arrived in the greenroom.

It was a dismal place. A lamp, attached to the wall at a crazy angle, was giving off just enough light to demonstrate that the greenroom had changed its function and become a dormitory for the men of the company. Beds had been made on the floor at close intervals and masculine clothing hung from nails on the wall. A large iron pot suspended over a small fire gave forth an aroma which might have been appetizing if it had been able to combat the other odors which filled the room. One of the bundles of bedclothes had an occupant, an unshaven young man who was sound asleep and snoring like a file of kettledrums.

"There!" said Samson, pointing at the sleeper. "That's the condition he come back in half an hour ago. I'll have to move Pinkie Kidweed into his part and let you have what he was down for. You'll play a drunk. You'll stay bubbed all through the piece and you'll wander on and off." He squinted suspiciously at Alfred. "Feel up to it?"

"But—but, Mr. Samson, do you mean I'm to play it tonight? Without any chance to get up in the part?"

"You go on in half an hour. Lissen, what's your name?"

"Alfred Carboy."

"All right, Curboy, here's what I'll do. I'll stay with you all evening. You don't be on long at any time and, before you step in, I'll rehearse you in what you got to say. I'll stand in the wings and prompt you if you forget. It's a good part because audiences always like drunks. All you got to do is come on and they starts to laugh. Can you do it?"

"I'll do my best."

"Good, Kirby." Having reached this corrupt form of address in two quick stages, the stage manager stuck to it thereafter and nothing could change his mind about it. "You better sleep here tonight, because the grand impressare-io ain't here and won't be until the morning rehearsal. The accummadation ain't fancy, as you can see."

Alfred said to himself that the accommodation was far from fancy but that he would be better off than sleeping in a hogshead in a warehouse or on a dank and weedy couch at the bottom of the river. He nodded his acquiescence in the arrangements and then asked about pay.

Samson sheered away from the question of money like a colt standing over a firecracker. "That," he said, "will be settled by Weeping Wally when he gets here in the morning. Now, Kirby, let's go over the first scene." He took a greasy book out of a pocket and began to leaf through it. "Here we are. You go on, staggering. You stagger right up to the footlights and you stare at 'em in a blank way. Then you say, 'Where am I?' Then you grin at 'em and say, 'I feel so fine that it must be that barmaid gave me a love potion.' From that moment, you've got 'em in your pocket. Very well. Kirby, show me what you can do with *that*."

Alfred went through the scene. Samson watched him critically and said at the finish: "Can't say it was in-spired exactly. But you'll do, I reckon. Now I'll have to get you made up. The costume will be a close fit but that will be good, specially if you should happen to break through in the rear during the purformance. I'm going to paint your nose so red it'll help to light up the house."

2

Alfred was careful to remove all his make-up before going to bed. When he wakened the next morning, however, he realized that the other male members of the cast had not been as particular as that. They were all snoring loudly with their painted faces turned up from greasy pillows. He found a tap and scrubbed himself vigorously. Then he went out on the stage to live over again his triumph of the previous evening.

He knew that he had been good and all the members of the company had been kind enough to confirm this opinion. And the audience *had* laughed.

He could hear still that gratifying chorus of guffaws which had come up to him over the footlights. It had been an intoxicating experience.

He said to himself: "An actor's life needn't be as bad as one would think from what goes on here. Perhaps I would soon be promoted to lead parts. . . . It would be fine to see my name in big black letters on the bills! Perhaps I might become famous and play in Europe. Perhaps Lolotte would come and watch me from the royal box. I might even be invited to supper at the palace afterward."

A cheerful voice hailed him from the wings. "Say, mister, what are you doing here?"

It was the soubrette of the company, whose name was Emmy Sweet. He recognized her at once, although a long skirt was concealing the perfect legs which had made her such a favorite with the audience the night before. Her hair was naturally red, apparently, for it looked real now in an unruly and rather pleasing way.

"I'm here because I'm a member of the company. At least, I was last night. I played the drunk."

The girl laughed in a pleased state of unbelief. "Hey nonny, mister! I don't believe it for a minute. Why, that red nose and that terrible squint! And here you're perfectly handsome."

"I recognized you at once," said Alfred. He was thinking, "She's pretty nice, I guess. My, what jolly red hair. And those wonderful legs!"

Emmy crossed the stage and stared up at him with a hint of awe in her round eyes.

"Oh, I do hope you're going to stay with us," she said in a dramatic whisper. "Has Wally talked to you yet about money? Don't let him talk you down. You were good last night. You were really very good. In that scene with me you almost made *me* laugh. Hold out for plenty when he does talk to you. If he gives in, it will only be a promise, of course, for no one ever gets paid in full. But it's some satisfaction to feel that your pay would be big if you got it; and when you tell people you're getting twice as much, it isn't quite as big a lie, is it?"

"I'd like to stay and learn to be an actor, Miss Sweet."

The girl giggled. "That's just a stage name and I won't tell you what my real one is. So just call me Emmy. What's your name, great big fellow?"

"Alfred Carboy. I'm from England."

"I'll call you Alfie. Alfie, have you any money?"

"I have a quarter. That's all. I intended to spend it on a seat last night. But then Samp saw me and got me to play the part."

"A quarter? A whole quarter? Why, Alfie, that's wonderful! That beautiful, round, shiny quarter will buy us both such a nice hot breakfast. If you want to take me to breakfast, that is."

Alfred tucked her arm in his. The depressed state of mind from which he had suffered so long had left him. He felt once more that the world was a good place in which to live. His companion was pretty and bubbling over with good spirits. What more could he ask?

"Come on, Emmy," he said. "I wish I had plenty of beautiful round, shiny silver dollars to spend on you. My, Emmy, you were pretty last night! You made the show."

Emmy giggled again. "Thank'ee, sir, thank'ee. Old Samp says I'm a great actress—from the waist down."

When they returned from breakfast, Alfred's pockets were empty but his spirits were as full as his stomach. He was so content, in fact, that he paid no attention to the scowl with which Samson greeted them at the stage door.

"Huh!" said the stage manager, looking them over with an accusing eye. "Late for rehearsal the first day! This won't do, Kirby, it won't do at all. Are you going to be a dishrupting influence on the company?"

"Aw, stow it, Samp," said Emmy in a casual tone. "We had breakfast together and I guess we had our sitting britches on."

The stage manager fastened his glance exclusively on Alfred. "Mr. Wallace is here and he wants to talk to you, Kirby. He got good reports of your work last night and he may be wanting to hire you on. He's a tough 'un and he's a close 'un. If you want to get hired, there's just one thing for you to do. Sing small. Don't go puffing out your Charlie Prescott at him. He's not used to well-filled vestkits."

"When does he want to see me?"

"Now. That's the one word in the landwidge that he seems to understand. Right now! Come along, I'll show you the way, Kirby. As for you, Mistress Sweet, get out of that snippy long skirt and into something sensible for rehearsal. You got two minutes to do it."

Marcus Aurelius Wallace had his office above the entrance. Alfred was surprised to find it so filled with furniture of all kinds that it was almost impossible to see the manager where he sat behind an ornate desk. Later he would learn that the room served as a warehouse and was kept filled with the better props which were not needed on stage at the time and which might be stolen if left in the wings. There was a continuous lugging of heavy furnishings back and forth and much profanity on the part of Samson and his aides.

The manager was a stout little man with suspicious eyes and an acquisitive mouth. He motioned to Samson to leave and then called to Alfred to present himself in the particular corner where the managerial desk stood behind a well-patched Chinese screen.

"Kirby," said Mr. Wallace, "you have a turn for comedy, but to me you look like a straight."

"My experience," said Alfred, "has been more in drama than comedy."

"Has it now? Where?"

"In England, sir. I played Bartlemy Band in *The Moated Ruin*."

"In Lunnon? Or on the road?"

Alfred decided he had better not play too exalted a tune. "On the road."

The manager took out a formidable-looking jackknife and began to cut

shreds for his pipe from a plug of cake tobacco. He had busy dark eyes
with which he kept glancing up as he plied the steel blade.

"We're in a slump," he said. "I don't know why. The company is good,
the plays are popular, and we have Cordelia Cadwallader as our star. What
more can I do? And yet people are not turning out. House is always half
empty. Wish I could use you. I can see looking at you here that you've got a
bit of manner. But how can I add another salary to the payroll? It's much
too big as it is."

Alfred remembered that he had been advised to sing small. "It's this way,
sir," he said. "I would like a job."

"You'd learn a lot with us," said Wallace quickly. "All you have to do is
watch my wife and you'll learn all there is to know about acting. You know,
of course, that Cordelia Cadwallader, the greatest all-around actress this
country has ever produced, honors me by being my wife?"

"I know how great Cordelia Cadwallader is," answered Alfred tactfully.
"But I didn't know she was your wife."

The little manager puffed out his chest. "I am the happiest and proudest
of men. As for Miss Cadwallader, she's equally great in tragedy or comedy.
Ah, Kirby, you should see her Lady Macbeth! The opportunity to play in
the same company with her, to watch how she achieves her effects, to—to
sit at her feet! Why should I pay large salaries to those who enjoy these
inestimable advantages?"

"I am sure the advantages are very great indeed, sir."

The manager had succeeded in lighting his pipe and was now drawing
on it with a deep soughing sound. He watched his visitor through the
smoke which soon gathered about him.

"There's a point about production"—puff—"which actors don't appreciate"—puff—"sufficiently. The need to find the money. It's costly putting on
a play"—puff, puff—"and I always say any successful theatrical manager
would make the perfect Chancellor of the Exchequer. He always has pressure on him"—puff—"to pay bills, to buy costumes and new scenery, to meet
the payroll, to—well, to match maximum demands with minimum resources."

For several moments there was silence while Wallace allowed his words
to sink in.

"I have said this many times, Kirby——"

"If you will permit me to interrupt, sir, my name is Carboy, not Kirby.
Mr. Samson heard it wrong."

"Very well, Carboy. As I was saying when you broke in so unexpectedly,
there is one point which is always overlooked. When business is poor, it
requires genius, sir, to keep a company going. I scrimp and save to keep my
people employed and paid." His eyes had filled with tears and he had to
reach into a pocket for his handkerchief. "You have no idea how I strive and
worry at a time like this." Sniff. "Even when things are prosperous on the
surface, there is still the same difficulty, the same pressure. I want you to

understand this, young man, that the theatrical business can at times be prosperous but—it is never profitable."

The manager gave his eyes a final whisking with the handkerchief before putting that useful article away. Then he leaned forward across the desk and shot a question at his visitor point-blank. "How much do you want? Come, out with it. I'm a busy man. Well, I see you hesitate to put a figure on it. You are perhaps afraid that you will ask less than a generous producer —and I am generous to a fault—would be prepared to pay. Very well, then, here's the best I can do for you. One dollar a week and found. Or three dollars and fly your own kite. The terms are handsome, Carboy. What do you say? Do you accept? Come, come, no hedging. Do you accept?"

"Yes," said Alfred, stunned by the smallness of the offer but realizing that he had no alternative. "Which—which basis do you think I should be on?"

"One and found," declared Wallace emphatically. "They're all on it. That way you always eat and you always have a roof over your head. The other way"—he seemed on the point of yielding to his feelings and reaching again for the handkerchief—"suppose there didn't happen to be three dollars in the till?"

"One and found," agreed Alfred. He was thinking there might be times when it would be impossible to find a dollar in the till. It seemed certain enough that no member of the company was receiving any salary at all at this particularly tight period of the company's history.

There was a rap on the door and a beautifully modulated voice said, "Wallace, may I come in?"

The manager sprang to his feet and ran to the door, crying, "Come in of course, my dear!"

The door opened to admit a lady in a green pelerine and a hat with an enormous black plume. Alfred knew at once that this must be the justly famous Cordelia Cadwallader, for the newcomer had "actress" written all over her. It was evident that she had once been beautiful but her face now showed the effects of a lifetime's use of grease paint. It was thin and leathery, and her nose, which had once been cast in the finest Grecian tradition, was sharp and lined. There could be no denying that she had fine eyes; they were large and dark and expressive. In one hand she carried a reticule and, despite the season, there was a fur muff in the other.

"Wallace!" she said in much the same tone that a queen might adopt in accusing a minister of treason. "I came back early. I was uneasy. The night before last I dreamed there were only eight people—eight, mind you!—in the pit and the boxes were all empty. I said to myself, 'Cordelia Cadwallader, it's a sign!' I knew I must forgo my brief moment of rest and return. Besides, not a soul in the hotel had ever heard of me! I couldn't breathe in such an atmosphere!" She gave both arms an impatient toss. "Well, here I am. Wallace, tell me the truth. Has the take been very bad?"

"Well, my dear, it hasn't been good. But last night we had one hundred and eight in the pit."

"One hundred and *eight?*" The voice of the once illustrious star became deep and dramatic. "Then it *was* a sign. It's a good thing I've come back. I'm needed here. I must be the new broom to sweep out," with a dramatic gesture, "all the cobwebs! Wallace, from now on I shall not be content to let you and the rest of these inanimate lumps decide what we are to put on. From now on I must be the one to make the decisions!"

"Cordelia!" protested the manager, who seemed to have started shrinking in stature as soon as she entered and had now become a very small man indeed. "You have always made the decisions."

"From this moment forward," declared the actress, raising the hand which held the muff high in the air, "my word must be law. Eight people in the pit! To see Cordelia Cadwallader!"

"We've had one bit of luck since you left," said Wallace in a low tone. He went on whispering so low that Alfred could not hear. He was sure they were talking about him, however, for in a few moments Cordelia Cadwallader strode over in the direction of the desk, saying: "Where is he? Show me this phenomenal young man who can make an audience laugh just by going out with a red nose. Produce him, Wallace, I am anxious to see this new miracle of the age."

She gasped when she saw Alfred standing diffidently beside the desk. After a moment's surprised scrutiny of his face and figure she turned furiously on her husband-manager. "Marcus Aurelius Wallace!" she stormed. "You blind earthworm! Never have I been so convinced of your limitations as I am at this moment. You let this young man, who is very handsome and has a fine straight figure, go on in the ragged trappings of a tramp and with his features disguised by a false nose! And you whisper to me that you are hiring him to play comedy bits!"

"My dear, my dear!" protested the manager, his eyes beginning to show signs of moisture. "I haven't seen him act. I decided last night, after the curtain went up and I had locked the cash away, to make a round of the other houses. One must keep abreast of the times, you know, my angel. When I returned, I found that Samp had pulled this young fellow out of some gutter and had put him on in the part. There seems no doubt he had made a hit. Samp punched the laughs on his program, and how many holes do you suppose there were at the finish? Thirty-seven!"

"Cease your babbling."

The onetime dramatic star was looking Alfred over from head to foot with what Samp had called her Haunting Eyes. She nodded her head finally and laid a hand on her husband's arm. "Wallace, don't you see in him what I do?" she demanded.

The manager gave the latest addition to the company a look which he strove to make searching. It was no use, apparently. "No, my dear. Frankly, I don't."

"Idiot!" cried Cordelia Cadwallader. "Don't you remember that great play, the one I wanted to do so much? The one where I played the daughter of an earl who disguises herself as a dairy maid and meets the curate who has run away from the gay life of the city?"

Wallace nodded. "*The Lady and the Curate.*"

"Yes. Oh, what a beautiful play! And we never did it because we couldn't cast it right. The curate defeated us." She looked at Alfred again and then said in a deep whisper to her husband, "He's the Rev. Horace Blennerhasset to the life!"

The manager looked startled. In deference to his wife's opinion, he treated Alfred to a close scrutiny. Finally he gave his head an enthusiastic nod. "My dear!" he exclaimed. "You have a genius for it. There's just no denying it. You see things no one else does." He nodded his head vigorously several times. "You're right. He *is* Horace Blennerhasset to the life."

One of the articles of furniture which filled the office at this juncture was a couch of considerable age which seemed to be suffering from rheumatism. Cordelia Cadwallader seated herself on one end of it and instructed Alfred to take the other.

"Speak," she commanded, "I haven't heard your voice."

"It's hard for me to think of anything to say," declared Alfred. "I'm so overawed at being in your presence."

"My dear boy," she said, her large eyes fixed on his, "you speak just as Horace Blennerhasset would! There's a good tone to your voice which can be brought out with proper training. I will take you in hand. It will be no harder for you than a young monk saying his aves and paters a hundred times a day. Lines like this—'Alas, when the western wind whistles like the wings of the wending whooping crane,' or 'Truly, 'twill be a twice twisting trip to Twiver.' You see, my dear boy, I am going to make an actor of you, perhaps an outstanding actor. Ah, how lucky you are that I saw you first in just the right light, with a shadow on your face and a hint of suffering in your eyes! Yes, yes, indeed, you *are* Horace Blennerhasset! We will play those parts together and so bring to the stage for the first time a great social comedy with undertones of tragedy. But not at once! No, no, dear boy. You will require much training. I will use you in smaller parts. But always with me. Perhaps as the brother in *The Williwaw* or as one who worships me silently from afar. I shall take the greatest pains with you because I am sure I can create out of the base clay I now see a being filled with the divine fire."

When Alfred was dismissed from the upper region where all the earth-shaking decisions were reached, he went slowly downstairs. His hand happened to encounter the two letters he had written the evening before, which were still in his pocket. He carried them down to the stage door and proceeded to tear them to bits. "That's the one I'd have sent Mother if I had been signed on a ship," he said to himself. "This one was if I had decided to jump off a dock and end it all." He dropped both into the barrel of refuse at the foot of the steps. "Now," cheerfully, "I'll write her an entirely different kind. I guess she'll be excited when she knows I'm going to be a great actor."

Emmy had seen him come down from the office and she ran away from the rehearsal to learn his news. She reached the top of the steps as he was tossing away the last of the torn sheets. The long skirt had been discarded and she was wearing a red cotton trifle which displayed her trim figure to the very best advantage.

"Well?" she said eagerly. "What did the old crocodile have to say?"

"I've been taken on," responded Alfred. "But I'm not to play comedy bits. Miss Cadwallader has come back and she thinks I should play straight."

"With her?" There was a sudden tensity in the tones of the little soubrette.

"Well—yes, I suppose so."

"I knew it!" cried Emmy. "I just knew it! She's the real crocodile around here. She'll devour you. Oh, I've seen it happen before." She was close to the point of tears. "I'm glad for your sake, Alfie, because you'll have it easier and they'll pay you more than one and found—that was what he offered you, wasn't it?—but, oh, Alfie, we'll be strangers from now on. You won't be allowed to speak to me. You'll belong to her." She began to do an imitation of a rehearsal in a deep voice surprisingly like that of the star. " 'No, no, dear boy, that's not quite it. We'll try it again. Come, put your arm around me and hold me tighter than you did before. And when you speak, dear boy, make me feel as well as the audience that you really love me.' "

Alfred started to laugh and, after a moment, the soubrette joined in. "Just the same," she said, "I wasn't exaggerating. Not a bit. You'll be dear-boyed to death from now on. That venerable bat, with her stringy neck and her eyes like burnt holes in a blanket! If that creaky skeleton ever did a prat-fall, they'd never be able to put her together again." But honesty compelled her to add to this unfriendly portrait: "But she *can* act. I've got to own up that the old ghost knows all the tricks."

3

The curtain went down to an outburst of applause which the newspapers next morning would characterize as "wild." *The Lady and the Curate* on this, its opening night, had been a great success.

When Alfred had removed his make-up and donned a fresh shirt and collar, he walked to the greenroom, wondering what he would do about a bite of supper. Emmy Sweet did not seem to be about. The whole company, in fact, had dispersed with more than the usual speed. Only the stage manager was still on hand.

"Kirby!" called Samp. "I want a word with you, young fella."

Alfred waited at the stage door. "It went well," he said when the general factotum of the company joined him.

"In a way, yes," said Samp. "In a way, no. I been watching the Great

Beauty. She's all set for a tantrum. It hasn't occurred to you, I reckon, that Weeping Wally is getting up his resolution to discharge you."

Alfred was so taken aback that he gasped and for several moments was unable to make any comment. He had been of the belief that he was indispensable and that Marcus Aurelius Wallace was fully aware of his value.

"I know it sounds crazy, Kirby. But it's true. And do you know why he's going to get rid of you? Because you don't make love to his wife."

Alfred found his tongue. "Samp," he said, "I think all your responsibilities are slowly driving you mad. Perhaps not slowly, either. Do you mean to stand there and say that Wally is going to discharge me because I *don't* make love to his wife?"

"Perzactly. You see, Kirby, this here manager of ours, this here squeezer of pennies, is afraid of his wife. And he wants her, poor little girl, to be happy. What does she need to be made happy? I'll tell you, Kirby; to get all the applause, to get all the praise in the press, to have a handsome leading man who's in love with her. Well, she doesn't get all the applause with you on the stage, she doesn't get all the praise in the papers, and worst of all you, her leading man, treat her like something washed up at Sandy Hook."

Alfred realized that there might be some truth in what Samson was saying. He had noticed that Cordelia Cadwallader was very cold to him and that she found fault with everything he did on the stage. There were a few dollars in his wallet but certainly he was in no position to regard the loss of his place in the company with equanimity. He frowned unhappily as he considered what the outcome might be.

"Samp," he said, "she's a fine actress. But, man, she's old! It's hard to make ardent love to a woman who must be thirty years older than you are. I play love scenes with her on the stage but I don't whisper sweet nothings of my own while I'm doing it."

"All the others did."

"I don't take her home after each performance and pretend to be mad with passion for her."

"All the others did. *You* go home with little Emmy."

"I don't write her notes and I can't afford to send her flowers."

"The others wrote her every day and sometimes they even managed to buy flowers for her. Kirby, get this into your thick skull once and for all. You've got to knuckle down to her. She's as mad as a hornet about you and Emmy and she's complaining to Weeping Wally about you all the time. He knows how valuable you are and it's going to break his great generous heart to lose you but that's exactly what's going to happen. He's afraid it's a case of losing you or losing his wife."

It did not take Alfred long to make up his mind. "He's going to lose me," he said.

4

Alfred entered Mrs. Paddy Gogarty's boardinghouse by the back door. He was surprised and rather discomfited to find Mrs. Gogarty herself in possession, with a broom in one hand. It looked for a moment as if he would feel the broom whistling about his ears. She discovered who it was in time, however, and let the end drop to the floor.

"Oh, it's you, is it?" she said. "And what do you mean, Mr. Corby, coming in by the back door at this hour of the night? I was thinking it was a burglar."

"Mrs. Gogarty, I must have a word with Emmy. Has she come in yet?"

"She's in bed and sound asleep, I'm sure, the poor lamb. What is it you want to tell her that won't keep until the morning?"

"It's a matter of business, Mrs. Gogarty. And it *won't* keep until the morning. Do you think you could arrange for me to see her here?"

"And hasn't it been arranged a dozen times or more?" demanded Mrs. Gogarty. "I've let the pair of you have me kitchen and you've stayed here and whispered and laughed and giggled like the loonies you are. Many's the time I've said to myself that I shouldn't have such goings-on going on in my house. It's scandal you'll be bringing down on me, Mr. Corby."

"Mrs. Gogarty, it's all about business. I'm afraid there won't be any giggling this time."

The boardinghouse keeper sighed gustily. "It's nothing I can be forbidding such a fine tall young man," she said.

A few minutes later Emmy came down the back stairs so quietly that he did not hear her until she reached the bottom and whispered, "Alfie!" It was clear that she had been in bed, for she was wearing a dressing gown of a frivolous blue and her hair was more tousled, and more fetching, than he had ever seen it.

They sat down together in the dark at the foot of the stairs and he put an arm around her shoulders. She laid her head against his arm and sighed happily.

"Oh, Alfie, you were so good!" she said. "All the women in the audience were mad about you. I was wishing I could go out through the pit from end to end and slap every one of their silly faces! And what I wanted to do to those in the boxes!"

"Emmy, why didn't you wait for me?"

"Because," she said in aggrieved tones, "Old Samp came to me and said, 'Git home, you!' He said I was causing you a lot of trouble. Alfie, am I causing you trouble?"

"If you are, it's the kind of trouble I like." He became grave then and began to talk about the play. "I'm glad it seems to be a hit because it's my last appearance on the boards, Emmy."

He could feel her body stiffen in his arms. "Alfie!" she whispered tensely. "Are you going home? Has your father relented and sent you money?"

"No. There'll be no relenting in that quarter, I'm afraid. I'll hand in my notice first thing in the morning to get ahead of Weeping Wally, who's going to discharge me."

"Oh no! Alfie, I don't believe it after the way things went tonight."

"It's because I don't make love to Cordelia. And how can I make love to her when I'm so busy making love to you?"

The soubrette giggled in the close shelter of his arms. "We *have* been rather going it, haven't we?"

"Well, her ladyship doesn't like having a leading man who doesn't pretend to be mad about her. She's demanding my head."

There was a moment of silence. Then Emmy got hold of one of his hands and squeezed it ecstatically. "Oh, what good news, Alfie! It's wonderful!"

"Wonderful! What's wonderful about it? I'll be back where I started when I played the drunk that first night. How am I going to make a living now?"

"I'll tell you how you're going to make a living, young Alfie, my lad. You're going to join up with another company. I'll go too."

"What are you talking about?"

"I'm talking about Hermie. Hermie Hanstock. You know him, don't you? He's forming a new stock company to tour the West—Buffalo, Cincinnati, Louisville, all those towns. He's got covered wagons to make the jumps in. He says the great West is hungry for drama."

"Has he approached you?"

"Five times," answered Emmy proudly. "He says my talents are wasted on a sophistic-something or other audience like we get here in New York and that a Western audience will really appreciate them." She paused to giggle. "What he means is my legs."

"Do you think he would want me?"

"Hermie? Want you? He'd jump at the chance to get you."

"What do you suppose he would pay?"

Emmy thought this over. "I think around five and found for the two of us. Say, three and a half for you and one and a half for me."

"What a relief!" exclaimed Alfred, kissing the top of her head and then crumpling her up even closer in his arms. "I expected I would have to choose again—between signing on a ship or jumping into the harbor."

There was a long moment of silence. "I'll tell Hermie that you *might* be interested and his coattails will crackle, he'll be in such a hurry to get over." Emmy sighed. "There's another reason why I'm glad you're willing to leave the Marcus Aurelius Wallace Company."

"What is it?"

The girl hesitated. "I'm glad we're sitting here in the dark and you can't see my face. There was another reason why I didn't wait for you tonight. I haven't been feeling well lately. Oh, how can I tell you? I want you to leave because, if you stayed here, you wouldn't be able to—to make an honest woman of me."

"Emmy! Do you mean——"

"Yes, Alfie." She sighed again. "That's exactly what I mean."

"Are—are you sure?"

"Yes. There isn't any doubt about it at all."

Alfred realized now that he faced the hardest decision of his life. If he married Emmy he would have to abandon all his prospects for the future. His father, whose patience was nearly exhausted as it was, would never forgive him if he brought home a nobody as a wife, an actress moreover. The best he could hope for would be to remain in America for the rest of his life on a small allowance. He would never share in his father's great fortune or inherit Beaulaw Hall. Isabelle would have children, and Samuel Carboy would see that they got everything.

He was neither selfish nor ambitious, and so he was disturbed more by something quite different. Marrying Emmy would mean an ending to all his romantic dreams. He would have to put Nell Groody out of his mind—he still thought of her a great deal—and the interlude at Point Breeze would be relegated to his dim memories. This would be a far remove from the kind of splendid romance he had always expected to share.

Not for a moment, however, did he have any doubts as to what he must do. And it might not be so bad after all. He was quite mad about Emmy. She was so gay always, dancing about the stage, laughing and teasing, and impudently tossing her mop of red hair. Life with her would not be dull. He was sure of that.

It took some time for these thoughts to pass through his mind, even though he had been certain from the start what course he must take.

"I'll be glad to see this Hermie in the morning," he said finally. "We'll make a deal with him as—as a team. Under all the circumstances, Emmy, I guess we should begin to think about plans for getting married, shouldn't we?"

CHAPTER SIXTEEN

1

Julian Grace was pleased to find that his duties were to be performed in the Admiralty Building at Whitehall. There were other navy offices scattered about the center of London but to be near the heart of things was some satisfaction, even to a man who had suffered so much that he looked on life with a disillusioned eye. He was given possession of one of a row of tiny cubicles not far from the historic room where Nelson's body had rested through the night preceding the funeral, and here he kept himself busy all day on matters of decidedly minor importance. A place had been made for him in one of the houses in Spring Gardens which were used exclusively by Admiralty men and their families, and so he had reason to feel that he had become a member of this great organization.

None of the houses in Spring Gardens was large or imposing but great associations clustered about them. Julian had been given two rooms in the house occupied by a Mr. Vincent Pardon who was something or other in the Victualing Office, and Mrs. Pardon was good enough, in fact eagerly willing, to provide him with breakfast and dinner. It was a pleasant arrangement, Mrs. Pardon being an excellent cook. She would soon have treated him as a son but the fact that he was related to the Duke of Outland kept her properly awed.

All the Admiralty houses were named after great naval victories and the occupants had labored, in their various ways, to give them a nautical air. One man had planted a cannon in his front yard and it was so small (the yard, not the cannon) that the snout reached out over the iron fence and was somewhat of a menace on dark nights. Another had at great personal expense built a walk on his roof and was in the habit of climbing up after dinner for a look at the stars through his telescope. Ships' models were displayed in front windows, and some of the curtains were red, white and blue. The house of the Pardons was chiefly distinguished by a motto in red brick over the front door: *For England, Home and Beauty*.

The Pardons were quite proud of the fact that their house was named Sandwich after the victory which, in the opinion of all scholarly navy men, was the first one of all, whereas the houses on each side had a *nouveau* look (to quote Mrs. Pardon), being called respectively Aboukir Bay and Copenhagen. There was a drawback, however, to the possession of this proud label. A former occupant had fancied himself an artist and had expended an incalculable amount of paint in covering the walls with scenes from Hubert de Burgh's great triumph over the French. The scene on the dining-room wall above the Queen Anne sideboard which Mrs. Pardon had inherited (the fact that two of the doors were cracked had, perhaps, made competition slight among the other relatives) was particularly unpleasant. The artist had chosen for this spot the execution of Eustace the Monk and had shown with gory detail how that dubious character came to his end with his head clamped down on the railing and the ax in the hands of an eager seaman. Julian faced this wall during meals and sometimes he found it hard to polish off his slice of mutton or finish his plate of trifle.

Mr. Pardon was tall and spare and spoke very little. He believed in practically nothing, it seemed, for Julian seldom heard him say anything but, "No, I do not think so." He sat at the head of the table, eating his food with a stern air as though only duty drove him to it, and threw his negations into the conversation with the flattening effect of navy shells. Whenever he spoke, Mrs. Pardon would look at Julian and nod her head and he knew she meant that something had now been settled for posterity. Sometimes Mr. Pardon would fall into a chatty mood and say, "We are hard put to it at the Victualing and somehow I do *not* think we will overcome our difficulties."

Mrs. Pardon labored under the impression that her husband was a much underestimated man. Once, when Julian had come in a little early, she waylaid him in the hall and spoke to him about this. "Mr. Grace," she asked, "what in your opinion are *they* going to do for Mr. Pardon?"

"They? Who are they?"

She answered with heavy emphasis. "The men who are above him in the Victualing. The lords of the Admiralty. The editors of the press. The members of the House. The prime minister. The peers, Mr. Grace, and among them your kinsman, the Duke of Outland."

"Ah," said Julian, lowering his voice, "would you by any chance, Mrs. Pardon, extend the list as far—actually as far as the Crown?"

"I would indeed, Mr. Grace. Now tell me, what do you think *they* will do for Mr. Pardon?"

Julian had not yet grasped her meaning. He frowned uncertainly. "May I ask, Mrs. Pardon, what *you* think they should do?"

"Young man," exclaimed the lady, "Mr. Pardon has worn out the seats of twenty-two pairs of trousers, sitting in the same chair and at the very same desk. *That* is what I mean."

"Oh, it's a matter of appreciation. Of promotion, perhaps?"

"Exactly, Mr. Grace."

"Did you say twenty-two pairs? It seems a great many."

"Twenty-two, young man. And as Mr. Pardon is a saving man, he never discards anything until the necessity is very great indeed. He has never given up a pair, Mr. Grace, until he could see an unfriendly glint in the eye of his immediate superior. That will give you no idea of the amount of patching I've had to do. I haven't all of them left to produce as evidence but I am prepared to go on any witness stand and swear to the truth."

Julian gave the matter some thought. "It hardly seems to me adequate to suggest that *they* might provide some kind of a tailoring and mending service. Let me think it over, Mrs. Pardon. Perhaps I'll find some kind of an idea for you."

A few days later he encountered his landlady in the hall at almost precisely the same moment, and gave her a gloomy nod. "Mrs. Pardon, I fear I have bad news for you. Twenty-two is in no sense extraordinary, ma'am. There's a man in our department who claims to have worn through the seats of twenty-four. And he hasn't been in the same office all that time. He's been moving steadily backward. There's a rumor also—but only a rumor so far, mind you—that a man in Navy Pay can claim twenty-eight. And it's said he can produce the evidence."

"What do I care?" cried Mrs. Pardon. "Just how important is your department, may I ask, Mr. Grace? And do we need give a single thought to Navy Pay? I want to tell you that the Victualing, and the work Mr. Pardon does there in particular, has been as vital to England as the very name of Nelson! Trafalgars are fought and won across his desk every day."

Julian was so startled that all he could manage to say was, "Indeed, ma'am, do you really think so?"

"I think so, Mr. Grace. I know it. *They* know it. *They* know how important Mr. Pardon is. Why don't *they* do something about it? Why don't the lords, for that matter, do something for your kinsman, Mr. Grace, who is said to have patches on the seats of every pair of trousers he has to his name?"

"Promotion, ma'am," said Julian, "is very slow in the Admiralty."

"Slow?" cried Mrs. Pardon. "Mr. Grace, there's no such thing."

2

It was well known throughout all the reaches of the Admiralty that Julian Grace had been disappointed in love. That he would keep to himself under the circumstances was to be expected and he did not suffer in popularity because of his standoffishness. Everyone was kind to him and even his superiors, who were very superior indeed, would sometimes give him a dignified half-smile as though desiring to convey comfort to him.

As time went on, however, and his aloofness showed no signs of abating, they began to talk about him in the dingy little offices and in the corridors. "He needn't be so damned sulky," was the general opinion. One of the younger members said: "So help me, Davy, I've been given the chuck by three gals and you don't see me blubbering about it." "I can't count the times I've been given the sack," declared another.

The talk always shifted sooner or later to Isabelle. They liked to recount her latest exploits and tell what they had heard about her. "They say the king chucked Lady Gardiner under the chin at a reception last night." "I saw her once and she's a beautiful bundle, that one!" "I hear she beat Nocky Prentice at tennis, and Nocky was playing for all he was worth." "She certainly is the rage!"

Julian knew what they were saying about him but he did not care. The loss of Isabelle, and the manner in which he had suffered his defeat, had broken his pride, he thought, as well as his heart. He suspected that his office mates were laughing at him secretly. He read intonations in their voices which they, being far from subtle, had not intended. This did not concern him very much, however. Since Isabelle was another man's wife, he did not care that life might have compensations to offer if he wanted to look for them. The face of his lost love was always in his mind; and in time he even began to enjoy a gloomy satisfaction in the fact that his loss had set him apart from his fellows.

One evening, when he had been at the Admiralty a matter of a year or more, Julian found himself with nothing to do. He had dined well enough in a small restaurant and had, for the first time perhaps, found it a matter of regret that he sat alone. When he had finished his coffee and paid his bill, he donned his light paletot (for the air had turned quite chilly) and set out for a walk, hoping that something would happen to relieve his tedium, even that his purposeless footsteps might lead him into an adventure.

Instinctively he turned eastward, for he loved the City when the turmoil of the day was over and the streets had been left to darkness and solitude.

It surprised him to find that the streets were not deserted at all. On second thoughts, however, the reason for this was quite clear. London was hungry and discontented. The depression which had been predicted at the end of the war had come belatedly, and because of that with greater violence. Factories and businesses had been closing down and a large part of the male population had no work. People were starving, the poorhouses were filled to overflowing with the indigent, the prisons were crowded with petty thieves who would probably die on the gallows. When men are idle and hungry, they do not sit around at home, if they have homes; they congregate instead in the streets and loudly voice their disaffection, and sometimes they make things uncomfortable for any well-dressed and well-fed people who venture among them.

This was what was now happening, Julian perceived, when his strolling feet brought him within sight of an establishment which was well lighted in spite of the hour. A party of young men of obviously high social rank (they all had beaver hats and they wore handsome blue coats over white waistcoats) seemed to be acting as a mounted escort for two ladies. They were riding slowly and laughing in loud voices, having dined well. The sound of their horses' hoofs on the cobbled street, combined with their high-pitched levity, had brought out crowds of the unemployed to jeer at them as they passed. Julian was both startled and alarmed to discover that the first of the two ladies, who rode in the van between two highly exhilarated young bucks, was none other than Isabelle.

The leaders came to a stop in front of the illuminated house and Isabelle's two immediate escorts sprang from their saddles to help her alight. She yielded herself to their upturned arms with some hesitation, for in their desire to do something different they had come from a formal dinner party and she was dressed in white satin with figured gauze draped over it. The necklace she was wearing was much too valuable to be flaunted openly in dark streets, and the same could be said for the pearl-decorated lace wrap she had thrown over her white shoulders.

"You will all stay here except Lady Betsy," announced Isabelle, when her delicately shod feet were safe on the pavement. "I won't have any of you hearing what Madame Martine may tell me. It would be all over London by morning if you did. Come along, Betsy, we'll keep our appointment with Madame. These gallant gentlemen will wait for us here. The fresh air will do them all much good, I'm sure."

"We'll count the seconds until you return, dear lady," said one of the escorts in a languishing voice.

Julian, standing on the opposite side of the road, was alarmed to find that the party of horsemen was now surrounded by men of anything but pacific intent. The onlookers had not yet resorted to any form of interference or violence but it was clear enough they would not long accept passively this open demonstration of the wealth and luxury which existed above them.

"What is that house across the street?" Julian asked a man standing beside him who did not seem to belong to the rapidly growing mob.

"Oh, that's where this fortuneteller lives. The one who's set all society agog," replied the man. "Her name is Madame Something-or-other and she's supposed to be absolutely clairvoyant. She tells people all about their pasts and sends them into spasms of amazement and delight with what she predicts of their futures. Her fees are damnably high, I understand." He then asked a question in turn. "Was it Lady Gardiner who just went in?"

"It was a lady and beautiful enough to be—the one you mention," answered Julian. "Does it occur to you, sir, that we are likely to witness a riot of sorts in a few minutes?"

"It *has* occurred to me," said the other. "And being a law-abiding citizen and the head of a family, I propose to take myself off at once and so avoid having any part in it."

Julian had recognized the young blood with the languishing voice as a fellow student at Clutterhaugh. He crossed the road and laid a hand on the blue-coated shoulder of his onetime friend.

"Delane," he said, "I've a word of advice for you. Collect your full party at once and get away from here. There will be trouble if you delay about it."

"Oh, it's you, Grace," said the other, recognizing him in the light from the windows of the fortuneteller's establishment. "Odd that you should be here. Or is it odd after all? Were you following us by any chance?"

"No," said Julian shortly. "It's pure coincidence that I'm here. I was out for a stroll and I saw you idiots come galloping down on some absurd prank or other. Who ever heard of riding in evening dress! The only reason I intrude myself on you is that I don't like the looks of this crowd. They are hungry and they are angry. If I were you, I would get the ladies out at once and escort them home while there's time."

"I'm sure, Grace, you have Lady Gardiner's best interests at heart." Delane gave a quick glance at the hostile faces staring at them out of the darkness and became convinced that quick action was needed. "By gad, you're right. I don't like the looks of this at all. Edgar," addressing the second rider who had been in the van, "I'm going in and drag her ladyship out. By force if necessary. What a pleasant task it would be, if I *had* to use force! Eh, Grace? We must get away from here, Edgar. We may be too late as it is."

Julian did not leave. If there was to be trouble, he must play a part in the safeguarding of Isabelle. He saw Isabelle emerge from the front entrance of the house, with Lady Betsy on one side and the partly inebriated Delane on the other. She was protesting at the interruption.

"This is absurd," Julian heard her say. "If you are afraid, Frankie Delane, go on back to the Veseys' and take your friends with you. Betsy and I are not afraid."

"I am," said Lady Betsy, taking one apprehensive look at the crowd.

The onlookers booed and jeered as the ladies were helped into the saddle. One of them stepped out from the rest and raised his voice above the din.

"Do you know who this beauchus creature is?" he demanded, pointing at Isabelle. "This one here in white with diamonts around her neck? She's the daughter of Samuel Carboy, the worst bloodsucker of the lot. She's married to a man what has millions. She's got four houses and hundreds of servants. That dress she's got on would keep our wives and childer in food for months."

The mention of the name Carboy brought prolonged groans and hisses from the mob but it also brought a second member to the fore. He stepped out and held up a hand.

"Wait a minute, all of you!" he shouted. "I got something I want to say. You're all wrong about Carboy. He may be a bloodsucker like the rest. Anybody what feeds and waxes fat off the labors of the poor *is* a bloodsucker, and that much I give you. But I want to call to your attention that not one of the Carboy factories has closed down. He hasn't chucked out a single worker. He hasn't been a hostrich with his head stuck in the ground like the rest of them. He's been working up trade in the U-nited States and now he's selling the goods he makes to them." The speaker looked about him belligerently, as though daring the others to disagree. "The time will come—and, oh, may it come soon, my friends and brothers—when there won't be any Carboys to skim off the cream. But until that time comes, I want to tell you this: I'd rather have one Carboy today than all the rest of them sewed up together—all the Smiths and the Jenkinses, and the Warrings and the Betgers. If they followed the example of Samuel Carboy, there wouldn't be none of us out of work today. And make no mistake about that."

The crowd seemed to have become more interested in the discussion than in the well-dressed interlopers. It was the right moment to leave. Julian caught Delane's eye and motioned to him frantically. The latter nodded and wheeled his horse about, calling to his companions to do the same. There was a hasty scatteration and a lane opened for the horses.

"Out of the way, gutter-lappers!" shouted Delane, his courage coming back.

But his confidence seemed likely to prove premature. One of the crowd, carried away by the sight of Isabelle's jewelry, dashed out unexpectedly and sprang on the neck of her horse, reaching with one hand for the necklace. The horse rose on its hind legs in fright, and the would-be thief would have been thrown off without more ado, but Isabelle was leaving nothing to chance. Julian, plunging through the ring of watchers, saw her double up her arm and drive her elbow into the midriff of her assailant. He gave up his hold immediately and, gasping for breath, dropped to the muddy cobbled road.

A second mobster had better luck. He had followed his fellow's example and had sprung at the neck of Lady Betsy's horse. When he was dislodged he kept in his grasp the rich cloth pelerine she had worn over her shoulders. With his booty tucked under an arm, he plunged into the crowd and was lost sight of at once.

When the sound of galloping hoofs was no longer heard, Julian resumed his walk, swinging his cane reflectively as he went. The streets grew darker and more silent. After a half hour of purposeless pacing he realized that he had no idea where he was.

"I'll ask for directions at the first light I see," he said to himself.

It was a long time before he saw the desired light but this did not matter at all. His mind was so busy that he did not care how far afield he might wander. What the second speaker from the mob had said had made a deep impression on him.

"It was true," he thought. "Samuel Carboy always knows the right thing to do. He never seems to make mistakes. I knew he hadn't closed down any of his factories but it had never occurred to me that this was important. I can see now that he's doing the country a real service. If all the heads of business were like him, the country wouldn't be in the state it is." He was finding it hard to make these admissions. Nevertheless, he went a step further. "I wish Father would stop digging at him in the House. People are beginning to laugh about it and say it's spite. Nothing came of all the pother in the House about the Tontine. In fact it turned out to be a feather in their caps."

Then he came to a full stop. All this time he had been turning over in his mind the things he had heard. Not once had he given a thought to Isabelle, although this was the first glimpse he had had of her since the wedding. Although the encounter had left him with plenty of room for speculation about his lost love, although he had seen her prove her presence of mind when attacked, he had allowed her to go completely out of his mind. Had her beauty and high spirits and arrogance become of less importance than what the poorer classes of London were thinking?

He remained still for several more moments, standing at a street corner and making no move to cross. "Can it be," he asked himself, "that I am getting over it? Am I actually cured? Is it possible that I'm like everyone else after all? I was certain I would carry Isabelle's image in my heart as long as I lived and never be able to forget her or put anyone in her place. Is it even possible that I may fall in love again sometime?"

He became aware that a light showed in an upper window of a building on the opposite corner. He crossed the street.

3

There was a sign over the door and the light from the window above enabled Julian to make out the lettering. It read:

A. BRINKER
Jamaica Merchant

He gasped with surprise. "Can it be the Ambrose Brinker I know?" he asked himself. It must be, he decided. It would be straining the bounds of credulity too far to believe there could be two of the same name in one thinly populated island. He gave a thump with the door knocker and almost immediately a figure appeared at the window above, cutting off most of the light.

"Who is it?"

"Are you Ambrose Brinker from Kingston?"

"Yes." There was a moment's silence and then the voice became eager. "I don't think I can be mistaken. Is it you, Grace?"

"It is. What a stroke of luck that I should choose this street blindly! Come down and let me in, man!"

It seemed a matter of seconds only until the door opened. Brinker, holding a candle over his head and looking in the dim light somewhat thinner and more gaunt about the eyes, stared out at the visitor.

"My dear fellow, my very dear fellow! What a splendid surprise. Come in, come in."

The downstairs rooms were all devoted to business and there was the same cool odor of molasses and rum in the air. Brinker led the way to a little counting office at the rear and ensconced his caller in a chair of considerable depth and corresponding comfort.

"I haven't Dunder with me but I can do almost as well myself. What is it to be? One of our special punches?"

"By all means. I've never encountered anything to equal them."

Brinker talked while he got out the ingredients and proceeded to mix them. It was with a deep sigh that he handed a glass to Julian.

"Poor Forster! I had your letter and it almost finished me. You will tell me all about it. But not now—not now! We mustn't mar our reunion with such sad memories. Particularly as there are depressing things I must tell you."

The animation which had shown in his eyes when he greeted his visitor at the door had vanished. He sat without moving for several moments. In the rather dim light of the candles Julian could see that his cheeks were thin and the lines about his mouth deep. He seemed in a highly nervous state, his face twitching, his long frame never still in the chair.

"My father is dead," said Brinker finally. "I sold the plantations at once—for reasons which I'll tell you later—and came here to London. He hadn't been in good health for quite a time but his end was very sudden. He toppled off his horse in the cane fields and was dead when the overseer reached him."

Julian expressed his regrets over this unfortunate occurrence. Then, thinking to take his host's mind into more pleasant fields, he asked Brinker how he liked life in London.

Brinker gave his head a shake. "I wasn't born for this sort of thing," he said. "I'm used to the soft air of Jamaica. All this rain and wind and rawness, not to mention the fogs, will be the death of me. I swear to you, Grace, that the poorest slave in the island has a fuller belly than these poor slinking devils you see on the streets of London. And *faugh!* The smells! Of course the life here is strangely stimulating. This business, which I've just started, is going very well. I may find it in time more profitable than the plantations.

But all in all it required an extraordinary reason to make me sell my island holdings."

He remained silent for a time and Julian did not speak, realizing that he must wait on his companion's moods.

"Did you know," asked Brinker finally, "that Constance Ballard is dead?"

Julian cried out in sharp disbelief: "No! You can't mean it! Brinker, it can't be, it can't be! She was so beautiful and gentle and fine."

"She's gone, poor child," said the other somberly. "She never recovered from the blow. She began to languish from the day your letter arrived and in a month she was like a shadow. It was quite clear that she had no desire to go on living."

The visitor had forgotten his glass, which rested untouched on the table. He regarded his host with unhappy eyes.

"They didn't send me word," he said. "Do you suppose that down in their hearts they resented me? That they couldn't forgive me for returning safely? I assure you, Brinker, the bullet which killed poor Cymric could have picked me off just as easily. We were not five feet apart when he went down."

"No, no, banish the thought. They have nothing but the deepest affection for you. I think, perhaps, they put off the writing, dreading the task, and let it go so long that they never did write. I'm sure that was it."

"She must have loved Cymric very much."

Brinker nodded slowly. "It was consumption which took her in the end. She seemed to get more beautiful all the time. I saw her a week before it happened and she looked like an angel. The poor child's mind had started to weaken and waver and she was sure he was alive and all her talk was of when he would return. She had her couch carried out on a porch where she could see the water; and there she lay, hour after hour, day after day, never taking her eyes from the horizon. She used to say, 'He will come tomorrow. I've seen the ship and it is sailing very fast because the captain knows he must bring my dear Cymric to me quickly.' At night she slept in the same place and they always built a bonfire close at hand, so that he would have no difficulty if he arrived in the dark." Brinker's voice fell to a lower pitch. "Mrs. Ballard is taking it very hard. Near the end the poor child knew she was going and she talked about it freely with her mother. She took messages with her for all the little Ballards who had gone before."

"The small sister is well, I hope," said Julian after a suitable interval.

Brinker looked up with a revived air of interest, even of good-humored slyness. "The small sister? Yes, the small sister is well. But, of course, no longer small. The years which have elapsed since you saw her have been good to Winifred. I hope you will see her sometime."

"Yes, I hope so," said Julian in a casual tone. "I seem to remember her as a bright child. I liked her. I liked them all."

They talked then about Julian himself and what he had been doing since his return from the Americas. He spoke of his disappointment and of Isabelle's marriage. When he mentioned who she now was, Brinker's eyes opened wide.

"Lady Gardiner!" he exclaimed. "So *she* is your Isabelle. I've been reading and hearing about her. What a swath she's cutting at court—and elsewhere."

"Ambrose," said Julian gravely, "I've mourned her loss for a year. You can't conceive of what a self-pitying, gloomy fellow I've been. Why, I've been a complete misanthrope! But something happened tonight. I saw her, and suddenly I realized that she wasn't very important after all. I didn't come away thinking of her. My mind was filled with other matters."

"My dear Julian!" cried Brinker. "I'm delighted to hear this. I've been so engrossed in getting my business started that I've made no effort to track you down. But I've thought of you a very great deal. I wondered how things were turning out."

Julian reached for his glass and took a long pull at its contents. "Capital!" he said with relish. "The first drink I've enjoyed since Isabelle told me she was going to marry her damned Tibby instead of me. I assure you, Ambrose, that food has been ashes in my mouth and that drink has tasted like hemlock."

"This really calls for a celebration," declared the young Jamaican. His spirits had been rising as quickly as Julian's but at this point he stopped. The look of gloom came back to take full possession of his face. "Julian," he said, "I must tell you the rest of my sad story. She is here—in London. But she refuses to see me. She doesn't answer my letters."

"She? Do you mean, by any chance, Mademoiselle Philline?"

Brinker nodded. "Yes, my beautiful will-o'-the-wisp is here. When we got her safely off the island, she went to the United States and lived for a time in Boston. I arranged for Boston newspapers to be sent me regularly, hoping I could keep myself in touch that way. It was through the papers that I learned she had attached herself to people who sought to abolish slavery in that country. She began to address meetings and the people of Boston were astonished at the fiery speeches made by this young and beautiful woman. They flocked out to hear her. Some time after I had a letter from her. It was short and to the point. She was leaving the United States. She had been advised to leave in order to avoid trouble. So she came here, after sending me a very brief note. I followed as soon as I could get my business affairs straightened out."

"What is she doing here?"

Ambrose motioned in the direction from which his visitor had come. "Did you pass a house on your walk which is being run by a palmist? It's always lighted up nights. They do an active business in the evenings."

"I passed the place. It's run by a Frenchwoman, I believe."

"Madame Martine. She must be very clever because everyone in London is running to see her. I've heard that even the Duke of Wellington has paid her a call." Ambrose paused and gave his friend a nod which suggested his inability to understand what he now intended to tell. "Madame Martine is none other than Mademoiselle Philline!"

"What a coincidence that I should find out about both of you in one night! Why do you suppose she has gone in for telling fortunes?"

"I discovered who she was by putting together little bits of information I heard. When I called at the house she sent out a note saying that she was afraid I would disapprove of what she was doing and that it would be better if we didn't meet. All the people about the place had some share of colored blood. Because of that, I came to the conclusion that she was raising money for the cause."

"Have you been back since?"

Ambrose Brinker gave his head a despondent shake. "A dozen times. The answer is always the same. She cannot see me. I write her letters and she doesn't reply. Perhaps the people she's with have decided it's unwise to let us meet and don't let her know when I call. Or it may be that they are up to something which she doesn't want me to know. Whichever it is, I encounter a cold and hostile silence when I go to the house."

There was an interruption at this point. A colored woman of mature years and some massive remains of good looks came into the room. She paused and shook an accusing forefinger at Brinker.

"M's'r Am'!" she said. "Yu fo'git what I tole yu. Win'ow up."

"But it's close tonight," protested her master.

"How often yu hear me say, 'Night come in win'ow, corpse go out door'?"

"It's so warm, Frass, that we must have fresh air."

Sassafrassa, to give her the full name her parents had coined, walked scornfully to the window and closed it down tight. "Night air got bref o' ghosts on it. It got ills and trubbles fum graveya'ds on it. Night air, h'it no good, M's'r Am'."

"Well," said her master, winking at his guest, "if we've got to do without fresh air, Frass, you will at least get us some food."

"No! No food. Too much food no good fo' young stummicks. No mo' eating tonight, M's'r Am'."

"I'm not hungry, I assure you," said Julian to his host. "I had a late dinner and a hearty one."

"Then let's do this. We'll celebrate our reunion with a really fine supper some evening soon." He added in a low tone, "I inherited this old termagant from my father. But she *is* a wonderful cook—when she's in the mood. I'll guarantee, Julian, that she'll be in the mood when you come and you'll have a supper which will quite transport you."

The cook was watching him with suspicion in every line of her countenance. Her hands were on her hips. "Wha' dat yu say, M's'r Am'?"

"I'm inviting my friend to have supper with me—next Tuesday."

Sassafrassa put her foot down, quite literally. "No! No sup' Tues'd. Weds'd, yes."

"Wednesday?" asked Brinker, smiling at Julian.

"Wednesday will be fine. I'll be glad to have supper with you. But now, Ambrose, I must be getting back to Spring Gardens."

Ambrose got to his feet. "I'll walk along with you," he said. "I'll go just far enough to catch a glimpse of the lights from her windows before turning back. You would laugh at me if you knew how often I do that."

CHAPTER SEVENTEEN

1

Julian dressed himself with particular care on the evening when he was to have supper with Ambrose Brinker. He avoided the excesses of the maca-ronis, however—the young bloods who disregarded the dictates of Beau Brum-mell and adorned themselves in all the colors of the rainbow—and wore a dark blue coat with very large silver buttons, a waistcoat of subdued fawn, and trousers fitting his calves as snugly as his skin and buttoned at the sides just above the ankle. He donned a tall beaver hat and, as his toilet had taken longer than he intended, took possession of a hackney cab.

Brinker was a little taken back by his elegance. "By gad, Julian, you put me right in the shade!" he complained. He was wearing a dark coat, it was true, but his stock was blue and his waistcoat a ripe lemon yellow; and, moreover, he wore breeches which were rather baggy at the knees and his stockings were *not* of silk.

The host led the way to a small room overlooking the street in which he kept his books and a few fine pieces of furniture which he had brought with him from the island. Julian's eyes took special note of a bookholder which was pyramidical in shape and which swung, rather creakily, on a round up-right support. He noticed that the top shelf, where the space was quite cramped, had false book backs of leather.

"I must explain about old Frass," said Brinker, looking cautiously first in the direction of the door. "She always kept my father on a pretty tight bradoon. She had been handsome in her day, so I was told, and he—well, he gave in to all her whims. Besides, she was the only cook he ever had who could make the tough meats of the island palatable. When I got my hands on things it was too late to do anything about Frass. She was the boss around the place. To keep the peace, I gave in to her.

"She met her match once," he went on, with a smile of pleased recollection. "That was when Mademoiselle was with us. Frass took one look at her and came right down off her high horse. She put off her airs and it was 'Yes, Missy,' the whole time. . . . Ah, Julian, how I long to see her again!"

"I can believe what you say about the old woman being a good cook," declared Julian. "I've been enjoying the most wonderful odors ever since I arrived."

"That's the hot bread. Yes, my good friend, it will be a fine supper. She'll have surprises for you. There's a white fish with a wine sauce, and cold mutton, and *such* hot bread, and *such* a pudding made of corn flour with plums and nazeberry jam, and all sprinkled over with white sugar and served with an orange sauce! Wait until you taste *that!*"

"Are we to sit down alone?"

Brinker shook his head and motioned toward the window, which was admitting the sound of carriage wheels and the shrill comments of curious neighbors. "Here they are now. Come and look out, Julian. Does that make you think of Jamaica?"

What Julian saw from the window was a glorified kittereen, with a fringed top instead of an umbrella and a colored man in a blue uniform driving with a fine flourish of the reins. Something about the driver's round face and small button nose and his roving eye stirred immediate recollections.

"Ambrose!" he cried. "I believe that's Noel."

"I believe it is," affirmed Ambrose, smiling. Then he added, "We must go down and welcome the ladies."

Julian was so delighted and puzzled at this unexpected encounter with the jovial servant who had done so much for his comfort in Jamaica that he allowed his host to welcome the two ladies who stepped down from the back seat of the kittereen while he spoke to Noel.

"You rascal!" he said. "How does it happen that you're here in London? Whatever the reason, I'm glad to see you."

"Yes, I'se N'le, m's'r. You goin' see plenty me, I guesses."

Julian turned and waited to be introduced to the ladies. One was a gentlewoman in slightly reduced circumstances with a pinched nose and an air of authority, which stamped her in his mind as a teacher in a private school, an impression which grew when he saw that her companion was young and fashionably dressed.

"Miss Alberta Hoxie," said Brinker, "this is Mr. Julian Grace."

The reduced gentlewoman inclined her head with the brevity and suspicion which constant chaperoning imposes on those of her kind. Julian bowed and said, "I am honored, ma'am."

"And this is someone you already know," went on Brinker. "I don't believe Miss Bordley would have allowed us the pleasure of Miss Hoxie's company and that of her charge if I had not been able to tell her that you had been a guest of Miss Ballard's parents in Jamaica."

Julian turned quickly to the girl who stood beside the teacher. She was slim and dark, with the cool beauty which comes from straight and simply dressed black hair and a skin as white as magnolia blossom. She was wearing a tiny leghorn hat and a long olive-green pelisse which allowed no further glimpses of her save of her small hands in Parma-violet gloves under puckered sleeves and the tip of a very small shoe.

"I know my papa and mama would have given me messages for you, Mr. Grace, if they had known I would see you in London," said the girl, in a slightly throaty voice.

Julian was recovering his wits with difficulty. "You are Miss Winifred, of course," he said. "Who else could you be? And yet—and yet——"

"Small girls *do* grow up, Mr. Grace," said Winifred with the most vagrant of smiles, and a coolness and poise which did credit to the training she had received at the fashionable establishment of Miss Gertrude Jane Bordley.

"Yes, of course," declared Julian, more at his ease. "I seem to remember an occasion when I had to convince you that this was what would happen to you. And at the same time I made a prophecy which I now realize was absurdly limited in its scope, and, in fact, most embarrassingly inadequate in every way."

The girl looked at him from under raised eyelashes. "Did you, Mr. Grace? Sometime you must tell me what it was."

The arrival of such an unusual vehicle was creating something approaching a sensation in the neighborhood. People had come out from the houses and were lounging on doorsteps, not making any effort to lower the voices in which they expressed their opinions. Boys were hammering at the spokes of the wheels with sticks and were shouting at Noel: "Hi, black fella! Ye think ye're pretty botty, don't ye?"

Ambrose Brinker escorted the ladies inside and Julian followed, after waving to Noel. The latter had brought out a whip of red leather and was preparing to depart.

Brinker led the way up the dark stairs, with the ladies following and Julian bringing up the rear. The latter was feeling a sense of disappointment. When he had stayed at the Ballard plantation and Winifred had been a small girl, they had been the best of friends; but now she treated him with polite aloofness. How lovely she had become! What a miracle, he said to himself, that eyes could be so soft and luminous and yet so intelligent. How slender and graceful she was!

When they reached the sitting room on the floor above, he had already come to a momentous conclusion. "It was all worked out by the fates," he thought. "It was ordained that I should empty my mind of Isabelle so there would be room for this lovely lady that little Winifred Ballard has grown into."

2

Despite the high expectations which had been raised in his mind about the supper, Julian barely knew what he was eating. He went through the meal in a dazed condition; but all the time he was acutely conscious of Winifred, who sat opposite him at the table. He was only faintly aware that the fish was delicate and the sauce superb but he knew every detail of her dress. There was in him the merest appreciation of the glory of the pudding but he was sure that her eyes, which had seemed black in the street, had become like the midnight blue of sapphires under the light of the candles.

He could not have enumerated later the topics of conversation which were introduced but it was evident at the time that he was bearing some share in the talk. At any rate the rest looked at him at intervals, and smiled or shook their heads before chiming in with thoughts of their own. It was an automatic function he was performing.

He found that she was called Freddie at school. Apparently she had refused to respond to Winnie, holding that it sounded soft and sentimental. It seemed to Julian that the new name suited her. He turned it over in his mind and reached the conclusion that he liked it. He learned also that the kittereen had been made in London on specifications that her father sent before he allowed his daughter to come over to complete her education. It had been in Timothy Ballard's mind that she would find the life at school too confining. It was maintained in the neighborhood of the school and the other girls fought for invitations to accompany her in it. Noel had been acquired through some curious train of circumstances and had been sent over to act as her driver, Mr. Ballard having no faith in the ability of London coachmen. Julian thought: "There's something curious about this. When I have a chance I must ask about it."

His feelings were achieving a sentimental maturity with dizzying speed. Never in all his years of devotion to the bewitching Isabelle had he been carried along on the crest of a positive flood tide of emotion as he was now. Little Freddie—— But Freddie was not small. She was, as he realized on more careful consideration, rather tall for a girl of her age and it was only her slenderness which made it possible to consider her small. The memory of Isabelle had left him just in time to admit someone else; and this girl from the golden isle had moved in and settled right down, and he knew that he would never allow as much as an inch to anyone else.

When coffee was being served in small stone mugs with cane handles, Julian recovered sufficiently to indulge in normal thoughts and speculations. He began to recall a conversation into which he had been trapped a few days before by Mrs. Pardon.

"Mr. Grace, it's a pity you take such little interest in the"—Mrs. Pardon had paused and smiled at him archly—"shall we say, in the fair sex? I've heard of a great chance for you. Oh, a very great chance indeed."

"How much a year does she have?" he had asked.

"*Mister* Grace! I'm not talking about a girl. You must find the right one for yourself. I meant that I know of something very interesting, *if* you had the girl. It's this, Mr. Grace. Santa Cruz is going to be vacated."

"Do you mean that neat little house at the end of the block which has no name on it?"

"Yes, Mr. Grace. It's really a dear little house. The gardens are nice, and the fireplaces all draw, and the dining room has the nicest cupboards. Oh, an ideal place really for a bride." She raised an admonishing finger. "You must take advantage of it. Find the girl, Mr. Grace, and I'm sure Santa Cruz will be yours. You see, it's named after a victory which is kind of looked down on because it was won in Cromwell's time—and nothing good must ever be said about *that* dreadful person. No one wants to have the house on that account. Do you feel very hard about Cromwell, Mr. Grace?"

"No. I don't."

"Then you ought to get married and take Santa Cruz. It was a little the same way when Mr. Pardon proposed to me. It was over twenty years ago and he was sitting at the same desk where he sits today, although at that time he had only worn out four or five—— Well, we'll not go into that. He came to me and said, 'My dear, if you'll say "Yes," I rather think I can get Sandwich.' It wasn't in real demand because of the paintings on the walls but I was sure Mr. Pardon would be moving up and up and up and that someday we might be able to ask for, and get, one of the very best. It never occurred to me I would have to get along on so very little. And so I said, 'Yes,' and here we've been ever since, looking at the beheading of that terrible Eustace at every meal and me spending all my evenings patching the seats of trousers."

"I'm not sure I like the moral to be drawn from this, Mrs. Pardon. If I find a girl who's willing to have me and they let me have Santa Cruz, will I sit at one desk for the rest of my life? And will my poor wife have to mend the seats of innumerable pairs of trousers?"

He began to think of this conversation as he sat opposite Winifred Ballard at the well-laden supper table—and to associate her in his mind with Santa Cruz at the end of the block in Spring Gardens. He could see her, wearing a jolly pinafore, in the dining room with the nicest cupboards, or kneeling in the garden with a pruner in one hand and rose scissors in the other. It would be wonderful to share such a trim house, even if it was associated with Oliver Cromwell. He was half disposed, in any case, to admire Old Noll, although this wrongheadedness was confined to the thinking which went on at the very back of his head.

At ten o'clock they heard carriage wheels approaching and then the voice of Noel saying: "Whoa dah, Pitt! Whoa dah, Walpull!" Miss Hoxie promptly began to draw on her pattens (they were strictly unnecessary because it was as dry as a bone outside). This much accomplished, she began to make motions to her pupil which meant, "Find your bonnet at once, my child."

Both young men accompanied the ladies to the street. Julian had no expectation of a relenting from the strictly correct attitude that the girl had maintained all evening. She would get into the carriage at once and he would be left with no more rewarding memory than a vision of the fringe of the kittereen swinging back and forth above the back of a neat leghorn hat. But things turned out rather better. Miss Hoxie got in first and then Freddie turned and held out a gloved hand to him. What was more she smiled, a warm and almost intimate smile.

"It's been so nice to see you again," she said in a voice very little above a whisper. "I've thought so much about the days when you and Cymric were with us."

"Come, child!" called the teacher impatiently.

"I must see you again," declared Julian in a discreetly low tone.

"Oh yes. You must."

The fringe swayed above the leghorn hat as they drove away but there

was a difference from what he had expected. The girl had turned her head
to smile back at him.

Ambrose Brinker had observed everything and he grinned appreciatively
in the darkness. "Well played, little Freddie!" he said to himself. "Well
played indeed!"

"And now," declared Julian, when the sound of the carriage wheels had
died away in the distance, "you will kindly explain how you managed to
arrange this wonderful surprise for me."

"Oh, I've seen the child several times since she came over," answered Ambrose in a casual tone. "I thought you might like to meet her again. She
has grown up, hasn't she?"

Words failed Julian. He was incapable of expressing his reactions to what
had happened to Miss Winifred Ballard in the process of growing up.

3

Miss Bordley's School for Young Ladies was a large and severe house in
the neighborhood of Berkeley Square, with an oval brass sign swinging above
the door and the most discreet of curtains on all the windows. Julian knew
it very well. He had, in fact, paid an unauthorized call there when Isabelle
was in attendance and had been sent about his business most promptly by a
minor teacher. But this time he was calling under the proper auspices. A
note had been dispatched to Miss Bordley and a reply had been received,
authorizing him to call on Thursday at four o'clock. And here he was now,
standing rather diffidently on the doorstep, attired in his long blue coat and
shoes of the glossiest black leather, and his beaver hat. His mind was in a
confused whirl.

He was admitted by a neatly dressed maid whose manners, on the most
favorable basis, could not be termed better than surface. At any rate she
winked at Julian as she stood aside to let him enter. Miss Bordley herself
swept into the hall in a positive susurrus of trailing silk to extend a greeting.
For, after all, was he not a kinsman of the Duke of Outland?

"I'm happy to see you, Mr. Grace," she said in a voice which suggested
she was holding in her mouth a collection of pearls, for of course it could not
be anything of less value. It was clear that she knew a great deal about him
and that she was curious enough not to let this chance slip. "Will you pardon
me, Mr. Grace, if I take it on myself to congratulate you without putting my
reason into words? You are indeed a lucky young man. She was pretty, I
admit, but never have I tried harder to instill into one of my pupils the
outward semblance of good breeding. Lady Gardiner indeed! Why she
even——" It was in her mind apparently to tell about Isabelle kicking her
on the shins; but after a moment's consideration she decided against this
disclosure. "Well, I had my troubles with her just as your father had with
hers. Dear, dear, I am being most indiscreet and that is exactly what I can't
afford to be. But that Isabelle Carboy! . . . And now, who is it you are to

see on this very fine afternoon? Oh yes, the Ballard child. Now this is quite different, Mr. Grace, *quite* different indeed. Winifred Ballard has good breeding and she came to me with more education than most of them have when they leave. Oh dear, what *am* I saying? They all have education when they leave, though how I manage to get it into the heads of some of them is a mystery. In fact I sometimes say it is a miracle. But Winifred Ballard had as much education when she came as any girl will ever need and I couldn't help wondering why she came to me at all. Unless she was weary of life so far away from civilization."

"Life in Jamaica is very pleasant, Miss Bordley," said Julian.

"Oh yes. You *have* been there. Quite." It was apparent a suspicion was growing in her mind. "Well, I'm sure you are more anxious to talk to Winifred than to me. I'll take you to the east drawing room where, no doubt, she is waiting for you."

Among the more outspoken pupils, and the least susceptible to the efforts of Miss Bordley to instill good breeding into her charges, the east drawing room was spoken of as the Mating Lair, because it was here that they always received their callers. When Julian entered the room in the wake of Miss Bordley, they found it filled with small tables, some of which were already occupied by young ladies with very young gentlemen in attendance, many of the latter in military uniforms. He could see that these weekly meetings were chaperoned with an iron rigidity. Not only was Miss Hoxie sitting in the center of the room, where she could see every one of the seventeen tables, and making no more than a polite pretense of reading a book, but there were maids in starched aprons and caps ready to carry around plates with sandwiches and cakes and cups of tea. Julian suspected also that Miss Bordley herself would never be far away and could be depended upon to appear in a trice in her swishing silk skirts if anything out of the ordinary happened.

"Ah, Miss Ballard!" Miss Bordley was shortsighted and she looked about her with a hint of very ladylike helplessness. As a matter of fact she was never known to be helpless under any circumstances.

"Here I am, Miss Bordley."

Julian felt his heart begin to thump when a slim figure detached itself from a group of girls in the rear, all of whom quite apparently were waiting for their respective swains to appear. Winifred walked toward them without any of the confusion so often displayed on such occasions. She was a picture of perfect poise, in fact, as she dropped a curtsy to Miss Bordley and then bowed to him. She spoke in a low and controlled voice. "It's so nice of you to come, Mr. Grace."

"Now let me see." Miss Bordley was staring about the room with a pretense of seeing everything. "Do you care where you sit, my child?"

"Oh yes, please, Miss Bordley. Could we have the corner table?"

"Well, now really, Winifred." The head of the school, quite clearly, was surprised at the daring of this request. "The corner table? It's generally reserved for those who have been here longest. However, as you seem to want it very much, and as I am going to be candid enough to say that I don't disapprove of Mr. Grace as a caller, perhaps you may have it."

The girl's eyes opened wide with pleasure. "Oh, thank you so much, Miss Bordley," she said. As she led the way across the room to the almost secluded nook where they would have their tea, she whispered to him, "Oh, *what* luck!"

The corner table undoubtedly had great advantages for those who occupied it. From there it was possible to see everyone else in the room while remaining secluded to quite a degree. It also had a disadvantage which was not likely to bother them much. The servants did not reach it as often as some of the other tables while carrying around the sandwiches and cakes.

"All the girls will be green with envy," she said as she seated herself beside him. She was thinking that the envy would be due in a small measure only to their possession of the prized table. She was certain that her caller was one of the tallest and straightest, and most decidedly the handsomest, of all the young gentlemen who had ever come to the Bordley School for Young Ladies on a Thursday afternoon.

"Do you like it here?" he asked.

"No," she whispered back. "The girls don't come here to learn. They come to be able to say they were at Miss Bordley's and to make friends. It's all rather stupid." She stopped abruptly and her eyes lost their animation. "Do you—do you know about my poor Constance?"

He nodded his head. "Yes. Ambrose Brinker told me."

"I haven't recovered from it yet," said the girl. "I know I never shall. I loved her so much!"

"You'll get over it in time, Freddie." He stopped short and looked at her with an apologetic air. "I'm sorry. The name slipped out. I don't want you to think of me as presuming—"

"I'm afraid we must stay on a formal basis when others are around for a while longer. But—we *are* old friends, aren't we? Please call me Freddie when we're alone. I'll love it. And perhaps I'll get my courage up to call you Julian."

The conversation came to a stop. It was not that the tea was monopolizing their attention; neither had taken a single sip of the rather weak beverage supplied them nor partaken of a crumb of cake. Julian was studying her with such complete absorption that talk had become impossible.

"Do you think, Julian, that you've looked at me long enough?" she asked finally. "Everyone in the room is watching *us* now. And I'm sure they're beginning to wonder."

"Not nearly long enough," he answered, collecting his wits with an effort. "I've just realized that, if I had the chance to look at you all through life, it still wouldn't be long enough."

Her cheeks had always seemed white and cool but now he saw for the first time a hint of color in them.

"Do you realize what you've said?"

He was asking himself why certain rules were considered right and proper and always had to be observed at the most important moment in a man's life. Why should he wait to ask her father for permission to pay his attentions to her when what seemed to him the right moment to tell her of his love had arrived?

"I know I shouldn't have said what I did. I'm breaking all the rules. I should speak to your father first. Or write to him, and get his consent. But an exchange of letters with Jamaica is a matter of many weeks and I can't wait that long. I'm sure I would go mad with the suspense. I must tell you that I'm in love with you. It—it happened as soon as I saw you step down from the kittereen. I knew then that my fate was sealed."

There had been many proposals made in the east drawing room of Miss Bordley's School for Young Ladies but it may be accepted as certain that none of the young ladies to whom the question had been popped (a truly frightful word which seemingly cannot be avoided) had possessed as much beauty and common sense as the girl listening to Julian Grace's declaration. Her superiority was displayed in her manner of receiving this highest of all compliments. She did not cast her eyes down, she did not blush or simper, she did not utter any of the "Oh, fies" or the "Really, sir's" which were supposed to denote a proper degree of maidenly modesty. Instead she sat very still and watched him with a direct and earnest glance.

"You will have to write to Father," she said after a long moment of eloquent silence. "And if you don't mind, Julian, I think I shall write too. You see, I know Father. He needs to be managed rather!"

"Does that mean—— Am I being too hasty and—er—optimistic in believing that you want him to say yes?"

"Julian," said Freddie, and now she did not look up but kept her eyes on the teacup in front of her, "do you want me to say exactly what is in my mind?"

"Yes. Of course." His tone suggested that he had suddenly become a prey to almost unbearable anxiety.

"Then there is a great deal I must tell you. You see, Julian, we all liked you very much, Papa and Mama and Constance and I. We get the London newspapers, as you must remember—very old and out of date when they reach us. But they help us to keep in touch with the world. About a year ago—after dear Constance left us—we saw the announcement of the marriage of your Isabelle. Mama felt very sorry about it. I remember that she shook her head and sighed. I wasn't sorry. I was glad. I never wanted you to marry her."

There was a moment's pause while she summoned up the courage to go more deeply into the matter of her own reactions. "I liked you from the first day you came. Do you remember what I said? I looked at you both very carefully and then I said, 'I think this one,' meaning you, 'is a more beautiful young man than the other one.' Do you remember now?"

"Yes." Julian was smiling broadly and happily. "I remember also that your mother was rather disturbed at your frankness."

"Well, when Mama had finished reading the long report of the wedding, she gave her head a shake and said, 'Some lucky girl will get him on the rebound after *this*.' I was terrified then, because—because I didn't want anyone to get you on the rebound." She broke off with sudden alarm. "Julian, you mustn't look at me like that. They are all staring at us now."

"My sweet child," said Julian tremulously, "I can't help looking at you like this. Because I think—because I am almost certain you've given me your answer."

She nodded her head slowly. "Yes. That is my answer. But you must now be perfectly frank with me. Do you love me because I *am* the lucky one to be here to catch you? Could it have happened if Isabelle hadn't married someone else?"

There was so much of a delirious sense of ownership in the gaze he turned on her that the girl at the next table said to her guest, a young man in the uniform of the Guards with a sandy mustache and no chin worth mentioning: "I know that I'm going to marry someday but I wonder if anyone will look at me the way he's looking at the sly young puss from that savage island away out west? Do you feel capable of anything like that, Osbald?"

"It's now over a year, my darling," Julian was saying, "since Isabelle's marriage. A rebound comes much sooner than that. It just happened that I found she had gone right out of my head. I saw her a short time ago and it was almost like seeing a stranger. Even then I didn't say to myself, 'Now I must find someone else to love.' I just went back to my normal state of mind. I had no inclination for romance whatever. What wonderful luck it was that you needed a final touch of education and so came here where I could see you and love you a thousand times more than I ever loved Isabelle."

"Oh, Julian, I wanted you to say that! I'm so happy!" She paused before going on. "You are going to find I always try to be honest about everything. Julian, I must be honest now, even though you may think ill of me. I didn't come to London to get an education. I came to get you." She began to laugh with a lack of restraint which had a touch of hysteria in it. "There, I have told the truth and I have no shame in doing it. If you don't believe I could be as designing as that, how do you suppose it came about that I brought Noel with me?"

"I've wondered."

"Papa was so concerned over me when I insisted on coming to Miss Bordley's that he thought of all manner of things to insure my comfort and health. He thought I needed a personal servant as well as a maid and it was then I mentioned how well you had thought of Noel. So instead of selecting one of our own slaves, as he had intended, he went to Kingston and bought Noel. I hoped then that—that Noel could be *your* servant and keep you comfortable all your life."

Julian was as completely happy as a man can be who has told a lady he loves her and has heard her acknowledge that she loves him but who cannot take her at once in his arms for the customary fervent kiss. He looked about him and saw that eyes, avid with curiosity, were still fixed on them from all parts of the room. An embrace was quite out of the question.

"There are times," said Freddie, "when Father thinks he has to be very businesslike. I'm sure this will be one of them. He'll want to know all about you. Not about your character. He knows already how fine you are. But about your—your prospects." She was looking quite worried. "Dear Julian, are you very poor?"

"I'm terribly poor, my darling."

"I think I'm going to be terribly rich."

"Will this make a great difference in your father's attitude?"

"Not in the end," declared the girl. "But he may be very disturbed and say many things he doesn't really mean. We will have to be careful and tactful about it, I'm afraid."

She sighed. "Hoxie has just caught my eye and nodded. That means our time is up." She looked at the table with a trace of dismay when she saw that everything had been left untouched, a mound of sandwiches, several raisin buns, a large wedge of spice cake and a gooseberry tartlet. "You may come to see me again. In a fortnight."

"A fortnight!" Julian's tone implied that this was close to eternity.

"And after that you mayn't come for another month. I never realized before how frightfully strict the rules are. Oh, Julian, what are we going to do?"

CHAPTER EIGHTEEN

1

It was several days later that Julian accompanied his friend Ambrose Brinker on a call at the fortunetelling establishment. A man with a colored skin stood at the door and in a melodious voice demanded to know their business.

"I desire to consult Madame Martine," said Julian.

The doorman looked at Ambrose as though recalling the many visits the latter had made and a doubtful look came into his eyes.

"I doan' know," he said. "We's moving."

Ambrose took things in hand on hearing this alarming piece of news. "Moving!" he said. "Are you taking another place in the city?"

The doorman shook his head. "No, suh. We's leaving country." Then he dropped his hand from the handle of the door which he had been holding zealously. "I's not goan' so it doan' mattah. You go in and ask man at desk. He's de boss heah. An' lose no time 'bout it. Dey's leaving soon."

There was every evidence inside to bear out what the guard had said. Domestics with skins varying from a light cream color to a positive black were hurrying from room to room, their arms filled with linen and clothing.

Loud voices could be heard everywhere and a sound of hammering came from the basement where, no doubt, goods were being crated for removal.

A young man with a highly intelligent face, which was white of skin but which might easily arouse doubts, sat at a desk in the reception room. Julian said to him, "I have no appointment but I'm extremely anxious to see Madame Martine before she gets away."

The secretary did not reply at once. His heavy brown eyes were fixed on Ambrose with hostile intentness.

"Now see here, this won't do," he said finally. "You don't ever give up, do you? Confound it, sir, I'll tell you for the last time that Madame Martine is not able to see you. And, as we are leaving today, there will be no purpose in coming back."

"Mr. Grace is an acquaintance of Madame Martine's," said Ambrose, keeping his temper with difficulty. "He's very anxious to see her."

The secretary smiled sleekly. "It's no use. Madame Martine has no time for callers today. You should have been convinced by this time that there's no use at all in coming here. Bringing acquaintances with you will not serve your purpose. I'm very busy so I'll say good day—and good-by."

"Not so fast, if you please. I insist that you send Mr. Grace's name in. It's certain that Madame Martine will want to see him." Ambrose added in a menacing tone: "You're quite the gentleman and you've been educated. But I'm not deceived about you. In fact I've taken pains to find out a great deal about you." He turned to Julian. "His name is Reuban Dupuis and he comes from Barbados. I know a *very* great deal about him."

The man at the desk scowled. "For the last time I tell you that under no circumstances will she see you. Oblige us by leaving."

Forcing their way in to see Mademoiselle was out of the question so they turned reluctantly. They had reached the door when they heard a feminine voice explode into laughter behind them. Both men wheeled quickly and saw that a maidservant had entered the reception room with a file of papers under one arm and that she was holding her other hand over her mouth. They saw also that the secretary had followed them with noiseless steps and that the maid had laughed because he was aping Ambrose Brinker. No two men could have been more unlike physically but the colored man had successfully achieved the Jamaican's gait and the way he carried his head as well as the brooding expression of his eyes.

Julian took a quick step backward and caught the man by the collar of his coat. "You are very clever," he said. "Does your employer know of this gift of yours and the way you use it to make light of her visitors? It's time she knew, I think."

"I have no employer," snarled Dupuis. "I'll have you know that I do what I like. It's my word around here, do you understand?"

"You're lying, you cheat and scoundrel!" Julian's anger was thoroughly aroused by this time. "I'll shake your bones loose if you don't notify Madame Martine at once that we are here."

A door behind the secretary's desk opened quietly and a feminine voice

asked, "What is going on, Reuban?" Both men recognized the voice. It was
that of Mademoiselle Philline. She stood in the doorway, a slender figure
in a dress of golden brown. Her face flushed when she recognized them.

"Mr. Grace! And you, Ambrose. This is indeed a surprise."

Julian crossed the room and shook hands with her, noting that she looked
very little different. There was, perhaps, a trace of fatigue in her eyes but
they were as large and lustrous as ever. The years, which take away so much
of the beauty and charm of women, had been kind to her.

"It is a great pleasure to renew our all too brief acquaintance," he said.
"It looked for a while as though we were to be denied that privilege."

Mademoiselle Philline turned to Ambrose Brinker with an air of con-
trition. "It may seem to you, my best of friends," she said, "that I am completely lacking in gratitude. But believe, please, that it is not so. I am fully
aware of what I owe you—and I am oh, so grateful, dear M'sieur Ambrose.
There have been—reasons. I cannot go into them now."

The face of the Jamaican brightened at this demonstration of her feeling
for him. "I have no complaints, my dear child," he said. "If you will never
forget, when you are in need of a friend, that I exist. That I exist for little
else than to help you." He hesitated and then continued: "Somehow I have
been sure that of late you have needed assistance. But you haven't called on
me."

While these remarks were exchanged the secretary had gone back to his
chair behind the desk. His face carried an open avowal of the deep resentment he was feeling. When Mademoiselle Philline turned toward him and
spoke in French, very rapidly and with a softly slurring accent, he frowned
and gestured violently to express his dissent. When she was through, he began a bitter harangue, the purpose of which obviously was to bring her back
to an acceptance of discipline. He motioned to the visitors to indicate that
she must send them away without further words.

"No, no!" she exclaimed. "It will not do. You are wrong, Reuban, and I
refuse to do what you want." She turned then to the two callers. "Will you
be kind enough to come with me? We must have a talk and it will be more
comfortable in here."

Reuban Dupuis did not look up as they passed him on their way to the
inner room but Julian observed that his fingers had taken hold of a long
paper cutter and that his knuckles were white with the intensity of his grip.

The house had been a residence of some distinction at one time and the
room into which they stepped had been used in its palmy days as a salon.
The ceiling was high and the stone of the chimney had been elaborately
carved by the hand of an artist. The hangings at the window and the French
rug on the floor had once contributed to the grandeur of the household but
now they were showing the effects of long usage. The curtains were drawn
so that the room depended for its illumination on candles in wall sconces;
an effect most useful for the purpose to which the apartment was now devoted.

Mademoiselle Philline seated herself behind a table with a handsome new velvet covering. It was completely bare of the usual trappings of the fortune-telling trade. The two men seated themselves in front of her.

"I wish to explain," she said in a low tone of voice, "that I have not been engaged in a money-making scheme. It is true that our venture here has been extremely profitable. I want you to know also that I believe in what I am doing. I have given my clients an honest picture of what they may expect of life. You see, God has placed on the palms of our hands a sure outward indication of what we have inside us. In our hearts and our minds. To that extent, at least, the palm is a key to the future."

"People have been talking about you all over town," said Julian with a smile. "I got the impression rather that you are a combination of the Maid of Kent, Mother Shipton and Cassandra."

"Make no mistake, messieurs," she said earnestly. "We could have continued here most profitably. But the proceeds go to spreading the word of the need for freeing slaves all over the world. None of us has profited from the money which poured in."

"Do you feel free to tell us why you are moving?" asked Ambrose, who had been watching with all his devotion in his eyes. "And where you are going?"

The young woman turned in his direction and gave him for the first time the exclusive attention of her eyes. "It is a matter of going where we can do the most good," she explained. "Did you read not so long ago of the colored servants who deserted a ship as soon as it touched port and ran with bare feet to the first piece of open ground they could find? The law that any slave whose feet touch the soil of the British Isles becomes free is not a new one; but that incident was a reminder that England is already in favor of abolition. We realized suddenly that we are not needed here. Your Mr. Wilberforce and those who worked with him have already guided the opinion of the country."

"Then where are you going?" asked Ambrose.

"It will take many years to free the slaves in the British dominions," she said. "In the meantime there are brave and devoted people leaving their homes here and going out to help the colored people. Doctors and teachers and ministers of the Gospel. We see now that it is our duty to help them." She paused as though reluctant to give him a more specific answer. "Well, you might as well know all about it. I am going back to Jamaica."

Ambrose leaned his arms on the table to bring himself closer to her. It was evident that her reply had both startled and dismayed him. "My dear child!" he exclaimed. "*Your* feet have touched the soil of England. You are free here. But if you go to Jamaica, won't you be in danger of immediate recognition and being sent back to the man who owned you?"

She nodded slowly. "Yes. There is that danger. But I must go."

At this point they heard voices from an adjoining room, many voices, raised in cheerful tones and accompanied by much laughter. The outburst was so sudden that the two visitors looked at her in surprise.

"Please, if you will go to that door and look in for a moment."

Mademoiselle Philline's suggestion was directed to Ambrose. He got up at once and opened the door into the other room for a few seconds, letting the animated sounds from the company there reach their ears in increased volume. Then he closed the door and returned to his chair.

"What did you see?"

"That was once the dining room, I judge," he answered. "All of your people are at the table and enjoying what seems to me a quite ample lunch. I saw a beefsteak-and-kidney pie, and a dish of boiled potatoes, steaming hot, and a plate of cold beef. When I said they were all there, I should have mentioned that the belligerent young man, whose name I happen to know is Reuban Dupuis, was not with them. I'm afraid our visit has spoiled his appetite."

Mademoiselle proceeded quietly with an explanation. "We are all equal. I have no privileges that aren't shared by the maids and the porters. We have our meals together. The money which comes in is as much theirs as mine. But, of course, none of us keep any part of it, except a very small allowance each week. My little Freezia, who sweeps and tidies this room for me and who's as black as the Queen of Sheba, gets exactly as much as I do."

"And who handles the funds?" asked Ambrose, although he was sure that he knew the answer.

"Reuban Dupuis. This was his plan. He got us together and he found the money to get us started. He considers himself the head—and has a right to —although he gets the same share as any of us."

"Are you sure of that?"

She responded with an earnest shake of her golden-brown head. "I am sure of it, M'sieur Ambrose. He is a fanatic in his loyalty to the cause."

"I have no right to ask this but—is he in love with you?"

"I—I rather think he is."

"My brave child," said Ambrose, whose face was clouded with uneasiness, "I know you well enough to be sure there is no use attempting to dissuade you from this course. You are gentle and sweet, and you get more lovely all the time, but at heart you're as much of a fanatic as he is. But what is this move going to mean? Do you realize fully the dangers you'll face? Are you prepared to take the risk of being sent back to the man who owned you?"

She returned his look with equal intentness. "I am ready to take any risk to be of service to these poor, persecuted people."

He reached out a hand abruptly. "Let me see your purse," he demanded.

There was a moment of hesitation on her part. Then she produced from under her belt a small purse of threadbare velvet. This she placed on the table in front of him.

He did not open it but, after a moment's study of its outward poverty and the flatness of its contour, he pressed it with the tips of his fingers.

"No bank notes," he said. "Only silver. And little of that. Two shillings, perhaps."

"About two shillings."

"Is that all you have?"

She nodded. "I need little. I have no expenses."

"You always dressed with great taste and discrimination. That dress you are wearing is neat but it's not new. Is it a fair sample of your present wardrobe?"

She flushed. "I am proud to tell you that it *is* my wardrobe, M'sieur Inquisitor."

"But it was your cleverness or intuition which brought all this flood of gold into the place. Are you sure this fellow outside is disposing of the funds honestly?"

"I have already told you that he is honest and devoted to the cause."

It was clear to both visitors that they could say or do nothing to change her mind. She was devoted to the cause, heart and soul. After a moment of thought, however, Ambrose Brinker opened the purse. "You must allow us one small privilege," he said. He nodded to Julian and they began to empty their pockets of the bank notes they had with them. Ambrose folded the notes carefully, placed them in the purse, closed it and then placed it in her hand.

At first she made a movement as though to refuse the gift. Then she hesitated, thinking intently with her eyes lowered to the table. Finally she took up the purse and replaced it under her belt. She favored them with a smile which was rather shamefaced.

"I will accept your kind gift," she said. "And I want to thank you both from the bottom of my heart. I know it is right for all of us who belong to share and share alike but—well, sometimes I can't help regretting that I have so little in my purse." She smiled then, the first real smile she had given them. "I confess it, my friends. There is a fine, warm feeling about having money in your pocket."

"Keep it for your own use," admonished Ambrose with sudden sharpness of tone.

On the way out he stopped at the desk where Reuban Dupuis was still sitting. He laid one hand on its surface and looked down at this man of whom he entertained such serious doubts. Dupuis looked up at him and for a moment nothing was said.

"M'sieur Dupuis," said Ambrose, "I don't like you and I don't trust you. If anything should happen to Ma'amselle Philline, I shall know about it. I have influence in the island which can be used to apply any punishment which may be deserved. Keep that always in your mind."

The man's eyes were filled with an implacable hatred. "You were once a slaveowner," he said. "Someday, some place, you'll be punished for that, M'sieur Brinker."

They walked slowly away together, making no response to the friendly, "Gooday, gemmum," of the outside guard.

"Well," said Ambrose finally, "I must now proceed to sell this tidy little business I've built up for myself."

"No!" cried Julian, seizing him by the arm and giving him a protesting shake. "You can go only so far with this quixotic attitude. She's beautiful and she's brave but she's cutting herself away from you, my friend. Get over it as I did when Isabelle gave me my congé."

"Do you think I would ever have any peace of mind if I did?" demanded the Jamaican. "I can't stay here and let her go back to the island to face danger and perhaps the loss of her freedom. No, Julian, my mind is made up. I'll sell out and return to Jamaica. I must be there to look out for her. To be on hand if she needs help at any time. It's my fate to do this. And, my dear old fellow, I ask for nothing better."

CHAPTER NINETEEN

1

Samuel Carboy was often at home these days. Things continued to go well with him in the world of business. The financial depression was worse than ever in the country but the Carboy interests were showing small traces of it. They paid little in the way of profits, it was true, and they had cut wages, but they continued to operate and to make their way. This, however, had nothing to do with the greater frequency of his periods of rest at Beaulaw Hall.

The truth of the matter was that he had so much money now that he had turned inevitably to surrounding himself with beauty. Knowing nothing at all of such things, of the value of precious stones, of what constituted the best in painting and sculpture, of tapestries or Georgian silver, he was still able instinctively to select the real from the spurious. "I don't know anything about rubies," he once boasted. "But put a handful of them down in front of me and I'll pick out the best every time. What's more, I'll grade them without a single mistake." "Buy when things are bad," was another remark he had often made. "When merchants need money, that's the time to pick up the things you want." As a result he was actively in the market for paintings and bits of marble sculpture, and rugs and old furniture. Beaulaw Hall was beginning to reflect the soundness of his judgment. He was particularly interested in the fine furniture of the previous century and was never so happy as when he had picked up, often at absurdly low prices, a beautiful desk, a breakfront, a drum table or even a mahogany wine cooler.

He was standing in front of his latest acquisition, a William and Mary escritoire, and practically drooling (to quote Mrs. Carboy, who did not sympathize with his new hobby and really preferred furniture with a high varnish finish and with lots of knobs and hand carving) over its splendid square lines and its spare display of inlay, when the butler came to him and said, "Lady Gardiner has arrived, sir."

Within a very few minutes Mrs. Carboy flounced into the room, followed by her daughter. "Mr. Carboy," she exclaimed, "this child of yours has left her husband!"

"Nonsense, Mama," said Isabelle. She was looking very cool and composed and more beautiful than ever. "You get so upset over trifles. I'm not breaking up my home. I'm just disciplining Tibby. He's so unreasonable. And when he gets angry at me he doesn't rage and get it all over with in one fine, jolly scene. Instead he just sulks. I can't bear sulkers."

"You little idiot!" said Mrs. Carboy. "I'm sure you've been flirting."

"Of course I've been flirting. My sweet Mama, why shouldn't I? Everybody flirts. Every man I meet whispers things in my ear. Tibby is too old-fashioned for words."

"If you weren't a married woman," said her mother, "I would send you up to your room this instant."

"You don't need to, dear Mama. That is exactly where I'm going. I'm going to get into riding clothes and go out for a little toot around the country."

It was late in the afternoon when Isabelle returned. Her father found her in the library where she was sitting in a deep chair with one slim booted leg crossed over the other. She had taken off her hat and her head was a mass of crinkling golden brown. Mrs. Carboy was sitting opposite and looking intensely critical.

"Hello, Papa," said Isabelle. "Who do you suppose I rode home with? Young Chip. He overtook me near Willikin Creek, coming thundering up on his hunter and shouting and waving his crop. He was delighted to see me."

"Your husband doesn't like Young Chip," declared Mrs. Carboy. "He dislikes all the men you ride with and golf with and sit with in conservatories and flirt with; but most of all he dislikes Young Chip. You know that, don't you?"

"Of course. He didn't mind Chip running around at my heels as long as he was a boy. But now Chip is growing up. My, my, how he's growing up!"

Her father had found this conversation very disturbing. To change the subject he asked how Young Chip had reported on the state of affairs at Outland Park.

"They're in the dumps," answered Isabelle. "As you know, they badgered poor Blettor into marrying that pottery widow and it turns out she's a regular nagger. Young Chip, who is positively amusing at times, calls her the Vinegar Virgin. That's kind of good, isn't it? And it seems she hasn't as much money as they thought. Not nearly enough certainly to put things right at Outland. Poor Old Sheppy never stirs out of the house now, he's so feeble, and he shudders whenever he hears his daughter-in-law's voice. He pays for his title, the poor old man. I must make him a visit tomorrow. I'm about the only one who can make him laugh any more."

"You'll do nothing of the sort!" declared Mrs. Carboy. "You want to go so you can see the grandson again. Besides, your husband will arrive on the evening coach."

"I suppose he will, and it will be such a bother."

"I hear the grandson's going to be married soon," said Carboy. "To the daughter of that banker in Birmingham. Avery Trask. I hear she's a plain little thing."

"Poor Chip!" Isabelle sighed sympathetically. "He knows he's in for it. It won't last long, that marriage. He kills off horses as fast as the Vinegar Virgin will buy them for him and he'll probably have the same way with wives. He was arguing with me most furiously today, as he always does. He wants me to divorce Tib and marry him."

This piece of information, so casually thrown out, drove Mrs. Carboy into enraged protest. She sat up straight in her chair and shook a finger at her daughter. "Isabelle! We'll have no divorces in this family. How would you like to have hostlers giving evidence in court and impudent maids telling what they've seen through keyholes?"

"Mama, *how* can you be so vulgar? One would think I had been having affairs with butlers and running around the country with bagmen. How can you conceive such things? It must be your father cropping out in you. Really!"

"Listen to me, young woman. All I have to do is repeat that remark to Grandfather Hanlon and he'll cut you right out of his will."

Isabelle gave her head an indifferent toss. "He's leaving almost everything to Allie anyway. Why should I care?"

Mrs. Carboy got to her feet. "I won't stay and be treated this way, young lady. I'm going to my own sitting room and you won't be welcome there."

But as she reached the door Fleck appeared, carrying a silver plate heaped with mail.

"Groody just came, ma'am," he said. "He gets later all the time. And drunker, ma'am, if you'll allow me to say so."

Mrs. Carboy took the letters, thumbed them through and then emitted a shriek of delight. "Here it is! I've been waiting for it so long. A letter from America, from my dear Allie. Oh, what a lovely surprise!"

She took her precious letter to a window embrasure and sat down to read it. "What a beautiful hand he writes!" she enthused. "It shows how clever he really is. You needn't try to tell me anything different, Mr. Carboy. My Allie will surprise us all someday."

Carboy was talking to his daughter. "Isabelle, did you read about the death of that old woman up in Westmoreland? She was the last survivor in Class F."

Isabelle looked puzzled. "Class F? I don't know what you're talking about, Papa."

"Class F in the Waterloo Tontine. You remember surely. It was confined to people of sixty and over and so it hasn't taken long to get finished. This old Mrs. Grabling did quite well during the two years when she had all the income to herself. Over six thousand pounds a year."

"Oh, that Tontine. I haven't given it a thought in years. It seems unimportant when I think of all the plans I have for myself."

"Isabelle! Are you serious?" Her father, it was clear, was very much taken aback. "I can't believe that you, of all people, would say such a thing. Isabelle, I will be dead before the payments from the Tontine become large and so I'm very much concerned about you. I will probably leave enough to make you the richest woman in the world but"—he paused, as though reluctant to suggest that anything concerned with him could go wrong—"but how can I tell what will happen when I'm not here to keep things in hand? You may marry again and your husband may play ducks and drakes with the money. Husbands have a habit of squandering the fortunes they've done nothing to earn. And money can shrivel, you know. It can fly right out the window. Times change. Even the wisest of people make mistakes. I want to see you protected from all such possibilities. The Tontine will do it."

"Papa, I expect to marry again—in course of time. But no husband will ever have a chance to play ducks and drakes with *my* money."

Carboy looked very much relieved. "I'm glad to hear you say that. I was afraid you had changed."

"But you must allow, Papa, that the Tontine is a small matter——"

"No, no! that's where you are wrong. The Tontine is firmly established —Sir Theobald and I have seen to that—and the interest will roll in, year after year. You'll be amazed how fast the amounts will grow that are paid out to each member. Do you know that seventy-six have died in your class since the last report? If you survive into the final stages—and I'm confident you will, my pet—the time may come when you'll look forward to the money from it, and you'll watch the health of the other survivors, and sometimes you may even say a prayer or two, 'Oh, kind God, let me be the one to go on living!' "

"My dear, big, successful Papa, don't you know that I appreciate money as much as you do? But there's something more important than money. Social standing. Do you remember when I said I wouldn't be content with a husband of lower rank than a duke? I meant it; and I'm going to marry a duke in the end. If no better one comes along, I may even marry Young Chip. Of course that's all in the future but you must realize, Papa, that when I'm a duchess it won't do for me to be concerned in anything as common as a tontine. Either I would have to sign away my share or turn the income over to charity as a gesture."

"It's a gesture you'll never make, child," said Carboy grimly. "I don't believe in handing over money to committees of impoverished nincompoops and climbing women. There's more malfeasance in charity than there is in government. People have to be helped—within reason—but I don't like so many lily-white hands dipping into the pot first."

"Come, come, Papa. You're taking me too seriously. I'm never going to be silly enough to give money away—unless there are strings to it."

"Good. But just the same I want to repeat what I said. Something keeps telling me that the Tontine will turn out in the end to be the biggest factor in your life."

"I'll remember, Papa. And I'll ease your mind on one point. I'll always keep my husbands under my thumb. They won't have any say about *my* money."

Carboy frowned somberly. "Just the same I wish—I wish I could always be here to look after things."

Mrs. Carboy had been sitting very still in the window embrasure. The letter had fallen into her lap. If her husband and daughter had not been so concerned with other matters they would have noticed that her lips were trembling and her face was white. Suddenly she got to her feet and gave the bellpull a nervous shake. When the butler appeared she said in a shrill voice, "Close all the windows, Fleck."

"Close the windows, ma'am?" Fleck seemed surprised at such an order, as well he might, it being an uncomfortably warm evening.

"Every one. Close them down tight. Draw the curtains, Fleck. And then close the doors."

The butler obeyed her instructions and the atmosphere of the long room quickly became almost unbearable. When he had left, Mrs. Carboy stood beside her chair for a moment, as motionless as a figure in bronze. Then she threw her arms above her head and began to emit moans and stifled cries, gradually allowing her voice to rise in volume.

Carboy looked in frowning alarm at his daughter. "Good gad, Isabelle, what's wrong with your mother? Has she gone mad? Hurry, child, send for a doctor!"

The outcries from the distraught woman continued, becoming louder. She had taken to running blindly about the room, bumping into chairs and tables and stumbling over stools. Her husband caught her by both wrists and tried to force her down into a chair, looking back over his shoulder as he did so in an appeal for help in this unprecedented situation.

"Isabelle, you must do something!" he cried. "Don't stand there staring at me. Get Fleck. Get her maid. Send for the doctor."

"I think she'll be better now, Papa," said Isabelle coolly. "You know how it is. She lets herself go when she has bad news. I think the letter from Allie must have some very bad news. Yes, I've seen her do this before."

Carboy unceremoniously seated his wife in the chair and stood over her, prepared to resist any effort on her part to begin again. "Come now," he said in a tone which he strove to make sympathetic. "Tell us what it is. We mustn't have any more of this kind of thing, you know. What will the servants think?"

"What has Allie done, Mama?" demanded the daughter.

"He's married!" Mrs. Carboy got the dreadful words out with considerable difficulty.

"I thought he was at death's door, the way you carried on, my dear," said Carboy. His first reaction to the news had been one of relief that it was no worse. On second thoughts, however, his choler began to rise. His cheeks became red. "Married? Good gad, who to? It couldn't be the Bonaparte woman. Is it—is it one of those Indian princesses?"

Mrs. Carboy was gradually getting herself under control, now that the extent of the calamity had been revealed. "Oh, how dreadful that I've got to say it. My Allie has married an actress. A little chit who—— Isabelle, bring me that letter. Here it is. He says she's pretty and gay, and has red hair, and the—the most beautiful legs in the world. What a dreadful thing for him to write to his own mother!"

"She sounds perfectly charming," commented Isabelle. "But not as a sister-in-law. Or a daughter-in-law either, dear Mama. I always thought something like this would happen, only I'd have laid my bets it would be a barmaid. Or a coachman's daughter like the Groody creature."

"Why, in God's name, did the boy do such a thing?" demanded the father of the erring Allie. "Speak up, woman. He must have made some explanation in that beautiful writing you were raving about."

"You'll be sorry you wanted to know, Mr. Carboy!" declared his wife grimly. "He was starving. Because his unfeeling father wouldn't send him any money and because he was too proud to ask for help. He was going to throw himself into the ocean and end it all but he was offered a chance to act with a company of theatrical players. So he took it in desperation, and he proved to be such a good actor that they made him the—the leading man. Don't look so astonished, Mr. Carboy. They have theaters in America, just the same as here. This girl was in the company and he fell in love with her, even though the leading lady was in love with him——"

Carboy's face had turned a curious mottled gray. "I don't understand it," he said. "I've done everything a father could for the boy."

"You were always hard and cruel to him, you cut him off, you starved him!" cried his wife. "This is all your fault and you needn't try to escape the blame."

"From coachman's daughter, to princess, to leading lady, to breeches girl," said Isabelle. "Allie has broad tastes, hasn't he?"

"Unfeeling child!" cried Mrs. Carboy. "I believe you're glad. I believe you're thinking that now your father will be cruel and monstrous enough to cut the poor boy off and that you'll come in for all the money. I know you, my girl."

Isabelle went to the bell and gave it an impatient tug. "Open the windows, Fleck," she said when the butler appeared. "Mrs. Carboy has recovered from her indisposition."

The butler withdrew and for several moments the three members of the family stared at each other in an unhappy silence. It was Isabelle who broke it. "Dinner tonight won't be a very festive occasion. Especially if Tibby arrives and is still in the sulks. I'm going to have mine in my room. And I want a good solid one. I need it after this demonstration of the idiotic strain which runs in our family."

"I won't be able to swallow a mouthful," declared Mrs. Carboy in a weak voice. "I'm going straight to bed."

Sir Theobald Gardiner did not come and so the head of the household sat at dinner by himself. He consumed dish after dish without pause and without relish. Then he began to drink. His thoughts, which had been unpleasantly self-critical while he dined, took a new turn. He became angry.

"An actor!" he said aloud, at a moment when all of the servants were out of the room. "My son, the son of Samuel Carboy who is turning the business of the Empire upside down to the benefit of all concerned, has become one of these strutting fools who caper and rant and make fools of themselves for a living! He doesn't get it from the Carboy side. We've been solid and sensible and hard-working for generations. It must come from the other side. They've got plenty of bad blood of one kind or another. Old Whip married his housemaid." He sat and glowered as his thoughts turned to the occupation his son had chosen; having no alternative, it was true. Finally, with the deepest scorn, he began to recite lines from plays which came into his mind. "'To be or not to be.' Gad, what tosh! 'The carriage awaits, m'lord.' Faugh! 'At last I have ye in my power, proud gel!' And that's the way *my* son is making his living!"

The brown line in the whisky decanter diminished and sank, and finally disappeared. When another had taken its place, the magnate's mood changed. He became sentimental, even a little maudlin.

"Was it all my fault, as my wife says?" he asked himself. "Did I drive the poor boy to this? Gad, I've a notion to take the first boat to New York and get everything straightened out. I could buy that redheaded baggage off and send her about her business. Then I would bring Alfred back and in no time at all the whole thing would be forgotten. I could take him in hand and make something of him." A tear of self-pity appeared in the corner of one eye. "But what in thunder could I make of a son like that?"

In the morning he realized that he could not spare the time to go to America. A hundred matters of the utmost importance pressed upon him. Instead, therefore, he wrote a crisp and peremptory letter, enclosing a substantial money order, demanding that his son return at once to discuss his future. Alone, he added. The baggage must be left behind.

2

A bagman came riding into Little Shallow in a red-wheeled cart piled high with goods. He was seeing to it that his horse kept up a lively gait and he himself whistled with a fine abandon. He gave every evidence, in fact, of being well content with life.

"Here I come, here I come, here I come!" he sang in a thin tenor voice as he opened the door of the Groody shop and walked in.

Nell issued out from the dining room beyond, looking very cool and neat and businesslike in a dress of Henrietta cloth. There were changes in her appearance and all of them for the better. She looked composed and sure of herself, although her dark hair had been given a titus cut so that it clustered on her forehead in crisp curls and made her look as young as on that never-to-be-forgotten day when she met Alfred Carboy at the ruined church.

"Good afternoon, Mr. Crashly," she said.

"Good afternoon, partner," said Mr. Crashly, eying her in a way which could only be called covetous. "You look extremely well, partner. I wonder if any further thought has been given to a certain suggestion I made—that you and I make it an out-and-outer? A partnership for life, no less."

"I haven't changed my mind about that." Nell was looking out the window at the smart equipage with red wheels. "And I never will, Mr. Crashly. And now about other matters. Business is good, I trust?"

"Business is good. Business, in fact, couldn't be better. The profits are growing all the time. Grimes buys the goods at low prices and I go out and sell 'em at high prices. When you invested your two hundred pounds with us, dear lady—and I concede we couldn't have got started if you hadn't and so you're entitled to your third—you picked two good horses to put your brass on."

"I was sure of that," declared Nell. "I knew Mr. Grimes was a solid businessman and that you, Mr. Crashly, were a born salesman. It's a good combination."

"I've two other investments in mind for you," declared the born salesman, with a wink. "First, a husband. Me. Ah, partner, what a good combination that would be! I know you aren't in a mood to invest in me yet but you'll come around to it in time. You can't remain blind to all my perfections forever. You're stubborn but you got a good head on you. I'm counting on that." He winked again. "This other one is a real investment. A man I've heard of down Reading way. He's got a bit of equipment he invented himself. It's a signal for starting and stopping trains. They tell me it's mighty clever and that none of these railroads will be able to get along without it. But he's as short of cash as a farm hand after a village fair. Someone's got to finance him or he won't be able to do anything about it. Thought you might like to know."

Nell had discarded her casual manner and was watching him with a serious air. "You've suggested several things to me, Mr. Crashly, at various times but I've never given any of them a second thought. Perhaps this is different. You see, in anything as new as a railway the people who finance the first construction are almost certain to lose everything they put in. I read all about it in a book. But those who hold patents on devices which have to be used, and paid for right from the start, they're the ones who make great fortunes. If this man has something really good, we might all make some money out of it. What's his name, Mr. Crashly?"

"Got it right here." The former bagman produced a piece of paper from a pocket. "That's his name and address. You got gold in your hand, partner. And, blow me tight, I was the one to put it there."

Nell put the paper away in a pocket of her apron. "And now that we're speaking of profits, Mr. Crashly, I have this thought to put before you. I'm sure you and Mr. Grimes can go on making money. But are we going to be as successful at keeping it? You seem to travel in high style. That cart, now."

"Oh, that! It pays to cut a good figure, my dear and very observant little partner. It brings in the business. I like you to come down on me like this, just the same. Makes me want to tweak that pretty little ear which hears so much and kiss those eyes which see so much. Ah, to have you coming down on me all the rest of my life!" He fumbled in the same pocket and produced, first of all, a letter he did not want seen. At any rate he stuffed it back again hastily and gave Nell a rather furtive look to see if she had noticed. What he finally brought forth was a balance sheet. "Here, dearest lady, are the figures; and I rather think that you won't want to come down on us about them. Do you wish to go over them now?"

"I do indeed," declared Nell.

Mr. Crashly was gone, after satisfying the shrewd young proprietress of the Little Shallow shop that her investment would continue to yield her good returns. The sun had sunk deeply enough in the west to make it difficult for Mrs. Groody's eyes, which were not as good as they had once been, to continue with her knitting. Nell was sitting at her desk, her hands folded in her lap, her thoughts far away.

Daniel Groody drove the mail cart into the yard and came into the shop on legs which were far from steady. He created such a loud jingling of the bell on the door that it might have been expected that some great merchant had come to offer a thousand pounds for the business; an offer, however, which Nell would never have accepted.

"Well, childie," he said. "It's glad I am to see you resting for once. I like to see my little girl just sitting there and enjoying the nice sunset and not worriting over books and papers."

Nell brought her mind back from wherever it had gone; the United States of America, one might have assumed. She studied her father with a somber eye.

"I see you've visited all the taverns, Father," she said. "And after the talks we've had!"

All trace of exuberance left Daniel Groody's manner and he looked very unhappy and penitent at once. He stood in front of her desk and fumbled with his cap.

"Yes, childie," he said. "It's all of them I've been to this day. But not for my own pleasure, I'll want you to know." He continued to stare down at her. "It's bad news I have for you. I don't like the telling of it and so I—well, I had to go in each of them and get my courage up a little."

Nell looked up at him slowly. Bad news! It must have to do with Allie

Carboy, she thought at once. Was he ill? Was he—was he dead? She felt so sick at heart as these possibilities took possession of her mind that she could not force her lips to ask a question.

"It's about this young Carboy," said her father. He swallowed before going on. "It comes to this, Nelly. He's married. He's gone and got himself another wife, the ill-begotten cur to treat my little girl so!"

"Married!" Somehow this seemed worse in the first few shocked moments than any of the dire surmises which she had conjured up. She had always been sure that Allie loved her. He was weak and thoughtless but she had never thought it possible he would love anyone else. She looked up at her father with so much grief and pain in her face that his eyes filled with tears for her.

"Married, Father? When, when?"

"I don't know as to that, childie. It's a long time letters take to reach us here from America. Weeks and weeks. The news has spread fast, my little Nelly. It was told me many places."

There was a long pause and then she asked in a subdued voice, "Who did he marry, Father?"

"An actress. A dancer, as light in the head as in the heels, no doubt."

An actress! Nell felt a slight amelioration of her grief. She was sure she could not have borne it if the girl her Allie had married had been one of the eligible kind, the daughter of a rich man, who rode to hounds and had an income of her own; the possessor, in other words, of all the advantages she herself had lacked. That he had shown enough courage to marry an actress brought her an instant pang (if he had remained at home, that same courage might have brought him finally to her) and at the same time a curious kind of pleasure. What would the Carboys, father, mother and sister, think of this? They would suffer also. For a brief moment she was almost glad of what had happened.

A very brief moment, however. The first reaction was followed by a realization of the irrevocability of what had happened. Allie was married. She would never see him again, never see him smile, never hear his voice. All the hopes she had secretly cherished were shattered. She knew now, if she had not before, that she could never love anyone else. All that life had to offer her was the dull routine of living, from hour to hour, from day to day.

"I'm going to my room," she said in a voice devoid of all expression. "Please, Father, see that I'm not disturbed."

Nell's parents discussed her at breakfast, hovering over a platter of bacon and speaking in low tones.

"It's no sleep she had last night, the poor child," said her father. "Twice I waked up and both times I heard her moving about her room."

Mrs. Groody gave her head an emphatic shake. "She's going to suffer for it. I warned her. I told her a hundred times to put him out of her mind. I said it from the very start."

"Words never rule the hearts of the young," said Daniel Groody. "Don't you see, woman, that the poor child couldn't help herself? She loved him. Holy Mother Mary help her now, for she still loves him!"

Mrs. Groody changed the subject abruptly. "You were drunk last night," she charged.

The ex-coachman did not deny the accusation or try to dodge the issue. "That I was. I hadn't the courage to face her and tell her the bad news. So I dropped in at this place and I dropped in at that one—and never an ounce of courage did I get out of it."

"You'll not be able to keep on the mail route," warned his wife. "There's plenty of talk about it already, Daniel Groody. People are complaining. You're always late and you're always a little tozie, and they don't like it."

His temper began to show signs of rising. "You don't know what you're saying, woman!" he declared.

"I know what people are saying—and that's what counts. They're saying they want someone who'll be on time and won't smell like a grogshop. They're tired of you, Daniel Groody, and that's the truth."

Groody's face showed the hurt of a boy who has stumbled on the fact that others do not like him. He began to defend himself, although it was clear there was little conviction in what he said. "But they're glad to see me. It's 'Hey, Dan Groody, and how are you?' And they laugh with me. At the Beau and the Britches, it's always, 'Here comes Dan Groody and he'll have a story for us.'"

"It's not your cronies I'm talking about. It's the people in the big houses who want the mail on time, and the merchants and the doctors and all the bigwigs. They're going to complain about it to the member. And if they do that's the last of you, Daniel Groody, because the member will go to the post office about it."

For a long time he made no comment but continued to sit very still, a stricken look on his face. Finally he gave his head a single nod and began to speak in the hopeless tone of a prisoner pleading guilty.

"I wouldn't hurt her for all the world. You know that, wife. And I want her to make money out of this farming of the mails. It's happy I've been, driving my neat little cart all over the country, but I'll drop out at once. I will indeed."

They could hear Nell's footsteps on the stair and so nothing more was said. They were pretending to eat bacon when she came into the room, and they looked up to say no more than "Good morning." Daniel Groody could see out of the corner of his eye that she was pale. Mrs. Groody got to her feet to bring another plate.

"No breakfast, Mother," said Nell. "I'm not hungry but you mustn't be worried. I'm going to survive." She sat down at the table, facing them. "I'm going to dread talking to people—for a time. So I'm going to let Nanty" —the little northern girl who helped in the store and waited on customers in the tea stalls—"take charge for a few days. There are some errands which will take my mind off things, I hope. Father, do you think you could turn the route over to someone today?"

"Yes, childie. There's Early Crackaday, who has a good hand on the reins and knows the country from the Vale to the Thames. But is it just for today we might get him? Or, perhaps, for all days?"

Nell looked at him intently and for a moment she forgot her own woes in the contemplation of his. "Father, we'll have to talk about that soon. I have some ideas. But all I want to do today is to have you drive me to Reading. There's a man near there I must see at once."

3

It was in the early fall of that year and the Vale had never looked more festive. The trees were a mass of yellow and red and the oak-beamed houses on the one street of the village had dahlias which seemed to reach to the slanting gables. Even the stubble in the fields suggested a bountiful harvest, so plentiful, in fact, that the men who had tilled the soil felt free to take an occasional moment off to look up into the hills and enjoy their beauty. Luke Finan, the philosophical landlord of the George and Charlotte, added to his reputation for queerness by remarking that the Horse itself "was a bit fat abat the ribs and demned if I don't think the beast has slowed daown to a jog trot."

One evening Early Crackaday returned with the red cart and old Barney, bringing with him as usual the letters he had accumulated on his rounds and which would be sorted and placed on the coaches the next day. He was fairly bursting with news, which made it very hard for Daniel Groody. The latter had insisted on giving up the route and had recommended Crackaday for his place. Once the change had been made, however, he had soured on his successor. He turned his back on him whenever they met and refused to say a word. It was Mrs. Groody who came out to receive the letters.

"There's trouble at Beaulaw Hall," said Crackaday. "Terrible trouble, I'm thinking it must be, Mrs. Groody. Though just what it is I don't know."

The voice of Daniel Groody reached them from where he was standing behind the half-open door of the shop. "He doesn't know what it is! Is he deaf and blind?"

"I ast questions but it was no answers I got," protested the new mailman.

"Woman, he must have more to tell us. Get it out of him. Pump him!"

"Come out and pump him yourself like a man instead of skulking there," replied Mrs. Groody, who had no patience with her spouse's idiosyncrasies.

"I'll tell you everything I know, Mrs. Groody," said Crackaday humbly. He stood in awe of his predecessor, expecting that Groody would demand the job back at any minute. "It started when the darter and hoosband arrived this morning on the Lunnon coach."

"Make him speak up, wife! I can't half hear."

"They come on the Lunnon coach," repeated Crackaday, raising his voice.

"Sir Ga'd'ner and Leddy Ga'd'ner. The car'ge from the Hall was waiting and off they went wi'out a word to anyone."

"How did they look?" asked Mrs. Groody.

"I don' know. I didn' see it but I hear 'bout it. Leddy Ga'd'ner had only two bags. Does that mean aught? Gen'lly she has six."

"It means a lot, Mr. Crackaday," answered Mrs. Groody. "If she had only two bags, it means she was fair upset about something. How many maids did she bring?"

"One."

"Only one! Then she's so distracted she doesn't know what she's doing, that's clear."

Daniel Groody spoke up from behind the door. "It's Mrs. Carboy. It's sick she is and no mistake." He added in a tone of deep regret, "It's a whole pund I'd give to have been at the Hall this day!"

"All the butler said to me when I asked him was, 'Git on with ye now.' Not a word would he give me."

"I'd have got it out of him," commented Groody.

Partly in self-defense, the new driver of the mail came forward now with another piece of information. "He was seen driving down the Oxford road. This ev'ning. 'Bout five-thirty."

"Who was seen? Are you lame in the brain, man!"

"Sam'l Carboy was seen. Driving in that car'ge with four horses, all smoking hot and covered with lather. They came at the gallop and Humpster was a-shouting at them and a-cracking his whip. And Jenny Taskery saw *him* looking out the window. She says he was white as a marr'ge sheet and he looked like Old Horny hisself."

"Perhaps it's Mr. Carboy that's ill," suggested Mrs. Groody. "Perhaps he has taken sick on his trip."

Daniel Groody brushed this aside. "It's Mrs. Carboy, I tell you. She's been moping for weeks and not eating a bite of food. Though it's said she has a fresh bottle of the stuff sent up each morning reg'lar."

"Did you talk to Jennie Taskery, Mr. Crackaday?" asked Mrs. Groody.

"No, ma'am. I got the news 'bout her at the Lonely Camel."

At this piece of information, Daniel Groody relinquished the role of bystander and, as he would have expressed it himself, got into the conversation with both feet. "So, you were at the Lonely Camel!" he said. "Let me tell you something, my man, for your own good. Though why I bother about you, I don't know. There'll be no drinking on this route, Mister Early Crackaday. Just fall into *that* habit and it's a new mail driver we'll be looking for."

Crackaday drew himself up with an attempt at dignity. "I had a letter for Sim Eavewright. And where else would I find him, Dan'l Groody, but in his own inn, may I ask?"

Unknown to any of them, Nell had been listening from the window of her bedroom above, having caught the word "Carboy." At this point, however, she ceased to be interested in what they were saying. It was clear to her that Crackaday had told everything he knew and, in any case, she was convinced they were wrong in their surmises about Mrs. Carboy. She was certain herself that it was not the health of that estimable lady which had brought Sir Theobald and Lady Gardiner by coach from London in such haste and had caused Samuel Carboy to come galloping down from the north at as mad a pace as the great Napoleon had ever demanded, shuttling back and forth over the roads of Europe.

"It's about Allie!" said Nell to herself. She went to a chair and dropped inertly into it. "I know it is! It can't be anything else. What can it be now? Oh, what has he done!"

She remained huddled in the chair for some time, speculating unhappily on the nature of the news which was causing so much commotion. "Oh, Allie, Allie!" she sobbed. "What have you done? Are you ill? Have you been hurt? Have you," hopefully, "run away from that terrible actress wife?"

But it was not his actress wife that Alfred Carboy had run away from. Sometimes, it must be said, he had given consideration to that idea: when Emmy had seemed unnecessarily scatterbrained or had flirted too openly with men in the audience or other members of the company. It was for a different reason entirely; but he had gone away.

The news reached the shop at Little Shallow late in the evening and it was brought by Dr. Moggridge. He had been summoned to Beaulaw Hall to administer sedatives to Mrs. Carboy and he was now to be disappointed in his main reason for driving three miles out of his way on the return trip. Nell Groody was not there to greet him when he entered the shop, her place being taken by Mrs. Groody.

"Evening, ma'am," said the doctor gruffly. He was a huge man and had always made his rounds on horseback until he overheard someone remark, "Dr. Moggridge kills as many horses as he does patients." Now he used a small gig which creaked and groaned under his weight.

"Good evening, Doctor. What are you needing, sir?"

"A spool of cotton." When Mrs. Groody went to rummage for it (she never had any idea where the stock was kept), he cleared his throat. "Sad news at Beaulaw Hall, ma'am."

Mrs. Groody suspended her search and straightened up. "Indeed, Doctor? We haven't heard."

"They've lost their son." The medical man's voice was absurdly high-pitched to issue from such a large frame. "The word reached them yesterday from America. Lady Gardiner was at a country house in Kent and Mr. Carboy was in the Midlands. There was a great to-do about getting them back. Mrs. Carboy is prostrated. I don't mind telling you, in the strictest confidence, that I am greatly worried about her."

Mrs. Groody had been staring at him with her mouth wide open in astonishment. It was with difficulty that she found her tongue. "What happened to the poor young man?" she asked.

"Well, it was a strange thing, ma'am. He was actually engaged with a company of touring players when it happened. You knew he was an actor?"

Mrs. Groody nodded.

"It seems the company decided to go on a tour of some of the places in the far West. I don't know any of the heathenish names, although one curious word seems to stick in my mind. Buffalo. Could that be the name of a place, do you suppose? Most highly unlikely, in my opinion. Well, they did their traveling in vehicles called covered wagons. Again I profess my ignorance. I have no conception of what a covered wagon is. Young Mr. Carboy was not accustomed to the severe cold they encountered while traveling in these strange carriages, whatever they may be, and he got taken down with pneumonia. Do you know what that is? An inflammation of the lungs. It's a serious business at any time, and it happened that they did not reach a town until he was pretty far gone with it. So he died. A very sad ending, ma'am, very sad indeed. He would have been a rich and prominent man someday. I always thought him a most attractive young gentleman."

Mrs. Groody continued to stare at him and made no comment.

"Your daughter is well?" asked the doctor, after waiting several moments for some verbal reaction.

"Well enough, Doctor. She's upstairs at her books. I'm thinking, Doctor, she may not be quite as well when she hears this news you've brought."

"I'm afraid not, ma'am. You will give her my regards? A very bright young woman, your daughter. I have grown to have quite an admiration for her. You will give her my *very* best regards, please."

He left them without waiting for the spool of cotton, so it may be assumed that it had been no more than an excuse for visiting the store with the news of Allie Carboy's death.

When the doctor had stepped into his gig and departed, Nell's parents sat down together and stared into each other's eyes. Mrs. Groody was in tears.

"Dan, I can't do it. I can't tell the child. It's going to break her heart this time. I've been watching her for the past weeks and it's clear to me she's not well. She doesn't eat enough to keep a bird alive."

In the face of this emergency, Daniel Groody seemed to achieve dignity and stature. He drew himself up with a suggestion of pride. "And who but her own father should tell the child?" he asked. "There must be no delay, so it's upstairs I'll go at once." He rose to his feet and stared at her solemnly. "It won't be hard, wife. *She knows!* I could tell from the look in her eyes when we told her of the commotion among the Carboys. She knew he was dead then. But I'll do my best to speak gently to her and not hurt her feelings."

CHAPTER TWENTY

1

It was a Sunday morning and Julian had been invited to share the Pardons' noon dinner. He knew that he would meet the leg of mutton at least four times during the ensuing week in various guises and so he was glad of the chance to see and taste it in its first glory. Mr. Pardon was giving the carving knife a final scrape on the stone sharpener when the familiar sound of Noel's whistle was heard in the street.

For several weeks Noel had been dividing his time. His mistress still had first call on his services but each morning at eight sharp Julian would issue out from the house and find the kittereen waiting for him, Noel on the box with a broad smile of greeting. The arrival of this equipage at the Admiralty naturally had been observed by all members of the staff. He had ceased to be Grace to his fellow workers and had become any one of many nicknames, including the Nabob, the Sultan, Croesus and Mr. Brads Himself.

Noel had much to learn but his good nature was so unshakable and his loyalty so complete that those he served had no desire to change him. One of the things he never got through his head was that England was not a land of wide-open doors and free-and-easy ways. He considered it quite proper to join in conversations and his head was as often turned to address his passengers as it was to the traffic through which he drove. He was full of curiosity and had no reluctance in asking questions. He enjoyed giving advice.

"M's'r Ju'," he would say, "you doan' wan' wear dat ole blue coat to wo'k three days in row." The habit which caused the most concern was his unwillingness to get down from the box and knock on doors to announce his arrival. Instead he would throw back his head and give forth whistled summons in four bars which to Julian sounded like the words, "Hurry, Come, Boss Man."

It was this message which reached Julian's ears as Mr. Pardon prepared to carve the roast. He looked apologetically at his hostess. "I'm afraid," he said, "that something has happened to demand my presence."

Mrs. Pardon, who had never seen Winifred but approved of her unreservedly because she was an heiress, gave him a smiling release. "If it's the pretty young lady, Mr. Grace, you must not delay," she said. "Hurry, you must not keep her waiting."

Noel was standing beside the horse and he bowed almost to the waist when Julian appeared.

"I'se to tak' yu, m's'r," he said, climbing back briskly to the box. "Us late now. Git in quick, m's'r."

"Is it Miss Winifred?"

"Yes, Mist' Ju'. Hit's Miss Win'fed. And Him, suh."

"Him? I don't understand, Noel. Who is with Miss Winifred?"

"The Brizzer, suh. The Great Say-so. Miss Win'fed's fathah, suh. Mist' Ball'."

"Mr. Ballard! Here? Are you sure?"

"Yes, Mist' Ju'. I'se suah."

It was a beautiful day with a sun high in a cloudless sky but Julian now felt as though the whole world had turned cold and clouded over. This sudden visit of Timothy Ballard's was ominous. It meant he had not been content to write his rejection of Julian as a suitor but had caught the first boat and had come over to deliver it in person. "This can mean only one thing," thought Julian. "He'll say no to me in no uncertain terms. Then he'll whisk my sweet Winifred away to Jamaica. And I'll never see her again."

"Noel," he said to the driver, "do you know that I—that I am much attached to your mistress?"

A grin spread over Noel's face. "Yes, Mist' Ju'. Ah knows dat."

"Do you know I want to marry her?"

"In cou'se, suh. Ev'body knows dat. Ev'body knows you goan' mah'y Miss Win'fed."

"Who do you mean by everybody?"

"Why, suh, people I lives wid at. Footsman at school. Man as keeps awster booth at cohner. Ev'body, suh."

"I always found you a good judge of things, Noel, and that's why I'm asking you these questions. How do you think Mr. Ballard is feeling? Does he seem angry?"

"No, Mist' Ju'. I hears 'im talk to Miss Win'fed. They's laff plen'y, Mist' Ju'."

Julian declined to accept this optimistic view. "He won't laugh when I get there. That's when the trouble will start."

"No, suh. He no haff Miss Win'fed wi' him if he mean mak' trub'. He keep Miss Win'fed out sight. He no let big roostah see nice lil lady bug."

2

The host of the Royal Kent Arms called to a passing waiter, "Here you are, Jonas, show this gent to seventeen." Julian knocked on the panel of room seventeen with a trepidation which Noel's words had done nothing to allay. A deep voice, which he recognized as that of Timothy Ballard, answered from within: "Come in! Don't stand there knocking!"

Timothy Ballard was sitting in a creaky armchair and it seemed on first glance that he was frowning in a most formidable way. Julian had no chance to form a definite conclusion on that point, however, for Winifred rose from a chair at the other side of the room and came over to greet him. It might even be said that she ran, for certainly she used up little time in reaching him. She threw her arms around his neck.

"Oh, darling!" she whispered. "Papa doesn't object. He's happy about it." She gave her arms a tug to bring his ear closer to her mouth. "Do you hear what I'm saying, my tall, wonderful husband-to-be? Don't you feel like shouting? Are you glad? Are you still in love with me? Papa's going to let me marry you. And I love you, I love you, I love you!"

Her father had risen from his chair and gone to one of the windows so that his back was turned to them. "I'll be glad to shake your hand, Mr. Grace," he said, "when my daughter has stopped monopolizing you. But of course there's no hurry about it. None at all."

"I'm happy to see you, sir," said Julian. "But I don't mind saying, sir, that I came in fear and trembling. I thought you were going to—to cast me into outer darkness."

"Never mind talking to Papa," said Winifred. "He can wait. We have so very, very many things to tell each other."

In course of time the three of them sat down together around a table which a waiter was preparing for a midday meal. The latter had already whisked the chenille cover off and replaced it with a linen tablecloth. Neither Julian nor Winifred had any idea how long it had been. Mr. Ballard had known to a second. It had been eleven minutes and forty seconds, and he had remained patiently all that time at the window, watching two men in the street below quarrel over a dog.

"I heard my daughter say to you, my boy, that I don't object," said Timothy Ballard, studying a bottle of wine which the waiter had deposited on the table. "That is not exactly accurate. As soon as the letters arrived I sat down and wrote one in which I poured out all the first objections and reservations they had roused in me. But when her mother and I had talked about it several times, I realized that I didn't object to the marriage as much as I thought at first. So, instead of writing a letter, I caught the first boat for England—and here I am."

"When did you arrive, sir?"

Timothy Ballard seemed happy to answer this question. In fact he quite perceptibly puffed out his chest as he said it was five days since he had reached the city. "You see, my boy," he explained, "I'm a believer in thoroughness. There were many things I had to do, and many questions I had to ask, before I could talk to you. For instance, I went into Berkshire and saw your father and mother. We had several long talks. I liked them very much and I am perhaps fatuous enough to believe that they liked me. Your father and I agreed on many points and he is not more than an inch or so taller than I am. I felt very comfortable with him and I can understand why he's making such a fine impression by his work in the House. They took me over to see the Duke of Outland, who spoke of you most glowingly. For some reason he seemed inclined to refer to you as Jasper."

"He had a younger brother named Jasper who went out and took up land in Canada."

"His mistake was due, I'm sure, to his advancing years and not to any lack of knowledge of your name. Need I tell you, my boy, that your parents are well disposed to the match? Although, of course, they haven't seen Winifred yet. I showed them a miniature of her which a colored artist in Kingston had painted—a really remarkable fellow. They were quite carried away by it."

"When they see Winifred, sir," declared Julian, "they will capitulate instantly, if they haven't already done so."

"I took the liberty of ordering the roast beef for all of us," said Mr. Ballard as the waiter began to carry in dishes. "We get so little good beef on the island that I've been devoting myself to it ever since I arrived. Ah, I see they have a steamed suet pudding instead of the Yorkshire. A sound combination." He returned to the recital of the affairs which had kept him busy since his arrival. "I went also to the Admiralty and there I saw both Sir Reginald Fettery and Sir Mainwaring Grant. Each of them gave a warm report of you.

"You will both be surprised, I think, to know that I've paid a visit to the little house they call Santa Cruz. It's not exactly what I would like for you but it's more or less an official matter, I judge. It may even be that you get it rent-free."

"No, sir. They don't go that far."

"Well, it may do for a while," said Ballard with a rather pompous air.

"Not for very long," contributed Winifred. "I think I'll take after Mama and have lots and lots and lots of children. The house hasn't room for more than one."

Having reached this stage in his story, Timothy Ballard seemed almost ready to burst with satisfaction over the accomplishment he proceeded to explain. "I thought of that," he declared. "The little house will do for a year but probably not a day longer. I've already found the ideal home for you."

Winifred looked up quickly and rather anxiously. "Where, Papa, where?"

"I don't mean a residence in the city. The important thing is to have a place in the county. I saw the perfect house when I went out to see your parents, my boy. It's not more than six miles from where they live. On the Thames but on an elevation which keeps it dry. The gardens run down to the water where there's a pier and a boathouse. It's Georgian, red brick, two stories high only, with charming wings, a parlor, a strawberry parlor, a library—a very handsome library and the books go with it—and a dining room and nice little studies, one for each of you. There's a garden, enclosed in a brick wall, stables and a fine stand of trees. Oak and elm, mostly."

Both the young people were breathing excitedly.

"It sounds much too large for us," said Julian in a reluctant state of doubt.

"I think it sounds fascinating," declared Winifred. "When can we look at it, Papa?"

"Any time at all, dear children," answered her father. "I bought it at once."

They began then to talk about the immediate future. The planter explained that he could remain until after they were married because Mrs. Ballard had gone to Barbados to visit relatives. Her health had been a little peaked, he said, and she had not felt equal to accompanying him, much as she had longed to come. Still, a short visit would do her good. He had no concern over the plantation because his new superintendent was handling everything in a most workmanlike way.

Winifred looked up quickly. "Who is it, Papa?"

"Clingman Rade. You remember when I had him in charge of the sugar mill? He ran it better than I could myself. So a short time ago I switched him to the rice paddies and he did just as well there. You see, my child, he has colored blood in him and so he understands the men working under him."

There was a long silence. It was clear that Winifred was worried. "Papa, I don't agree with what you've done. I never liked Clingman Rade."

Her father laughed easily. "Why not, my small one? As I say, he's capable and he knows his place——"

"I'm not sure he does. There was always a look in his eye I didn't like. Papa, I dreaded the sight of his feet. They were so large and broad and flat. I always had the feeling that wherever he planted them down—anywhere, in a doorway, in a room, in a position of trust—nothing would ever move them. You know, Papa, he *did* put those feet of his in other men's doorways."

"I've talked to him about that. No more philandering, I said. He had to leave the wives alone and not have his men hating him and waiting for a chance to cut his throat with a hatchet. He promised. I have every confidence in him now."

His daughter was still far from content but she said nothing more. The meal progressed to a steamed pudding which caused the planter to roll his eyes toward the ceiling. Then came a final course, consisting of a sharp cheese with apples. It was not until all their appetites had been satisfied that Timothy Ballard settled back in his chair and began to talk.

"The whole face of life is changing, my dear young people. Perhaps I'm better able to see it than anyone who has been here all the time. On my last visit I found London full of redcoats and I heard fifes and drums everywhere. It was all war then. The press gangs still roamed the streets and picked up men for the navy. Would you believe it that a pair got hold of me one night?" He looked a little sheepish at making this confession. "I'd gone out for a stroll alone after attending a dinner of bankers. The dinner had been a good one and I was hardly able to defend myself when a pair of them swooped on me with their swords out. They dragged me to the inn where the bosun in command was having a jovial evening. I fairly blasted him and he took one look at me and said to them, 'Lumme, ye've thrown your net over a queer fish this time.' He realized the magnitude of their mistake when I told him who I was. I was apologized to handsomely and asked to overlook it. And one of my captors went along to see me back safely to my quarters, whining the whole time."

"Why, Papa, I've never heard you tell about that."

"My child, I'm not particularly proud of it and I don't enjoy telling about anything as cruel as this. They call the country a democracy and yet they send out ruffianly sailors to seize young fellows with honest employment and perhaps wives and children, and put them into the navy. They put them into hell holes and beat them unmercifully for any mistakes. They feed them on wormy bread and nauseous salt pork.

"There are no press gangs at the moment," he went on, "although another war would bring them out. But the point I started to make is how vastly England has changed. I haven't seen a redcoat since I reached London. I don't hear a word about war or the Battle of Waterloo or Nelson. It's all trade and commerce now. Everything I hear has to do with building railroads and launching steamships and raising new factories. It's a new age. Is it going to be an improvement? It's hard to tell. At the moment there's more interest in this Samuel Carboy than in the old Iron Duke. That worries me.

"This morning I took a turn in St. James's Park and I saw a tall young fellow with black curls sticking out from under the tallest silk hat ever worn on a human head. He had a monocle and a collar which hid his ears. His coat was fawn and hung almost to his knees. His trousers were so baggy he could have stuck both legs into one and the cloth was a glaring bottle blue. What's more, he was wearing spurs though I think he's probably never been on a horse in his life. That sort of thing worries me too."

Winifred had been listening although her eyes had never left Julian's face. "But, Papa," she asked, "life hasn't changed in the important things, has it? People still fall in love and get married. And they can still be so happy that it doesn't matter what's going on in the outside world. . . ."

Timothy Ballard smiled broadly. "I'm going downstairs to attend to some matters of business. From the look on our young friend's face, I can see he's ready to answer your question."

CHAPTER TWENTY-ONE

1

Three years had passed. Another fall had rolled around but it was not as bright and bountiful as the autumn when the news of Allie Carboy's death had reached the Vale. It was a dark autumn, rainy and dank and decidedly unpleasant. The kind of winds which belonged by rights to winter were howling through Little Shallow and whistling about the stone walk at Beaulaw Hall where the ghost of someone's wife or mistress or daughter (no one was quite clear about this) was supposed to issue forth at night. If the shade of the unfortunate lady was doing penance for some sin by flitting about the courtyard, she was paying a high price for her wrongdoing in life.

One Sunday Samuel Carboy had a group of business associates at the Hall. They had all driven over for lunch and there was a curious collection of vehicles along the drive, including a stanhope which had a seat at least seven feet in the air. They had been given a fine meal and were emerging from the dining room with red faces and a general air of repletion when Fleck sidled up to his master's shoulder and said in his ear, "A lady to see you, sir."

The great industrial leader had partaken of one drink of whisky too many. He looked at Fleck with a rather glassy eye.

"A lady? How in thunderation did she get here?"

"She got off the Lunnon coach at Wantage and had herself driven over, sir. She has a boy with her."

"I can't imagine who it is. What name did she give, Fleck?"

The butler hesitated. "She says, sir, that her name is Mrs. Alfred Carboy."

The head of the house might be a step over the line from sobriety but it required no more than the briefest unit of time for him to grasp the full significance of this announcement.

"Ah! So that's it! Well, it was to be expected." He paused and frowned thoughtfully. Then his eyes came back to Fleck with a fierce intentness. "What did you say, Fleck? A boy? Good gad, I didn't expect *that*." Another pause. "Fleck, take the lady and the boy to my study. I'll be there directly."

When Carboy reached the study, after settling his guests elsewhere and seeing them well supplied with everything they might need in the line of drinks, he found the woman who called herself his son's widow sitting near the window and looking out into the drizzle. A boy of perhaps three stood beside her. He was dressed in a velvet suit and was wearing a blue bow tie and trim leather shoes laced up over his ankles and tied with tasseled laces; a very nice-looking little boy indeed, with light hair and blue eyes.

All Mr. Carboy's attention was being given to the lady. She was small, with red hair, which had once been more red and more vibrant, and a pert face. He was surprised to note that she was quietly dressed in dark blue and was wearing a hat that could be described almost as prim. Her skirts, which were so full that they spread out as wide as a peacock's tail, did not permit as much as the point of a shoe to show.

"The butler tells me," said Carboy, "that you gave him the name of Mrs. Alfred Carboy. That means you are the widow of my son. Or that you *say* you are his widow."

Emmy had been dreading this interview with her father-in-law. Allie's references to his father had left the impression of a household tyrant who demanded his own way in everything, a family ogre, in fact. She looked up at Samuel Carboy, who had drawn in his lips and was watching her with hostile eyes, and decided that the picture had not been overdrawn. She began to tremble.

"Alfred and I were married, Mr.—Mr. Carboy," she said. "He wrote to his mother about me."

"Yes. I saw the letter."

"He wrote twice. I wanted him to do it oftener but he would promise me and then not do it." She hesitated. "No one ever wrote to me."

"Certainly not. You may be sure we didn't approve of what he had done. We were informed later of his—of his death." Carboy was almost as ill at ease as she was. He kept moistening his lips and his eyes seldom met hers. "You have brought your proofs, of course?"

"Proofs, Mr. Carboy? What proofs do I need? Everyone in the company will tell you that we were married, and so will the minister who performed the ceremony, and his wife and daughter. We gave a little supper after— just sandwiches and beer and a beautiful cake—and we invited the stage hands and a writer from a newspaper. There was a very nice piece about it in the paper the next day. Do I need any other proofs, Mr.—Mr. Carboy?"

"I was not a member of the company," declared the magnate. "The minister is thousands of miles away, no doubt. I did not go to the supper. I did not partake of the sandwiches or the beer or the cake. I did not read the piece in the paper. You may be Alfred's widow or you may not. How can I be sure unless you can show me your marriage certificate?"

Emmy was very much disturbed. She placed an arm around the small boy's shoulder and drew him closer to her. "I had a marriage certificate, Mr. Carboy. And a birth certificate for little Sammy——"

"Who?" demanded Carboy. "Who did you say?"

"My little son. I named him after you, Mr. Carboy, because my Alfie always said he wanted the child named Samuel if it turned out to be a boy. I promised him before he died and I lived up to it, though I don't like the name, and never did."

Carboy was studying the boy without any indication of a more friendly feeling toward him. The child looked at him once, a level glance from his large blue eyes, and then lowered his head. The scrutiny of this old man was making him very uneasy, it was clear.

"You brought no papers with you, then?"

"No, sir. No, Mr. Carboy." Emmy suddenly drew herself up indignantly. "And supposing I didn't? Does that make any difference? It's no crime to forget where you put papers, especially when you're on the road and moving every day, or nearly every day. I don't suppose you've ever been with a road company, Mr. Carboy, but I want to tell you that after weeks of packings and unpackings you just throw things into your bag and buckle it tight. How can you keep track of papers when you're living that way?"

"There are some papers one never loses, my girl," declared Carboy.

He was saying to himself that her neglect to bring the usual documents was suspicious in the extreme. She might be as careless as she made out but what she had said sounded like a cock-and-bull story. At the same time, he had to confess to himself that she was not as bad personally as might have been expected. She was quiet in both manner and dress. Her voice was not good, of course, but what could you expect of an American?

"You want me to believe that this is Alfred's son and to accept him as such?"

"He *is* Alfie's son!" cried the mother. "Are you trying to put a slur on my character?"

"No, no!" said Carboy hastily. "How old is the boy?"

"He was born two months after his father died. And he's been such a good little boy. He's never known what it is to have a home, Mr. Carboy. I've been on the road from the time he was a month old. He has to sit in a hotel room all day long and I take him to the theater at night and put him in the wings. He never complains or makes a noise, the little pet. I was very extravagant to get him a velvet suit and cap but I wanted him to make a good impression.

"You have no proofs of his parentage and so I'm telling you candidly I have my doubts about all this. The boy doesn't look at all like my son Alfred. I've been watching him and I haven't detected a single point of resemblance."

Emmy's face had become flushed with resentment. She got to her feet and faced this man she knew to be her father-in-law but who seemed determined to repudiate her and her son.

"He may not look like his father now but I hope he will later because my Alfie was the handsomest man that ever lived. If you'll take a good look at him, you'll see that he resembles you, more's the pity!"

Despite a rather startled moment of close scrutiny, Carboy failed to detect any resemblance in the now very much embarrassed boy. Young Samuel was refusing to look up and was limiting himself to the study of a very small segment of carpet. With an air of sudden impatience, Carboy reached over and pulled the bell cord.

"Fleck," he said when the butler appeared, "will you ask Mrs. Carboy to come down?"

In the few minutes which elapsed Samuel Carboy gave some serious thought to the situation. It was quite possible, he conceded, that the girl would turn out to be his son's widow. She seemed to fit the description they had received and it was clear she belonged on the stage. On the other hand he had been finding it continuously necessary to raise his defenses against the demands made on him. He was already being called publicly the richest man in the world and this brought beggars buzzing around him like flies at a mutton bone. They pestered him on the streets, they climbed on the steps of his carriage and thrust their faces in at him with every kind of demand. Veterans in rags claimed to have fought at Waterloo and armless sailors swore to have seen Nelson fall at Trafalgar. He received scores of letters a day, begging, whining, demanding, threatening. How could he be sure this was anything more than a phase of the daily pattern?

"Tell me this," he said abruptly. "Why did you wait so long? My son has been dead for three years."

Emmy had been thinking also and was on the point of an outburst of tears over the kind of reception she was receiving. She had been so sure that her little son, looking so fine in his expensive velvets, would win the hearts of the grandparents at once. There was a new vehemence in her reply, because of this, while she dabbed at her eyes with a handkerchief.

"I have to make a living for myself and my son," she said. "It takes more money to cross the ocean than I can make in a year. It was only because I got this chance to appear at a London theater that I could afford to come."

"You're playing in London now?"

"Yes. At the Criterion."

"Oh. You're that one. I saw the billing. They call you—let me think, the Scintillating Salome and the Lissome Lilliom." His frown grew dark and heavy. "They tell me, young woman, that your act is disgraceful. You appear in almost nothing and display your body to the gaze of the idle and vulgar."

"That's not true!" cried Emmy. Her red hair seemed to bristle, her eyes flashed angrily. "It's true I wear tights but that's nothing new. Breeches girls have appeared on the stage in tights for centuries."

"I don't consider that an excuse."

Fleck returned at this point. "Mrs. Carboy has fallen asleep, sir, and her maid refused to have her disturbed. She has not been at all well today, sir."

"She mustn't be disturbed. But let me know when she wakens, Fleck."

Carboy began then to pace up and down the room, frowning uncertainly. It was clear that he was finding it hard to decide on the proper course to pursue. "This is the most disorganized human being I've ever encountered," he said to himself. "I can't believe Alfred would have fallen so low." Finally he came to a stop in front of the boy.

"Well, young man," he said, "and what's your name?"

The boy had sensed that this ugly man was angry with his mother and he did not raise his eyes.

"Sa—Sa—Samuel, sir."

"How old are you?"

"I'm nearly three, sir."

"You're a small boy for three. When I was three I could swing an ax around my head. Can you swing an ax around your head?"

"I—I don't think so, sir."

"Where do you live?"

"On the road, sir. We are always on the road."

"Do you think your mother is a good actress?"

"Oh yes, sir. My mother is lovely."

"Do you remember your father?"

"No, sir. My father is dead."

"What was his name?"

"Alfred, sir."

"Where were you born?"

"I don't know, sir."

The boy had continued to keep his head averted. Carboy put a hand under his chin and turned his face up so that he could study it.

"You're a good enough looking young fellow," he commented. Turning toward Emmy, he asked, "How does it happen he has such good manners?"

"He must have been born with them," declared Emmy, giving her head a toss. "It's certain he couldn't have got them from me." Her temper flared up. "I have no manners. I'm just a cheap little actress, and an American to make it worse. But let me tell you this, Mr. Samuel Carboy, my manners are as good as yours. You're a horrible, cruel man! You're just as mean as my poor Alfie said you were."

Samuel Carboy became angry in turn. "Now you listen to me, young woman. Don't you suppose I would be happy to know that my son, the only one I had, left a son to take his place? Nothing would make me happier. I would be quick to claim him, to receive him into the family and to figure that in time he would follow in my footsteps. There's nothing I would like better than to believe this young codger *is* my grandson." He turned and scowled at her. "But how can you expect me to believe your story? You come over here three years after my son's death. I've never had a line from you in all that time, not even an announcement of his birth. You don't come direct to us. You go into a London theater and make a spectacle of yourself. Finally you come down here, bringing a boy with you. You haven't a scrap of paper to prove who you are or to back up your story. You're most conveniently vague about everything. And the boy doesn't look to me to have as much as a drop of Carboy blood in his veins.

"It comes down to this," he continued. "I can't accept you at face value. Suppose I did and it turned out later you were an impostor, and the real widow came along! That would be a pretty fix, wouldn't it? Well, here's what I'm going to do. I'm going to start an investigation over there at once. I suppose it should have been done before but somehow I've overlooked it. Now I'll hire the best lawyers in New York and we'll get at the facts in no time at all. We should have all the facts in a few weeks."

"Don't you intend to do something at once for your grandson?"

"I intend to do nothing for him until I know he *is* my grandson. I have a decided aversion to being taken in."

Emmy's reddish-brown eyes were growing redder as her resentment mounted. "Then you expect me to support him in the meantime by continuing my—my disgraceful performance on the stage?"

This was a poser. Carboy gave the point careful consideration before answering. "I think I see a way to make a test out of this. If your son is my Alfred's boy, we couldn't have you appearing on the stage. You know what the truth is; and so, if you keep on playing, it will be an indication to me that you don't expect the report from America to be in your favor. On the other hand, if you agree to give up acting and live on the small allowance I'll make you temporarily—and it will be a bare subsistence, because I won't allow myself to be imposed on—I'll feel reasonably certain you've been telling the truth."

"And if I accept this allowance, where are we to live?"

"Wherever you like, except that you're to keep out of sight. I make that a positive condition."

"And what will happen when your lawyers find that I *am* Emmy Sweet, that my little boy *is* your grandson, that everything I've told you *is* true?"

"Your son will be acknowledged at once as my grandson and as my ultimate heir."

"And what about me?"

Carboy made an impatient gesture. "How can I tell at this point? It would depend on so many things. Oh, you would be looked after, of course. That goes without saying."

"I would have to give up the stage?"

"Naturally. This sort of thing couldn't be allowed to go on any longer."

"You might even prefer me to return to the United States and leave my son in your care."

"Perhaps. It would depend, I think, on whether Mrs. Carboy liked you or not."

"I don't believe, Mr. Carboy, that you like me."

"No. I'm always frank. I don't like you."

"In fact you would be ashamed to have me around as a daughter-in-law."

"If the occasion ever arises for me to feel that way," declared Carboy, "you will have yourself to blame. What you are doing—all this prancing and kicking and flaunting of yourself—will be hard to live down. In fact I'm sure you will always be remembered as the—the Scintillating Salome."

"That's all I need to know." Emmy got to her feet and took her son's hand in hers. "Come on, sonny. We're going back to London."

The boy asked eagerly, "Will they have four horses?"

"I expect so. You take after your father, don't you? He always liked horses."

"I'll hear from you of course," said Carboy indifferently.

"No. You'll never hear from me again. As soon as the run is over I'm returning to the United States."

Carboy indulged in a broad grin. "The test seems to have worked," he said.

There were foreign faces in the group Carboy was entertaining and at this point the possessor of a visage which suggested middle Europe appeared in the door. Behind him was a short and very stout man with a fringe of red hair clinging in tight curls around the bald dome of his head, none other than Baron Menzies, a prominent figure in the industrial world.

"Carboy," said Menzies, giving a twirl to the beaver hat he held in his hand, "Princep and I want a word with you. In private, you understand."

"About the Greek contract . . ." began the foreigner.

Carboy winked at him and inclined his head in Emmy's direction. "I have company, Prin. But the lady is going at once."

Emmy crossed the floor, leading her small son by the hand. The man with the red curls and the bald head recognized her and gave a pleased nod.

"I've seen you, young woman. In a play in London. You're a dancer. And a *very* good one."

Emmy strove to answer in a properly dignified tone. "I'm glad you liked our play."

"Oh, it was you I liked rather than the play. *How* you kicked! I didn't recognize you at first because of the—he, he!—the long skirt you're wearing."

Emmy's temper began to assert itself. "Sir," she said, "will you do me a favor?"

The stout man nodded his head emphatically. "Of course, dear lady. I'll be very glad to do you a favor. Anything—within reason, of course."

"Please hold your hat up as high as you can."

The financier giggled and lifted his hat in the air. Emmy took her skirts in both hands and raised them above her knees, thereby proving that every-thing in the way of praise which had been lavished on the share of her anatomy thus revealed had been in the nature of understatement. The man named Princep whistled loudly and the stout Englishman's eyes rolled in their sockets. Carboy was hunting for some papers on his desk and did not notice.

Raising herself on one toe, the dancer from the United States flashed up-ward with her other leg and sent the hat flying right to the ceiling.

"Brava!" cried the foreigner.

"Now I call that kicking," commented the Englishman, "though I'm sorry it had to be my hat. It's a new one."

"There, Mr. Carboy," said Emmy, "I've disgraced myself and justified your bad opinion of me, haven't I? Not that I care, Mr. Carboy. What I've done expresses my feeling about you and your family and your friends, and the whole English public for that matter."

Emmy led her son from the room. "The toe of my boot to the lot of you," she said.

2

News has a way of circulating quickly in the country districts and it was not long before word reached the Groody shop of what had happened. It was an exaggerated version which was poured into their ears by a domestic from Beaulaw Hall who had kept up an acquaintance with Mrs. Groody. "Mr. Carboy ordered her out of the house, saying as it was plain she was telling nothing but a pack of lies. The hussy said she wouldn't go. She said he would hear from the prisidint of the U-nited States about the way he was treating her and there might be trouble atween the two countries. And she kicked the hat off the head of one of his guests and made a hole right through it—the hat, not the head. I didn't set eyes on the creature but I got a glimpse of the boy in the hall and I must say he seemed a very nice and quiet little kincher."

The reference to the boy was all that Nell believed. When the visitor had gone, she sought out her father, who was enjoying a pipe in a rocking chair back of the house. "Get yourself ready," she said. "We're going to London, you and I. There's just time to catch the afternoon coach."

Neither of them had been in the great city before and they were very much excited by their first glimpse of it. They arrived late at night, however, and so they missed seeing London in its picturesque daytime mien. The streets were dark and seemed like a succession of yawning holes into which it would be dangerous to venture. The massiveness of the place caused them to wonder if they would ever be able to find their way out again. This maze of winding streets and small squares was a hundredfold more mystifying than the minotaur's lair. The incessant noises of the day were not in evidence but the dark city could not be called silent. It rumbled and growled and muttered about them, and each deserted mews seemed alive. Fortunately the stars were out and they caught sudden glimpses which caused Nell to grasp her father's arm in ecstatic interest; the dome of St. Paul's, the bridges arching out over the river, the gloomy turrets of palaces, the four-square menace of the White Tower. The latter caused Daniel Groody to say, "It's a smell of blood I'm getting, and plenty of it Irish."

The theater was dark but a uniformed runner happened along and advised them to try an inn in the neighborhood, the Cibber Arms. Here they were given rooms and told that all members of the Criterion company were staying there.

"Is there a Miss Sweet?" asked Nell.

"The dancer? She's here, with her son. They say," in a confidential whisper, "as he's the son of a hurl. It might be, the way the nerbility hangs around the opery houses these days. She's in sixty-two."

It happened that the Boots had not visited the east corridor and there

were shoes of all sizes, shapes and conditions outside the doors. At sixty-two
there was a pair with tasseled draws which had been made for a boy of three
or thereabouts.

"The little faller puts 'em out every night," said the waiter who was escort-
ing them to their rooms. "And he's allus up and peeking out the door when
Boots brings 'em back in the morning. Boots says the boy's smirk is as good
as the tuppence he doesn't get from 'em."

Nell stopped and looked down at the tiny shoes. Then she dropped on one
knee and touched them with trembling fingers. "The nice little boy," she
said to herself. "I love him already. I'm certain he's Allie's son. How sad
that Allie did not live to see him!"

When their bags had been deposited in their rooms and the waiter had
been tipped (Nell attended to this, as her father believed only in incoming
tips), Nell followed him out into the corridor.

"Where would I find Boots?" she asked, offering him an additional six-
penny piece.

The man pocketed the coin. "I hears his step now, miss. He'll be in a
veecious mood, 'cause the house is full and he'll have more'n enough to do;
and from my sizing up o' the guests, it's little he'll get in the way o' tips."

Nell confronted the Boots some distance down the corridor where he was
marking numbers on the soles of shoes with chalk.

"Mr. Boots, have you the boy's shoes from number sixty-two?"

The man squinted at her and said in a grumpy tone: "In course, miss.
I gets 'em every night. They're not easy, cause I can't get a hand inside 'em."

"Would you like to earn two shillings?"

Boots stared at Nell. He was not accustomed, apparently, to dealing in such
astronomical figures. " 'Ow many o' the guests is to be choked in their blooming beds wi' pillers, miss?" he asked.

"I want you to bring that little boy's shoes up to my room, seventy-two.
Bring brush and polish with you. I want to do the shoes myself."

"For a shilling more, I'll let you polish all of these, even including your
own, miss. If it's polishing you've got your mind set on."

Nell was so deft and careful that she finished the tiny shoes without getting
a single stain on her fingers. Perhaps she regretted this and would have been
glad to have polish smudges to wash from her hands. There was a tear in
the corner of each eye as she handed the shoes out the door to the waiting
Boots.

"I'm sure he's a very nice boy," she said.

"I thought you knew the young'un. A nevvy, perhaps."

Nell shook her head. "No. I've never seen him. Is he a nice-looking little
boy?"

"Nice enough, miss, as young varmints goes. He's a towheaded boy."

"Of course," commented Nell in a breathless tone.

"No in course 'bout it, miss. The mother's as redheaded as a parrot."

"But his father was fair. Very fair, Mr. Boots. And very tall."

"Ah!" said Boots with a knowing nod of his head. "Well, it's the easiest two bob I've ever made. I hopes you visits us offen, miss, and that you allus wants to take the job off'n my hands. And I'll have nought to say to the young varmint's mother about this."

"Please don't, Mr. Boots."

Nell saw Emmy Sweet the next afternoon. It was a matinee day and the little dancer came down to the stage entrance between acts, looking young and beautifully lithe in the very shortest of skirts and the very tightest of stockings.

"You wanted to see *me?*" she asked, looking Nell over with a surprised air. It was a warm afternoon and the grease paint glistened on her cheeks and forehead.

"Yes," said Nell, whose eyes had been in danger of popping right out of their sockets at all the strange things she had been seeing. A tall man walking on stilts had been the last to enchain her attention. "My name is Nell Groody. I knew your husband although I don't suppose he ever spoke of me."

"Oh, you're *her*." Emmy's interest was aroused at once. "Of course he spoke of you. He made no bones about it at all. He told me how much he'd been in love with you. I'm sure he always liked you better than any of the rest of them."

"The rest of them!" Nell gasped as she repeated the phrase.

"Oh yes, Miss Groody. Allie bowled them over. Not his fault, perhaps, though he was never one to run away from them. There was the princess, of course. And there was the Divine Cordelia, the painted old cradle snatcher! I watched her mooning over him. And there was Miss Violet Nash, who swooned away in the front row of the pit, and the veterinary's daughter, who sent him notes every day." She became aware that she was making her visitor unhappy with this recital of Allie Carboy's triumphs. She adopted a new tack. "Oh, Allie couldn't help it. He was born to be adored by women. Switch me, if I didn't nearly go into a swoon myself the first time I set eyes on him. But I'll say this in all honesty, Nell Groody. I think he liked you better than all the rest of them. Even including me, perhaps."

Nell's heart began to thump exultantly. This was honest evidence and she could accept it and remember it always, and draw upon it when she was low in mind. Allie *had* loved her. He had always kept her in his mind. He had preferred her even to the woman he had married.

"I want to have a talk with you," said Nell when she found it possible to speak. "Could you have tea with my father and me after the matinee? We're staying at the same inn. Number seventy and seventy-two. I'll go back now and see about having a very good tea, if you'll oblige me by coming."

"Why, yes. It's very kind of you."

"And bring your son, please."

"Of course. But he's a great eater. A regular little stuffer, that one. When he gets the chance, that is."

"And," added Nell breathlessly, "thanks for what you told me! Thank you a thousand times! You were very kind and generous to say it."

3

The tea was a huge success from every standpoint. As soon as Nell saw the boy entering the room with slow steps and clinging to his mother's hand, she knew that he was Allie's son. It was a resemblance which required an eye for small likenesses, the variations of the line of the mouth, a flash of expression in the eyes, the tilt of the nose when glimpsed at a certain angle, the unmistakable fact that there was a touch of Samuel Carboy in the shape of his head; this all added up to a feeling of certainty about him.

"Well, Sammy," she said, shaking his hand, "I'm glad to see you. I think that velvet suit is a very nice one."

The boy looked down as he answered, "Yes, ma'am. It's nice. A boy in Buffalo was in a box with a—a——"

"A governess," prompted his mother.

"Yes. And he wore one like it."

"He told me after the show that night," said Emmy, "that he would like one. I had to visit half a dozen shops in New York to get it. And, whew, was it expensive!"

The tea turned out to be a most substantial meal, planned around a large capon which had been roasted brown and crisp. The boy did not take his eyes off it from the moment it was placed on the table and Nell said to herself she would never forget the look of pleasure he showed when a whole drumstick was put on his plate.

"May I eat it all?" he asked his mother.

"If you've got the room for it."

It was soon apparent that he had the room for it. He made quick dispatch of the drumstick and then turned his attention to the prawns. It was clear he had never tasted them before, because he emitted an exclamation of startled delight at the first taste.

"Just one more," said his mother hastily. When he had taken the second prawn she promptly removed the dish to the other side of the table. "I don't want you doubling up with pain in the wings while I'm smiling away at the audience and trying to make them like me. Which is hard enough to begin with, because English people don't seem to follow my way of speaking."

"How long are you staying in London?" asked Nell.

"The show closes in two weeks. I'll have my passage back paid—that was in the contract. Then, I guess, I'll have to go on the road again."

"Do you plan to take your son with you when you go out on the road?"

"What else can I do?"

Nell had been watching the boy with a longing to take him into her heart which amazed her by its overwhelming force.

"It's not a good thing for a boy his age," she said. "Is there no family which might take him for a while?"

Emmy gave her head an emphatic shake. "I've no relatives left. And from what I remember of them, I wouldn't trust a chipmunk into their keeping.

No, Nell"—they had reached the use of first names already—"I'll just have to take him along and make things as comfortable for him as I can."

While they talked Nell never took her eyes from the boy. She was now observing with delight the avidity he was displaying in his attack on a bun, a very fancy bun with icing on top and raisins and nuts all the way through. "He won't be as handsome as Allie when he grows up," she was thinking, "but perhaps it's just as well. It doesn't do for men to be too handsome." Suddenly she found herself putting into words the thought which had been in her mind from the first moment she had seen the small shoes in the hall of the hotel.

"Leave him with me for a while. Until you get sufficiently established and won't have to go on the road. You'll be playing with one of the good New York companies soon, I expect."

Emmy seemed doubtful of the chance of becoming established in New York. "They take to me more on the road," she said. "The reviewer in Utica wrote a poem in praise of—well, what I dance with. It was quite a cute poem. I get good notices all the way out to Louisville and as far south as Richmond. But I don't seem to do well in New York. To be perfectly honest, I didn't do very well here." She looked at her son, who was finishing his meal with a glass of milk. "Young man, what would you think of staying for a while with the pretty lady?"

Daniel Groody had been following the talk with an eager interest in his sharp dark eyes. He decided now to take a hand in it. "It's been in my mind, child," he said, addressing Nell, "that we're a bit cramped where we are. The little shop should be used for business only. Now there's the Old Rectory. I hear the Reverend is going to live in Carnwood and the old place will be looking for tenants. My head isn't one for figures and it's mixed up I get when there's talk of money. But you have a way, child, of forking out whatever we need in that line. If we took the Rectory, it's a fine stable it has. We could keep old Barney there. And if the boy should come to visit us, I know where a pony could be got for a trifle."

"A pony?" There was an ecstatic note in the boy's voice.

"Yes, sir, a pony. An Irish pony, bedad. A black little fellow with just a smidgin of white on his nose. And such a tail! You've never seen the like of that tail."

The boy was listening to the Irishman with fascinated absorption. "Would I be let to ride the pony?"

"Well," said Daniel Groody, "we'd have the looking after of him, you and me. We'd feed him and put the currycomb on him and take him out for runs around the yard. And you could sit on his back and get the feel of riding in your hands and knees. In another year I think it's old enough you'd be and strong enough to start riding him."

The boy had been giving thought to the drumstick and the prawns and the rich bun, and now he was thinking with a wild surge of interest of the pony. He turned to his mother. "If you think I might, Mother. If you wouldn't mind, I'd like to stay for a while with the nice lady and the nice man—and the pony."

CHAPTER TWENTY-TWO

1

With an approving eye, Daniel Groody watched the boy as he attended to his black pony. "Git the little fella good and dry," he said.

"Yes, Mister Groody," said Sammy politely. "I look after Turk well. Turk's a fine pony. He's the best pony in the world, isn't he?"

"Well, now, in the whole world, you say? Well, now, that's going it a bit. But Turk's a good pony, right enough."

"I'll be glad when I'm big enough to ride real horses. But I'll always like Turk as much as I do now. Is he to be allowed oats tonight?"

"It's meself will attend to the feeding of him." Groody broke off and looked apprehensively in the direction of the main road curving down through Little Shallow. "It's him! Your grandfather. Look at the way that Humpster is driving! It must be the devil's coattails they're trying to catch."

The boy walked to the door of the stables and looked up the road. "My grandfather always drives fast," he said. There was a hint of pride in his voice. "Is he coming here, do you think?"

"If he is, it'll be to get you," declared Groody. He looked down at the intent face of the boy. "Is it thinking ye are that ye'd like to go and live with him?"

"No!" cried Sammy. "I'd rather stay here. With Turk and you and Aunt Helen and Mrs. Groody. I like it here."

"Then I'll tell you what it is, young fella. You'd better get up and hide in the haymow. If he comes for ye and he asks me where ye are, I'll say ye've gone away. I'll say ye've gone on a long churney all by yerself. To France or Egypt or Prushia."

"Tell him," said the boy, with his foot on the first step of the ladder leading up to the fragrant blackness of the haymow, "that I went to America like my father did."

The swaying carriage came to a stop in front of the Old Rectory. Samuel Carboy stepped down, followed by Jonathan Bade, the latter with a well-stuffed barrister's bag over his shoulder. The titan looked up at the well-lighted rooms of the square old house and then took in the activity at the stables.

"Horses eating their heads off," he muttered. "Candles burning away at a ruinous rate. How does she manage it, Jonathan?"

"She's a clever woman, Samuel. She doubles her money every time she forks over for something. I tell you, Samuel, she's got the Midas touch too."

Nell received them in the room she used as an office. She had been working at her books and correspondence for hours but she looked as neat and fresh as though she had been doing nothing more taxing than lifting a teacup. Carboy looked at her and noted, perhaps for the first time, the deep blue of her eyes and the striking effect of the single white lock in her black hair. "The woman's damned pretty," he said to himself.

Nell knew the errand on which they had come and her heart threatened to stop. She said, with trembling lips, "You've heard from America?"

Carboy nodded. "That Sweet woman was telling the truth. It's galling to admit it because I've always prided myself on knowing the spurious article from the real. I thought she was lying." He turned to the lawyer. "Explain things, Jonathan."

Jonathan Bade seated himself at the table and began to draw documents from his bag. "Our correspondents in New York have sent us the facts, Miss Groody," he said. "It's taken them a long time but they've finally got through with it. Here we are—the affidavits from members of the theatrical company about the marriage, the birth certificate of the boy, the death certificate of Alfred Carboy. Everything is in order."

Nell looked up quickly. "Everything?" she asked.

"Well, practically everything."

"I think there may be one lack, Mr. Bade. But we'll speak of that later."

Carboy looked at her suspiciously. "It's good enough for me. I'm satisfied with the evidence."

"There's plenty at any rate," declared the lawyer, "to prove that the boy is the son of the late Alfred Carboy and the grandson of my client."

"Of course," said Nell. "I knew that from the first. And little Sammy gets to look more like his father every day." She turned to Samuel Carboy with sudden vehemence. "And now you've come to claim him! You want to take him away from me."

Carboy nodded. "Naturally. Now that I know he *is* my Alfred's boy, I mean to see to his raising myself. That's natural, isn't it?"

"Quite natural. I wouldn't expect you to feel any other way. But—but there are others to be considered too."

Carboy answered in grumbling agreement. "You mean yourself, I suppose. You've got attached to the boy."

"I'm so attached to him," she cried, "that I'll want to die when he has to leave me. As I know he will. But I meant his mother. She plans to send for him as soon as she's in a position to look after him."

"That silly creature! She'll never be able to take him. It's more than likely you'll never hear from her again."

"I've had several letters from her. I like her and I'm sure she means well. One came a fortnight ago. She's still playing on the road—that means they go from town to town—and so there's no chance that she'll want him back soon." She hesitated, as though doubtful of the advisability of giving further information. "I think she's likely to marry again. To a member of the company. She acknowledged she was giving it some thought. He plays villain parts."

Carboy gave his head a contemptuous toss. "Mark my words, that flutter-head will have one husband after another. I wouldn't permit my grandson to be placed in her charge again."

"Indeed?" Nell spoke in a rather incisive tone. "May I ask what you could do to prevent it?"

"How would I prevent it? By due process of law, young woman. The law is very clear in giving children into the care of the father. I stand in this matter in lieu of my son."

Jonathan had been listening with some anxiety. At this point he deemed it wise to intervene.

"There are points of law involved, Miss Groody. In a case of this kind it would not be hard for the grandfather, who is in a position to give the boy the best care and who moreover offers prospects for the future of the most substantial kind, to be awarded the custody. If he took the case to the Court of Chancery."

Nell turned to the lawyer. "I understand the legal aspects and I don't agree with you. As the father of the boy is dead, the mother has the guardian-ship *in nurture*. She has transferred that guardianship to me."

Samuel Carboy took a few steps which brought him closer to where she was sitting, and looked down at her; "glared" would perhaps be a more accurate word, for the Colossus was becoming decidedly impatient.

"You say she transferred the guardianship to you?"

"Yes, Mr. Carboy. That's what I said. I stand in that relationship to your grandson until such time as she sends for him."

"Do you think that an English court of law would accept an arrangement between two foolish women in the face of my undoubted rights in the mat-ter, and my capacity, and great desire, to do things for the boy? The two of you reached a verbal agreement, no doubt."

"No, Mr. Carboy. The two foolish women knew better than that."

"What do you mean?" He was towering over her as he spoke and his face had taken on a belligerent expression.

"Just this. Your daughter-in-law went before a magistrate in London and swore out a paper, declaring her desires in the matter. The paper was duly witnessed and attested."

Carboy turned and looked questioningly at his lawyer. Jonathan gave his head a quick shake to indicate that his employer should now leave matters in his hands.

"You have the paper, Miss Groody?"

"One copy. The other is in the mother's hands."

"Was it her idea to have the document drawn up and signed?"

Nell gave her head a shake. "No, Mr. Bade."

Carboy could not restrain himself, in spite of the warning looks that Jon-athan continued to send in his direction.

"This is all due to your meddling, young woman!" he exclaimed. "You were determined to get the boy into your hands. You brought him here to live with you where everyone would know who he was. You flaunted your defiance of me in the face of the whole Vale. I knew what you were trying to do. You saw a chance to strike at us—at the parents of the man you wanted to marry. I've known that right along."

Nell kept her composure in the face of this heated charge. "I took the boy, Mr. Carboy," she said, "because otherwise his mother would have taken him back to America. You refused to do anything for them. Do you realize what kind of a life he would have lived there?" She rose to her feet and faced him. Her color was high and her eyes were filled with defiance. "His mother would have taken him on the road with her. Traveling from town to town in drafty covered wagons. Living in cheap little inns. Spending every evening in the wings of a theater. Never knowing the comforts of a home and having no chance to get an education. When you washed your hands of him I stepped in. I couldn't let him go back to that kind of life."

Carboy realized that he had put himself in the wrong. He took another tack at once. "Overlook what I said. I'm in an upset state of mind. And you must realize that I can do everything for him. He will live in the greatest luxury with us. I'll engage a tutor at once for him. When he's old enough he'll go to one of the best public schools. Dammit, young woman," becoming belligerent again, "don't you see that you can't stand in the boy's way? I intend to make him my heir. He'll be a rich man, one of the richest in the world. You must be ready to give in for his sake."

"I've had him with me now for nearly a year," said Nell in a repressed tone. She was holding her head down to conceal the intensity of her feelings. "I love him. He seems like my own son. But I have no intention of standing in his way. I know only too well that he must go to you in time. I—I love him enough to step aside tonight and let you take him away. But I haven't the right to do that without his mother's consent. That was a part of the agreement we signed; because, you see, she thought you treated her badly. She was furious over the way you spoke to her. She said you'd never get him. She still feels that way about it. And I must have her consent in writing."

"Humph! *That* won't be hard to get." The Colossus laughed easily. "I'll buy her consent. I want the boy. He's my grandson and he must be with us where he belongs. Now that I know he's Allie's son, nothing is going to stand in my way. I'll have my New York lawyers see her at once and offer her enough to bring her around."

"She isn't in New York. Her letter reached me from Cincinnati."

"Never heard of the place. Where is it?"

Nell was thinking hard. "Little Sammy belongs with his own people. I must accept that fact sooner or later. But, oh, if I could only have him a little longer. I can't let him go yet."

"Well, young woman, where is this place you mentioned?"

"I think it's many weeks' travel from New York. It's on a great river in the West. You have to go on horseback."

Carboy turned to Jonathan. "Could you persuade our New York man to ride that far?"

"From what I've heard of Spurlock, I doubt it. He's not young, you know, and he's well provided with tallow around the waist. He likes his own bed and his fireside. A letter might get there as quickly as he would."

"I want quick action, Jonathan! I'm not content to sit around for months waiting for this silly creature's signature."

"It's hard to reach traveling companies by mail," declared the lawyer. "They never stay long in any one place and they change their plans all the time. Letters seldom catch up with them."

"Then we'll begin action at once to have this delegation of guardianship set aside," said Carboy emphatically.

Nell's mood of reluctant compliance left her at this point. "I don't think that would be wise, Mr. Carboy. A study of the documents might reveal something you would rather not have known."

"And what do you mean by that?"

Jonathan Bade raised a hand and shook it emphatically at his employer. Carboy said in a grumbling tone, "All right, *you* do the talking then."

"Miss Groody," said the lawyer, "you have made a statement which will bear examination. Are you prepared to tell us what you *did* mean?"

Nell hesitated. "You won't believe me perhaps," she declared, "when I say that I'm thinking only of little Sammy and what is best for him. His mother said something which raised my suspicions. I questioned her about it and what she told me was quite—quite disturbing."

Jonathan knew what was coming.

"We believe you, Miss Groody," he said, "when you tell us that you have the boy's best interests at heart. But we think we are entitled to know what you're talking about. I am certain it has to do with the minister who married them."

Nell nodded her head, unhappy at this need to raise doubts. "His mother told me, after I had questioned her closely, that she didn't get a marriage certificate from the minister. She didn't seem to attach any importance to it. But I couldn't help wondering if—if he had the right to give one. You see, he belonged to some religious sect. Emmy—the mother—had forgotten what they were called. They believed the world was coming to an end soon and that when it did they would be the only ones allowed to rise from the grave. I'm sure from what she told me that the man considered himself a minister in the sight of God and therefore free to perform marriages. The sect seems to have ignored the law in everything." She looked first at Carboy and then at the lawyer, sensing the feelings she had aroused in both. "You needn't be afraid! I won't do anything to let it be known. The boy mustn't be hurt. I feel as badly about it as you do. But you'll have to be careful what action you take while this doubt remains."

Carboy laid a hand on Jonathan's shoulder and led him to a corner of the room.

"She's right," he whispered. "I wondered why there wasn't a certificate. What's your opinion?"

"In the first place, Samuel, I think she means what she says. She won't hold this over our heads. Her sole concern is for the boy. But it will be better not to go into court until we've explored the matter further. For one thing you can't demand custody of the boy if the marriage was not a legal one. Certainly you couldn't get him until he's fourteen."

"But, damme, look at her!" exclaimed Carboy. "She's downright handsome and she'll be getting married one of these days. It stands to reason that anyone as attractive as that won't remain single all her life. Suppose she marries some fellow who doesn't share her scruples? Suppose she tells him all about it? That would put us in a pretty fix. The whole story would come out. Shouldn't we press for a settlement before anything of the kind can happen?"

"Samuel," said the lawyer earnestly, "we can't go into court. This affidavit she was smart enough to get has settled that. We have no case."

"Then," said Carboy after some thought, "there's only one thing to be done. You must go to America and look into it yourself. I can't wait for this fellow Spurlock to hoist his backsides out of his chair and get to work. I want action. Find the mother and pay her whatever she asks. Ah—within reason, that is. Find the minister, if you have to travel to the pole, and get that point cleared up."

Jonathan Bade nodded in assent. "It's the only way, I'm afraid. I'll drop everything and go."

Carboy looked cautiously in the direction of Nell. "And in the meantime what happens here? What do we do about *her* and the boy?"

"Nothing. We must wait until I've had a chance to clear things up."

Nell had been watching them with the merest hint of a smile on her lips. "Now that you've decided not to drag things into court—as I'm quite certain you have—would you like to see your grandson, Mr. Carboy?"

The financier nodded in assent. He tried to be casual about it but it was evident that he was eager to see the boy. "I caught a glimpse of him a week or so ago. The little rascal was riding a pony; and doing an oncommon good job of it, back straight, head up, just like his father. It made me feel badly, even though I wasn't sure at the time he was my grandson. It made me realize that I—well, that I had been hard on the boy—on Allie, I mean."

Nell looked at him with quickened interest. "If you feel that way, Mr. Carboy, it will be much easier for me to give little Sammy to you when the time comes that I must." She walked to a side door and called: "Sam! Where are you? There's someone here to see you."

It was Daniel Groody who came in response to her call. He stood in the doorway and shuffled his feet uneasily as he looked at Samuel Carboy.

"I'm glad to see you, Groody," said the latter. "We parted in anger but that's all forgotten and in the past now."

"That fella ye've got in my place," said Groody. "I'd enjiy a word or two with *that* fellow. He's hard on the horses."

"Father, where is Sammy? His grandfather wants to see him."

"He's gone away."

"Papa Groody! He has *not* gone away. What foolishness is this?"

"He's gone on a churney. To Rooshia."

"I know you, Daniel Groody!" exclaimed his daughter. "You've hidden him somewhere."

"He's gone on a churney, I'm telling you."

"He's gone no further on this journey than the haymow. And it's not necessary. Mr. Carboy isn't thinking of taking him away."

A wide smile took immediate possession of the Irishman's face. "Indeed, and in that case, it's not to Rooshia the boy's gone. It's to the haymow, just like you suspectioned, childie. I'll tell the boy it's safe to come down."

"Are you teaching my grandson to regard me as an ogre?" demanded Carboy when Groody had left. "Have you made him afraid of me?"

"No, Mr. Carboy. I've tried instead to make him properly proud of what you are and what you've done. If there's any feeling it's with the boy himself and my father. Sammy is happy here, Mr. Carboy. He doesn't want to be taken away."

When the boy came in, followed by Daniel Groody, who seemed determined to make sure that nothing happened, Carboy walked over to Nell. "What a difference this year has made!" he said in a low tone. "He's my boy all over again. There can be no doubt any longer about that. Miss Groody, I meant what I said just now about my treatment of Allie. I *was* unfair to him. I was sharp and harsh; and I suppose you can say that I was responsible for the way he died. Well, I'm going to do right by his son. That much you can be sure of. I'm going to make up to him for all the things I didn't do for Allie."

"Sammy," said Nell, her voice showing a tendency to choke up, "you know this is your grandfather, don't you? Are you going to speak to him?"

"How do you do, sir."

"I'm quite well, my boy." Carboy paused, not knowing what to say. He finally adopted the obvious course. "Would you like to have some money if I should be lucky enough to find some right here in my pocket?"

"Oh yes, sir."

"Supposing now that I give you five pounds, say. What would you do with it?"

"I think, sir, I would spend some of it on new gear for Turk. He's kind of shabby, sir. And the rest I would put away."

"Now then, let's get this straight. How much of it would you spend on gear and how much would you put away?"

"I think, sir," said the boy after some thought, "that one pound would be enough for the gear. I would put all the rest away."

"And how much would that be?"

"Oh, Mr. Carboy," said Nell, "that isn't fair. He hasn't got to division yet."

"I think, sir, it would be four pounds left."

"There, you see!" cried Carboy triumphantly. "He knows. This grandson of mine can figure by instinct. And he intends to spend one pound only and put four pounds away. I can tell, my boy, that you and I are going to get along fine!"

BOOK III

The Colossus

CHAPTER ONE

1

TEN YEARS have passed.

In those ten years many things happened in England. George IV died, mourned by very few, and a brother took his place on the throne as William IV, to reign a few years only and then pass on to the valhalla reserved for sea kings. The responsibility was then assumed by a girl of eighteen named Victoria, a rather plump and rather pretty young lady; and the people of the country began to hope at once that the era of regal disreputability had come to an end with the passing of the last of the sons of poor old George III.

There had been political upheavals. An overwhelming demand for reform had resulted in sweeping electoral changes. This was a good thing for the country but a very bad thing for George Ninian Grace, because rotten boroughs had been done away with and, of course, Little Grimditch had been high on the list. Regretting that he no longer had a seat in the House, Grace took to Causes and making speeches at public meetings, taking pains to bring in the name of Samuel Carboy at every opportunity, in far from complimentary terms.

The country was in a state of change apart from politics. Railways were being built (with Carboy taking no more than a wary financial interest in them) and the lighting of city streets by gas had ceased to be a novelty. Buildings were being torn down to make room for Trafalgar Square and all London was very much concerned about a shortage in cemeteries. A law had been passed that no apprentices under sixteen years of age could be employed as chimney sweeps, the whole nation having become aroused to the iniquity of that method of keeping home fires burning; but as chimneys were seldom large enough to admit boys of sixteen, and they *had* to be cleaned, there was a great deal of winking at this particular law.

Old Sheppy had died, for the time comes when even dukes must leave their grandeur behind them. Young Chip, therefore, had moved a step nearer the stage when he would have that title to dangle before the eyes of Isabelle. He had married but did not seem to be taking matrimony seriously. Mrs. Carboy had died, lacking both strength and will to continue living after the loss of her beloved son. Mrs. Groody also had passed away, not because of her rheumatism nor for any reason the doctor could put a tongue to, unless it was her heart; a very quiet death in a rocking chair. Out on the western rim of the world, on the island of Jamaica to be exact, still another lady, Mrs. Timothy Ballard, had flitted to a higher sphere, to join her much-loved Constance and the six infant Ballards in their identical white bonnets and strings of blue ribbon. To the list of those who had joined the majority must be added the names of the brothers Beck. Samuel Carboy had attended the funeral of Heaven Beck, who had been the last to go, and had caused amazement by offering a pound to anyone who would give a home to one of what might be termed the bereaved pets. His foresight had come to his assistance in time to make the stipulation that one half would be paid at once and the balance at the end of a year; a precaution which insured them a home. When asked his reason for this unusual exhibition of generosity, Carboy had been at a loss to explain himself. Did he love pets? he was asked. No, on the contrary, he was disposed to dislike them, particularly dogs. Had he been in the debt of the brothers Beck? No, they had been in his debt. Finally he had satisfied himself on the score of his reason, although he did not put it into words. Beck had been associated in his mind with the greatest moment of his life and this had been a bond between them.

Samuel Carboy now owned so many factories that it was difficult to find sufficient labor, although almshouses and parish schools were looked over to find children old enough (eight years was satisfactory) to begin twelve-hour-a-day employment. He controlled as many ships as the Admiralty, and he had plantations in both east and west, and godowns in China and copra sheds in the south seas. He was powerful and rich but sometimes he found it hard to shake out the barbs planted in his hide by his old partner. Twice the question of a knighthood had been discussed by the Cabinet but each time the opposition had been too great.

Mrs. Carboy had died before Jonathan Bade returned from his investigations in the United States and so she never knew that Emmy Sweet had agreed to have her son transferred to the care of his paternal grandfather. Emmy had become thoroughly tired of the portrayer of villain roles, and faced the necessity of involving herself in heavy expense for a divorce. She was not as slender as she had been and the symmetry of her legs was commented on less frequently. But she was still romantically inclined and she had her eye on the new juvenile who appeared on the bills as Chauncy Dawlish but whose real name was George Mash. Accordingly she accepted the money that the English lawyer dangled before her eyes, and betook herself and her legs and her new husband out of the story for good and all.

Jonathan had discovered, moreover, that there was some shadowy possibility that the minister who had married Alfred Carboy and Emmy Sweet had been within his rights. It was agreed among all the parties concerned that this flimsy bit of justification should be accepted and never again referred to for the same reason that sleeping dogs are allowed to lie. Nell Groody relinquished her beloved Sammy to his grandfather. The boy agreed to go when she said that he could take Turk with him. The pony lived out his last years in ease and plenty at Beaulaw Hall, for young Sam soon took to riding horses. He would canter down the main street of Little Shallow, with a groom at his side, and stop at the Old Rectory for a visit with the diminished Groody family. One very sad day he rode by to tell his aunt Helen, as he continued to call her, that he was leaving the next day for Eton.

But while life had been churning and changing in England, the members of the cast of this story had found existence during these ten years, except for what has been related, somewhat uneventful. This is not surprising. After all the excitement he had shared with his three musketeer companions, D'Artagnan stood for twenty years in the anteroom of the French king and nothing happened to him. Life has a way of packing much into short spaces of time and then pausing to rest and catch its breath. The ten years had been so humdrum, in fact, that at this point, when it becomes the duty of the narrator to pick up the threads again, it is necessary to begin by telling of two games of whist. Many readers will accept this as proof that life was indeed dull and monotonous.

2

Two hansom cabs stopped in front of Brooks's Club in St. James's Street at exactly the same moment. It was well past the dinner hour and there was not a star in the sky. The first of the two passengers to alight peered dubiously into the gloom and finally said: "Ah, it's you, Sir Theobald. A minute ahead of time."

"We are punctual men, Father-in-law," answered Gardiner. Closer inspection than the darkness made possible would have shown that he was thin and that his face had new lines and creases.

"Have to be," declared Samuel Carboy. "Seconds are precious gold to me and I assume that other men's time is equally valuable. 'Tain't, of course." He looked sharply at the baronet. "You're a bit run down, ain't you? Are your years catching up with you?"

The unwillingness of all men of advancing years, who have young and beautiful wives, to acknowledge the inroads of time brought the baronet quickly to his own defense. "Not at all!" he said. "I'm in excellent trim. I've been three times this season at the Green Man with the golfers. Didn't you know that my wonderful Isabelle and I were partners the last time and came in far ahead of the field? I feel younger every day."

Carboy waited for his companion to lead the way into the club. He asked: "Will there be any ceremony to go through? I mean, will I have to face a committee or something of that kind?"

Gardiner shook his head. "You'll have to stop and pay down your membership guineas. That's all. We made a rather neat thing of getting you through. A single blackball does the trick, you know, and there were three members of the committee who swore to block you; all of them living off their own land and so not open to pressure."

"I'm not so sure of that," said Carboy grimly. "There's always a bank you can use to get at them."

"Well, there they were, these stubborn three, and all of them itching to drop the blackball. We saw to it that each of them received a late invitation to a rather special tea this afternoon. They went. I suppose each of them thought the other two would be on hand to attend to you, Samuel. I'd like to have seen their faces when they met at the tea and realized they'd been done."

Carboy was not pleased that there had been so much difficulty in getting him elected. He frowned heavily as he followed his companion up the steps of the famous club. "Someday," he was thinking, "those three stiff-necked Tories will feel the weight of my dislike. I'll not rest until I've paid them back a hundred times over."

Carboy had heard of the splendors of the great salon in the club but he could not suppress a grunt of surprise when he stood under its immense arched ceiling and saw that on the floor stood, seemingly, all the great men of England. Having been sternly tutored by his son-in-law, Carboy had reluctantly encased his gristly legs in black breeches and the sleekest of silk stockings. He was glad that he had yielded, for there wasn't a pair of trousers in the place.

"They wouldn't admit the Duke of Wellington one night," whispered Gardiner, "because he had made the mistake of not wearing breeches."

Two men, who were progressing arm in arm through the crowd, came to a sudden stop when they saw the great industrialist. One of them looked down his nose at Carboy and scowled in a most superior way.

"What are you doing here, sir?" he demanded to know.

"I am a member of the club, sir," answered Carboy.

"If you are, sir, there has been some highly reprehensible juggling of the rules. If men in trade are to be members, then I for one shall be quick to tender my resignation, sir."

"I had no idea, sir, that my election would prove so beneficial to the club."

The objector, who was a certain Lord Creatley, had a round head covered with stiff black hair like a scrub brush. He spoke to his companion.

"Mark my words, Gussie, my boy," he said. "We'll have haberdashers as members before long. And hatmakers and cheap little clothiers and snide drapers. I swear, Gussie, we'll soon be making bets against our own valets if this sort of thing keeps up."

His companion laughed. "Gad, Artie, you're in rare form tonight. You are indeed, old boy. That about betting against our valets, now, that was capital. I'm going to repeat it, if you don't mind."

"Son-in-law," said Carboy, leading Gardiner to one side, "am I to assume that I'll always have to take this kind of treatment? Is there something shameful about being in trade? The prosperity of England is based on her foreign trade. For generations the family of Carboy has been in the eastern trade. It's an honorable business. My family has been an honorable one. I'm an honorable man. I don't deserve this kind of thing."

"Don't give the matter a thought," protested Gardiner. "Creatley is a mean little fellow. No one pays any attention to him."

"It's time," declared Carboy, "that this kind of snobbishness was stamped out. I'll have a chance someday perhaps to do the stamping myself. What should I do in the meantime? Should I get hold of this fellow and throw him bodily out of the place?"

"No, no!" cried Gardiner. "That would be a very great mistake. No violence, if you please. My advice to you, Father-in-law, is to forget the whole matter."

Carboy's debut became much more pleasant after this opening episode but he noticed a certain reserve nevertheless about all of the members he met. He knew most of them and had often had dealings with them; but here they were on their own ground and not on his, and they showed it in many ways. Even those who were almost obsequious in business were a little standoffish here. The difference was hard to define but it was noticeable in the tone of their voices, in the ease they displayed, and in a faint condescension about everything. He was sensible enough to make no effort to break down the barrier; but he filed a few mental notes away for future use. "I won't forget," he repeated to himself several times.

Only when he encountered a member of Parliament, one Richard Brinsley Wolfenden who was reputed to be close to cabinet stature, did he find everything normal again. The parliamentarian wanted his opinion and so discarded any sense of social superiority he might otherwise have felt. Buttonholing the financial giant (who loomed so large in the world of trade even if he dragged his feet slightly in the halls of privilege), the member drew Carboy to one side of the room.

"My dear Mr. Carboy," he said. "I am sure you follow the course of international affairs as closely as if you sat in the House yourself. What do you think of the Frenchman?"

"I think ill of all Frenchmen," answered Carboy. "Which one do you refer to in particular?"

"Why, sir, Louis Napoleon, of course. Did you know he has come to this country?"

"I heard something about it. He's in London, I hear. And being taken up socially."

"Exactly. And now, sir, will you condescend to give me your opinion of the man?"

Carboy indulged in a snort. "He has the ambition of the great Napoleon but lacks his genius. And yet this obstinate young man makes a wonderful tool for us. He's a born troublemaker and he'll go on stirring up dissension until he gets the throne of France. Then, sir, he'll be most uncommonly useful to us. He'll ruin France and in doing so he'll cause a great deal of trouble for all Europe, particularly Germany. I despise the little creature, of course, waddling about in shoes too big for him and his head swallowed up in a three-cornered hat. But we ought to pay him a fat pension not to give up his ambitious ideas."

"Why do you think he'll be useful to us if he's going to start the Napoleonic Wars again?"

"Mr. Wolfenden," said Carboy, "do you realize that England, which was a maritime and agricultural nation, is now becoming an industrial nation as

well? Have you seen the smokestacks rising in the Midlands? Do you know
how much we're exporting to all parts of the world? The French and the
Germans are better fitted for this sort of thing than we are but we're starting to leave them far behind. I don't believe they know yet what is happening
to them."

"I see your point, Mr. Carboy."

"That is where this dull little drum-thumper comes in. He's going to steal
the throne of France and keep the Continent in a turmoil while we coolly
pocket the trade of the world."

The member had been listening to every word with the greatest concentration. "The government must decide whether he's to be allowed to live in
England. Ever since the Strasbourg incident—they hustled him off to America
after that, you remember—the French government has made it clear they
would rather we wouldn't harbor him. They haven't taken a stand yet but it
may come to that. Now, what are we to do about it? Your opinion, I judge,
is that we should allow him to stay."

"Not only that, sir," declared Carboy, "but we should butter him up with
praise and stuff him full of belief in his own greatness. They tell me he's
susceptible and so the best way is to see that he meets all our most charming
ladies—and instruct them to make him believe he's greater than his uncle."

The member said to himself, "There's no one in England better suited
for *that* than your own daughter, Mr. Samuel Carboy." At this point Sir
Theobald Gardiner joined them to ask whether the new member desired to
try his luck at the faro table. This game of chance was still the most popular
one at Brooks's and a huge round table, which could have accommodated
King Arthur's knights, was devoted to it, whereas all other games had small
tables along the walls or in corners.

Carboy shook his head. "I don't care for gambling. But I would enjoy a
game of whist, if it could be arranged."

Gardiner looked along the nearest wall and his eye lighted on a table
where three men were sitting, engaging in what, most clearly, was a desultory
attempt at conversation. "I think perhaps they're waiting for a fourth player
over there. But I strongly advise against cutting in."

The member looked in the same direction and indulged in a low whistle.
"Decidedly not. Those three are the best players in the club. They play for
very high stakes."

Carboy did not know any of the trio but he seemed quite unimpressed by
the reputations they enjoyed. "I'm willing, if they're in need of another, and
will take me."

"Samuel!" exclaimed Gardiner. "Those birds of prey will turn you inside
out. They will skin you alive. It will be like throwing a child into a pool of
crocodiles. I assure you, they'll take more out of your pockets than you'll enjoy
losing."

"I play whist," said the member. "Perhaps I could find two others and
give you a game."

Carboy thanked him but insisted that they must not go to so much trouble.

"Just lead me over and introduce me to those three vultures," he said. "I'll take my chance with them, if you don't mind."

Two hours later the baronet returned to the table where his father-in-law had been doing battle with the three most expert whist players, and the toughest, in all London. The game was breaking up and to his amazement he saw that the trio were passing large mounds of bank notes across the table to Samuel Carboy. He heard the latter say, "Thank you, gentlemen," as he pocketed the notes. "It was a most pleasant game."

"For you, Carboy," said one of the three. "Not for us. Are you Midas come back to earth, with his touch unimpaired?"

Gardiner looked at Carboy in astonishment as they made their way to the cloakroom. "Did you actually win all that money from them?" he asked.

"Son-in-law," said the financier easily, "I take it you will agree that Isabelle is a very fine whist player?"

"A wonderful player. But then she's wonderful at everything."

Carboy grinned. "Will it surprise you if I say that I taught her the game?"

3

Sir Theobald Gardiner sat at his desk frowning over a pile of mail. It was still very early—ten-forty, to be exact—and he was wearing a handsome dressing gown of scarlet, befrogged and becuffed in silver.

Isabelle came to the door, crop in hand, riding hat on head. She seemed in a decidedly impatient mood. "Mudge said you asked for me."

The baronet laid down a letter and looked at her with a wary eye, as though striving to analyze her mood before proceeding with what he had to say. "Yes, dear child. I knew that if you once got away I might not see you until dinnertime. Who is to be your riding partner?"

"Gertrude Umpstead. With grooms, of course."

He seemed relieved. "I don't like the woman. She's a flirt, a liar and an arrant gossip. But it's better to be with her than the men you generally honor with your company in the park."

"You don't care to ride yourself, you know," she reminded him.

"I believe it's a relief to you that I don't. You seem to prefer the company of other men."

Isabelle's eyes hardened. "What has brought on the sulks this time, my very dear husband?" she asked.

He did not retreat at once as was his usual habit. Instead he leaned back in his chair and studied her closely.

"I have been most forbearing," he said. "Your flirtations are the talk of London but so far I have—I have done nothing. It may be that I've kept my eyes closed to unpleasant truths. I don't want to believe anything bad about you, my very dear wife." He sighed deeply. "But I wish you to understand that from now on I am going to protect my good name. I don't intend to have all London laughing at me."

Isabelle began to tap the side of one boot with her riding crop. Her eyes had turned a red-brown.

"And what do you propose to do?"

"I shall insist in future on knowing your plans for each day. I am going to refuse to let you see certain people. To begin with, I shall give you a list of those you must not see again."

"How interesting! How *very* interesting! What makes you think I'll consent to have my husband become my jailer?"

His resolution showed a slight tendency to waver. "Isabelle, it's the only way!" he exclaimed. "You must see that we're riding head on for trouble. I can't keep my eyes closed any longer. You must come to your senses, my dear, before it's too late. Do you want to be barred from court? Do you want people calling you an immoral woman?"

Isabelle seated herself so that she faced him. "There's something I must tell you," she said. "You don't seem to know how hard it is to be the young wife of an old man. We haven't a single taste in common. I love to dance. You don't. I like to stay out late. You want to go to bed early. You don't ride, you don't play cards, you don't do any of the things I like."

He nodded sadly. "I realize it fully, dear Isabelle. That is why I have been so long in speaking to you." He picked up an opened letter and seemed on the point of quoting from it. Changing his mind, he dropped it back on top of the pile. "I want to help you, my dear. The situation we've drifted into may harm you more than me." He sighed again. "I introduced you to Prince Louis Napoleon because your father thought he should be taken up—for reasons that you understand as well as I do. But I did not mean you to become one of the prince's confidantes. You see him much too often."

Isabelle said to herself, "It's a good thing he doesn't know how often I've seen my little Boney."

"Unfortunately," he went on, "we must attend his reception this evening. It's even more unfortunate that I have another engagement which can't be broken. I shall escort you there, pay my respects to the prince, and leave. I'll return to take you home early. At eleven o'clock. I shall expect you to be on your best behavior while I'm gone." After a moment he added in a voice of considered decision: "I have no intention of letting you get involved any further with that lot. The prince is as promiscuous in his habits as his famous uncle. The men around him are cheap and dangerous opportunists."

Isabelle got to her feet. "There's no time now to discuss this further, dear lord and master, but I shall have a great deal to say to you later. As for this evening, it shall be as you say. I'll be ready to return with you at eleven o'clock like any plump little country wife. I won't be happy about it. And you won't be happy over what I shall say to you later."

He picked up a slip of paper from the desk. "Here is the list I mentioned."

Isabelle did not turn her head as she left the room. "I am not interested in your list, my dear Tibby."

An open carriage, with two footmen up behind and an eagle painted on the side panels in a bright blue, turned out of St. James's Park. In it rode a stoutish man, with a good brow and a goatee, and a lady of quite remarkable beauty.

"My little Isabelle," said the man, accenting the words accurately, although it was quite clear that he was not English, "it was a most pleasant coincidence that we met in the park. And it was very kind of you to be persuaded to have the groom take your horse on, so I would have the privilege of driving you home."

"Yes, a pleasant coincidence indeed," answered Lady Gardiner in a low tone, "if we overlook the note I had from *your most exalted Excellency*, and the note I sent to Gertrude Umpstead to say that I could not ride with her." She indulged in a light laugh. "And if I am not very much mistaken, *my great and supreme Emperor-to-be*—don't look disturbed, none of them can hear a word I'm saying—I am not to be taken home. You will get out at Carlton Gardens and have them drive me on from there."

"That is indeed my intention, my little Isabelle."

He was verging on the middle years and, inasmuch as he had taken into his own hands the baton of leadership of the Bonaparte family, he was often compared to his illustrious uncle, Napoleon. Actually the resemblance was not very marked; he lacked the look of concentrated power, the light in the eye. It might more accurately have been said that he looked, as far as his features were concerned, like a certain brilliant young man in the Conservative party whose name was D'Israeli or, even more, a still younger man whose name was Dickens and who was bringing out in monthly installments a novel called *Nicholas Nickleby*.

"Was it only the pleasure of my company you sought in sending me the note, *my most charming and exalted and all-powerful et cetera?*" Isabelle was speaking in the mocking tone she often employed in the talks they shared. His eyes twinkled in response. A satisfactory basis of relationship had been established between them since the pretender to the French throne had come to England to live and had acquired the handsome house in Carlton Gardens which belonged to Lord Ripon. "Or," she continued, "did you have something to tell me? Have you, by any chance, reached a decision?"

"A decision, sweet Isabelle? My child, I make scores of decisions every day."

"Don't bandy words with me, *O King who will, I trust, live forever*. There is only *one*, as you well know."

Prince Louis Napoleon stroked his glossy goatee. "*The* decision? Perhaps I have made it. But it will not happen for—for a very long time."

Isabelle was disappointed. "I've heard you say the time is ripe. Why then delay?" She drew her handsome brows together in a frown. "I can hardly wait for it to happen. I'm going with you. You needn't look at me with that stern Napoleonic eye, O Prince. I have made up my mind. I want excitement and I want to play a part in historic events before I settle down into middle age—when it will be too late."

"Should I feel flattered that you are ready to stake so much in my behalf? Your life even?"

"Every other man I know would be bitterly opposed to having me take such a risk."

"A wife could accompany me, of course," said the prince. "A mistress, perhaps. But a spectator, no matter how beautiful? No, my dear Isabelle."

"I wouldn't be a spectator. I would wear, perhaps, an officer's uniform like that lovely little creature who was with Napoleon in Egypt."

"I think you mean La Bellilotte."

"Yes, that was the one. The emperor had such a power to compel the devotion of lovely women! Do all the Bonapartes have it?"

Prince Louis Napoleon preened himself. "In some degree, I think. But, dear Lady Gardiner, I must draw the line at certain manifestations of this devotion. There will be no wearing of uniforms like La Bellilotte when I put out to sea."

"I must have a uniform of some kind. Ah, I have it! A *vivandière*."

"No, not a *vivandière*. It will be rough work, and no place for a lady." The smile vanished from his face. "I may change my mind about making the attempt. An invasion is a great risk under the most favorable circumstances. Can we be sure the army is anxious for a change? Are the people of France tired of the stupid usurper who now occupies the throne? All this must be considered, for the fortunes of the Bonapartes will be risked on a single cast of the dice." He went on after a moment's thought: "I know, dear Isabelle, that I can depend on your discretion. Otherwise I would not fill your pretty ears with so much dull political talk."

Isabelle answered with an eager rush of words. "Excellency! My devotion knows no limits. I could not be guilty of the crime of repeating a word spoken in my hearing!"

The smile with which he received this declaration of allegiance had a slight touch of self-consciousness about it. "I am well aware, dear Isabelle, how completely you are to be trusted. There is no one I rely on more." He reached over discreetly and gave her hand an approving pat. "How lovely you are this morning! You seem to grow in beauty every moment. You will be with us this evening?"

"Yes, Excellency."

"And your husband also, I trust?"

The carriage had turned into Carlton Gardens and the horses came to a stop. The footmen sprang down to assist the alighting of the French prince.

"My husband," said Isabelle, "will fetch me here at nine and call for me at eleven."

The prince smiled at her before lowering his head to kiss her hand. "An excellent arrangement, dear Isabelle. I shall make the most of those two precious hours."

4

But the head of the Bonaparte family was to see little of Isabelle that evening. When she arrived, escorted by her husband, he was standing in a brilliant group, made up for the most part of the loveliest women in London. "I am happy to see you, Lady Gardiner," he said, kissing her hand. "And Sir Theobald also. Though I am told, sir, that you do not intend to stay. That you are generous enough to permit us the honor of your wife's company is the very finest compensation for your own absence."

"Your Highness does not seem to need much in the way of compensation," said Isabelle, looking rather critically at the group about him. Her husband had already bowed and departed. In a low voice she added: "You look positively radiant, *my Grand Cham and exalted Lord.* It seems you are happy to have so much beauty about you. But where is the prettiest of them all, the one who is never spoken of by any other name than Miss Howard? She is high in your favor, I am told."

"She is not here," answered Louis Napoleon in a tone which hinted that he was a little vexed. "She is never asked for large receptions, as you know very well. Because of this, I do not hesitate to ask a favor of you. That you will play in a game of whist this evening. Am I asking too much?"

Isabelle's first reaction was one of annoyance. She had dressed with particular care, selecting one of her favorite gowns. It was of black velvet and displayed her shoulders to the fullest advantage. In several respects it was a departure from the mode of the moment, and so courage as well as pulchritude was required to make an appearance in it. The sleeves were not so extended that they had to be held out by wicker frames but fell instead in graceful folds close to the wrists. On the other hand the skirt was longer and so much more wide and voluminous that she had found it necessary to practice walking with the shortest steps to avoid setting it to swaying like the inrolling waves of the sea. This was not a costume to be tucked under a whist table, to go unnoticed for the whole evening.

"I see that it does not much appeal to you, my little Isabelle."

She responded by asking who would make up the table.

"Lord Henricot and Colonel Teeple. To make the fourth, I have already bespoken Claude de Launy, who is, I think, known to you."

Three men! That, she conceded mentally at once, would be some compensation. She had a slight acquaintance with the first two named and was sure they would be prepared to play for a substantial stake. Her interest was now aroused, for she loved the excitement of high play and performed at her best under such circumstances. Claude de Launy was a young Frenchman of good family who was often at the receptions of the prince and was reputed to be an excellent cardplayer. He had the wide white brow of a poet and the physique of an athlete. Isabelle knew him very slightly and had always felt she would enjoy a closer acquaintance.

"You said, *O great Prince,* that we would make the most of our two hours," said Isabelle. She gave him, nevertheless, one of her most brilliant smiles. "Ah, well, I understand. You must be gracious to so many. Because I feel a little sorry for you, I shall let myself be banished into exile. Send me to your island of detention, your salt mine, your whist table. I shall strive to make the best of it."

The prince smiled. "My sweet Isabelle! It would be easy for me to fall in love with you."

"It is very easy," she declared, "for Your Highness to fall in love."

The eyes of the three men who were to share a table with her lighted up when she joined them. Lord Henricot said, "What luck, I say, what great luck!" Colonel Teeple bowed from his great height and remarked, "It is a privilege indeed but will we be able to keep our minds on the game?" Claude de Launy kissed her hand and murmured fervently, "At last! At last!"

Isabelle said to herself as she gave the young Frenchman an intent look, "He's the handsomest creature I've ever set eyes on." He was more than that, it developed as the game went on. He was gay and had the pleasantest manners and his smile was nothing short of devastating. At first she wondered if it would be possible for *her* to play her best game but after the first hand the habit of concentration resumed its hold. She played as well as ever, which was very well indeed. It was enough to make Lord Henricot drop his gallant way of addressing her, such as "Dear Lady Gardiner, I am desolated but duty to self and partner compels me to take this trick" and to become even a little abrupt. Colonel Teeple gnawed the ends of his sandy mustache and glared down at the table where the cards were making him the sufferer of many mischances. The young Frenchman played brilliantly but in bad luck.

At the end of two hours, the time she had stipulated for the game to end, the three men drew out their reluctant wallets and built up high piles of bank notes which they then pushed across the table toward her. Lord Henricot was not happy about it and, from the look in the hot brown eyes of Colonel Teeple, it was a good thing he was not presiding at a court-martial. The two older men then rose, bowed and took their departure, leaving the impression that as far as they were concerned chivalry had its limits and that being beaten at cards by a beautiful woman was not an experience to call out their most gracious sides.

Isabelle leaned her black velvet sleeves on the table and looked across at the young Frenchman, who had remained seated. He seemed distrait and unhappy.

"Monsieur Claude de Launy," she said, "I am of the impression that you lost more this evening than you can afford."

The young man flushed. He did not answer at once and it was apparent that he did not know what to say. "It is true, Lady Gardiner," he answered finally. He gestured at the pile of notes and gold coins he had passed across the table to her. "My pockets now are empty."

"But you play a great deal, m'sieur."

"Yes, Lady Gardiner. I am, as you will perhaps be lenient enough to concede, a good player. Of course, I am no match for you but I am good enough to win in almost any company. I might as well confess to you that I make my living by playing whist."

"I'm beginning to realize," said Isabelle, keeping her eyes fixed on his, "that I've been interested in you from the first time I saw you. I'm sorry to know that you're in financial straits——"

"I've been this way before, Madame. It's not a new experience. When you live by your wits you become accustomed to both ups and downs."

"But it was my impression that you belonged to the French nobility and could afford to follow Prince Louis Napoleon into exile as a matter of duty."

"I am of a good family," answered Claude de Launy. "But my father was an ardent Bonapartist and at the restoration all his property was confiscated. You couldn't believe the hardships my brothers and I suffered in the process of living and growing up. We all had to make our own way in the world. I chose the easiest—but the most uncertain."

"I'm discovering that I'm quite fond of you."

They sat in silence then for several minutes, looking into each others' eyes. "I can't believe it," said the Frenchman. "You! The lovely Lady Gardiner. I have worshiped you so long from a distance. Such a distance!"

Isabelle's fingers were busily collecting the notes and the gold and silver pieces into one pile. She then made a quick gesture and shoved the money to his side. "You must not be angry with me. As I said before, I like you; and that gives me privileges. I can help you. You must accept this money— your own, and the losses of our late and rather unpleasant opponents."

"Lady Gardiner!" cried the young Frenchman.

"Your eyes tell me that you like me," said Isabelle. "I have already confessed that I like you. Surely, then, there's no reason for me to stand aside and see you suffer inconvenience." She paused. "It's truly remarkable how the Ripon House has been transformed. It has always been gracious but now our good prince has turned it into a bit of France—Napoleonic France. M'sieur, take me about the room and explain things to me. They are mementos of Napoleon, I think."

"Yes, my lady. I shall be proud to act as your guide. And happy, also, and excited. Ah, my lady, how very excited!"

Isabelle had risen to her feet. "It will even be a way of avoiding all these people until my husband arrives."

"A bitter reminder that you have a husband. For the moment I had forgotten him."

So Claude de Launy, his dark eyes glowing and his manner proof that he was emotionally unhinged, guided her about the great drawing room. "The emperor, my lady," he said, stopping in front of a portrait. "But not, I think, one of the happiest. It is a little dull, don't you think?" His voice fell to a whisper. "My lady is not very much interested."

"No, m'sieur, not very. But let us go on. We can talk of other things also."

"This is a portrait of the empress."

"Josephine?"

"Yes, my lady. The lovely Creole. She *was* lovely. At least she seems so when I look at the painting and not—not at you, dear lady."

"You are very sweet."

"This," rather hurriedly, "is the prince's mother, Queen Hortense of Holland, the daughter of Josephine. They say she was most charming. Tied, unhappily, to the stupidest of the Bonaparte brothers."

"She looks rather tragic."

"So much for the portraits. Here in this nest of fortunate velvet is a very great reminder of the glorious days. It is Napoleon's coronation ring."

On the wall beside one of the huge fireplaces was a long scarf of cashmere. The young Frenchman paused in front of it. "The emperor wore this at the Battle of the Pyramids," he said in a tone of awe.

Isabelle did not look. She whispered to him. "How very unfortunate that my husband has just come in. I shall have to go. But, m'sieur, we must see each other again."

"Yes, oh yes!" declared Claude de Launy. "If my lady will tell me how—and when and where——"

"You can't come to me." Isabelle was whispering. Her cheeks had flushed. "My husband is jealous, being so much older than I am. Our London house is—well, Tibby says it's like a coaching office. People coming and going all the time. My dear M'sieur Claude, I shall have to go to you."

"My lady!" The Frenchman's eyes had become more luminous than the three-candle sconce under which they stood. "Will you deign to come? Ah, gracious and lovely lady, my rooms are neat but they are small and in a very poor neighborhood. I am not sure I can allow you to come."

"All the better," declared Isabelle. "The poorer the quarter, the smaller chance of being seen and recognized. You must be prepared to greet someone plainly dressed."

CHAPTER TWO

1

The new duke occupied Outland Park with his waspish wife and so it had been necessary for Young Chip to find other quarters for himself and his rather plain spouse. Scorning the Dower House, which was in an advanced state of disrepair and suffering from chronic drain trouble, he had persuaded his wealthy father-in-law to buy them a house on the floor of the Vale within sight of the White Horse.

There is no land more fertile and green and pleasant than is to be found in the Vale; but their new habitation, which was called Strothe House, seemed singularly out of harmony with the gentle meadows from which it rose. It was a tall and quite ugly pile of gray stone, set in a clump of high trees over which a single window in the one gable seemed to squint at passers-by like an inquisitive woman. At the back there was good stabling, which unquestionably had been a factor in its selection. A very small stream trickled by one side of the property from which trout could sometimes be taken.

It was to this rather ungainly residence that Sir Theobald Gardiner drove one night some four months later, accompanied by a close friend, Colonel Frisbie of the East Anglian Fusiliers. It was now late in the fall and a heavy rain was falling. The lash of the storm against the sides of the carriage caused the baronet to sigh heavily. As they came in sight of the house he said to his companion, "If this is to be my last night, it might have been arranged for the stars to be out. I would like another look at the moon."

"Come, Tib," said the soldier, "why be so down in the mouth? The Frenchy is probably an abominably bad shot. By the way, you haven't told me anything about yourself. Are you good with the shiny little fellows?"

"I've fired a pistol only once in my life," confessed Gardiner. "And that was by accident."

The colonel frowned in sudden exasperation. "Damme, Tib, I don't understand this at all. Why are you fighting with pistols if you know nothing about them?"

"What else was there to do? I'm the challenger."

"Of course. But there are ways, you know. We could have dodged the need to use pistols."

"It's better as it is." Gardiner drew another deep sigh. "My lack of skill with a sword would have made me ludicrous."

The colonel did not address his companion again as they crunched up the drive but grumbled bitterly to himself about wives who got into affairs with foreigners and made it necessary for their husbands to fight them.

Young Chip was playing alone in the billiard room when they arrived, slamming the balls around and grumbling at his lack of an opponent, and even tossing the mace on the floor when he was through with it. He came out to greet them with a cue in his hand.

"Hallo, what's up?" he asked, his eyes taking in the grayness and fatigue of the man who was married to the woman he himself coveted. "You look a bit slaggy, I must say."

"Can you put us up for the night?" asked the baronet in a weary tone of voice. "We'll be off at dawn."

"At dawn?" Young Chip looked first at one and then at the other as understanding grew in him. "Look here, what are you two up to? Is it a duel?"

Gardiner nodded. "Yes. I'm meeting a Frenchman named Claude de Launy. The authorities got wind of it in London and I was informed we would be arrested on sight if we tried to break the law. Knowing we would be watched, it was decided we would have to get as far away as possible. In fact, that we would have to select one of the least likely places in all England."

"On the White Horse slope," said Colonel Frisbie.

Young Chip's round black eyes were now glittering angrily. He had heard veiled rumors of Isabelle's infatuation for some "damned French sponger" but he had refused to believe it. Now he realized it was true and he was as furious as Isabelle's husband had been when convincing evidence had been brought him. The future Duke of Outland was so angry, in fact, that he wished he could change places with Gardiner and take on the punishment of the Frenchman himself.

"Tib," he said, "you can't shoot straight. You couldn't hit a haystack at ten paces."

"No," agreed the baronet. "I'm helpless with all weapons."

The future duke began to swear in loud and furious tones. "This mangy fellow, who deserves to be filled with good English lead, will get off scot free. Tib, there must be some other way of doing this. Do you suppose he would agree to let me take your place? I could put a bullet right through the miserable cadger."

Colonel Frisbie took it on himself to answer. "Sir, most decidedly not. Sir Theobald could not be guilty of such a confession of inability to face up to his own responsibilities."

Young Chip squared around to face the officer. "I suppose you're acting as second?"

Frisbie nodded. "I'm serving in that capacity."

The future duke struck the floor so savagely with his cue that it broke in two. "Our hands are tied!" he exclaimed. "I can do nothing. I must stand by and see this beggarly cardsharp, this leech, get off without a scratch on his white skin! Do this much, Tib: let me drive you over in the morning. If the chance arises—oh, it might, he could be guilty of some beastly breaking of the code—I'll take a hand myself and horsewhip him within an inch of his life."

Sir Theobald had ensconced himself on a settle beside the fire. "It's good of you, Chip, to be so concerned about me. But right now I'm afraid there's only one thing you can do. You can get some supper for poor Frisbie, who hasn't had a bite since noon."

Their host tugged at a bell cord. "There's some cold roast beef and probably something in the way of a custard. My wife is sickly and has to be fed on that kind of pap." He turned back to the principal in the case. "There must be something we can do, Tib."

"I'm afraid not. I have some letters to write. If you could have me shown to a room, I would be glad to get at them. One of them is going to be difficult. I won't want any supper."

"Brandy?" asked Young Chip.

The baronet shook his head. "I may need a drop before we start in the morning. But not now. I'm a duffer with weapons but there's nothing very wrong with my courage."

2

When Young Chip came down at four o'clock the next morning, yawning prodigiously and carrying a candle in each hand, he found that his two guests were ahead of him. It was clear that Sir Theobald Gardiner had not been to bed, for his coat was rumpled (perhaps for the first time in his life) and his cravat was loose, and his eyes were sunk in hollows of sleeplessness. He was, however, in an easier mood and greeted his host with a warm smile. Colonel Frisbie had nothing to say and it was evident that he was in the grip of hunger.

"They'll be down immediately to attend to us," said the future duke. He looked at the principal in the impending encounter. "How are you feeling?"

"Quite well," answered the baronet. "I think I'm reconciled to anything which may happen. And the letters are written, which is a load off my mind. I believe I've attended to everything." He produced a bundle of letters addressed in a handsome script and handed them to Chip. "Will you attend to them? The one on the top is not to be entrusted to the mails and must be delivered personally, if you will be so good, Chip. You understand that they are to be delivered only if I—if I suffer certain consequences."

"You've done nothing about seeing a lawyer," declared Colonel Frisbie.

Gardiner gave his head a shake. "I'm not changing my will. The bitterness I felt at first has gone. I'm not blaming Isabelle very much. I'm an old man and not a satisfactory husband for one so young and beautiful. And there is this to be remembered: she gave her life into my keeping and she belonged to me through the last stages of girlhood and the first sweet years of her maturity. She was a lovely and captivating wife, even if she was capricious at times and with a will of her own. I was very happy and proud, and I still feel that I am in her debt." He paused before adding, "And there's this to be said. I urged her to cultivate the prince for political reasons. It was in part my fault. No, Frisbie, I have no thought of making changes in my will, of cutting her out of it. And I am glad that you and Chip are here to learn my reasons."

The rain had stopped when they set out. It had fallen so heavily during the night that the woods were wet and the trees dripped as they passed. They crossed the Ock and found that usually placid little stream roaring under the narrow bridge in unexpected plenitude. The sky was still heavy and it seemed clear that there would be no sun to witness the scene in which they were to play parts. The future duke handled the reins with a skilled hand, giving vent to his feelings occasionally by cracking the whip in the air as though he were applying it to the shoulders of a certain Frenchman.

Dr. Sweetland met them at Uffington with an instrument case in his hand. "Good morning, my lord," he said, getting in with them. "The White Horse has seen many great and strange things but I wonder if its eye has rested before on anything quite like this. You, sir, I suspect, are Sir Theobald

Gardiner. I've seen you here and about. But you and I," turning to Frisbie, "are strangers, sir."

Gardiner introduced them. The doctor nodded. "You are acting as the second, then. This, I judge, is not as new for you as it is for Sir Theobald."

"No," answered the officer shortly. It always took a long time after wakening for him to regain any degree of amiability. "I've served in both capacities, as principal and second. Many times. It's all very familiar."

They were climbing now and the pace of the horses had slackened. It was evident that every foot of the ground was familiar to the surgeon. When they took a sudden turn northward he sat up at once.

"We are going, then, to the foot of the Manger?"

"That was the arrangement made," answered Frisbie. "The Frenchman's second has been over the ground and it was his suggestion."

"It will save us some leg work. At my age I am happy to go it easy." The doctor swung around and spoke to Gardiner. "Your first venture, Sir Theobald? I mean on the field of honor?"

The baronet nodded his head. "My first, sir. And I am persuaded to think it will be my last."

"Of course. You are a man of peace. This is a grim and terrible business and you will be glad to be over with it."

They were beginning now to encounter some signs of life. Birds were singing their matins in the dripping treetops and barnyard activities reached their ears faintly. From the direction of the hills they heard an early shepherd calling "Teg, Teg, Teggy!" They reached Woolston but did not take the narrow road which would lead them up to the point where the mysterious Horse stretched its limbs on the crest of the hill. Instead they turned over to a still narrower road. A stout woman with her hair bound up in the kind of snood called a cockernony stared at them from behind a gate. She had a milking pail in one red hand. "OO-ay!" she said. "Sirs, it's early it be to be going up there."

The doctor said in a low tone: "Too bad it had to be Mrs. Gramp. She's the worst gossip in the whole Vale." He looked ahead of them to where a high stand of trees cut off their view of the western half of the hill. "I take it we're going to that bit of flat land this side of the Manger?"

Frisbie nodded. "The Frenchman's second suggested it. He's some kind of a scientist or other and is interested in the Horse."

Another carriage was laboring up the steep Woolston approach, the horses floundering in the mud. Young Chip glowered at the party. "Stinking foreigners! Why do we let them come in?"

They came to a level piece of land which had been under cultivation but had been so thoroughly harvested that a stubble goose would have starved on the remains. Frisbie looked the location over with a jaundiced eye. "I suppose it will have to do," he said. "It isn't as smooth as a cricket crease exactly. But if the sun does come out—which seems pretty unlikely—there will be no advantage for either man. We'll face them north and south."

Young Chip drove to the east end of the open space and the other carriage, as a matter of course, took the opposite end. He threw the reins to the groom who had accompanied them and sprang to the ground. Taking a few steps forward, he fixed his eyes intently on the party of three alighting from the second carriage. One of the new arrivals was a tall young man who had discarded his hat and who advanced a few strides in the direction of the level ground in the center. The future peer studied him with a hostile eye.

"That's the Frenchman!" he said to himself. "I can tell it in every line of him. His heaviness of thigh, his damned poetic hair, his manner. I hate him on sight!"

Chip observed now that the seconds and the surgeon had moved together into the center ground and were discussing the rules. A countryman in a tattered smock had materialized from nowhere, seemingly, and was watching with a lethargic interest. Certain that his movements would not be noticed, Chip skirted the open ground and arrived at the shoulder of the young Frenchman.

"Monsieur," he said.

Claude de Launy was suffering apparently from taut nerves. At any rate his shoulders twitched noticeably at the unexpectedness of the salutation. He turned and stared at his accoster.

"Who are you?" he demanded in a belligerent tone.

"My name is George Louis Gorse and someday I will be a duke and sit in the House of Peers. You, I am sure, are Monsieur Claude de Launy."

"Yes."

"I am a friend of Sir Theobald Gardiner's and there is something I must say to you before you come to the point of exchanging shots."

"You have no right to be here. It is not my desire to speak further with you."

"I come to give you a warning," declared Chip grimly. "My friend is a great gentleman as well as a man of peace. If anything should happen to him, I declare my intention now to call you out myself. You will never get out of this country alive. That much I most solemnly swear."

"I regret the necessity of being here," declared Claude de Launy. "But I am a man of honor. When he sent his seconds to me I had no alternative."

"Are you a good shot, monsieur?"

"I—I have some skill."

"Is it your intention to shoot straight?"

The Frenchman turned about and stared at his questioner. His handsome features were pale and his lips showed a tendency to quiver.

"He hates me," he said in a low voice. "I can feel even at this distance the desire in him to bring my life to an end. To protect myself, I must aim well."

"I, standing off at one side, will be in as much danger from his marksmanship as you will. My friend has had a pistol in his hands only once in his life."

"It is easy for you to say that!" cried the Frenchman. "But how can I tell if there is truth in what you say?"

"I give you my word of honor, Monsieur de Launy, that you will be perfectly safe if you fire in the air. Allow me to point out also that it would be a fine and generous gesture on your part. You have given him mortal offense. You left him with no honorable course but to call you out. Surely you can afford to be generous."

The Frenchman's face twitched spasmodically. "Go away!" he cried. "You have no right here. You are breaking all the rules. I refuse to listen to another word."

Very much downcast at his lack of success, Young Chip made his way back to his carriage at the other end of the field. He watched the seconds as he did so. They had completed their discussions and were now measuring off the ground and placing the toe stones. The Comte de Lussac, a man of such strong Bonapartist convictions that he preferred exile to the immunity at home which had been tendered him, was acting for Claude de Launy. He had a deserved reputation for fairness and it was clear that he was not enjoying his role. The future peer heard him say to Dr. Sweetland, "Claude sets such value on his life that he will not accept as much as a fraction of one per cent of risk."

"That coward!" thought Young Chip with mounting bitterness. "He'll shoot to kill. Nothing will count with him but the safety of his own precious skin."

The principals, on receiving the word from the seconds, advanced to their stations. The Comte de Lussac, his handsome face set and grave, addressed them in a tone which seemed to contain a note of pleading.

"We have reached the moment, messieurs, when a reconciliation must be made or a compromise reached, if such is your desire."

A silence followed. The comte looked first at his man and then at Sir Theobald, who was holding his silver-mounted pistol with an awkwardness which bespoke unfamiliarity. He turned then to his fellow second.

"Colonel Frisbie."

The colonel cleared his throat. "It is my duty, as second for the challenger, to ask the challenged party if he is prepared to make reparation in any other form."

Claude de Launy answered, "I see no way, m'sieur."

After a still longer silence the Comte de Lussac began to speak of the rules.

"Messieurs, my brave and honorable friends, if I am permitted to so address you, you are to remain where you are. At the distance agreed upon, which is twenty yards. The toe stones are at your feet. You may rest your advanced foot on them but under no circumstances are you allowed to step closer. You have witnessed the placing of the white handkerchief at an equal distance between you. When my colleague draws it away by means of the cord attached to it, you will fire." His voice rose. "One shot only, messieurs. After the first exchange, a consultation will be in order."

The sun came out with a suddenness which startled them all. Every line of the Horse above them became clear to the eye.

A complete silence fell on the field. Frisbie looked at the baronet and then at Claude de Launy. With a brisk movement of his hand, he pulled at the cord.

Sir Theobald raised his pistol and fired straight into the air. His opponent may not have rested on his aim, which was against the code; not, at least, in the fullest sense of the word. But it seemed to the watchers that he was somewhat deliberate. There was the briefest interval between the two shots.

Young Chip saw the baronet fall slowly forward on his face. He was at least twice as far away as the surgeon but he reached the prostrate figure on the damp turf almost as soon as the frantically hurrying Dr. Sweetland. The latter turned the inert form over and made an examination with hands which did not seem too steady. He was deliberate, however, in reaching a conclusion and it was several moments before he rose to his feet.

"Gentlemen," he said, "the bullet touched the heart."

Colonel Frisbie drew in his lips and frowned uneasily. "Is there anything to be done?" he asked.

"Nothing, sir. Death was instantaneous."

The future Duke of Outland watched the members of the other party climb into their carriage with a haste which reflected a desire to remove themselves beyond the reach of the law. The Comte de Lussac raised a hand in solemn greeting as they turned onto the road. Claude de Launy was leaning forward to speak to the driver and paid no attention to them.

"He'll get away," said Young Chip to himself with the deepest bitterness. "By night he'll be across the Channel and safe in Belgium. It's certain he'll never come back to England." Aloud he said: "I want to call attention to the fact that the fellow wore a suit of green. He was taking no chances at all."

Dr. Sweetland looked at them, his manner solemn, his face white. "You must leave now. Both of you. Later you will be called for the inquest. What follows immediately is my unhappy responsibility."

3

Most young widows look well in their weeds, particularly when they have been at great pains to fashion them after the latest style. Isabelle had neglected nothing; and she looked as prepossessing as ever, even though her brows were tight in concentration as she studied the sheets spread out on the ormolu table at which she sat. Jonathan Bade, watching her intently, said to himself that nothing would ever affect her adversely. She took life, its misfortunes as well as its brighter sides, in her stride.

It was a Sunday and so the lawyer was dressed in an appropriate black dress coat and a dark satin waistcoat. He had noticed that the hammercloth on the carriage at the front door (Isabelle, apparently, was going on somewhere as soon as she was through with him) was as black as sable.

Isabelle laid the sheets down finally and gave him an approving smile. "I agree with everything you've done, Jonathan," she said. They had finally reached the stage of using first names. "What a grasping little beast that

Cousin Dirk is! You would almost think it was his money to begin with, that he had made it, instead of my dear papa, who more than tripled the Gardiner estates. Well, Master Dirk seems to have recovered some degree of sense at last."

"Very unwillingly, however," said Bade. "It was only when I hinted that the entail on Wimperley could be revived that he began to see reason, the dear fellow. You see, under entail the property would go to that dull clod of a Cousin Avery and that was something Dirk could not thole. The two cousins, with their thin shoulders and their spidery little legs, are like a pair of male sparrows chiffering away at each other on one branch."

The lawyer had been puzzled by the unusual silence of the room. Sir Theobald had been fond of canaries and had kept them in fine brass cages in all parts of the town house. None of them were left. Had Isabelle ordered them removed or had the butler carried them to the back quarters as a part of Sunday observance?

"As a matter of fact, Jonathan," said Isabelle, "I'm rather glad to be rid of Wimperley. It's a cold big barracks and I despise all the neighbors. Such incredibly stupid people! Do you know that Lady Wiston talked to me for a whole evening on the use of manure in rose gardens?" She folded over the sheets of the financial report and put them away in a purse bespangled with diamonds and pearls. She looked appreciatively about her. "*This* was what I wanted from the first. I love it. I really think it the most pleasant and convenient town house in all London, even if Mecklenburgh Square is not *quite* as good an address as some others."

"Dear Cousin Dirk," said Bade, "is not sure he can keep up Wimperley on his share of the income. He was quite dark and gloomy about it the last time I saw him. It's only the insistence of his great fat wife, dear Cousin Dulcinea, which brought him to it."

Isabelle's temper rose, creating a hard gleam in her eyes. "I hope they go smash!" she said. "I hope the sheriff sells them out! It would be pleasant to attend the auction. I might bid in that four-poster with the cupid border." Observing a disapproving expression on his face, she gave her head a toss. "Now you're angry with me."

"Of course I'm angry with you, indulging your spite in this way."

"You don't care for me any more."

The lawyer sighed. "I'm afraid I care for you a very great deal. But in a very unusual fashion."

"You are always saying things like that," pouted Isabelle. "You have never approved of me, have you?"

"No. I've never approved of you. Strangely enough, I didn't disapprove of your conduct in the recent unpleasantness as much as you might expect. I happen to know the whole sad sequence of events. Your father wanted you and your husband to be kind to the exiled prince. It was your husband who introduced you to Louis Napoleon. It was in the prince's house that you met the fellow De Launy. There was an inevitability about the whole thing. You were caught in the web as much as the rest. I can't in all honesty lay the entire blame at your door. Except that you made such a rancid choice."

"I'm afraid Claude behaved badly that—that morning."

"From what I hear, he conducted himself like a rank coward."

Isabelle sighed. "I know. I'm as severe with myself as you are. But he was *so* handsome."

"Now that we're on the subject, I feel I should say that you've been very lucky," declared the lawyer. "The queen is too young to assert herself in such matters but, unless I've misjudged her character, she will be very strict and stern later on. It has been your misfortune to be caught out in a—a little peccadillo, but I think you'll succeed in living it down. Let me give you a piece of advice, my—my very dear Isabelle." He lost control of himself for a moment and permitted too much feeling to show in his voice. "You are aiming high. You'll never reach the heights to which you aspire if you don't show the closest regard for what goes on in the mind of this new queen."

"You are quite right, Jonathan. I had already reached that conclusion."

The lawyer rose to leave but had not gone more than a few steps when he turned. "Isabelle," he said, "why don't you go to see your father? He's feeling the tension between you very much."

Isabelle looked both penitent and impatient. "Papa has been very angry with me. He still is. He sent me a note as soon as he heard of the duel. I thought he should have come to see me. Of course he happened to be out somewhere in the wilderness at the time and was too busy to return at once. It was a bitter letter and not very understanding. He put all the blame on me and, as you've just said, Jonathan, he started it himself. I felt quite hurt and I didn't answer him. I've not been to see him since."

"I think the time has come to go. He misses you. In fact he talked about little else the last time I saw him."

"Did he ask you to speak to me?"

"He hinted that I might take it on myself. It seemed to me he was drinking too much."

Isabelle dismissed the last suggestion casually. "Drinking won't hurt Papa. He has the hardest head in England. Well, I suppose I must make the first move. I think he's the only man in the world I really love. Husbands—well, that's a different matter. I don't believe it would ever be hard to get over a husband. There are so many to be had. Now that I am baring my innermost thoughts to you, Jonathan, I might as well tell you that I rather think you come second."

He looked both surprised and deeply pleased. "I am very happy to hear you say that. But of course what you feel for me is a different matter also. I fall somewhere between a father and a husband—and much nearer the father relationship than the other, I'm afraid."

Isabelle was listening intently. "Perhaps," she said. "But I think it's more a case of having a quite special place of your own."

He asked with some hesitation: "Does it seem to you possible that circumstances might move me to a new position in your esteem? Not quite so close to the fatherly side of things?"

She shook her head immediately. "No, Jonathan. You will always remain in your own special place."

"Then that is settled forever and a day." He sighed deeply. Almost at once, however, his expression lightened. "Not forever. There is still the future and reincarnation. Will we come back to this earth in new guises? I'm sure the same accident couldn't happen to me a second time. If I walk again in a new era, it will be with a face I won't need to hide. You know, Isabelle, there will be great changes in the future. Other nations will rise to greatness. Germany, and perhaps even Russia with its uncounted millions of voiceless people. . . . If that happened—who knows?—I might be a ruler in Muscovy and you a Slavic slave." He indulged in a brief laugh. "This is foolish talk. Pay no attention to my absurdities, my dear Isabelle."

A church bell began to ring from somewhere close at hand. The street below was already filled with people walking arm in arm to the services.

"I know," said Jonathan, "that you have gone out very little since the tragedy. That has been wise but the time has come, I think, to face the world. You would find, at any rate, that the anonymity of a thick veil would be respected in church."

The butler entered the room in his Sunday black silk stockings and black plush breeches, carrying a tray on which reposed a single letter. "The gentleman who brought it, my lady, is below. He desires to see you for a few minutes."

Isabelle sought her companion's consent with a lift of her eyebrows and then proceeded to slit the envelope with a gold-handled knife. The lawyer was so fascinated by the grace of her movements as she did so that he failed to note the expression which took possession of her face as she read what the note contained.

"Jonathan, what do you know about the Comte de Lussac?" she asked after a moment.

Bade brought himself back from a brief glimpse into a life where he would never be separated from the owner of the white hands. "The comte, of course, was Claude de Launy's second," he said. "He's in his late fifties, I suspect; a courtly and rather handsome man. They tell me he has a very nice turn of wit. I've never met him."

"I understood he had left the country with Claude," commented Isabelle, putting the note into her purse. "But I must have been misinformed. He is downstairs now. I'll have to see him. Thanks, Jonathan, for getting all the estate tangles straightened out. I'll sign the papers."

Isabelle found the Comte de Lussac standing before a portrait of some long-gone Gardiner in a huge wig.

"Good morning," she said, advancing toward him. "I am Lady Gardiner. Sit down, please."

The comte contented himself with a rather cold bow. "I come, milady," he said, "to keep a promise made to M'sieur de Launy before his—his rather hurried departure. I bring a letter." He produced it and held it out to her. "He gave me other instructions of which I shall speak later."

Isabelle took the letter in her hands, giving it no more than one hurried glance. It was addressed in a sprawling script. "Claude had no culture," she thought. She held the envelope gingerly, not knowing what to do with it. Finally she laid it on the table beside which she had seated herself.

"M'sieur le Comte," she said, "I don't think I want it. I know I won't be able to bring myself to read it. What, then, am I to do? Will you think badly of me if I give it back to you?"

"No, milady," answered the comte. "I think I can understand your reluctance to receiving it. But I would prefer not to take it. It may be a long time before I see that young man again." He paused. "Are you certain you wish to be relieved of it?"

"Oh yes, yes!" Isabelle shook her hands as though to rid them of the effects of contact with the letter. "I am afraid of it. I am afraid of what he may have said."

"Then," said the comte, "I shall tear it into small pieces for you and put them here on the hearth. Your butler can attend to burning them. I shall report what happened to it when I see him on the Continent."

Isabelle had been sure that seeing this particular caller would be a painful duty but now she realized that she was liking him. He had the cool manners of the true aristocrat and the hint of an inner warmth which does not always go with the first. His face was long and, although his features lacked somewhat in regularity, he was rather handsome as Jonathan Bade had said.

"I was told you left with him," she said after a moment's silence.

"It was impossible for me to get away at once. I have property interests here in England and so there was much to be settled first." He smiled rather bleakly. "Needless to state, I have been living—how is it you say it?—ah, yes, I have been under cover. I am sailing tomorrow under an assumed name."

"I am sorry to have been the cause of so much inconvenience to you."

The comte was studying her face. "It is strange we have never met. You have been to see the prince many times. And I, as you perhaps know, am an ardent Bonapartist. I am devoting my life, my energies and my talents—such as they are—and my property, to the cause. I live only to see my country enjoying again the glory that the great emperor won for France. We may never meet again, milady, and so I have no excuse for venturing on a personal remark. But this I must say: I am gaining a different impression of you than I had when I came."

Isabelle said to herself, "He likes me better," and was surprised to find that this pleased her very much. She did not want him to go away disliking her.

"I hope you will return to England," she said, "and that your opinion of me then will be influenced less by what has happened."

The comte smiled. "I expect to be allowed to return. The worst mistake that anyone involved in a duel can make is to be caught. I intend not to make that mistake and so perhaps the law will come to holding a more lenient view toward me. I shall return when I can be sure that the mood of leniency has manifested itself."

"Colonel Frisbie will get off with a fine, we expect." Isabelle's tone carried the faintest hint of impatience. "He has no money at all, so I suppose it will have to be paid for him."

The comte was thinking, "Well, that much of what I was told about her is true. She's like her father in money matters. What a pity!" He was quite sorry to discover this flaw in her, for his admiration had been rising with each moment spent in her company. "Why," he demanded of himself, "are widows so attractive? Especially when it has been demonstrated that they possess a certain degree of frailty? It's a good thing I am going to be away so long. I must succeed in forgetting this lovely little creature."

It was time for him to go. He said as he rose: "It is not necessary for me to convey any of the messages he confided to me since I know your feeling about his letter. I am particularly certain that you will have no message for me to take to him."

"No, Comte. The only message I could send"—she suddenly dropped all reserve—"would be that I hate him! He did not need to kill my husband. Everything I have heard makes that clear." She paused in an effort to get her emotions under better control. "I have told you how I feel but I would prefer not to have him know. I am certain, Comte, that I can depend on your tactfulness when you speak with him."

She held out her hand and this time he raised it to his lips. "I will return," he said. He had already forgotten his resolution. "In the spring, perhaps. And it is my hope that I shall have the privilege of seeing you then."

CHAPTER THREE

1

It is one of the greatest traits of the English people that they can oppose an innovation to the bitter end and then turn around, after it has been forced on them, and espouse the change, whatever it may be, with almost complete readiness. London had not opposed the railways as savagely as the people of the counties nor railed as angrily at Samuel Carboy (who got most of the blame although he was no more than an investor in the new roads) but all Londoners had expressed hatred for the "belching abominations" almost up to the time that regular services began. Already the Londoner who had a home in the western counties hurried cheerfully on Fridays to the terminal which the Great Western had erected at Paddington and set off to spend the weekend in Bucks or Berkshire or Wiltshire without a passing regret for the stagecoaches which had once served him.

Julian Grace had been converted early, because he could get to his home in much quicker time. A porter would accompany him from the Admiralty to Paddington, carrying the supplies which he always took home with him. At Maidenhead, which was as far as the railway had been completed, he could take one of the connecting coach lines (Carboy-owned and -operated, and always on time, of course) and reach his place in no time at all, comparatively speaking.

One Friday afternoon in early October he was standing on the platform with an assortment of bags and containers of all kinds. There was a neat basket filled with small parcels, the result of a list of needs which Freddie had pressed into his hands when he departed his home on Monday morning. There was a hamper with the delicacies which could be obtained only in the great city, bottles of special wine, jars of potted meats, and such exotic items as olives and oranges. There was also a small barrel of oysters and two bags containing his clothes.

The responsibility of getting all these articles safely assembled and ready to be transferred to the train had kept him occupied so that he had paid no attention to a very gay party nearby. Someone, a great favorite obviously, was departing on this same train and friends had assembled to say good-by. He did not look in their direction until a familiar voice reached his ears. It was Isabelle's voice. Turning quickly, he discovered that she was standing not more than a score of feet from him. She was looking, moreover, most slender and lovely, as lovely, he was sure, as when she had been sixteen. Her face was framed in fur and her arms were filled with hothouse flowers. A well-groomed man of perhaps fifty winters was standing beside her and monopolizing most of her attention. Julian recognized him as the Comte de Lussac, whom she was to marry within a few weeks, according to a recent announcement in the newspapers.

Isabelle recognized him at practically the same moment and invited him to draw nearer with a somewhat imperious motion of her head.

"Julian!" she said when he had obeyed the summons, carrying a portfolio of navy papers under one arm and a newspaper in the other hand. "It's a long time since I've seen you. A very long time."

"Years," said Julian rather tactlessly, and not caring.

"You are married and have a family," she went on. Her eyes took in the bags and parcels which belonged to him. "But I had no idea you were *quite* such a family man."

The comte had walked away and was talking with other members of the party. Isabelle lowered her voice. "I'm marrying again. Did you know?"

"Yes. I saw the announcement. I hope you'll be very happy, Isabelle."

"I expect to be quite deliriously happy."

As a pause threatened to develop, he asked, "Will you continue to live in England?"

"Oh no. Hippy"—it should be explained that her prospective husband's full name was Hippolyte Raoul René de Beyne, Comte de Lussac—"is an ardent Bonapartist, as you probably know, but there's nothing to prevent him from going back to France. He won't, of course, until that stupid king

they have over there has been tumbled off and the Bonapartes restored. We
expect it will be very soon."

Julian restrained himself from saying that it seemed highly improbable
to him that she would ever get to France under those circumstances. A
clangor of bells was giving warning that the train would soon be starting.
The instinct of obedience was already developing among those who traveled
by train and Julian was no exception. Without regret he ducked his head
toward the beautiful woman he had once loved so devotedly, and turned
hastily away to see that the porter got all his goods aboard.

"Good-by, dear Julian," Isabelle called after him in a voice which suggested she had been both surprised and hurt by the unceremonious nature
of his departure.

He secured a seat in the first coach (there was a general belief that the
rear coaches might be lost like the last skaters in a line of crack-the-whip)
and had the satisfaction of seeing that all his belongings had been carried
in and deposited about him. It was not until then that he became conscious
of something in the nature of a coincidence. Once, quite a number of years
before, in fact within the first year that he and his wife had taken blissful
possession of the house Timothy Ballard had found for them, he had caught
a stagecoach on an early Friday morning and had turned over to the guard
an identical assortment of baggage. There had been a basket full of the
articles his passionately loved Freddie had wanted, a hamper filled as full of
food as the one he was now taking and, actually, a barrel of oysters of exactly
the same size.

There had been nothing casual about that homeward trip, however. He
had been filled with such intense anxiety that he had not been able to stand
still on the cobbled bit of courtyard where the coaches started. This, of
course, was before there had been such a thing as a railroad. He had been
convinced they would be late in getting under way and had observed the
slow movements of the driver and his aides with mounting indignation. He
had consulted his watch three times in as many minutes and was no better
informed as to the time than he had been before.

"Look at them, the sluggards, the quatters!" he had said to himself. "Perhaps I ought to explain to them that it's a matter of life and death!"

They had started on time, of course, but there had been small consolation
in that. Every delay on the road threw him into a frenzy of impatience. The
cheerful sound of the conversations carried on at every stop almost drove him
mad. It was not until they reached his stopping point that he was able to
feel any sense of relief whatever; and this was owing to the fact that he was
greeted by Timothy Ballard and that the latter had whispered to him,
"You're in time, my boy, but it's going to be a close-run thing."

"How is she?" he had asked.

"Bright and cheerful," his father-in-law had answered. The latter was
neither bright nor cheerful, however. Although he had been through the
births of eight daughters, he had insisted on crossing the Atlantic to be on

hand for this memorable occasion. He shook his head doubtfully and said to Julian: "He's been here since nine this morning. The doctor, I mean. I ordered him from London on Wednesday and he's been on call at the village inn ever since. Whenever I look at him I have doubts. He's so damnably cheerful, he *can't* be the best one in London. He smiled and grinned and rubbed his hands when he arrived this morning, and I nearly sent off post-haste for someone to replace him."

2

Julian's thoughts turned backward and he found himself going over everything which had happened on that most memorable of days.

If the doctor from London had been full of good cheer earlier, his mood had changed when Julian and his father-in-law reached Three Gables. He came down to speak to them immediately and his face looked grim as well as tired.

"Not an easy case, Mr. Ballard," he said, giving his bald dome a shake. "But it's over, I am happy to tell you. Your daughter is resting well." He glanced at Julian. "If you are Mr. Grace, sir, and I presume you are from the expression you wear, I wish to extend my congratulations. You are the father of a healthy boy."

They were standing in the hall and the afternoon sun was visible through a door at the rear. In his first feeling of exultation, Julian thought of rushing out through this door and shouting the wonderful news for the whole world to hear. He said to himself, "There must be champagne for dinner, the brisk, bubbling kind, and we'll invite neighbors in to drink the health of my son, and there must be fireworks on the hill." Then a more sober reflection took possession of his mind. He pawed at the doctor's arm: "My wife, sir! My wife! Is she well? Has she come through it safely?"

But the doctor was watching Timothy Ballard, whose emotional reaction was being more vigorously expressed. The new grandfather had taken the rusty sword which hung from a suit of armor in the hall and was waving it above his head. "A boy!" he was shouting. "A son, a male heir in the Ballard family at last! Not a girl, beautiful though my daughters have always been, but a fine, strong boy. I wish my voice could be heard all the way to the island. I wish they were all listening to me in the clubs of Kingston. I wish they could drink my grandson's health in every plantation. I wish they could sing in the slave quarters tonight, 'A son, Massa' Balla'd, has been added on to you.'" He dropped the sword on the floor with a loud clang and seized the doctor by the hand. "Sir, you *must* be the finest doctor in London! I will give a written certificate to that effect to anyone who is interested. I shall proclaim you, sir, the greatest doctor in the whole world!"

He turned his face, which was almost of the redness of a beet, in his son-in-law's direction. "Julian, I was promised a boy eight times. Old Dr. Cobbledick would always say to me, 'Sir, it must be a boy this time or I'll refuse to believe in common justice or the law of averages!' But it never was. Eight times it was a girl. I loved them all, of course, but Shakespeare himself couldn't put into words the longing I had for just one son!"

A high and unmistakable wail reached them from the floor above. Julian clutched his father-in-law by the arm. He knew what it was. It was the voice of his newborn son raised in entreaty, expostulation, pain, relief, or whatever emotion it is which fills the souls of new arrivals in this vale of sorrow. He listened intently. The sound stopped. He turned pale and his hand trembled. But it began again, in greater volume if possible.

"Sir," he said, solemnly, to his father-in-law, "that sound you hear is being made by one Timothy Ballard Grace."

Mr. Ballard stared eagerly into Julian's face. "Do you mean it, my boy?" he asked. "Is this great honor to be mine?"

"It was settled long ago. Freddie and I talked it over many times. We agreed from the very first that if it was a boy he would be named after you. If a girl, Constance."

"Yes, yes, of course. Our poor dear Constance! But I'm happy, my boy, that it has turned out to be a son. When Noel drove me over to the coaching office to meet you, he said he knew it was going to be a boy. I demanded to know why he thought so. All he would say was, 'Ah doan' know how, m's'r, but ah just does.'"

Julian had forgotten all about the new arrival, even though it happened to be his own son. Anxiety was plucking at his heartstrings again. He turned to the doctor. "When am I to be allowed to see my wife?" he demanded. "You said she was resting. That frightens me. Are you sure she is all right?"

"Of course, of course. But as to when you may see her—well, soon, I think, soon. I must be certain that she's feeling strong enough."

The young husband's face turned white with fear. "Doctor, I can't stand this suspense. Are you holding something back? Come, sir, I must know. I demand to know!"

The doctor seemed very uncertain what he should say under the circumstances. "Mr. Grace," he stated finally, "there's something I must tell you sooner or later. Perhaps the present would be the best time. Let's step in here."

He led the way into a small room which Freddie used as a household office. It was a neat, white-painted apartment, lined with shelves for account books and small cabinets for papers. The desk was flat-topped and displayed no more than a pen and a container for ink and a tiny ship's model which served as a paperweight. There was an excellent oil painting on the wall, a view of the kitchen garden, which the young wife had painted herself.

"Now, Mr. Grace, you mustn't go jumping to conclusions," said Dr. Weatherly, over the rim of the glass of rum which Noel had placed in his hand. "Never insist on conclusions, sir; erroneous things, conclusions, always. And never, never jump. You see, Mrs. Grace has had a rather bad time of it. There was a condition which I won't explain because, sir, it's quite technical. Not now, at least. But there it was—and it's not uncommon at all, sir. I must tell you this: a second venture of this kind would be a serious mistake. I feel I must say it straight out that your good lady would never survive bringing another child into the world."

Julian walked to the one window the little office contained. The room was wedged in between the front hall and the dining salon and it looked out on the drive. He was surprised to see Timothy Ballard running toward the road to intercept a passing vehicle. To tell the wonderful news, no doubt.

"Dr. Weatherly," he said, turning back to face the physician, "I won't mind about the blow to our plans—my wife, sir, hoped to have at least six children—if you can assure me that her health will be good. Will she have any permanent ill effects? That, sir, is all that counts."

"It will take her some time to get her strength back. But it *will* come back. I give you my most solemn assurances on that point. I have a slight suspicion—very slight, sir—that her lungs are a little delicate. But then, of course, most lungs *are* delicate."

"Does she know what—what you have just told me?"

The doctor nodded reluctantly. "I'm afraid, sir, that she does. I make it a point not to tell them at first. Sometimes they go into hysterics or cry themselves into a bad state when they hear. But it seems that Mrs. Grace has a quick pair of ears. She caught a chance remark I made to the nurse and she took right hold of it, sir, and in no time at all she had it out of me."

The proportions of the catastrophe had at last come home to Julian. He took a chair and sat in deep silence for several moments, his eyes on the floor. He seemed to find the asking of questions on such a sacred matter most difficult.

"How did she take it, Doctor?"

"Bravely, sir. And quietly. She hasn't said much since; but there was no weeping or repining or laying of blame."

"May I see her now?"

The doctor gave the point some thought. Then he rose to his feet and drained the glass. "I'll go up and have a look at her first. If it seems wise, I'll come to the head of the stairs and nod to you. If she asks you how much you know, say that I told you. She mustn't be allowed to tell you herself. And now, sir, strive to be cheerful. You must match her in fortitude, sir." He added as an afterthought, "Very few husbands do."

This was the story which ran through Julian Grace's head as the train ran smoothly and with what seemed amazing speed over the newly laid tracks between London and Maidenhead. He remembered every detail as clearly as though it had been the day before and not a matter of fourteen years—the exuberance of Timothy Ballard, the solicitude of the doctor, the sadness in the dark eyes of his wife.

They had been good years, with some advancement at the Admiralty and a raise or two in salary. Three Gables, under Freddie's care, had been an ideal home. The boy had been healthy and normal. What more could he have asked?

3

When the train pulled in at Maidenhead, Julian roused himself from his thoughts of the past. "As we're to have only one child, we're lucky to have such a fine son as young Timothy," he said to himself. He looked out of the window of the coach as this thought crossed his mind; and there on the platform, to his very great surprise, was young Timothy himself. It was the first time that the son of the house had seen a train (the line had been opened a few months only) and his eyes were the size and shape of oysters. He was a handsome and rather gentle-looking boy, with his father's broad brow and wavy black hair; and he was clutching a cricket bat in his hand. Julian stepped down to the platform and ceremoniously shook hands with him.

"Well, son, are you off to play an important game? I must say I didn't expect to find you here."

"I'm taking the game up, sir. Old Brinsley says he wants every man in our house to begin at it seriously. He wants to beat the other houses, sir."

"A most commendable idea. But what are you doing here, if it's not too deep a secret to share with your father?"

"Mother sent for me, sir. And it's been so exciting, sir. Engines are wonderful, aren't they? I don't think there's anything I would rather be than an engineer when I grow up."

"But why did your mother send for you, Timmy? I'm worried about this. Is she ill? Has there been bad news of any kind?"

"I don't know, sir. I'm to be told later. After Mother has talked with you." The boy's eyes went back to the engine, which was still puffing and emitting steam. "It's the most wonderful thing I've ever seen, sir. I'll bet it could go faster than twenty horses all hitched up together."

Julian was tempted to question him further but decided that it would be better to wait. That, clearly, was his wife's wish in the matter. He looked about him and asked, "Where's Noel?"

The boy suddenly exploded into delighted laughter. "Oh, sir, you should have seen him. When the train came puffing into the station, he was frightened to death. His eyes got so big I thought they were going to burst. He didn't say a word to me but he just turned and ran. He was yelling, 'Lawd save us!' "

"Where did he go?" asked Julian, smiling.

"I don't know, sir. I think perhaps he's running still."

"Well, the first thing for us to do, Timothy, is to find him. Which direction did he take?"

The boy indicated the waiting room. His father waylaid a porter. "Bring all this stuff along with me. And did you see a colored man running away from here a few minutes ago?"

The porter grinned broadly. "Yes, sir, I see that colored boy. But he wasn't doing no running, sir. He'd sprouted wings and he was flying."

It developed that Noel had taken sanctuary behind a pile of trunks in the baggage room. He stuck out his head. "M's'r," he asked, "did dey git it stopped?"

Julian nodded. "It stopped of its own accord, Noel. There's nothing to be afraid of."

"Is it stopped snortin' and belchin' out smoke?"

"It's as quiet as a horse at a hitching post. Come, now, no more of this foolishness. Get yourself out of there. We have a long drive ahead of us."

Noel came out from behind the trunk and walked toward his employer gingerly. He kept looking about him. "I'se no meant fo' mixing wi' devils, suh," he said.

The whole world outside seemed in commotion. Across the road, where the Dumb Bell Inn stood, there were stagecoaches waiting to take the passengers in all directions and many private carriages as well. Drivers were inviting patronage by loudly announcing their destinations, grooms were giving the horses a final rubbing down, luggage was being hauled across the road in furious haste. There was much drinking of beer and ale and munching of sandwiches and meat pies in preparation for the long journeys ahead. Above all there was much argument going on because the stagecoaches were allowed the space along the road and private vehicles were relegated to positions farther back.

Noel took the road which ran under the tracks. They bore off then to the southwest, along roads lined with Elizabethan cottages, still in good repair and looking very snug behind their high hedges. It was a pleasant drive and when they came in sight of the river and could hear the water rolling slowly over the weir the boy stood up and gave a loud cheer. If it had not been for the anxiety which possessed him Julian would have done the same.

Three Gables faced the river, which took a slight and brief turn northward at this point; and, as a result, the late afternoon sun shone in all the front windows. The plum trees were leaning their heavily laden branches on the brick top of the red wall enclosing the kitchen garden. The land in front, sloping down to the water, was blazing with fall flowers. The iron rooster stood dead still on the front gable of the stables. It was a picture of complete peace, and Julian gave himself an admonitory thought: "Put aside all worry and unhappiness, ye who are lucky enough to enter here."

A maid met them at the front door and curtsied to Julian. "It's always nice to see you back, sir," she said. "And, Master Timothy, your mother says some friends have arrived for a game of cricket in the meadow behind the barn. But she says you can play for no more'n an hour because you still got lessons to do."

Timothy gave his bat an excited twirl over his head. "That's great! I have some new strokes to show these country quatters." He vanished at top speed around the side of the house.

"Where is Mrs. Grace, Annie?" asked the master of the house, his eyes on the last glimpse of his son's coattails.

"She's in the summerhouse, sir. There's been such a warm sun and she's been out there nearly all afternoon."

His wife heard him as soon as his hand touched the iron latch of the garden gate. She called, "Julian?"

"Yes, darling."

"I'm so glad you're here. It's been such a very long wait. My dear, there—there is something to tell you."

"I judged so when I saw that Timothy was back from school. Is it bad news, then?"

There was a pause.

"Yes, my dear one."

He walked into the summerhouse where Freddie was lying on a rather dilapidated old couch. Leaning over her, he placed his hands on each side of her face and kissed her hungrily. Every time he returned from his labors in the city it was as though he were coming back from a trip around the world or a cruise on distant seas.

"Have you been well, my darling?" he asked after a moment.

"Yes, of course. I'm always well." But she coughed as she said it.

"Have you been coughing very much?"

"Not—not very much." She looked up at him with tragic eyes. "Please, dear one, there's a letter on the table. Will you read it?"

Her tone was the final proof that trouble of serious proportions was visiting them. He picked up the letter, which lay beside his wife's sewing and a bottle of medicine. He saw at first glance that it came from Jamaica and bore the familiar name of the law firm which handled Timothy Ballard's affairs.

"Since Cousin Jeremy died last summer, we have no relatives in the island," said the young wife in a hushed tone. "And so this is from Mr. Thistlewood."

Timothy Ballard was dead. The old lawyer had striven to break the news with kindness and tact but Julian realized the truth from the first sentence. His wife's father had died in Kingston where he had gone to consult his attorneys. It had been very sudden. He had dined the night before with the Thistlewoods, the father and his three partner sons, and had seemed in as good health and spirits as was possible in view of the business which had brought him to the big city. The next morning he was found dead in his bed.

Julian dropped the letter after reading no more than the first page. "Freddie," he said. "It's so terrible and so sudden that I can't believe it. I feel the same way I did when I sat beside the body of Cymric; I couldn't believe that he had left me for good. Your father was so well when he was here last. And he took such delight in the company of young Timothy. I can see him yet, bowling away at the wickets so the boy could improve his strokes. It was hard to tell which was the younger of the two, the way they whooped and laughed together. Young Timothy is going to take it very hard." He stopped and it was several moments before he could say anything more. "I find some consolation, my darling, in the fact that he passed away in his sleep. It is small comfort, I know, to offer you."

Freddie responded in a voice which was measured and slow. "He was glad not to waken that morning. Read the rest of the letter, please."

The proud and once successful planter had left his affairs in very bad shape; so bad, in fact, that it was doubtful if the assets would do much more than clear off the debts. This depreciation in his position had not been sudden. Things had been getting worse steadily for a number of years. The lawyer had no hesitation in laying the blame on the new manager who had served during that time, a sharp individual named Amos Bingley, and on the overseer, Clingman Rade. He stated his conviction that the pair had been working together and that they had systematically looted the estate. They had vanished immediately after their employer's death, taking a boat to the United States. He was certain they had carried away with them everything they could get their hands on; and that, probably, was a very great deal. But no matter where the blame was to be laid, the fact remained that the once lordly Ballard domain was a thing of tattered financial shreds. The old lawyer held out little hope of any substantial salvage.

"The saddest part of what has happened," declared Julian after a long spell of silence, "is that this cloud hung over him in his last days. He was so proud, and I'm sure he fought bravely to the last, striving to save what he could. For us. That is the real tragedy. And it doesn't matter so much to us——"

"It does, it does, my dear one!" cried his wife. "I feel like lying down and dying myself when I think of my poor brave father battling all alone against those robbers and thieves. But we must be practical about what this means. It matters so much to you and me and to poor little Timothy. Can we go on living like this? Can we keep Three Gables?"

Julian gave the problem some moments of rueful thought. During this brief spell of silence they could hear the shouts of the boys playing in the meadow behind the stables. It was apparent from the tone of their voices that they were having a good time. Cricket is such a quiet and gentlemanly game that everything they heard was in one vein: "Well played!"; "Well bowled, Jerry!"; and "Well tried, man!"

"I think we can count on that increase in my Admiralty pay," said Julian finally. "Sir Darcy Bale was speaking to me about it this week. But it won't be very large. A hundred a year perhaps. And I've—I've worn out quite a few pairs of pants waiting for it, haven't I? Of course you'll never have to worry the way poor Mrs. Pardon did. I'll have to go on letting my parents have the twenty-five guineas we send them each quarter. Father has been unfortunate in an investment again and they couldn't get along if we didn't." He gave his head a shake. "I'm afraid not, Freddie. We won't be able to manage it. It takes quite a pot of money to keep this place up, my dear. We won't have enough. We'll have to sell."

"That dreadful word!" cried the wife. She roused herself from her reclining position on the couch and sat up, facing him resolutely. "Sell! The most dreadful word in the language! Julian, there's the money Mother left me. It isn't large, I know; but it's secure and nothing can ever disturb it. It will go a long way in keeping the place up—if we are content to live quietly. I can get along with one woman in the house and a boy to help in the gardens, and Noel, of course. I could manage, I really could. And, Julian, my dear, I must try. I can't bear to think of leaving here. I would die if I couldn't see the river from my bedroom window, and the boats going up and down. I love every blade of grass in the garden and every leaf on the trees. We came here, dear husband, when we were first married. Could any other place be home to us?"

A long silence fell between them. Julian's mind was busy, calculating, adding, subtracting, considering this and discarding that. The same cheerful shouts came from the meadow, the same friendly "Well tried!" which meant that someone had dropped the ball or had failed to protect his wickets. When Julian looked again at his wife, who was sitting up on the couch dry-eyed and determined, it was clear to both of them that they had reached a decision.

"We'll try it," said Julian.

"Yes, my wonderful husband. We'll try."

"And if we get a cropper, I'm sure Timothy will be kind enough to say, 'Well tried.'"

CHAPTER FOUR

1

Samuel Carboy should have been in a happily occupied frame of mind. He had completed a very thorough renovation of the dining room at Beaulaw Hall, turning it into a splendid apartment of high white walls, with an Adam fireplace of sheer perfection and six tall niches containing the best samples of Grecian art he could obtain. A new dining table of almost honey-colored mahogany, capable of seating thirty guests, supplemented the note of color supplied by the doors, which were of the same wood with massive brass handles. He had decided, most properly, to have neither paintings nor hangings to detract from the austere note of the room.

But in spite of his inability to find a flaw in the finished Hall, he was far from happy. He was tired, to begin with, having just returned from one of his long tours of inspection. The carriage he had used, although identical with the first one in all respects, was the third of the kind, the Carboy activities being such that no vehicle could serve him for more than three or four years.

He was seriously disturbed about Isabelle, who had come to Beaulaw Hall to spend the weekend with him, leaving her second husband alone in

London. There was a rift developing in the happiness of the newly wedded couple, which did not surprise her father, who had been against the match in the first place. "A foreigner!" he had said to her a dozen times. "Marry an Englishman, any Englishman, or even a good Scot or a particular Irishman, but, damme, child, don't take a Frenchman. They're a queer lot, I'm telling you."

The Comte de Lussac was proving a queer lot in one respect. Isabelle, having married him finally without letting her father know, had neglected to pin her bridegroom down in advance in the matter of property adjustments. When they got around to discussing it after the honeymoon, she had found there were queer ideas in the handsome head of her elderly spouse. He did not intend to alter his will in so far as his French estates were concerned!

"I can squeeze him, if you say the word," declared Carboy, going to a window of the library and staring out at the cold rain. "Oh yes, there are ways of doing it. I can get at him through his French bankers. And nothing, my child, would give me greater pleasure."

"You've never liked Hippy, have you?"

"Your Hippy is too proud and distant to suit me. To listen to him, you'd think the French are the only people with brains, sense or character in the whole damned world."

"I think he'll change his mind in time," declared Isabelle, still convinced that she could twist her husband around her little finger if she really tried. "Don't squeeze him yet, Papa. I'll let you know if it becomes necessary."

"Keep us apart in the meantime. If he looks at me down his nose again, I'll be tempted to knock it off his face. To put it plainly, child, I despise him."

And then there was the matter of a crusade which had been launched to get better conditions for factory workers. It was reaching wide proportions. Meetings were being held in all parts of the country and things were being said which Samuel Carboy did not enjoy at all. He, of course, was the chief butt of the speakers and it was getting so that he dreaded to open a newspaper, unless it happened to be one of the group which he controlled. To make matters more irritating, George Ninian Grace was in the forefront of the movement.

He discussed this situation with his daughter at lunch. "Isa," he said, "they sent a deputation to talk to me before I left London on this trip. Who do you suppose was the chairman?"

"Mr. Grace, of course," said Isabelle, making good headway on her cutlet.

"Mr. Grace, of course. He was smirking all over his face. It was the first time we had met since we split up and I hardly knew him. He looks like an old man. Well, they had come to offer me terms. They had a long list of demands and I had to meet every one of them or they would get legislation to compel me to knuckle under."

"What did you do?"

"I looked them over and saw that there wasn't a businessman in the lot.

I pointed this out to them. I said, 'Send men to talk to me. I can't discuss a matter like this with a lot of visionaries who've never escaped from the nursery. I can't talk factory management with nincompoops who don't know a bill of lading from a basting spoon!' And then I asked them, 'Can one of you tell me what a bill of lading is?' And, damme, Isabelle, not one of them could. If George ever knew, he had forgotten. They slunk out at that."

"But they go on holding meetings still and drawing large crowds," pointed out his daughter. "Papa, I think the time has come for action. You must hire men to break up the meetings. The speakers must be driven off the platforms."

In spite of his gloomy state of mind, Carboy had brought a good appetite to the table. At this point, however, he laid down his knife and fork and stared at Isabelle.

"Do you know what you're proposing?"

"Of course I do. I'm well aware it would lead to riots and fighting. People might get hurt. But something's got to be done." She helped herself to a chop and a heaping spoonful of mushrooms. "I hate him. I think I've always hated him. He patronized me, even when I was a little girl. He thought I wasn't good enough for his son. Well, I guess I've shown him something on *that* score."

The Colossus had started on a slice of cold roast beef. "You are right in one respect, Isa, my dear. I must change my attitude toward Grace. So far I've considered him a bothersome gnat buzzing around, or a mosquito. Now he's getting really troublesome."

Isabelle proceeded to make it clear that she was taking a more completely realistic attitude than her father. "You must make a deal with Common Jack," she said.

"Common Jack! Do you mean the fellow who's supposed to be the leader of the London crooks?"

"Yes, of course. I hear he's often paid to break up political rallies. His price would be high, I suppose."

Her father stared at her over the rim of a glass of whisky. "Do you think I would jeopardize my position in society, my whole future perhaps, by involving myself with organized crime?"

"Papa! You don't have to do more than drop a hint and someone will take the matter in hand. Not even as much as a hint. What was it that king said?"

"Which king do you mean?"

"Oh, the one who wanted to get rid of a chancellor or an archbishop or something."

Carboy pondered the point. "I think you must mean the one who said, 'Who will deliver me from this lowborn priest!' That was the time four knights came over to England and killed Thomas à Becket."

"All you would have to say is, 'Hasn't the time come to do something about these meetings?' Then one of your bright men will take things in hand and he will go to London and see Common Jack."

Carboy was watching his daughter with a puzzled look in his eyes. "I believe, Isabelle, that under your beautiful surface you are of tougher fiber than your father."

Isabelle had reached the dessert stage and was occupied with a plum tart and a piece of cheddar. "Of course, I am, Papa," she said.

The Colossus lighted a cigar and carried his glass back into the library. He was in a more disturbed state of mind than ever and turned to inspect his latest acquisition in the hope of relief. It was a Carlton House writing table and a very remarkable piece of furniture indeed. It had been fashioned by the famous firm of Gillow's in Lancaster and, as they had made no more than ten of them, he could be certain that its value would continue to increase over the years. He ran a hand along the smooth surface of the coved ends, and studied the satinwood inlay and the taper legs. Not finding that this absorbed his mind as he had expected, he wandered into the billiard room where the clink of balls announced the presence of his daughter. Isabelle was practicing cannon shots and was so intent that she did not turn when he entered.

"I wish young Sammy was here," said the head of the house. "He would give you a game."

Isabelle looked up. "Papa, your Sammy is a child. I could beat him with one hand tied behind my back. Really, you're getting absurd about that boy."

"He might surprise you." Carboy indulged in a sigh. "I wish he didn't have to go to Eton. It's dull here without him. Did you hear about him shooting both of the eyes out of a monument in St. Mary's? There was a lot of trouble about it."

Isabelle did not answer. She had been making it clear since the grandson of the family had been brought to Beaulaw Hall that she was not pleased. She was particularly grim whenever her father spoke of the boy as his heir.

2

The stormy period of Hark Chaffery's leadership in the nether world of London had been followed by ten years of debonair dominance by a flamboyant young man named Silk Finucane. When Silk vanished one night (the river gave up his body later) an individual of a far different stripe took his place. The new man was a stolid and plain fellow who was known at first as Jack the Crunch and afterward, because he was so different from Silk, as Common Jack. Once his authority had been established, he went into a seclusion which amounted almost to disappearance. No one saw him again, with the exception of his three closest lieutenants. The rank and file of the nether world would have been amazed to know that Common Jack had a double identity.

He sat through every working day in the president's office of a concern called John W. Common and Co., Liquor Importers. The office was a glassed-in cubicle from which he could survey his spirituous kingdom. There he supervised the business to the very last detail. At night he vanished into a private world of his own; and not even the confidential trio knew where he lived.

The members of the staff believed that the continuous stream of messages which they saw put into the hands of the man behind the glass panels dealt with the prices of rum and the sale of gin. They would have been startled into speechlessness if they had known that most of them had to do with his overlordship in the world of crime. He was a man of quick decision. He would give no more than a glance at the paper, say a few brisk words to the messenger, and then crumple up the slip and toss it on the grate fire; and some nefarious enterprise would quickly get under way.

It is possible that one of the slips thus handed in to him had contained information about a desire on the part of certain industrialists to discourage public meetings for the discussion of employment ills; in which case the decision he had sent back had set a very high figure for the services required. It is certain, at any rate, that one day in December, when it was too early for minds to be fixed on roast beef and plum pudding but late enough for a snowstorm to turn London spotlessly white, a paper was placed in his hand which caused the cruel line of his mouth to become even more tight and set. He got to his feet and retired to the anteroom through which the handers of notes reached him.

"Sloop," he said to the furtive lieutenant he found awaiting him there, "I don't like this."

"Trouble," affirmed the taciturn Sloop.

"Not that the man amounts to much," went on the leader. "The public soon gets tired of these rouser-upper boys. But I warned against violence. You remember what I said, Sloop. Why did they start throwing stones?"

"To get results."

"It's a damnably unlucky thing this fellow had to get his head in the way. What's the last word from the hospital?"

"Gone."

The mob leader considered the situation with an angry frown. His nose twitched, a sure sign that someone was going to suffer for what had happened.

"Who did it?" he demanded.

"You mean, who chucked the stone?"

"Of course! What else could I mean?"

"It was Creeper Close."

The leader's scowl deepened into an expression of positive ferocity. "A damned undependable fellow, the Creeper. Not an ounce of brain and a tongue like a sieve. He's an ale-head, ain't he?"

The messenger nodded. "Spills everything he knows after the first pint's down the hatch."

"See he's got rid of." Common Jack made Sloop the recipient of a steady stare which was full of unspoken meaning. "Get him out of my way, see? For keeps."

Sloop looked rather startled. "I'll pass the word on, Jack."

"All the rest are to be called in. Fast. No more disturbances on top of this. Let their damned meetings alone. There'll be enough of an uproar as it is." He glared at Sloop almost as though that rather weak individual had been responsible himself. "Get this through your head. Through all their heads. We've had nothing to do with this business. If there's trouble, the big money boys can have the whole blame."

3

The meeting at which the tragedy occurred was held in a Midland town where factory conditions were said to be particularly bad. George Grace had gone up by stagecoach and had been dismayed to find the countryside blanketed with snow. The committee in charge, which consisted of the vicar of a local church, a newspaper editor, and half a dozen ladies, had been very pessimistic about the prospects.

"The wind's rising," said the vicar, blowing his nose. "The people won't turn out. I suggest we postpone the meeting until the spring. If you don't want to do that, Mr. Grace, we could hold it in the church hall."

"How many will the hall hold?"

The vicar became a little vague. "Well, now, we could put in extra chairs or we could throw open the doors into the passage. But, of course, we wouldn't do either. There would be drafts from the passage. There won't be enough turn up to fill the regular seats. Well, Mr. Grace, forty perhaps. Or say fifty."

George Grace was annoyed. He had gone to the extreme inconvenience of winter traveling, coming over one hundred miles by stagecoach. The speech he had prepared was an excellent one. He had been promised that a report would be sent to the London newspapers. He rather thought that what he had to say would stir the country up.

"Postponement is out of the question," he said testily. "And I think you are being pessimistic about the number we may expect to attend. There must be a very deep interest here in factory reform."

"Not in this kind of weather," said the newspaper editor. "It's the pubs get the call."

"If we hold the meeting outside, we'll catch our death of colds," declared the vicar unhappily.

Nevertheless the meeting was held on the market square as originally planned. They had one visitor they could have done without, a blustering wind from the northwest. A handful of hardy people gathered in front of the platform and a few more clustered in the shelter of doorways on the square. The vicar was extremely brief in his introductory remarks.

Quite apart from the cold and the sparseness of the attendance, George Grace found that he was speaking under difficult circumstances. A torch had been lighted and fitted into a socket at the side of the platform and the wind whipped the flames about so unexpectedly that he had to keep watching and be prepared to move fast. Finally the torch was wrenched out of the socket and blown off the platform. The same wind took hold of the speaker's notes and distributed them across the square.

George Grace found himself now in a serious difficulty. He was not a good extemporaneous speaker and the loss of his notes left him with little to say.

"My good friends," he began, striving to make himself heard above the roar of the wind, "my notes being lost, I fear that I can give you a poor version only of what I had intended to say——"

A burly individual, covered up to his ears in a red woolen muffler, decided that he was not going to be needed on this occasion. From the far side of the square he watched the ranks of the spectators thin as some of them decided to go home. He was thinking longingly of the comfort of the bar from which he had emerged to carry out his duties. Deciding that a hint of trouble would probably bring this dismal occasion to a quick close, he stepped out into the square.

"Go home, ye conycatchers!" he shouted in a raucous voice. Picking up a fragment of stone, he threw it haphazardly across the square.

George Grace had been an unlucky man all his life and now he was to experience the final buffet from the hand of his unkind fate. The sharp piece of stone, so carelessly thrown, traveled unerringly in his direction. As there was no light left he did not see it coming and it struck him in the temple. His voice stopped and he crumpled to the platform.

4

Samuel Carboy told himself that he was not guilty in any degree in the death of George Grace. It was true that he had thrown off a casual remark on the order of his daughter's suggestion. It was at a meeting of his personal staff. He did not follow the remark up and no discussion followed it. He forgot what he had said and it did not come back to him until he saw the report of George Grace's death in the morning paper. He sat for several moments in a stunned silence, his eyes fastened to the first sentence.

The death of his former partner affected the Colossus in various ways. In the first place it raised a highly disturbing question in his mind. Had the throwing of the fatal stone been part, then, of a concerted campaign to make such meetings impossible? There were moments when he said to himself that Grace had deserved it, that for years he had been venting his spleen gratuitously, without any sense of sincere interest in the causes he espoused. Grace, moreover, had placed himself athwart the pathway of progress, a stubborn and futile figure, raising his voice about things he did not understand. When this point came into his mind, Carboy felt a deep indignation, for he was firmly convinced of the value of what he was accomplishing. This was followed quickly by a sense of regret. He remembered George Grace as a boy, a rather ingratiating boy, and then as a young man when they had been taken into the business together. Grace had charm then and, at first, a sense of his shortcomings as a businessman. He had been in the habit of bringing his problems to Carboy, who had fitted into the business from the very first like a hand in a perfectly made glove. It was not until they assumed joint control of the business, and Grace had somehow become convinced of his greater importance even in the face of accumulating evidence of his lack of fitness, that the breach between them had started.

"He deserved what he got," Carboy said to himself.

The death of George Grace was never out of his mind in the days which followed. He was aware that it had aroused the public to violent abuse of industrial leaders generally and himself in particular. The press did not dare charge him with the crime but went to the length of dark innuendoes. He knew that he was widely held to have been responsible.

It was a matter of a week before Isabelle came to Beaulaw Hall. She seemed somewhat subdued in manner but had nothing to say about the tragedy. The greeting she gave him, in fact, was entirely casual and she talked of everything else. Watching her, and listening to her rather aimless chatter, he reached the conclusion that, back of her apparent ease, she was seriously disturbed.

It could not be passed over without a word. The next morning at breakfast, when they shared the table between them and the servants had withdrawn, he forced himself to face the issue.

"I had no part in it!" he said abruptly.

She looked up with a pretense of surprise. "Why, Papa, what do you mean? What didn't you have a part in?"

"You know what I mean. Georgie's death. I tell you I had nothing to do with it. All this vicious talk going on, all these hints in the newspapers, are false and unjust." His voice rose to an excited pitch. "I tell you, it's wrong, wrong!"

"Keep your voice down, Papa. Do you want the servants to hear what you're saying?"

"I'm sorry, child, but I couldn't keep it in. I've kept it all bottled up inside me and never said a word. I'm sure that even you have been thinking things. You've believed that I said something to start all this. I didn't, I tell you. What I said couldn't be construed as an order or even a desire for something to be done. It was no more than a remark thrown off in the course of a general discussion. I forgot it as soon as I said it. I meant nothing by it."

There was a long moment of silence. "What was it you said, Papa?" she asked in a small voice.

"I'm not sure just what it was. We were discussing the report of a meeting held at Birmingham. The speaker had let himself go and had laid the blame for everything on my shoulders. I got upset and said something like 'There should be some way to stop this.' Nothing more than anyone would have said. I meant nothing and it's hard to believe that anyone there took it seriously."

"But," said Isabelle after a moment of deep thought, "things did start to happen. Do you suppose that one of the men with you thought—well, you know what I mean."

"Absurd! Impossible! Absolutely impossible!"

"It seems so. And yet—you know what people are saying, don't you, Papa? It would make things worse if they knew what you said. The worst construction would be put on it."

"I'm aware of that. I've thought of little else since this happened. Wasn't it just like George Grace to get his head in the way of the only stone thrown the whole time? He succeeds in causing me trouble even by the way he gets himself killed."

"Papa, we must be *very* careful."

"I know it, child. And yet I can do nothing. I can't go to the men who were with me at the time, and caution them. I want them to think I have no recollection of ever having said a thing."

"They'll keep quiet. They may be up to the ears in it themselves." Isabelle's face had turned pale and it was certain she was afraid of what might be ahead of them. "Papa, when I spoke to you that day——"

Samuel Carboy responded in a tone of bitter dissent. "What are you talking about, child? You said nothing to me. Not a word!"

"Are you quite sure that you—that you didn't misconstrue something that I spoke about?"

"Get this in your head. What we're saying now is the first talk we've ever had about George Grace. Not a word passed between us before. I'm prepared to swear to that on a stack of Bibles as high as the gallows of Haman."

Isabelle shuddered at this reference to the gallows. "I'm glad, Papa, that I'm not in any way responsible. I've been frightened that—that——"

Carboy regained control of himself at this point. He even turned back to the food on his plate. "This is the last time we'll discuss it, my dear. It's a closed issue. We had nothing to do with what happened to Georgie. Neither of us said as much as a word. Is that understood?"

5

Shortly after the accident a caller put in an appearance at the Carboy offices, announcing himself as a police inspector. He was shown in at once to the office of the president.

"Mr. Carboy," said the inspector, looking a little disturbed over the nature of his errand, "I have some questions to ask you. You understand, sir, that this is an official matter."

"Sit down," said Carboy, motioning to a chair beside his desk. "Well, now, what is it you want to know?"

The inspector, whose name was McMurdle and whose accent made it quite easy to guess the part of the kingdom from which he sprang, decided to come right to the point.

"Sir, it is being said openly in the streets, and guardedly in the news-papers, that your organization, or some subsidiary branch thereof, hired men from London to break up meetings being held throughout the country in the interests of factory reform."

"That, sir, is not true. If such a step had been contemplated, I would have heard of it. It is my way to keep closely in touch with everything going on in my rather extensive organization."

"And you heard nothing of such a move?"

"Nothing. If any plan of that kind had been brought to me, sir, I would have squelched it immediately."

The inspector hesitated. "It is being said that a certain individual who is reputed to be the leader of all criminal activities in London, name of Com-mon Jack, was paid to provide gangs of rowdies to break up the meetings."

"My denial covers that point also. I know nothing of such an arrange-ment. I am positive, sir, that none such existed. The manufacturers of England, sir, would not join forces with criminals under any conceivable cir-cumstances."

"Do you know Common Jack yourself?"

"I most decidedly do not."

"Does any member of your organization know him?"

"Impossible, sir. I can conceive of nothing more unlikely."

The inspector then changed his point of attack. "It's true, of course, that you and George Grace were partners in business at one time?"

Carboy nodded gravely. "Yes, Mr. Inspector. The firm of Grace and Car-boy was one of long standing and, I may say, of unblemished reputation."

"Why did you and Mr. Grace dissolve the partnership?"

"For the same reasons, I judge, which bring nearly all partnerships to a point of dissolution sooner or later. A certain degree of personal incompati-bility figures in the decision. The real reason, however, was my conviction that my share of the rewards did not equal my—well, my contributions to the management."

"Is it true that you forced him to retire?"

"Most decidedly not. I set a fair price at which I was willing to buy or sell. It was his choice. He elected to sell."

"Is it true that there has been a feud between you ever since?"

Carboy considered the point carefully. "If you insist, Mr. McMurdle, on applying the word 'feud' to the relationship after the dissolution of the firm, I must tell you that it was one-sided. I have been too busy to give much thought to the past. I did nothing to create bad feeling between us nor did I fan any of the flames he sometimes started."

"This one-sided feud, to use your own expression, led to bitter feelings between you, I believe?"

"The bitter feeling was all on his side. I would soon have forgotten the differences of the past if it hadn't been for the persistence of his attacks upon me."

"He made it clear that his feelings ran deeply. Did you hold any hatred for him?"

"None!" answered Carboy emphatically. "Sometimes I was annoyed, and amazed, by the things he said openly, feeling them to be completely baseless and unfair. If you check the records, however, you'll find that on no occasion did I reply to his attacks."

"Did you feel any desire to adopt means which would compel him to stop?"

"Certainly not. You may find this hard to believe, Mr. Inspector, but to the very end I held a certain amount of regard for him. The liking I had for him as a boy never entirely left me. I was sorry for him, even when he was most vituperative in his public remarks."

The inspector got to his feet. "Thank you, Mr. Carboy. You have answered the questions I was instructed to ask you. You understand, of course, that there is no evidence of collusion on the part of your organizations with the criminals of London. There have been hints in the press about it but we have not uncovered anything to suggest that those who interrupted the meetings were imported for the purpose. We have failed to find any clue to the identity of the individual who threw the fatal stone. Good day, sir."

If there was any further investigation, Carboy did not hear of it. The veiled fulminations in the press gradually died down. In due course the incident was forgotten.

CHAPTER FIVE

1

Julian Grace was not present at his father's funeral. In the late morning of the day previous he received a note which caused him to turn suddenly white. It was from old Dr. Crandell, who had charge of the health of the family at Three Gables. Stumbling blindly, he went in search of his mother. His concern was so great that he found it hard to believe she could be systematically going over lists for the ceremony. She was so deep in the task, nevertheless, that she did not look up at first.

"Mother," he said in a tense voice, "I must go home."

"What did you say, son?"

"I said that I must go home. I won't be able to come back at once."

She frowned up at him absent-mindedly. "Go home? Why, Julian, how can you think of such a thing?"

"Mother, Freddie isn't doing well. I'm afraid from what Dr. Crandell says that I may lose her. At any minute."

Mrs. Grace adjusted her glasses and looked up at him sternly. "I'm sorry, Julian, that Winifred is worse. But this doctor may be frightening you unnecessarily. Nothing will happen between now and the time when we lay your father in his grave tomorrow."

"I'm terribly afraid that something will happen."

"Julian!" said his mother sharply. "Your duty is here. You *must* remain for your father's funeral. I must have you beside me in my moment of great trial. I won't hear of you going away."

"You don't seem to understand, Mother," said Julian, trying to speak calmly. "Dr. Crandell says I must go at once. He isn't sure I'll get there in time as it is. It nearly kills me to put such a thing into words but—my wife is dying."

Mrs. Grace rose to her feet. She had never been on the best of terms with her son's wife, not because of any fault in Winifred but simply because she herself lacked the character to be a good mother-in-law. From the first she had been openly critical about small things. That there had never been a breach was owing to the young wife's forbearance. Mrs. Grace now drew in her lips in a manner which Julian had learned to dread.

"If Winifred is as sick as the doctor says, it becomes a question of loyalties, my son. I say that your first duty is to your father and me. Your father lies in the parlor in his coffin, and I am alone to face the world as well as I may. I need you with me."

Julian said in a low tone: "My wife needs me. Nothing can keep me from going to her."

"What will people say? What will they think if you are not here with me when your father is laid away?"

"If we are to be concerned about what people say, what do you suppose they would say and think if my wife died alone in the house her father bought for us and where we thought we would live happily until the end of our lives?"

"If you go, I'll never forgive you. I mean it, Julian."

"It seems then that I'm not only losing my father and my wife but you as well. Because, Mother, I'm riding back to my own home at once."

The water in the weir was singing when Julian reached home and the sun was still shining into the gardens and even reaching the windows in the square annex. The ground floor of the annex had always served as the library but it was now being used as a bedroom for Winifred. Lacking the strength to climb the stairs, she had been glad to have her bed moved in among the books and the maps which they had been collecting as a joint hobby. Julian met Dr. Crandell, coming from the library, as he entered the house.

The doctor was in his late middle years, with a tousled head of reddish hair and a preoccupied manner. He was so well liked that no one cared how he looked; but it had to be admitted that his trousers had attained the very extreme of bagginess, that his shoes were muddy even in the best of weather, and that his cravat was not entirely above reproach in the matter of stains. He wore, nevertheless, a shiny new stethoscope around his neck with an air of conscious pride. They had been in use a short time only and were very hard to obtain. The good doctor, always a forward looker, had contented himself before getting the instrument with making a hollow tube out of newspapers and listening to his patients' breathing through that.

"I had your note," said Julian, swallowing hard. "I've been praying all the way down that you're not right. But if you *are* right, how—how long is there?"

"You must be prepared for the worst," said the doctor. "It's hard to tell you this but I don't believe she will last the night. Right now she's in a happy mood. She says she's feeling better and she has the nurse in there with her, doing her hair so she'll look well if you should come. But, my boy, that means nothing." He shook his head sadly. "Nothing at all. They have their ups as well as their downs almost to the end."

The two men faced each other in silence. Julian's face was drawn and he looked as though nothing was left for him in life. "I've always treated death lightly," he whispered finally, "but now it has come into my own family and I know at last how terrible it is. I feel guilty, Doctor. Somehow I should have been able to save her. When Timothy was born, the doctor from London said he thought her lungs were delicate. Why didn't I start then and move heaven and earth to help her? Surely the disease could have been checked if I hadn't been so passive about it."

The doctor shook his head. "Nothing can be done once the disease touches the lungs. You mustn't blame yourself, Mr. Grace. You were never in a position to help her. Well, I must be on my way. Old Mrs. Tassy has a cut on her hand which needs dressing. I'll return sometime during the evening. And, my boy, try to carry a cheerful face into the sickroom. The poor child still hopes, you know."

Julian's attempt at a smile was a ghastly failure. "I'll do my best."

The doctor had been on the point of leaving but he paused, pondered a few moments, and then turned back. He laid a hand on Julian's shoulder. "My boy," he said, "someone *is* to blame for this. I am. I have been a coward.

"I'm not content," he went on, "with the way phthisis is treated, in spite of the fact that every authority agrees. The patient is believed to dread the chill of the air and so is kept in a hermetically sealed room with a fire going at all times of the year. To keep an even temperature, they say. It is my belief that the disease comes through lack of fresh air, among other things, and that the way to cure it is to see that the weak lungs are kept fed on the fine, clear air the Lord has provided." He looked earnestly at Julian, his face drawn into an expression of pain by the conflict within himself. "But who am I to say such revolutionary things? A humble country doctor. If I had seen to it that your lovely little wife slept out in the open—well tucked in but with her face exposed—and she had died, I would have been charged with killing her. I could not bring myself to experiment with a life as precious as hers. And now"—he spread his hands in a gesture of despair—"and now she is dying anyway. The regular methods have failed. Gracious God, they always fail! And yet the medical leaders won't change their minds. Perhaps I should have risked criticism, and the criminal action which probably would have been brought against me, in a desperate effort to save the child. But I didn't, and I'm not sure I'll ever be able to forgive myself!"

Julian tapped on the library door as soon as the unhappy physician had betaken himself off. A voice from inside called excitedly: "Come in, dearest Julian! Oh, it is you, isn't it?"

"Yes," he said, opening the door. "I rode over to see how you were."

The room was very hot. Not only were all the windows closed but a Franklin stove had been set up in the fireplace and was sending out so much heat that Julian felt a tendency to gasp as he stepped inside.

"Isn't she pretty, the darling?" said Mrs. Shannigan, the nurse, who was busying herself at the table.

Winifred was more than pretty; she had an almost ethereal beauty, due to the sparkle his arrival had brought into her eyes and the hectic flush of her cheeks. She was propped up in bed with a fascinator of wool, trimmed with blue ribbon, over her shoulders for further warmth. It was strange to see a bed standing in the middle of a room where books covered all the walls and the corners were occupied by reading desks and globes and a ladder for reaching the upper shelves; strange and terrifying, because it was a device of expediency which would be employed only in the most desperate crisis.

"Julian, Julian! You shouldn't have come. It's such a long ride for you. But I'm so happy you did!"

He seated himself on the side of the bed and placed his face against her cheek. "My dear one!" he whispered. "I couldn't stay away from you any longer. If you're better in the morning, I'll ride back in time for the ceremony."

She laid a hand on his head. It seemed to have no weight at all and he found it difficult to choke back a sob as he realized this.

"I'm better now. Really, Julian, I'm so much better. I took a glass of sherry an hour ago and I had a soft-boiled egg and even a little toast. Do you know what I think? I think perhaps I'm turning the corner."

She grew too weak to talk any more, however, and contented herself with watching him as he rose and stood beside the table. The surface of the table was covered with the things which sickness seemed to make necessary —a bottle of oil from the liver of a cod, another filled with carbonate of iron, a metal receptacle which he knew contained some derivative of opium (opiates for Freddie! A dreadful thought), and a basin containing a sponge soaked in vinegar and water which Mrs. Shannigan would use during the night. He felt an impulse to sweep everything to the floor. What good had these foolish medicines done her?

"You mustn't talk any more, my darling," he said, drawing up a chair beside the bed. "Even though you are so much better, you haven't much strength yet, you know. So I'll sit here and do all the talking. I'll mention only pleasant things. I had a letter from Timothy a few days ago. It was before we knew about—about my father—and it was a real topper of a letter. I'll read it to you tomorrow. He seems to be doing well now. I think he'll be a good student when he gets to Oxford. And I'm told the new family of kittens are all healthy. One maltese and two gray tigers."

Winifred began to speak in a very low voice. "When I wasn't doing well and was getting so discouraged, I always had one consolation. All the Ballards would be together—father and mother and my sweet Constance and the six little sisters I never knew. I couldn't help worrying about the arrangements made for them up there. Do you suppose, Julian, they're allowed to stay as a family, all by themselves, with a house of their own in heaven? It would be made of gold, wouldn't it? But perhaps it's just one big family up there. I don't think they would like it as much if that was the way."

"Whichever way it is," said Julian, "we can be sure it's the right way."

Her voice gave out at this point and in a few minutes she fell asleep. The nurse, a bony woman in a black dress, came over to the bed and studied the motionless figure.

"I'm not liking the way she breathes," she said, shaking her head. "It's a bit more ratteldy than it should be. The poor little one."

Yes, she was very small, he agreed in his mind; smaller even than when he first saw her as a schoolgirl during his stay at the Ballard plantation.

2

Julian could hear his sick wife's voice as he came downstairs the next morning. It was high-pitched and it went on and on, almost without a break.

"She's delirious," whispered Mrs. Shannigan, meeting him at the door. "They often get that way."

"Good morning!" called the patient when he entered the room. "Oh, Julian, I'm feeling so much better. I'm really in high spirits, you know, so I must be going to get better. And it's just in time. I'm down almost to skin and bones. I'm ashamed to have anyone see me, I'm so thin."

"It's wonderful you feel so well," said the husband, mustering up a smile which would have done credit to an emotional actor. "But you mustn't overdo it, my love. You must foster your strength, you know."

"Oh, nonsense, my dear, dear, dear one! I'm so well that I've been making plans. For the future, when I can be up and about again. It's going to be simply grand. I think, my husband, we must build greenhouses because I want to raise all the flowers we can't grow in the gardens—acres of greenhouses, and so much glass you won't see anything else hardly. We'll have to take all the land back of the stables—— No, that wouldn't do, would it? We can't take Timothy's cricket grounds away from him. Well, we'll just have to buy land, won't we? Acres of land, whole miles of land."

"Yes, that will be the best way."

"We'll need so much land. I really think we'll have to own as far as the Cotswolds because there are some flowers which only grow at high elevations. But we'll be able to afford that, won't we?"

"Of course, my love."

"I've been thinking too that I may be a new woman when I get well. Why not? Won't I conquer everything that's been wrong with me? It may be— Julian, it may be I'll be able to have more children then. I've been thinking about that a great deal. I want three more boys and four girls, to even things up. Eight would make a really nice family, wouldn't it? I've been thinking of names for them. George for your father—is he getting better, Julian?—and Julian for you and Albert for the queen's husband. And, oh, I've got such nice names for the girls. Victoria and Constance and Charlotte and Juanita. That last one will be for a little friend I had when I was very young in Jamaica. Julian, your mother has never liked me and I don't think I want to name one of the girls after her. Do you mind, Julian?"

"No, my sweet one. You must choose the names you want for all four of our little girls."

Winifred was silent for a moment. "I have some ideas about the gardens too. Do you think you could carry me to the window so I could see if they are possible?"

He looked at the nurse. She gave a nod and then brought a warm blanket in which they proceeded to wrap the patient. He lifted her in his arms and his heart sank when he found how light she was. It was like carrying a child.

He walked slowly to the window, taking each step with the greatest caution, knowing that nothing must be allowed to disturb the feeble functioning of the wasted body.

"The sun is so strong," she said, in the first tone of complaint he had heard her use. "I can hardly see."

The sun was strong in a sky devoid of clouds but where they stood her eyes were shaded from it. Julian looked at the nurse and she gave a lugubrious nod which confirmed his fears.

"Can you see as far as the weir?" he asked.

There was a pause. "Yes," she said in a low voice. "I can just make it out. I can see the water tumbling through. Oh, it's so lovely here. Julian, you must never take me away, never as long as I live."

"Of course. This is our home. Your father liked it so much he bought it the first time he set eyes on it. And we both loved it the first glimpse we had."

"I couldn't think of living anywhere else."

"Of course not. I think, my darling, we should go back to bed now. I mustn't keep you up too long and exhaust your strength."

"The sun wasn't very strong after all," she said with a sigh. "I wasn't able to see the gardens clearly."

She closed her eyes when he deposited her in bed and seemed to be resting. Julian walked over to the nurse and said he thought the doctor should be sent for at once. Mrs. Shannigan agreed and he had started for the door when he heard the sound of hoofbeats on the drive.

"She's exhausted now," he whispered to Dr. Crandell when the latter appeared in the door, with his black bag open and the precious stethoscope already in his hand. "But she was talking a great deal before. She wanted to see the garden and I carried her to the window. Was that wrong?"

The doctor's head shook in denial but Julian had a feeling that he meant it did not matter at this stage, that her wishes might as well be carried out. Without speaking, the man of medicine walked to the bedside and gazed down at the wasted figure. "Very weak," he whispered, after taking her pulse. "Thready, in fact."

There was silence in the room for several minutes and then Winifred opened her eyes. She gasped.

"Julian! Is a storm coming up? There must be. The room is dark. Julian, I can't see anything!"

The sun had made its way around Tofter's Spinney on the other side of the river and was now filling the room with warm light. Julian sank into a chair and his shoulders shook as grief swept over him. There could be no doubt of what this meant.

"Julian, why is the room in darkness?"

"I think it must be a storm coming up, dear one."

"I can't hear what you say."

"I think it's a storm."

"Why—don't—you—answer?" There was silence for a moment and then she began to whisper. "It's hard—to speak. I think it means—I'm—I'm going away from you—after all."

In a few moments, during which time there had not been a sound in the room, the doctor crossed to the bedside and lifted her hand. He seemed reluctant to accept the truth and it was a full minute before he turned around. He nodded to Julian without a word and walked from the room.

3

Winifred was buried in a corner of the nearest churchyard. It was shaded by the old stone walls, and rosebushes stood at both head and foot. Julian stood by the raised mound for several minutes after the rest had left, struggling to regain his composure. Then he straightened up and said to his son, who was waiting for him: "Come, Timothy. We're starting on a new kind of life, you and I. We must make the best of it, mustn't we?"

The boy's eyes were filled with tears. "Yes, Father," he said. "But it's going to be hard."

Julian's mother had not come to the funeral, nor had she written him a note of any kind. It was clear she had meant what she said when he made his choice. He thought of this now and it seemed to him that he was standing alone in the world. All the props he had depended on had been removed.

"Why didn't Grandmother come?" asked Timothy as they turned and walked down the narrow path between the aging gravestones.

"I think she must have been too tired, son. You see, I wasn't there to help her when my father was buried."

There was a moment of silence. "Father, I don't like her very much."

"Timothy! You mustn't say such things."

"Well, perhaps I shouldn't. But I can't help thinking them."

They drove home in complete silence. Julian's mind was back in happier days, the boy was thinking about a problem which had to be settled and which he had not yet discussed with his father. Noel, holding the reins, had hardly spoken since the mistress died, except to say, "Yes, m's'r," on necessary occasions.

When they reached home, Julian said: "I think the time has come for a council of war. Come and sit near us, Noel, when you've stabled the horses. You're a member of the family."

When they were all together again, sitting on the grass of the first garden terrace, with a towering oak tree shading them from the sun, the head of the family began to discuss the future. He was not sure they would be able to get along without the active supervision that Winifred had supplied. Should they sell the place and get something smaller?

Timothy was against this. "Mother would know," he said, "and it would make her unhappy. I think I see a way, Father."

Julian was smiling now. "That was what I wanted to hear, Timothy. If you really want to keep the place, and you're willing to bear a share of the burden, then I'm in favor of keeping it."

Noel said, "I'se got no need fo' what I'se paid, m's'r."

The boy got to his feet. "I've something to show you," he said, and made his way into the house. When he returned, he was carrying an unframed picture on canvas. Noel scrambled to his feet when he saw it and started to run. "No, no, M's'r Timpty!" he cried. "I'se can see de sperets starin' out at me. Take dat away!"

It was a picture of Winifred, done in oils with bold strokes. Fault could have been found with the work which had gone into it but it could not be denied that it was a remarkable likeness. The soft dark eyes, the black hair, the whiteness of the skin, the delicately modeled features; all were there.

Julian took the canvas in his hands and studied it in a state of wonder. "When did you paint it, son?" he asked. Then he added, "It's wonderfully good."

"Yesterday. I never stopped."

"It's all from memory, then. I'm very proud of you, my boy. It's a remarkable likeness."

"Why did Noel holler like that and run away?"

"Where he comes from," explained Julian, "they're afraid of pictures. They think they're full of spells. Noel has lots of beliefs like that. He told me yesterday that he saw two angels with long white wings standing beside the coffin." He paused and swallowed hard to control his feelings. "Perhaps he did. It would make us both happy to think the little mother was so well protected, wouldn't it?"

"Father," said the boy, plunging into his problem, "I don't want to finish at Clutterhaugh. And I don't want to go to Oxford at all. I want to attend an art school. If I did that, I could be at home a lot of the time and I could sort of look after things here."

"Timothy, you mustn't think of giving up your education in order to make things easier at home. That isn't necessary."

"But, honestly, it's what I want to do. I don't care about Latin and Greek and trigonometry. I want to be an artist. I'm—I'm good at it, don't you think?"

"You have a great gift without a doubt, my boy. But you were born a gentleman, and a gentleman must go to one of the universities and get the right kind of education."

"It wouldn't be the right kind for me, sir. I want to paint. I think of nothing else. It's in my blood, I guess. Didn't Grandfather Grace do some painting once?"

"Yes. But painting's only a hobby, you know."

"Father, you're wrong about that. The great artists all gave their lives to their work. They painted all the time. And that's what I want to do."

Julian shook his head. "But, son, it's going to be necessary for you to make your own living, you know. I won't have much to leave you. And certainly you can't make a living as a painter."

"But you can, sir. Particularly when you do what I've got in mind. I want to be a portrait painter. If you get a reputation in that field, you make large fees."

Julian gave the matter some thought. "Well, that's true enough. Reynolds and Gainsborough and Romney were paid tremendous fees. But you've got to get into the front rank." He frowned thoughtfully. "Well, we must give it some consideration, Timothy. It isn't necessary to decide as important a matter as this right off. Your whole life depends on it, you know. One thing I insist upon, you must finish at Clutterhaugh. You're a senior and it would be foolish not to graduate with your friends."

CHAPTER SIX

1

Carboy was at home and expecting a visit from Jonathan Bade. He was expecting also that there would be trouble between them. There were plans under way for further developments which were likely to arouse the rather tender conscience of the lawyer.

"He won't like what I've got in mind," said the Colossus to himself. But this time, he added, his own mind was made up. "If Jonathan is too obstinate," he thought, "it will be the sticking point with me. I'll take no more from that young man. He obeys my orders from this time on or we part company."

It was Jonathan's way to bring a present when he was not in a compliant mood. When he rode up the drive between the long rows of straddle stones, there were half a dozen bottles of choice wine in his saddlebags. Carboy, standing in the entrance, looked at the gift and drew a long lip.

"This is going to be a battle to the death, it seems," he remarked. "You've never been so generous before."

"It may be a battle," said the lawyer, dismounting. He was both tired and stiff, for it had been a long ride over from Maidenhead and he was not a good horseman. "But I'm hoping it won't be to the death. I'm anxious to win you over to my way of thinking."

"I'm not in a mood to be won over. You might as well know it."

They went at once into the library. "Let's not wait," said Carboy, helping himself to a whisky and forgetting to suggest that his guest do the same. "I can see you've got that godly look on your face again. Good gad, Jonathan, what's upsetting you now? What have I done wrong? What blasted, noncomformist nonsense is preying on your mind? Don't try to evade me. I know what it means when you get that sniveling Jeremiah look."

"Something has just come to my knowledge which has—well, Samuel, it has shaken me up." The lawyer rose and stood over the financier, who had ensconced himself in a deep chair and was pawing at his boots in an effort to get them off. "Samuel, do you know about labor conditions in our textile mill in Rixby?"

"Before we get to talking, ring the bell for that fellow. He'll have to pull these boots off for me."

When the butler had performed this service and had brought carpet slippers for his master, Carboy relaxed in the chair and took a satisfying pull at the glass.

"Now we can talk. Before we go into what's troubling you, I want to have my say. Sadie Coaster is on the warpath again. She's going through the Midlands and holding meetings and creating a great uproar. I want you to go up there and stop it. We can't lie down and let this agitator walk all over us but I don't want to build up the miserable woman's importance. You go and look the situation over. See what the factory owners up there think should be done."

Jonathan was silent for a moment. "Very well, I'll go," he said. "Samuel, what I had to say to you concerned our plants in one of the Midland towns. Rixby. Do you know about a bargain that your people made with the Rixby workhouse?"

"Let me see. We agreed to provide employment for all children over a certain age. It's been the custom for the local boards to pay employers who take children off their hands. We waived that."

"But it may be that you're taking it out on the children."

Carboy said: "Bah! I've been told that a hundred times."

"And you've never listened. What was the age set?"

Carboy puckered his brow in thought. "Eight, I think."

"Samuel, I have an earnest request to make of you. If I go north to Rixby to see how much truth there is in the story I've heard, will you come with me? And if we find it *is* true and that these wretched children have been treated like slaves on a plantation, will you put a stop to it?"

Carboy splashed more whisky into his glass. "Jonathan," he said, "are you going to preach at me like these damned, black-gloved reformers? Are you going to say the children work too long hours?"

"That's part of it. I've been told they've been taken away from the orphanage and lodged in a miserable lean-to on the factory grounds. The conditions there are appalling. They are fed like poor little pigs bleating at a trough. They are worked like beasts of the field. No play for them and little sleep. Samuel, Samuel, listen to me! It's a fearful and dreadful thing! I rode over from Maidenhead this afternoon and I thought of nothing else all the way. I wondered what could be done about it—what I could do about it—"

"Saul on the road to Damascus!" declared Carboy with more than a hint of a sneer in his voice. "Listen to me. This is an old story. Even at our board meetings some sissified director gets up and splutters about the poor children in the factories. Get this into your head: there's nothing we can do about it. All our competitors employ children. Are we going to let them cut under us in price because we're too lily-fingered to do the same? Damme, man, they get clothing this way and they don't starve, and sometimes they keep their parents from starving. We can't let weak sympathies get the better of us. We've got to accept as our motto, Let well enough alone."

"Let well enough alone! That seems to be the slogan of the nineteenth century. Don't change a thing because it might upset conditions which are so easy and pleasant for those on top. It's going to make this century the most cruel and hypocritical time the world has ever seen. It's going to lead to trouble and bloodshed and revolution." He stopped for a moment to catch his breath. "Samuel, I'm going to see these things with my own eyes. Will you come with me?"

"No. I'll waste no time on your silly little crusade, Jonathan."

Carboy looked at his lieutenant. His eyes hardened. "No need to go to extremes, Jonathan. You and I are a good team but I could get along without you. Could you get along without me?"

Jonathan paused before answering. "You've made it clear that you intend to do nothing about child labor. If I find it necessary to change sides while I'm there, I'll notify you at once. In the meantime I go as your legal representative. I promise to keep an open mind and to study the situation from all sides."

"And now for dinner. We'll crack one of those bottles you brought."

The lawyer shook his head. "I can't stay. I must be on my way."

Carboy looked at him with suddenly aroused apprehension. "Damnation, Jonathan, you've got an odd look in your eyes. Are you really serious about all this? Are you likely to walk out on me?"

"It's possible. I'm deeply concerned about the things I've been told. If I find them as bad as I suspect——"

A sudden anger took possession of the Colossus. "Get up there then and make up your mind. If you want to break with me, it may be all for the best. I'm tired of all this preaching and prophesying. Just send me word so I'll know where I stand."

2

It had started to rain when Jonathan Bade mounted his horse and cantered down the drive. By the time he reached the inn at Little Shallow he was soaked to the skin. The landlord peered through the door at him and shook his head. "Storm coomin' filled a' the rooms. Could hook you up to wall like quatter of beef. Nathin' else, sur."

"How far is the nearest inn?" he asked.

"Six miles, sur. You'll not care for the bed."

The lawyer saw windows twinkling with light from a house on the turn of the road. "The Old Rectory," he said to himself. "Perhaps Miss Groody will take me in."

He was given a warm welcome. A trim maid in a gray uniform admitted him and showed the way to the parlor where Nell and her father were sitting in front of a fire. Nell had not changed much through the years and she seemed to the lawyer a charming and attractive woman. Daniel Groody had shrunk until he was no more than a bag of old bones. Curled up in his chair, he looked like an ancient leprechaun.

"We heard you were at the Hall, Mr. Bade," said Nell. "It's a surprise to see you starting back so soon, and in such dreadful weather."

Bade looked ruefully at the dampness he had brought into the room, then smiled back at her. "I've seen enough of you, Miss Groody, to know that I can trust you. It's possible I may never be at Beaulaw Hall again."

Nell's eyes widened in surprise. "That's hard to believe."

"I came to you tonight hoping you'd give me shelter," he said. "But there is another purpose lurking in the back of my mind. You remember, I'm sure, the talks we've had when it's been necessary for me to see you on legal business. I carried away the impression from them that you had a deep sympathy for the people, for the downtrodden poor. You seemed sympathetic to the idea that something should be done for them and that you would like to help. It's possible that the time has come when you can achieve that desire."

After the evening meal, with Jonathan in an old dressing gown which barely came to his knees and a pair of trousers much too small, they adjourned to the parlor. Daniel Groody had already gone upstairs to bed. Jonathan told her then of the visit he proposed to make through the country where the industrial development had been greatest and of his double purpose in going.

"If I find things as bad as I suspect, and if Samuel doesn't change his mind," he said, "I am going to devote myself to factory reform and the abolition of child labor. In that event, will you help? I'll need you. I'll need many like you. This isn't a task for one person or a small group. Public opinion must be aroused and that will take a large body of workers. Yes, Miss Groody, there will be plenty for you to do if you really mean what you've said."

She leaned forward to lend emphasis to her words. "It's like an answer to prayer," she declared. "I've been feeling the need of a new interest in life. It isn't enough to run my little business here and look after my investments. I can't just sit and let life pass me by. I must find myself some kind of a mission and perhaps this is the answer."

Bade had been watching her as they talked. The one notable change in her was the suggestion of culture which time had brought. Her voice was lower and any hint of dialect which had clung to her speech when she was a girl had vanished. What she had to say, moreover, showed the effects of the reading she had begun when the care of Young Samuel had been confided to her.

Her dress was quiet in style although she had allowed herself a daring venture in the matter of color. It was a red not far removed from crimson and had an oriental hint about it, with narrow bands of black at the neck and waist and a myriad of gold tuckers at the wrists. This was the age of petticoats and it was certain that Nell wore at least the six that custom demanded. Her skirts were very full, certainly, and one of the petticoats must have been of silk, for there was the pleasantest rustle whenever she moved.

Watching her intently, Jonathan Bade said to himself, "Galatea has come to life without a Pygmalion to affect the transformation."

"I'm going into the Midlands at once," he said after a moment's silence. "I plan to visit Rixby first!"

Nell leaned forward eagerly. "Let me go too. You've so aroused my interest that I can't be content with waiting and watching."

The lawyer thought this suggestion over and then gave his head a negative shake. "What I intend is a quick visit. I must see things for myself, and I must see everything. If you were to go, it would mean taking a party in and I don't see how we could escape Sadie Coaster. You know all about the militant Sadie, of course."

Nell nodded her head. Everyone knew about Sadie Coaster, the mill hand's daughter who had been crusading in the Midlands for years for an improvement in working conditions, A slender young creature with auburn hair, she had been the darling of the plain people at first. There was no denying, however, that she carried things with too high a hand and that her tongue had such a sharp edge to it she made more enemies than friends. As her hair lost its luster and her figure thickened, she became a redheaded virago whom people flocked to hear but whose message no longer won adherents. Whether she realized this or not, she continued to tour the country, going everywhere that smokestacks stood and brazen whistles summoned workers to their looms and treadles in the small hours of the morning. Lately she had entered into the holy state of matrimony, her husband being a certain Mr. Regulus Dengate who had some small property in Yorkshire. He went with her wherever duty called her, trotting silently and obediently at her chariot steps.

"Anything that Sadie has a hand in now is doomed to failure," declared Bade. "It would mean public meetings and violent speeches and beating of drums; and the police rushing in to put a stop to it. It would be dangerous for Sadie to hear about what I am to do. I shall have to gather evidence quickly by myself. And that means, I'm afraid, that you can't take any part at once."

"I'm disappointed," said Nell. "But I'm sure you know best. I shall have to be content to wait and watch and, perhaps, pray. Woman's invariable role. I hope you will let me contribute to your fund, at any rate."

"Not yet," said the lawyer. "I don't need help at this stage. But later, I'm sure, we'll need money badly. Depend upon it, you will have plenty of chance to take an active part after the first guns are fired. It will be war, Miss Groody. The most ruthless kind of war; a war on their part to protect profits. No holds or weapons or measures are barred when the sanctity of dividends is at stake."

Nell's eyes were sparkling with excitement. "I want to enlist. You can use me as little or as much as you like, and whenever you want. I place myself in your hands and all I expect is to march in the ranks with the rest of the privates. But I *am* in a position to help you with money. I have been very lucky with my investments."

Bade smiled. "I know a great deal about your investments and I'm sure 'lucky' is not quite the right word." He nodded vigorously. "The fight has begun. I count myself fortunate to have won your interest and support at the very beginning. I rather think, Miss Groody, that you and I will see many remarkable things before we reach the end of this struggle against the powers of wealth and privilege."

CHAPTER SEVEN

1

The mill town of Rixby stood on the edge of the moors. To say that it stood is perhaps misleading, for there was nothing elevated or forthright about the place. Perhaps "crouched" would be more fitting, because the houses huddled together and were small and mean to begin with, and even the church spires seemed apologetic in their puny efforts to reach up into the skies. Nothing in the way of winds ever seemed capable of disrupting and driving away the pall of smoke which hung over Rixby. The people did not seem to mind. They were accustomed to it; most of them, in fact, had been born in it and married in it and they were content to die in it. A local poet had written sonnets to it, praising it above the blue of normal skies. The owners of the mills did not mind. On the contrary, they were proud of the smoke because it was a sign of continuous industry. "Look at Rixby," they would say. "Now there's a busy town, a producing town, a profit-making town, a really fine town."

The owners were quite right on one count. Rixby was a profit-making town. But all the profits went into one set of pockets, the capacious pockets of the owners and investors. The prosperity of the mills did not alleviate the lot of the people who lived under that perpetual pall. The inhabitants of Rixby, which did not include the aforementioned owners and investors, who were careful to live a long distance away, existed in squalor and want and found it necessary to send their children into the mills as soon as they were able to take a thread or pump a treadle. Their wages enabled the people to patronize the local pubs rather well but it hardly needs saying that the greengrocers found their profits were all on the slate and the community doctors were a philanthropic lot, content to take their pay in a sense of spiritual satisfaction.

Jonathan Bade shuddered when he reined in his horse at the edge of the black cloud under which three of the most prosperous of the Carboy factories were located. "How blind all these new millionaires are," he said to himself. "They think this will go on forever, if they let well enough alone and see that no one else is allowed to tamper with the orderliness of poverty and starvation. Don't they see the beginnings of another Reign of Terror in pestholes like this? Revolution breeds faster in a welter of smokestacks than in forest glades or country crossroads. Those shrewd eyes of Samuel Carboy see Rixby only as a home of patient helots, and even he doesn't realize that the sun which finally breaks through this smoke may be blood-red."

Having thus oracularly expressed the thoughts aroused in him by the grim aspect of the town, he rode to the nearest pub. He asked the landlord, "Where will I find one Peveril Cullen, a preacher of sorts?"

The landlord grunted. "You look like a man as has his wits about him, stranger, so why do ye want to see Pev Cullen? But you're right about him, stranger. Pev's a preacher of sorts. Not my sorts, mind ye. He ain't what ye'd call a comf'table preacher, Pev ain't. We live, he says, under the smoke and when we die, he says, we go down into the flames. And soon, he says. This preaching the end of the world ain't good for business, stranger. It don't set people thinking, 'If it's hell I'm headed for, I better stoke up with cool beer afore I'm heaved into the flames.' Naw, sir, that's not the way it works. It starts 'em thinking they better behave theirselves. My trade has fell off since he started it."

"I must see him nevertheless," said Bade.

"He's hard to find, is Pev Cullen. If ye'll promise as much as a penny, I can get a boy to show the way."

The boy proved to be sharper than the landlord and stood out for double, one penny down and one when the task was finished. With the first coin in his pocket, he set off whistling and led his charge a considerable distance down the main street (a pitiful conglomeration of poverty-stricken shops displaying the dingiest of goods) before taking off into a maze of lanes. At the very end of the very last lane he knocked on a door and held out a grimy hand. "Rev'und lives 'ere, mister. T'other penny." With two coins to jingle in his pockets, he was off like a shot.

The Rev. Peveril Cullen, who came to the door, had a light in his sunken eyes which could only be supplied by the fires of fanaticism. It was clear that he found the shepherding of a small nonconforming flock a far from profitable endeavor; at any rate he was so thin that his shoddy clothes hung on his frame like a scarecrow's.

"Your name?" he demanded of the visitor.

"Jonathan Bade."

"Jonathan Bade!" The dark eyes seemed to burn right through the new-comer. "The devil's advocate who guides the carrion hand of Carboy. Do you come here to inspect your handiwork? Will you be proud when you see how these poor sodden creatures live?"

"I've come to see things. I want improvements made in working conditions. I come to Rixby, I assure you, with an honest purpose. To begin with, I am here to see about child labor with my own eyes. *There* is the starting point. I was told to come to you; that you would know what I should do to acquaint myself with all the facts."

The gaunt preacher shook his head. "My friend, I am half inclined to believe you. There is a light in your eyes which I understand. But you are too late. Still, if you will come in I will tell you whatever I know."

They traversed a narrow hall covered with a green oilcloth and came to a small parlor which contained no more than two chairs, a table and a shelf with six books. The windows were bare.

"The Lord makes sunshine and men hang up curtains to shut it out," declared the preacher. "I have never had a curtain in my home. Not that it matters here where the sun is closed off by the smoke belched out of stinking chimneys." He took one of the chairs and motioned to his visitor to occupy the other. "I said you are too late. You cannot do anything for the poor children who are lashed to work like the slaves of an Eastern potentate. You can't, I say, because the Lord is going to attend to all that soon." The deep voice stopped for a moment while its owner leaned forward and fixed the visitor with an almost mesmeric eye. "Don't you know that the Second Coming is near at hand? Has no whisper of that dread fact reached your ears? I saw the light four years ago. It leaped at me from the pages of the Book. I calculated and checked, I prayed and beseeched guidance, I fasted and studied. And the truth came to me then in full measure.

"For the last four years I have forseen the End," he went on. His face had lighted up and he looked like a prophet of the Old Testament. "I know the day when the Voice will be heard from heaven, as the voice of many waters and as the voice of a great thunder. Nothing has happened to change my mind. The proofs that my calculations are inspired have been accumulating." He paused and pointed a finger at Bade. "Brother, the End is near at hand. The Lord will come in His glory and wrath in six weeks and two days."

The lawyer's mind had been busy. "How long have you been preaching this?" he asked.

"Two months only. I waited for certain things to come to pass. They have happened, exactly as I said. I waited for a sign. Brother, I have had the sign!"

"Have you preached the end outside of Rixby?"

"No. It is an unfortunate thing that I lack the means. I have preached only in my own small chapel, which was once a paint warehouse. It holds no more than forty people. My followers, brother, are poor people. A few shillings a week is all they can contribute. I live on that but I am happy and blessed. One does not think of luxuries when the vision of the golden gates is so clear in the sky. But I can't do any traveling."

Bade got to his feet and walked to a window which looked out on a yard where not a single blade of grass sprouted. There was one tree, a drooping specimen which resembled a fowl at molting time. Dreary windows faced him from the other side of the fence.

"I have an idea," he said finally, turning back to face the expounder of doom. "Are you sufficiently interested to put on your hat and take me to see the Carboy factories?"

Cullen rose also. "Gladly, brother. It won't be a cheering sight. But you are prepared for that. I am greedy to save souls before the End and so on the way I will expound my reasons and produce my proofs. Perhaps you, Jonathan Bade, can be snatched like a brand from the burning."

The Slasher and Welldon Mill, which belonged to Carboy although his name was never used officially, was reached by descending a steep street and crossing a canal. This purely utilitarian waterway had been cut recently (with Carboy the moving spirit, of course) to connect all the industries of the town with the Wasey River, which avoided the place by a safe margin of six miles. When the railway came, a matter of perhaps five years, the canal would lose some of its importance. At the moment it was a busy artery with freight boats moving up and down it and occasionally a body to be dredged up when another Rixburian decided to give up the struggle.

Bade and his guide stood on the swing bridge across the canal and looked at the teeming mill which produced so much wealth. It was a great jumble of buildings, all of them old and covered with grime, with a glass cupola which had been raised above the main building as an architectural conceit but in which every pane had been broken long since. The high fence which surrounded the plant (some patriotic Rixburians boasted that it took a mile and a half of fence to accomplish this) hid much of the squalor of the yards; but nothing could conceal the fact that not since the cupola had been raised as a gesture of completion had a moment's thought or an hour of labor or a single shilling been devoted to upkeep or repairs. The hum of continuous industry came through the open windows and, when the figure of a workman was seen in the crowded and muddy yards, he always moved at the double quick.

Peveril Cullen pointed a finger at a corner of the yard where a small frame structure leaned against the side of the noisiest of the wings.

"There," he said. "That's where they are kept."

"The children?"

"Yes, the poor little creatures are slept and fed in that palatial home." Cullen turned his glittering dark eyes in the direction of his companion. "You see, Mr. Jonathan Bade, this town is noted for its high percentage of orphans. Parents don't seem to last very long here. The hours of labor and the liking they have for the pubs does for them sooner than their Maker intended. They all leave children, of course, and not as much as a penny for their keep; so into the workhouses they go. The taxpayers of the town find the cost of supporting all these orphans somewhat excessive. It used to be the custom to pay men of the town to take them as apprentices in any capacity whatsoever, which enabled the town to wash its hands of them. But the Carboy industries had a better idea. They agreed to pay the parochial board for the right to take all the children over eight years of age—or even a little under when the records could be safely falsified. They take them away from the workhouse and keep them right on the premises and continue to benefit by their labor until they are fourteen years of age. Each child who survives that long receives then the accumulation of the wages laid aside for him."

"How much is that?" asked Bade, who had never removed his eyes from the lean-to where the orphans of the town were lodged.

"Well," said the minister, "it must be taken into consideration that this money requires quite a little handling. Bookkeeping and so forth. It dwindles some in the course of time. Each male graduate gets twenty shillings. Each girl fifteen. And a fine handsome sum it is. Or don't you think so?"

"Very handsome indeed."

The two men looked at each other with somber eyes. It was clear that Bade had not expected to find anything as bad as this. Perhaps he was thinking, "Part of the money I have accumulated with Carboy has been gained by the slavery of these unfortunate children."

"What about this building where they are kept? Is it comfortable?"

Cullen answered in terse phrases as though he did not dare risk more extended description. "Hot in summer and cold in winter. As dark, I would say, as the town jail. One stinking latrine to serve both sexes. Two dormitories with beds wide enough for three *and* all of them fully occupied. A small kitchen where cockroaches keep company with a slattern who prepares unappetizing meals. As she does it on contract, they are always close to the point of starvation. Is there anything else you want to know?"

"There is much I shall need to know later," said Bade. "At the moment I am too stunned and unhappy to ask questions."

"A thought occurs to me. In addition to the kitchen, these opulent quarters have a scullery with an open hatch looking out on the room where the children are fed. It is used after the meals for the washing of the dishes, a quick and very casual matter. A brother of this slattern belongs to my chapel. If you desire to see what goes on with your own eyes, he could manage to get you into this unoccupied corner."

"When could it be done?" asked Bade with sudden eagerness.

"Why delay? Tomorrow morning. It would mean arriving at the plant before the hour of four in the morning. The brother could get passes for us." Cullen nodded to his companion. "I would like to go with you. If you have no objections, of course."

2

A few minutes before the hour of four the next morning the two men, with passes in their hands, approached the main entrance to the plant. Rain was falling in soggy insistence and they had to dig their feet out of the mud at each step. The watchman held a lantern up to stare at them.

"Pev Cullen, is it." His tone did not convey any sense of admiration. A long study of the pass by the light of the lantern ensued. "Well, ye're to go in. It says so here. Though why is more'n I can figger out."

"We are here on a special errand, Dick Slider," said the preacher.

"Goin' to pick out the spot where the lightnin' of the Lord will strike?" asked the watchman with a cackle. "Well, then, git along in. An odd-lookin' pair ye are, I mus' say."

The brother, whose name was Melchiel Burns, joined them in the rubble and confusion of the yard.

"Ready for us, Mel?" asked the preacher.

The man nodded. "She's in a ugly mood," he said, referring quite clearly to his sister. "She's a-stirring the porridge and a-pouring in sawdust to make it go farther. We better get in without her seeing us or she'll be at us with that iron spoon of hers."

They made a quiet entrance through the rear door and achieved the seclusion and darkness of the scullery without attracting the attention of the honest woman who was preparing breakfast in the kitchen next door. She was singing a hymn as she worked, a singularly inappropriate one, it seemed: "And the Lord Shall Feed Them."

"She's at her ugliest when she gets to singin' hymns," whispered the brother. "She'll beat time on their heads wi' that spoon."

A clock struck from somewhere high in the factory. The hymn ceased abruptly and the iron spoon was employed in beating on a tin pan. Bang! Clang! Bang! A childish voice from somewhere in the darkness said, "Measy, get up, Measy." The answer, also in a youthful voice, was accompanied by a tired sob: "Oh no, Addie! Not so soon. Addie, I'm awful sick."

The slattern raised her voice. "Come on, now, the whole kit and bilin' water of ye! Ye don't want Mr. Joe Middles comin' in at ye with that gad of his, do ye? Any as isn't up and dressed in ten minutes will be a-feelin' of it!"

The preacher said in a whisper to his companions: "Joe Middles! The hardest man in Rixby. He used to be the most hated sergeant in the army."

Sounds of stirring came from the rooms beyond. The voices of children could be heard raised in despair, vexation, protest and anger. Standing back in the darkness of the scullery, the watchers could see through the open hatch a line forming outside the latrine, with much pushing and shoving and shrill complaints. Most of the children had tumbled into bed without washing from the previous day's work and their faces and hands were black. The gray uniforms they wore were shapeless, sleazy and in many cases worn to tatters. Although a nervous reaction from lack of sleep made their voices shrill and loud, there was little hint of energy about them. Their bodies showed thin and bony under the misfit of the uniforms.

Some dropped out of the line to sit on the floor and rest their drowsy heads against the unplaned planks of the partition. "Let me alone, I want to sleep," was the response when any of them were disturbed.

The cook kept striking her tin pan in the kitchen and calling shrill admonitions. "Now then, stand on yer feet, charity brats! And I'll have less noise!"

"Look!" whispered Cullen tensely.

Two girls had come within their range of vision. The older of the pair walked with hanging head and with pigtails of brown hair which seemed limp and lifeless on her shoulders. It was the smaller girl who had attracted the preacher's attention, however. She was hobbling along on a crutch and, to judge by the twitches of pain which crossed her face, was suffering a great deal.

"Surely that poor little thing is not going to be sent in to run a machine all day," said Bade in a tense voice.

"You'll find them smaller than that, I'm very much afraid."

"Measy," said the girl with the crutch, "I'll ask Mr. Joe Middles if he won't send you to the doctor."

"No!" There was panic in the taller girl's voice. "I'm afeared of Doctor. He goes punchin' at me and he makes me take awful medicines."

"But, Measy, he'll make you better."

"He won't. He'll make me worse."

A tall boy of perhaps thirteen or fourteen gave the older girl a shove as he passed them and said in a voice pitched high in derision: "Please, Addie, I'm so turrible sick! I gotta headache, Addie, rub me for'ad fer me. Wash me face, Addie, I'm too sick to raise meself offen the piller."

"You leave my sister alone, Mat Blunt!" cried the cripple.

"Measy, Measy, Measy!" taunted the boy. "She's a big lummox and you're a spitfire."

"Get along now or I'll hit you with my crutch!"

The boy stopped and scowled ill-naturedly at the two girls. "You just hit me with that thing," he said, "and I'll break it over yer back. Don't think I'm afraid to hit ye just becus ye're a cripple. I've slammed plenty cripples."

Without hesitation the girl raised the crutch and gave him a vigorous rap on one side of the head. The boy retreated in sheer surprise. "She hit me!" he exclaimed. "Didya see that? She slammed me on the snook." Then his anger got the better of him and he clawed at her with both hands. "I'll fix ye for this, ye whally-eyed little toad! Ye'll need two crutches when I gets through."

At this moment a man in a high choker, and a hat which had been worn so much in the rain that it looked like a deflated balloon, came briskly through the entrance.

"Joe Middles!" whispered Mel Burns. "He's a thorough nasty one. If he caught us here he'd boot us all off the place."

Mr. Middles had just breakfasted because there were crumbs on his chin and for the moment he seemed disposed to be amiable. This changed when he perceived the altercation going on.

"What's this!" he said in threatening tones. "H'arguing, is it? Making trubble, is it? What right have ye got to be a-behavin' this way? Don't Slasher and Welldon give ye beds and food and treat ye kind? Don't Mr. Samuel Carboy hisself lose sleep at nights thinkin' o' ways to make life easy fer all o' ye?"

"She hit me!" said the boy. "Slam bang on the snook."

"On the snook, was it? Well, Mat Blunt, 'ere's one on the jaw to even it up. Now, none of yer blubberin', ye pesterin' little sneak. Get in to yer fine, warm, nourishin' breakfuss. We don't want anyone late for work, mind ye." He turned his attention to the cook. "Here, Mrs. Weany, get the food on the table, woman! We'll be late agin and Mr. Billy Isbester will be comin' down on me. What ye got for the little angels? Porrich and bread? Ain't ye cuttin' it pretty fine, ye old bloss? We'll have a talk if ye get to makin' too much pruffits and keepin' it all yerself."

In a few minutes the children had filed into the room where the food had been laid out on a long trestle table. There must have been thirty of them in all and, in spite of the meagerness of the fare, they made considerable noise. The cook interrupted herself in the course of carrying in trays with mugs of very weak tea to say to Mr. Joe Middles: "She's wuss. That aggravatin' Winly child. Don't eat and don't seem to sleep. Allus a-crying she wants her dear mumma. Why can't she get it through her head that her dear mumma is dead and she's a h'orphan like the rest?"

"How old is she, Mrs. Weany?"

"Must be eight or she wouldn't be here, would she?" The broad and somewhat squashy face of the cook contorted itself in a wink. "But I must say she don't look it."

"I'll change her over to the treadles," said Joe Middles. "That'll keep her so busy she won't have time to think about nothin'."

A bell sounded from the factory tower. The ex-sergeant raised his voice to shout, "Ten to five!" The children came pouring out from their meal with pieces of bread in their hands which they had clawed off the plates before leaving. "Line up now, the lot o' ye. Two and two as usual. You lead off, Mat Blunt, ye're the oldest."

The children began to file through a door into the factory. The two sisters were near the end of the line, the older one with her cheeks damp from tears, the smaller one hobbling along beside her and striving hard to cheer her up. Mr. Middles counted them as they walked past him.

"Hey, what's this?" he shouted as the last of them went by. "We're two short. Where are they? Have they burr'ed down under their dirty blankets to get more sleep?" His face reflected the outrage to his feelings the prospect of such a thing was causing. "This is a nice state o' things, this is!"

"Purhaps they's gone and run away on us," suggested the cook.

"They wouldn't dare. Not them. They know the drubbing they'd get if they tried *that*."

A search of the dormitories produced no results. Mrs. Weany then looked into the stale room where the food had been served and let out a shrill burst of annoyance and triumph. "Here's the tru'nts!" she said.

A little girl was sitting at the table with her face in her arms on the board. She was a very small girl, smaller even than Addie. It was apparent at once from the annoyance on the face of the cook that it was the aggravating Winly child.

A square-built boy with a round head and a turned-up nose was leaning over her, with a puzzled desire to help evident on his face.

"You!" exclaimed the cook, taking the girl by the shoulder and shaking her. "It's a good whupping ye need."

"What's this? What's this?" demanded Mr. Middles. "Ye heard the order. Why didn't ye fall in with the rest, eh? Now lissen to me. I give ye five secunks and no more to catch up with the line."

"Oh, why doesn't my dear mumma come and get me?" said the small girl in a muffled voice.

"How many times must ye be told she's dead?" exclaimed the cook.

"She's not dead, Mrs. Weany! They told me she wasn't. They said she had gone away. My aunt Martha said she would come back soon."

"And a nice one she is! Doin' nothin' fer ye!"

"I need my mumma so much! Oh, why doesn't she come back?"

Joe Middles took the child by the ear and almost dragged her to the door. "Git!" he said. "And don't go blubberin' that way into the factory. They'll think ye're not treated right."

The small girl walked through the door, trying hard to check her tears.

"And now, you," said the ex-sergeant, turning to the boy. "What d'ye mean skulkin' in here when you's ought to be up in the line?"

The boy answered slowly, "I was sorry. For her."

"You was sorry, eh! Well, ye'll be sorry for yerself if this kind o' thing keeps up. And while I got ye, I'm goin' to ask ye again. Have ye remembered yer name yet?"

The square-built boy nodded. "Yes, sur. H'r'l'd."

Middles looked at the cook. "Sticks to it, don't he now? H'r'l'd, he says. That ain't a name. It's more like a cough or a hiccup." He threw back his head and laughed loudly, the cook joining in. "Now see here, young H'r'l'd, ye've been with us two weeks. You was found on a doorstep, a respect'le doorstep right here in town. Nearly starved, wasn't ye?"

The boy nodded his head at once. The condition he was in at the time was something he was not likely to forget.

"Ye've been here ever since and ye ain't give us yer name. It stands to reason ye've got a last name."

"No, sur. H'r'l'd. That's all."

"Don't ye remember yer father and mother?"

The boy shook his head.

"Where d'ya come from?"

The boy motioned vaguely. "Farm," he said. "Big farm. Hosses."

"How long was you there? Surely ye can tell us that much."

The boy looked bewildered. He could not tell them that long years of hard treatment as a drudge on a farm in the north country had left him with little mind and less memory. He had only the faintest recollection of the night he climbed from an upstairs window at night and ran away. It was a black night and only the need to escape from the heavy and pitiless hand of his master had induced him to venture out into it. The blind tramp which followed, begging at farmhouses (and getting little but sharp words and threats), was no longer anything but an ugly dream.

All he could do was to look even vaguer than usual and shake his head again.

"No use askin' this ninakin!" Mr. Joe Middles shook his head in disgust. "Here, git into the shop. And git this through that thick skull. I want h'industry today, and plenty of it!"

The silent and unsuspected spectators of this depressing scene had taken advantage of the chance to leave. They had tiptoed out by the back entrance and were already making their way slowly through the mud of the factory yard.

"Rev. Peveril Cullen," said Jonathan to his companion, "I'm beginning to think you are right after all. This is the kind of world which ought to be brought to an end. I'm sure I'll be happy to see the Lord come down to earth in six weeks and one day. It will mean the end to this sort of crime."

Cullen sighed deeply and unhappily. "What horrors are allowed to go on because well-disposed people know nothing about them! Or, knowing, are prone to sit back and wait for others to do something about it. Sometimes they don't do anything because it would cut into their income. Let well enough alone! I'm afraid, brother, that the Lord will be very hard when He sits in judgment on the let-well-enough-alone-ers."

Jonathan was in a thoroughly chastened mood. "I've been one of those who sit down and wait. To my great shame I acknowledge it. But," and his jaw set itself at a pugnacious angle and the gleam of battle began to show in his eyes, "from this day forward I shall devote every moment of my time, every bit of energy in this body of mine, every shilling I've accumulated, to the purpose of uprooting this dreadful selfishness and making the world a more decent place in which to live."

When they had passed out through the gates, breasting a steady stream of workmen pouring in to begin the labors of the day, and had crossed the canal drawbridge, Jonathan asked his companion a question.

"What's the biggest hall in town?"

"The Opera House. It seats six hundred. And standing room for two hundred more."

"Is it hard to rent?"

Cullen looked both shocked and startled. "Rent the Opera House!" he said. "The price they ask is nothing short of col-ossal."

"I don't care about the cost," declared Jonathan. "We'll rent it this morning. Outright. For six weeks and one day. You can hold your meetings in it every day and all day long if you desire. You can put the fear of the Second Coming into them and bring them sobbing to the seats of repentance. I shall make one condition only. I want the use of the hall for one night. One big, memorable night. A plan has taken possession of me and I'm going to need your help—and the help of the Lord who you say will come down out of the skies to judge us."

"I can promise for myself," said Cullen. "And I'm sure the Lord will be on your side."

CHAPTER EIGHT

1

Jonathan Bade had been right in his prediction that Sadie Coaster would arrive on the scene as soon as she caught the scent. She reached Rixby on the morning of the day when the all-important public meeting was to be held; a tall and stringy woman of indeterminate years, with an unruly mop of violently red hair and the face of a conqueror or a born troublemaker, according to the views of the onlooker. Her husband was with her and acting, as usual, under her orders. "Mr. Dengate," she said when they reached their rooms at the Dairy Maid and Bucket, "give the man tuppence. Nothing more, mind you. He's been insolent." A little later she said: "Mr. Dengate, hire a carriage at once. I must make some calls on prominent citizens in this most downtrodden of towns. I have much to say to them."

Her husband did not need to be told this. He was certain she would say a great deal and that every word she uttered would be full of invective, malice and incitement to libel action. Without pause or question, however, he engaged a carriage and a driver, and they set out on their rounds. From each call the stern leader of causes emerged with a red and triumphant face, her open reticule (she was always snapping the catch to get some article out and forgetting to close it) dangling on her wrist. "Well, Mr. Dengate," she said each time, "you can be sure of one thing. I left nothing unsaid."

When he had returned her to the inn, however, Mr. Dengate started out alone on the same route, calling on all of the men and women his wife had seen. He had one speech which he delivered to each of them. "Sir," he would say, or "Madame" as the case might be, "I have come to express my regrets. My wife doesn't know I am here. It is only my personal conviction that she has been perhaps a little too frank which brings me to see you. My wife, sir, follows one principle in life, she leaves nothing unsaid. It may be a fault but it is the fault of a great and courageous soul. I am certain, sir, that you are broad-minded enough to realize that. Whatever she says should be considered as nothing more than—in a sense—rhetorical."

Sometimes those who had borne the brunt of her rhetorical assault would laugh and say, "Oh well, we *know* Sadie Coaster." Sometimes they were still burning with righteous wrath and showed him promptly to the door.

He returned in time to hear the last of an interview, which apparently had been a stormy one, between his wife and the two promoters of the emotional shocks which were rocking Rixby, Jonathan Bade and Peveril Cullen. His wife was having the last word.

"I will have you know, gentlemen," she was saying, "that the name of Sadie Coaster is synonymous with the cause of factory reform. She was the first"—it was her way to speak of herself in the third person—"to point out to the people of England the horrors of child labor, of the factory system. She was the first to hold public meetings and to attack the heads of privilege. She has been thrown into prison countless times for the vigor of her attacks.

"Do you think, sirs," she demanded in conclusion, "that Sadie Coaster will permit a meeting, such as you propose, to be held without her voice being heard? If you think that, sirs, you do not know her. Let me tell you this: persist in your refusal to have her speak and she will hold another meeting at the same time; on the public square, sirs, with much excitement and cheering and the police in attendance. Your meeting will be interrupted, drowned out, blanketed, stifled, suppressed, done in, reduced to the size of a board meeting or a session of churchwardens. And that, sirs, is Sadie Coaster's last word on the subject."

Jonathan Bade took Mr. Regulus Dengate aside in the corridor.

"Sir," he said, "you have the appearance of a reasonable and fair man. I would like to explain to you why this meeting is so important and why we must conduct it along certain lines; an explanation we have already made to your wife with, I regret to say, no results. Sir, we are going to present the case against child labor in a way which will bring it to every pair of ears in England. We believe, sir, that we can make an end of the terrible conditions which exist. But we must be allowed to proceed in our own way. We cannot have interruptions or disturbances.

"I have been writing letters," he went on earnestly, "for the last three weeks. I have written over three hundred letters—to the leading citizens in this part of the country, to all people of established good intent, to leaders of state and church and trade, to people of social standing, to men and women of Christian convictions. I have implored them to come to this meeting tonight, I have tried to make it seem a matter of duty. It is already certain that many of them will be in attendance. Enough of them have signified their intention to come to fill the hall. Sir, we must have the chance to convince these people who have it in their power to destroy this monstrous thing. That is all we ask, the opportunity to present our case to them without violence of any kind."

Mr. Dengate had listened attentively. At the finish he gave his head a negative shake. "It is no use, sir. No meeting of the kind is complete without Sadie Coaster. She cannot in fairness to herself permit it to be held without the sanction of her presence and the sound of her voice. You have told her she will not be permitted to speak. Then, sir, she will hold her own meeting outside. That she will do so, sir, is as certain as the tides, as certain as life and death. Her resolution is iron, her will is steel. She has made up her mind and nothing in the world can change her."

"Even though she may prevent the wonderful results I foresee?"

"Child labor," declared Dengate, "cannot be abolished without Sadie Coaster. Child labor must *not* be abolished without her."

Jonathan gave his shoulders a shrug which showed the bitterness he was feeling. "Very well, sir. There is nothing more to be said."

"She will have her meeting," went on the faithful husband. "It will be held on the Court House Square in front of the Opera House. There will be sound and fury and such denunciations and naming of names as the world has never heard. You, sir, will be named, I am certain; and without the least hint of good will. The Rev. Mr. Cullen will be torn to shreds and tatters. The town government will be condemned in no uncertain terms. The government of the country will be attacked. I am even disposed to think"—he dropped his voice to the low level of apprehension—"that the members of the royal family will come in for some words of censure!"

"All this is what I feared," declared Jonathan. "It explains why I begged your wife to forgo any active part on this occasion."

There was more than a hint of smug satisfaction in Dengate's final words. "She will be arrested, of course. She will go to prison. She wants to be arrested. She welcomes the chance to be incarcerated in the town jail. But, sir," with the shake of a forefinger raised above the level of his eyes, "for one night only. Her willingness to face martyrdom is always appeased by one night behind bars. For that reason it is necessary for me to keep myself so successfully in the background that I am not taken into custody with her. I must be at large the next day to negotiate her release from durance vile." He paused and the raised forefinger came into play again. "I am telling you this in full frankness, sir, so that you will be convinced of the inevitability of events in case you persist in your resolution not to have her filling the most prominent place on your platform and her voice raised once more while all England listens."

"And our plans shrivel and the cause gets another setback." Jonathan's temper had been rising as he listened. "Very well," he went on. "She may have her opposition meeting and she may go to prison for all we care. I will not say, sir, that I hope your efforts to get her out of jail will be in vain; but the thought hovers in my mind that it would be a wonderful thing if you *never* get her out. It is a great tragedy, sir, to see the chance to strike a telling blow for the cause endangered by the thirst for publicity of one stubborn woman."

2

Nell Groody stepped off the stagecoach at Rixby around noon, looking excited and happy. Jonathan had gone to meet her and his greeting had a touch of solemnity about it.

"You look like Joan of Arc, ready for the stake," he said. "Have you much luggage?"

"One bag only." She paused and her eyes lighted up. "That's exactly how I feel, like Joan of Arc or Anne Askew. I'm ready for anything, and happy that you've called on me."

"That's good." But Jonathan did not seem entirely satisfied, for he gave his head a shake. "It may prove a very rough and trying experience."

Nell completed the committee he had picked to bear the brunt of the day's happenings. Six men and three women assembled in his sitting room at the Maid and Bucket, all of them looking as excited as Nell, some of them clearly a little apprehensive.

"You all know in general what it is we have to do tonight," said Jonathan, watching them closely as he talked. "We must get into the factory grounds and lead the children out without being seen or stopped. It's to be hoped, of course, that we can get them to the carriages before an alarm is raised. The old man who looks after the east gate has been persuaded to desert his post for a sufficient time to let us carry out our plans. The gate unfortunately is one of the new kind which close of their own weight. It has been declared that entering through gates of the kind constitutes entering or, to put it bluntly, burglary—simple burglary, of course. Under One Victoria, Chapter 85, Section 2, the penalty for simple burglary is no longer hanging but transportation for ten years to life or three years' close confinement. Provided, of course, that the millowners should be sufficiently vindictive to demand the full penalty under the law."

"Oh!" said a feminine voice faintly.

"I don't understand," said one of the men. "We are not stealing anything."

"Yet it amounts to theft. The arrangement entered into by the parochial board with the mill makes the children the property of the company. I'm telling you this so you'll go into it with your eyes open. I don't think they'll transport us to one of the Indies. In fact I'm very strongly of the opinion that they wouldn't dare. However, Boisterous Billy Isbester is a tough citizen. You can never be sure what he may do."

There was a long silence. None of the committee members spoke but it was clear to Jonathan that some of them were wavering.

"There is another phase of the law which we must understand," he went on. "If anyone on the other side, an employee at the factory, for instance, is hurt or roughly handled while we are removing the children—even if we as much as lay a hand on one of them—then our offense becomes a full felony."

"And what," asked a timorous voice, "is the penalty for that?"

"The penalty in that case, under the statute already quoted, is hanging."

"Do you actually mean that we could all be hanged for doing a charitable act?" asked a male voice.

"The law would permit the extreme penalty to be exacted," declared Jonathan, "if—if the owners demanded it. I don't think they would dare. There would be such a wave of protest from all over England——"

"But," said the same voice, "we might be hanged while the protest was going on. It's—it's not a pleasant prospect, is it?"

The result of the discussion which followed was that three of the committee begged to be excused and betook themselves from the meeting on hurried feet. Jonathan looked at the remaining six and nodded his head with pride and satisfaction.

"To be honest," he said, "I didn't think we would have as many as this left. I extend my respects to all of you—my brave friends and comrades. And now to discuss plans."

When the meeting came to an end Jonathan drew Nell to one side. "Are you quite sure?" he asked. "Are you staying in this without any reservations?"

The sparkle in her eyes conveyed the answer. After a moment she whispered: "I'm hoping for the very worst. It would set the country into such a blaze that never again would they be able to treat children like this."

"The trial of the seven bishops would be nothing to what might happen if they did try to exact the full penalty," declared Jonathan. He shook his head soberly. "Yes, I'm prepared for it. But, of course, I don't think it is going to happen that way. I'd rather that none of us become martyrs if it can be avoided."

3

Part of the committee in charge of the meeting sat in the greenroom of the Opera House and listened rather nervously to the sounds which reached them from the square. It was becoming more apparent every minute that Sadie Coaster was making good her threat to hold a noisy rally outside in defiance of the gathering within.

"The square is black with people," said the latest member of the committee to arrive. "You ought to see the banners she's unfurling above the carriage where she's going to speak. *Sadie Coaster Won't Be Kept Down* and *Sadie Is the Only True Friend of the Downtrodden*. The police are out there already. A whole squad."

Peveril Cullen was pacing up and down nervously. Having no watch of his own, he paused every few minutes to ask the time of one of the other members. "How ridiculous to be thinking about minutes and seconds when the Lord will come in six days to usher in eternity," he said. Nevertheless, he continued to ask. When told that it was ten minutes to eight, he gave his head a satisfied shake.

"Well, it's under way," he declared, addressing the whole committee.

"They're in by this time. If everything goes according to our plans, they'll have the children out of the grounds and into the carriages in a very few minutes. They should be here not later than ten minutes after eight."

An apprehensive voice asked what action might be expected on the part of the owners of the mill. Would they make an effort to break up the meeting and regain possession of the children?

"From what I know of Boisterous Billy Isbester, there is certain to be violent retaliation. Those who have been responsible for entering the plant and taking the children away will be placed under arrest without a doubt. They expect it. I am certain that Jonathan Bade will be disappointed if they don't have to go to jail. It's going to take a lot of noise to waken the people of England."

A somewhat nervous silence fell on the sponsors in the greenroom and nothing more was said until Jonathan Bade entered with a brisk step. He wore an air of triumph.

"Everything went smoothly," he announced. "The children are here. They are hungry and tired, and some of them are sick, and none of them knows what it is all about. But they came willingly. No prospect could seem worse to them than staying where they were." He paused to smile at Cullen. "I'm happy with the way things have gone; and I don't care now what Boisterous Billy may do." He asked anxiously, "How is our house?"

"The place is filled," said Cullen. "Unless I'm mistaken, we have every voter in the riding upstairs."

"The square is black with people. Everyone who couldn't get in here is outside to hear Sadie. I expect she'll open fire in a few minutes."

The last play produced at the Opera House had been a military piece and the greenroom was crowded with wooden muskets, drums, uniforms and flags. Jonathan lifted a sword and gave it a swish in the air.

"Tonight it has been like Napoleon's best campaigns," he said exultantly. "We thought of everything. The whole program was carried through without a hitch. That press man we hired is upstairs now, working on his report of what happened at the factory. As fast as he finishes a sheet, six clerks make copies. They'll go right on with the story of what occurs now. The six copies will be sent off posthaste to newspapers in London, York, Edinburgh, Birmingham, Manchester and Liverpool. Wait, we must have another copy for the west. Bristol. We must have all England reading about it in two days. And if Isbester has us sent to jail, they'll get that story too. We'll have the trial reported in the same way."

He began to sing in a low tone the song which swept the country at the time of the trial of the bishops.

> And shall Trelawney die, and shall Trelawney die?
> Then twenty thousand Cornish boys will know the reason why.

"Perhaps," he added, "they'll be singing songs about us and printing cartoons and pamphlets. Of one thing I am certain. The harsher they are, the quicker we'll have an end to child labor."

As Cullen had intimated, the pit and the boxes were filled with people in broadcloth and silks and there was a certain mixture of elegance even in the shoddy of the gallery. When Bade rose to speak, the light from the large gas chandelier was reflected back at him from monocle and lorgnette; and this convinced him that the people he needed to reach were sitting out front.

Those who had their first glimpse of him from his good side were impressed with the strength and symmetry of his face but when they saw the other side they were startled. It was as though two men stood on the platform. He had been seen little in the town and they whispered among themselves, "What strange manner of man is this?"

Bade knew what they were saying but for once he did not care. "I am not going to make a speech tonight," he began. "The time has passed when the power of the human tongue can advance the cause. Not even the sound and fury which we hear rising from the square below us will be of any avail. In the face of impassioned oratory such as this, conditions in the factories have grown steadily worse. Therefore we will not strive tonight to convince you through your ears but rather we will address our evidence to your eyes." He turned toward one side of the stage. "Are you ready?"

A curtain was parted and Helen Groody stepped out on the stage. She was somewhat flushed but otherwise seemed to have full control of herself. She held the curtain back. "Come, children, if you please," she said.

Mat Blunt, as the oldest and tallest, was the first to appear. He took one

look at the faces staring up from the pit and terror took possession of him. "Swipe me!" he muttered. "Where am I?"

"Come, Mat," said Nell. She took him by the arm and led him to the other side of the stage. "You're a big stout fellow and you're not afraid of anything."

The rest of the thirty-two began then to file out, walking hesitatingly as though they expected to be publicly whipped by Mr. Joe Middles. They formed a line stretching from one wing to the other. Never in the entire history of stage and opera had such a chorus as this been seen. The children were too stunned by the things happening to them to realize where they were or what they were supposed to do. They stood with bent backs and dangling arms and looked out at the people beneath them with lackluster eyes. Their faces were black from the day's toil and their tattered clothes hung limply on their emaciated frames. Little Addie was there, leaning on her crutch; and the Winly child, crying a little and rubbing her eyes with blackened knuckles; and at the far end of the line the dwarfish figure of the runaway from the north whose only name seemed to be H'r'l'd.

Jonathan advanced to the front of the stage.

"Ladies and gentlemen," he said, "these children, these sad little waifs who have ceased to know kindness and compassion, and who seem almost to have been forgotten by God, were born here in Rixby. They were unfortunate. Their parents died and they became public dependents. The care of orphans is a trust laid on each community. What do you think of the way this town is carrying out that solemn obligation?

"You, ladies and gentlemen, have children who live in comfort and warmth and plenty. They are happy and safe in the love and care you lavish on them. Can you spare a thought to these unfortunates who live in dread of the foreman's whip and are the slaves of a relentless factory clock?

"These poor little people were roused from sleep at four o'clock this morning. After a breakfast of sour porridge and thin milk they were herded into the mill at five o'clock—and there they remained all day in heavy toil until half an hour ago when the factory bells struck eight and that terrible working day of fifteen hours came at last to an end. In a brief interval at noon they were fed a meal of cold broken mutton which only famished stomachs could tolerate.

"If we were to take them back to their filthy, crowded quarters at the mill—and I assure you that we do not intend to—they would have a few hours of sleep and at four o'clock tomorrow morning, their minds drugged with fatigue, their lids heavy, their hearts empty of hope, they would begin again on the same treadmill."

He turned back abruptly to his helpers and said: "The children are hungry. Please see they have the warm meal which is ready for them. Then they must have baths and go to sleep in comfortable beds—and when the hour of four strikes tomorrow they will sleep blissfully through it. Take care of them at once, please."

As the children were led away, Jonathan moved up to the front of the stage.

"And now what is to be done about this?" he asked. "Good citizens as I know you all to be, if there is one among you who thinks it is the sole responsibility of the owners of the mill, let me say this to you: The man or woman who has seen these children and is not willing to fight in their behalf will be as guilty in the sight of God as those who profit from their labor."

There was an interruption at this point. A loud voice sounded from the back of the hall. "No one is to leave. Keep your seats, ladies and gentlemen."

The owner of the voice, an officer in uniform, stepped out of the shadows at the back, followed by half a dozen of the rank and file. They walked down the center aisle until the leader was immediately under the stage.

"I have warrants for the arrest of seven people," he announced. "There's no sense any of 'em trying to get away. They'll step for'ward as they hears their names called out. Now then. Jonathan Bade!"

"I am here," said the lawyer.

The officer lifted a paper and checked off a name on his list.

"Miss Helen Groody."

Nell walked out on the stage and took her stand beside Jonathan. "Here," she said.

The officer went down the list and each person named came forward to the front of the stage.

"We'll take ye out the back way. The audience is requested to remain in their seats until we've had a chance to leave."

End of Volume One